OUR CHOICE OF GODS

OUR CHOICE OF GODS

Quisque suos patimur manes.
—VIRGIL

Richard Parrish

A Birch Lane Press Book
Published by Carol Publishing Group

Copyright © 1989 by Richard Parrish

A Birch Lane Press Book
Published by Carol Publishing Group

Editorial Offices
600 Madison Avenue
New York, NY 10022

Sales & Distribution Offices
120 Enterprise Avenue
Secaucus, NJ 07094

In Canada: Musson Book Company
A division of General Publishing Co. Limited
Don Mills, Ontario

Manufactured in the United States of America

Library of Congress Cataloging-in-Publication Data

Parrish, Richard.
    Our choice of gods / Richard Parrish.
      p.   cm.
    "A Birch Lane Press book."
    ISBN 1-55972-002-6 : $19.95
    1. Jewish-Arab relations--Fiction. I. Title.
  PS3566.A75709   1989
  813'.54--dc20

                                              89-10036
                                                 CIP

This is a work of fiction, a product of the imagination. Now and then historical characters enter the story. In all cases, their roles are entirely fictionalized, although a very few of the scenes in which they appear resemble events which actually occurred. The dates of historical events are correct, except that the tragedy at Deir Yassin was April 9, 1948, the curfew killing at Kafr-Qasim was October 29, 1956, and the massacre of the Maronites at the church in Ain Rumanneh (Beirut) took place on April 13, 1975.

The stanza from Naomi Shemer's *Yerushala'im Shel Zahav* ("Jerusalem of Gold"), © 1967 by Naomi Shemer, was translated by Richard Parrish under license granted by Chappell Music, Ltd., all rights for the Western Hemisphere controlled by Chappell & Co., used by permission. Quotations from the *Shulchan Aruch* are from *Code of Jewish Law*, translated by Hyman E. Goldin, reprinted by permission of the publishers, Hebrew Publishing Company © 1963, all rights reserved. The Nuremberg Trial summation of Sir Hartley Shawcross is excerpted from *Nuremberg Diary* by G. M. Gilbert, © 1947 by Gustave Mahler Gilbert, renewal copyright © 1974 by Gustave Mahler Gilbert, reprinted by permission of Farrar, Straus and Giroux, Inc. The 1977 victory speech of Menachem Begin is the English translation from *Menachem Begin*, by Eitan Haber, © 1978 by Michaelmark Books/Zmora, Bitan, Modan Publishers, reprinted by permission of Delacorte Press, a division of Bantam, Doubleday, Dell Publishing Group, Inc. The quoted material from the New York Herald Tribune and the translation of the "Bar-Lev Line" Mapai advertisement, are from *A History of Israel: From the Rise of Zionism to Our Time*, Howard M. Sachar, © 1976, Alfred. A. Knopf, used by permission of the publishers. The translation of *Hatikvah* is from *Terror Out of Zion*, J. Bowyer Bell (St. Martin's: New York, 1977), used by permission of the author. Excerpts from the *Qur'an* are from *The Koran*, translated by N. J. Dawood (Penguin Classics, revised Edition, 1974), © N. J. Dawood 1956, 1959, 1966, 1968, 1974, reproduced by permission of Penguin Books Ltd.

Quotations from the Hebrew Scriptures are an amalgam of the King James Version and my own translation, essentially limited to modernizing the archaisms. No pains have been taken to adhere to technical rules for transliterating Hebrew and Arabic terms. Some usages are conventional and would be almost unrecognizable if rendered technically (*imam* instead of *'imaam*). Others are transliterated to attempt to reproduce sound for an English reader that will not look too frightening (*aroo* instead of *'aruub*). The properly transliterated Arabic was supplied by my friend Hamdi Qafisheh, and I took great license with it. *Mea culpa.*

To my eleven-year-old son Joshua, who will not yet be able to read and understand this novel, but who will understand the blessing of Isaac, Genesis 27:27-28: "And he came near and kissed him, and he smelled the smell of his garment, and said, 'See, the scent of my son is of a golden field which the Lord hath blessed; may God grant thee of the dew of heaven, and the fatness of the earth, and plenty of corn and wine.'" And to my wife Pat, my son Michael, and my parents Pearl and Jerry. Always first and foremost.

To Rabbi Alfred Gottschalk, President of the Hebrew Union College-Jewish Institute of Religion, who started me on this path.

To Ralph and May Ziskin, without whose love I could not have endured my Nuremberg trials.

To Hamdi Qafisheh, Professor of Arabic in the Oriental Studies Department of the University of Arizona: Palestinian Jerusalemite, my teacher, my friend.

OUR CHOICE OF GODS

BOOK ONE

THE LAST MALINEH

"Is it of no concern to you who pass by?
If only you would look and see:
Behold, there is no pain like unto mine,
    which is visited upon me,
    wherewith the Lord hath afflicted me."

—Lamentations 1:12

Chapter One

April 1946

The dreams stood around her cot again, the golems, the dybbuks, grotesque gargoyles waiting for her to sleep, so that they
could gorge themselves on the flesh of her heart, the blood of her
veins. And as Leah fell unwillingly into exhausted sleep, the
gargoyles hunched close around and their fangs tore into her.

*Leah finally receives the stamped and approved permit to attend High
Holy Day services at the Gaon Synagogue in Ghetto Two. It is already the
afternoon of Kol Nidre, the day before Yom Kippur, the most austere of the*

Jewish holidays. She races to the squalid apartment and washes herself in the bucket of freezing water that serves as their wash basin. She went yesterday to the mikveh *[ritual bath] to cleanse herself from the "uncleanness" of her period which ended a week ago. She can now make love to her husband as a clean and pious Jewess, but not unless she reaches him well before sundown. Because from an hour before sundown on Kol Nidre eve until an hour after sundown tomorrow, Yom Kippur, both she and her husband must refrain from sex or even such thoughts.*

She puts on her prettiest long-sleeved, full-length white dress and wraps herself in a heavy black woolen stole. She runs to the gate between the two Ghettos and shows her pass through the guardpost window slot. A Jewish policeman looks it over and rings his field telephone. Leah impatiently shifts from foot to foot, rubbing her arms for warmth, waiting endless minutes. Then the guard comes outside, takes her by the arm and leads her into the guard shack, seating her on a wooden stool.

"I am sorry, Mrs. Arad. There is some problem with the Gestapo. Your pass has been held up. I just called the Chief of the Judenrat Police, and he is trying to solve the problem. Please be patient. I am sure that everything will be all right."

Leah sits in despair. Other Jews present their passes and are allowed through the gate. Old white-bearded men with long payess *[prayer curls] framing their faces, wrapped in their woolen shawls, their wives in old* shaitels *[wigs] and shapeless black woolen coats, shuffling behind their men. Now and then young men, with and without wives, and a few boys who must have been yeshiva* bucherim *[students] when the world was still right side up. Still Leah waits, and the short fall day begins to darken. She is desperate.*

Jewish Police Chief Isaac Krens comes into the guardhouse. "I have finally straightened everything out, Mrs. Arad. You can go through now."

Leah runs through the opened gate. Krens smiles, revealing brown-stained, rotten teeth. It is too late for this beauty to make love to her husband now. Kol Nidre is about to begin. With great satisfaction, Krens strolls back to his office. Someday, he vows to himself, he will have this golden-haired beauty.

Leah rushes to the Gaon Synagogue. It is almost dark. The pews are filled with a thousand men wearing white linen robes, since custom requires that a man wear a kittel *on the most important days of his life—and his burial day—for the Talmud teaches that all Jews must present themselves before God as equals to be judged strictly for their merit and not for their money or jewelry or fine clothes.*

Daniel is not at the elevated reader's table in the center of the huge synagogue. Nor is he on the dais on the east wall, in one of the throne-like chairs next to the ark of the Torah. Leah rushes down the outer hallway to the stairway which leads down to the large study rooms and the living quarters of the rabbis. Daniel is just emerging from a door at the far end of the hallway. She runs to him and they hug hungrily. But it is too late for kissing. He rubs her back under the shawl. He caresses her. She shudders with pleasure and holds him tightly.

He pushes her away, gently. "Leah, when must you go back?"

"My pass is good for two days."

"Good. Then we will have tomorrow night. Come, we must go now." It is already Kol Nidre, too late for sex or thoughts of love.

They walk upstairs, Leah behind her husband. He walks through a side door onto the dais. She continues on, goes through the main door and walks behind the mechitzah *in the back of the synagogue. All the women have to remain behind this wooden screen, about five feet high, which separates them from the men, so that no thoughts except of God will enter the men's minds while they pray.*

The cantor climbs the small steps to the reader's platform, opens his prayerbook, and begins the ancient chant which ushers in the Day of Atonement:

"Kol nidre, vayessaray,
vacherumay . . . ."

He has a wonderful tenor plaintive weepy voice. The chanting of the prayer goes on for ten minutes, since it must be repeated three times.

Daniel stands alone on the dais beside the ark. His curly brown beard is short in the modern style, his prayer curls are tucked over and behind his ears. He is radiant with the religious fervor of this most awesome of holy days and with the relief of seeing his wife healthy and strong. He is resplendent in his white linen kittel.

Leah gazes at the stately man who is her husband and the father of their son, Nachman. She is filled with loving him, and her mind is flooded with the sensual verses of the Song of Songs, even though it is Kol Nidre, and she is not supposed to have such thoughts or stirrings:

"My beloved is all radiant and ruddy,
    the chief among ten thousand.
His head is the finest gold:
His locks are wavy, black as a raven.

His eyes are like doves beside springs,
   bathed in milk, fitly set.
His cheeks are like beds of spices,
   yielding sweet fragrance.
His lips are lilies, distilling myrrh.
His body is ivory work, overlaid with
   sapphires.
His legs are marble columns, set upon
   bases of gold...
His speech is most sweet, and he is
   altogether desirable.
This is my beloved and this is my friend.
O daughters of Jerusalem."

At first no one notices the German soldiers with machine guns quietly entering the synagogue and lining up along the side wall. Then a few people see them and stare open-mouthed. The cantor sees them as the clack of their heels on the wooden floor breaks through everyone's reverie. He stops chanting. A deathly hush falls over the congregation.

An SS officer strides briskly past his troops and up to the dais. He turns to face the congregation. He is standing in front of Daniel.

"You are enemies of the Third Reich, and you will all be taken to Lukiszki Prison. Please follow the orders of the guards."

A shocked murmur begins among the congregation. Daniel Arad is aghast at the desecration of the synagogue on this holy night. He is beyond restraint. He steps forward and swings his forearm up into the officer's back, sending him toppling off the dais to his knees on the floor below. Almost instantly there is a short burst of machine gun fire from one of the soldiers. Daniel, a puzzled look crossing his face, slumps to the floor. His crimson blood pours down the white linen kittel and puddles on the floor. His dead eyes stare at nothing.

Leah screams from behind the mechitzah. Others start moaning and screaming. More bursts of gunfire. Leah starts to run to where Daniel has fallen. But two old women hold her back behind the mechitzah. More gunfire. A few men lie on the floor, some moving and groaning, others motionless.

The SS officer remounts the dais. He draws his Luger and fires twice into the air. "Attention! Attention! Be orderly and go outside or you will be killed right here," he barks.

No one hears him. Pandemonium and terror sweep the Jews. They know that Lukiszki Prison means the firing squads in Ponar Forest. If they stay here and refuse to go, they will also be shot. The certainty of their impending death makes them fight blindly for life. They tear at each other to get out the door through the line of soldiers. They jump over the bodies of their dead and wounded brethren and attack the soldiers with fists and prayer books. Machine gun fire roars seemingly from everywhere.

Behind the mechitzah is a door concealed from the Germans' view. It is the women's door which opens to the back of the synagogue. Some women start running through it. Leah is dragged, pulled, the two old women are trying to help her. She finally comes to her senses. Daniel is beyond help. She must save herself, she must save her baby. She runs into the grounds behind the synagogue. It is dark, and the overcast sky blackens everything. There are no street lights or auto lights. German soldiers are firing at the front of the synagogue as doomed men manage to reach the outer doors. But there are no soldiers at the back. Leah runs with twenty or thirty other women toward the gate at Niemiecka Street.

When they reach it, an old woman in front pleads with the Jewish policeman on the other side to open it. He will not. To do so would be committing suicide. Several women begin pounding on the gate. Leah and a few others break off behind and start running along the fence in the pitch blackness. One of them yells "Here!," and falls to her knees to struggle through a hole where several of the staves have been broken away. It is a small hole which must be used by the Ghetto smugglers to get from one Ghetto to the other. Leah crawls through the opening, shedding her heavy woolen stole to enable her to squeeze through.

She gets her bearings on the other side. She is stunned and fearful, but she wants to live, to get to her baby. She runs through side streets and alleys to her apartment. Since it is Kol Nidre, not even the Ghetto policemen are on the streets. She hears shots coming from the direction of Niemiecka Gate, but she is safe. She sprints up the stairs and into her apartment breathless. Her mother is asleep on the couch.

She rushes over to Nachman to see if he is all right. He is sleeping soundly. She slumps on the floor beside his crib, and the horror of her husband's murder consumes her. Daniel, Daniel. He had been her only love. And she had been his "fairest among women":

> "Whither has your beloved gone, O fairest
>   among women?...
> Upon my bed by night, I sought him whom my
>   soul loves;
> I sought him but found him not;
> I called him, but he gave no answer."

Leah lies in a daze on the floor next to Nachman's crib. Daniel can give no answer, not ever again. She is in a state beyond tears. Perhaps tears will come later, to wash away the blood of her murdered husband, to cleanse her soul, to make her well again. But now there is just silence and staring, wide-eyed staring. She reaches up softly to touch Nachman, to feel his life—

"Wake up! Wake up!" the old woman from the next cot was hovering over Leah, shaking her. "Another dream, almost every night the same. Get out of here and let us sleep. We have to sleep." Her voice was more mournful than angry, as weak as a sparrow's twitter. In the murky dawn light, her face was the color and texture of a walnut shell.

"I'm sorry," murmured Leah. She swung her legs over the cot and wrapped the threadbare olive drap army wool blanket around her shoulders. She pulled on the scuffed combat boots and left the laces to dangle as she walked outside into Regensburg's frigid spring dawn. A shroud of mist enveloped her like the linen *tachrichim* they used to clothe the dead.

She went into the children's tent, where she went most mornings after being shaken awake from her dreams, to see him, to try to reaffirm life. The woman attendant in a brown woolen army overcoat was asleep on her cot. The old man was not there, probably at the wash house. She went over to the boy's bunk and watched his lips twitch and listened to him groan in his sleep. She touched his cheek softly, a mother's fingertip caress, and he started to breathe undisturbed and the twitching stopped.

"Come. Come," the old man whispered behind her, his voice hoarse and distant. He took her gently by the shoulders with frail hands like quavering butterfly wings and led her out of the tent. "Let him sleep. It is too early yet." His eyes were hollow, rheumy, staring at her from that emaciated corpse he still called his body.

She nodded softly and walked back to her tent, to sit, to stare endlessly at the walls of the six-woman tent, like all the other days, the tens and hundreds of days, waiting with dimming hope for the British to issue her a visa into Palestine, her last *malineh*.

Chapter Two

Captain Matthew Jordan shook the frigid rain from his overcoat and stamped the dripping water from his soaked shoes. His brown woolen trousers, saturated to the knees, emitted a musty camphor odor. His heels clicked hollowly down the narrow south corridor of the *Justizpalast* to the small back door of the trial hall.

The MP saluted smartly. "Real pisser out there today, ain't it Captain Jordan?"

"Never saw anything like it. Three straight days." The Captain removed his overcoat and hung it on a hat tree by the door. "What's happening in there?"

"I think they're about done," said the MP, checking his wrist-watch. "Had a recess over two hours ago. Won't go on much longer."

Jordan pressed his shoes against the brown cement floor, trying to squeeze out more of the rain. "Goddam shoes are ruined," he muttered to nobody.

The MP opened the door and the Captain entered the back of the immense trial hall. He walked quickly to his chair at the prosecution table.

Justice Robert Jackson, the United States Supreme Court Justice who had been appointed chief prosecutor for the American contingent at the Nuremberg Trial, was just beginning his cross-examination of Hans Frank—former Governor General of Poland for the Third Reich.

Jordan watched as Justice Jackson eased politely into his questioning, asking about little things, seemingly inessential things. Jackson was the consummate examiner—always creating a mood, always aware of the mood he was creating. An excellent teacher for a young lawyer like Matthew Jordan.

Suddenly, Jackson bristled like a winter starved mountain lion stalking prey, and his eyes became cold. He grabbed the rail of the witness stand and leaned in toward Frank. "Aren't you," he demanded, "personally responsible for the death of millions of Jews?"

Hans Frank drew back, his mouth falling open in shocked silence, a wild pig trapped in a thicket of thorns. He looked around the hall, as if for help, obviously startled by the abrupt change in Jackson's demeanor. No one rose to defend him. He was all alone, fresh meat for the rapacious lawyer.

"Certainly not, sir," he finally stammered. "I killed no one. I am personally responsible for nothing."

Jackson pressed in, his voice hard edged and rasping. "But you saw Jews die in the camps, you watched them, you were the senior officer of the Nazi occupation government of Poland. Wasn't it you who really killed them?".

"Not at all, sir." Frank looked down, whimpering, as so many had done before him. And, as so many had also done before him, he carefully repeated the cover story he had endlessly rehearsed. "I was an *administrator*, sir, the *civilian* governor. I had nothing to do with the killing centers, neither the ones used for the Jews nor those used for the Poles. In fact, all of those terrible places were directly under the command of Himmler and the SS, and I was not even *aware* of them until near the end of the war. They were entirely outside the scope of my duties as Governor General."

Justice Jackson responded with angry sarcasm. "Are you telling this tribunal that you had no part whatsoever in crimes against humanity, that you weren't even aware that in your own district, the killing centers of Belzec and Majdenek and Treblinka and Sobibor were murdering literally millions of Jews and Poles and Gypsies?"

"That is precisely what I am saying, sir. I truly did not know." Frank was a tall man, heavy and dissolute, wheezing from emotion, and his paunchy jowls pulsed like empty water bladders.

Justice Jackson smacked his thick sheaf of papers down on the prosecution table, then addressed the tribunal over the dramatically diminishing echo. "Your Honors, perhaps this is an appropriate point to recess until tomorrow. It's almost five, and I can see that my cross-examination of Mr. Frank will require several days."

The judges conferred briefly, and the Chief Judge adjourned the session with a quick bang of his gavel. The MP's led the prisoners from the dock, and the huge trial hall slowly emptied. Justice Jackson and his three military assistants—including Captain Jordan—remained seated at the prosecution table.

Jackson was in a frustrated rage. "First that foul scum claims that everything he did was simply following orders, and now he says he didn't even know about the camps! We have *got* to prove that he *did* know!"

He examined his three aides with dark, troubled eyes, and they sat quiet, uneasy under his scrutiny.

Jackson tapped his finger down on the stack of prosecution papers, many of which Captain Jordan had himself prepared. "What evidence have we gathered that he was ever actually *at* one of the killing centers?" Jackson's low, broad forehead gleamed with perspiration as he studied his aides. His intense eyes were demanding, imperious. Again there was silence.

Finally, Captain Jordan cleared his throat and spoke. "We actually have no documentary evidence, Justice Jackson. But we may be able to find a refugee in one of our DP camps who could testify as an eyewitness."

Jackson peered at Jordan from under bushy black brows, then began nodding his head excitedly, as he did whenever an idea appealed to him.

"We have just about ten days to find out," he bellowed, still looking straight at Jordan. "If it's agreed that we have no other proof, then you'd better get to work."

The other aides could provide no alternative. "Okay, Jordan. Find us a witness." Justice Jackson grimaced, got up from the table heavily, and walked out of the trial hall.

Matt Jordan frowned as his boss left the table. Well, Matty boy, he mumbled to himself, that's a hell of an idea you had there—but just where you going to find this witness? He groaned inwardly, stuffed his papers into a leather satchel, and walked slowly to his cubbyhole office with the stenciled sign on the door: "Capt. Jordan, JAG."

After the war had ended, when he had desperately wanted to return to the States, he had received orders to leave Patton's Third Army headquarters in Wurzburg and to report to the Nuremberg JAG. With Patton, he had been the legal officer in charge of court-martialing lonely G.I.'s for fraternization with German girls. It had actually been a step up from his earlier job on Patton's staff, court-martialing frightened soldiers who had fled from the combat areas. He needed to get away from this senseless mess and go back to the real world. But then he had been ordered to Nuremberg, to help with the war trials, because he spoke Yiddish and pretty good Hebrew and was needed to get Jewish witnesses ready for trial.

It was a crummy irony. His father had made him go to Hebrew school as a boy and had forced him to study the Bible and even a little Talmud, because this was how a decent Jewish boy put himself in good with God. And his father and mother had always spoken Yiddish at home so that Matt would be able to speak Yiddish, which was—as they would often say—the only really Jewish language. And then he had studied Hebrew in college, taking it for a full four years. And what had it gotten him? Extended in the Army for month after month in the bombed out rubble of Nuremberg, listening to the endless accounts of Nazi atrocities and the equally endless Nazi excuses, while everyone else had long ago gone home. A hell of a way to serve God! He was bored sick with it all. As far as he was concerned, it was time for this war to end.

He looked over the roster of the displaced persons camps. He hoped that somebody there would be able to help him, if not as a witness, then at least to give him a lead to other possible witnesses. He took out a military cable request form:

"To: All Commanders, Displaced Persons Camps, American
      Zone—April 11, 1946
Subject: Trial Witnesses

Please query inmates to determine if any witnesses to presence of Hans Frank, former Governor General of Poland, at any concentration camp, preferably killing center. Advise immediately."

Three days later, he received his only reply. The commanding officer at Regensburg Camp reported that a Jewish woman named Leah Arad had personal knowledge of Hans Frank's presence at Treblinka and that she wanted to make a deal. In exchange for testimony, she wanted a railway ticket to Marseilles, a ship ticket to Haifa, and a visa issued by the British government for permanent entry into Palestine.

Palestine? Matt frowned to himself. Hasn't this woman had enough war? And how was the U.S. Army supposed to get anyone a visa from the British?

He took the cable and walked down the hall to Justice Jackson's office. Jackson was preparing for the afternoon court session and looked up impatiently when Jordan knocked twice against the open door and entered the office.

"Sir, I just got a reply on that cable I sent out about the Hans Frank witness." He handed the half sheet of paper to the Supreme Court Justice.

Jackson read the cable and looked up. "Have you talked to her yet?"

"No sir. I thought I'd better clear it with you before I made her any promises. If she's really adamant about that visa—"

"Well, first things first," Jackson said, waving his hand, dismissing any possible obstacles between himself and his quarry, Hans Frank. "Get down to Regensburg and make sure that she's legit and can give us what we need. If so, call me immediately, and I'll contact Shawcross and see what he can do for us." Sir Hartley Shawcross was the chief prosecutor for the British contingent at the Nuremberg Trial. "I don't think it's beyond our doing if Sir Hartley backs us up."

Matt drove his jeep fast over the potholed Autobahn enclosed on both sides by towering hills brocaded with spring lush birch trees, silver green and white mammoths pushing their lofty tusks lustily toward the newly warm sun. More of these horror stories to listen to, he thought with chagrin. Day after deadly day of half-dead men testifying and half-dead women moaning from the witness stand about murder and torture and demented cruelty. And Justice Jackson fuming and pointing and accusing. And night after night of grinding trial preparation, always too many documents to read, too many wretched Jewish Ichabod Cranes to get prepared to testify. God, will this never end? Did he have to do this until he shriveled up and his juices dried to dust, and he just crumbled into the blood colored mud of Germany? What would he be doing back at home, he thought inanely. Maybe listening to a baseball game on the radio, the mighty Yankee Clipper knocking one right into the seats, maybe eating supper in that little Greek restaurant with the great moussaka that even now made his mouth water, and that waitress who made his mouth water even more, with eyes as black as amphissa olives and hair like a wet mink, and the rest of her, the best of her, a puckered plump red bell pepper, sweet, glistening—

Bang! He hit a pothole and the jeep swerved, and he fought to get it under control. Wow! That was a close one! Just take it easy, jerk, keep your mind on living through this and getting back home, otherwise you're never going to get a taste of that red pepper.

Finally he arrived at Regensburg Camp, a rippling lake of grass with faded olive drab canvas tents scattered about it like wilted lily pads. He was ushered into a Colonel Livazer's office in the Headquarters quonset hut and shook the Rabbi's hand. Livazer sat on the edge of his desk—portly, bald, no more than five feet tall. His face was round and plump, and he chewed the gnarled butt of a long-dead cigar.

Jordan sat attentively in a straight chair in front of Livazer. The Rabbi pushed the cigar to the side of his mouth. "It was two days," he said, "before this girl came to see me after I posted copies of your cable all over camp. I have to tell you she is very reluctant to testify. None of these people want to talk about what they've lived through. The only reason she's even considering it is because she wants to go to Palestine. Now if you can't honestly provide that visa for her, I don't even want you to talk to her." He looked at Jordan sternly, chewing intently.

Captain Jordan shifted in his chair. "Sir, I had a talk with Justice Jackson about it. He thinks that if she's really got the testimony we need, he can get the head of the British prosecution team to push for a visa. Justice Jackson is not a talker. If he says he'll try, he'll try. But I certainly can't guarantee anything. Anyway, I have to interview her first so I'll be able to confirm to Jackson whether we really do need her."

Livazer wrinkled his eyebrows and worked harder on the cigar. He jutted his face forward and glared at the captain. "All right, son. But be careful with this girl. She's been through more than most of us could stand."

"Yes, of course, sir. I'll keep that in mind." Whenever people uttered statements like that—and it happened often here in Nuremburg—Matt felt himself wanting to say, "Hey, it's been a tough war on everyone." The Jews of Europe had lived through hell, no doubt about it, but a lot of Matt's friends had paid an awesome price, too. There was no monopoly on pain.

"I'll go get her," Livazer said. "I think she's in English language class."

Minutes later, the elderly Rabbi returned, followed by a young woman clad in faded, much too large battle fatigues.

"Captain Jordan," said Livazer, "this is Leah Arad."

She looked tired, maybe a little sick, but as Matt held his hand out for hers he could somehow feel that she was stronger than many of the others. Less defeated. She looked capable of providing hard, useful testimony. Matt realized that he was staring at her, but he couldn't stop himself. What a face!

"*Gutten morgan*," she said softly in Yiddish. Then she smiled briefly, perhaps unconsciously. Her smile washed over Jordan, softened him. Matt tried to remember the last real female smile he'd experienced. Wurzburg? London? Way back in Tucson? He couldn't remember, but it had been too long. Thank God the trial is almost over. It's really time to go home.

"Why don't you go over to the mess tent, Captain," Livazer suggested. "You'll have some privacy there for a couple of hours until five o'clock. If you need some more time after that, you can use my office."

"Thank you, sir." Jordan saluted. A sudden sweet sense of possibility welled unexpectedly inside him. This woman, with her smile, might finally help put an end to things for the *Captain* Jordan in Matt. The war *was* finally getting over, and he could stop being a soldier, just be a man again.

"*Tavo-i iti, bevakashah*," he said to her, showing off his Hebrew. He knew that most east European Jewish girls couldn't speak Hebrew, just Yiddish. He held the screen door open for her.

"*Todah rabah, seren* Jordan," she replied in Hebrew, another soft smile flirting with her full lips.

They walked slowly to the mess tent and went to a small table in the corner. Matt watched her walk, sit down, wipe a crumb off the wooden table. After months and months of apathy toward everything, he suddenly couldn't stop looking. The war was over, and he was with a woman, Leah: endless gray eyes with black rings around the irises. Alabaster skin. Thick blond hair framing her face. Strong and delicate at once. Remarkable.

Matt could see that his staring made her feel uncomfortable, and he was a little relieved. Livazer was right, after all. Leah had been through the worst of the war, and it might have left her brittle, unfeeling. Or worse, too frightened to react at all. But this was not the case. She looked back at him—curious, open, maybe even interested.

But there was work to do. "Chaplain Livazer tells me you actually saw Hans Frank at a death camp. Is that true?"

"Yes." Leah turned aside coldly, no longer looking interested.

Matt had to press. "Can you describe him?"

She could. Matt Jordan listened to the description, down to the side on which Frank parted his slick black hair. Leah Arad was obviously a very observant woman.

"Where did you see him? Which camp?"

"Treblinka," she said. The word, once so bright, so musical, had in these past months taken on a dirge-like darkness. No longer just a sleepy hamlet by a sparkling river, Treblinka was and would always be a death camp.

Matt looked at her and nodded, smiling encouragement. "Would you tell me about your background, how you came to be sent to Treblinka?"

She looked down at her hands in her lap, squeezed her eyes shut for a moment. How many putrid memories pushed their way back? How many were there? Matt could only guess.

"I'm sorry," he said softly. "I realize how difficult it is for you to talk of these things. But with your help we might be able to convict that—that Nazi scum." He spoke as gently as he could, and he knew that his bookish, biblical poetic Hebrew imparted a quaintness to his speech, unlike the coarse modernized Hebrew he had heard spoken by the Palestinians who worked in the Regensburg Camp. Leah appeared to be disarmed by his gentleness.

She spoke quietly. "I was born in Vilna, Poland, on August 7, 1922. My father Saul became the owner of the Baltic Trade Bank in 1934. It was Vilna's third largest bank and had been started in 1911 by my grandfather. After the 'numbers clause' prevented the Jews from attending regular schools in 1936, I was educated at home by tutors along with my youngest brother, Jonathan. Vilna had been back and forth occupied by Germany and Poland and Lithuania, so in addition to our studies of the Bible and the Talmud, we were tutored in German and Lithuanian and Polish. At the time, it was a normal education for wealthy Jews in Vilna."

She spoke evenly and without animation, not letting any emotion show through her words.

"I had three older brothers. Two of them started a branch bank in Bialystok in 1937, and my oldest brother, David, went to Palestine as a 'pioneer' in 1931. I had two sisters, one of them died in childbirth, and the other now lives in New York City with her husband. When I was seventeen, in September 1939, I married Rabbi Daniel Arad. He was nineteen. We lived in my parent's home and my husband continued his studies at the Gaon Yeshiva. I gave birth to a son, Nachman, in October 1940."

Matt shifted in the uncomfortable straight-backed wooden chair: a husband, a child? He couldn't help wondering, perversely, he realized, if they were dead or alive. Was that why she wished to go to Palestine—to rejoin her family? Despite his growing feelings for her, he really did hope so. For her sake.

Leah's voice had lowered, almost broken, as she spoke her son's name, and she paused and closed her eyes as if to blink away the memory. She swallowed hard, and her creamy skin turned blotchy with pink patches. Perspiration beaded on her brow. A Degas portrait of a sad ballerina, Matt thought. She looked at him—and he felt himself blushing, feeling guilty for having romantic thoughts at a time like this.

Abruptly she stood up. "I'm sorry, Captain. I don't think I can go through with this testifying. I thought I could—I want the visa—but I was wrong."

Matt had interviewed dozens of witnesses during the last few months, and he was not surprised by Leah Arad's sudden leaving. Most of the survivors were unwilling—at least at first—to lower the barriers that they had erected within themselves to protect themselves, to keep from reliving the horrors, to enable them to go on living. Sometimes it took two or three interviews before the story began to emerge. Sometimes it was never told.

Since there were no transient barracks at Regensburg Camp to house temporary personnel, Matt had to drive across the only bridge left standing over the Danube—a rickety wooden span—to the heart of the medieval town of cobblestones and square cut stone houses with red shingle roofs, to look for a small pension in which to spend the night. As he drove, he promised himself that with this particular witness he would try as hard as he possibly could to draw the story out. The last thing he wanted was to cause Leah Arad pain, but at the same time he was sure that he could not let her go. This thought made him wrinkle his forehead and squint hard and puzzle it over. What the hell is going on? Just get it over with, he reprimanded himself, and get the hell back home where you belong.

Chapter Three

At eleven o'clock the next morning, he arrived back at the shabby camp. Leah was working in the orphan's tent, the WAC told him, and she would not be available till after lunchtime. With two hours to kill, Matt strolled around the huge camp, trying to imagine a place like this as home. It wasn't easy—and until this day, he reflected, he had never even felt the urge to *try* to imagine a place like this as home. It was a camp for lost souls, lugubrious Rip Van Winkles, perplexed and terrorized, just now awaking from their almost endless night. They were people he interviewed but rarely actually felt for, Europeans, foreigners. But now there was Leah, and the awful place became more personal to him—and he hated it all the more. Perhaps her intense craving to find a way to Palestine wasn't so crazy after all.

Along his walk he heard the shouts and whoops of children playing, and he followed the noise to a small playground where he saw Leah and two other women with about twenty small children. Leah held one end of a long frayed jump rope while one of the older girls held the other end. Little kids jumped happily through the swinging arc. Then, two of the children pushed a five or six year old boy into the middle. He seemed less willing to join the fun, and he quickly stumbled and fell to his knees. He didn't blink, he didn't yell or cry. Matt thought the kid looked too old to be a child— almost like an old man, he was so bent and tired. His hair was close cropped and as soft and white as cygnet down.

The rope stopped swinging. The children quieted down for a moment and watched. The little boy simply got up and rubbed his knees, walked to a corner of the playground and sat down. He was wearing short pants, and Matt could see blood trickling down both of his shins.

Leah called another of the older girls over to take her end of the rope, and the game resumed. She walked to the injured boy and sat down beside him, putting her arm around his shoulders, whispering to him. At first he pulled away and sat down ten or fifteen feet away, stoney faced, but after repeated attempts Leah seemed to get him talking, and soon a hesitant smile stole across his smudged face.

Matt walked over as the boy shuffled off, downcast, to rejoin the others. "Good morning," he said and smiled.

Leah looked up, startled. "Captain"—not returning his smile—"I thought you'd already left."

"I don't need to be back till tomorrow, so I thought I'd look the camp over today. These interviews normally last a day or two. No one will miss me. Mind if I sit?"

She scratched at the ground, and he took a seat in front of her. "Yesterday you said you had a son, Nachman. Is that boy Nachman?"

She turned her face away from him.

"Leah, I'm sorry. I didn't mean to—"

"It's all right," she said slowly. "It's all right."

"I want to help you," he whispered. "That's all. I can help you get to Palestine. Please let me try."

"Captain Jordan," she said very quietly, "why don't you meet me in the mess tent at two o'clock. We'll talk then." She got up slowly and walked back to the children, to the little boy with the scraped knees, and Matt returned to the Headquarters to wait. He would try again.

About three hours later, Leah sat down at the long mess table, pushing a hot cup of coffee in Matt's direction. He smiled and nodded thanks and sipped. "If I testify," she asked, "you will get me a Palestine visa?"

He held up his palms. "All I can promise is that I'll do everything I can to get it for you."

She looked hard at him, and he could tell—or at least he hoped he could tell—that she believed him. Her eyes reddened and her face became taut. She began to speak slowly.

"A few days after the Nazi invasion in June 1941, my father was arrested and taken to Lukiszki Prison. We heard nothing from him for four days. We had no idea what was happening. Our whole world had overturned. The Nazis had restricted Jewish travel on public streets, so we were afraid to leave the house. Finally, we simply had to find out what had happened to him.

"Since I looked like a Christian and spoke German, my mother sent me to Lukiszki Prison to find out about my father. I managed to get there and was taken into Kommandant Schlegg's office. They brought my father in. He looked—I could hardly believe it was my father. Schlegg then took a walking stick and beat him to death, right before my eyes."

Matt listened grimly, and although he had become at least partially immunized to the deep shock and horror that the first such tales had aroused in him, he could not suppress the intense feeling of pain and frustration that arose in him.

"Was that before the creation of the Vilna Ghettos?" he asked, trying to draw her out, to get her to speak freely.

"Yes. We were still living at home then. A few weeks later, we were forced to leave our homes and go live in two Ghettos in the old Jewish slum in the center of Vilna. The Ghettos were separated by a fence, and there was no free movement between them."

Matt was reluctant to ask the next question—afraid of any kind of response to it. But he had to ask. "Was your husband with you then?"

"Yes," said Leah. "But he was sent to Ghetto Two, because the Gaon Synagogue was there, and he was one of the junior rabbis. My mother and I and my son Nachman and my brother Jonathan were sent to Ghetto One. On the eve of Yom Kippur, I got a pass to attend Kol Nidre services at the Gaon Synagogue." She paused for a moment, swallowing hard before continuing. "In the middle of the services, an SS detachment entered the building and started shooting everyone. David—my husband—was killed on the dais. I was behind the *mechitzah* in the women's section at the back of the synagogue, and several of us escaped back to Ghetto One."

She spoke evenly, without emotion, and the only sign of the toll it was taking on her was her deep, measured breathing. "The Ghetto's most powerful Jew was Isaac Krens," she continued, her voice rising with the mention of his name, "the Jewish Police Chief of Ghetto One. My husband had been well known, and when the news of his death spread through the Ghetto, Krens called me to his office in the *Judenrat* and told me that the Nazis were issuing 'family passes,' over which he had complete control. Anyone without a pass would be rounded up in the next Nazi *Aktion* and taken to the Ponar Forest where they were forced to dig trenches and the Lithuanian *Ipatingas* executed them right there in their freshly-dug graves."

Leah stopped and lightly rubbed her eyes. "I had to save what was left of my family," she said quietly. "I had to become the *kurveh* of Police Chief Krens."

When she said the word "whore," her voice finally broke. Matt Jordan felt a stab of pain as he listened to this delicate and beautiful girl tell her story. He looked away from her and fought the tears pressing against the backs of his eyes. He felt oddly embarrassed, listening to the recital of such horrors by this girl, as if he were reading some forbidden diary. For the first time, perhaps out of growing affection for her, he was able to connect these awful horrors to a real live person. She—Leah—had lived through the worst of them. It made Matt feel sad, guilty, ashamed, and hopelessly frustrated all at once. This, he thought, was what it would feel like to be a Jew from now on. Nothing could ever be the same again. The old safe world he had grown up in was gone.

"Despite Krens's promise to give my mother a family pass," Leah went on, "he didn't. In the next *Aktion*, she fled to a *malineh*, a refuge. There were hundreds of *malinehs* all over the Ghetto where our people without passes hid and lived like starved rats, but at least they lived. It was late December and a snowstorm came that night, and the *malineh* was just a hollowed out closet behind some shelves in the basement of the building my mother lived in. She froze to death. I had to stay with Police Chief Krens anyway, because he told me that if I left him he would take away my work pass and my brother Jonathan's, and we would both be killed in the next *Aktion*."

Leah stopped again, but Matthew Jordan could not look up. He stared at his hands, not at her, and when he finally raised his face there were tears in his eyes.

"Colonel Karl Mencken was appointed military occupation Kommandant of Vilna. He came to the *Judenrat* to give orders to Krens to ferret the Jews out of all of the *malinehs*. Since Krens didn't speak German, he asked me to translate for the Colonel. After Mencken gave his orders, he told Krens to go down to the street and wait for him. Then"—she gasped, sucking in air to gather what strength she had left—"Mencken raped me."

Matt longed to reach out to her, to soothe her, to tell her it was all right. But it was not all right. He was powerless to erase her pain, he could say nothing to make it easier for her.

"Two weeks later, in the next *Aktion*, Mencken's *Totenkopfstandarten* [Death Head Regiment] rounded up over three thousand Jews from the *malinehs* and executed them in the Ponar Forest. He also murdered Chief of Police Krens personally. He took me and Nachman to live with him in his mansion. I never went outside. This was for Mencken's protection, of course, since cohabiting with a Jew was illegal and considered perversion."

Matt looked at her. Perversion? That it could ever be perverse to live with this breathtaking woman showed just how insane the Nazi world had become. What was their deep sickness that turned beauty to foulness, goodness to evil? He didn't want to hear any more. He could not. He felt sick to his stomach.

They sat in silence across from each other at the narrow table. The spring chill pervaded the mess tent as the sun lowered to the horizon outside, and a dusky gloom began to settle on Regensburg. Leah stood up and walked around to Jordan and placed her hand softly on his slumped shoulder. With her touch, silent tears began streaming down his cheeks. Then Leah quietly left and went back to her tent.

Matt stood up and slowly walked back to his jeep. It was late afternoon, already getting dark. He drove across the purpling Danube to Regensburg to the same small pension and closed the door to his room. He lay on the thick goose down quilted bed, more alone than he'd been the entire war. This woman had suffered the worst horrors that man had ever been capable of visiting on his fellow man, and yet she had drawn forth from somewhere the strength to console *him* because of what *she* had been through. She was twenty-three years old and he was twenty-nine. But she was a woman, and right now he felt like a little boy.

In the morning, he telephoned Justice Jackson and told him that Leah Arad was indeed the witness they needed to hang Hans Frank. Now they needed to have assurances from the British trial contingent that a Palestine visa would be provided. A half hour later, he received a phone call from one of Jackson's other aides. Sir Hartley had cabled the Foreign Office and they would have their answer the next day.

Matt drove back to the headquarters of the displaced persons camp and asked the WAC clerk to send for Leah Arad. He now had to get her ready to testify. When she came into the headquarters a few minutes later, he had the same stunned feeling he had experienced twice before. No one had ever engulfed him like this before, simply by being with him, by looking at him. Her doleful gray eyes were bottomless, haunting.

"Have you made contact with your people about a visa and travel arrangements for me, Captain Jordan?" she asked, acting more distant than he'd expected.

"Yes, yes I did." He couldn't stop staring at her. He felt changed, widened, and yet at the same time all alone. To him, there was no background, no furniture, no room, just this woman. Just himself and Leah Arad.

"Are you certain the visa will be issued?"

"Almost certain. We'll know tomorrow for sure." He suddenly felt chilled, panicky at the thought of losing her. "Is there somewhere we can go to discuss your testimony?" His voice was soft, tentative. He had so much more to say to her, but he couldn't find the words, the way.

"Well," she said quietly. "I suppose we can go back to the mess hall again. It's empty until eleven-thirty." She looked at him with steady eyes, more trusting than before. He smiled, feeling the gap once again closing. He could feel the tug between them, the rapidly growing need. She smiled too. "Or we could walk on the bank of the Danube," she said. "It's a lovely day. There's no reason to stay cooped up inside."

Together they walked slowly and silently past the yawning American MP through the back gate and up the grassy bank strewn with scarlet mohn and orange daisies. Across the river, below the other bank, was a desiccated wood dock crowded with old motorboats and rowboats. The river was pregnant with the melted snow of the Bavarian Frankische Schweiz Mountains. Butterflies and bees took turns gorging on the honeyed cores of the myriad perfumed blooms resurrected by the spring sun. Squirrels darted along the limbs of budding birch trees, and crested bluejays pranced on the ground, feeding on the new life taking root.

Matt took off his woolen tunic and spread it on the dewy grass. Leah sat down on it, and he sat on the grass. Suddenly, romantic visions were once again crowding into his mind. Every time he was with Leah, it was as though the background were fuzzy, not quite focused. They were figures in a French Impressionist painting, "Luncheon on the Grass," or "The Boat Basin at Argenteuil." Was she feeling this too?

"Well," he began, "I'm sorry to say that I've got to hear the rest of the story. I hate to put you through this, but it's the only way to hang Hans Frank."

"For that, it's worth it," she said bitterly. She gathered herself and again picked up her story. This time she needed no prodding from Matt Jordan.

"We lived in Vilna until May 1942, when Mencken was rewarded for his success in destroying Vilna's Jews by being sent to Treblinka, to supervise the building of a killing center and become its Kommandant. He brought me and Nachman with him, and we lived in a new stone house on the edge of Treblinka Village a few miles from camp. As a favor to me, Mencken brought my twelve-year-old brother Jonathan to the camp, to save him from being destroyed along with Vilna's other Jews.

"Mencken's nickname in the camp was the *moloch ha'movos*, the Angel of Death, the Prince of Darkness. He was the absolute giver of life and death, and to all of us he was more powerful than God—and much closer. Nachman and I almost never went outside the house. We had no papers, and there was nowhere we could go anyway. If we had escaped and anyone ever saw that Nachman was circumcised, we would be killed, by the Nazis, by the Poles, by the Cossack partisans in the forests. So we stayed.

"Mencken was an alcoholic. He would work all day killing Jews and then drink half the night with his officers. Then he would come home and beat me. But he never touched my baby. That was all that mattered to me by then—that my Nachman live."

Matt heard the pain in her voice, and he knew that nothing in the world meant more to Leah Arad than her young son.

"After we'd been at Treblinka for about a year, Mencken's superiors set up an inspection schedule for the killing centers in the district. Hans Frank was the man in charge of the tours. He came with Globocnik and Hoess and a whole entourage I can't even remember, and we wined them and dined them, and then Mencken led them all on a tour of the extermination center.

"About ten days later, Mencken was summoned to Frank's headquarters. He told Mencken they had found out that I was a Jew, and they ordered him to get his house in order." Her voice weakened, and she spoke haltingly, almost in a whisper, softly weeping, her entire body shaking as she told of Mencken's return to Treblinka.

Matt listened grimly to the story and felt that he could hardly breathe, like a great stone was on his chest suffocating him. Minutes passed. Then he looked up at her, and he was so injured by her own pain that he couldn't say a word.

"Then I just pedaled as far as I could, away from Treblinka. The only thing I could think of was the prayer *Ayl molay rachamim.* Do you hear that, Captain Jordan? *God full of mercy!* What a terrible lie that is! What a sick joke He played on His chosen people!" Her eyes were ablaze. "I ended up in a tiny medieval village called Brzka, isolated in a great Pine forest, and I stayed there for two years until the war ended."

They sat on the placid beautiful bank of the Danube, the river of fable and minstrel songs and poets. But it could not wash away the haunting memories. They sat together, close, looking at the river and silently experiencing one another, merging without touching, fusing together.

Matt had to get back to Nuremberg to report to Justice Jackson. In mid-afternoon he left, with Leah still sitting on the bank of the river. There were other Jews from the camp, strolling or sitting or lying back on the bank under the bright sun, baking their memories until they would turn to dust and sift out of their souls.

As he drove out of the camp, Matt could see, on the other bank of the river, the Regensburg side, several Germans fishing in the water with wooden poles and string and safety pins for hooks. He could make out their gaunt faces and venomous stares as they watched the "lucky" Jews. *They*—the Germans—did not have all the food they could eat, he imagined them thinking to themselves, like these *verdammte* Jews ambling along the other bank like tourists. *They* had nothing to do with Hitler; they were good Germans. Their fathers and sons and lovers and husbands had all fought on the eastern front, against the barbarous Russians, not against the Americans.

This, Matt knew, was the story they would hold to from now on, no matter who raised his eyebrows. And these reports about death camps run by German soldiers? *Quatsch!* It must have been the Russians or the Poles. These Jews were doing what they had always done, sucking the teat of anyone who would feed them for nothing, taking food from decent Germans.

Despite any past indifference he might have felt, Matthew Jordan now felt a seething hatred for the Germans overtake him. He realized that, in reality, he had won nothing during this war. As an American soldier he had emerged victorious, but as a Jew he was worse off than ever before. His own people were lost, "displaced," with nowhere to look but skyward, where no God seemed to reign. There was nowhere else to search for succor—or to go—except to Palestine, the Promised Land.

Chapter Four

Leah had been at Regensburg Camp for eight months now, waiting with a growing realization of hopelessness for a Palestine visa which the British were refusing to issue to the Jews. And over the months, the ever recurrent nightmares had become a little less frequent. Sometimes she went for two or three entire days and nights on end without being paralyzed by the memories. But telling the story to Captain Jordan had rekindled the scorching visions. And as she sat on the river bank, she was seized by the shimmering gargoyles which were always perched eager to rend her soul.

Mama and Leah and Daniel sit in the parlor and listen to Professor Dovidov summarize the events of the past week. Once again nothing makes sense, nothing adds up. What will come of the prisoners in Lukiszki Prison, Leah's father among them? No one knows. And it is impossible for a man to find out. Without a Nazi-stamped work pass, no Jewish man can walk the streets at all, and even the pass doesn't protect him after three o'clock.

Leah feels the heat of their indirect glances, their silent suggestion—and though she is very afraid to leave her home she volunteers to go to the prison to find out what she can. She is the logical choice—beautiful, blond, Christian-looking, and there are no reports of the Nazis or the Ipatingas murdering women. And, of course, she can speak German.

After a sleepless night, she begins her two-hour walk to the prison. Normally, Lukiszki would be barely fifteen minutes away by auto, but earlier in the week all Jewish-owned vehicles were requisitioned by the German Army. First they took half the men, then all the cars—what could be next?

An acrid sulphur stench from the recent bombings still hangs in the air like a fearsome emblem of the German presence. When she arrives, a dull-eyed Nazi guard leads her through the prison courtyard into a huge hallway and down it to a door where he knocks, waits a moment, then pushes the door open for her to enter. Just inside the door is another German guard, this one standing silently with a machine gun.

A friendly voice calls out: "Ach, gnädige Frau!" *The man emerges from behind a large steel desk, moving out of the shadows created by the bright day beyond the room's narrow windows. He is short, stocky, and apparently very pleased to see her.*

"Please sit down," he says. "I'm so sorry, but I've just been too busy to send word about your father. In just a moment Feldwebel *[Sergeant] Kohler will bring him here to visit." He motions toward the armed guard who immediately leaves the room. Leah sees the colonel's nameplate—* Standartenführer *Erwin Schlegg—then glances around the large bare room, which has but one chair besides the desk and desk chair. In a corner is a hat and coat rack with an officer's wool hat and tunic hanging from it. In the umbrella stand, Leah sees, is her father's ebony walking stick with the silver lion's head. Unmistakeable.*

"I am Erwin Schlegg, the Commander," he says to her, smiling very broadly, moving back to his fine leather desk chair. He has a plump, round cherubic pink face and fine brown neatly combed hair. "I'm afraid it's been a real madhouse here since our soldiers started rounding up traitors and bringing them in. But your father, of course, is no traitor. We have indeed decided to release all of the Jewish detainees. So it is very fortunate that you've come just now."

His kindness and avuncular manner help melt away some of her dread. "Thank you very much, Herr Kommandant," *she says. "We have been so worried. I'm sure you can understand." She is about to ask about her father's*

*walking stick, when the door swings open and her father is thrown to the
floor behind her.*

*"Herr Doktor Brod, how very nice to see you again!" Schlegg rises,
walks briskly around the desk, and stands next to Leah, his quick breath
heavy in his nostrils. Leah turns in her chair and looks down at her father.
His once immaculate red hair and beard are matted, his hazel eyes flat and
glazed. His tailored trousers are filthy with caked feces. The odor is
nauseating and clogs the room. His starched white shirt is gray and splotchy
with dried blood and dirt. His cuffs and collar hang loosely because the gold
cufflinks and collar pin are gone. He looks starved, fifteen pounds lighter
than he'd been a week ago.*

The Sergeant turns the bolt on the door.

*Seeing his daughter, Saul Brod struggles to his hands and knees. Leah
jumps out of the chair and takes her father's arms, helping him to stand. She
is frightened and cannot speak. They look into each other's eyes.*

*"My God, why have you come, why have you come?" he moans through
broken lips. Fresh scabs cover his mouth and nose and forehead. Several of his
teeth are gone. Leah steps back from him and gasps, stuffing the back of her
left hand into her mouth to stifle her sobs, her eyes blurring over with tears.
She has made a terrible mistake. She closes her eyes but the room will not go
away.*

*Schlegg has gone to the umbrella stand and picked up Saul's walking
stick. Without a word he swings the stick in a wide arc, and Leah watches
for a moment as his eyes shrink to tiny, angry red dots—and then she is
smashed across the bridge of her nose and along her eyebrows. She sinks to her
knees, paralyzed, blood gushing from her nostrils, her brain gradually
draining. She feels she is dreaming, entered into a strange, horrible world
she has never even imagined could exist.*

*She remains conscious—and because of this she knows this must be real,
this must be shaol—hell. She watches Schlegg press the stick under Saul's
chin and push up. "Take off your pants, Jew Pig," he grunts through
clenched teeth.*

*After four days of starvation and dehydration and beatings, Saul cannot
resist any order. He undoes the buttons of his pants and they slide to the floor.
His undershorts are caked black with dried excrement. "Take them off,"
shouts Schlegg, his breath coming now in rapid gusts.*

*Saul pushes down his shorts and they too fall stiff around his ankles.
Schlegg is very excited, wheezing, spittle welling in the corners of his mouth.*

Blood is pouring into Leah's mouth from her broken nose, and she must gag and cough to keep from suffocating. Schlegg pushes Saul up to his kneeling daughter. Saul's flaccid penis hangs an inch from her face. "Suck his cock, Jew bitch." Schlegg is enraged, screaming. Neither Saul nor Leah move.

The Kommandant *pushes Saul away and pulls Leah to her feet. He pulls off her suit jacket. He rips off her silk high-buttoned blouse. He rips her skirt buttons and it falls to the floor. He tears the straps of her full-length slip and rips it off her body. Her firm breasts stand out naked. He tears off her panties. "On the floor!" he screams. "On your back!"*

Leah kneels and lies back slowly on the floor. Schlegg kicks her legs. "Spread them!" She spreads her knees, still spitting blood from her mouth, and the Sergeant presses her father down on all fours between her legs. Schlegg comes around and pushes Saul down to his stomach. Schlegg's fat face is purple now, and he is sweating heavily. Saul tries to lift himself to his knees, his face turned sideways, but Schlegg swings the walking stick straight down on his head, and Saul's face falls between Leah's loins. Schlegg swings again and again. Still on her back, Leah vomits. She pulls her blood-soaked legs away from her father's mutilated head and turns over and retches—blood and bile flowing out of her, pooling on the hardwood floor.

Silence shatters the air.

Leah sobs, coughing, while Schlegg returns to his chair behind the desk. "Please help her up," he says conversationally to the Sergeant.

Sergeant Kohler pulls her to her feet. He hands her the jacket and skirt, studded with blood and bits of her father's flesh. She puts them on in a daze. Her nose bleeds steadily, the trail winding around her mouth and over her chin.

"Now go back to your family," Schlegg says calmly. "Tell them we have come to make Vilna and all of the east Judenrein. Auf Wiedersehen, gnädige Frau."

Sergeant Kohler leads Leah outside to a jeep and gives instructions to the driver. She is driven to Semenov Avenue, where she's pushed out on the curb in front of the Brod mansion.

Chapter Five

Two days after speaking with Matt Jordan, Leah was told that the visa had been approved. Colonel Livazer assigned an MP to drive her to Nuremberg. They drove the sixty miles in silence, since the MP could not speak Yiddish and Leah was only to the "x" stage of her English lessons at Regensburg Camp's school. Apple, cat, house and xylophone did not combine for a very stimulating conversation. So they just looked at the road and countryside and thought their own thoughts.

In downtown Nuremberg, they turned onto *Fürtherstrasse*, paralleling the meandering Pegnitz River about a half-mile to the right. On the grassy pastures along its banks, shepherds roamed with their flocks, grazing their sheep as though their lives were immune to the demolition of warfare all around them.

Leah and her driver came up to the fifteen foot high wrought iron and stone fence in front of the *Justizpalast* where the war criminals were jailed and where the trial was underway.

There were two buildings to the Palace of Justice; Leah was directed to the west wing. She showed her pass to the numerous military policemen and was eventually directed to the corridor of Justice Robert Jackson's prosecution team. The place bustled with uniformed men and women. Leah, too, was uniformed, but the women here wore skirts and blouses and short heels, not faded battle fatigues and scuffed boots. For the first time in many months, she felt a twinge of shame at her appearance.

She was finally ushered into Captain Jordan's office by an MP. It was Monday morning, and she'd be testifying on Wednesday. She hadn't seen Jordan since he left Regensburg camp last Friday, and now she felt awkward, silly, when their eyes met once again. He had lambent brown eyes, piercing. His face was rugged, etched lines running from the sides of his nose down his cheeks to a strongly dimpled chin. His hair was seal brown and wavy, now tousled over his high forehead. He got up from his desk and took her arm, the first time he had ever touched her, and they walked back into the corridor. To her disappointment, he seemed all business today, telling her matter-of-factly that they would first go over to the main post exchange at William O. Darby in Fürth. There were some women's clothing and shoes sold there for the nurses and secretarial pool personnel. She'd need something to testify in.

He gave Leah a small booklet of coupons, already signed by the post commander, and told her she could spend up to $50. He said he'd wait in the cafeteria in the basement. The salesgirls were all local German girls, so she would have no problems with the language. Just come down and get him when she was through.

That was it; he went down to the basement. Leah felt more than a bit disappointed. She'd expected more from this man—but now she reminded herself that her real goal was Palestine. There she'd have plenty of chances to rediscover her warmer side, her femininity. She'd rebuild her life from the innermost soul to the outermost fingertip—and she could start right now by finding some new clothes, free of charge thanks to the U.S. Government.

At the exchange she found a red corduroy skirt and a fitted white cotton sleeveless blouse. The tight-fitting material felt luxurious after these months in fatigues. She bought some silk stockings—her first in four years—and black leather heels. In front of the fitting-room mirror, she combed out her blond hair from the bun she'd been wearing and applied a small bit of rouge to her lips, then some mascara to her lashes. In her former life, back in Vilna, she had never used cosmetics or been a careful dresser—she had been a rabbi's wife. But now she felt great pleasure in renewing herself.

Matthew Jordan obviously noticed the difference. As she strode down the steps to the cafeteria, she saw him sitting bored at a small table, sipping a soft drink. But when he looked up at her, he bolted upright out of the chair and practically gasped, whispering something in English. His eyes opened wide as he stared at her.

"Well, Mrs. Arad," he said, regaining his Hebrew. "Would you like a little lunch? We have some time before getting you over to the nurses' quarters at the hospital. That's where we're putting you up for the week."

Leah was glad to see the change in him. "I eat kosher if I can, Captain Jordan," she said. "Is there any possibility of that around here?"

"Not really, but there *is* a vegetarian restaurant in downtown Fürth. We could eat there."

"That'd be fine," Leah said, holding a long slender arm to him, watching him take another look at her. He softly took her arm as though he were afraid to bruise her, and they walked out of the complex.

It was Indian summer and quite warm. The cafe downtown was a tiny hole-in-the-wall across from a large, grassy park. Captain Jordan ordered the food and it came after a long wait: purple stuff and green stuff and yellow stuff, greasy in the German manner. But it was good and spicy and after just a few minutes Leah felt happy and relaxed.

"May I call you Leah?" asked Jordan. "And please call me Matt."

"Did the visa come?" she asked slowly. She had hesitated to ask. She didn't really know why. Had the growing importance of Matt Jordan reduced the lure of Palestine?

He frowned and unbuttoned his shirt pocket and withdrew the folded green card. He passed it across the table to her and she held it carefully, examining the fancy seal on the outside, the English and Hebrew on the inside, and the official-looking stamps and signatures.

"It's the real thing, Leah, a ticket to Palestine."

She put it in her purse. "Thank you, Matt."

"But still," he said, "I can't really understand why you want to *go* there. You've already been through six years of war in Europe, and you want to leave the flames of hell and jump right into a boiling cauldron? What's the big attraction?"

Leah answered very solemnly. "It's to fulfill a pledge I made in my heart to a man who helped me after the war. I can't explain it so well. I met Yussel Pinsker in Warsaw. We were both starving beggars. He was a simple man, a pious man like may husband Daniel had been. And somehow, Yussel gave me the will to live again, even after what I had done to survive. I had degraded myself, lost everyone and everything. I had nothing left, no hope. And then I met Yussel, a tiny seventy-year-old cripple, emaciated from disease and starvation. But still he had something to live for, one great hope: Palestine. Sadly, he didn't live long enough for that. He died in Poland, just days after we met. His soul passed into mine to make me whole again, to make me want to live." Leah looked at Matt closely to see if he was amused by her, scoffing at her naiveté. He wasn't, or at least didn't seem to be. His face was clear and honest. She could feel his compassion.

"I really believe that," she went on, feeling more willing to share her thoughts with him now. "I really do believe that the soul of Yussel Pinsker has enabled me to survive. He died with his one dream left unfulfilled, to get to Palestine, to feel the Jewish sun, to pray at the Wailing Wall. I must do it for him, fulfill his still-empty dream."

Matt shook his head kindly. "But it's really not a Jewish sun, Leah. It's Arab. And as far as I can tell, the British have no intention of giving up the Mandate. You'd be better off in America, and I can get you there."

Leah looked at Matt intently. "What's America to me? I have no connections to *it*. Palestine is the last refuge, the last *malineh* for the Jewish people. In Deuteronomy, it tells of Moses gathering the Hebrews about him after they had wandered in the desert for many years and before they were permitted to enter the promised land, and Moses talks about the evil things that would befall the Jews before they entered the Land of Israel. We would recite this passage in Vilna every Shabbos: 'The Lord shall scatter thee among all people, to the ends of the earth. . . . And among these nations shalt thou find no solace, nor shall the soul of thy foot have rest, but the Lord shall give thee a failing of heart and failing of eyes and sorrow of mind. And thy life shall hang doubtful before thee, and thou shalt fear day and night and have no certainty of thy life. . . .'

"The truth of the condition of the Jews in Europe is that passage from Deuteronomy. I have experienced it. If there is a war in Palestine and I have to fight in it, at least I will be a free Jew fighting for my own country."

Leah studied the rugged face of the man sitting across the table from her. She imagined his touch, and—again for the first time in many many months—her body stirred. She wanted to know more about him, what he felt, what he was and wanted to be. She wanted him to understand the importance of going to Palestine, the Promised Land. But most of all, she wanted him to touch her.

"And you, Captain," she said. "How about you?"

"Matt, please call me Matt. Come on, let's walk in the park by the Pegnitz. It's beautiful there."

He took her arm and escorted her across the broad cobblestoned avenue. They walked to the glinting blue river and slowly strolled along it on its bank of voluptuous green dichondra.

"I was born in Brooklyn, New York, in 1917. My parents both came from Odessa, Russia. My father's name was originally Jordanovitch, but it was changed to Jordan by the immigration people at Ellis Island. It was easier for them to spell. My father and mother were tailors and worked in a sweatshop in the garment district. When the Depression started, my father decided the land of cowboys and Indians had to be better than our Brownsville tenement, so we drove out to Tucson, Arizona. My father, my mother, my big brother Budd, and our dog 'Rabies,' a little wire-haired terrier." Matt smiled at the memory.

"Tucson is very far from New York?" Leah asked.

Matt laughed. "About three thousand miles far," he said.

"And was it nice?"

"Well, there weren't any cowboys, and the Indians didn't look like they did in the movies. But it really was better than a Brooklyn slum. We lived in a tiny adobe house smack-dab in the middle of nowhere. Across the street was a water tower, and then desert stretched for miles to the Rillito River, which only had water in it in March or April, when the snow would melt down from the Catalina Mountains.

"There was a little synagogue in town, too far to walk to. So we would drive to services, even on Shabbos. The rabbi was an old Orthodox guy from the Lower East Side, and I went to Hebrew school every day after school. Dad and Mom opened a tailor shop downtown and eked out enough money to feed us. I got through the University of Arizona there on a scholarship and working nights as a desk clerk at a motel. Then I got a scholarship to study law in New York, at Columbia, so I picked up extra money teaching Hebrew to rich kids on Central Park West, and I managed to get through to my degree. My mother died of tuberculosis, and my father died of a heart attack, both within just a few months of each other. That was when I was in my second year of law school.

"When I graduated from Columbia, I went back to Tucson and became an Assistant County Attorney prosecuting criminals, and I'd still be there if I hadn't been drafted in 1943. So here I am, in Nuremberg, Germany."

"I'm glad you were drafted," she smiled, feeling very close to this Jewish fellow from the Wild West.

"I guess we better get you over to the hospital," Matt said, showing some hesitancy at the thought of leaving. "If you get there too late, the quartermaster will probably be gone and you won't be able to get sheets or a pillow."

They walked back to the jeep and drove to the hospital. Matt went with her to the supply office to get her linens, so there would be no language problems, no hassles. Her quarters were a small tent with three nurses. Not much different than Regensburg Camp, except here each bunk had a foot locker and a standing wall locker. There was no need for such things in Regensburg, since no one had anything to store or lock up. Leah opened her locker and hung up the clothes she'd bought at the PX and put the shoes on the floor. Jordan sat on her bunk, and she felt his probing eyes, and it felt good.

He stood in front of her before leaving, suddenly becoming quieter, more embarrassed than before. "Would you like to go out to dinner tonight?" he asked. "We could go over your testimony, if you want."

Leah felt flattered—amused by his awkward excuse—but she was very tired. Even the military bunk looked inviting after the cots she'd grown used to over the past months. "Maybe I'd better just stay here tonight and meet the nurses I'm living with," she said.

"Oh, don't worry about that. I'll get you back in time for that. Lights out isn't till eleven, and I'll get you back early, I promise."

Leah looked into his limpid brown eyes, and she deeply felt the need to be with him.

"Then first let me get freshened up and find my way around this place," she said to him. "How's that?"

"Great," he grinned. "I'll be back at six."

Alone, Leah eased onto the bed and relaxed, feeling full—both with food and with hope. New things were happening and would continue to happen. Her dream of Palestine was becoming reality, and now, a less expected dream had also entered the picture. Matthew Jordan. She thought of Daniel, her murdered husband, the man whose name she still carried, and she said a prayer to him. She had not forgotten him, and she felt sure that he had not forgotten her.

"You understand me, Daniel," she whispered. "I need to feel alive again."

Chapter Six

Matt shuffled papers in his office at the *Justizpalast* until the hands of the clock finally showed five. Then he hurried back to the Officers' Quarters at William O. Darby Post, showered, shaved off his afternoon stubble, and put on a clean uniform. For added flair, he even wore the red scarf of the paratroop contingent of the Third Armored Cavalry. As he tucked the scarf in, he hoped it might make him seem taller somehow—as if that might persuade Leah to stay behind with him. He stretched his neck and lifted his shoulders and examined the result in the mirror. Oh what the hell. Same old Matt. He smiled, saluted himself flippantly, and went outside to the jeep.

Down the road at the commissary, he bought a couple of tins of corned beef, a loaf of bread, some mustard, a large can of peach halves in syrup, two forks, a corkscrew, and a bottle of red wine. He drove to the nurses' quarters at the hospital and knocked on the thin wooden door of Leah's tent.

"Come in," hollered someone—not Leah.

Leah was leaning close to a small mirror, dabbing her lips with that same ruby-red lipstick. On another bunk, Matt noticed, a fat, homely nurse sat watching her, no doubt as awed as Matt himself.

"Hi-ya, Matt," said the fat nurse.

Matt pulled his eyes off Leah, finally recognizing the face and voice. "Ginger, it's you!" This Ginger had platinum hair all right, but she sure as hell was no Ginger Rogers. Matt had met her weeks before under rather odd circumstances. After he'd been out in the field for a long stretch, constantly on the move, he'd developed a painful and persistent case of jock itch. So he'd gone over to officers' minor sick call and was examined by Major Adams— whom everyone knew as Ginger. She told him to drop his pants and shorts, and then she fondled his penis and testicles in both hands like an avid milkmaid and held them up while she examined the underside of his crotch. Rather overly personal treatment, but Matt figured at the time that this was probably her only real contact with men, even in the middle of this battalion of horny G.I.'s.

"You're in for a real treat, honey," Ginger said, winking up at Leah and giggling. Matt felt the blood rise in his cheeks. Leah didn't understand, but she smiled at Ginger and tried out her new English phrase for the day: "See ya."

Alone again with Leah, Matt drove to the small lake near the *Stadion*, the parade ground and stadium for Hitler's mass rallies. Next to it, the incomplete red brick shell of the huge building that was to have been Hitler's new headquarters loomed with halted possibility, an unnerving reminder of what might have been. Next to it was the lake, nature's creation, in the middle of the wooded park, serene and lovely against the backdrop of the multicolored spring leaves and the luxuriant carpet of grass and ivy. A concession near the bank rented pedal boats, and farther up, a small carnival offered a ferris wheel and a merry-go-round and, of course, a beer tent. There were a few Germans with their children around the rides and a larger number sitting in or near the beer tent.

Matt spread an Army blanket on the grassy lakeside, and the two of them sat down, and he placed before them the things he had bought. "We," he said to her in English, "are having a *picnic*."

"Picnic," she repeated, then tried the word several times. "I won't forget that one." She caught Matt's eye and smiled. "This is very nice of you, a lovely farewell."

The idea of her leaving knifed at Matt, but he let the subject drop, and they ate quietly and hungrily. The wine helped warm them against the evening chill. They chatted like kids on a date— about everything and nothing, getting to know each other. His life had been quite simple, he told her. No battles waged in the streets of Tucson, no ducking from killers in the forests, no tragic loss of family or home or property. Then she told him more about herself, about her childhood in Vilna and her important father, and even about her husband, the rabbi.

After dinner, they rented a pedal boat and drifted around the lake. They sat close in the small seat, and Leah's lightly perfumed scent intoxicated him, even more than the wine. She let him wrap his arm around her, and she rested her cheek against his shoulder, and for those few moments he was able to forget about her imminent departure. Tonight was all there was. But soon it got late and quite cool, and neither Matt's arms nor Leah's thin sweater could fight off the German spring, and they finally had to pedal back to shore.

He drove her back to the hospital. In the jeep, he tenderly stroked her hair and neck. They kissed softly, hesitantly, then more intensely—but only briefly. She went into the darkened tent, and he drove back to his quarters, full of the brisk night and the stars and the future. If only he could feel there would be one for them.

The next morning, he picked her up in his jeep at eight-thirty and they drove to his office. Something about the warm pink glow on her cheeks when she looked at him, her hair like a palomino's mane whipped by the cool breeze, made him catch his breath.

She'd be taking the stand tomorrow, and Matt wanted her to get the feel of the courtroom and see how the trial was conducted so it wouldn't come as a shock to her when things got underway. Matt had worked with many witnesses, survivors of the Holocaust, and they were often petrified when they first began testifying. He wanted to do his best to preview the scene for her so she could prepare herself for it.

They entered the huge trial hall and walked to the American prosecutors' table where Justice Jackson was preparing for the morning session. Jordan introduced Leah to the United States Supreme Court Justice, then escorted her to the back of the rapidly-filling spectators' section. Leah's face contorted with disgust and hate as the Nazi defendants were led by MP's through a side door into the docks.

They sat in rows, like sullen schoolboys—the leaders of history's greatest machine of mass murder, sitting silently in somber business suits, shorn of the emblems and trappings and hauteur of their former horrific power. In their stiffness, in the still-too-prideful lift of their chins and brows, Matt could see lingering there the gold braid of field marshals, he could hear the rattle of razor sharp sabers in gilded scabbards, he could feel the impudent mindset of men trained to love war, carnivores, impalers of the enemy in battles down the ages from Junkers to Janissaries to Achilles and Agamemnon. But something had gone desperately wrong, become terribly twisted, and the would-be noble warriors were but putrid piles of sick meat, not human—inhuman—jackals with the faces of men, wearing ties.

At noon, the court recessed until one-thirty. Matt walked with Leah to the Army Transportation Office in the east wing of the *Justizpalast*. The Palestine visa was useless without the means to travel there, and she had only the $20 which had been issued to her by the Jewish Welfare Board representative at Regensburg Camp, not enough to purchase tickets.

The military transportation officer, Captain DiGeorgio, looked Leah up and down, then winked appreciatively at Matt Jordan. He shuffled through a stack of papers and produced a package with her name on it. Inside were a series of rail tickets which would get her to Marseilles as well as a ticket on the *Ideleton*, a Greek freighter with several passenger cabins, which was leaving Friday afternoon for Haifa. If she took an afternoon train from Nuremberg tomorrow, she would make the connection. Everything was set.

Leah did not appear nearly as thrilled as Matt thought she would be, and though that seemed encouraging he felt depressed as well. Neither of them spoke. They walked to the Army commisary in the basement and passed through the lunch line with their trays. Leah didn't know what most of the food was, and she had little appetite anyway. She got some chocolate pudding and a small salad. Matt had lost his appetite at the transportation office, with the realization that in one more day she would be gone. He sat glumly at the little table, drinking bitter instant coffee and clacking a spoon on the table.

"Matt, please. That spoon."

He looked up at her in surprise and put the spoon down. "Sorry, Leah. I didn't even know I was doing it."

"What's wrong?" she asked him.

He felt like an injured child. "You know what's wrong, Leah. I don't want you to leave tomorrow. I want you to stay here."

"I can't." Her voice faltered, pleaded. "We've been through all of this. You know I *must* go to Palestine."

They sat somberly, silently. After their meager lunch, they walked slowly back upstairs to the trial hall where the afternoon session was set to begin. The morning had been taken up with technical matters, nothing very interesting. But now a little old man took the stand. His shriveled, gray, waxen skin contrasted cruelly with the richly polished black walnut-paneled witness stand. His testimony was gruesome: he'd been part of the medical experiments at Auschwitz, one of the human experimental animals. First one testicle had been removed and then the other. To achieve what scientific goal, nobody was quite sure. Not even the Nazis could explain it. Then he was injected with various disease germs into the bone marrow of his legs. As the litany of bestiality was revealed through the little man's testimony, Leah became increasingly pale, her hand in Matt's became increasingly cool. The testimony continued unrelentingly for over four hours.

As they left the trial chambers, Leah was very subdued. The reciting of the revolting torture of the witness, the sight of the unflinching Nazi leaders sitting in the dock—all of this had overwhelmed her. She didn't want to go out for dinner. It was too cold to have a picnic or walk by the river. Matt drove her to his quarters on Darby Post. He closed the door to his room behind them.

There was nowhere to sit, just the bed. She sat on it and wept quietly. He sat beside her and helped her off with her coat. Then he held her, smoothing her hair and kissing the tears from her cheeks. He wrapped her in his arms, not wanting to lose her, to let her get too far away.

Suddenly she pulled away from him and leapt out of bed with a scream. She backed up to the wall of the darkened room and her body shook with uncontrollable sobbing. She spread her arms to her side and pressed back against the wall, her face contorted with fear and pain. Matt sat on the bed, riveted in place by her fear, by her sudden loss of contact. . . .

Standartenführer *Mencken sits at Isaac Krens' desk in the Jewish police chief's office. Krens stands at attention in front of this Death Head Regiment Colonel and trembles. Mencken has straight blond hair, piercing blue eyes, a square, ruddy face. He is tall and powerfully built. His black uniform stretches tightly across his broad shoulders and slender waist and hips. His black kidskin boots are spit-polished to a mirror shine.*

The Colonel speaks neither Yiddish, Lithuanian, nor Polish. Krens speaks no German. Leah is therefore called in to translate. She enters the office, leaving the apartment door open so she can hear if Nachman stirs.

Leah looks at Standartenführer *Mencken, and immediately she is terrified. She has seen that leer before on other faces, and she looks quickly away so as not to encourage him. Krens sees the fear in Leah's face and the quickened look in Mencken's eyes. His trembling increases.*

Mencken turns to the Ghetto Chief of Police and speaks slowly as Leah translates into Yiddish. The refuges must be discovered and destroyed. No malinehs for the Jews. The Jewish policemen must help the German Einsatzkommandos find all of the unregistered Jews. . . .

Mencken stands and comes around the desk. "Wait for me on the street by my command car." Krens shudders but instantly obeys, leaving Leah alone with the German. The Colonel motions for her to sit in one of the chairs and he takes the other.

"Are you that pig's wife, that pock-faced Police Chief?"

"Oh no Herr Standartenführer," *answers Leah, taking her blue pass out of her skirt pocket and handing it to him. "I am his daughter."*

Mencken looks at the pass and laughs. "So you Jews play the same games with family passes that they did in Kovel. Well, we will soon fix that." His voice becomes harder. "Are you that pig's woman?"

Leah nods, afraid to lie, afraid even to speak because she isn't sure that she still has a voice.

Mencken stands and walks to her and pulls her up. He leads her into the apartment. Nachman sleeps soundly, bundled in his blanket. In the bedroom, Mencken seats her on the bed and lifts her sweater over her head and arms. His face is drawn, his eyes as hard and lifeless as billiard balls. He pushes the straps of her slip over her arms and pulls the slip down to her waist. He kneels and sucks with thin, cool lips on her nipples as he fondles her breasts. Involuntarily her nipples harden. His spatulate fingernails scrape against her large areolas. She feels a wave of nausea overwhelm her.

Mencken shoves her back on the bed and pushes her loose skirt up, pulls her panties down. Her legs are bent over the edge of the bed. He kneels again on the floor between her knees and spreads her thighs, and she feels his tongue and his lips.

He stands and pulls her to a sitting position on the edge of the bed. He unbuttons his heavy uniform trousers. He presses himself to her lips and holds her head, forcing her, and he rocks back and forth in her. He finally comes with great groans, and just as suddenly she spits it on the floor and runs into the bathroom, slamming the door. She vomits into the toilet.

She weeps for a moment, horrified, sickened, but presses her mouth and nose so that he will not hear her. She rinses her mouth and composes herself and wipes her face, but she can still smell him on her, in her. She pulls up her

slip and replaces the straps on her shoulders. She attempts to will away her
terror, but it has gripped her, paralyzing her.

She returns to the edge of the bed and sits down next to Mencken, afraid
to look at him. He is sitting quietly, his pants buttoned. He slaps her hard
across the face. "Don't you ever spit me out!"

Matt Jordan was frightened, he had no idea what to do. Slowly
he eased off the bed and tried to soothe her. "Leah. Leah, it's all
right. It's okay, you're safe." Her shoulders still shook, and when he
reached out to touch her she spun away with a cry of pain and
slumped to the floor, hiding her face in her hands, unable to stop
weeping.

"I'll take you back to your quarters," he said gently, afraid to get
too near, afraid to touch her. She stood slowly and put on her
overcoat, looking at him blankly as though she could not recognize
him. She walked shakily out of the room. In the corridor she
stopped again, and her shoulders shook with soft weeping.

This time she accepted his comfort, turning slowly into his
arms, hugging him. She held him tightly and put her face on his
chest and wept.

"Oh God," she said. "I'm sorry, Matthew." They stood in the
chilly darkness for minutes until she stopped crying. Then she took
his hand and led him back to the room. Exhausted, they lay
together on the bed, fully clothed.

"Hold me, Matthew. Just hold me."

Matt felt muted by her pain, engulfed in her helpless suffering.
He longed to kiss her and make it better, like his mother had done
for him when he was a child and had scraped his knee or cut a
finger. But what could he kiss away? Leah's injury was too deep, too
piercing, far beyond his capacity to heal. They lay there clasped
hard to one another, and they dozed fitfully through the night.

In the morning, he drove her to her quarters to shower and
change and get ready to testify. When she came out, he winced
when he saw that she had with her a small cardboard valise. She
really was going to leave for Palestine.

They drove to the *Justizpalast* and went directly to the trial hall.
Justice Jackson took her and Matt aside and spoke to her, with Matt
as interpreter, about the general outline of his questioning. Then
the trial was convened, and she was called to the stand as the
prosecution's witness.

She was in control of herself, and Matt's fear for her gradually decreased as she unfolded her story. Minutely she described the three times she'd been within the walls of Treblinka's headquarters. Then the lunch recess was declared. Leah accompanied Justice Jackson to his office so they could prepare for the afternoon session. Once again, Matt went along as interpreter. They ate sandwiches and drank bitter Army coffee. Leah was holding up well.

They went back into the trial hall at one twenty-five, and the prisoners were already in the docks. Hans Frank was in an animated discussion with his attorney at the glistening walnut railing in front of the docks. When Leah came in, he looked away from her as if to hide his face. She stared at him with stony hatred as she walked to the witness stand. The trial resumed. She testified in Yiddish, since there was no official Army Hebrew interpreter. Most of the participants in the courtroom listened through headphones to one of the simultaneous translations being done in Russian, French, German, and English.

"Had you ever seen the defendant Hans Frank before you first came into these chambers yesterday?" asked Justice Jackson.

"Yes, sir."

"Where was that?"

"At Treblinka killing center."

There was a rustle in the courtroom.

"When was it?"

"It was in the spring of 1943. I do not remember the exact date."

"Can you identify him today?"

"Yes, sir. He is the third from the right in the second row."

Frank squirmed nervously in his chair but looked straight ahead, not turning his head toward the witness. The other defendants seemed almost imperceptibly to shift in their chairs away from Frank, away from the witness' accusitorily pointed finger.

"On what occasion did you see him?"

"He was making an inspection tour of Treblinka with an entourage of other killing center commanders."

The rustle among the spectators turned to a murmur of surprise. "Do you know who some of the others were?" asked Jackson.

"I only remember two names. Hoess, the Auschwitz commander, and Globocnik, the commander of Belzec and Sobibor."

The murmur from the onlookers became a loud gasp. Hans Frank was finished! Several of the large corps of reporters rushed out of the courtroom to cable the news to their agencies. The chief judge rapped his gavel to restore order.

Under further questioning, Leah described the luncheon that she had served to Hans Frank and detailed the technical talk of mass killing that had absorbed the Nazis. Then she testified about the visit that Mencken had made to Krakow two weeks later, to report to Hans Frank's headquarters.

"What happened when he returned?"

Leah looked down at her hands and her composure broke. The spectators were hushed. As she began to recite the rest of her story, she wept uncontrollably. Matt Jordan could not watch her suffering or listen to her story again. His pain for her was so choking that he had to leave the courtroom. Nauseated, he needed air, air not filled with the stifling stench of the sick Nazi scum sitting in the docks and trying to look bored and detached. Matt quickly left the courtroom.

Down the corridor he started running for the side exit of the huge building. He rushed outside into the mild spring air and breathed deeply, then sat down on the cement steps at the side door. Gradually he began to feel better and the sick feeling left him. He got up and walked past the line of flowering oleanders and out of the rear courtyard of the *Justizpalast* onto the broad northern bank of the Pegnitz River, splendid with blood-red poppies and startling edelweiss and rich emerald-mantled oak trees. He walked along the clear gurgling river watching the ubiquitous shepherds and the grazing bleating flocks of pure white fleeced sheep. How different was this Germany from the one pictured in the courtroom inside. How peaceful and picturesque and bucolic was this Nuremberg, not the city of Nazi Party rallies and jackbooted stormtroopers of just a year ago.

It was three-thirty, and Matt estimated that her direct testimony would be well over by now and the cross-examination would be in full swing. He felt somewhat revived, and walked slowly back into the *Justizpalast* down the huge echoing corridor and into the trial hall. It was empty.

Leah! Gone already? He ran back to the prosecution's wing and asked the WAC secretary when the afternoon session had ended. She said that the defense had waived cross-examination of Leah and that the trial had recessed over an hour ago. Mrs. Arad had waited for Jordan, then Justice Jackson had detailed an MP to take her to the *Hauptbahnhof* to catch a train. At least thirty minutes ago.

He ran out to his jeep and gunned it toward the main railway station three miles away. He parked at the curb and took the broad stone steps two at a time into the immense high-ceilinged station. There was one train in, and a small group of people milled about getting ready to board. He saw Leah sitting on a bench.

"My God, I thought I missed you!" he blurted.

A look of relief spread over her face. "Oh, Matthew, I'm so glad you came! I looked for you and waited, but finally I had to leave."

"Please, Leah, don't go." He sat beside her and took both of her hands in his. "I can't let you go. Please." How had it happened so soon, that he needed her so deeply?

She leaned forward and kissed him softly. "Matthew," her voice was faint, trembling, "you and I are from different ends of the universe. I know that you can't understand why I must go to Palestine. I know you think that because you and I found something together that all of our problems are solved. Love conquers all, like in the movies. But this isn't the movies. Inside me is the soul of Yussel Pinsker, a little tortured Jew, just like that man who testified yesterday about the medical experiments at Auschwitz. And Yussel's soul, yearning for Palestine, is what made me able to stay alive. I must go." She stood up. The people on the platform were nearly through boarding. Matt stood with her, looking forlornly into her tortured gray eyes.

"Goodbye, my sweet, loving Matthew," she said softly, kissing him again. She walked slowly across the platform and up the steps into the car. He stood there, petrified to the spot, unable to stop her, unable to do anything but drown in surging emptiness and watch Leah Arad leave his life.

Chapter Seven

Leah sat on the hard bench as the train rolled slowly out of Nuremberg, and she watched the city's buildings turn to a blur through teary eyes. She cried for her family—for father and Daniel and Nachman, for her mother, her brother Jonathan, and all the others whom she had loved so much, all of whom were now part of Europe's dust. Leaving Europe, Leah was leaving behind most of her life. All of the familiar sights of Vilna, all the sounds and smells and feelings, all of that would be gone now, and she wept a bitter farewell to that part of her life. Gone. Those people would live through her, she promised them, in the Jewish state soon to be established in Palestine.

The horror-laden memories roiled in her soul. The tears were for all of her family, for all that had been. But that was done, and she had managed to go on, to live. And now, somehow, she knew that the pain she felt most at this precise moment, the tears that fell the hardest, were for Matthew Jordan.

Perhaps she'd made a mistake in leaving; perhaps she'd find no other man as loving and as gentle and innocent as he. But Nuremberg was a town of ghosts, filled with the desecrated, maimed remnants of war. And America held nothing for her. Palestine was the Promised Land, and she willed herself to believe that it was filled with *promise* of every kind. She thanked God for sending Matt when He did. But now she must go on, to her last *malineh*.

Days later, in Palestine at last, Leah disembarked and began the process of officially entering this exotic land. First there was British customs to go through, but that didn't take long since Leah had only a small canvas bag and six American dollars to declare. Then came Jewish customs and a questionnaire to be completed. She gave a skimpy account of her odyssey from Vilna to Haifa, and she listed David Brod, Kibbutz Na'on, as her only known relative in Palestine. The Jewish customs inspector quickly scanned the form, looked hard at Leah, and asked her to wait in a small office.

The young inspector returned after ten minutes. "Your brother David has asked us to see you safely to Tel Aviv. We have a car outside and a driver will take you. Your brother will meet you there."

Leah was thrilled—and more than a bit surprised. She had not seen David since she was nine years old. He'd left Vilna for Palestine in 1931 at the age of twenty. She remembered him as a tall, robust man, like their father, but she really couldn't remember exactly what he looked like.

A military jeep pulled up—with a large white Star of David painted on the door, Leah noticed—and the driver helped her and her baggage into the back seat. This man was quite a contrast to the men of Europe, particularly those of the past five years. He didn't stare or leer at her. Rather, he treated her politely, almost diffidently. He called her *"g'veret nichbada"* [Dear Madam], and in the car he kept his eyes trained straight ahead, watching only the road. Leah had no idea why, but she supposed that David must be some kind of important man. She was very excited about seeing him again, and very happy about having found him so easily.

They drove sixty miles to Tel Aviv, then down to Arlosoroff Street to the corner where Ben Yehuda met Hayarkon, to an unimposing dilapidated stone building three stories high. For a moment, Leah thought she'd been all wrong; this didn't seem like the office of a very powerful man.

Then a tall, well-built redhead in army fatigues came springing out of the front door. Leah stepped out of the jeep, recognizing her brother at once, as though she had seen him for the last time just yesterday.

"Leahleh, Leahleh, what a woman you've become!"

They hugged each other, holding each other hard and close.

"I never thought I'd see any of you again, Leahleh," David said, his eyes rimmed with tears. "Come into my office and rest for a while."

He put his arm around his sister, took her cardboard valise, and they walked through the front door held open by a young soldier. They walked down a hallway to a small shabby office, sparsely furnished with an old metal desk and three folding chairs.

"What are you, David? What is this place?"

David grinned. "I am an *Aluf* [General], Assistant Chief of Operations for the General Staff of the Haganah. When I dropped out of school to come to Palestine, did you ever think I'd become a General?" He laughed and smiled at Leah.

"Let me start from the beginning," he said. "I have no idea how much you know."

"Tell me everything," Leah told him. "I want to hear it all."

"Okay. First of all, as you know, I was one of the founders of Kibbutz Na'on in 1931. I and about thirty other settlers from Poland and Lithuania set up tents in the middle of this malarial swamp and started draining it and fertilizing the earth as it dried. We were all teenagers or in our early twenties, and we were young and strong enough to overcome the onslaughts of mosquitoes and locusts and one hundred thirty degree winds called the Hamsin, and drought and famine and flood and disease.

"We improved the land all right, but in 1933, Kibbutz Na'on decided it needed real expertise in farming if it was ever really going to survive. We decided that one of us had to go to school. Unfortunately, the Haifa Technion's tuition and dormitory fees exceeded the total wealth of Na'on. So I wrote to father and asked for the money. He immediately sent a certified letter of credit to the Technion, and I was admitted. In May 1937, I graduated as a mechanical engineer with a sub-specialty in hydrological engineering. From my experiments with various irrigation systems, Na'on was able to begin its cotton farm and pear orchard. The sprinkler factory was an offshoot of my solution to the watering of the alfalfa fields on which our small herds of cattle and sheep pasture."

"That's fantastic," Leah said. It all sounded so exciting to her. Her brother was a real pioneer of the Holy Land. "But what does farming have to do with being a General?"

David raised a finger and continued. "I served in a special Jewish commando unit organized and trained by a British Captain named Orde Wingate. He chose a few members of the Haganah and trained us as 'Jewish Special Night Squads.' We conducted guerrilla warfare against marauding Arab villagers in Lebanon and Syria as well as 'active defense' against Palestinian Arab terrorists under the Mufti Haj Amin el-Husseini. Wingate's training created a corps of highly trained officers, and several of us have risen to the leadership of the Haganah." He paused and looked closely at his sister. His gray eyes were just like hers, bottomless, sad—but at this moment triumphant as well.

Then he darkened a bit and looked down. He had hesitated to ask, fearful, expecting the worst but hoping for good news. "And you, Leahleh, can you tell me about our family? I have heard from Chava and Josef in New York, but they also know nothing of the family."

There was no other way for Leah to say it. "Everyone is dead but me," she said, looking into her brother's eyes. She told him the things that she had lived through, the fate of their family. David sat with his face buried in his hands, his elbows on his knees. Several times he wept openly. Then she told him about her resurrection from the dead with the help of Yussel Pinsker and Matthew Jordan. Sweet, loving Matthew, whom she had left just six days ago.

David was unable to speak for several minutes after she finished her story. The worst had been confirmed. He stood and walked around the desk and gently held Leah's teary face in his hands.

"You will come live with me and my wife, Deena," he told her. "We have a small extra room, and we'll move the baby's crib into the parlor." He paused and looked earnestly into her eyes. "I cannot tell you how happy Deena and I will be to have you with us." This last gesture meant everything to Leah: she had almost no family left, so to be unconditionally accepted into David's home helped her feel needed, and situated, in this new place.

David took her by the hand and picked up the suitcase, and they walked into another office down the hall. He told a young soldier to drive Leah home, and he kissed her on the forehead and hugged her.

"I'll call Deena and tell her you'll be there soon. I'll be home later."

Deena, it turned out, was a "sabra," a Jew born in Palestine. Named after the fruit of the prickly pear cactus, the sabras were typically rough and abrasive to strangers, and mushy and sweet and loving to their family and friends. Deena was born in Degania Kibbutz, on the Sea of Galilee, in 1918.

In 1940, David and Deena had met, and they were married in 1941. Their first son died in a cholera epidemic in 1943. Their second son Jacob was born in 1946. He was dark like his mother.

Deena Brod was as black-haired and olive-skinned as Leah was blond and alabaster. She had big piercing black eyes and short glistening hair. She was tall and slender and as sleek as a sable. She spoke with the throaty contralto tones of a torch singer. As soon as Leah stepped into the house, Deena took her in her arms and hugged her as though she were her own sister. She had already taken the baby's crib out of the little bedroom and put it in a corner of the parlor. Exhausted from the emotions of landing in Palestine and finding her family, Leah hugged Deena once again then lay down on the small bed and dozed off for almost two hours. Peace at last. When she awoke, she felt alive again.

David was already home, changed from his general's uniform to the customary shorts and thin cotton shirt of summertime Palestine. The Brods lived in a small stone house on Herbert Samuel Street, across from a grassy park and the beautiful white sands of the Mediterranean seashore, where Jewish Tel Aviv met the northern edge of the ancient Arab seafaring city of Jaffa. Because of David's high position in the Haganah, he had rated what were considered rather nice accommodations in the cities of the Yishuv [Jewish Palestine]—two bedrooms, a large parlor, a separate kitchen and dining area, and a little garden of dazzlingly fragrant orange trees and multicolored petunias behind the house.

They sat around the small kitchen table and ate herring and tomatoes and cucumbers.

"Next Tuesday, Leah, I have a meeting with a mutual friend of ours," said David with a smile spreading over his face. "I got word to him today that you were coming. I'm sure he'll be delighted to see you. Rabbi Israel Sassover."

David winked, but Leah was puzzled for a moment, unable to place the name. Then she brightened as it came to her: Menachem Begin.

"That's the same alias he used in Vilna six years ago," Leah said, "when he used to come to father's house for donations to help support his Zionist youth group." She paused a moment, squinting. "The 'Betar,' I think it was."

David nodded. "He told me that the alias had served him well for a long time, Israel Sassover. I guess he was right."

"Back then," Leah went on, "he was in hiding from the Russians. They declared all Zionist groups subversive. Father helped him with money and influence as much as he could, but Begin was arrested in 1940 and thrown into Lukiszki prison. Then we lost track of him."

"Well, he ended up being freed by the Russians, and he joined the Free Polish Army and was sent as a Private to the detachment stationed in Jerusalem. That was 1942. Then he joined the Irgun Tzvai Leumi [National Military Organization] and became its leader a year later. He's been in hiding for two years with a price on his head, and most Jews now consider him a cold-blooded terrorist."

"I don't get it," said Leah. "You're a General in the Haganah, and you're meeting with a 'cold-blooded terrorist'?"

"Yes, politics." David shrugged his shoulders. "From time to time, Irgun and the Haganah mount combined campaigns to steal British arms or blow up bridges or supply trains or military installations. And then again, from time to time the Haganah is ordered by Ben-Gurion to help search out and arrest Irgun members. It has to do with a couple of things."

"Yes," piped in Deena, who was busy feeding Jacob. "Mostly that the Old Man—Ben-Gurion—hates political competition, and he sees Menachem as a potentially popular leader, so he'd like to see him get killed off by the British or the Arabs!"

"Come on now," chided David. "Don't be so cynical." He turned back to Leah. "Maybe that *is* a part of it, but there's a more important part. The Irgun's emblem—Begin's emblem—is an arm holding a rifle over the map of Palestine and Transjordan, with the motto '*Rak Kach*' ['Only Thus']. That's the real problem. Begin sees the issue of a Jewish National Home as the fulfillment of the Biblical promise that God made to give the Jews *all* of Eretz Yisrael—the *Biblical* Land of Israel—and that means that Begin wants a Jewish State in all of the British Mandate, all of Palestine including Transjordan. But in reality, we're never going to get it. We'll be lucky if the United Nations gives us just a wrinkled little ribbon of land."

Leah looked thoughtfully at her brother and sister-in-law. "I can't say I disagree with Menachem," she said. "I mean, this is *our* promised land, and I didn't do what I did to survive and come all the way here to hunker down to the goyim like a boot-licking dog, and accept almost nothing, particularly after what they've done to us over the last ten years."

"Look, Leah. Maybe you and Begin are right. I don't know. But all I am is an officer in the Haganah. That means I work for Ben-Gurion and the Jewish Agency. I follow their policy of *havlaga* [restraint]. I'm not sure who the hell's right about everything—whether it's Ben-Gurion or Begin or someone else we haven't even heard from yet. But nobody asked me. They just told me to be the liaison officer between Irgun and Haganah, and that's it. I leave all the rest to the politicians."

Four days later, David and Leah dressed nondescriptly in the shorts, sandals and white short-sleeved shirts of the Yishuv, and took a bus through Tel Aviv to Bin Nun Street. They walked quickly through alleys and streets, David continually checking to see if he could spot any surveillance. There was none. They entered a back gate into an overgrown garden of unruly orange honeysuckles and wild yellow and red zinnias and knocked softly on the frail slatted kitchen door of a tiny dilapidated wooden house. Most of its once white paint had long since chipped off or sunburned to gray. Aliza Begin opened the door a crack, then pulled it open all the way, smiling at David as at an old friend.

"*Baruch haba*, David. And this must be your sister, Leah. Thank God at least you lived through the Holocaust." She hugged Leah warmly and continued. "Menachem is expecting you. He will be so pleased."

They walked through the parlor into a tiny back bedroom which Begin had converted to his study. He rose and looked at Leah and broke into a wide smile.

"Leah, *baruch hashem*, God has brought you back to us healthy and safe. I was so happy yesterday when I heard you had managed to enter Eretz Yisrael. Please sit. We'll all have some juice."

As in most of the Yishuv, citrus juice substituted for alcoholic beverages in the entertaining of guests. The slivovitz of Eastern Europe was too expensive in Palestine, and the Jews tended to shun whiskey and gin because it was drunk by the hated British. Aliza brought in a pitcher of grapefruit juice and three glasses. She left the room and closed the door.

David handed Menachem the message he was carrying from the Haganah commander:

> You are to carry out as soon as possible the "chick" and the house of "Your Slave and Redeemer." Inform us of the time. Best to do both simultaneously. Don't publicize identity of force used, even by implication.

Begin struck his thigh with a tight fist. "So the Haganah has finally agreed to bomb the King David Hotel. This will be the biggest blow yet to the British." Irgun had long proposed the bombing of British Military Headquarters and Colonial Civil Headquarters in the southern wing of the King David Hotel in Jerusalem, as well as the neighboring building carrying the name of the builders, the David Brothers. The code name "chick" was short "malonchik" [little hotel], and "Your Slave and Redeemer" was the code for the David Brothers' Building, used as the headquarters of the British Military Police and the Special Investigation Bureau.

David put down his juice glass. "We want those British intelligence files at the hotel destroyed, Menachem. They're potentially damaging to all of us. But the Old Man wants to be absolutely sure the bomb goes off when no one's around. He doesn't want a bloodbath."

"We are not the Stern Gang, David," Begin said defensively. "We'll give the British warning after we plant the explosives so they can clear out their personnel, but not so long that they'll have time to remove the files."

"Right," said David. "Let us know the plan and the time so we'll be prepared. There's bound to be a major crackdown by the British police."

"And you, Leah," Begin asked. "Are you ready to help us win our freedom?"

Leah looked at her brother, and he nodded.

Chapter Eight

Three days after her reunion with Begin, Leah Arad walked into a small dark Arab cafe in Jaffa, anxious to join the active struggle for Jewish freedom. She had been in Palestine for a week.

She'd been instructed to meet a man named Yisrael Levi, part of the Irgun team. He would recognize her. She looked around the crowded, smoky cafe, unsure of herself, unsure of what to do, trying to look like an average Jewish settler and not an undercover Irgun freedom fighter. Just as the cafe owner approached, smiling expectantly, a young man at a distant corner table waved her over. He was sandy-haired and freckle-faced, in his early twenties. In the thin lighting his skin looked too pallid and finely wrinkled for so young a man, and when he stood to greet her Leah thought that his hunched, gaunt frame and hollow cheeks betrayed consumption.

They greeted each other loudly, as though they knew each other well, and she sat down.

"I sure hope you're Yisrael Levi," she said, scraping her chair in under the small table.

"Yes—but let's leave here. It's too risky to talk."

They walked slowly to the bus stop to wait for the sightseeing tour to Jerusalem, saying nothing. The young man coughed continually into a soiled handkerchief.

"Tuberculosis?" Leah asked.

"No, no, no," he reassured her. "Just bronchitis."

She felt somewhat safer, but she wasn't sure that she believed him. The last thing she needed was to survive the Nazis and catch TB in Israel.

"So how much experience do you have?"

Leah shook her head. "None."

He stopped coughing, looked with earnest eyes over the dirty handkerchief. "Scared?" he asked.

"Yes, I really am. I've never done anything like this, even in Europe during the war. Everytime I look around I think there must be a British policeman there to arrest me."

"Don't worry," said Levi. "I promise we'll be okay. I've been working on this plan for weeks. We won't even be near the place when it blows."

His assurance did little to settle Leah's nerves. "Where are we going?" she asked.

"The Regency Cafe at the King David Hotel. I've got to look the place over good and make sure it'll work."

The sightseeing bus picked them up a few minutes later, then drove slowly through the rough hills around Jerusalem which the Bible calls "the Shephelah," and finally to the old walled city, where it stopped at Jaffa Gate near the Tower of David. Leah and Yisrael Levi took the walking tour with the rest of the tourists, mostly British and American, and walked the Via Dolorosa through St. Stephen's Gate, down the Kidron Valley and up the hill on the other side through the Garden of Gethsemane to the panoramic view from the Mount of Olives. Though Leah was here for other, more important reasons, she enjoyed the tour because she was, after all, still a newcomer to this wondrous city. After lunching in a tiny restaurant run by a Russian Orthodox monastery, the group retraced its steps back to the bus, pointing and chatting and pointing some more.

Leah and Yisrael got "lost" in the Arab market place, the souk, and missed the bus. They wandered around the souk stalls for a short while, then sat for three hours at an Armenian cafe drinking tea and eating humous, a thick gruel made of ground chickpeas and sesame seed oil.

Finally, at seven o'clock, they went to the Regency Cafe, a popular watering place for Palestine's rich and powerful Arabs, Jews, and highly-placed British officials, both military and civilian.

Leah looked around the gracious room. "David told me about this place," she said. "And he was right. These people look awfully rich."

"Well, if not rich, at least better off than us," said Yisrael a bit ruefully.

"What do we do, just sit here?" she asked.

"No. We dance, we watch, we wait. I have to find the right moment to go into the kitchen and check it out. It's right under British Headquarters, and the pillars supporting the whole south wing of the hotel are in the kitchen."

He got up and extended his hand to her. It was a slow foxtrot and he held her closely. He was a poor dancer, and she didn't want to be held by him. Consumption or not, his constant coughing continued to bother her. And each time she looked at Levi, the only man she wanted to see was Matthew Jordan.

"Listen, just take it easy," he whispered in her ear. "I'm not here to try and shtupp you, but we can't attract any attention. The best thing is just relax. We'll dance a little, drink a little, dance a little. I've got to wait till the time is right, then I'm going to take a look in the kitchen and we can leave."

She forced herself to loosen up, and pressed herself to him like a young lover on a date. Over the next five hours, she had several martinis and managed to relax.

"I'm going to the kitchen now," he said. It was a little after midnight. "If there's any ruckus, just get the hell out of here fast and go back to Tel Aviv."

She walked back to their table, becoming very nervous again. Levi went quickly through the swinging doors into the kitchen. Just a few moments later he was back.

"Well," he said loudly, startling her, "I guess Kamil isn't coming in to work tonight. Might as well leave."

They left the cafe and walked another four or five blocks to the

Irgun safe house. Three other Irgun members were waiting for them there.

The next morning, Leah and Yisrael and the three other Irgun members hijacked a milk truck, bound and gagged the driver, and drove to the Hotel. Leah didn't do much, just sat quietly and fearfully. It was well before lunchtime when they arrived at the Regency, and only a skeleton crew was in the kitchen. Leah held a submachine gun on the petrified staff while the others bound and gagged them. Despite her resolve, she held the gun unsteadily with trembling hands, not knowing if it was actually loaded, or if she could get herself to pull the trigger even if she had to. Yisrael set explosives next to the major weight-bearing pillars in the Cafe kitchen directly under British headquarters, and then the employees were untied and told to flee.

The Irgun team drove a few blocks away, stopped at a pay phone, and Yisrael made a telephone call to Sir John Shaw, the Secretary to the British Palestine government, at his office in the King David Hotel, to warn him that they had just thirty minutes to evacuate the Hotel before it would be leveled. Indignant, Sir John took the warning as a mere prank, screaming petulantly "I don't accept orders from Jews! I give the orders here!" Yisrael Levi slammed the phone down.

Thirty minutes later, a massive explosion rocked Jerusalem. Dozens of Englishmen, Jews and Arabs were killed, with well over a hundred others seriously injured. The whole southern wing of the King David Hotel was reduced to blood-splattered rubble.

A British manhunt immediately began. The Irgun terrorists scattered into hiding. With her brother David and his small family, Leah fled across the desert to Kibbutz Na'on, where there was a network of underground bunkers used to hide weapons and Jewish fugitives during the all-too-frequent British searches.

Chapter Nine

Matthew Jordan listened to the closing statement of the Chief British Prosecutor, Sir Hartley Shawcross. The only sound in the huge courtroom, besides Sir Hartley's stentorian voice, came from the prisoners in the dock—trying to appear bored, yawning and shifting in their chairs, flipping through pages of transcripts to keep their faces downcast.

"I am confident that this honorable tribunal well remembers the description of a mass execution by one of Himmler's 'action commandos.'" Shawcross fixed the judges with his jutting chin, his Oxford don's demeanor, as he read from the transcript of a Nazi soldier's prior testimony.

"Without screaming or weeping, these people undressed. They stood around in family groups, kissed each other, said farewells, and waited for a sign from another SS man, who stood near the pit, also with a whip in his hand. During the fifteen minutes that I stood near, I heard no complaint or plea for mercy. I watched a family of about eight persons, a man and a woman both about fifty with their children of about one, eight and ten, and two grown-up daughters of about twenty to twenty-four. An old woman with snow-white hair was holding the one-year-old child in her arms and singing to it and tickling it. The child was cooing with delight. The couple were looking on with tears in their eyes.

"The father was holding the hand of a boy about ten years old and speaking to him softly; the boy was fighting his tears. The father pointed to the sky, stroked his head and seemed to explain something to him.

"At that moment, the SS man at the pit shouted something to his comrade. The latter counted off about twenty persons and instructed them to go behind the earth mound. Among them was the family which I have mentioned. I well remember a girl, slim and with black hair, who, as she passed close to me, pointed to herself and said, 'Twenty-three.' I walked around the mound and found myself confronted by a tremendous grave. People were closely wedged together and lying on top of each other so that only their heads were visible. Nearly all had blood running over their shoulders from their heads. Some of the people shot were still moving. Some were lifting their arms and turning their heads to show that they were still alive. The pit was already two-thirds full. I estimated that it already contained about a thousand people.

"I looked for the man who did the shooting. He was an SS man who sat on the edge of the narrow end of the pit, his feet dangling into the pit. He had a tommy gun on his knees and was smoking a cigarette. The people, completely naked, went down some steps which were cut in the clay wall of the pit and clambered over the heads of the people lying there, to the place to which the SS man directed them. They lay down in front of the dead or injured people; some caressed those who were still alive and spoke to them in a low voice. Then I heard a series of shots. I looked into the pit and saw that the bodies were twitching or the heads lying motionless on top of the bodies which lay before them. Blood was running away from their necks."

Sir Hartley finished reading the transcript and glared at the prisoners in the dock. He slowly removed his spectacles.

"What special dispensation of Providence kept these men," he bellowed, sweeping his arm at the Nazi prisoners, "ignorant of these things, as they claim. For these are the mad animals who perpetrated these very outrages."

Kaltenbrunner remained, as always, expressionless. Goering supported his head on his hand and looked bored, then stirred uneasily in his chair and changed position, looking away from Shawcross. Hans Frank muttered viciously, *"Dass verdammte Englisher!"* ["That damn Englishman!"]

Sir Hartley turned disgustedly away from the prisoners and walked toward the tribunal, stopping but a few feet in front of the railing. His voice was soft, tremulous: "Mankind itself—struggling now to reestablish in all the countries of the world the common simple things—liberty, love, understanding—comes to this court and cries, 'These are our laws, let them prevail!' You will remember when you come to give your decision, the story of this mass execution. But not in vengeance. In a determination that these things shall never occur again. The father—you remember—pointed to the sky, and said something to his son."

Matthew Jordan was emotionally overcome by Shawcross's shattering summation. Tears filled his eyes as he walked heavily back to his office. He sat at his desk gritting his teeth. He finally could really comprehend what Leah and the others had been forced to do just to survive and why she had abandoned the Gentile world and sought refuge in Palestine. Not a single Christian leader, not Roosevelt or the Pope, had lifted a finger to help the Jews.

Try as he had over the weeks and months, Matt could not forget Leah Arad. For some reason, he couldn't purge himself of Leah's image, those sad deep gray eyes, the magnificent face, the tall slender body. And that night he'd held her in his arms, both of them bundled in their overcoats, that was the best night of his life. More than he needed to go home, back to the real world, he needed to see her again.

Matt put through his separation papers. The prosecution summations had ended his job here. He was free to leave the Army, become a civilian again. He asked Sir Hartley Shawcross's senior assistant to see if he could find out where Leah Arad was living in Palestine, at least where she was officially listed.

In early August, the assitant British prosecutor handed him a sheet of paper with David Brod's address on it. Two days later, Matt went to the Army Transportation office in the Palace of Justice.

He was met there with disbelief. "What are ya—outta your fuckin' mind?" Captain Tony DiGeorgio held the transit request papers at arm's length.

"Just show me the MATS list, Georgie."

"Hey man, I don't know what you're thinking. We ain't got no goddam flights to no Palestine. There's a fuckin' war goin' on over there!"

"C'mon, Georgie, just gimme the goddam list."

DiGeorgio reached for the clipboard hanging next to his desk and handed it to Matt. "Does this maybe have something to do with that blonde with the great ass you was in here with a few months back?"

Matt studied the list of regular Military flights leaving Nuremberg. "Looks like I have to go to Paris, then try to get a hop down to Marseilles."

"Naw, let me show ya." DiGeorgio grabbed the clipboard. "Best is to go to Genoa. 'Bout every two weeks we got a supply ship goes from there to Cyprus, then you can get a commercial freighter anytime from there into Haifa."

"Okay, write me up for the Genoa flight tomorrow."

DiGeorgio studied Matt's face. "Hey, you're really serious about this."

"You got it, Georgie. I took a European discharge yesterday."

"What are ya—out of your fuckin' mind?" This time his surprise was more genuine. "You and me was both at the fuckin' Battle of the Bulge. That wasn't enough for ya? I lost three goddam toes to frostbite."

"It doesn't snow in Tel Aviv," Matt said lamely. "Just gimme a break and write me the chit."

"Jesus fuckin' Christ..." DiGeorgio breathed out slowly. "Lemme give ya a little advice, huh, Matty boy?"

"Okay Georgie, get it off your chest."

"I mean—I feel I owe ya, after how ya helped me with the old man after I spent a little time with that Kraut broad." He winked conspiratorially at Matt.

"So if you owe me, pay me," said Matt, holding out his hand, palm up.

"Listen to me! I'm payin' ya off with advice!"

"Debts like yours gonna make me rich, Georgie."

"Seriously, man. Where you from, Phoenix, Tucson, somethin' like that?" He didn't wait for a reply. "You're a goddam lawyer. You can go live in a big house in the foothills with a big pool in your backyard and you'll have goddam pussy wrigglin' all over your pool deck all friggin' night long. You'll be a big shot rich guy! But all you're gonna get in Palestine is your goddam balls shot off!"

"Listen Georgie, try to comprehend this." Matt was getting annoyed with this moron. "I'm a *Jew,* and there's a war going on for a Jewish state. *My* state, *my* people. And I also happen to want to see a certain woman again."

"What the hell's the sense in that? I'm a Catholic, right? That mean I'm supposed to go live in Rome and suck spaghetti all day long in fronna St. Peter's? Shit, man! Remember what Rome was like when we got done with it? Fuckin' pile of rocks, kids beggin' all over the place, twelve-year-old girls havin' to sell nookie for a meal. I'll be damn happy to forget Rome an' go back to the good ol' U. S. of A. and be a *plenty good* Catholic!"

"It's different," was all Matt could say, not entirely sure what the difference was; in fact, not sure about anything at all except that he had to see Leah Arad again.

"Yeah, the only thing different is it's a helluva lot more dangerous where *you're* goin'."

"You don't understand."

"Hey, I understand. You're a love-sick som-bitch!" DiGeorgio laughed, not very happily. He crossed himself dramatically. "Requiescat in packy, baby."

Matt finally arrived in Haifa late in August, on a dank oppressive day when even the giant sunflowers were curling up and bending over like they were looking for shade. He immediately hired a taxi for the short trip to Tel Aviv. Since he was still in his military uniform, he wasn't detained long at the three British roadblock checkpoints along the way. The color of Germany had been green, all shades of green. From the brilliant lime of the Linden trees to the forest green of Aspens to the deep emerald of the oak foliage and dense rye grass and low shrubs which grew everywhere. Israel's colors, however, were shades of brown. The drab yellow-brown of the stone and wood houses, the many hued beiges of the miles of untilled dirt which lined the highway, the browns of the Aleppos and Mediterranean pines, even their needles sunburned from green to rust in the relentless sun.

Matt gave the driver David Brod's address, and soon the taxi pulled up in front of a small stone house. He asked the driver to wait.

There was no answer at the door. The drapes were drawn, and Matt saw that dust had settled on the doorknob. The small grass lawn was overgrown and parched a pale brown. He walked to the neighboring house and knocked on the front door. An elderly man opened it, looking suspiciously through the footwide crack.

"I'm looking for Leah Arad. She was supposed to be living next door with her brother."

"Who are you?"

"Matthew Jordan. I'm a Jew from the United States. I met Mrs. Arad when she was in Nuremberg. I was a lawyer with the American occupation forces."

"What do you want with her?"

"I—" He couldn't think of anything that might persuade the old man that he was safe, an ally. "I just want to see her," he said, deciding on simple honesty. "I—I just have to see her again." He felt very stupid.

The old man's wife poked her head into view. "Are you that American lawyer she met at the trials?"

"Yes! That's me. My name's Matthew Jordan."

"He already told me that, woman," the old man said, pushing at his wife. "Get back in there." He turned back to Matt and squinted through thick lids. "They don't live there anymore," he said. "There've been manhunts for weeks for leaders of the Irgun and the Haganah. David is a high officer. That's all I can tell you. He must be in hiding."

Matt knew he was getting closer—but not yet close enough. "How can I find them?"

"David lived at Kibbutz Na'on before coming here. Maybe they'll know." He started to shut the door.

"How do I get there?"

"Ask the taxi driver." With that, the old man disappeared, and the door clattered shut.

Matt got back in the taxi. "Driver, have you by any chance heard of a Kibbutz Na'on?"

"Sure I have. But listen, friend, I'm already over sixty miles from home. Na'on's another fifteen or so. You want me to take you, it'll be another ten American dollars."

"Let's go."

They drove through the scorching countryside, farther and farther from the sea, and the heat descended like a wide, burning umbrella. Just like Tucson, thought Matt, but a lot more humid. They drove through Rishon le-Zion, one of the Yishuv's first settlements in the 1890s, and then through Rehovot, a dusty, poor desert town. They drove a few miles farther down the rutted narrow asphalt road and then turned off onto a cart track. The taxi drove slowly about two miles through expansive fields of ripening cotton. They came to a circle of giant cottonwood trees shading a small brown wooden building with a Hebrew sign that read "Eating Hall." Lavish beds of glossy white trailing roses lapped at the sides of the unpainted eating hall walls of decaying wood.

"This is Na'on," the driver said, glancing back. "Last stop."

"What the hell do I do now?" Matt asked, surveying the run-down spread before him.

"That's your problem. I can't wait. After six P.M., I can't be on the highway without official British orders, which I don't have. So you're going to have to stay or come, and right now."

Matt looked around uneasily at the poor buildings—shacks—of this desolate cotton farm. He didn't move.

"Listen pal," the driver said reassuringly, "even if you don't find what you're looking for, they'll still put you up for the night. These kibbutzniks won't throw anybody out. So take a shot."

Matt Jordan paid the driver, pushed his duffelbag out on the ground, and watched the taxi bump off back to the highway.

Suddenly eight or ten people came toward him, seemingly right out of the trees. "Who are you? What do you want here?" asked a young man while several other kibbutzniks surrounded Matt.

"I'm a friend of Leah Arad. I was told she may be here with her brother David Brod."

"Come with me," the young man ordered.

Four of them walked Matt over to a small weather-beaten wooden shack with a sign that read "Secretariat." A few moments later, a tall, powerfully built red-haired man came through the door and studied Matt.

"You're Matthew Jordan?"

"You're David Brod?"

Each man scrutinized the other. David slowly extended his hand to Matt and smiled. They shook hands.

"I'm very glad you came. I'll put your bag in a room. Go over to that building over there." David pointed beyond the trees to a barracks-like building in a grassy field. There were several other barracks and cottages beyond it. Several plows had been parked on a dirt path leading up to the set of buildings, and numerous sprinklers were watering the field of grass.

Matt walked down a flagstone path fringed by narrow beds of pink verbena, then up the front steps of the wooden barracks. He stopped at the door and looked through the screen. There were two rows of cribs against the walls. At least thirty children ranging from several months old to four or five were playing everywhere on the floor. In the far corner, sitting on a wooden stool surrounded by three- and four-year-olds sitting cross legged on the floor, was Leah.

He opened the creaking screen door and walked in slowly. The bright light through the doorway made her squint, and she apparently couldn't make out who it was. But she recognized something; her hands stopped in mid-clap and she stopped singing. The children turned to look at the intruder.

Leah got up and said something to another woman standing nearby. She walked down the aisle and took Matt's hand. They walked outside, without a word, and stopped beside the building, just beyond the range of the sprinklers. She stepped closer to him, almost his height, and looked into his eyes. Her eyes were wet with tears, and her upper lip quivered slightly. They kissed and held each other hard for several minutes. Tears ran down both their faces. Thirty small pairs of eyes watched them from the nursery barracks windows, and they soon heard the children's giggles.

It had happened to him again, he thought to himself as he held her and looked at her. She was Ingres' haunting *Odalisque*, Botticelli's *Venus*, tantalizing, pulse quickening, evanescent. She had a paralyzing effect on him, as if she held him locked in her magnetic field. This time there could be no doubt: they belonged here, together.

Matt held her face, his voice a breathless whisper. "I missed you, Leah. I needed to see you again—to be with you."

Leah sniffled and nodded. She wore a simple white tee-shirt and a pair of blue shorts and sandals. The Palestinian sun—her Jewish sun—had lightly bronzed her and bleached her hair almost platinum. She took his hand and together they walked through the wet grass, directly under the spray of the sprinklers.

They went to her small cottage. Matt looked over the metal frame double bed, a straight backed chair, a rickety table, and a tiny bathroom. His duffelbag had been dusted off and was sitting in the corner.

"Let's get washed up for supper," Leah said. "It's at six-thirty." She wasn't looking at him.

Matt peeled off his perspiration-soaked Eisenhower jacket and his uniform shirt and tie. He felt shy, embarrassed, as though their months apart had been years. Now that he was here, he realized how little time they'd actually spent together.

"I guess you'd like to take a shower," she said, her voice a bit deeper than before. She looked up at him. He nodded, afraid of frightening her. He vividly remembered what happened on the night he'd touched her the first time.

She read his mind. "It's okay," she said, smiling softly. She pulled off her tee-shirt and unbuttoned and unzipped her shorts, letting them fall to the floor. His heart, he was sure, beat almost audibly, and the front of his uniform trousers began to stir. He undid the buckle and the button and zipper and the trousers fell to the floor. Still he was afraid to move, fearful of frightening her.

She stepped to him. "Matt," she whispered, "I'm so glad you're here." She pressed her body to him. They caressed and stood holding each other tightly. She took his hand and he stepped out of his shorts and pants and they walked into the small bathroom.

The shower consisted of a nozzle attached to a rubber hose attached to a spigot in the wall. There was no hot water, but in this weather there was no need for any. They stood pressed together in the three-foot nook in the floor with the water drain in it. Matt held the nozzle over their heads and the sun-warmed water played over their bodies. Leah lathered the soap and washed him, gently, lovingly massaging the soap all over his body, and then he rinsed himself. She held the nozzle over herself and he painted her body with soap suds and she too rinsed off. He turned off the water. They stepped dripping out of the bathroom, and they toweled off together.

"I love you, Matthew. I need you very much," she said, caressing his face with both hands.

"I love you, Leah," he said in a whisper, hugging her tightly and kissing her. She was more delicious than he'd let himself remember.

Leah pulled down the faded bedspread and they lay on the coarse sheet. She lay back and closed her eyes and felt his hands and his lips on her, and she forgot time and place and moved rhythmically to his pressure. This time, there were no looming specters from her past, no searing visions of Isaac Krens or Karl Mencken sweating on her, hurting her, no stabs of pain and fear. There was only Matthew Jordan. Nothing else mattered. She and Matthew were together.

And Matt held her close, merging into her body. And they lay there deep in each other and their own new world.

Chapter Ten

Like most of the other buildings on the kibbutz, the eating hall was constructed primarily for efficiency: unadorned plaster walls, a high ceiling to reduce the heat, and ten long dining tables leading away from the industrial kitchen. At the far end of the hall a raised stage had been built, for official kibbutz meetings and recreational stage presentations. Everyone at the kibbutz ate together here at every meal.

Matt and Leah arrived that evening for supper, joining David and Deena and a dozen others at one of the long tables. Matt felt conspicuous, not only because he was new, but also because he felt certain that his and Leah's afternoon pleasure could be seen from every corner of the room. Leah's face had a healthy-looking blush to it, and his felt very warm as well. He sat down quickly and sipped from a glass of fresh juice.

The big bald man whom Matt had seen at the Secretariat door came over to the table and shook his hand.

"I am Giora," he said. "Welcome." Kibbutzniks used only first names, an effort to keep a hierarchy from forming within the kibbutz social structure.

"I'm Matt."

"What can you do, Matt?" asked Giora.

Matt was puzzled and looked questioningly at David. "He means," David explained, "do you have a trade we can use on the kibbutz. You've had your vacation. You start work tomorrow." Both Matt and Leah blushed, and several of the nearby women chuckled.

"Well, I'm a lawyer," Matt told Giora. "Do you need a lawyer?"

Everyone at the table broke into laughter. "Only if you can pick cotton," Giora said, shrugging his shoulders. "I'll put you down for the cotton fields. You meet your group at six o'clock in the morning in front of the eating hall. I'm very pleased to have you with us." Matt shook Giora's offered hand.

"From all of us," said David lifting his glass of milk in a toast. The others at the long table joined in the toast, proffering glasses of milk or orange juice or water.

After supper, when the sun had finally set, the temperture "cooled" to about eighty-five degrees. David, Deena, Leah and Matt strolled over to the Brods' cottage, one of the largest on the kibbutz since David was a *vatik* ["veteran"] of Na'on and rated the best available housing. It had a large front porch and was surrounded by Deena's carefully tended rose bushes. The four of them sat on creaky metal lawn chairs and swatted flies and drank pear juice made from last winter's harvest of Na'on's own orchards.

"Maybe we ought to celebrate your first night in Palestine with something a bit stiffer than pear juice," said David, getting up and disappearing into the dark cottage. He came back a minute later with two bottles. "Brandy from the Rothschild vineyards at Rishon le-Zion," he said, holding a bottle in each hand. "Let's see if they've gotten the hang of making brandy yet. Their wine isn't bad, but the last batch of brandy gave me heartburn and a two-day hangover." He laughed and twisted the cork out of one of the bottles and poured glassfuls for all four of them.

"I'm not used to hard liquor," said Matt. "This'll probably knock me cold."

"Good! Then maybe my sister will get some sleep tonight!"

"David—stop that!" Leah giggled, and David laughed. Matt looked down at his lap, feeling his face turn even brighter than before. He took a long swallow of brandy and felt the blood slowly come down from his face. They all sat quietly, drinking and listening to the sounds of the kibbutz—a radio playing on another porch, a dance record spinning on the victrola in the recreation hall, youngsters playing tag in front of the children's barracks. Matt felt as if he'd known David and Deena for years.

"So what are your plans?" asked David after they had drunk enough to feel well-loosened.

Anesthetized by the drink, Matt answered sternly and with a slight lisp. "Whither Leah goest, I shall go. Her people shall be my people."

"Oy vay, a biblical poet," laughed Deena. She turned to Matt, smiling, and he felt close to her. Accepted.

Leah rose from her chair, walked over to Matt and sat down on the porch in front of him. She put her head in his lap, and he bent over and kissed her hair. They sat in silence, drinking in more of the brandy and the peaceful night.

* * *

The next day, Matt and Leah went to breakfast at five-thirty sharp. Again, everyone was there. As an effort against the heat of the desert, work on the kibbutz began promptly at six o'clock. They worked till one, then had lunch and didn't go back to work until four. The workday ended at six in the evening.

David, Matt learned after breakfast, was a tractor driver. Attached to a tractor outside the eating hall was a cotton bin about thirty feet long, ten feet wide, and six feet high. It was empty. The field crew jumped into the bin, and David drove about a mile to a ripe field which had been partly harvested. David pulled up beside another cotton bin.

"Here's where you get off," he said to Matt.

"What the hell do I do?" Matt asked, feeling lost.

"We load the bin and you jump up and down on the cotton to compact it."

"You serious?"

"That's it. We only have two bins, but we harvest enough cotton to fill six every day. So we have to compact it. Then every afternoon we take the bins over to the gin about ten miles from here."

"Sounds like a heck of a job for a lawyer," said Matt with a laugh.

"Don't worry, you'll love it. Fresh air, exercise, just what a man needs."

Theoretically, that was true. But by one o'clock, when David detached the plow to drive the crew back to the eating hall, Matt could hardly open his eyes. They were swollen shut and tearing constantly. His nose ran, and no amount of blowing stopped the flood. David told him to go over to the infirmary before lunch.

The nurse at the infirmary laughed.

"Well, I'd say you've got a cotton allergy." She smiled and gave him an injection and a small packet of antihistamines.

He walked back to the eating hall and joined Leah and David at a table. His face was resuming its normal shape and his eyes and his nose had stopped running.

"I feel like an idiot," he announced. "I guess I really am just a lawyer at heart."

"Don't feel that way at all," David told him. "A lot of us here have the allergy. You can live all your life next to a cotton field and never sneeze, but once you start touching it, you get what happened to you today. Take the afternoon off and take the pills. You'll be okay tomorrow."

"So what'll be my job now?"

"Talk to Giora at supper. He'll give you a new assignment."

Matt passed the afternoon lying on the bed in the cottage, letting his body slowly return to normal. When he and Leah went to supper, Giora waved him over to his table.

"Tomorrow morning, report to Margalit at the sprinkler factor. She'll give you a new job."

Matt went back to the table where Leah and David and Deena were eating. It was roast chicken and dumplings and assorted boiled vegetables. The kibbutz breakfasts of herring, cucumbers and tomatoes were hard to take, and the lunches were simply sandwiches and fruit, but suppers were always good. They raised much of their own food, and what they did not have was generally bartered with the other nearby kibbutzim and villages. Matt was still a little queasy, so he left early to go to bed.

The next morning, Matt presented himself to the sprinkler factory foreman at about six-fifteen.

"We start work on time around here," said the very large middle-aged woman, staring hard at Matt. "No one has privileges in Kibbutz Na'on, not even American lawyers." She spoke gruffly, loud enough for some of the other workers to hear.

"I'm not expecting any privileges," Matt said, returning her testiness. "I won't be late again. Now what's my job here?"

Margalit marched to one end of the long factory building, which screamed and clanged with machines at work. They came to a huge pile of brass shavings, at least ten feet high and twenty five feet across.

"These are the waste shavings and filings from the production process. You have to shovel them into the wheelbarrow and wheel the loads down to the melting pot. We re-use all the tailings. It's more work than stomping cotton," she added, with just the beginnings of a sneer, "but I don't think you'll be allergic to metal." Margalit lumbered away, leaving him the Alpine mound of brass slivers, a flat-bladed shovel, and a deep wooden wheelbarrow.

By nine o'clock, Matt's hands were both bleeding through broken blisters, and his back was pulsing with radiating pain. A bell rang, and all of the work stopped. He followed the other thirty or forty workers downstairs to a basement cafeteria. There was a selection of foods, as much as one wanted, and Matt was happy to discover that it was much better than breakfast. There were even sweet rolls made by a baker on the factory premises. The kibbutzniks gathered in their own cliques, not shunning the new man but exerting no particular effort to make him feel at home. Matt sat alone at a small table. At nine-thirty, the bell rang again and everyone went back to work. This time he moderated his shoveling, and the aching in his back got only a little worse. He knew there was nothing he could do for his hands. After enough days, they would get tough and calloused.

The bell finally rang at one o'clock, and he went over to the eating hall. He washed his burning hands at the trough outside, letting the soap seep into the battered blisters. He went inside the kitchen and asked one of the servers for a clean dishrag. He tore it in two and wrapped half around each hand.

The others at the table noticed but said nothing. Not even Leah and David. This was the kibbutz way. Toughen up like everyone else and you would be one of them. Break down and you weren't needed here. Matt forced himself to laugh and tell jokes, performing gaily for all to see. This kibbutz would need him, he would see to that.

Chapter Eleven

Matt's hands healed, as he knew they would, within a couple of weeks, and the back pains slowly subsided as well. The days began to shorten and the cotton was harvested. Then, rain came to awaken the dormant clumps of wild yellow daisies and orange honeysuckle, and snowy white cyclamen.

Matt and Leah lay stretched out on a blanket, enjoying a warm afternoon work-break. "I've got an idea," she said. "Let's go to Tel Aviv tomorrow."

"Terrific," said Matt. "I'd love to see it."

"We can go to the beach. It's still warm enough."

The next day, they borrowed one of the kibbutz jeeps and left after breakfast. It was Saturday, and Tel Aviv was quiet, since no public transportation operated on the Sabbath. The shops in Dizengoff Square were shuttered and dark.

"How about going into Jaffa?" said Matt. "The Arab shops will be open."

Leah nodded, excited. "Let's go to David's house on Herbert Samuel Street! It's right across from the beach, and it's just two blocks from the Jaffa Open Market. There are all kinds of things there—ceramics, fabrics, antiques."

They parked in front of the small house where Matt had first looked for Leah, several weeks before, and from the street they could hear and see the *mu'etheen* chanting in the minaret of the Hassan Bek Mosque just a block away.

The air in the house was thick and stale. No one had been in it for months, since the manhunt began after the King David Hotel bombing. Leah and Matt opened most of the windows, and the cool Mediterranean air began to wash away the mustiness.

"It's not warm enough to swim yet," said Leah. "Let's walk over to the market."

They strolled hand in hand past the mosque, and they could hear the growing clamor from the market square. The streets were a potpourri of cultures, Arabs and Europeans in business suits, Arabs in flowing robes, women in long black dresses, many wearing veils. The open stalls had fish and butchered blue-dyed carcasses of lambs with gaping eyes, and souks overflowing with every kind of merchandise. The narrow streets were cluttered with donkey carts and taxis and cars and bicycles and an occasional horse being clucked forward, its harness bells tinkling as it clacked down the cobblestone lanes.

They looked and touched, and they haggled and bartered with the merchants. The sun was high, and the day gradually became warmer. They walked arm and arm back to the house and went into the small bedroom to change into their swim suits. Matt couldn't be happier, here in Palestine, on a perpetual vacation with his most beautiful woman.

Leah sat on the bed, while Matt stood beside it, pulling his swimming trunks up past his knees. He stopped when he saw Leah's eyes, staring at him. She smiled and crooked her finger, beckoning for him to come closer. She delicately wet her lips with the tip of her tongue and slid her hands around to the back of his thighs. She brought her mouth toward—

A loud banging on the door. "Open in the name of His Majesty's Colonial Police!" The bellow was in heavily accented English.

"What the hell—" Matt quickly pulled his trunks up over his rapidly retreating bulge. Leah pulled on her bathing suit. Repeated banging reverberated through the house.

Matt went to the door and opened it. Two Arabs with sten guns stood on the porch, dressed in officers uniforms of the British Constabulary. They quickly pushed past him. One of them—a tall blond with a million freckles and striking blue eyes—held his submachine gun on Matt, and the other searched quickly and came out of the small bedroom pulling Leah by her hair.

"Hey, get your fucking hands off her!" Matt roared, lunging at the policeman holding Leah, slugging him square on the chin. The short, dark, pimple-faced policeman staggered, gingerly fingering an angry purple welt on his chin and daubing at a trickle of blood running from his split lip.

The other Arab clubbed Matt on the back of the neck with the barrel of his sten gun, and Matt sank to the floor, stunned. He rubbed the back of his neck and stood slowly, shakily.

"David Brod, you are under arrest for subversion against the King."

Matt shook his head, regaining his senses. "You fucking idiot," he seethed. "I'm an officer in the United States Army. I don't know who this Brod fellow is, but your fucking ass is finished." He stabbed a shaking finger at the Arab.

"This is David Brod's house. We've had it under surveillance for months. You are David Brod, and this is a warrant for your arrest." The Arab brandished some papers which he'd pulled from his back pocket and looked victoriously from Matt to Leah.

"This house belongs to the Jewish Agency," Leah said. She had quickly understood the gist of the English. "Captain Jordan is on an official visit to Palestine, and the Agency has assigned me as his tour guide." Leah smiled at this last phrase and winked slyly at the Arabs. She spoke in Hebrew, uncertain that either Arab understood, but she knew they'd understand the suggestive wink.

The Arabs looked at each other.

"If that's an arrest warrant, it's got to have this Brud's description on it," said Matt. He eyed them viciously. "You better make damn sure you got the right man before you make the biggest mistake of your fucking lives."

The Arab with the warrant visibly lost his assuredness. He thumbed through the papers and his face whitened as he compared the description of red-headed, six-foot-three Daivd Brod with the man standing in front of him—dark brown hair, several inches shorter, an American accent.

"If you are an American officer, show me official identification." The Arab's bravado was rapidly fading.

Matt was escorted into the bedroom. He picked up his trousers from the bed and took out his wallet. Thank God he had kept his military ID, he thought. He handed it to the Arab, who scrutinized it, comparing the photo and the man.

They walked back into the living room. The Arabs spoke together in agitated whispers.

"We have to check on this," said the policeman, trying to sound very officious, saving as much face as possible. The two Arabs left hurriedly.

Matt watched from the window as they drove away in their land rover.

"Let's get the hell out of here before they come back," he said. They got out of their swim suits and dressed quickly. They ran out to the jeep and drove fast out of Tel Aviv. When they had left the city, and Matt could detect no tail, he eased up on the accelerator and turned toward Leah.

"What was that about?"

She looked back at him intently, hoping that he would understand. She did not want him to leave her. Please God, don't let him leave, she thought. I need him so. "Matthew," she said. "You know I'm a member of the Irgun, and you know that David is a General in the Haganah."

"So?"

She paused. "Did you read about the King David Hotel bombing while you were in Nuremberg?"

"Yeah, sure. Some terrorist group." He was watching the road, driving easily.

"It was the Irgun," she said quietly. "I was part of the group, and David helped plan it."

Matt slowed the jeep and pulled it to the shoulder of the road. There was very little traffic. He'd heard about the more violent excesses of the Irgun, but he'd always considered them to be mistakes—accidental incidents blown out of proportion by the Gentile press. But suddenly he was very somber, stunned. Could David and Leah support such violence as the King David Hotel massacre?

"Okay, I'm listening," he said.

Leah's voice remained steady, steeled against the possibility of rejection. But she had to tell the truth; she knew she had nothing to be ashamed of. "I knew Menachem Begin in Vilna," she explained. "And I joined his Irgun when I got to Palestine last April. When we planted the bombs at the hotel, we telephoned the British Commissioner and gave him half an hour's warning. I was there, and I swear we warned him. But he thought it was some kind of practical joke, so he didn't clear the hotel. That's why there was so much bloodshed."

Matt couldn't believe what he was hearing. Leah involved in bombing, in cold-blooded murder. He turned to her, looked into her kind, sad eyes. "You're a terrorist, Leah?" His eyes were wide, his mouth open.

She looked at him resolutely and put her hand on his shoulder. "I don't care what they call us, Matthew. But we're *not* terrorists. This is *our* Jewish nation, and we're simply trying to make the British keep their promise to us. Killing people is not our thing. But proving to the British that we're willing to die for a free country is." Tears filled her eyes. "I didn't want to have to tell you about the King David, Matthew. At least not until you joined us, or at least until you saw the horrible struggle that's facing us. I didn't want anything to make you stop loving me."

Matt sat deep in thought, looking at her. DiGeorgio, back in Nuremburg, had warned him. Out of one war, into another. It was a far cry from poolside living in Tucson, Arizona. He just wasn't sure he could take another war.

Tears rolled down Leah's cheeks. Moments passed.

"Nothing will ever make me stop loving you, Leah," he said softly. "Nothing." They touched hands, saying no more. Then he shifted the jeep into gear and pulled back onto the road.

* * *

The only clothes that Matt had were his Army uniforms, some crumpled old suits and shirts, and his kibbutz work shorts and shirts. Leah and he decided that he could wear a tan short sleeved shirt with the insignia removed from the collar and epaulets, a pair of khaki trousers, and his brown dress shoes. Leah had some clothes made by the kibbutz seamstress.

Saturday night, mid-November, a pleasant seventy degrees. At five minutes to seven, Matt walked over to the eating hall, stepping high to keep the dust off his freshly polished shoes, feeling more nervous than he'd expected. He'd been through law school, through a world war, but still he couldn't contain his nerves for an occasion such as this.

The tables had been folded and stacked in a corner, and the chairs were set up auditorium-style, facing the stage, leaving a large empty area for dancing. Many of the kibbutzniks were already there, dressed in their finest, scrubbed and shined. Matt stood at the back of the hall. Still no Leah. By about seven-thirty, the kibbutzniks had all arrived, as well as probably another three hundred people from the nearby kibbutzim. Then the rabbi came in, an old man with a flowing white beard that trailed over his dark business suit. At a signal, one of the children ran out of the hall.

Five minutes later, Leah was escorted into the hall by her brother David, wearing his uniform as General of the Haganah. Leah wore a pale violet jersey blouse with a scoop neck and no sleeves and a dark violet velvet skirt. She had a garland of dwarf, pale purple, angel-face roses which she wore as a diadem over her long wavy blond hair. Her arrival sent a buzz of admiration through the hundreds of kibbutzniks. Matt came to the front and took Leah's arm. The rabbi mounted the stage and the crowd hushed.

The ceremony was a short one. Leah forced away the memory of her first wedding and concentrated on her new husband, Matthew Jordan. Matt, meanwhile, was completely enveloped in Leah's beauty. As he looked at his lovely new wife, the only thing in his mind was the line from the Bible, recited at every Sabbath service: "A woman of valor, who can find; her price is far greater than rubies." After he crushed the small wine glass, the hall erupted into cheers and everyone began filing outside where twenty-five lambs were already turning on spits over charcoal barbecue pits. On the grass field, some of the boys and girls had started a game of soccer.

A huge line of well-wishers formed, shaking Matt's hand and kissing Leah's cheek. Then, near eight o'clock, Giora had two of the boys wheel up a wheelbarrow loaded with bottles of slivovitz. Everyone who wanted some took a tin cup off one of the tables and got a healthy dollop of the plum brandy. Many went back for seconds, and not a few for thirds and fourths.

The lambs were ready too, and the people passed by with tin plates while butter-soft chunks of the savory meat were sliced off for them. They picked their own baked potatoes out of the coals. Everyone ate with his fingers; there simply weren't enough implements to go around. In addition to the slivovitz, Giora had brought back a hundred bottles of red wine from the Rothschild Vintners at Rishon le-Zion for which he had bartered some irrigation equipment. For anyone to have gotten drunk at a public celebration like this would have been socially intolerable on the kibbutz, but almost every adult and even some of the stealthier teenagers put on a pretty good glow.

Then the music began. An accordionist, three guitarists, and a trumpet player started playing the rousing folk music of the Yishuv. Groups began dancing the hora, in larger and larger concentric circles, with Leah and Matt and David and Deena dancing in the middle. Then some of the better dancers danced a cherkassia while the others stood watching and clapping.

Suddenly the festive flow of the evening came to a glaring halt: pulsing klieg lights flooded over the five hundred revelers. The spotlights came from every side.

The kibbutzniks squinted into the lights, blinded by them, trying to see what was happening. The dancing and music stopped.

"In the name of His Majesty's Colonial Forces, I order you to stand peacefully where you are. We are conducting a search for illegals and weapons. If you stay calm, no one will be hurt, and we will leave quickly."

Leah felt panic grow within her. She'd heard this warning too many times before. She and Matt clung to one another, pressing against the other frightened kibbutzniks. A ring of British military jeeps with mounted machine guns surrounded the group. At least a hundred soldiers had fanned out into the barracks and cottages and were searching them. Atop an armored car, a British officer held a microphone attached to two tall loudspeakers.

"When the search is over in the living area, you will pass single file to your left for personal inspection. No one will be harmed."

The people stood closely together like a weird roll call of ghosts in the shadowy light from the fading campfires and the pulsing generator-driven spotlights. David crouched in front of Matt and Leah and removed his Haganah tunic. He pulled the insignia of rank off the epaulets and threw them in a little hole he'd kicked out with his heel in the soft ground. He toed the dirt back over the hole and let the tunic drop to the ground.

The hundreds of kibbutzniks filed past the cordon of British soldiers under the glare of the spotlights. Leah and Matt passed through and began walking slowly to their cottage, looking back to see if there would be any trouble.

"You there, step out of line," blared the voice over the microphone.

Two soldiers pushed Deena to the ground and grabbed David by the arms and pulled him to the armored car. Deena was pulled up roughly by another soldier and pushed toward the cottages. She stopped and turned and started walking back to David. A soldier blocked her way and pushed her backwards. "Now there, dearie, off ya go. We'll take good care a yer ol' man, ya can be well assured a that!" He had a lilting, leering brogue.

Everyone in the hushed camp heard the next announcement, over near the armored car: "David Brod, you are under arrest for subversion against His Majesty's Government."

Leah and Matt froze and watched. Deena rushed up and joined them, tears of fear streaming down her cheeks. The other kibbutzniks stopped where they were, and the lead officer picked up the microphone and yelled into it: "Everyone keep moving! Anyone who does not keep moving to his quarters is subject to immediate arrest!"

The kibbutzniks shuffled slowly away from the British soldiers. Leah and Matt and Deena remained standing in the darkness, about forty yards away, straining to hear what was happening with David.

"Where are your weapons hidden?" the officer demanded. David stood silent. "Where is your weapons stash?" the officer bellowed, directly into David's face, six inches away. Silence.

The officer struck David across the face with his riding crop and brought his knee sharply up into David's groin. He fell to his hands and knees, gasping. Silence. Two soldiers hauled him to his feet.

"I'll beat your bloody brains out if you don't answer me immediately, you sodding Jew bastard."

"Get a move on there, come on," yelled a British soldier walking up behind Leah and Deena and prodding Matt with his tommy gun. Their last sight of David was watching him fall backwards when the British officer once again swung the crop across his face.

They went sullenly into Matt and Leah's cottage and it was a shambles, mattress turned over, drawers pulled out, the contents strewn about the room. They slowly put everything back into place, brooding silently.

Matt sat on the bed, forlorn and confused. "I don't get it," he said. "The British are perfectly civilized people—America's closest and best allies. I've never seen anything like this before."

"I have," Leah whispered.

Fear etched Deena's face. "What will they do to him?" she gasped between sobs. "What will they do to my David?"

Chapter Twelve

The telephone rang in the secretariat office on Na'on.

"Hello, this is Rabbi Sassover," the caller said to Giora.

"Yes sir, what can I do for you?"

"Please ask the family of our friend to pick up the package at the *Strassenbahnhaltestelle*. It will arrive around six o'clock this evening."

Before Giora could respond, the line went dead. He got up from his desk and made his way to the nursery, where Leah worked with the children. He called her aside.

"Menachem Begin just called. He wants you to go to the main bus station in Tel Aviv this evening at six o'clock. Someone will meet you there."

That afternoon, dressed as kibbutzniks, Leah and Matt were driven out to the highway on a tractor and waited for the Egged Bus to Tel Aviv. It came at approximately hourly intervals. They caught it at three forty-five and were at the main Tel Aviv station by five-thirty. They loitered around the snack counter and had some sardines on stale bread.

Matt bought an evening newspaper, and the headlines read, "CID Capture Haganah No. 3." The story related the raid at Kibbutz Na'on and the capture of Aluf David Brod. He had been linked to the massacre at the King David Hotel by CID double agent Martin Berman who had identified him as the Haganah's liaison officer with Irgun. The British were convening a Court under emergency police powers to try Brod as a terrorist. The effect of his trial as a terrorist would make the death penalty available if he should be convicted. A Court not invoking the Emergency Powers Act could not sentence a prisoner to death.

Matt showed the story to Leah and watched her blanch as she read it. "It's very strange for me," Matt told her, "to read about the British as the enemy."

"We have many enemies," Leah said, her voice dull and hoarse. "That's why we're here. That's why we fight." Just then, she caught the eye of Yisrael Levi, her partner from the King David Hotel. He'd grown a thin mustache and combed his hair differently and colored it darker as a disguise. But it was the same sickly, thin-chested, hunched body, the same feline carriage. He started walking away from the station into the residential section and Leah and Matt followed a half-block behind. The streets were busy and crowded, since people were just now coming home from work.

They lost sight of Levi's gaunt figure in the crowd, but they kept walking. A few minutes later, a small car pulled up next to them at the curb. Levi was driving. Matt got in front and Leah in back, and it rejoined the heavy flow of traffic.

Matthew and Yisrael shook hands. They drove about twenty minutes to a slummy neighborhood where they maneuvered in and out of small cobblestoned alleys and parked in a ramshackle shed next to a crumbling brick apartment building. Levi closed the shed door, and they went through the back door of the apartment building to the top floor. Begin stood on the landing.

"I heard you drive up," he said. "Any trouble?"

"No sir," said Levi.

"Come inside."

They followed him into the spacious apartment which covered the entire third floor. Windows on all sides gave a 360 degree view of the neighborhood outside. Short partitions separated the room into a kitchen, two bedrooms, and a parlor. Only the small bathroom was fully enclosed.

"Menachem, this is my husband, Matthew Jordan." The men shook hands warmly.

"I'd like you to meet Dov Gruner," said Begin, introducing the tall, stocky young man who stepped forward and shook hands with Matt and Leah.

"Dov is from Hungary and was a Betar member. He served in Europe with the British forces as an armory sergeant. He was demobilized in London and has just joined us here. He knows British tactics and procedures, and he's in charge of the plan to free David. Dov will explain."

"We have information that David's being held in Ramat Gan police station, awaiting transfer to the military court in Jerusalem." Gruner's Hebrew was poor, so he spoke to them in Yiddish.

"Ramat Gan is in the north of Tel Aviv, and we have a hiding place set up at Petach Tikva about five miles from there. Matt, you speak English and can affect a British accent."

Matt shrugged, not quite understanding the comment.

"Will you join us in freeing David?" asked Begin.

"Of course I will," came Matt's instant reply. David was not only Matt's brother-in-law, but over the past several months he'd become Matt's closest friend. "What should I do?"

"Good!" Gruner straddled a chair and explained the plan. "Matthew, you'll dress as a British Captain, and I'll use my Sergeant's uniform. We have three other men who'll dress as riflemen. We will enter the police station at five o'clock tomorrow morning before the full contingent of police come on duty. We'll neutralize them, and our sapper Schmulik will blow the cell door. It should take less than five minutes, if we do it right. Matthew, you and I will go now and reconnoiter the area."

"That's fine," said Begin, allowing a smile. "Leah can remain here with Aliza and me until everything is done and David is free."

Matt, Gruner and Levi left. They walked several blocks away through narrow dark alleys. Matt felt more like a soldier now, here in Tel Aviv, than he ever had in Europe. There, he'd been a lawyer; here, he felt like a spy on a secret mission. Which, of course, he was.

Gruner stopped and pulled open an old shed door. Inside were the rest of the Irgun team, three men dressed as British soldiers and a stolen British army truck. It had a canvas van behind the cab, big enough to carry six or eight people. Gruner would drive and Matt would be the passenger in the cab. The others would ride in the van. They had already hidden an old civilian truck in an orange grove just outside of Petach Tikvah. In it were civilian clothes for all the men. As far as Matt could tell, the rescue was very well planned. All it had to do now was work.

None of them slept that night; they played cards and talked politics, and discussed the crops at the various kibbutzim. They talked about the imminent success of their plan. After driving by the Ramat Gan police station twice, and driving through the sparse neighborhood, checking everything, they knew that with a little bit of luck the rescue would come off as scheduled.

They started for the station at four forty-five in the morning and parked in front of it at exactly five o'clock. Matt put on his best British officer's look, tucked the inevitable riding crop under his arm, and strode with his sergeant to the front door. The riflemen followed smartly. They entered the station and a sleepy desk sergeant stared in surprise. His mouth was quickly taped shut and his hands and feet tied. The team moved down the hall to the cell area. Another guard, this one wide awake and holding a sub-machine gun, asked for Matt's orders. Matt swung the crop up, catching the guard under the chin. He fell back against the wall and struck his head, slumping to the floor. The outer gate to the cell area was locked. The unconscious guard did not have the key.

The sapper set a small explosive on the gate's lock and blew it. The noise was deafening. They rushed down the hallway toward the cells. Three other guards sprung up from a bench in the cell area. Before they could react, Gruner leveled them with a short volley from his sten gun. Matt stepped past the dying men, trying not to look. He reached the three cells first and found only a few frightened Arabs. There were no other cells. David Brod was not there.

Without a word, they ran back down the hall and out the front door. By now, the policemen who slept in a small barracks behind the station were running out carrying their sten guns. Levi hopped into the driver's seat and quickly started the engine. Matt jumped in beside him. A burst of gunfire split the early-morning stillness of the neighborhood, and one of the Irgun men was killed before

reaching the van. Schmulik and Gruner leapt into the back as
the truck careened off down the street. A steady stream of sten gun
fire was exchanged by a pursuing jeep of British policemen and the
Irgun men in the back of the van. Then there was an explosion, and
Matt looked back and saw the police jeep engulfed in flames. One
of the bullets must have ignited the gas tank.

They drove as fast as they could to the hidden truck in the orange
grove outside of Petach Tikvah. Levi and Matt jumped out and ran
around to the back of the van. Gruner was not inside. Schmulik lay
dead in a pool of blood. He'd been shot in the chest.

Stunned, Matt followed Levi and the others to the civilian truck
as the sun began to rise in the orchard. They quickly changed into
civilian clothes and drove about twenty minutes to the hiding place
that had been prepared for them. The operation had been a
complete failure, a disaster.

Matt was almost literally in a state of shock. All of this pointless
violence, bloodshed. He had never imagined that they would have
to kill three British soldiers, and for what? David hadn't even been
there. And Dov Gruner was gone.

Matt felt queasy. My God, he thought, what have I gotten into?
The struggle for a Jewish homeland was one thing, but this other
business was completely different. Anyone—even he—would call
this terrorism.

Huddled in the beat-up shack where they hid, Matt felt the
distant tug of America, his home, pulling at his conscience. He
thought of the gentle quiet streets of Tucson, where nothing worse
than two-car collisions ever seemed to happen. His father had taken
his family to that new land, for their chance at freedom and dignity,
and now Matt was halfway around the globe, fighting a war no real
nation had declared. What would his parents say, if they were still
alive to see him? Their nice Jewish son, blowing up British
soldiers. Surely they wouldn't understand this. He was a terrorist.
The realization came suddenly to him, clawing at his soul like a
ravening hawk. There was no other way to say it. It burst on him
with shock and disgust: he was a goddam terrorist.

Chapter Thirteen

Dov Gruner, it was soon learned, had fallen wounded out the back of the van. A CID patrol picked him up and brought him to the infirmary in Ramat Gan, but facilities there were insufficient to help with his serious wounds, so they tranferred him to the Government hospital in Jerusalem. The British wanted at all costs to keep Gruner alive so they could put him on trial with David Brod. He lived, but his jaw had been so badly shattered that he could eat only through a straw, and for several weeks he could barely speak. So David's trial was postponed.

Finally, on January 17, 1947, both men stood in shackles in the British Military Court in Jerusalem. It was a small room, with only six seats behind the railing for very select observers from the very select British press. The walls were dingy gray plaster, smeared with sweaty handprints and squashed mosquitoes and flies. The judge read the indictment for murder and accessory to murder and terrorism against both men and asked how they pleaded. Gruner stared straight ahead, remaining seated, saying nothing.

David rose to his feet and addressed the periwigged, stolid judge. "We do not recognize your authority to judge us. This court has no basis in law since it is appointed by an oppressive and illegal regime without basis in law. Where there is no legal government, and its replacement is a government of oppression and tyranny, it is the right and even the duty of the citizens to fight that government and to overthrow it." David resumed his seat.

Neither the judge nor the prosecution seemed particularly ruffled by this, and the trial proceeded swiftly. Witnesses were heard one after another without cross-examination, since neither Dov nor David had permitted attorneys to be appointed for them. Several days later, both men were convicted. The presiding judge pronounced the death penalty on them both.

Dov Gruner stood, faced the judge, and recited a line from a Betar poem he had learned as a youth: "In blood and fire Judea fell, In blood and fire shall Judea rise."

That same day, they were taken to the Jerusalem Central Prison and issued the red pajamas of the condemned. The British Commanding General confirmed the sentences on January 24 and set Gruner's execution for January 28 and Brod's for January 31.

Back at Irgun headquarters, no one—least of all Leah and Menachem Begin—sat patiently to see what might unfold. They knew they needed to retaliate, to show they could not be broken by a single publicized trial—and they also needed to save David and Dov from the gallows.

Matt attended every hastily called meeting but said little as Leah urged Begin into action. "They have two of our very best people, Menachem," Leah argued. "Our response is simple: we must take two of theirs. It's an eye for an eye."

On January 26, the Irgun kidnapped a British intelligence officer and a Tel Aviv district judge. As hoped, the British promised an indefinite stay of execution if the Englishmen were released. Begin complied. Gruner and Brod were moved from Jerusalem to the condemned cell at Acre Prison.

Almost three months later, on the evening of April 16, Leah, Matt and Deena sat around the radio at Kibbutz Na'on, listening as usual to the British news of the day. There had been nothing on the Irgun prisoners since the move to Acre. But this night, they leaned closer to the small speakers, straining to hear, as the name of the prison caught their attention. Matt placed his hand on Leah's shoulder as she stooped in front of him, her ear practically touching the radio. Deena stroked Jacob's hair, her eyes wide, concentrating.

The news came fast, like gunfire: sometime before dawn that morning, without any prior notification or formal announcement, Dov Gruner had been taken out of his cell and hanged at Acre Prison.

The next day, Begin was furious. "These are the deals they make with us," he said, pacing back in forth in front of Matt and the others."We cannot delay any longer, for David's sake. And for the sake of our freedom, we *cannot* make any more deals!"

He assigned Matt and Ami Carmel to lead the escape, and though Matt listened as Begin described his basic plan, his own enthusiasm was beginning to wane. He was still trying to get over the jailbreak fiasco. Of course he wanted to free David, of course he wanted to help free the Jewish people, but the idea of all this incidental killing wasn't easy to take. He'd said nothing to Leah; he really didn't know what to say. He'd already tried to rescue David once, and had ended up taking part in the killing of three guards—men, soldiers like himself. It was war, and he knew that, but it was also terrorism, and he had to think that part of it through, come to grips with it, and up to now he just hadn't been able to.

"Matthew, you need to find a couple of troop carriers—"

Matt looked up, focused on Begin's intent face, on his slightly bulging eyes. "Yes sir," Matt said slowly.

Begin continued, and Matt forced himself to pay closer attention. He was again being called upon to help his brother-in-law. And once again he agreed. There was no time for the luxury of contemplation. They had to free David now, before it was too late, and he could worry about the meaning of it all later.

Matt Jordan once again donned a British officer's uniform, but this time he decided to promote himself to paratrooper Lieutenant Colonel. He was accompanied by twelve paratroop riflemen, all in their red berets, and a sapper—their explosives man. They'd picked up two stolen British troop carriers in a tiny Arab village outside of Acre, and as they drove toward the prison, they hurriedly changed into their uniforms. At dusk, they arrived in Acre. The prison was the thousand-year-old Crusader fortress of St. Jean d'Acre, immense stone parapets protecting crypts dug into a solid granite cliff overlooking the Mediterranean.

On a corner a block away from the prison's south wall, two of the Irgun men jumped from the lead truck and bound and gagged the attendant at an Arab gas station. While the trucks drove on, the new gas station men pumped hundreds of gallons of gasoline onto the two streets coming from the prison, so that once the escape trucks had safely returned, a covering explosion and fire could be laid down to prevent pursuit.

The two trucks drove slowly to the prison and backed up to the wall, stopping about fifteen feet away. Within minutes, the sapper had set his charges. Everyone lay flat on the beds of the trucks as the charge was detonated. A mountainous explosion ripped a gaping hole in the wall. In just seconds, Irgun and Stern Gang prisoners were clambering excitedly into the back of the trucks.

Matt, standing outside and directing the escapees, waited for

David. Finally, he stumbled through the rubble, half-blinded by the dust, and Matt pulled him into the cab of the truck. The trucks were filled and they sped away on the escape route.

The second truck slowed at the gas station for the two Irgun men, who hopped in. One of them tossed a lit firecracker behind them as the truck drove away, and the two streets and the gas station erupted into a volcano of flame.

About a block ahead, in the cab of the first truck, Matt held David around his shoulders, smiling at his brother-in-law for the first time in nearly half a year. David, looking weak and much thinner than before, managed a wan smile in return. "Dov is dead," David said. "Have they announced it?"

"Yes," Matt said. "Four days ago. We knew we had to get you soon, or maybe—" He didn't finish the obvious. "Let's talk later, David. There'll be plenty of time. Deena's waiting for you." They sped down the coastal highway, highlighted by the giant conflagration leaping into the sky behind them.

Then came the hitch, the surprise: several British soldiers, who must have spent the afternoon and early evening on the nearby beach, drinking and swimming, taking a break from things here in war-torn Palestine, who were in any case now hitchhiking back to their barracks, tried to flag down what appeared to them to be a British troop carrier. Matt tensed in his seat, told the driver to keep on driving. The truck sped by, but as it passed, one of the Irgun men in the van sprayed the soldiers with his sten gun.

"Aw, shit—" Matt leaned across David and caught a glimpse of the fading images in the side-view mirror. Two of the soldiers lay on the road, the other four or five had spread out and dropped to the side of the road, their weapons drawn.

The second truck approached. Matt could do nothing to warn them, to stop them. The British soldiers took aim and fired. A barrage of machine gun fire shattered the windshield, killing the driver instantly, and blew out the front tires. The truck veered crazily off the highway and spun over on its side.

"Keep driving!" Matt screamed, as David strained to see past the truckful of soldiers and escapees. The driver punched the accelerator, but the truck sputtered and hestitated. Matt screamed again, "Goddam it, let's get out of here!"

They managed to escape unharmed. Behind them, bodies live

and dead flew in every direction. The ones who were not killed by
the crash were killed or captured by the British soldiers.

Several miles later, as the surviving truck neared its first escape-
route meeting point, David turned his drawn and pasty face toward
Matt. "Who'd we lose?" he asked. "How many besides the prisoners were in the truck?"

"Yisrael Levi," was the only one Matt could think of. He
coughed a weak laugh. "The man who introduced both Leah and
me to—to all of this. Several others, three or four. I don't know. Too
many."

"Agreed," said David slowly. "Much too many."

They abandoned the truck six miles from the prison, where the
men were picked up by two small civilian vans and taken to
Kibbutz Daliya. It was almost midnight. Later, after the news had
spread and plans were discussed, David Brod slept a free man for
the first time in almost six months. But there had been a terrible
price.

Less than a week later, David and Matt were back on Kibbutz
Na'on, David trying to get back in step with family and military
life on the kibbutz, Matt just trying to get back in step. The
inevitable rounds of retaliation began, and all Matt could do was
watch and listen. He no longer felt like taking part, at least not for
the moment. Leah, meanwhile, felt as strongly as ever—and for the
first time in all the time he'd known her, he felt separate from her,
distanced. He didn't like the feeling.

To keep his mind off Leah—off the fact that he found it
increasingly difficult even to speak openly with her—Matt worked
hard physically and kept careful track of the political events as they
unwound. First, the British hastily convened a military court for
the three men captured during the prison breakout. They were all
sentenced to be hanged and their executions were confirmed for
July 15. Leah wrote in Irgun's underground newspaper that if the
British were determined to line Palestine with "an avenue of
gallows," the Jews would "see to it that in this there is no racial
discrimination." The Jews, she said, were the legitimate government of Palestine. They therefore also had the right to conduct
official executions.

Irgun plastered posters on walls proclaiming that God's law of
retribution would be solemnly obeyed, that it would be "an eye for

an eye," and that if the Jews were hanged in Acre prison, then British soldiers would also be executed. No deals. Just equal reaction to every British action.

A week before the scheduled hangings, two British CID Sergeants left the Rose Garden Cafe a little after midnight in the seaside resort of Netanya. A black sedan pulled up alongside them, and before they could react, they were clubbed unconscious and piled inside. Sergeants Clifford Martin and Mervyn Paice were driven to a hideout under a Netanya diamond factory. It was an underground bunker, about ten feet square with a three-foot dirt roof. The bunker was so airtight that it had to be provided with two bottles of oxygen. The prisoners were also supplied enough food for a week and a canvas bucket for a toilet.

Matt and the others kept both ears to the radio. As they expected, the British reaction to the kidnapping was immediate and intense. "Operation Tiger" was launched. Netanya and twenty outlying settlements were put under martial law, and thousands of soldiers conducted house-to-house searches. A twenty-four hour a day curfew rendered Netanya a ghost town. Irgun's underground radio announced that if the Irgun soldiers' death sentences were commuted, the Sergeants would be released.

Ben-Gurion denounced the kidnappings and sent a message to Begin ordering him not to go through with his "eye for an eye" reprisals. Haganah soldiers were detailed to go along with the British to intensify the search for the hostages. Still the hideout could not be found.

At two o'clock in the morning of July 15, a rabbi visited with the condemned prisoners at Acre Prison for the last time. Yisrael Levi and the other two men were hanged at four o'clock that morning. The remaining Jewish prisoners pressed against the bars and sang Hatikvah, "The Hope," the Zionist anthem:

> "As long as within the heart a Jewish soul
> yearns,
> And forward toward the east, an eye turns
> to Zion,
> Our hope is not yet lost, our hope of
> 2,000 years,
> To be a free people in our land,
> The land of Zion and Jerusalem."

Early the next morning, British radio announced the executions. It also announced that a nationwide curfew would be imposed by eleven o'clock that evening, and no Jewish traffic would be permitted on the streets for two days to avert the threat of violence.

Menachem Begin sent Ami Carmel to Kibbutz Na'on to pick up Leah and Matt and bring them to an Irgun high command meeting at Begin's Tel Aviv hiding place that afternoon.

Carmel got to the kibbutz during the mid-morning work break, at about nine-thirty, and found David and Deena and the Jordans sitting glumly together over cups of ersatz coffee at the rear of the eating hall.

"The roads are crawling with British Tommies and CID agents," said Carmel, sitting down at the table. "I don't think there's any way to get through if David comes along. His picture has been plastered all over Palestine for weeks. We're sure to be spotted."

"But those men died saving my life," David said, rising in his seat, stabbing savagely at his chest. "This meeting is about me and I must go."

"Please, David," Leah said, her voice soft and soothing. "You know Ami is right. If you come, we'll all be caught." She looked over at Matt. "Matt and I will go," she went on, keeping her eyes on her husband. "We will see that justice is done."

Matt chose again not to think. It was all he could do to keep from stopping altogether. He and Leah got up quickly from the table and went outside to the little Morris 8. Two hours later, they reached Begin's *malineh*. The Irgun high command meeting was in grim session.

"We have decided that we must execute the Sergeants the same way our three men were executed this morning," Begin told them as they entered. "They must be hanged." He looked hard at Matt and Leah.

No one spoke. Matt Jordan wanted to scream out in protest, but he was a newcomer here, and he had little fight left in him anyway. He had taken part in the military operations to free his brother-in-law, but when it came to cold-blooded, premeditated murder, he wanted no part of it. The other members could do what they wished.

And then he heard his wife speaking and he couldn't believe what came out. "Those men gave their lives saving my brother from the gallows," she said. "I will hang the prisoners." Her voice, oddly unfamiliar to Matt, was rough, wooden. Her face showed nothing.

Begin acted not at all surprised, nodding slightly toward Leah, agreeing to her plan. He then began to draw a detailed map on a large sheet of paper draped over the easel at the front of the room.

Matt stood near the back, stunned. He wanted to grab Leah by the shoulders and shake her hard, to wake her and himself out of this melodramatic dream. But he could do nothing in this place, before this group of men and women who were so different from himself, such different kinds of Jews. They were Ghetto Jews from Europe, the ones who'd barely escaped death in the Holocaust, and they had been tempered in the flames of Hell. This was their battle to survive, and among them Matt felt like an unwanted interloper, like a visitor from another planet.

He could leave for Tucson tomorrow, be a country lawyer in a powerful, endless, gentle nation, and the only danger he would face each day would be getting sunburned if he stayed outside too long. But Palestine was a different world. Every Englishman and Arab was potentially his executioner. Here Matt was a *Jew*, not a Jewish lawyer or an American Jew. Just a Jew. In Palestine, it was his sole identity, and being a lawyer was meaningless and being an American was superfluous. And here, Jews were in great danger.

Begin handed Leah the car keys. "Take the Morris and go back to Na'on as soon as you're done. Go back to your brother. Stay there until it's blown over."

She stood and walked quickly out of the room. Matt followed her wordlessly, feeling small, alien, unimportant. *Go back to your brother.* Suddenly he felt oddly embarrassed by Menachem's words, implying that Leah was more closely tied to her brother—her real family—than to him, her *American* husband. He was, and always would be, the outsider here.

They got into the car. Leah didn't look over at Matt. It was one thing, he thought, to be a heroic freedom fighter struggling for right, truth and justice. That was romantic, an ideal. But what Leah was about to do was another thing altogether, not at all in keeping with anyone's romantic, idealistic notions. It was plain, cold, premeditated killing: hanging two innocent English soldiers as a reprisal for the hanging of three Jewish terrorists who had broken British law. This was not the stuff of storybook romantic heroism. But then, this was not a storybook.

"Leah." Matt touched her arm lightly, trying to rekindle with a touch their love and closeness, but she said nothing and simply looked ahead. He tried to recall Nuremburg, and their lovely afternoons by the Danube and the Pegnitz.

Leah cautiously turned her head and stared into him—then she started the car.

They drove a roundabout route to Netanya and reached the diamond factory hideout after almost an hour. They didn't say a word to one another. As Leah stopped the car, Matt reached out for her again. This time he touched her arm and held it.

"Are you going through with this?" he asked quietly, watching her steadily.

"Yes." She looked back at him and held his stare. Her nacreous eyes were moist. She spoke very softly and quietly, almost a whisper. "They killed three of our people who did nothing worse than rescue David—*our* brother David—from being murdered. We promised them an eye for an eye. If we do not do this, then we have no right to be a nation."

Matt said nothing. He felt ashamed and afraid—looking at his beautiful wife in this horrible place, connected to this terrifying event. How could she be doing it so coldly?

"I guess I just don't know what to say," he stammered, shaking his head. "I just can't take a rope and hang two British soldiers— two *men*. They never did a thing to us. They're as innocent as David. We don't have any right to do this."

Leah held his hand in both of hers. Her face had become florid with nervous perspiration, her eyes bore tearfully into his. He knew she was suffering and that whatever she believed, she believed it fully, with all her heart. "Matthew," she said, "we have suffered for two thousand years. We are Jews—both of us. I've been through the worst, and you've seen it. We *all* have to feel it, remember it. We finally have a chance to break the chain of misery: we have a nation. The Jews are the legitimate government of Palestine. This is Eretz Yisrael, the Land of Israel of our Bible, our birthright from God. We are still no better than fuel for the Nazi ovens unless we prove that the Jews have learned to make the world reel with agony whenever it takes the life of one of our people."

Her eyes gained strength and burned into his. Her cheeks quivered slightly and her voice broke into a hoarse whisper. "We must no longer try to prove that we are morally better than the rest of the world. We're just the same, and our oppressors must burn in Hell each time they cause us pain."

Matt breathed deeply, trying to calm his pounding heart. These were strong, awesome words, and despite his hatred of what they were doing, he understood their purpose: to convince him that two British soldiers could never compare to two thousand years of Jewish hopelessness. About that, Leah was right. The Jews could no more fight the British with prayers and biblical morality than they could use these to protect themselves from the Nazis. Suddenly he knew that he really had no choice.

He got slowly out of the Morris and took the hemp rope that was coiled on the floor at his feet. Leah followed him as he lifted the heavy trapdoor over the pitch black subterranean dungeon. The stench of excrement rose, sickening. Leah held the flashlight and they climbed down into the Sergeants' cell. Both of the men were unconscious from lack of oxygen. Matt placed the prepared nooses around their necks. He and Leah struggled to prop the Englishmen against the short ladder.

The fresh air streamed through the open trapdoor and the men slowly regained consciousness. They were still partially dazed, and Matt tied their hands securely behind them. With a steady voice, he ordered them up the ladder and they walked shakily to the Morris. "In the back seat," Matt told them.

They drove to a eucalyptus grove at the deserted and remote village of umm Uleiga. Matt ordered them out of the car and they stumbled out, still dazed, still unable to perceive their situation. The two men never uttered a word of protest—whether out of courage or confusion Matt would never know. He hooded them both and pushed them to a large tree with a broad limb stretching some ten feet off the ground. Leah got a rickety, folding, wood-slatted camp chair out of the trunk of the Morris. Matt stood first one and then the other Sergeant on the chair, secured the rope around the limb, and kicked away the chair. It was over in minutes.

Leah and Matt stood back from the bodies, and Matt began to say the kaddish, the prayer for the dead. Leah walked toward the Morris. Matt's voice cracked, barely audible, as he stood in awe before the bodies swinging gently in the afternoon breeze. Was this murder? Was it justice? Who decided?

Matthew Jordan sank to his knees and vomited. Behind him, the tiny Morris engine sputtered and turned over, stalled once, then turned over again. In front of him, the dead soldiers continued to swing back and forth against the darkened Israeli sky.

Chapter Fourteen

"How could you do such a thing? How could you believe that this could help us?" David Brod looked searingly at his sister and Matt Jordan, who sat next to Deena on the little couch in the living room of their home. Matt felt like a sixth-grader being scolded by his angry father. And just maybe he *had* acted like a child, doing what he knew was wrong. But was it?

Leah was silent, blank, definitely less regretful. As David looked down at her, she reached down and dangled a baby rattle before the tiny outstretched hands of giggling Jacob, who was lying on the floor in front of the couch.

David Brod stalked back and forth. "Now we have British soldiers going through back alleys, shooting indiscriminately at everything that moves." He stopped in front of the couch. "Just today," he bellowed, "five people were killed and over a hundred injured!"

"Okay, David," soothed Deena, "we can all hear you just fine."

When the red-headed giant was angry, only his wife could cool him down; it was as though he was careful not to scorch her with his heat. David stopped pacing and thrust his hands into his pockets.

"If Ben-Gurion ever gets an inkling that you were the killers, he'll throw us all in jail."

"Then we'll go," said Leah quietly. "And when the Old Man gets into his next political jam with the British and he needs something done, he'll quietly open the cell door and let us out to do his dirty work for him. So much for everybody's morality. We did more for Israel in five minutes than he has done in five years."

"My God, I don't believe what I'm hearing." David held up his hands. "You're killers. You have lowered yourself lower than the British."

"Stop it, David," Matt said. "You know better than to say that. We didn't kill for pleasure or for thrill. We executed two prisoners because nothing else was appropriate. It's as simple as that."

David simply shook his head. "But you can't do that. You have no right to execute prisoners. Begin, the Irgun, have no right."

"I don't understand you, David," said Leah, turning more acidic. She pointed a finger, moved forward in her seat. "The very day I came to Israel, you told me I should go with you to a meeting with Begin. And when he asked me to join the Irgun, it was with your blessing. Now what are you telling me?"

"I'm telling you that since that time, the Irgun has begun to engage in real terrorist acts. The Haganah doesn't approve. The Jewish Agency doesn't approve. This terrorism violates our policy of *havlaga* [restraint] and it's going to bring extremely serious British reprisals."

"I can't believe this nonsense!" Leah hissed. "The Haganah approves the bombing of the King David Hotel—the *bombing*, David, with explosives—but just because someone gets killed, Ben-Gurion is all aquiver. And these other actions resulted directly from our attempts to rescue *you*"—she pointed an accusing finger at her brother—"and you preach *havlaga* to *me*!"

"I never asked you to *murder* anyone!"

Leah turned her head, then spoke slowly, deliberately. "You know what the rabbis of the Talmud say. In a forest full of wolves, the only sin is to have no teeth." She looked at her brother, her cheeks quivering with her intensity. "I cannot endure what the British are doing to us. I've had enough, David. We engaged in a symbolic act, one that had to be done. We finally showed our teeth."

"Shhh, shhh," said Deena softly. "Jacob is falling asleep."

They all looked at the pink little baby, who despite the argument had begun to snore faintly. Deena smiled.

"Do you know what the London press is calling us?" David spoke in a raspy whisper and looked from Leah to Matt. "They called us 'vile Nazis.' Can you believe it? They called us Jews Nazis!"

David slumped into the small overstuffed chair next to the sofa. All of them looked grim.

"They used to call us shopkeepers and moneylenders and usurers and scum," Deena said softly. "Now they call us Nazis. Who cares what they call us? Just so they leave us alone. The mandate must end. Then the killing can stop. We've all had enough."

Deena looked at her husband and her eyes implored him to stop. David calmed himself. His voice became beseeching.

"There has to be a difference," he said, "between murder and self-defense. And I don't just mean what you call it. Somehow the killing of someone who is not trying to kill you has to be wrong. You can't just take hostages and execute them to make a point." David looked for help from Leah and Matt. Neither said a word. "How can we have any moral claim to this land of ours if we lower ourselves to the level of our oppressors? Acts like this will plunder our souls."

Leah responded in a whisper. "We are Jews, David. If we fight for ourselves, the whole world will call us criminals. If we execute British soldiers just like they execute ours, we are lawless. Who cares, David? Who cares anymore what the rest of the world says of us. Only one thing matters, to make this place our home, to destroy those who would hurt us." She stopped abruptly as Jacob woke with a startled cry.

"He must have wet himself," Deena said, rising from the couch, holding Jacob at arm's length. "And he's probably hungry."

"Let me," Leah said, reaching across Matt's lap for the crying baby. "I'm the one who woke him." She took the child in her arms, soothing him. "Come, mameleh," she said, "let's get you changed and fed and put a stop to all this foolishness." She stood, rocking Jacob softly. "You're the one we're doing all this for, little baby, so that nothing bad will ever happen to you." She looked over Jacob's downy little head at David, who turned his face away and sighed.

Chapter Fifteen

The struggle finally achieved a modicum of "success" in November of 1947, with the United Nations partition vote. Palestine would be divided into separate states—one Jewish, one Arab. Great Britain grudgingly established May 14, 1948, as the end of the British Mandate and the beginning of Jewish independence. The manhunts came to an end. David and the other Israeli "terrorists" were no longer wanted men. But the struggle was far from over: Jewish Palestine was only to be a fragment of the Promised Land, an affront to the will of God; and six Arab states readied their armies to invade Israel on May 15, its very first day in almost two and a half thousand years as a full-fledged nation again.

The Arab build-up was no secret, and both the Haganah and Irgun armies went about preparing for the inevitable battle. New weapons were now being smuggled into Israel despite the British embargo, and World War II arms slowly replaced the antiquated, undependable single-shot rifles which had long been Israel's only defense.

Menachem Begin had been in hiding in various places for several years, but when the fifteenth of May came, he finally left his hiding place undisguised and attended an Irgun rally in Mograbi Square in Tel Aviv. Leah went with him and together they stood proudly among thousands of other Jews, all exercising their rights as full citizens. Matt was back at Kibbutz Na'on, and Leah missed his presence on this important day; but then, it almost seemed fitting that she should celebrate this first day of Jewish independence alone—filled with the memory of her family, her first husband and child, and the weak old man who'd inspired her to fight so hard for this Jewish homeland, Yussel Pinsker. Leah thanked God for all these people who'd helped shape her life. She also thanked Him for all He'd done for her and her new family over the past year.

After some time, the mob grew restless and began to chant slogans denigrating David Ben-Gurion's government. Many of the words, to be sure, were vicious—but Leah quietly agreed with them. To her mind, a Begin government would be much better for the new nation, and it was clear that many others felt the same way. In response to the jeers, several loyal Haganah soldiers threw hand grenades into the startled crowd, seriously injuring a number of random onlookers.

Begin was outraged. At this rate, the Arabs didn't have to fire a shot. The Jews would wipe themselves out for them. Later that day, he demanded a meeting with Ben-Gurion. They needed to discuss things. The Old Man agreed.

Menachem Begin and Leah Jordan went to the meeting place.

Ben-Gurion and David Shaltner sat drinking juice. They all shook hands and sat down.

"You look pale, Menachem," said Ben-Gurion wanly.

"Years away from the sun, David. But I think it was worth it." Neither man smiled.

Ben-Gurion continued. "I have brought David Shaltner with me, because I have just put him in charge of the consolidation of our armed forces. That's what's foremost on my mind at the moment."

David Shaltner had been a Sergeant in the French Foreign Legion and was one of the few Jewish survivors of Dachau. He was an intensely loyal follower of Ben-Gurion, and it was for this reason, Leah knew, and not for any military prowess he might possess, that Ben-Gurion had given him the critically important job of unifying Haganah and Irgun. Shaltner also hated Begin, another trait much admired by Ben-Gurion.

"Menachem, it is time for us to bury the hatchet. We can't afford to have Irgun fighting the Haganah. As a nation, we must have a unified army."

"I entirely agree with you, David," Begin said quickly. "And I'll issue orders to that effect immediately, on one small condition." He paused. "I want our Irgun soldiers to go into the Haganah as a separate branch, just like the Palmach. But we will take our orders from the Haganah high command and the Jewish Agency."

Ben-Gurion and Shaltner whispered together for a moment, and Ben-Gurion said, "We agree." He began to stand up to leave the meeting, but Begin waved him back to the sofa.

"There's one more matter we must discuss, David. Last November, Irgun acquired a ship through American Jewish donations. We have named it the *Altalena*." Begin stopped and let the effect of this sink in. "Altalena" had been the pen name of Zeev Jabotinsky, the founder of the Betar movement which Begin had converted into the Irgun, and Jabotinsky had been Ben-Gurion's most viciously outspoken critic until his death a few year's back.

"The *Altalena* is a four-thousand ton LST capable of making fourteen knots while fully loaded with a thousand troops and their equipment," Begin went on. "It is now anchored off the coast of France. The French have agreed to supply us with a huge assortment of heavy and light weapons for a token payment of $250,000."

Ben-Gurion sank deeply into the overstuffed armchair. His eyes narrowed to slits and his look turned venomous. Leah sat calmly and watched him, waiting for his response, enjoying the fact that Begin had managed to grab the upper hand. As she and Begin had discussed on their way to the meeting, Ben-Gurion had no safe way to respond to this request: on the one hand, if he granted Begin the control of the ship and all the weapons, he'd be losing much of his own military advantage, practically risking civil war—and a tough war it would be, fighting against such an artillery; on the other hand, if he denied the request, Begin would have good reason to withdraw his allegiance to Haganah, and the civil strife Ben-Gurion sought to halt would merely continue.

Ben-Gurion sighed, pressing his fingertips together below his chin. "I'm very sorry, Menachem, but our coffers are empty. We haven't a grosh left to buy anything. But I will certainly look into the matter." Ben-Gurion stood quickly and offered his hand to Leah. They'd met several times over the past year when she'd accompanied her brother to Tel Aviv on Haganah business. She smiled politely at the cunning old fox, and he stalked silently out of the room without so much as looking at Begin.

Alone, Leah and Menachem sat tensely, enraged over this refusal to recognize Irgun's legitimacy, over Ben-Gurion's devious and weak-willed commitment to unification only to help fight the Arabs but not to achieve the ultimate prize, the restoration of the Third Temple, the Biblical Land of Israel.

"Well, what do we do about the *Altalena!*?" Leah asked.

"We bring it over any way we can," Begin hissed. "Irgun needs the men and the weapons."

"The Old Man won't let us, Menachem. We both know that was only a fancy excuse about having no money. The truth is, he hates you and he'll destroy us the first chance he gets."

Menachem rose from his seat. "Then it will start a civil war! I'm not prepared to let Israel be sold out by the Jewish Agency. Many of our people are ready to fight to make Judea and Samaria and Transjordan part of the Land of Israel, just as it was during the kingdoms of David and Solomon. Our people have suffered too much in the last ten years to let the British and the Americans dictate to us that all we can have is a tiny sliver of infertile land and the Arabs get most of the Land of Israel. Never! I don't care what the Old Man says—we will bring in the *Altalena* and the men and the weapons!"

In the past months, Leah had become one of Begin's closest confidants. Part of the closeness went back to the early years in Vilna, when Saul Brod had done so much to help Betar. But that was long ago, and now there was a new Leah, not the timid ultra-orthodox rabbi's wife of the stetl. Now she was full-grown and independent and she shared Begin's political messianic vision of Israel as a mighty Jewish colossus astride both banks of the Jordan as God had promised. She agreed with him about the ship, about finding a way to procure the weapons, and together the two of them would lead the fight to regain their homeland, with or without the blessing of David Ben-Gurion.

Several days later, Begin signed the formal agreement with Ben-Gurion to effect the merger of Irgun into Tzahal. Begin decided not to complicate matters by telling Ben-Gurion that a deal had been finalized just two days before between himself and the French government for all the requested military equipment. Two weeks later, the loading of the *Altalena* with the new recruits and weapons was complete: nine hundred trained soldiers, five thousand rifles, three hundred heavy machine guns, one hundred fifty artillery pieces, five caterpillar-track armored cars, four million rounds of ammunition, several thousand bombs, and an assortment of additional weaponry. The *Altalena* set sail for Israel.

On June 15, Begin met again with Ben-Gurion, this time to let him know about the impending arrival of the *Altalena*. Leah waited anxiously at the Tel Aviv headquarters, knowing full well that civil war could break out any day. After several long hours, Begin returned, and his reddened face told her much about how the meeting had gone.

"What happened, Menachem? What'd he say?"

Begin snarled through gritted teeth. "Well, he called me a lying snake, to start with. Things degenerated from there."

"I see," said Leah with a sarcastic smile. "I take it he didn't like your plan to land the *Altalena* in Tel Aviv."

"No, he didn't. He told me I was a carrion-eating vulture just waiting for him to make one false step, so I could rip out his liver with my teeth and feed it to the ragtag bunch of criminals I call an Army!" Begin was deeply humiliated and still angry, his temples throbbing. "That bastard wants us to land at Kfar Vitkin! Can you believe it? So he can store the weapons at the Haganah warehouse there!"

Kfar Vitkin, twenty-three miles north of Tel Aviv, was a *Mapai* [Labor Party] stronghold, totally loyal to Ben-Gurion. If the ship landed there and the Mapai troops took control of the unloading, none of the Irgun units in Tel Aviv would receive any of the weapons.

"That's absurd," Leah said. "Did you tell him we couldn't do that? We must land at Tel Aviv! These are *our* weapons, not his!"

"I told him," Menachem said. "It didn't do any good. We argued some, then I left. I've had enough cat-and-mouse, Leah. I'm ready to fight." He thought for a moment. "Have as many units as we have available report as soon as possible to the beach at Kfar Vitkin. The ship should land in three or four days. We'll be ready for it."

On June 19, when the *Altalena* was two-hundred twenty miles offshore, Captain Fein received his landing instructions from Begin: Kfar Vitkin. That evening at nine, the *Altalena* hit extremely rough water about fifty yards off the pier and had to return to open sea to avoid breaking up.

The following afternoon, Captain Fein once again maneuvered the *Altalena* to the Kfar Vitkin pier. All around the pier, up the side streets, from sidewalk cafes and market-stands, soldiers of both camps watched and waited. The ship was moored fast, and the Irgun soldiers, fresh from Europe, disembarked.

Several of the Irgun high command stood near the pier, surveying the collection of soldiers before them. A little over four hundred Irgun regulars had shown up over the past few days, and now nine hundred fresh recruits had been added. It was the largest gathering of Irgun soldiers ever assembled.

Leah gestured toward the Haganah units, who'd slowly lined the area. So far they'd done nothing to interfere with the operation. "Everything seems so quiet," she said, looking at Begin. "If we can get those weapons unloaded, we might get out of here without a hitch."

Begin shook his head. "No, this can't be it. Ben-Gurion's up to something—I just don't know what."

"We can't just *stay* here," said Leah. "We've got almost two thousand soldiers standing around staring at each other. Sooner or later something's going to snap. Someone's going to shoot."

Begin slapped the fence-rail he'd been leaning against. "Let's send all but fifty of our men to our installations in and around Tel

Aviv. If we do have any casualties here, let's be certain we're not completely wiped out. Those who remain can begin unloading the weaponry after nightfall. Then we'll see what the Old Man's planning."

"And in the meantime?" Leah asked.

"If trouble starts, we simply pull out and dock at Tel Aviv as we originally planned. If we're going to have a civil war, we ought to start it there, where we're strongest. And by waiting now, we force Ben-Gurion to make the first move. It will be his war, not ours. And in Tel Aviv, we'll crush him."

The Haganah lines broke to allow the Irgun troops to pull out. Dozens of trucks drove untouched out of Kfar Vitkin, and by six o'clock, Begin and Leah had boarded the ship at the dock to supervise the nighttime unloading.

As they were set to begin, a Corporal ran aboard ship with a message for Begin. "Sir, the Palmach batallion just arrived and they're replacing the Haganah units."

"The Palmach?" Begin looked at Leah. "What's Ben-Gurion thinking now? Is Yigal Armon out there, Corporal?"

"He is, sir."

"Damn." Armon had been one of Begin's other rivals since the battle for independence had begun. There was no love lost between the two men—and Ben-Gurion obviously knew that.

The Corporal shifted uneasily. "He gave me a message, sir. Here it is."

Begin read the slip of paper silently, then handed it to Leah. It commanded the Irgun units to surrender and informed them that the *Altalena* was being confiscated by the Palmach.

"We will *not* surrender!" Begin's forehead burst into a crimson red. His chest and arms began to tremble. Leah watched helplessly, fearing the worst—that Begin would start the war here and now. She knew that to him to be forced into retreat by that bastard Ben-Gurion would be the ultimate dishonor. But what other option did they have? They were down to fifty or sixty troops. They simply could not fight.

As it happened, there was no decision to make. After ten, maybe fifteen seconds the first mortar shells from the Palmach unit hit the ship. They exploded just forward of the small deck cannon in the bow.

Captain Fein leapt from his seat. "My God, those lunatics are trying to kill us!"

Chaos broke out among the troops. Leah ran with Begin to the deck gun to return the fire. Three soldiers were lying dead around it. Another mortar shell exploded about twenty feet away. Leah sprawled on the deck, Begin next to her.

They jumped up and ran back into the ship's control room. On the beach there was a battle raging between the Irgunists and the Palmachniks. The ship's units were outnumbered ten to one.

"Weigh anchor!" Begin shouted over the noise of the battle. "Let's get out of here before they kill us all!"

"Where the hell to?" yelled Fein, his eyes wild with fear.

"Tel Aviv!" hollered Leah.

"Right, right!" shouted Begin. The Palmach won't start a civil war right in the middle of Tel Aviv!"

After regaining twenty-five of its men, the Altalena slowly pulled away from the Kfar Vitken pier. The shelling stopped, and after a tense night of navigating, the ship anchored two hundred yards off the beach at Tel Aviv. It was six in the morning.

Begin had been wrong about Ben-Gurion: Armon and his Palmach battalion had regrouped on the beach and were waiting as Begin caught sight of land with the first light of new day. Crates of grenades filled the docks and several artillery pieces had been set up along the shore.

Begin ordered a motor launch to be loaded with supplies for a test run at the beach. He and Leah watched through binoculars as the launch reached the shore and the men unloaded the crates of weapons. No incidents. The launch returned to the Altalena and was reloaded. At one o'clock, it started out again for shore.

When the launch was about twenty yards from landing, Armon ordered his troops to open fire. Machine gun fire at close range swept the launch, killing all four men aboard. The launch blew up as its ammunition was ignited and bullets sprayed everywhere for ten minutes. Mortar fire pummeled the deck of the Altalena. More men fell. No fire was returned from the ship. Leah and Menachem ducked behind the bridge rampart. They knew that they were doomed.

The firing stopped. Irgun men extinguished the fires on the Altalena. Above the piers, U.N. observers at the Kaete Dan Hotel took their lunch on the terrace restaurant and watched the civil war show with the enthusiasm of fans at a Sunday soccer match. Thousands of Tel Aviv citizens formed curious crowds on the seashore.

"Ben-Gurion has gone mad," Begin said through clenched teeth, his jaw muscles working nervously.

"He's showing everyone that he's the boss and there is no leader but him," said Leah. "He wants to prove to the U.N. observer team"—Leah pointed at the luncheoners on the terrace of the Kaete Dan Hotel—"that he can keep order, even if it means killing his fellow Jews." Her eyes clouded with fear and her eyelids twitched with hatred.

"So what do we do? We desperately need this ship and these weapons," Begin said.

"I say we go right into the pier and unload. Ben-Gurion can't be crazy enough to kill us in front of half of Tel Aviv."

"God help me, I think you're wrong, Leah. I think he'll do just that. He wants me and the Irgun dead so he has no real competition as head of the government. I think he'll use the *Altalena* as proof that Irgun wants a civil war, and he's going to try to kill us all."

Leah and Menachem looked grimly at each other.

"And I'll tell you what else," Begin said. "I think when we're dead, that crazy bastard is going to call in the Haganah and try to get them to wipe out the Palmach. In one day's work, he's trying to destroy all of his competition."

The sun had dropped behind the *Altalena*, casting a golden sheen over Tel Aviv. The Irgun was trapped, helpless—and the battle for control over Israel was at hand.

Chapter Sixteen

Throughout the morning and early afternoon of June 21, David Brod listened to reports of the battle over his military radio. He'd been placed in command of the Haganah troops in the Galilee and the situation there was stable. Today, all the action was in Tel Aviv: Palmach attacking Irgun—with the Haganah watching from the wings. It was unbelievable. Ben-Gurion had certainly played this one strangely, if in fact he was the man behind it. The whole episode seemed almost comical, it was so bizarre.

But no one, least of all David, dared take the matter lightly. It was more than a political chess game; it was civil war. The Arabs— the Jews' legitimate enemy—had nothing to do with this conflict, and David's overriding concern had to be with the very survival of the Jewish state, now some five weeks old.

And then there was Leah. David hadn't been contacted about her whereabouts, but he'd heard Begin's name mentioned several times throughout the morning, and since they were almost always together, he knew she was probably on board ship with him. As the second exchange of gunfire heated up that afternoon, David no longer felt capable of keeping his post. He had to get to Tel Aviv.

He got into his staff car and ordered his driver to the Ritz Hotel in Tel Aviv. They sped through sporadic sniper fire and a half-hearted Arab roadblock near Nablus, then had a clear road into Tel Aviv. It was two o'clock and the sun was high, but a night-like hush pervaded the city. The car moved freely through the narrow streets to the Ritz Hotel—where Yigal Armon's Palmach had set up temporary headquarters.

David jumped out of the car and ran into the hotel, taking the elevator to the top floor. He burst through the staff room door. Inside, Yigal Armon was standing at the window, watching the *Altalena* through binoculars. For the moment, the battle had stopped.

"What the hell are you doing, Yigal?" David demanded. "We have a goddam civil war on our hands! I've heard reports that Irgun units are leaving their posts all over the country!"

"Calm down, David!" Armon said, turning away from the window and reaching for a cigarette from the humidor on his desktop. "I can explain everything."

As Assistant Chief of Staff, David Brod was not accustomed to this kind of talk from subordinates. He leaned across the desktop and spoke directly into Armon's bland, flat face. "Just who the hell do you think you're talking to?"

Armon struck a long wooden match, listening casually. The two men had never been friendly, and for David this was too much. He glared menacingly at the Palmach commander and raised his voice another notch: "I want to know *right now* on whose authority you're conducting this operation!"

After lighting his cigarette, Armon waved the match out, looking up with large, false, apologetic eyes. "David Ben-Gurion called me at five o'clock this morning," he said. "These are his direct orders."

"The Old Man himself? Has he gone crazy?" David backed away from the desk, looked out through the window. The *Altalena* rested quietly some two hundred yards off-shore. "It's civil war, goddammit. What's got into him?"

"It was a cabinet decision, David. Call Moshe Yadlin. He was there. He'll confirm it."

David turned again toward Armon, pointing roughly at the ship. "My sister's on that ship!" he screamed. "Do you hear me? My sister is on the *Altalena*!"

Armon finally showed some concern, falling forward from his relaxed position, stubbing out his unsmoked cigarette. "But David—I have direct orders. God help me, I can't defy orders from the Cabinet."

David sank into a chair, deflated. He thought for a minute, then reached for the telephone and dialed Moshe Yadlin's private office number. The Commander-in-Chief answered: "I'm sorry, David, it's out of my hands. This is the Old Man's direct order. You'll have to call him."

David dialed the National Council Headquarters, but Ben-Gurion was not available at the moment. Yes, they would have him call as soon as possible. David hung up. Fifteen minutes passed like a decade, and the phone rang.

"Aluf Brod." Ben-Gurion's voice was stern, formal. David wondered what it meant; high officials of Israel rarely addressed each other with such formality. "We've got a problem?" asked Ben-Gurion casually.

"Sir, I'm sure that my sister is on the *Altalena* with Begin. I called to see if we can grant a cease-fire, just long enough for me to get her off, provided she's willing to leave, along with any of the others who want to call it quits."

Ben-Gurion was quiet for a moment. "They could have called it quits last night, David," he said. "We offered them a chance to surrender."

"I know, sir. But I'm sure that by now they've reconsidered their position. If I could just speak with my sister...."

The Old Man paused again. "Okay, I don't suppose that could hurt anything. We just want to end this thing. Put Yigal on the line."

David thanked him. Armon took the phone, listened for a moment, said "Yes, sir," and hung up. "There will be a cease-fire until four o'clock," he announced. "Everyone who wants off can get off on the remaining launch from the *Altalena*. Go down and tell Isaac Rubin to pass the message to the ship."

David took the elevator down and ran to the command post on the beach. "Isaac, the Old Man has ordered a cease-fire until four o'clock so anyone who wants to leave the *Altalena* can come in unharmed. Send a motorboat out to deliver the message to Begin."

A motorboat was rigged with a white flag of truce on its radio antenna and sped out to the *Altalena*. After just a few minutes, the sailor reported back that the *Altalena* would send out its wounded and anyone else who wanted to leave.

David decided to stay ashore as the unloading operation got underway. Slowly, the men on the *Altalena* loaded their wounded into the launch under a flag of truce, and David watched closely through his binoculars, searching for his sister Leah.

She hadn't yet emerged from the cabin when Isaac Rubin's field telephone rang with a message from Armon. David lowered his binoculars and watched Rubin take his orders. Rubin hung up and immediately contacted his artillery commander.

"Prepare to open up with mortar and artillery fire on the ship," he said. "Stand by for further orders."

David grabbed Rubin by the lapels. "Countermand that order, you son of a bitch! We've got a cease-fire!"

Two Palmach military policemen guarding the command post hustled inside and pulled David off Rubin. The two Privates stared in clench-jawed fear as they restrained the Assistant Chief of Staff of the entire Haganah from throttling the much junior Assistant Palmach Commander.

Rubin glared at David. "I've got my orders! Armon just spotted the Irgunists setting up fifty-caliber machine guns on the deck—pointed straight at the Ritz and all the soldiers we've got stationed out here. What do you want us to do, let them murder us, just because the white flag's flying?"

Rubin grabbed his telephone and issued the firing orders.

Instantly, the deep booms of the artillery and the pops of the mortar shells went off in volleys. Everyone on the beach watched as the shells hit the *Altalena* and the ship burst into flames.

David shook free of the guards and ran outside. He saw Irgun soldiers jumping off the *Altalena* and swimming toward shore. Several Haganah men got into rowboats and rowed out to pick up survivors. David joined them.

As they neared the ship, which now was nearly engulfed by flames, David still could not spot Leah. Finally, he saw the ship's captain bodily removing Menachem Begin from the cabin and pushing him overboard. Despite the deadly situation, David knew that Begin, incredibly stubborn man that he was, had undoubtedly refused to abandon his sinking ship. Suddenly, David saw Leah jumping into the churning topaz water, and he directed his boat toward her and the seething, bobbing, silent Begin.

An Irgun craft approached simultaneously, and as David's crew gathered Leah out of the choppy water, the Irgun men pulled Begin into their vessel and sped off toward Netanya. Begin wasn't about to offer himself into the hands of the Palmach.

"David, thank God!" Leah reached out for him, and they hugged each other. "The Old Man's gone crazy," she whispered. "I thought we'd had it. I thought it was finally the end."

"We've all gone a little crazy," David said. "I don't know what's going on." He soothingly touched his sister's bruised, reddened cheek. "But I know it's not the end."

The next day, David read the National Council directive, signed by Ben-Gurion, out loud to the family gathered around the kitchen table: "Effective immediately, the Palmach and Irgun commands are disbanded. All Palmach and Irgun soldiers are now members of *Tzahal* [the Israel Defense Forces] under the uniform command of *Haganah* [Army] Chief of Staff Moshe Yadlin."

No one said a word. Leah tore the paper from David's hand and viciously crumpled it, then threw it on the floor.

She raised her hands to the ceiling, screaming out in frustration: "Ben-Gurion, that no-good bastard! He's stolen Israel!"

Chapter Seventeen

David Brod now had to be in Tel Aviv full-time to carry out his new duties as Haganah Chief of Operations. Matt Jordan had had three years of military duty in Europe as well as combat experience in Sicily and the Battle of the Bulge, so with David's strong recommendation, Matt was appointed a Major in the Haganah and assigned to the operations staff. The two families moved from Kibbutz Na'on to the house on Herbert Samuel Street in Tel Aviv.

As the summer wore on, the Arab/Jewish edge of Jaffa/Tel Aviv became a virtual firing range: Arab snipers in the high stone minaret of the Hassan Bek Mosque in Jaffa laid down a deadly barrage of machine gun fire into Herbert Samuel Street and the park and beach across the street. Just a half-block south of the house now shared by the Brods and Jordans, the Haganah erected a barricade of stone and sandbags, and Haganah soldiers patrolled the area behind the barricade and prevented any Arab attacks from Jaffa through to Tel Aviv. Arab and Jewish families alike tried to maintain a normal existence as best they could—but the city was at war and tensions were explosive.

On the last Saturday in July, 1948, the Grand Mufti of Jerusalem lit the fuse by giving an impassioned speech over the nationally-broadcast Arab radio station. As Mufti, one of his principal duties was to administer *waqf* funds for the protection and maintenance of Muslim holy places, including the Mosque of Omar in the Old City of Jerusalem. The Mosque was built on the ruins of the Second Temple of Jerusalem, the holiest shrine of the Jews, and was bounded on one side by the "wailing wall," the outer courtyard wall of the Second Temple.

In his address, the Grand Mufti accused a mob of Hasidim of desecrating the Mosque of Omar. When the Arabs heard this, their grinding hatred of the Jews erupted into an orgy of violence in Jaffa and Haifa and Jerusalem. The uprising was as spontaneous as it was brutal. Arab irregulars stormed through Jewish neighbor-hoods, killing and looting and pillaging. The Jewish radio station was silent for the sabbath, so there was no warning of the outbreak of violence.

On Herbert Samuel Street, a hundred angry Arabs assaulted the eleven Haganah soldiers stationed at the barricade. Seven of the soldiers fled in panic. The other four were captured by the mob. They were stripped, held down on their backs on the ground, and castrated. Their eyes were gouged out and their tongues sliced, and the hysterical Arabs danced and cheered as the Jews choked to death in their own blood.

David, Matt and Leah were all at work that day. The only ones home on Herbert Samuel Street were Deena and Jacob.

Across town, Matt and David got word of the Jaffa riot at Haganah headquarters. It was a little after ten-thirty. David panicked immediately, becoming wild with fear for his wife and son. Matt quickly radioed the commander of the Haganah platoon that was stationed at the Great Synagogue on Allenby Road and was told that the main group of Arabs had already been repulsed. A mopping up action was underway. He and David wouldn't be needed for a while.

He ran downstairs to the basement armory and got two Bren guns, heavy British machine guns. Then he ran back outside to David, waiting in the jeep at the curb. They careened around the corner of Hayarkon to Ben Yehuda and sped through the open market square onto Herbert Samuel Street. The place was barely recognizable from that morning, just a few hours before. Several houses were afire. Women and children ran through the street, wailing and moaning, their houses ruined, their loved ones gone.

David skidded the jeep to a lurching stop in front of the house, and he and Matt raced through the open doorway. Just as Deena's name began to form on Matt's lips—to call out for her—he saw her lying on the floor in the middle of the living room, a pool of blood outlining her naked body. She'd been grotesquely mutilated: her breasts cut off, her eyes gouged out, her body slit from her chest to below her navel. Her bloody, oozing intestines had been scooped out of her and heaped by her side.

Jacob lay headless beside her. His tiny body had been emasculated. Jacob's penis and testicles had been stuffed into Deena's mouth. Jacob's dark, bloody head lay in a corner of the room.

Matt put his arm around David and pulled him out of the house.

David slumped to his knees on the lawn, pitching forward on his face. Matt knelt beside him. There was silence except for the women's crying and the occasional calls of the soldiers on the street, searching the houses for casualties. Matt waved over a Lieutenant, who came out of the house directly adjacent. The Lieutenant walked into the Brod house, then came out an instant later, staggering and gagging. He steadied himself and walked over to David's jeep and used the radio.

Moments later, a military ambulance drove up and parked. David was now sitting up on the grass, staring vacantly. Matt still knelt beside him, too shocked to speak or move. He only wanted to provide some sort of comfort for David, but he knew that there was none. He watched dumbly as the two medics walked into the house, and a moment later one of them returned to the ambulance, took two rubberized canvas bags out of the back, and re-entered the house.

Tires screeched on the street. Matt looked over and saw Leah in the tiny Morris Minor belonging to Menachim Begin. Her eyes found the two of them, kneeling on the lawn, and her look of panic changed to horror. She climbed out of the car, just as the medics filed out of the house, and gasped when she saw them. One had a large bag slung over his shoulder. The other cradled a much smaller bag. Both men were covered with blood.

"David," Leah said quietly, walking up to her brother and putting her arm on his shoulder.

Matt got slowly to his feet. Leah said, "I heard about it just a few minutes ago. I—" She held back her tears. "All I heard was that a mob worked its way down Herbert Samuel."

Matt felt distant—not from Leah, but from his own body, his own feelings, as if his outer layer of skin had gone dead and he had begun operating mechanically. He felt neither warm nor cold, just nothing. He spoke without emotion. "Deena and Jacob were mutilated," he said. "We found them inside."

"David?" Leah collapsed down next to her brother, touching his face with both hands, beginning to sob. "David, are you all right?"

David nodded slowly. His body shook uncontrollably, but no sound came from him and no tears fell from his eyes. Matt again knelt beside him and hugged him hard to stop his shaking.

One of the medics approached hesitatingly. "Do you want to

come with us?" he asked gently. "Does Aluf Brod want to come?"

David stared at nothing. His body slowly ceased shaking. He looked up at the medic and forced his eyes to focus. He shook his head slowly.

Matt stood up. "I'll go with Deena and Jacob," he said quietly. "Maybe we should all go back to Na'on tonight. I'll see you at the Haganah Hospital." He hugged Leah, kissing her softly on the lips. "Stay with David," he whispered to her and walked to the ambulance.

Leah didn't need to be told. She felt her brother's loss as strongly as she'd felt her own. This, too, was her loss, although right now David could not feel or even imagine that. Leah knew there was nothing to say, and nothing to do. She simply sat with him as he stared blankly out at the street. She refused to let her own crippling memories possess her and disable her. David needed her strength, not her weakness. For more than an hour they just sat, then David finally stood up. He was shaky at first, but then he put his arms straight down at his sides and stiffened militarily.

"I'll drive myself to Na'on," he said. "I want Deena and Jacob there with me. Will you and Matt see that they're brought there as soon as possible?" He still didn't look at her; his voice was no more than a distant whisper.

"Of course, David. We'll be there tomorrow morning. And we'll stop in Rehovot to pick up Rabbi Shatzkin for the funeral."

David walked slowly to his jeep, leaned against it for a moment, seemingly to catch his breath, then got in and drove slowly away from the little house.

Leah walked into the house and saw the pools of blood and several small pieces of intestines and skin which the medic had carelessly failed to scoop into the bags. She ran to the kitchen and vomited into the sink. After a couple of minutes of empty heaving, she reached a bottle of brandy from the cupboard and filled her mouth with it and gargled and spat it into the sink, running some water to clean the mess into the drain. She walked into David's bedroom and packed his old suitcase with his civilian clothes and Army uniforms. Most of his clothing and belongings were at Na'on. She packed nothing of Deena's or Jacob's.

She went into her and Matt's room and packed Matt's dufflebag with the few clothes they had brought here from Na'on. Then, forcing herself not to look down at the floor, she walked out of the house forever, put the valise and dufflebag in the back seat of the Morris, and drove to Begin's *malineh*.

Leah and Matt slept on the floor in the Begins' apartment that night, as they had many times in the past. Leah thought all night, through fitful bouts of sleep, of Deena, and little Jacob, and how horribly they'd been killed. She remembered the evening not so long ago, when Deena had voiced the one dream that the whole family shared and dreamed of every day: that the killing would soon stop. That night, they'd all looked at Jacob as the hope for a better future, a safe and secure and richly promising future. But now he was dead.

Late the next morning, she and Matt took a bus to the morgue, and Matt handed the officer in charge the temporary requisition papers for an ambulance. The two plain pine coffins were placed inside, one large, one small, and they drove slowly through the parchment desert. They picked up Rabbi Shatzkin and headed to Kibbutz Na'on. The sun was a lurid blood stain spilling onto a shimmering crimson horizon. Myriad wildflowers stood mournfully at parade rest beside the road where Deena and Jacob passed.

The ceremony at Na'on's graveyard was not elaborate. Death was no stranger to the Yishuv or the people of the kibbutz, especially since the War for Independence had begun two and a half months earlier. Na'on had already buried four of its sons and one daughter. But this time there was an added element of grief. The coffins could not be opened to let Deena and Jacob be seen just one last time. As the rabbi chanted the centuries-old prayers, the pine coffins were lowered into the earth.

David picked up a handful of dirt and threw it on the large box and he did the same with the small one. Then he walked slowly across the barren cotton field to his cottage in front of the pear orchard.

Chapter Eighteen

Matt and Leah stayed on in Na'on with David. The first few days, David stayed alone in his cottage. Leah brought his meals, left them steaming on his small work table—only to return with the next meal and find the first one cold and barely touched. There was nothing Leah could tell him; she could only hope that soon David would rise up out of his gloom and find his own life again.

On the fifth day after the funeral, David showed up at the large eating hall for dinner and quietly ate his meal with the rest of the kibbutzniks. Afterward, he joined Matt and Leah for a walk around Na'on. The three walked silently, drinking in the warm air and the heavy fragrance of the tiny white grapefruit flowers which covered the budding trees in the small emerald green grove. The gloomy half-light of dusk descended on them, and they walked to David's cottage.

"Stay with me awhile," David said.

"You sure you don't want to go inside and rest?" asked his sister.

"I'm all rested out. I don't feel like being alone."

Leah was relieved. The worst of the grieving was apparently over. David looked strong, and the haunted, vacant stare that he had worn for almost a week was gone.

"Come on. I'll get the brandy," he said. "We could all use a drink. It's been a long time."

They sat in the quickly deepening darkness and sipped the raw brandy from Rishon le-Zion. The memories of the missing pair drifted conspicuously on the evening air. Two ground squirrels cavorted merrily on the leaf-strewn, untended lawn in front of the cottage. The same old barn owl sonorously hooted a melancholy pavane from its perch on the great sycamore tree.

David cleared his throat, then spoke deliberately, as if he'd rehearsed: "We could have prevented what happened to Deena and Jacob."

Neither Matt nor Leah said anything.

"It's true," David continued after a pause. "Our entire policy toward the Arabs has been wrong. The Christian Arabs are okay, the ones in the Galilee. The Muslims hate them more than they hate the Jews, so the Christians have always sided with us. But they're a small minority. There are a million and a half Palestinian Muslim Arabs and less than half that many Jews—about six-hundred fifty thousand. If we keep going like we have been since November, we're simply going to be wiped out by the Muslims, like Deena and Jacob."

The mention of his brutally slain family made David turn his face away, and he stopped speaking. He sighed deeply, took a long swallow of the brandy. Still Matt and Leah said nothing. They just sat listening, relieved, at least, that David had conquered his grief and come back to them. But Leah felt a bit frightened as well. The robust good-naturedness of her brother was gone, not even a shadow remained, and in its place was a brittleness and a bitterness which he had never before had.

"Many of our people have lost all of their families and loved ones over the last decade. First the Germans and the Poles and the Lithuanians slaughtered us. Now the Arabs slaughter us. We made a terrible mistake in the Holocaust. Our people didn't fight back! They just became humbled victims, singing religious songs while they marched passively into the ovens."

The only light was from the sliver of pale moon, partially smoked over by a high, thin washboard of clouds. Leah could only see her brother's form, his hunched, still outline, in the dissipated light.

Leah now understood the direction of his bitterness. He, too, had grown tired of Ben-Gurion's policy of restraint. "Now you sound like Menachem Begin," she said to him. "That's exactly what he's been saying— 'Only thus!'" Leah held up her clenched right fist holding an unseen rifle, the symbol of Irgun. "No more eye for an eye. A *hundred* of their eyes for every Jewish eye they gouge out! Let them pay ten times in mutilated dead for every one of our people that they slaughter!"

David nodded. "How can we continue to practice *havlaga* [restraint] after what we've been through? The Arabs only understand people who're willing to rip their livers out with their teeth. There's no other way to reach them. We know; we've tried."

Matthew would once have been shocked by such thinking, let

alone such violent talk coming from his friend David and his own wife, Leah. But the last two years had changed him. He had come to believe—to know with grim conviction—that counter-terrorism was the only defense the Jews had against Arab atrocities. Matt had not wept at the gravesides of Deena and Jacob; here in Palestine it was wasteful to cry over the deaths of family or friends or anyone, for there was too much death. It dried up all the tears and left you parched, filled with hatred of the killers, with a voice that screamed forth for vengeance from your very soul.

David Brod's voice broke into the silence that had fallen over them. "I've come to the conclusion that the Jewish Agency policy of peaceful coexistence with the Palestinian Arabs is wildly wishful thinking."

Matt walked over to the door jamb and switched on the dim yellow porch light. Immediately it was swarmed around by an eager, darting coterie of translucent, veiny winged bugs.

"The surrounding Arab countries have a zillion square miles of empty space," David said solemnly. "I think the Palestinian Arabs ought to go there to live."

"And just how do you think we can accomplish that?" Leah chided him gently. "Shall we just ask them to leave?"

"No, of course not." David stared ahead into the darkness, possessed by the demons of the past, haunted by the ghosts of the future. He had clearly had enough. He wanted to change the way of the future. "There's only *one* way," he said, his voice vicious, grating. "We go through their villages and destroy their homes. We go through their towns and destroy their buildings. They'll have nowhere to live. They'll *have* to leave. And they won't be able to go anywhere in Israel. So they'll go to the Arab states. It sounds foolishly simple, I know, but I've been thinking about it a long time. It's the only way."

Matt wished Deena was still here; if she were, she could calm David down. No one else was capable of it—not Leah, not Matt, certainly not David himself.

David stood up from his chair, his voice baleful, his body tensed and poised like a threatened adder. "If we mount severe reprisals against the Arabs each and every time they massacre any of our people, we'll be able to plant fear in their breasts. As it is now, they're used to murdering helpless Hasidim and women and children, without ever suffering any real consequences. We never take revenge, because we're such a holy people. Bullshit! It's time we do unto others what they have been doing to us! We can't let any notions of biblical morality make us afraid to protect ourselves. We have learned well how to die. It's time we learn how to live, and in this world, that means that we have to learn how to kill!"

BOOK TWO

EXODUS

"When the Lord thy God shall bring thee into the land to possess it, and shall cast out many nations before thee, the Hittites, and the Girgashites, and the Amorites, and the Canaanites, and the Perrizites, and the Givites, and the Jebusites, seven nations all greater and mightier than thou; and when the Lord thy God shall deliver them up before thee, thou shalt smite them; *then* thou shalt utterly destroy them. Thou shalt make no covenant with them, nor show mercy unto them."

—Deuteronomy 7:1-2

Chapter One

September 1948

The Company of Israeli soldiers watched and waited nervously as the brooding stone walls of the ancient village of Deir Yassin slowly took shape against the dry, rocky hills west of Jerusalem. At first, the morning's slow dawn only deepened the slate-gray pall; then the sun's first beams finally cut through and melted the sepulchral gloom of mist off the slumbering village. It was six in the morning.

Three millennia of conquerors had struggled to control this bleak heap of rocks; since the reign of King David, Deir Yassin had been the key to Jerusalem. It commanded the most strategic heights on the road from Jaffa/Tel Aviv into the capital. And now, the Israeli Army needed the heights to protect Jerusalem from Arab attack.

Leah's job was simply to drive the makeshift armored car to the edge of the village, where Ami Carmel would announce the siege over the car's loudspeaker while the villagers awoke. He would announce that the way to Ein Kerem, five miles south, was open, and that no one would be harmed if they immediately loaded their belongings on their donkey carts and left Deir Yassin. The "resettlement" of the Arab villagers was slated to be swift and efficient. Routine.

Eighty Irgun soldiers crept behind the armored car, as slow and plodding as a yoked water buffalo, as Leah steered it up the road to Deir Yassin. Fifty-two Stern Gang soldiers approached from the other side. They were now all members of the Haganah, serving in a unified Tzahal to tighten Israel's control over the Shephelah.

About fifty yards from the village, Ami Carmel began his announcement. The loudspeaker screeched, then his voice came over loud and clear, in fluent Arabic: "Attention! The village of Deir Yassin has been requisitioned by the Israel Defense Forces. No one will be hurt. Remove your belongings and evacuate immediately to Ein Kerem. All structures in this village will be demolished in two hours. Repeat, all structures will be demolished in two hours."

Ami waited. Sleepy Arabs began emerging from their homes, shouting to each other in confusion and disbelief.

"Repeat it, Ami," Leah said. "Make sure they understand our—"

Suddenly, the armored car she and Ami were riding in struck a land mine and was blasted into the air—smashing back to the ground, rolling over on its side. Leah heard the popping of gunfire: Arab sentries, apparently frightened by what they thought was an artillery attack, had opened up on the approaching soldiers. As the car rocked to a stop, Leah checked herself—she was unhurt—and shook Ami back to consciousness. He looked at her, confused, then heard the gunfire and began kicking at the jammed car-door. It finally burst free and the two of them grabbed their submachine guns and climbed out of the wreckage.

They saw pandemonium. The Irgun and Stern Gang men, steeped in the tactics of terrorism but never before exposed to a more conventional battle, had panicked. Firing had broken out from every side, overwhelming the limited defense of the village. Whatever Arabs had started shooting were now dead. The Israeli men ran from house to house, breaking out windows with their submachine guns and firing indiscriminate bursts into the houses. A sapper planted charges against several buildings and explosions filled the air with blinding dust.

Leah ran toward the center of the village, looking for the Irgun commander in charge of this fiasco. She stumbled over the bodies of dead Arabs, old men with canes, babies splattered with blood, old and young women, a little girl still clinging to her mother's severed arm. In front of one house, an old man lay face-up to the rising sun, his empty eyes peering eerily from the dark cloth of a woman's scarf—a quick costume that obviously hadn't worked. Beyond him, and throughout the village, Arab men of all ages, some with rifles and machine guns, some not even armed or dressed after jumping out of bed, littered the dusty ground.

In the village center was an ancient stone house, painted turquoise to ward off evil demons—two stories, many rooms, elegantly decorated around the door jambs and windowsills with colorful ceramic tiles. It was obviously the *mukhtar's* [mayor's] house. A Stern Gang soldier holding a heavy machine gun had lined several Arabs up against the outer wall. The first, an old man in a flowing *keffiyah* [headdress] and gray beard, looked like the mukhtar. Next to him shivered a tiny, shriveled white-haired woman covered in a traditional black gown, and next to her, a tall, handsome young man stood only in his baggy pajama bottoms, his back turned, his arms raised. A young girl—just six or seven years old—cried out beside him, and finally, at the end of the line, a terrified, beautiful young woman, heavily pregnant, clutched a small baby in her arms.

As Leah ran toward them, the soldier opened fire, spraying the group slowly from left to right. Leah stopped, horrified, and without a second thought, she put the butt of her submachine gun against her hip and fired a short blast. The Jewish murderer fell in a bloody heap.

Leah ran to the people against the wall. They were all dead, except the dark young woman holding the baby. The shots meant for the mother had shattered the baby's skull, and the woman's dress was covered with the blood and bits of the bone and flesh of her child. In the woman's cobalt eyes Leah saw blank terror, uncomprehending stark terror. Leah pulled the shattered baby out of her arms and placed it down by the wall. She grabbed both of the woman's hands and pulled her up off the ground, where she'd fallen from the force of the blasts against her child.

Leah held tightly to one of the young woman's hands and started running toward the edge of the village. When they were just outside the village, Leah pointed south and shouted, "Ein Kerem, Ein Kerem," looking the woman in the eyes to see if she understood what was happening.

"Ein Kerem! Ein Kerem!" Leah yelled again, still pointing in the direction of the safe village.

The woman gasped and looked down at herself, at her empty arms, at the bloody mess on the front of her dress. *"Ibni? Wain Ibni?"* she cried, holding up her hands pleadingly. Leah could not understand the Arabic, but she knew the look, the gesture. The vision of the Prince of Darkness swinging Nachman by his legs exploded before her eyes.

"Ein Kerem! Ein Kerem!" Leah yelled again, pointing. The woman slowly began to realize her situation—looking back at the village once more, then at Leah. Finally she turned, ran down through the ditch and up the other side to a grassy meadow and began running toward Ein Kerem. By now other Arabs were also fleeing across the open field.

Leah ran reluctantly back into the village. She couldn't imagine how this kind of carnage could have happened, or how she and the others would explain it to Ben-Gurion and the rest of the world. She knew it wasn't planned or ordered; they were simply supposed to evacuate the village. The men had just gone wild.

The firing was at last dying down. The Irgun commander was running from soldier to soldier, screaming at each to hold his fire. Carmel was doing the same. About forty of the Jewish soldiers were wounded and a few were dead, but some two hundred and fifty

Arabs—men, women, children and babies—were dead, many in the streets, many still in their beds and cradles.

Leah rushed up to Ami Carmel and asked him to locate a Koran in one of the houses and meet her at the edge of the meadow next to the village. He looked back at her, confused but saying nothing, then nodded gently. "Two minutes," was all he said.

She ran to the *mukhtar's* house, wrapped the Arab woman's dead and bloodied infant in his blanket, and met Ami in the meadow. He said nothing, just watched as Leah kicked out a small hole in the soft earth and laid the baby in it, covering him with the loose soil. She didn't know which tears were for her own baby Nachman and which for the tiny infant lying before her in his fresh grave—but it didn't matter. The tears simply came for them both, senselessly destroyed. She could see Nachman now, those big blue eyes. . . .

"Read something appropriate for a funeral, Ami," she gasped between sobs. Carmel paged through the Koran for a few moments, then started reading in Arabic:

"*Bi-smi'llahi'r Rachmani'r Rachim.*" [In the name of Allah, the Beneficent, the Merciful.]

For the unbelievers we have prepared fetters and chains and a blazing fire. But the righteous shall drink of a cup tempered at the Camphor fountain, a gushing spring at which the servants of Allah will refresh themselves. . . .

They shall be served with silver dishes, and beakers as large as goblets; silver goblets which they themselves shall measure; and cups brim-full with ginger flavored water from the Fount of Selsabil. They shall be attended by boys graced with eternal youth, who to the beholder's eyes will seem like scattered pearls. When you gaze upon that scene you will behold a Kingdom blissful and glorious. . . .

Leah fell to her knees by the side of the grave. A deathly silence settled over everything. She clutched her aching swollen belly, the new life that was growing there, and she began shaking uncontrollably. "My God, what have we done?" she wept, her head sagging on her chest. "What have we done?"

Her mind reeled with the ghastly stench of death all around her and the horrific vision of the shattered, bloodied Arab baby in his grave. She couldn't stop the piercing memories which followed her, drowning her, suffocating her. Nachman's baby blue eyes, his terrified wail, his tiny, shattered skull....

The Nazi armies are stymied by the Russians. The Thousand Year Reich is teetering on the edge of disaster. For the moment, the killing centers are needed for their slave labor factories, to turn out supplies for the German Armies, rather than merely to kill Jews. Treblinka's crematoria pits vomit forth much less of the blood and bone and sinew of the Jewish people—foul smelling soot which clings to everyone and everything within miles. Only two or three hundred Jews are being slaughtered each day.

Governor General Frank orders his adjutant to set up an inspection schedule for the killing centers to find ways to increase productivity and the quality of workmanship in the slave labor factories. Frank himself will conduct this vital mission, to see if significant improvements can be made, and he will be accompanied by General Odilo Globocnik, who has set up the killing centers of Belzec and Sobibor, as well as Rudolph Hoess, the commander of Auschwitz.

The entire cadre of Sonderkommandos *at Treblinka is put to work making the place spotless for the coming inspection. The carpenter shop produces a beautiful sign for the top of the camp entrance, with "Treblinka" hand-etched into a huge pine beam. The factory extends its workday from twelve to fourteen hours to increase the number of German uniforms already clogging the warehouse by the railway station. Bodies and pieces of bodies which have not been fully incinerated in the pits behind the "shower" room are soaked with gasoline and burned. Everything is in readiness for the inspection.*

Leah and Colonel Karl Mencken have lived together for a year and a half. Nachman is just turning three years old. He speaks only German, knows no one but Leah herself. Leah only permits him to call Mencken "Herr" [Sir], never "Vati" [Daddy]. The Colonel is in his office or in camp headquarters from dawn till late in the evening. He gets drunk almost every night in Treblinka with other senior camp officers, so he almost never sees Nachman. Leah prefers it that way. She knows that whatever Mencken touches, he befouls. She, meanwhile, lives reclusively in the spacious and comfortable quarters, never going into the camp, dreaming of the days back in Vilna when she had her freedom and her family. Twice a week she goes shopping for groceries in the village on her bicycle, but only for short moments. It cannot compare to those wondrous spring days when she'd wander through the narrow streets of Vilna, picking out new clothes for the summer. Instead, she sits at home and waits for Mencken to finish his nightly drinking, after which he joins her in bed and rapes her, or beats her, or both. Leah's old life is over—and she has no way of knowing how long this new one is going to last.

Jew or no Jew—and he is the only one, God willing, who will ever know—Karl Mencken is proud and covetous of his beautiful young mistress, and he looks forward to showing her off when the high military personnel come for their inspection. She's as delicate as French lace and the most permissive lover he has ever known, though it never occurs to him that her permissiveness comes from his constant beatings.

On the Saturday before the scheduled inspection, Mencken announces to Leah that he wants her to have a new outfit to wear for the dignitaries who are coming to inspect Treblinka. Later that morning, he, Leah and Nachman drive to Warsaw, about sixty-five miles away. There, in Paderewski Square, the stylish boutiques of Warsaw import the finest gowns from Nazi-occupied Paris for the wives and mistresses of the senior Nazi officers of the Generalgouvernement.

They park among numerous other German staff cars at Paderewski Square, and Leah steps foot on strange turf for the first time in eighteen months. Though still enslaved by Karl Mencken, she can't help feeling some of the excitement of this modern city. Mencken takes her hand and they begin to stroll the boulevard.

As they window shop along the broad avenue, they blend in well with the many other Nazi officers strolling and shopping with their wives and girlfriends, many holding little children by the hand. It's a wonderfully sunny day, not too hot, and Mencken feels exuberant being away from the sooty death at Treblinka. They sit at an outdoor table of a fancy little restaurant and order lime ices. Nachman claps his hands at the prospect of a treat.

As Karl chats amicably with Leah, and Nachman dribbles sherbet on his shirtfront, a short stocky officer stops on the sidewalk in front of the table and walks up to Karl.

"Karl, how are you?" blurts Standartenführer *[Colonel] Erwin Schlegg, slapping Karl on the back. They shake hands effusively.*

Leah looks at him and smiles sweetly. She has long since learned to hide the infinite terror which suffuses her from time to time. She has instantly recognized this animal who beat her father to death before her eyes less than two years ago.

Karl stands and introduces Leah and Nachman to Schlegg, calling them "Lara" and "Milos." Nachman continues digging at a small, slippery ball of lime sherbet with his fingers. Leah extends her hand limply to Schlegg, saying in a muffled voice, "Sehr angenehm." She looks away quickly.

Karl and Erwin stand and talk about their assignments, the old days in Vilna, their prospects. Again they clap each other on the back and shake hands. Schlegg turns toward Leah and clicks his heels, bowing slightly. He says nothing, but his black eyes linger on her, quizzically, trying to place her, to remember where they met. His hairless eyebrows pucker as he scrutinizes her. He walks away, and Karl resumes his seat, goes on chatting.

Leah thinks better of telling Karl that Schlegg might have recognized her. She doesn't know what Karl would do to her and Nachman if he thought there were the possibility that they might injure his career. So she says nothing.

They shop at a very elegant boutique, as planned, but Leah is too frightened now even to pretend to enjoy herself. The city has turned gray for her. It has, like the rest of her horrifying, nightmarish life, gone Nazi. Oblivious to her misery, Mencken cheerfully chooses a dusky rose silk dress that clings slinkily to her hips and shows her firm nipples. She'll knock their eyes out, he muses to himself. They'll go crazy over her. He also buys her a pair of red peau de soie *heels and precious silk stockings. Then he spends perhaps a bit too much on a tiny bottle of rare French perfume—but he is jubilant, doesn't care about the money. On the drive back, he drinks from a bottle of French cognac he has just bought. Everything is going well. He is very happy.*

The inspection team comes on Wednesday. Leah stands back from the window and watches two armored cars with SS soldiers escort the five Mercedes staff cars to the front of the house. Governor General Hans Frank wears a black suit and black homburg befitting a former judge. General Globocnik wears his newest SS uniform and Rudolph Hoess wears a green Bavarian hunting coat and hat and gray knickers. They are surrounded by a fluttering covey of fawning aides.

The three are introduced to Lara. She serves them an elaborate luncheon, which has been in preparation all week. She dips and dawdles, always smiling, and makes a dramatic show of love for Mencken. She is behaving as instructed—but also because she's terrified of these very powerful men. More than ever, she knows that she must never be found out. Her very existence— and that of her son—hangs on that thin thread. All goes well, and all the men agree that Mencken's woman Lara is positively enchanting.

After lunch the men rejoin the waiting aides and get into the cars for the three-mile drive around to the railway platform and the gate. They inspect the factories just inside the camp and head for the high point of the inspection. A load of Jews is processed for the showers and then shoveled into the pits for cremation. Hans Frank is very impressed at the marvelously efficient camp operations.

All in all, a fine camp, says Hans Frank, an excellently run killing center. Standartenführer Mencken has every reason to be pleased with the job he is performing. A fine officer, Frank says to him, and sure to attain the highest ranks of the Army. After the inspection, Mencken entertains Frank and Hoess and Globocnik in his quarters. They drink freely of the Polish vodka and effusively congratulate Lara on her man's brilliance and likewise extoll the prowess of Mencken for having acquired such a magnificent mistress. As afternoon darkens into night, the inspection team finally drives back to Warsaw, since there is nowhere fine enough for them to spend the night around Treblinka.

Mencken is delighted. It has all gone beautifully. Maybe now he will be promoted out of this remote spot to Warsaw or even Paris. Wouldn't that be great, he bubbles drunkenly to Leah: Paris.

Meanwhile, Ludwig Bielasc—the inmate control officer under Mencken at Treblinka—is also very pleased with his camp's performance. That night, he gets a little less drunk on Polish vodka and gives himself a special treat. He enjoys all six of his "girls" two at a time. Yes, life is sweet when you get the recognition you deserve.

A week later, a single Gestapo officer comes to Treblinka unannounced. He has orders from Hans Frank's chief of staff to conduct an inspection. He tells a puzzled Mencken nothing and spends less than an hour in the camp with only his driver by his side. They leave without a word. Mencken watches them go, his hands clasped nervously behind his back. Nothing unusual, he tells himself. The Gestapo has its own vital mission to pursue and often acts secretively.

Ten days later, the long-awaited reward for Karl Mencken's loyalty and hard work is delivered by messenger. He's ordered forthwith to go to Krakow to Governor General Frank's personal headquarters for further instructions. Karl is gleeful. He leaves the next day, bringing Leah and Nachman along for the triumphant ride and then a day of celebration.

Sergeant Schnebel drives the Mercedes staff car. When they arrive, Mencken tells Schnebel to drive Leah to the shopping square and he leans through the back window and kisses her, giving her plenty of money to spend. With his promotion, Mencken is sure to get a raise—so right now money is easy to let go.

Frank's castle headquarters is truly opulent. Polished black marble floors sparkle with reflected light from clustered crystal chandeliers. The lovely German girl at the reception desk scans a list and points Mencken up the main spiral stairway. He is directed to a large waiting room with a reception desk in the center. He gives the Major his name and is told to be seated and wait.

And wait he does. He waits a total of six hours—but of course it doesn't take him that long to figure that perhaps there is some bad news as well as the obvious good news he will surely receive. Mencken begins to perspire under his heavy uniform. At two o'clock, he asks the Major if he might go somewhere to have lunch, but the Major frowns and answers brusquely that the commissary is not open for personnel in transit. Mencken sits and waits with increasing uneasiness.

Late in the afternoon, he's finally asked to go in by the Major, who holds the door for him. He enters Governor General Frank's dark, musty office and salutes. Frank, sitting at the desk, looks up from the file folder in his hands and motions for him to take a seat, neither smiling nor greeting him. As he sits, Mencken is surprised to see that standing in the shadows near the ceiling-high drapes, looking intently out the window, is an elderly officer of medium height, totally bald, cadaverously thin and hunchbacked, his face a jigsaw puzzle of lines and creases, his nose a crooked hawk's beak. He looks important, and dangerous. Mencken clears his throat and waits.

"This is Dr. Gunther," says Frank, pointing to the officer who turns around and faces Karl. Karl has never had the chance to meet Dr. Gunther, but his reputation is well known. He is the Gestapo General in charge of SS and Police Court XI, the group assigned to exposing and prosecuting corruption among guards in the concentration camps and killing centers in Poland. Gunther is one of Himmler's favorites, a one-time professor of philosophy at the University of Berlin, a devout Nazi theoretician, and an expert on the Jewish Question.

The SS Police Courts do not deal with the issues of murder or torture, since these are the reason the concentration camps exist in the first place. Rather, the courts are concerned with what they define as "gross excesses" of behavior. The principle is to keep the concentration camp Nazis from being contaminated by the Jewish filth they have to deal with on a daily basis. "Gross excess" is a mass orgy or repeated sexual perversion with a Jew. Such behavior goes to the very heart of the dilemma—how a man can remain a pure and idealistic Nazi while at the same time working among the many Jews of a concentration camp. The Jews are devious and wily, and lapses are bound to occur. Such "lapses" from the Nazi ethic are personally abhorrent to SS and Gestapo Chief Himmler, whose responsibility it is to run the camps.

Dr. Gunther nods, moving out of the shadows and into the solid beam of afternoon sunlight angling through the tall set of windows. "We have heard some very disappointing news about your Treblinka camp, Mencken," *he says, standing next to Frank's desk, folding his arms across his narrow chest. Mencken tenses, gripping the arms of his chair, and listens grimly.*

"Your inmate control officer, Bielasc, is a pervert who keeps six young Jewish boys in the headquarters building." *The pitch of Gunther's voice goes up, along with his eyebrows. His eyes remain fixed on Mencken's.* "They receive special food and clothing and do no labor." *Gunther pauses and studies Mencken. Silence.*

Mencken speaks carefully in response. "Yes, Herr Doktor, *but Bielasc does a superb job as my next in command. I have thought it best to permit him his pleasures." He's aware that "excesses" are widely and variously defined by the Gestapo Courts. He feels that he might be able to convince Dr. Gunther that given Bielasc's value as an inmate control officer, and the obviously masterful way that Treblinka is being run, certain small defects in this one officer's character might profitably be overlooked.*

Gunther nods reasonably. "But Mencken, when we couple your lack of judgment in this Bielasc matter with the fact that you are yourself living with a Jew pig, your value as a senior Nazi officer enters into serious doubt."

The Angel of Death sits gaping at Gunther, and he suddenly feels very sick. The man who has sold his soul to the Devil for a pittance is looking into the fiery eyes of one of the Devil's own apostles, and he is about to be consumed by the blaze.

Hans Frank and Dr. Gunther look at Mencken, studying his reaction. Mencken reaches for the emergency story that he has prepared in case this most dangerous confrontation should ever occur.

"A Jew?" *he gasps in disbelief.* "It can't be. It isn't possible. Lara, A Jew?"

"Yes, Standartenführer *Mencken. There is no doubt. She is a Jew." Dr. Gunther's tone is hard. Hans Frank studies Mencken closely. Gunther continues:* "Standartenführer *Erwin Schlegg, who commanded* Einsatzkommando *Nine in Vilna when you were there, reported that he was certain that the woman he saw with you in Warsaw some weeks ago is the daughter of a Jewish banker from Vilna. He met her when she came to visit her father at Lukiszki Prison before he was 'resettled.'"*

Mencken has managed to recover his senses, and now feels fully in control of himself. He is intent on carving his way out of this; he must protect himself, make them believe his story.

"I simply cannot believe it," he says again, shaking his head. "I was introduced to her at a party by my own adjutant, Oberleutnant *Schwarz. She can't be Jewish. She surely doesn't look it. She speaks Lithuanian and Polish and German. Her father was a sympathizer with the Lithuanian Nazis and her husband was a simple workman. They were both killed in the bombing of Vilna when we liberated it. At least, this is the story I was told by both Schwarz and Lara." No problems here, Mencken knows, since Schwarz was killed in the battle of Leningrad. "I am truly devastated,* Herr Doktor. *I simply don't know what else to say."*

Hans Frank, who seems sympathetic to Mencken's story, turns to Gunther. "It's true, Herr Doktor, *the girl looks Aryan, and she speaks perfect German. I can see how our friend Karl could have been duped." Pausing a moment, he turns back to Mencken and says, "Please wait outside. We'll discuss this matter."*

Mencken retreats to the waiting room, feeling gravely ill. How else can he feel? The alternatives are unacceptable. In five minutes, the buzzer sounds on the Major's desk and the young man lifts the intercom and listens. Mencken is ushered back into the office and stands stiffly at attention in front of the desk.

"You are too good an officer with too fine a record to be wasted, Mencken," Frank says. "Here are your orders: you are to straighten out Bielasc's problem. We want to hear nothing more of this. And take care of your own situation. We will not put this in your official record. We believe you. But, please, do not disappoint us."

Frank extends his hand cordially and shakes Mencken's hand. Mencken also shakes Gunther's sweaty hand, then Gunther walks him to the door and puts his arm around his shoulders in a fatherly gesture. "We good Nazis must guard the treasure of our ideals, Herr Standartenführer," *he tells him. "You are one of us, Karl. Do not let yourself be led astray, even inadvertently. We old heads know that the future of our Third Reich rests with men like you." Gunther stops and clicks his heels. "Goodbye,* Herr Standartenführer." *Mencken clicks his heels in return, salutes smartly, and flees the building.*

He returns trembling to the motor pool behind Frank's castle. The staff car is there waiting for him. He is livid with ill-suppressed rage, almost apoplectic. In the car he says nothing, just fumes silently. Leah sits in deepening dread during the long drive back to Treblinka. The terribly long day of waiting has made her very, very worried.

Halfway home, Mencken turns to her and speaks." The trip has not gone well," he says, then little by little he tells her what has happened. His rage builds as his story emerges—the waiting, the lying, the narrow escape. Leah is desperate with terror.

It's midnight when they reach their house in Treblinka. Leah carries the sleeping Nachman inside and Mencken locks the steel padlock on the outside of the door, leaving her trapped inside, unable to move, forced to await his return.

He drives to Treblinka Camp and sprints savagely up the stairs to Bielasc's sleeping quarters. The door is locked. He kicks it twice, until the jamb shatters and the door flies open. He switches on the light. Bielasc— "Lialka" ["Babydoll"] to the inmates—sits up in bed, bleary-eyed from drink, musky sweat streaking the folds of flesh on his chest and belly and upper arms. Two young, frightened boys try to pull the sheets over themselves, to hide, to escape.

"Get out of bed, you pig-faced scum." Mencken approaches the bed and grabs Bielasc by the arm and pulls him to his feet. Lialka stumbles, standing up shakily.

Mencken draws his Mauser and shoots a few bursts into the bundles under the sheets. Blood spreads, overtaking the clean white cotton. He pulls the naked Bielasc with him and enters the side door into the "girls'" room. The remaining four boys are sitting up in bed terrified, wide-eyed.

"Line up in the center!" Mencken screams. "Kneel!" The four boys jump out of bed and kneel in front of the two men. Mencken holds his pistol out. "You do this one." He hands the weapon to a quickly sobering Bielasc. The fat man hesitates, looking entreatingly at his commanding officer. "Do it!" shouts Mencken. "Or I'll do it to you!"

Lialka "the Babydoll" quickly shoots the four boys in the face. Jonathan Brod, Leah's brother, lies under the sheet in Lialka's bed, already dead. Mencken grabs his pistol away from Bielasc and strides out of the headquarters building, leaving the grotesque pervert alone with his tender corpses.

He walks back to his staff car and drives directly to his quarters in Treblinka Village. In the kitchen, he takes a bottle of Steinhäger out of the cupboard and drinks thirstily. He sits at the table and drinks most of the bottle. He is reeling. He staggers into the bedroom. Leah is lying in bed, wide awake with terror. She heard him come in thirty minutes before and slam the door, and she has listened in growing dread to the sounds of his increasing drunkenness. They are sounds she knows well.

Mencken lifts a heavy hand and points unsteadily, propping himself against a small table. "You fucking Jew bitch. You and your dog-shit son have almost cost me my career." He pushes himself away from the table, stands framed by the kitchen light in the doorway of the darkened bedroom.

"I have just killed your Jew brother, and now I'll take care of your fucking puppy and you."

He reels out of the doorway down toward Nachman's room, and she hears him open the door and stumble in. Wild, terrified, she runs into the kitchen and grabs a meat cleaver off the hook next to the stove. She enters Nachman's room just as Karl swings the baby by his legs and smashes his small skull against the rock wall. At the same instant, she sweeps the cleaver over her head and down on Mencken's shoulder. He growls and straightens up, stunned. He drops Nachman and turns around, looking at her in dull surprise. Leah swings again. The cleaver buries itself in Karl's forehead. He heaves backwards against the wall and falls to the floor on his back.

Leah switches on the light and runs over to Nachman, kneeling over him. The top of his head is shattered, crushed, a pulpy red oozing mass. She is splattered with the blood and flesh of her baby and her baby's murderer. She is wild with an agony that she cannot release. She cannot scream, she cannot weep, she can hardly breathe. She stands up slowly, too shaky to move any faster, and walks out of the room. She changes out of her nightdress into a simple frock, then re-enters Death's bedchamber and picks up her shattered baby, bundling him in a small wool blanket.

She walks out of the main door of the house and gets on her bicycle. She puts the bundled body of her son in the basket and pedals in the pitch darkness away from the gates of Hell. After several miles she stops and takes the bundle into the forest. On her hands and knees she scoops out a small hole in the soft moist loam and lays her baby in it. Sobbing uncontrollably as she covers him, she gasps out loud the words she has been repeating over and over for the last hour, by which she has forced all other thoughts and images from her mind:

"Ayl molay rachamim
Shochayn bamromim,
Hamtzay menucho nechono
Tachas kanfay shechino...."

[God full of mercy, grant everlasting peace to the soul of Nachman ben-Daniel, who has passed to his eternal resting place; may he be under the Lord's divine wings among the sanctified and pure who sparkle as brightly as the heavens....]

Suddenly two rifle shots rang out. Leah lept to her feet, jarred back into attentiveness. Ami Carmel looked at her silently, his eyes filled with sympathy. She fought away the disabling, crippling memories. The firing again stopped and a hush was over the village. She leaned against the scabrous bark of an olive tree and scraped her shoulder hard against it, trying to blot out the agony in her soul with physical pain. Of course it didn't work. It never worked.

Chapter Two

Nadia Attiyah ran terrified across the newly plowed watermelon fields and through the olive groves that belonged to her father-in-law, Mukhtar Muhammad ibn-Walid Attiyah—now a dead man lying in bloody tatters against the outer wall of his own home, no one left in the village even to bury him. Everyone still alive now fled across the fields, running for Ein Kerem. Nadia stopped to catch her breath a couple of hundred yards from the village and looked back. She saw the Jewish woman with pale golden hair like spring wheat and another soldier holding a book, standing with their heads bowed, their shoulders slumped, in the flowery meadow by her village. In her heart she knew that Sami was being sent by this Jewess to eternal bliss with Allah. She did not understand this strange woman, why she would do such a thing as save her, or bury Sami, after riding into town in a machine of killing with all those other murderous Jews.

She was running from the only village she'd ever lived in, which had suddenly been blasted to broken bits and thoroughly ransacked. Life as she'd always known it had ended—her entire family had just been slaughtered.

Exhausted, she slumped against the gnarled trunk of an ancient olive tree and slid into a sitting position on the dewy ground. The early morning chill of the Jerusalem hills turned the perspiration on her face ice cold. Her thin cotton night dress was wet with blood and perspiration and she began to shiver.

Nadia watched for a moment and only vaguely felt her body trembling. She was in a state beyond tears. Perhaps tears would come later, to wash away the blood of her murdered son, daughter and husband, to cleanse her soul, to make her well again. But now there was just silence and staring, wide-eyed staring.

She had lived in Deir Yassin all of her twenty-five years and had grown up the village beauty, Deir Yassin's Helen, Cleopatra, renowned among all other villagers of the countryside for her shiny long black hair, her luminous, riveting cobalt eyes, and her satin, almond-colored skin. At sixteen, she had married Farid, son of the Mukhtar Muhammad Attiyah, who owned all of the watermelon fields and olive groves surrounding Deir Yassin for miles. The Attiyah family had tended these fields for a millenium. They'd beaten back the European Crusaders who forcibly and foolishly had tried to convert the Muslims. Others in the north, in the Galilee, had succumbed to the Crusaders' swords. They'd become Christians, and the Christian Arabs of Nazareth and Maghar and Tiberias had ever afterwards been scorned as traitors by their Muslim brethren who had held fast to the true Faith of the Prophet. Deir Yassin had held to that faith.

Deir Yassin and its hereditary line of rulers from the Attiyah clan had survived and flourished through centuries of invasions by Mongols and Mamluks and Ottomans and finally the British. But now, in the month of Nisan, in the Muslim year 1367 since the Prophet Muhammad left Mecca on his *hijra* to Medina, it was suddenly over. Every male member of the Attiyah clan had been senselessly and brutally murdered by the Jews, the latest European Crusaders intent on subjugating the Arab infidels. The Mukhtar and his mother were dead. Nadia's husband and daughter and son were dead. The only one left who could carry on the name and tradition of the Attiyahs was the life growing in Nadia's body: she was seven months pregnant.

She walked the rest of the way to Ein Kerem. She'd known everyone there her entire life; her sister Widad was married to the principal of the high school that served about fifteen Arab villages around Ein Kerem, including Deir Yassin. Nadia went up to Widad's house. The shutters on the windows were locked. She knocked softly.

The door opened a crack, then Widad el-Rashid opened it wide, quickly pulled Nadia inside, and barred the door. She gasped when she got a full look at her sister.

"What happened? We heard shooting. Are you wounded?"

"Our village," Nadia said, her voice breaking. "The Jews murdered everyone in the village. I was holding Sami and they shot him out of my arms." She held her empty arms out.

Widad let out a short wail of pain and pressed her hands over her mouth to suppress her sobs. The two sisters were quiet for a minute, absorbing the reality of the loss. Widad stood, murmuring prayers and invectives against the Jews and took Nadia's hand. She led her to the bathroom and sat her on the edge of the claw-foot tub. "Sit, Nadia. You must relax and heal."

Widad's voice turned weak, fearful. A morning of strain and sorrow showed on her forehead, like cracks in the earth after too long a drought. "We heard the explosions," she said. "And a few of the villagers already arrived before you, so we knew. This is a terrible day." She paused. "Do you think they'll come here?"

"The Jewish woman who saved me said Ein Kerem would be safe. I don't know."

Widad pulled back, frowning. "Jewish woman? What are you talking about, Nadia? Who is it who saved you?"

"Just as I say," Nadia told her. "A Jewish woman saved me from being shot." Even to her own ears, it sounded impossible. "One of the animals had broken in the door and forced us all outside. Everywhere there was shooting, screaming. Everywhere there were bodies. He lined us up against the house and before we really understood what he intended to do—he just opened up on us. He killed Muhammad first, then worked right down the line, past Farid, to—" She lowered her face and began to cry.

"Okay, okay," Widad whispered. "Not now. Let's get you cleaned up." She reached out and unbuttoned her sister's dress, then pulled her to a standing position to let the blood-crusted dress fall to the floor. "You must bathe, Nadia. I'll get water."

Nadia stood naked in the bathroom, not moving, not really seeing what she stared at, just standing limply. Widad returned and lit a gas burner that heated a tank of water hanging over the tub. She poured a large bucket of hot water, which was always kept heating on the stone oven in the kitchen, into the tub. She held Nadia by both shoulders and shook her gently. "Get into the tub, Nadia."

Nadia lay against the inclined back of the tub, her feet up on the rim of the other end, and Widad scrubbed the dried blood off her with scouring soap. "Go on, Nadia," Widad said. "Tell me more."

"Before the Haganah soldier could finish me off, he suddenly crumpled into a ball, dead. This Jewish woman had shot him down. She then took Sami from my arms and made me leave the village. And then she buried him in the meadow."

Tears rolled down Widad's cheeks. She too had children, and as a mother, she understood the horror Nadia was trying to describe. She leaned back on her haunches, sobbing, and handed Nadia the soap. Nadia started rubbing her breasts and belly hard, too hard, as if to wash away the soiled memory, and Widad immediately took the soap back again. There was nothing more for either of them to say. Nadia lay in the hot water, and more heated water began to come out of the tank into the tub. She lay there until the water became tepid. Then her sister pulled the plug, pulled Nadia to her feet, and as the water gurgled through the pipes, she dried Nadia with a large towel.

She led her to a sofa in the small sitting room, laid her on it and covered her with a down comforter. Nadia stared and dozed and stared. Widad sat with her, holding and patting her hand, saying nothing. Widad's round face was drawn, her gleaming black eyes dulled by fear. Her short black hair was covered in a gray lace kerchief, and she wore the traditional gray caftan. She wasn't as tall as her sister and she'd become a bit stout as she entered her mid-thirties, but she was an attractive woman, and she had a fine family and a luxurious home here in Ein Kerem.

At noon, Widad's husband Samir drove up in his Land Rover and rushed inside. The two sisters sat motionless on the sofa. Nadia looked up. Samir el-Rashid was built like a high stone pillar with no taper at either end. His head was a granite block, square and dark with close curly black hair. His cheeks were made purple by a heavy beard which, despite his efforts, looked perpetually unshaven. In the center of this rugged rock face was an incongruous soft spot: pale blue eyes, evidence that somewhere deep in his family tree there lurked a French or English ancestor—one of the Crusaders who invaded these rolling Jerusalem hills a thousand years ago.

"I heard about it on Jordanian radio," Samir said darkly. "How about Muhammad and Farid and the children? Are they all right?"

Widad looked at her husband. "All dead but Nadia."

"May Allah protect us," gasped Samir. His eyes betrayed his deep fear. "The radio said it was a brutal massacre. Hundreds dead. And they think the Jews will do the same thing to all the villages surrounding Jerusalem so they can take over the city, despite the United Nations decision to internationalize it."

"What are we going to do, Samir?"

He stared back at her, then shook his head. "Right now, I just don't know." His eyes dropped, perhaps in shame for having no ready answer for his wife. But Widad understood: there simply was no ready answer. She wanted to call him over to her, hold him, but before she could say anything he'd already opened the door. He looked back and held up the keys to the Land Rover. "I'm going over to the school to pick up the children," he said. "I don't feel right without them today. I want them here with us."

Chapter Three

Samir picked up their four children, ranging from age six to fourteen, and packed them into the Land Rover. Only the oldest boy, Zuhayr, seemed to understand what was going on in the Arab community that day—and Samir felt a mixture of pride and fear for his young son. Soon Zuhayr would be involved in all family decisions, and even the larger community decisions like the one Samir and his neighbors would have to consider over the coming days. And just as soon, Zuhayr would be old enough to become a soldier—to place his life on the line for the cause of freedom.

Samir reached out and jostled Zuhayr's shoulder. "Don't be so glum," he told him. "We have nothing to worry about, as long as we keep our heads. Our village has lasted a long, long time, and we're not about to lose it now."

The other children listened quietly, sensing the air of seriousness in their father's voice. Something unusual was happening; that's why they'd been let out of school.

Zuhayr turned toward his father, his dark eyes squinted in determination. "I want to join the fight, Father," he said as gruffly as his young voice would allow. "We need more soldiers and more guns. The boys at school said the villagers of Deir Yassin were gunned down like tin cans, without so much as putting up a battle. They said the Jews will destroy us all if we just roll over and let them!"

Samir shushed him, while the youngest little girl, Zina, began to cry softly. The others held their eyes low, waiting, as the Land Rover rumbled over the sandy road through the sycamore trees with their brilliant yellow blossoms. Frayed clouds cluttered the cerulean sky. "Settle down, all of you," Samir said. "No one's going to invade our village. There was a horrible tragedy today at Deir Yassin, but it was surely a mistake. Many lives were wasted, but that doesn't mean the Jews are going to enter every village in all of Palestine and do the same thing. It just wouldn't make sense."

Zuhayr had crossed his arms. "We have to be ready for them, in case they do attack," he said. "That's all."

"We'll be ready," was all Samir could think to say. "And it's not the concern of you and your schoolmates, Zuhayr. The Mufti and the village counsel will be far more knowledgeable in their decisions. You can be sure of that. Now, let's not worry about this any more. Your mother's waiting for us, and Nadia has come to stay with us for a while. We need to be nice to her."

Samir looked over at Zuhayr, who nodded his head sadly. The other children were cheered about Nadia's visit, unable to guess the reason for it. Zuhayr knew better. Samir smiled at him, feeling very proud to have such a strong-willed and courageous son, even if he could be a bit rash at times. Someday, Samir knew, Zuhayr would be just like his father.

Back at home, the four children piled out of the Land Rover and ran inside. Traditional Muslim Arabs commonly had ten or fifteen children, but the el-Rashid family was a modern, educated and cultured family, and remained smaller in the current fashion. Times were changing the Palestinian Arabs. Widad, for one, was unwilling to be a pinched old hag by the age of thirty-five. She was more modern and educated than that. She had, in fact, been permitted to attend the teacher's college in Jerusalem at the age of sixteen. That's where Samir had met her. He'd been one of her teachers, and when they were married not so very long after, he had moved the two of them back to his family's village of Ein Kerem.

As custom dictated, his father, a Jerusalem contractor, had built onto the family home another two sumptuous rooms for his son and daughter-in-law. As their children were born, another room was added, then another. And now that his father was dead, Samir, the eldest son, was the head of the family. His younger brother Munif also had a room in the family house, and they kept the construction business going in Jerusalem. They were an influential family, and the marriage of Farid Attiyah to Widad's stunning younger sister Nadia had also been a strong political and economic move, for it linked the Attiyahs, the leading family of Deir Yassin, to the el-Rashids, the leading family of Ein Kerem.

Over the last several months, Samir and Farid had for their part been vary careful to maintain a non-aggressive relationship with the Jews in the nearby kibbutzim and Jerusalem. They knew that when war broke out, as was inevitable after the Partition vote, their villages would be strategic to both sides. And in a decision made by Mukhtar Muhammad and strongly supported by the villagers of Deir Yassin and Ein Kerem, they had refused to permit Arab irregulars to be stationed in the villages. Despite this, despite their risky attempts to stay clear of involvement in the war, the Jews had decimated Deir Yassin and probably had the same plans for Ein Kerem. What Samir had told his children had been, of course, only wishful thinking. More realistically, it looked as if the Jews had only one objective: to take control of the entire country and drive all the Arabs out in the process. Zuhayr and his schoolmates were probably right. This was a far cry from the publicized plan for a "shared" Arab and Jewish state.

Samir fretted at home all day, fearful of venturing onto the Jerusalem road in daylight lest the patrolling Jews murder him in cold blood. No matter how much he thought about it, there seemed to be no sure way to avoid the continuing violence. All he and his family had ever wanted was peace—but now that appeared to be an incredibly difficult and elusive goal.

His brother Munif came home a little after four o'clock. "Is it true what happened?" he asked.

Samir nodded.

"Farid? Nadia?"

"All dead but Nadia. She's here with Widad."

Munif was tall and gaunt, "scarecrowy," as his mother had lovingly described him. He had a thin, straggly beard, prematurely graying, and short salt-and-pepper hair. His brooding black eyes were set deep under wild bushy brows, which at the moment were twitching nervously.

"Well, I'm glad we finally decided to stash the money," Munif said, a hint of triumph in his voice. Samir hadn't thought it necessary to place their construction company accounts in a Lebanese bank for safe keeping, but Munif had prevailed upon him to take 20,000 pounds sterling and put it in an account in the *Banque du Liban* in Beirut. And now it was clear that Munif had been right.

"What now?" Munif asked.

Samir was slow to answer. "Well, I'm going to the Dome of the Rock in Jerusalem tonight. We're going to get a report from Kamal el-Husseini, the Mufti's cousin. Then we'll know better what to do. You stay here with the family. We'll have to get the shotguns out. You may need them."

On hearing this, Zuhayr rushed eagerly to the back room to retrieve the family shotguns, which were kept encased inside a heavy trunk. Samir called out to him: "Those guns are for the protection of this family, Zuhayr. You're forbidden to so much as touch a trigger unless your uncle tells you to. The last thing we need is an accidental shooting. Is that clear?"

"Yes, Father," Zuhayr said, returning with two long Egyptian shotguns. "I'll be careful."

"Okay." With that, Samir resumed his nervous pacing in the main room, while the family spread out around him, lying down or sitting, quietly watching. Munif sat in a straight-backed chair, staring intently at nothing, deep in thought. Occasionally, one of the children would begin to chatter, but for the most part the household was very quiet that afternoon and evening.

Finally, at six o'clock, when it was dark, Samir buttoned up his sheepskin coat and drove alone to the Dome of the Rock, one of the most important landmarks in all of Palestine. Built high on Mt.

Moriah in the old city of Jerusalem, the mosque housed a rock sacred both to the Muslims and the Jews. The rock, said the Jews, was where Abraham brought his son Isaac and tied him up to sacrifice him at God's command. The rock, said the Muslims, was the place whence the Prophet Muhammad ascended to heaven on his magical winged horse, with a woman's face and a peacock's tail, and you can still see the hoofprint in the rock if you look closely. Thus, the Dome had become the most sacred mosque in Palestine, and the *mu'etheen* who called the faithful to prayer from the nearby minaret was also the most important teller of news to the Arabs, who would stand below and listen to him chant the latest news bulletins.

The Dome of the Rock was filled with Arab notables waiting to hear what was really happening and what they could do about it. Samir parked his car near the mosque, took off his shoes next to el-Kas fountain, sprinkled water on his feet, and walked into the Dome. As always, the magnificent tapestried walls and the high, distant dome humbled him, for he was in the presence of Allah.

Hundreds of men sat cross-legged on the ornate Persian carpets. After several minutes, Kamal el-Husseini mounted the beautifully carved speaker's stand. The crowd hushed.

"*Bi-smi'llahi'r Rachmani'r Rachim.* I am here to tell you what is happening to our people. I must begin by informing you that what I have to say is not good news." He looked around the mosque. "The British left three months ago and the Jews have already begun their campaign to destroy our people." El-Husseini's face was drawn, his skin blotched and pale. Despite the chilly air, his stark black hair was matted down on his brow in sweaty ringlets. Samir listened intently.

"This morning the Jews attacked the village of Deir Yassin without provocation or warning and despite the fact that Deir Yassin has consistently proclaimed neutrality. Three hundred of our people were killed, many while they slept. Our women were raped and cut open. Our babies were smashed and murdered. The Jews piled the bodies into the well to hide them and then their sappers blew up every building in the village."

The listeners had heard most of this as rumors all day long, but this was the first confirmation that it was really true. Gasps of grief and hatred spread through the mosque.

"The Jews have sent loudspeaker trucks through the cities of Haifa and Jaffa and Safed, ordering our people everywhere to leave their homes or be killed. The Greek Orthodox Primate of Haifa, Archbishop al-Hakim, has already moved twenty-five thousand woman and children to safety in Damascus and Beirut. Another twenty thousand left during this week from Haifa alone. We have confirmed reports that over six-hundred thousand of our people have fled their homes all over Palestine and are seeking refuge in Jordan and Syria and Lebanon and the Gaza Strip. As our people leave, the Jews blow up their homes so they cannot return.

"*Al-jamia al-'arabiya* [the Arab League] has given strict orders for all Arabs to remain in their homes and fight the Jews!" screamed el-Husseini. "These are orders from King Abdullah himself and Azzam Pasha himself!" Azzam Pasha was the Secretary General of the Arab League and King Abdullah of Jordan was its most respected spokesman.

"We must preserve our *'awda* [homeland] in Palestine. Our Arab brethren from Egypt and Lebanon and Jordan and Syria and Iraq are even now attacking the Jews and driving them into the sea!" The speaker's stand shook from el-Husseini's pounding fists. He was tall and stocky, a looming, forbidding hulk. The listeners erupted in an explosion of clapping and cheering. The speaker held up his hands to restore quiet.

"Stay in your homes, my friends, and kill the Jews before they kill you," he said, his voice calmer, quieter. Then he lifted his arms above his head and thundered out his last line, to the rising eruption of passionate applause that once again filled the mosque: "This is *jihad*, this is holy war, in the name of the Prophet!"

Chapter Four

Nadia, of course, had first-hand experience with the way Jews treated Arabs, even the helpless and the aged and the infants. So when the rumors started two months later that the Jews would be clearing the Arabs out of all of the villages of the Latrun Pass, she knew they would have no choice, they would all have to leave Ein

Kerem or be killed, slaughtered like rats and cockroaches. There was no alternative but to flee, to join the growing ocean of hundreds of thousands of Muslim refugees who were living in squalid tent cities and shanty towns that had reportedly arisen on the alien fringes of their Palestine homeland.

But Samir refused to budge. Ein Kerem had been his ancestral home for over forty generations, and he would not abandon it like a whipped puppy. No amount of pleading and reasoning and begging and explaining by Nadia and Widad had any effect on him. Ein Kerem had laid down its guns, Samir would answer, and the Jews would leave them be. They were miles off the road to Jerusalem, just a sleepy pastoral village lost in the hills of the Shephelah, and they would be safe.

November 9, 1948—a bitter winter morning in the Jerusalem hills. The frost chilled the last life from the brittle leaves of the bougainvillea and wisteria that hugged the stone houses. The puddles from yesterday's frigid rainfall had sheeted over with ice and the children on their way to school walked stiffly with mincing steps to avoid slipping.

Nadia awoke from her recurrent nightmare—a slow ballet of death frozen in slow motion, a detailed reliving of what had actually happened at Deir Yassin, real life having far exceeded what her imagination could ever dream up—and she was drenched with perspiration. A throbbing ache moved slowly up from her swollen vagina through her back and surrounded her distended belly in clawed bands. The pain made her stiffen and grip the sheets and clench her teeth. And then it passed.

He was coming, Allah be praised. The seed of her husband had lived and matured and was now about to emerge, to grow, to wreak vengeance on the Jew oppressors. She winced again as another pain traversed her midsection. The contractions were coming very close together—just two or three minutes apart.

"Widad!" Nadia called out. She had heard the children leave for school a few minutes earlier, which meant that Samir had already left as well. "Widad!" she called out louder, as another contraction clawed at her womb and percolated around her, sending darting pains toward her kidneys.

Her sister rushed into the small bedroom and opened the shutters to let the gloomy gray light in. One look at Nadia answered

Widad's question, and she rushed to the side of the bed, reaching
for her sister's sweat-soaked face.

"How often are they coming?"

"Less than five minutes. Faster. They're going fast now," answered Nadia.

"I'll run for the midwife."

"No! There's no time—" and Nadia gasped. Her water had
broken. Some of the pressure inside her released and she felt better
for a moment. She sighed, enjoying her brief respite.

Widad pulled down the bed's heavy quilt and threw it on the
floor. She took the pillow from under her sister's head and propped
it under her hips. Widad had seen a score of babies born and
assisted at more than a few. There was no panic or fear in her. She
knew exactly what to do.

Bearing babies was the calling of a woman in obedience to Allah's
will. And this baby was not waiting at all. Widad kneeled between
Nadia's legs and pushed Nadia's knees back. "Hold on to your
ankles!" she ordered.

Nadia obeyed. This was her third baby. She too was no ingenue.
She gripped her ankles and held her legs spread and bent and she
groaned as she felt her vagina stretch and there was a shot of searing
pain and then suddenly it was over. Just like that. The baby
plopped out like a slippery watermelon seed snapped between two
fingers, and the pain was mostly gone.

Widad held up the tiny purple boy covered with a sticky white
protective cream, and he immediately gasped and cried out with
anger at being wrenched from his warm and watery home and
being cast into the inhospitable chill of this wintry morning.
Widad laid the baby on Nadia's bosom and busied herself gently
persuading the placenta to be delivered, pulling steadily on the
cord. Then Widad ran out of the room and returned with a wooden
clothespin and a basin and a pair of scissors. She pressed the
clothespin over the cord an inch above the baby's belly and snipped
the cord two inches from the pin. She gingerly placed the placenta
and the rest of the umbilical cord into the basin and put it carefully
in the corner of the room. Custom demanded that it be buried
reverently, for it too was a vital element of life.

Nadia placed the baby on her bare swollen breasts, heavy with
milk to nurture the Attiyah seed, the scion of the thousand-year-old

hamula [clan] which the Jews had virtually destroyed. She had already named him. He was "Hamdi," meaning "Thanks" be to Allah for preserving the Attiyah *hamula* despite the tragedy, war, oppression and exile which Nadia knew would inevitably come. She relaxed, peaceful for the first time in a month, and she synchronized her own breathing to that of her son, and together they slept.

But there was no time for resting. No time for healing. Before sunup the next morning, as Nadia lay half-asleep in her adopted bed, softly cooing the name of her newborn son, a dry, grating, mechanical sound jarred her out of her peaceful twelve-hour reverie.

She peeked through a crack in the window shutters, and saw what she first hoped was a nightmare vision, some kind of awful mirage. But she knew it was real: out of the nearby hills and down into the shallow valley of Ein Kerem, a line of armored cars came crunching over the thin ice of yesterday's mud puddles. The first trucks were already roaring slowly down the center of the village's only street. Nadia stiffened, looked back toward the bed trying to think of hiding places for Hamdi, imagining all the horrible things that could be done with so small a body. Just a day old.

And then the loudspeaker started: the same voice, or one very similar, blaring the same bland message: "This village has been requisitioned by the Israel Defense Forces. No one will be hurt. No one will be hurt. Please remove your belongings and evacuate immediately. All structures in this village will be demolished in two hours. Repeat, all structures in this village will be demolished in two hours."

This time, however, the speaker added an ominously effective extension to his warning: "If you fail to cooperate, the fate of Deir Yassin will be yours. Do not resist. Please remove your belongings and evacuate immediately."

The household bustled into action; in the front room, Samir pulled on his trousers and grabbed his sheepskin coat, whispering directions to Munif and Widad. He rubbed the sleep from his eyes and stepped into his shoes. Widad lit the kerosene lantern for him, and without another word, he went out the front door into the growing dawn.

Nadia rushed back to the window, pushing from her mind the memories of her last morning with Farid—he, too, had stepped outside alone, and she, too, had failed to say good-bye. By the time she was able to get near him again, he was seconds away from being murdered by that Jew monster. They never did say it to each other: a simple good-bye. As far as she could now remember, his last words to her had been, "Keep him quiet," about the baby Sami, back in the house before he'd left.

There were three armored cars in the street. Samir was dazed. He stood in front of the doorway as the Jewish sappers got busy planting charges against the walls of all the buildings of the village. Soldiers with submachine guns stood wary guard around the armored cars as the other Palestinians began emerging from their homes. Samir watched a Jewish soldier calmly hammer out a chunk of the cornerstone of the el-Rashid house and nestle a satchel in it.

"Ya Samir, ya Samir!" yelled the scrawny village *imam* [preacher] as he ran up half dressed, a coat thrown quickly over his nightshirt. "You said they would not come, that we were safe!" His eyes were round and frantic in his leathery face.

"Be still, ya Yusuf!" Samir told him. "They must be trying to frighten us. They have no reason to hurt us." The sappers continued to set their charges. "Just be still. Let me talk to them."

Samir walked up to a tall, thin soldier who had gray hair and wore spectacles and looked a little older and more important than the others.

"You must have made a mistake, sir," Samir said in careful English. "We are a neutral village. We have no arms. We do not give aid to the irregulars. Please leave us alone."

The Jew eyed him cautiously through thick, round, steel-rimmed lenses which grossly magnified his black eyes. "My orders for clear Ein Kerem," he said in broken English. "So. This Ein Kerem?"

"Yes, this is Ein Kerem," Samir answered stiffly, through clenched teeth, turning away from the oafish Jew as if to keep from striking him. Nadia watched from the shuttered window, sharing his hatred.

"You have less of two hours clear out."

Samir opened his arms, his voice growing plaintive. "But I told you we have done nothing, we are peaceful here." Unable to restrain himself, he stepped forward, directly in front of the soldier. The Jew lowered the submachine gun barrel to Samir's chest.

"Stay!" he ordered.

Next to Nadia behind the living room shutters, Zuhayr whined softly as the submachine gun was pointed at his father. For a moment, he bounced excitedly on his toes, looking around the room in a frightened panic, then he ran to the closet and got out the old British Enfield rifle they used for shooting the deer that occasionally wandered into the village from the thick scrub. Before Nadia or anyone could stop him, he chambered a cartridge and bolted out the front door.

"Zuhayr, no!" Widad reached impotently for the door, then fell to the floor of the living room, sobbing. "Come back!"

Nadia hunched down and looked back out the window. Another Jewish soldier, fifteen feet away from Samir and the oafish man with the glasses, leveled Zuhayr with a short burst. Just like that. Samir turned and ran to him with a long wail of anguish, cradling his dead son in his arms.

Widad shrieked in pain as she heard the shots, then rose in a blind panic, her gown raising like the hackles of a rooster on the block. She looked furious and desperate—capable of trying something senseless in order to save her son. Before she could try anything, Nadia grabbed her and wrestled her back down to the floor. Both of the women cried, heaving together in anguish over the loss of this boy. The other children hid in their bedroom in fear, listening silently to the chaos that enveloped them.

Outside, Samir stared in horror at the crimson smears on his sheepskin coat and his blood-splattered hands. Blindly, almost stuporously, he reached for the rifle, but before he could touch it, a soldier kicked it away and smashed Samir across the back of the head with a billy club. Samir toppled unconscious over his dead son.

He came to hours later, the sun already high over the horizon, feeling a severe pain in the back of his skull where the blood was crusted in his hair and his scalp was too tender to touch. He looked around in confusion. He was lying on a flatbed trailer belonging to the el-Rashid Construction Company, and next to him was a large roll of carpet. He saw the head of his firstborn son protruding from the roll and he was immediately stabbed by the memory of what had happened. The flatbed was lumbering behind a stake truck, and he could see through the rear window that the driver was his brother Munif. The bed of the stake truck was loaded with some of the belongings from the el-Rashid household. Nadia was sitting seemingly placidly on a sofa, suckling her baby. Widad was driving the Land Rover, following close behind the flatbed, and their other three children were with her. Behind the Land Rover were donkey carts and some other cars and three more of the construction company trucks. To the rear of the slow caravan was a huge el-Rashid Company bulldozer tacking and bucking like a barque on rough seas along the dirt highway on its fixed axles.

Nadia saw Samir sit up stiffly and wince with pain.

"Are you all right, ya Samir?" she called out to him.

"Yes. Where are we going?"

"To Gaza City. That's where the Jews told us all to go. They wouldn't let us go to Jerusalem."

Samir tried to stand and was jolted back down. He tried again without success.

"Just wait, Samir," Nadia called out to him. "We've been on the road for two hours. We'll be there very soon."

The Gaza Strip was officially under Egyptian control, and a few miles after the caravan rumbled past the drab, dusty Israeli settlement of Yad Mordechai, they passed a short wooden flagstaff from the top of which dangled a limp, faded Egyptian flag. Another twenty minutes, and they drove into a huge camp of motley rows of tarpaper shacks and tents and corrugated tin hovels—the new homes for over fifty thousand of the Gaza Strip's one hundred and twenty thousand Palestinian refugees. They saw rows and rows of tents, hundreds of people milling around. It looked almost like a Friday in Jerusalem or some other large city. There was even a sort of town square, in the original center of the camp—just a clear area where people stood and talked. Further out, the new arrivals staked their claims and started building. Nadia could see that expansion here had been rapid; tents and shacks coiled around open sewer pits, which had undoubtedly once been on the outskirts of the settlement. It was a giant makeshift city of castaways—constructed in sad despair, but still maintained in staunch hope.

Over the next day and a half, Munif and two of the workmen from the el-Rashid Construction Company built four connected huts from rolls of tarpaper and wooden four-by-four beams they had brought with them. They chose a location far enough away from any sewage ditch that the stench was not continuous. It did, however, come in waves on the afternoon breezes. They'd have to get used to that; this was not a place to be choosy or demanding, and the whole family considered itself lucky just to have a solid structure to live in, rather than a mere tent.

That afternoon, just thirty-six hours after Zuhayr's brutal death, they gathered at the cemetery outside Gaza City. The Egyptian *'alim* [holy man] from the mosque recited appropriate passages of the Koran as they sent Zuhayr, wrapped in his shrouds of old, rolled carpeting, to blissful repose at the camphor fountain of Allah.

As Nadia stood next to Widad and they ululated their deep grief, she pressed Hamdi to her breast and felt the fierce, absolute certainty that this tiny new Attiyah would become the redeemer of the Palestinian people. Hamdi would be the new *Salach al-Din* [Saladin], the warrior who would restore the sacred city of Jerusalem to its rightful inhabitants the Muslims, the Defender of the Faith who would destroy the Jewish infidel crusaders in a *jihad*—a holy war for the glory of Allah—just as the first Salach al-Din had destroyed the Christian Crusaders eight hundred years before. Nothing else was more certain in Nadia's heart, and nothing else mattered more. They must repay every one of the Jew scum who had murdered them, degraded them, turned them into homeless rootless rabble without dignity. If that revenge meant destroying the Jews, then so be it. It would be a lesson they would never forget: the Palestinian people could not be so easily routed from their homeland.

Chapter Five

The quickly-constructed tarpaper shack they lived in was like nothing Nadia had ever imagined. A sharp chemical smell seeped out of the paper and pervaded everything, the clothing, the food, the very air they breathed. And with the war raging against the Jews, there was very little else to do but breathe and talk and eat. No escape was possible, at least not now. There wasn't a home or village in all of Palestine that was truly safe. And of course no real business could be done here in the camp. For food everyone relied almost entirely on U.N. handouts and the meager fruit of whatever small gardens they could manage. Schooling was practically out of the question. The el-Rashid family desperately needed the 20,000 pounds sterling that Munif had stashed in the *Banque du Liban* in Beirut, but until the *jihad* was won against the Jews, it was simply too dangerous to go to Beirut to get the money. So life—if it could be called that—ground on day by day in the huge garbage dump they were now beginning to call a "refugee camp."

Try as the "refugees" might, they could not make this hastily gathered city of fifty-thousand citizens work as smoothly as the much smaller thousand-year-old villages which has operated under the *hamula* system. First of all, no one had ever imagined that the camp would grow so large, so no one had found the time or money to establish any kind of sewer system. With fifty thousand people, this quickly became one of the major problems. The first rainstorm of the season literally transformed the camp into a cesspool. The almost rainless Gaza strip received in a year only a handful of thunderstorms, which deposited two or three inches of rain in as little as half a day. The ground, baked hard by the sun and glazed smooth by the winds, absorbed very little, and the runoff collected in huge muddy ponds which bred millions of mosquitoes. So there was the certain promise of malaria. And then the overflowing of the sewage and animal waste which ran in rivulets through every major street of the camp resulted in typhus borne by lice and rat fleas. The epidemic typhus dysentery which visited almost every squalid shack added to the stench and disease and the awesome toll of the dead.

While Samir and Munif met with the other men of the camp to discuss the ongoing war, the women attempted to run the tarpaper shacks as much as possible like homes. But with only a truckload of belongings to work with, and no reliable water supply, and the vermin that ran rampant through the camp, Widad and Nadia had their hands full.

Every day there was a new crisis, and every day it got to be more and more difficult to bear.

"Get away!" Widad screamed late one afternoon, cowering back against the wall as two rats crept into the "kitchen" of the hut.

Nadia grabbed a broom and tried to smash them, but they scurried toward the bedroom and she couldn't keep up.

Samir rushed in from outside in response to Widad's scream and he managed to crush one of the rats with his heavy boot. The other ran into the pile of rags that made up Samir and Widad's bed, and Nadia followed behind it and smashed it with the broom handle. Samir gingerly picked it up by its limp tail and flung it out the doorway.

They went back into the kitchen—a corner of the main room with three rough shelves stacked with pots and dishes and an old Saudi oil drum they used for food storage. On the floor they had a small tub, a raised wooden board for chopping—where Widad slaughtered the rare chicken the family managed to find—and a thin metal flour sifter, made from an oil can.

The day was warm, and the breeze carried with it the ripe stench of the pits. "We need DDT," said Samir, wiping his chin. He'd said it many times before and it never did any good, but somehow it always felt better to say it again. "We need oil to kill the mosquitos breeding on the cesspool ponds. We need medicine." His sweaty face was mottled with desperation.

Nadia sighed, touching with her foot the rusty tub that was half-filled with much-used water. "And clean water," she said. "We only have that one bucket left from yesterday." She pointed at the gallon wooden jug under the shelves. "We can't get more. They closed the well this morning, said it was polluted from the cesspool seepage." She slowly raised her arms to the tin roof, as if in prayer: "We need water to drink. We cannot cook or even wash. What are we going to do?"

She looked at her sister and brother-in-law forlornly, but she knew none of this was within their power to change. They'd been over all of these complaints dozens of times before—every day, really, since they'd come here. The complaints didn't feed the children, or kill the mosquitos, or bring back Farid or any of the other dead family members.

But things were getting worse. Now, it was the water. Water they needed to live. The situation seemed hopeless. Nadia felt tears come as Hamdi, bundled in rags on the thin rag bed, wailed ominously in the next room.

"So what do we do?" asked Widad. "There's nothing in Gaza City. I heard there might be water trucked in, but what about the other things we need?"

They shuffled uneasily on the mud floor, looking to one another for any suggestion, any hope.

"How about El Arish?" Samir asked. "It's the biggest Egyptian town in the Sinai. Maybe they have some."

Everybody agreed that they ought to try. Otherwise, what else was there to do but sit and die? There was no water in the camp, so someone had to venture elsewhere. If DDT and medicine were also available, so much the better.

That afternoon and evening, Samir spoke with some of the other men of the camp. He told them about his plan, about how much they needed to find a reliable source of fresh water. But the men were engrossed in their own heated discussions and they couldn't make time for this new topic. They looked at Samir and scoffed. The Jews are at fault, they told him. Ask them for some water! Why should we run further into Egypt for water and supplies when we have everything we need just over the border in Palestine?

Because tomorrow we'll have nothing to drink, Samir answered them. But it did no good. Tomorrow was not important to the men of the camp. They were too worried about today, and today they were stuck in this miserable pest-ridden hell-hole a hundred miles from home. And the Jews were to blame. That was all that mattered. They had been cornered by the Jewish "beaters," and now they were wounded Bengal tigers, crouching in hiding, waiting to sate their blood lust on their hunters, the Jews. They could focus on nothing else.

The next morning, after waiting in line with their ration cards for two hours at Gaza City's only gas station, Samir and Munif set out alone for the city of El Arish. They were allotted just ten gallons of gas, but that would be more than enough for the ninety-mile round trip down the coast and back.

They bounced down the narrow pot-holed asphalt highway through Khan Yunis and Rafah and out of the Gaza Strip into the Sinai Desert. The landscape changed from the flat, crusted, weedy desert to shifting hills of barren yellow sand. Before long, Samir realized that he and Munif were in trouble: the same thunderstorm that had made a morass out of the refugee camp two days earlier had washed sheets of sand across the highway and obscured it for miles ahead. The road was soon impossible to see or follow. With no other option, Samir simply pointed his Land Rover west and guessed where the road might be.

It didn't work. Suddenly, they were fender-deep in a shifting sea of sand. The engine coughed and sputtered dead. The engine wouldn't restart and no amount of pushing by the two men could budge the car.

It was ten o'clock in the morning. As Samir and Munif worked at digging the sand away from the wheels, the brilliant sun effectively obliterated all but the exhausting work before them. Even if they'd looked, they probably wouldn't have seen the figures of three men walking over a hillock to the east of the Land Rover, approaching in an odd, spread formation as if wary of gunfire or some other form of attack.

"*A'salaamu alaykum*," called out one of the three men.

Samir looked up with a start, blinded by the sun directly in his eyes. He squinted and shaded his forehead with his open hand and made out the three slowly approaching figures. They were Bedouins, dressed in baggy once-black pants and long loose shirts, their heads swathed in filthy white *keffiyehs*. They carried single-shot Springfield rifles of pre-World War One vintage.

"*Alaykum salaam*," responded Samir slowly. Munif came around the vehicle to stand next to his brother. His face was waxy, ashen, and his brows twitched rapidly, as they always did when he became anxious.

The oldest of the three Bedouins smiled at them, his eyes mere slits, revealing tobacco-stained gapped teeth. He said something, but Samir could not understand.

"We do not speak Badu," Samir said in Palestinian dialect.

The Bedouin broke into peels of laughter and said something to his smiling companion. Samir noticed that the third man had disappeared, but before he could even look around Munif grunted and fell forward, the back of his head smashed with the butt of a rifle. Munif sprawled on his face, unconscious, a puddle of blood forming under his head in a hollow divot of sand.

Samir spun back against the Land Rover. Before he could move again, the oldest Bedouin shoved the barrel of the rifle directly onto the bridge of his nose, right between his eyes. The man snarled something at Samir, but again Samir could not make out the words.

The Bedouin quickly lowered the rifle and shot Samir in the right shoulder. Dazed, Samir thought briefly of dying, here in the middle of the Sinai desert, hours and hours from home, from his family's burial ground in Ein Kerem—then his consciousness faded, and he blacked out from the pain.

The sun was high in the eastern sky when he awoke, pain suffusing his right side. The bullet had gone through the cap of muscle on his shoulder, but it had apparently broken no bones, and the wound had almost completely coagulated up front. The back of his shoulder, however, was still oozing steadily. Samir sat up very slowly and saw his brother rolling equally slowly onto his side. The Land Rover was gone—rich booty—but at least they had survived.

Munif propped himself on his side and touched the back of his head gingerly. The blood from the gash was dry. He slowly and painfully got to his feet, walked over and knelt by Samir to examine the shoulder.

"Okay, not a serious wound, *alhamdillah* [thank God]," he said. "Can you stand?"

With his brother's help, Samir stood, feeling with each movement a shocking stab in his injured shoulder. Both brothers staggered for a moment and then steadied themselves against each other. The desert spread before them, as deep as the winter sky, as wide as the endless Mediterranean. Without another word, they began their journey home.

It took them almost four hours to walk the five or six miles back to Rafah. From there they hitchhiked, finally catching a ride sitting atop crates of powdered milk on a rickety truck which took them all the way back to the refugee camp. The sharp bouncing opened Samir's shoulder wound and he was again bleeding steadily when Munif laid him down on his sodden rag bed in the tarpaper shack in the refugee camp.

Widad covered him with their only quilt, but he remained cold-skinned and sweaty throughout the night. He was in shock from loss of blood, and the filth of the bedding infected the wound, and by morning it had begun to suppurate.

The el-Rashid family still had no water, and now on top of that they needed penicillin for Samir, otherwise he might die. They needed DDT and oil and typhoid vaccine as well, otherwise they all might die.

Nadia, Munif and Widad sat outside their shack, leaning against the wooden beams, while Samir groaned quietly through the thin walls. The rest of the camp continued on as before—a day shorter on water, but no less willing just to point angry fingers at the Jews across the border and to do nothing.

"We can't get to El Arish," said Munif. "The road is out and I'd never get through even with the stake truck. Anyway, we're just sitting ducks for the Bedouin."

"How about Lebanon?" said Nadia. "Maybe in one of the small fishing boats with an outboard motor. It's only about a hundred miles."

"No, we'd never make it past the Jews. We couldn't go far enough out from shore to avoid their patrol boats. They aren't content to kick us out of our own country, you know. They want to make sure we die of disease and thirst as well. Lebanon is off limits, as far as they're concerned." All hope had leaked from Munif's gravelly voice.

"Well, then one of the bigger kibbutzim in Israel," said Nadia. She knew they had to find help somewhere; they couldn't give in to the situation, no matter how bad it became. Her own hope remained alive in the shape of her baby boy, Hamdi—the future redeemer of the Palestinian nation—who suckled calmly at her breast as she talked. For his sake, she was unwilling to quit.

Munif smiled weakly. "What do we do, just drive up like tourists and ask for a little medicine?"

"What do we have to lose?" was Nadia's shrugged reply.

"Only our lives," said Munif, turning away solemnly. Then, after

a moment's thought, he grimaced. "Right now that doesn't seem
like very much."

"Don't be so defeated, Munif," scolded Nadia. "We have everything to live for. We'll soon take sickles and gut the same Jew pigs
who stole our *'awda* [homeland] from us." She heard the forceful
pride in her own voice, she felt her eyes deepen and burn into
Munif's—and she saw him straighten against the wall and catch his
breath in response. She meant what she'd said.

"I'll go with you, Munif," she went on. "And we'll get what we
need from the Jew scum." Nadia smiled at her words, so strongly
phrased to have come from a woman. But they felt right, coming
from her. The matter was too important for any of them to keep
quiet about. The old social rules about a woman's place no longer
seemed to apply.

Hamdi finished suckling and abruptly pulled away from Nadia's
swollen nipple.

"You can't take Hamdi with you, Nadia," Widad said. "How am
I to feed him when you're gone?"

Nadia thought for a moment. "How about that midwife I've seen
walking around the camp? Muna, I think is her name. She's fat and
young and can give suck. I'll go right now to see if she can stay here
and help." She got up carefully and handed the lightly snoring
Hamdi to Widad.

Fifteen minutes later, she was back with the midwife. Muna was
homeless and without family, having left everything behind when
she fled from Jaffa. Her husband had been killed, like thousands of
others, in a battle with the Jews. Her six-month old daughter had
just died of typhus. She was in dire need of the protection of a
powerful family and would be delighted to be a midwife for the el-
Rashid *hamula*. To prove her eagerness, she picked up the sleeping
baby and nestled him protectively in her very ample breast.

"Okay, then," said Munif. "Tomorrow morning early, we'll go to
the nearest kibbutz and find our medicine. Which is it, Yad
Mordechai?"

"I think that's it," Nadia told him, the strength still deepening
her voice. "It's just a few miles from here, and if we find nothing
there, I remember seeing another pretty big one ten miles beyond it
called Gan Artzi. We'll be fine."

In the morning, they once again had to endure the ritual of the gas station. This time the wait stretched to two and three-quarters hours.

"So far, Nadia," Munif whispered to her, "our luck is far from good."

"That will change,"Nadia said. "First we have to get out of Gaza. Our bad luck is here."

Finally, they made it to the pumps and got their ten gallons, so they could begin the drive toward Yad Mordechai. It was a beautiful winter day, about eighty degrees and sunny, and the sight of the fertile fields of tomatoes, onions and carrots lent surprisingly vivid color to the otherwise dreary wilderness.

The stake truck had the name El-Rashid in English on the driver's door, as well as the old British Mandate contractor's license number stenciled beneath it. Nadia and Munif hoped these two marks of official validity would keep their truck from seeming too ominous or dangerous to the kibbutzniks who looked up from their field labor and stared at the two Arabs as they made their way onto kibbutz property.

At the entrance to the main living area was a small guard shack. The Israeli soldier stationed there waved the truck to stop and eyed the two of them warily. He said something quickly in Hebrew.

Munif motioned that he didn't understand. "Doctor?" he asked hopefully. The guard said nothing. He walked around the back of the truck and came to a halt by the driver's door.

"Gan Artzi," the soldier said evenly, and beckoned with his rifle for Munif to back up the truck and leave.

"Go ahead, Munif," Nadia told him. "They have no doctor here. He must be telling the truth, otherwise he wouldn't suggest the other kibbutz. We'll try there."

Munif backed the truck and turned it around on the narrow dirt path and drove slowly back to the highway. They lumbered in silence another eight or nine miles, and came to the graded dirt road to Gan Artzi. There was a large stand of eucalyptus trees denoting the center of the kibbutz about two miles away. They drove past a mile-long cotton field which had been picked clean and now lay grayly barren. Then came a series of small pastures housing sheep and goats and a long chicken house which gave off a foul, pungent ammoniac odor. All of these signs of village life seemed sweet to the homesick visitors. Nadia prayed that someday she would once again taste the fruit of her own family's fields. But first, they had to outlast this war. That was all that mattered.

Again they approached a guard shack. Four soldiers sat next to this one on a long bench that had been placed as a barrier across the narrow road. As the truck approached and geared down to a stop, two of the soldiers moved into the guard shack and the other two walked to each of the cab doors and opened them.

"Get out," ordered the soldier in Hebrew, pointing his rifle at Munif.

Both Munif and Nadia climbed down from the truck. They didn't need a translation to understand the gestures with the rifles. The soldier on the driver's side gestured to Munif to turn around and face the truck, and then he patted him down for weapons.

The soldier standing by Nadia walked directly in front of her. He was much taller than she, skinny, pimply and clean shaven. A kid, really, Nadia thought—no more than 18. A heavy odor of onions drifted from his body as he stood a foot in front of her. He smiled at her suggestively and slowly rubbed his free hand over her breasts and down her body, over her stomach and crotch. He pinched the skin of her vulva, winking slowly, his face an inch from her nose. Laughter came from the other soldiers in the guard shack.

"We need a doctor, please," Munif said in heavily accented English to the soldier who had finished frisking him. "We need medicine." He towered over the Israeli soldier, but kept his eyes as low as he could. He knew they couldn't afford to seem confrontational. They were here for help.

"Levik," the soldier called out loudly to the other one, who was still absorbed in his probing search of Nadia's body. "*Tikach et ha' isha lamirpa'ah.*"

The pimply-faced soldier smiled broadly. He stopped his frisk and gestured for Nadia to walk with him. The other soldier pointed his rifle to the bench, and Munif walked over to it and sat down. His black eyes glistened and his muscles tightened in his cheeks like wales as Nadia and the Jew walked away down the dusty path.

Nadia felt odd that she was not frightened, though she knew full well what was about to happen. She sensed that the soldier with her would not harm her—he seemed too young for that—but he certainly was not leering at her as an expression of selfless medical philanthropy. But by now it didn't matter to her. She had a desperate reason for being here; all that mattered was getting the medicine and DDT and oil.

There were no kibbutzniks on the short path that led between two rows of wooden buildings. A few soldiers milled about in front of the eating hall and one of them called out something to the soldier with Nadia. He waved to them and laughed conspiratorially. Then he stopped at a small wooden cottage at the end of the street and beckoned her inside.

It was some kind of medical house. An old steel examining table stood in the middle of the only room and three walls had drug and instrument shelves, very poorly stocked.

The soldier reeked of fresh onions, probably from working one of the kibbutz's many fields. He moved close to her in the small room, pressing toward her, his scuffed army boots shuffling against her thin leather sandals. She wore nothing but a thick, unbelted, loosely flowing black cotton caftan, which began to feel like too little. She was getting frightened. At the same time, she sensed a little fear in him, some timidity. Maybe he really wasn't an experienced rapist or killer. Really just a kid.

"Typhus," she said to the soldier in English. "Infection. Need penicillin." Munif had told her to say these words.

The soldier drew back and scrutinized her, obviously to see if it was she who was afflicted with these maladies, but he could see that she was not. He took her hand and drew her toward the examining table.

She pulled her hand away and stepped back from him, fear creeping into her voice: "Medicine, medicine, penicillin." She implored him and pressed her hands together in the sign of all prayer—his, hers, it didn't matter.

The soldier walked to a shelf filled sparsely with small boxes and viles and carefully took down two different boxes. He put them on the small sink counter and turned back toward Nadia. He gestured toward the two boxes and then toward the examining table, smiling.

She went to the table, sat on the edge, then lay back slowly. She covered her eyes with her forearm and waited, trying to think of nothing but the medicine—of Samir's shoulder getting better, of the children being safe.

His hand moved from the inside of her knee up her leg, lifting her dress as it went, and she spread her legs farther apart to accommodate him. There was no use in fighting him, or angering him.

He crawled onto the table between her legs and she felt him trying to get into her, but she was dry and he was very small, and the examining table was not meant for this sort of examination. He grunted and backed away for a moment, then got off the table.

Nadia propped herself on one elbow and took him in her hand and rubbed hard. It didn't take long: the young soldier groaned weakly and came in short bursts, spilling onto her hand and naked thigh. He turned away from her, breathing quickly, excitedly. She patted herself with a swatch of her caftan, got off the table, picked up the drugs from the counter, put them in her pocket, and walked out of the infirmary to the truck, not once looking back for the pimply-faced soldier.

Munif was still sitting on the bench. Beside him was a large full bag which looked like a bag of cement. Nadia got into the cab of the truck. With the soldier's permission, Munif shouldered the heavy bag, hoisted it onto the truck bed, and got into the driver's seat. He didn't look at Nadia or say a word, and she just looked out the window. The soldiers waved them off and they drove silently back to the refugee camp.

Munif unloaded the bag of DDT and they walked to their shack. He ripped the top seam off the bag and started shaking the chalky powder on the ground around the perimeter of the hut.

Nadia excitedly went inside to Widad, who was sitting cross-legged next to Samir. He looked a little better than he had the night before, though pain still showed on his face.

"What'd you get?" Widad asked calmly, restraining the note of hope in her voice.

"I don't know," Nadia told her, reaching into her pocket and pulling out the two small boxes. She couldn't read any of the English on them, so she handed them to Samir.

He squinted at the first package. "Mercurochrome." He squinted at the second package and groaned. "Bicarbonate of soda."

"Worthless?" Widad asked. Samir nodded gravely.

Nadia stood up slowly and stumbled into the other room where Muna was rocking Hamdi to sleep and sat in a corner on the muddy floor. Muna saw the sick, hollow look in Nadia's eyes and gestured to her to see if she wanted to hold her baby. Nadia shook her head and looked away, her lips drawn bloodlessly, tautly across her teeth. She rubbed her hand in the mud of the floor, trying to cleanse away the filth.

Chapter Six

In other, better times, the unseasonal heat wave that hit the beleaguered camp early that spring would have been cursed and hated, but this one dried the reeking cesspool ponds and the mud in the streets and under the shacks and was treated universally as a great gift from Allah. Deep freshwater wells were augered at the north edge of the camp. DDT was brought to the camp from Egypt, and finally the rats and fleas and lice stopped their deadly visits to the refugees. The total death toll from the epidemic had reached the thousands, and huge pits received the bodies of the dead. For health purposes, these were cremated and the entire area was covered with lye and recovered with earth.

An herb poultice of lupine, scrounged from somewhere and made by Muna, had drawn the infection from Samir's shoulder, and he recovered fully. Munif had a permanent lump on the back of his head to remind him of his meeting with the Bedouins. Otherwise, time moved on for the people of the camp, and Palestine remained as far away as ever.

Since no police force had been assigned or established in the refugee camp, minor crime, burglary, assault and muggings were as epidemic as the typhus had been. The only protection was provided by the clans themselves and this was limited by the unwieldy number and random distribution of the refugees. The simple rules of social order that had worked for hundreds of years were inconsequential in this giant pest-hole.

Traditional Palestinian society consisted of stratification along *hamula* lines. Villages typically arose that way. First, there'd be a single family of parents with ten or twelve or fifteen children. And as the sons married, the family would build another room onto the home and the new husband and wife would live there. When the new husband and wife had too many children to be housed in the one room, they would either start building additions or build another new house right next door. It in turn would grow by the addition of children. Thus did the extended family *hamula* system develop.

The strength of the *hamula* was in large part its size; sons, therefore, were much more prized than daughters, because in this intensely patriarchal society sons would remain in the family village and bring the wife into the *hamula*, while daughters would move away to another village and be lost to their parents' clan. In larger villages with several *hamulas*, the government was traditionally composed of a council of the eldest male from each clan, which then elected a *mukhtar* to preside as chief of the council. There was no need for a police force, since the men of the separate *hamulas* formed protective walls around their family and possessions. When crimes were committed, punishments were direct and simple and carried out communally. A thief would have his hand cut off. A rapist would be killed by the victim's father and brothers. An adulterous wife would be stoned to death—while no punishment ordinarily befell her partner, because to be horny and indiscriminate was deemed proper for a man in this quintessential man's world, as long as he did not defile a virgin and thus destroy her bride price.

Bands of wild family-less children and teenagers roamed the sprawling refugee camp like jackals. They had no schools, they had no jobs, they had no money for food, and they were reduced to stealing and eating garbage just to survive. The border with Israel had become a barbed-wire barrier patrolled by Jewish soldiers with dogs. The border with Egypt was sealed by Egyptian soldiers to insure that not a single Palestinian entered to take a job or slice of bread from an Egyptian or to add to the growing unrest against King Farouk.

The Palestinian refugees were hermetically sealed into these wretched, sprawling shantytowns by both Jew and Arab alike. Their only news came from a few aging shortwave sets that could pick up the static-filled broadcasts from Cairo and Beirut.

That spring, they heard a few tantalizing details about an armistice conference that was going on between the Arabs and Jews on the Island of Rhodes. At first, they had been excited, but as 1949 progressed and nothing happened, they realized that all the talk and promises of repatriation had been meaningless, and that they were all alone in their fetid, verminous, Egyptian world, without help or hope.

One balmy evening, Samir and Munif listened with several other men to the crackling shortwave set in the mosque in Gaza City, a favorite hangout for the *hamula* leaders from the refugee camps. They sat cross-legged on threadbare carpets and shared a nargilah with the others. The men puffed deeply of the precious tobacco, and clouds of humid smoke spread like cirrus in the tepid air.

The sterile voice from Cairo droned on with its news: "King Abdullah of Transjordan has decided to consolidate his new, so-called 'Hashemite Kingdom of Jordan' by issuing new decrees which will be effective January 1, 1950.

"His decrees will abolish the status of the so-called 'West Bank' as a separate Palestinian state, which had been established by the United Nations in its 1947 Partition vote, and will forbid any resident of the new Hashemite Kingdom, including the West Bank, from using the term 'Palestinian.' From January 1st on, all of these people are to refer to themselves as Jordanians. The use of 'Palestine' will be banned from the press and the radio."

Shouts of "Kill the traitor" instantly filled the mosque, and even out in the streets they could hear the news having an immediate effect. The Palestinians were being made illegal! Their very peoplehood was being legislated out of existence.

Samir realized that there would be demonstrations at the camps, perhaps riots. He and Munif had to protect their family.

"Let's go," he said, and both of them ran outside to their truck, along with many of the other frightened, angry Palestinian men. The streets had already come alive with protestors.

By the time they reached the camp just ten minutes away, there were crowds of rabble chanting and hollering along the dirt paths and streets. Samir parked the truck as close as he could get it to their shanty. It was nearly dark, and bonfires were being built on the fringes of the tinderbox shantytown by the rapidly forming groups of refugees.

Luckily, that night, no one in the camp had a military handgun or rifle. Many had shotguns, however, and those began to appear from the dark innards of the huts. There were a few solo shots, just enough to convince Samir to prepare for the worst. He went to the large ornate trunk at the foot of his and Widad's rag bed and withdrew the intricately engraved H&R .12 gauge shotgun that had escaped the Jewish searchers back in Ein Kerem. The shotgun had been one of his father's carefully maintained treasures; bird hunting had always been a great sport among Palestinian men.

There were two live shells in the double barrels, but Samir had no other ammunition. He went outside the shanty and stood in the doorway, standing guard against anyone who might try to enter, to dare intrude upon his *hamula*. Munif took a rake with heavy steel teeth and stood beside his brother, trying to appear as ferocious as he felt. Both he and Samir were tall, and Samir was stocky as well. They were a brooding, fearsome pair of Cerberuses guarding the gates of their own private Hell.

Hours passed, and the expected riots never materialized. The torches wielded by the firebrands around the bonfires were not thrown into the huts or carried recklessly through the tinder-dry camp. Finally the fires waned and a torpor settled over the camp, a kind of sullen malaise of helplessness and despair. They could do nothing about the actions of King Abdullah. Their country was gone, their identity as a people had been ripped from them.

Samir and Munif finally sat back against the doorjamb of the shack. They were exhausted from their tense vigil.

"How many more such nights can we stay here," Samir whispered, "until the rabble burns down the entire camp?"

"All it will take is one spark on a windy night," was Munif's reply.

From the thick darkness of the interior of the tarpaper shack, Nadia emerged slowly and silently, carrying Hamdi nestled to her breast.

"You can't blame the protesters," she said. "Now Abdullah has stabbed us in the heart." She was fighting back tears and her voice broke.

"Nobody blames anyone," soothed Samir. "But one of these days they will be unable to contain their grief and pain, and there will be much death here."

They sat in silence.

"It's time to go to Lebanon to get our money," said Munif matter-of-factly.

Again silence.

"And who goes?" asked Samir. "How do we get through Israel or through the Bedouins to Cairo?"

"Well, maybe a fishing boat to El Arish and then a coastal trawler to Alexandria and then to Beirut, and back the same way," Nadia said slowly.

They sat pensively, and there was suddenly a palpable spark of hope, a possibility to get out of this squalid camp and live in one of the sprawling stone villas in Gaza City. If nothing else, money could do that much for them—provide some comfort against the misery of their exile.

"The only one who has a chance is me," whispered Nadia, saying what they all knew. A man couldn't possibly travel as safely as a woman.

"With Hamdi with me," she went on, "it's unlikely that anyone will harm me or even take much notice of me. The Jews have undoubtedly created many Arab widows."

"Yes," said Samir slowly. "It's our only chance."

There was no reason to wait. All the planning they could do had been done that night, in those few moments. So Nadia left the next day, clutching Hamdi close to herself. Samir drove her to the ramshackle fishing pier just outside of Dayr el-Balah. It was before sunrise, and the Egyptian fishermen were readying their twenty-foot skiffs for the morning's foray into the Mediterranean.

A tiny, wizened fisherman was delighted to accept the offer of five pounds sterling to carry the widow and her child to El Arish. Nadia stepped carefully and uncertainly into the narrow boat and sat on the large rolled-up net in the bow. The Egyptian started the outboard motor and the skiff eased swiftly away from the dock into the hyacinth waters.

Nadia looked back at Samir and couldn't help thinking of her own murdered husband. How her life had changed in the months since his death! Now she found herself embarking on a plan that a year ago would have seemed far too outlandish even to imagine, going alone with her baby to Beirut! She prayed that Farid was watching over her.

Chapter Seven

Nadia had never actually lived anywhere but Deir Yassin and the refugee camp. But she was no primitive. She had ten years of schooling at a *madrassa*, strictly for upper-class village girls. She had learned the Koran almost by heart, she knew the traditional history of Islam and the empires of the Muslims. She knew arithmetic. And she had even made a habit of reading the Arabic newspaper that her father-in-law the Mukhtar Muhammad had picked up in Jerusalem every Thursday.

But nothing that she had ever read or studied prepared her for the rusted creaking freighter with the Greek name on the side and the tower of Babel complement of sailors and roustabouts who walked half-naked on deck in filthy, oil-impregnated shorts and sandals. It had cost her fifteen pounds sterling to purchase passage in the one separate cabin on the ship. She had inquired at a dozen ship offices in El Arish, and finally she had found this old freighter which was heading directly to Beirut, just a two-day voyage. Just one night in this putrid, oily dungeon they called a cabin.

She'd boarded the ship in dread, draped in the full-length *shaddur* [veil] she never wore in Palestine. *Shaddurs* were for the old women, for Saudis and Bedouins. But here, she knew, the veil was her friend. On this creaking tub, locked in the airless dank cabin, she was just a faceless old Arab hag with a baby. No one bothered her. They docked the next afternoon in the Port of Beirut, and she stepped onto Lebanese soil.

She'd never seen such a large, modern city before. The shiny gray buildings looked to her like polished stones, like ancient pieces of gigantic jewelry, basking in the mild sun of the afternoon. Glittery as they were, the buildings were not beautiful to her: they reminded her of the Western intrusion that had ravaged the Arab nations and brought the merciless Jew Crusader hordes that had taken over her beloved homeland.

Nadia finally unwrapped the heavy *shaddur* and shook her hair free and felt better. It was a perfect day. She took a taxi from the port to the *Banque du Liban*, but it was closed. She'd forgotten: it was Sunday, a regular weekday to the Muslims, but the sabbath for the Maronite Catholic banking gentry of Beirut. In fact, this was the principal reason why Beirut had become the banker for the Middle East; it was why she was here. Muslims considered it a violation of Koranic law to charge interest—usury—and banking was therefore a discredited institution. Among the Lebanese Maronite Catholics, however, no such prohibition existed, and they had become the bankers for all of the Muslim states.

Nadia asked the taxi driver to take her to any nearby pension suitable for a traveler such as herself. He smiled at her and rushed into traffic. She had never before been to a hotel or pension, but Samir had told her to do this. A pension, he had said, would feed her and be more homey than a big-city hotel.

The driver pulled up beside a stately two-story stucco building with mock-marble pillars and the facade of an ancient Roman temple. The taxi driver opened her door and escorted her through ornate wooden doors into a large reception room padded with thick Persian carpets, with sofas and armchairs of red plush, and they went up to the desk. No one was there, but the driver told her to wait. He went into a small room to the right.

A moment later he emerged, smiling, followed by a very fat bleached blonde of at least fifty years. The driver grinned at Nadia and pocketed something the fat lady gave him, but only after she had looked Nadia over. The driver left without asking Nadia to pay for the ride—something Samir had not prepared her for. But she figured that the pension must have some sort of business agreement with this and other taxi companies, so the fare was paid by the fat woman.

"Oh, what a lovely little boy," the fat lady purred in a soft, sweet voice, taking Hamdi from Nadia and admiring him like a doting grandmother. Hamdi, however, began to cry and Nadia had to take him back into her arms.

"And what brings you here, my dear?" the fat lady asked in that very soft voice.

"I have some business for my family," answered Nadia. "I'll only be here a day, I believe."

The fat lady suddenly looked sad. "Oh, my dear, I see you're from Palestine. What a terrible time you must have had at the hands of the Jews." The woman had apparently recognized Nadia's accent. She clasped her hands to the large gold crucifix hanging from her necklace into the cleavage of her huge breasts, as though she were soothing her aching heart. Nadia didn't know what to say, so she simply nodded.

"Come, my dear, I have the perfect room for you," the fat woman purred. She pulled a foot-long skeleton key down from a hook behind the desk and led Nadia up the stairs and down a wide hallway on the second floor. There were ten or twelve numbered doors, Nadia noticed, and they entered the one numbered "6."

The room turned out to be spacious and clean and had a large four-poster bed and a small divan. Compared to the refugee camp, this was a palace. On the wall behind the bed was a large crucifix of filigreed silver with a skillfully carved olivewood Jesus.

"Dinner is downstairs in the dining room at six-thirty," the woman said, smiling sweetly and closing the door behind her as she left.

It was already after five. Nadia placed Hamdi on the bed and lay down beside him, easing on to the soft cushion of the lush bedding, feeling softer and more pampered than she had in many, many months. They both fell quickly to sleep.

After what seemed like seconds, she awoke to the sound of a woman's voice announcing dinner. There was loud knocking on several other doors and then on her own. She stretched happily, already feeling hungry for the food downstairs, and picked up her baby, and the two of them went to the end of the hallway to the dormitory-style bathroom. It too was clean and well-kept.

Downstairs there were a number of people milling about in the reception room. She went into a large room on the other side where a long table stretched length-wise, piled high with various plates of food, around which ten women were seated. The food looked delicious and plentiful, and Nadia drank it all in as if it were a dream. Platters of roast capons and squabs, glazed lamb, trays of kibbah and yellow and saffron pilafs and coucous, plates of cut watermelon and honeydew and red grapes like great cabochon rubies, and bright green apples cut in half, with moist pure white flesh.

More than ever, she wanted to get that bank money so she and her family could get out of the camp, move to Gaza City, so they could enjoy food like this. This was the way things should be.

The fat lady rose from her chair and came over to Nadia. Her bleached-blond hair fell about her thick bare shoulders. She was heavily made-up with violet painted eyelids and rouged cheeks. She wore a beautiful emerald green silk evening gown and her huge cleavage squeezed over the top of the gown. The big gold crucifix bounced on her breasts as she walked.

"Oh, my dear, it's so nice to have you with us," she gushed in that purring voice. "Look, everybody," she said, turning to the others. "This is Nadia and Hamdi. They come to us from Palestine."

The other women looked up and smiled and called out "hellos," then went back to eating and chatting. The fat lady pulled out a chair for Nadia, and Nadia put Hamdi into the high chair that was already next to it. Several of the other women also had babies in high chairs. Nadia busied herself feeding Hamdi, and they both ate well of the handsome food.

The woman on her right was a petite blonde wearing a seductive red jersey sheath which followed the curves of her body. Nadia spoke a few words to her in Arabic, but the girl shook her head and answered something in some other language. The fat lady was laughing heartily at the head of the table and carrying on an animated discussion in French with three of the ladies.

The woman on Nadia's left was wearing a traditional caftan. She was very dark, maybe Sudanese or Ethiopian, thought Nadia, and very subdued. She ate quickly without looking around at all and she left the table only a few moments after Nadia arrived.

Nadia finished eating, picked Hamdi up, and walked out of the dining room through the now-crowded reception room and out of the pension. It was a marvelous spring night, cool and still and starry, and she walked the two blocks to the boulevard which ran by the beach and walked along the broad sidewalk. There were many benches along the sidewalk, and she laid Hamdi down on one and sat next to him. It was very pretty here, peaceful, and she felt happy and confident. Beyond the boulevard the city glowed with thousands of lights, no less busy than it had been this afternoon. It was quite a place, Beirut. Tomorrow she would get the money and leave. Then another short freighter ride and back to her family. She sat a long time and listened to her baby's soft snoring. Things were going to be fine.

It soon grew more chilly, and Hamdi awoke with a short cry.

Nadia hugged him to her and walked slowly back to the pension, ready for a long night's sleep. The reception room was almost dark, just a few dim candle lamps flickering, and several groups of men and women standing around sipping on drinks and laughing together in a gaggle of languages. Nadia walked upstairs, and there was a huge rhinoceros of an Arab in a business suit sitting on a chair on the landing, holding a rifle across his lap. He smiled and nodded very politely at Nadia, and she smiled back and went into the bathroom at the end of the hallway. Then she carried Hamdi into their room, laid him down on the divan, and sat next to him until he fell asleep.

It was late, she didn't know how late, but a high opalescent moon shone through the sheer curtain of the large window. Muffled sounds came from below, laughter and Victrola music. It was a pleasant backdrop. People here certainly enjoyed themselves, no matter what time of night or day. Nadia undressed and got under the thick goose down comforter and felt deliciously warm and fell asleep almost immediately.

Shortly after—it literally felt like seconds—she awoke with a start. Someone had pulled the comforter off her. A man was crawling on top of her. He smelled of whiskey and sickeningly sweet cologne. She tried to push him away—she punched him in the face. She started to scream. Struggling, he clasped one hand over her nose and mouth and slapped her hard with the other. She wriggled beneath him, trying to jostle him off. He was small and she finally managed to push him away. She jumped out of bed and ran toward the door, but he caught up with her and punched her in the back, in the kidney, and she slumped against the door in pain, gasping for breath. He pulled her back and threw her on the bed.

She regained her breath and screamed shrilly. Hamdi woke up and started crying. The door flew open and the rhinoceros with the rifle came in, followed closely by the fat lady, who rushed not to Nadia or Hamdi but to the short, naked man—who in turn began to shake his fist at the fat lady, yelling at her in furious gutter Arabic. The fat lady wrung her hands and apologized and soothed and implored.

"I'll give you much better," she purred. "I have much better. I have a black who is an ebony Cleopatra. She will make you feel like a sultan," she said, wringing her hands and smiling hopefully.

Finally the yelling stopped. The man put on the clothes that were on the floor beside the bed and left the room with the huge Arab. Nadia had dressed and was sitting on the divan cooing to Hamdi to settle him down. The fat lady came over to her and slapped her hard across the face. The soft purring voice had changed to steel wool.

"How dare you treat my honored customers like that, you homeless Palestinian scum!" The woman seethed with indignant anger.

Nadia felt oddly calm. If she had a knife, she would kill this fat Maronite whore. But now nothing mattered to her but getting that money tomorrow. Nothing mattered but leaving this modern, angry city and getting back to her *hamula*. She picked up Hamdi and walked out of the room, out of the pension, and back to the beach.

She wrapped herself and her baby in the *shaddur* and rocked him to sleep and slept off and on through the night. When the sun finally rose, they went to a small elegant cafe near the *Banque du Liban*, and Nadia drank coffee and they ate pastry until nine o'clock when the bank opened.

She got a bank letter of credit, "unstealable," Samir had told her, put it in an envelope, taped it to her belly, wrapped herself in the *shaddur*, and walked to the port to find a ship bound for El Arish. She had gotten the money—and that was all that mattered.

Chapter Eight

"It will destroy us," Samir breathed out slowly, eying his brother Munif with concern.

"I only know what all the talk is," said Munif, "and I think it's absolutely true. The Nashibis want the construction contracts for all of the Gaza Strip. Now that the United Nations is going to construct refugee camps, the contracts will be very lucrative. The Nashibis have decided to bid for them."

"But *we* need those contracts. Without them, all of this suffering, all of this work, will simply have been in vain." Samir lifted his hands from his desk and gestured around the spacious el-Rashid Construction Company office, located just outside Gaza City. They had finally been able to move into a spacious stone and stucco villa in the fashionable quarter of the City. "The housing contracts we got from the American Friends are just not enough. If we don't get the U.N. contracts, we'll be ruined."

Munif said nothing, just stared grimly at his brother.

"Those fucking traitors," seethed Samir. "The Nashibi family refused to back the Mufti against the Jews, and because of them, the Mufti is now in exile and the Nashibis are getting rich in Jerusalem along with their Jew friends!"

The radio in the background was blaring happy music, and Samir reached back to his mahogany credenza and switched it off.

"What do we do?" Samir asked.

Munif sat a moment deep in thought, then shrugged his shoulders. "The Nashibis sent one of their construction company officials here four days ago. He is the one who is going to present the bid tomorrow at the construction meeting at U.N. Headquarters. He is staying in a rented room down by the Corniche where the sailors hang out with their tarts. Maybe we should have a talk with him."

Samir studied his brother. Munif's bushy eyebrows were twitching wildly, the way he got when he was doing some very serious thinking.

"What do you mean?" Samir asked slowly. "We sure as hell don't have enough money to bribe him. The Nashibis are the richest family in Jerusalem. What is there to say?"

"I'm not talking about bribes. I wouldn't pay a dime of our money to the treacherous Jew-loving Nashibis, even if it would work. I have something more definite in mind."

Samir studied him and began to scowl. He nodded. "But how do we do it?"

"Well, I've been thinking about that too. He spends his evenings in that bar on the Corniche, the one where the expensive whores hang out. He gets drunk and leaves with a girl...."

Again Samir scrutinized his brother, pursing his lips and squinting, seeing the scene unfold before his mind's eye. "But we don't know any of the girls, and who could we trust even if we did?"

Munif's answer was one carefully spoken word: "Nadia."

"*Ya Allah!* [My God!]" Samir breathed out in a shocked whisper. And then he looked hard at his brother and his breath caught in his throat, and then he breathed a long sigh and nodded.

"You can't really want me to do this!" she blurted again.

Samir merely sat still in front of his sister-in-law in the parlor of the villa, and he made no reply.

"Let some strange man touch me?"

"You need not do that", he said reassuringly. "You need only spark his interest in you and bring him to your room. We will be waiting. Nothing more."

"But it is unseemly."

"This is for our family. We have no other way. The Jew-loving traitors will underbid us and destroy us. It is not unseemly, it is our only choice. It is for all of us, for Hamdi."

"And how can we possibly be undetected? I will be found out."

"That is not so. We have rented a room in one of those whorehouse hotels. Munif was wearing a *keffiyeh* and a robe and nobody could ever recognize him. And when the deed is discovered, no one will care, no one will even investigate. Our people hate the Nashibis and their ilk, and they will simply write this off as another faceless prostitute murdering a rich man for his wallet."

She breathed deeply and took the twenty pound note which Samir pressed into her hand. She had to buy a dress, in that phony French boutique down on the Corniche where they sold those sinfully scanty dresses to the girls who frequented the bars and nightclubs in the area where the sailors came.

Nadia thickly rouged her cheeks and blued her eyelids and hennaed her hair in disguise. She put on the turquoise satin evening gown she had bought, with the low cut bodice and tight-fitting skirt. She wrapped herself in her black gauze caftan and *shaddur* so no one would see how she was dressed, when she left the villa and got into the Jaguar sedan with Samir and Munif at eleven o'clock that evening.

She had never been in a bar. It was very smoky and smelled of stale bodies and strong drinks. A trio of musicians filled the large room with raucous sound, a clarinet, a trumpet, cymbals and drums. She spotted the elegant looking man in the gray silk suit with the slicked-back black hair, sitting at a small table near the stage where the trio was playing. Munif had described him to her perfectly. A very big-chested, auburn-haired woman sat at the table with him. Her large round face was dark and smeared with heavy patches of cosmetics, her full lips were glossy with violet lipstick.

Nadia passed close by the table and caught the man's eye. He looked at her with great interest, swaying slightly from too much drink.

She sat on a stool at the bar, next to an aging drunk whore, wearing a beautiful red silk evening gown. A moment later, she felt a rough hand on her bare shoulder.

"You're the prettiest pussy in the whole place," the elegantly dressed man said to her, breathing the stink of cheap cognac into her face. "How come I've never sheen you?" he lisped, drunk.

"I guess I've never been lucky enough," breathed Nadia, giving him what she hoped was a convincingly seductive whore's smile of anticipation.

"Come, shit with me," he giggled at his own intoxicated lisp and took her roughly by the hand. He led her to the table.

"What the Hell do you think—" the whore at the table said.

"Get out of here, bitch!" The elegant man spoke menacingly through his gapped teeth to the woman, who looked carefully into his eyes, considered the situation for a moment, picked up her pocketbook off the table, and stumbled to the bar.

He sloshed the rest of his drink into his mouth, spilling some of it on his obviously expensive green silk tie. He flicked absently at the droplets and then turned toward Nadia. "Lesh go fuck."

"Maybe I'm too expensive for you," she said demurely.

He burst into laughter and pulled a wallet out of his coat pocket. He withdrew two crisp new fifty pound sterling notes and laid them in front of her. She picked them up and folded them and stuffed them in her bodice, the way she had seen once in a Turkish movie she had snuck into in Jerusalem. She stood up and began walking out of the bar. He followed closely behind her like an anxious hound dog.

They walked into the dark, overcast night. "Where to, honey?" he lisped, swaying unsurely.

"Come on, I have a room," she said, letting him put his arm

around her shoulders and prop himself up so he wouldn't fall down. They walked a block to the dingy apartment building and walked with difficulty up two flights of creaky wooden stairs to the landing of apartment 3.

She unlocked it, and they walked inside the pitch black room. She quickly pushed his arm off of her shoulders, and she felt him being pulled away by unseen hands.

"What the—" is all he managed to say.

She pulled the bills out of the bodice of her dress and threw them on the floor. She ran through the door, slammed it behind her, ran down the stairs and out the back door of the building into the alley where the black Jaguar was parked. She got into the back seat and waited, her heart beating painfully, her breath coming in wheezes.

Moments later, Samir and Munif came silently out the back door of the building. Samir was carrying a long rolled up bulky carpet. Munif opened the trunk and Samir stuffed the bundle inside. They quickly climbed into the car.

"I thought you were just going to leave him there," said Nadia in a weak, thin voice.

"I had a better idea—safer," said Samir. "We're going to leave him at the garbage dump to the south of the city. By morning, after the rats are through with him, no one will be able to tell whether it was a man or a dog."

A half hour later, they quietly returned to their splendid villa in Gaza City.

BOOK THREE

GENESIS

"How lonely doth the city lie, that was once so full of people. She that was once great among the nations, a princess among the provinces, how she is become enslaved!

"She weepeth bitterly in the night, and her tears are on her cheeks. Among all her lovers she hath none to comfort her. All her friends have dealt treacherously with her, they have become her enemies."

—Lamentations 1:1-2

Chapter One

February 1949

Leah Jordan awoke abruptly with wrenching pains in her loins, and the sheet was drenched with fluid and blood. She felt as though a hyena had its claws embedded in her womb. She shook Matt awake. He was instantly alert.

"Are you okay?" he whispered.

"Yes," she breathed out slowly as a contraction clutched her.

Matt jumped out of bed in the chilly dawn and quickly pulled on his work clothes and boots. "I'm going to the secretarial office to telephone the obstetrician."

Leah had started spotting two months ago, and she was afraid that she would miscarry. The obstetrician from Rehovot had ordered her to bed with her legs elevated, and she had slavishly obeyed the doctor's every word. She wanted this baby. Oh God, oh God, oh God how she wanted Matthew Jordan's son, for he would be one of the new Jews. Not a stetl Yid uprooted from his home and transplanted in the midst of violence and murder, but an *Israeli*, born in a Jewish State, proud, free, never to see his loved ones and his people slaughtered before his eyes by the Germans or the Poles or the Lithuanians or the Arabs or any other aspirant to the throne of Satan.

Leah had returned to Kibbutz Na'on the day after the massacre at Deir Yassin and Matt had implored her to stay out of further action. When the war finally ended, Matt too had returned to Na'on.

Matt had brought Leah's meals on a tray from the eating hall and made her tea and puttered around the tiny cottage and fretted so much that finally Leah threw him out of the cottage and told him to go back to work at the sprinkler factory and quit driving her nuts.

She had stayed in bed for the last two weeks of January, and by the end of February's first week, she knew that she was ready. February 6, 1949.

"Dr. Cohen is on his way. Fifteen minutes." Matt was puffing hard from his run to the Secretariat. He knelt on the bed beside Leah, patting her arm. "Should I boil water?" he looked at her very solemnly, and despite the pain she couldn't help laughing. Dear sweet Matthew, tender Matthew, oh I love you so.

"What would you do with boiling water?"

He answered very gravely: "I saw it in a movie once. I cut up strips of the sheet and I sterilize everything with boiling water."

"How do we get boiling water, Matthew? We have no stove, we have no hot plate, we have no fireplace." Another contraction made her arch her back and grip Matt's hand tightly. The pain slowly subsided.

"Yes," he said slowly, "I guess you're right."

"Just hold my hand and love me," she looked into his worried eyes. "Everything will be fine—" Again she arched with the pain of the contraction and beads of perspiration gathered on her forehead.

Deep in her soul Leah knew why she was having so much trouble with this childbirth. It was the abortion. It had injured her somehow, she had always felt that. It was the one thing that she had never told anyone, not even Matt. She couldn't. She stiffened with the searing pain, and she saw it all again. So real, so near....

Leah misses her period. She carefully studies the calendar. No mistake, she is ten days late. She waits with mounting fear and dread. Another week, another week, and another week. She is pregnant. The mere thought that her womb could be the breeding place for the seed of Karl Mencken, the Prince of Darkness, fills her with disgust. She feels filthy.

A few weeks after she is certain, Mencken leaves on a trip to Lublin to attend a conference of concentration camp commanders. It is past midnight. Leah bundles Nachman in a wool blanket, places him in the bicycle carrier, and peddles into Treblinka. She goes as silently as possible to the rear door of the cottage where the village midwife lives. After a few furtive knocks, the ancient hag opens the door a crack.

"Please, I need help," whispers Leah, holding Nachman in her arms, sleeping.

"What is it, who are you?" asks the old woman opening the door wider to see if she can recognize the visitor in the moonlight, squinting at Leah's face. "Ah, Pani Pulkownik *[Madam Colonel]," she says, recognizing one of Treblinka's celebrities and opening the door wide. "Come in, come in."*

She closes the door behind them and lights a kerosene lantern in the dingy, squalid one room cottage. She looks at Leah inquiringly.

"I am sure that I am pregnant and I do not wish to have the baby."

"Here, let me take your baby. Oh, what a sweet little child." With bony hands like quivering birds, she lays Nachman on the wooden table. Her voice is a high thin Robin's cheep. "Now my dear, we cannot go against God's will. Jesus loves all of his children, even those we ourselves don't love. I do not like to take part in such a thing as this."

Leah pulls out a small bag of coins and empties them into the old hag's hand. It is more money than the midwife has seen in many months. She opens her eyes wide and smiles at Leah.

"All right, my dear. Let it be on your head. How long have you been pregnant?"

"Not more than ten weeks."

"Then we will try first the easy way. I have some herbs. You will drink them with a glass of vodka. In an hour you should start hemorrhaging. I will stop the bleeding. If that doesn't work, we will take the next step."

The midwife busies herself at the cupboard and mixes her potion. She gives it to Leah to drink and tells her to lie down on the bed. The old hag then takes a pair of scissors out of a drawer in the table next to the sleeping Nachman. She cuts strips of cloth and lays the scissors and some uncut cloth on the table in case more should be needed.

After five minutes, Leah becomes extremely nauseous and begins to gag. The midwife holds her hand over Leah's mouth to keep her from vomiting up the concoction. Then Leah dozes dizzily, dulled by the vodka. The hag pulls up Leah's dress and stuffs rags under her to absorb the mess.

About an hour later, Leah feels severe cramps in her abdomen and blood begins to flow slowly. Then she erupts with a copious flow. She feels very sick. When the major hemorrhaging is over, the midwife presses a plug of rags into Leah and elevates her buttocks and legs by piling a thick quilt under them. Leah begins to doze again as the pain subsides.

She awakes to Nachman's crying and looks over to him on the table.

"He has wet himself," says the midwife. *"I'll change him so he'll go back to sleep."* She unwraps the blanket and unpins the diaper. "As she pulls the diaper off, she sees his circumcized penis and freezes, staring at it and then at the mother.

Leah, dulled by the vodka and the pain, does not realize what has happened until the midwife begins backing toward the door, away from the naked infant, a look of horror on her face. Leah forces herself out of her fog and off the bed and grabs the long scissors on the table. She reaches the midwife just as she starts to pull the door open, and Leah plunges the scissors in her back, again and again.

Leah steadies herself holding onto the table and waits for the room to stop spinning. She rediapers and wraps Nachman and goes outside to her bicycle and pedals quickly back to her house.

It is pitch black on the highway and the lights are out in the house. She rushes inside and closes the door softly. Not a dog barks anywhere, not a light or a flashlight has gone on outside. She is safe. She nestles the sleeping Nachman in his crib and slumps beside it. She is suddenly overwhelmed by exhaustion. She knows what she has just done, but none of it is vivid. It is veiled and misted over by the herbs and vodka she has drunk. It is dulled by the panic that gripped her when she looked into the horrified eyes of the *midwife. Leah cannot remember stabbing the hag with the scissors. All she remembers is blood, a great dancing sea of blood, and the thud of the scissors going into the flesh again and again. But none of that matters. Nothing matters to her but Nachman's life. She will kill anyone to preserve him. God will not punish or condemn her for that. He would not, He could not . . . .*

Leah heard a car drive up outside and footsteps on the porch, and Dr. Cohen walked in carrying his black bag.

"Major Jordan," he said with mock sternness, "please wring your hands outside. This is not a place where a frightened husband can do any good."

Matt walked out of the cottage obediently. He sat down on the wooden stoop to watch the sun crawl up the pear trees and the light frost steam off the ground.

He was still sitting there two hours later, chewing his thumbnail down to where blood oozed, when he jumped to his feet at the sound of a baby's cry. He ran inside the cottage as the doctor laid the pink and wrinkled tiny boy on Leah's naked, swollen breasts. The baby instantly fell asleep. Leah was exhausted and her face was ashen. She looked at Matthew and smiled her miraculous madonna smile.

"You'll be unable to have any more children," said Dr. Cohen quietly.

Leah looked at him in alarm.

"You will almost certainly miscarry if you get pregnant again. And the hemorrhaging would probably kill you."

Tears began to shimmer in Leah's eyes. But this was no time for sorrow.

The doctor left.

Matt sat on the edge of the bed and leaned across his son and his wife and put his arms around her and lay his face lightly on her breast. Matt licked Leah's nipple and took it in his mouth tenderly and sucked lightly, drawing from his wife the sustaining milk of life. And Leah stroked his hair and held both of her men tightly. She would never let them go.

Chapter Two

Menachem and Aliza Begin came to Na'on for the bris. Everyone gathered for the circumcision ceremony in the eating hall. They all rose as Matthew came into the hall carrying his son on a pillow cased in white velvet. The crowd parted and he brought the infant to the center where David was sitting and waiting. Matt placed the pillow and his son on David's lap and stepped back to let the mohel approach closely to the baby.

David held the baby gingerly, trying to keep his thoughts from meandering to the day of Jacob's bris, to the day of Jacob's death, to seeing the headless emasculated body of his son lying next to Deena. Tears rolled down his cheeks as he held his godson and he summoned all his strength to keep from running away.

Various benedictions were intoned by Matt and the mohel and the Covenant of Abraham was completed. The mohel then chanted the ceremony of naming: "... preserve this child to his father and to his mother, and let his name be called in Israel *Yehoshua ben-Mattityahu Yardenn*—Joshua ben-Matthew Jordan."

Matt and Leah had carefully chosen the name Joshua for their son. Joshua had been the leader of the Israelites, appointed by God to lead the chosen people to the Promised Land after the death of Moses in the wilderness. It had been Joshua who had finally led the Jews across the alien mountains and the plains and into the Holy Land, to occupy it from the Shephelah to the Arabah, from Canaan to the Lebanon, from the Mediterranean Sea to the Euphrates River, as God had commanded.

The bris ended as the mohel chanted: "This little boy Joshua, may he become great. Even as he has entered into the covenant, so may he enter into the Torah, marriage, and good deeds." The mohel passed a cup of red wine to David, who drank deeply. Then David dipped his fingertip in the cup and put it in Joshua's mouth and the squalling infant quieted and sucked the ritual wine. The wine was passed to Leah and she emptied the cup.

A cheer went up from the kibbutzniks and David stood and

handed the pillowed infant to Leah. He left quickly, unable any longer to contain his grief. The other celebrants lingered for only a moment and then left to go to their jobs. This was a workday and there was much to do.

The Begins walked to Matt and Leah's cottage. Matt carried his sleeping son. The other three sat on the porch in the early spring warmth of southern Israel as Matt put Joshua in his new newly white painted old wooden crib. He came out and joined them.

"The Irgun Tzvai Leumi has served its purpose," Menachem was saying as Matt sat down next to Leah on the creaking two-seater porch swing. Leah was still a bit drawn and tired, not fully recuperated from the difficult months just past and not yet at peace with the knowledge that she could have no more children.

"We have left the underground and disbanded as an army. A few of us have decided to form a political party: 'Cherut' [Freedom]." Begin beamed.

"That's great, Menachem!" said Leah with genuine pleasure. "But you'll never beat Ben-Gurion in an election."

"We don't have to, Leah. The National Council has decided that Israel's government will be like France's, a parliamentary democracy with party lists. So long as our party wins a respectable number of seats, we will someday have the opportunity to try to form a coalition with several of the other parties and become the main party in the ruling coalition. It's certainly not out of the question."

Matt went inside and opened a large can of grapefruit juice, put it on a tray with four glasses, and served them all.

"What are your plans, Matt?" asked Begin.

"I am going to join the Foreign Ministry to be the legal advisor for the American desk. Leah and I and Joshua will be moving to Jerusalem as soon as Leah is fully recovered."

"That's fine!" said Begin. Then he looked at Leah and studied her closely. "And you, Leah, what are you planning?"

"To be a mother. Just to be a mother and a wife, at least for a few years. Too many of my best years were torn from me in that other life. I also think I'll study at the Hebrew University of Jerusalem. Maybe get a degree in History. But first and most important just to be a mother and a wife."

"Cherut would like you to be on our party list to run for a seat in the Knesset [Legislature]," Begin drawled slowly.

Leah looked at him in surprise. "Run for the Knesset? What in the world makes me qualified for that, Menachem?"

"You have the same qualifications as the rest of us. You fought for Israel. And I'll be perfectly honest with you, we think you'll be a real attraction for the women's vote. Married, a mother, a survivor of the Holocaust, a fighter in the War of Independence." Menachem ticked off the several attributes on his fingers as he spoke. "Anyway, you're better looking than any of the rest of us." They all chuckled.

"Cherut really needs you. I need you to be with us."

Leah was genuinely surprised. And she looked at her husband and he raised his eyebrows and shrugged, telling her with the gesture to do whatever she thought best.

"I can see David Ben-Gurion's face, when he picks up the newspaper and reads that the wife of one of his Foreign Ministry employees is running for the Knesset in Menachem Begin's party! He'll take a lion out of Hadassah Zoo and let it tear Matt's heart out on the steps of Government House!" They all erupted in laughter. "But I can't do it, Menachem, not just yet. I need more time to rest, to be a wife and mother."

As one of his "perks" as Deputy Assistant Foreign Minister, Matt was assigned an old army jeep, and in mid-March, he and Leah piled their meager belongings in the back and bundled up Joshua and drove to Jerusalem. The Latrun Pass had been cleared of rubble and gutted tanks and armored cars as soon as the war ended, and they drove quickly through the flowery Shephelah toward Jerusalem. On both sides of the Pass, Leah could see the ghosts of the ancient Arab villages which had been evacuated and leveled to insure that no marauding bands of Arab terrorists would ever find shelter there again, to murder any Jew who drove through the Pass, to cut off Jerusalem and sever the heart of the Jewish people.

Matt had already scouted a few possible homes in Jerusalem, ones that would be affordable and far enough away from the green line closing off Arab East Jerusalem so that they could live safely. Leah had been sightseeing in the hills that composed Jerusalem only once before, on the King David Hotel "scouting mission" with

Yisrael Levi. But then she had been too frightened to savor it fully. Now, she was drawn to its extreme starkness. Everything was shades of gray. Virtually all of the buildings and houses were created of rough hewn grayish yellow limestone, square buildings, dull tile roofs, geometric blocks of massive stone that felt overpowering, relieved only occasionally by small parks with silvery, gnarled olive trees and ragged copses of Jerusalem pines and thin grass. It seemed to her that all of Jerusalem floated above the surrounding countryside under an azure sky reflected from the hyacinth Mediterranean just fifty miles away. They drove through the winding hilly streets into the Yemin Moshe quarter, but as they passed the bombed out south wing of the King David Hotel, Leah decided that she didn't want to look up and see her handiwork every day. So she told Matt that the little stone house was too cold and forbidding.

Across the city they went to the Geulah quarter, and it was much more to Leah's liking. The centuries-old stone buildings looked like ponderous elephants looming over narrow cobblestone streets. Hasidim from Mea Shearim a few blocks away hurried here and there, to the many little synagogues or the yeshivas or the butchers or the bakers. Signs and wall posters announced their messages in Yiddish and Hebrew, and the entire Geulah quarter looked like it had been lifted intact out of the Jewish section of pre-war Vilna or Warsaw or Lublin or Bialystok. It was quaint and familiar, and it immediately struck a nostalgic chord in Leah. Here they would live.

They rented a second story flat right on Geulah Street. It had two bedrooms, a large, homey living room with old style European overstuffed furniture, and a dining room with a walnut table and six hard cushioned chairs done in a strange mix of Louis Quatorze and New Empire. The kitchen was spacious and had a large window opening directly over Geulah Street and facing east so it would catch the morning sun. Leah felt immediately at home.

Days became weeks and then months. Leah enrolled as a freshman at the Hebrew University. She studied history and political science. Matthew was busy from dawn till dusk at the Foreign Ministry.

Joshua grew out of looking like a pink prune and looked more like his father and mother every day. He had a shock of strawberry blonde hair and deep brown eyes and dimples which pierced his cheeks whenever he laughed, which was always. Leah and Matt swore that he would never know the pain of being a Jew, the death and suffering that it engendered in so many generations. Joshua was an Israeli, as clean and fresh and new and bright as this resurrected land. And Joshua and the thousands and thousands of children like him were the future of Israel. They would be strong— very strong. And they would be free.

Chapter Three

At Gaza's open air market one scorching morning in August, the sun resembled the belly of a blast furnace spewing forth streams of molten yellow white steel. As Nadia was shopping for vegetables, she saw a man standing on a vegetable table in the next souk, fulminating with outstretched arms to a growing crowd of listeners. She walked closer, curious to hear.

"*Bi-smi'llahi'r Rachmani'r Rachim.* It is the Jews who have imprisoned us in this ghetto where we must live as impoverished landless fellahin without hope of ever returning to our homes in Palestine. We must form an underground army to battle the Jews, the same way their underground fought against the British and forced them to leave Palestine."

The speaker was a young man with sparkling deep black eyes and a fierce intensity that made his chocolate dark face glow with the ardor of what he was saying.

"We are the *fedayeen* [self-sacrificers]. Whenever Islam has been threatened by unbelievers, fedayeen have risen against the infidels. Now we must do it again. We have started an organization called the General Union of Palestinian Students and we shall regain our homes and our homeland!"

He was now screaming to a crowd of hundreds. Most of them were young and jobless refugees who hung around the markets everyday, eating the vegetables which spoiled in the sun and could not be sold, and waiting—always waiting—for any work truck to come along and pick up two or three or four of them to do a day or two of field labor.

"Our principles are simple and the very core of our lives," the speaker was now at the top of his form, magnetic, glowing, charismatic. "We believe in *'awda*, a complete resettlement of all of the refugees in our homeland, Palestine. And we know that to achieve *'awda* there is but one way, *'al-tariq al-fida'i'* [the way of the fedayeen]. And the *way* is *futuwwah* [guerrilla warfare], just as the Haganah and Irgun and the Stern Gang defeated the British through guerrilla warefare, so must we defeat the Jews."

The last statement was shouted in his great booming deep voice, slowly, emphasizing each word, and then he repeated it three times, even louder, even more fiercely. The crowd was cheering and clapping. Nadia stood transfixed, glued to the ground, absorbed into the most gripping event of her life since Deir Yassin.

Now he had everyone's rapt attention and he raised his arms to quiet the crowd. "We who are true fedayeen will meet tonight at the Mosque al-Malik at Rafah at seven o'clock. It is safer there than here, because Egyptian troops are stationed there in force and we will have no threat from the Israelis. Come all of you, men and women, Palestine needs you all. Come and learn the way of the Palestinian refugees."

With a flourish, he jumped off the vegetable table and made his way slowly through the cheering crowd. He got into a jeep and drove south on the Gaza Road toward the towns of Dayr el-Balah, Khan Yunis and Rafah, there to make the same speech to other crowds.

As the crowd cleared, Nadia noticed a small table set up next to the vegetable stand. She recognized the man sitting behind it with a notebook and writing down the names of many of the crowd of onlookers who had lined up to join the organization. Nadia waited in line. There were a few other women but mostly men. When she reached the table after about half an hour, she said, "Nadia Attiyah."

The man behind the table looked up in surprise. It was her brother-in-law, Munif el-Rashid. His bushy eyebrows worked up and down nervously at Nadia. His intense eyes studied her.

"I thought you were at home with Hamdi, Nadia."

"And I thought you were at work with Samir."

"This was important today."

"I agree. I wish to join the organization. Will they take women?"

"Of course, Nadia. They will take everyone who is a true Palestinian. I'll put your name down here. We'll talk later when I get home."

Nadia did the rest of her shopping and returned home to the sprawling villa to supervise the cleaning women and the cook. She felt a surging of new life in her soul, and she began to feel fully alive again for the first time since she had seen her husband and daughter and son murdered before her eyes almost six years ago.

At about two o'clock, Munif came home for the afternoon break. It was too hot to work from two till five every day, and this was the Mediterranean siesta time.

"So, Nadia, you think that the way of the fedayeen is your way?" He studied her closely, quizzically.

"I think so, I want to go to the Mosque al-Malik tonight and hear what they have to say. All right?"

"Of course." Munif eyed her and tilted his head, squinting at her with a sly smile. "There isn't maybe a little interest in the man you saw today?"

Nadia blushed crimson. She did not have to answer. Munif laughed.

"That was Hassan abu-Sittah. He was born in Jerusalem, but he's a student in Cairo now. He and another student there, Yassir Arafat, are starting General Union groups in all of the Palestinians' towns and camps. Hassan is quite a man, isn't he?"

Nadia smiled softly and then excused herself. There was work to be done before the rest of the family came home for dinner.

Quite a man, she thought to herself as she scurried around the house. Quite a man.

Munif drove one of the company's stake trucks into Gaza's central square and picked up about twenty-five men waiting for a ride to Rafah. With Nadia next to him in the cab, they bumped along the old asphalt road the fifteen miles to Rafah and parked near the Mosque. They entered the courtyard through a huge wooden gate and their names were checked on a list by a fatigue-uniformed guard. There were at least three hundred other men and a few women milling about awaiting Hassan abu-Sittah. When Hassan came, it was already beginning to grow dark and lanterns were lit and placed on the fountain in the center of the courtyard.

Hassan went up to Munif and held hands with him, and they kissed each other on both cheeks. Munif gently pulled Nadia forward.

"I would like you to meet Nadia Attiyah, my sister-in-law. Her husband was the son of the Mukhtar of Deir Yassin who was murdered in the massacre in 1948. Nadia lost her entire family there except for her son Hamdi. She heard you today in Gaza and would like to join the fedayeen."

"The General Union will be honored to have another member of your family, Munif," said Hassan, scrutinizing Nadia. He bowed low to her and then he raised his head and shoulders slowly, looking her over from foot to head. Nadia was embarrassed by his attention in front of all these strange men, but she was once again hypnotized by the intensity of his face, his eyes. He was of medium height and slender, sinewy. His piercing black eyes seemed to plumb the very core of her, and his eyes lit up his dark face and high cheekbones and thick black wavy hair. He was not a handsome man, a pretty man, but his magnetism instantly drew her to him.

"The General Union practices *futuwwah*, and it may not be something you will find to your liking," Hassan said softly to Nadia.

"Regaining our homeland is my life. Any way it must be done is to my liking," Nadia looked straight into his eyes, exuding her own power, refusing to let herself be overwhelmed by his intensity or wilted by his heat.

"Then we have found another of the true fedayeen. Munif, please come with me to the fountain. I want to introduce you and make sure that everyone knows that you are the General Union's Lieutenant in the Gaza Strip." Even as he spoke to Munif, Hassan did not take his eyes from Nadia.

The two men walked up onto the stone-and-mosaic tiled fountain. The fedayeen sat cross-legged on the grass and listened as Hassan began to speak.

"My brothers and sisters, we must all be ready to fight and die as true believers for *'awda*, for this is the way of the fedayeen. Standing with me in Munif el-Rashid. He is my next in command in the Gaza Strip. He will be your commander. He has spent two years as an officer in the Egyptian Army and he is highly qualified.

"Our overall commander is Yassir Arafat. He is establishing groups of fedayeen in Cairo who will soon join us in Gaza to fight the Jews.

"Our only absolute rule is to obey the commanders. Otherwise, we will dissolve into a rabble army unfit to fulfill our sacred honor. When your commander, Munif, gives you orders, they have come from me and from Yassir Arafat. Our plans to harass the Israeli kibbutzim along the Gaza Strip are not just the idle daydreams of children. We intend to create among the Israelis such a sense of fear and uncertainty that they will be forced to imprison themselves together into large fortress-like towns and desert their scattered kibbutzim. This will be the beginning of our victory in our war."

Hassan introduced four more General Union commanders to the crowd. These would be unit leaders serving under Munif and responsible for the four designated sectors of the Gaza Strip.

Then came the high point of the meeting for all of the eager fedayeen. They were going to receive their weapons. They were Russian machine guns and had been supplied by Egypt.

"The fedayeen in the courtyard of the Mosque al-Malik hoisted high their machine guns and their bundles of clips, pridefully showing their jobless, penniless brothers and sisters that their lives now had new purpose, genuine meaning. They would fight as martyrs for 'awda. And these were the weapons they would use, the way of the fedayeen.

Munif and his four section commanders went through the crowd kissing cheeks, hugging the fedayeen, meeting those few they did not already know. Each of the four commanders called out for a separate group of men and women from his particular sector to gather round him for further instructions. As the several hundred fedayeen separated into the four corners of the courtyard, Munif and Hassan and Nadia stood together on the tiled fountain.

"What are your plans for the night, Hassan?" asked Munif.

"I have no firm commitments for the next two days," Hassan said. "Then I have to do some more recruiting in the villages of Jabaliya, Nazla and Beit Lahiya."

"My family would be honored to show you the hospitality of our house, Hassan. Please stay with us for the next few days," said Munif.

Traditions were rapidly changing among the refugee Palestinians. While women were still protected by their families, and social contact was limited with single men, nonetheless a widow might well be permitted—and permit herself—to meet discreetly and innocently with an important Palestinian leader like Hassan abu-Sittah. Nadia looked at Hassan and she felt sure that he was very attracted to her, that it wasn't just because she was Munif's sister-in-law that he was so attentive.

"I should be most displeased if I caused anyone discomfort by my intrusion on your household," said Hassan.

"Be assured that it is no intrusion in the slightest, Hassan. It is an honor. It is settled. I have to return the fedayeen to the town square in the truck. Why don't you and Nadia drive directly to our home?"

Nadia was looking away, visibly busying herself watching the groups of fedayeen, hiding her burning cheeks from Hassan's searching eyes. A soft smile of excitement, anticipation, flickered on her face.

Hassan drove his jeep rapidly, jerkily, over the potholed road to Gaza. It was a warm, vividly starry night, a typical Mediterranean night sky of twinkling diamonds against a black velvet matte. Nadia felt as though she could reach right up and pluck the stars and make a necklace to adorn her throat and a sparkling garland for Hassan's glistening black hair. There was almost no traffic on the road and they drove several miles in silence.

"You survived Deir Yassin, Nadia? You are but one of the few."

"I was saved by a Jewish woman. She actually killed the Jewish soldier who had murdered my family, and she pulled me out of the village. But for her, I would also have been killed."

"There are good Israelis and bad, Nadia. But this is *jihad*. To the fedayeen, all Jewish Israelis are the enemy. They are the occupiers of our homes, our land. We will never let up while one of them usurps our *'awda*."

"Hassan, I don't need any convincing about our struggle for our homeland."

They rode further in silence. It was not of war and martyrdom that Nadia wished to speak. She wanted to know more about Hassan himself. But she had not been with a man in many years and she felt awkward and embarrassed.

"Where are you from, Hassan?"

"I was born in East Jerusalem during Muharram in 1921."

They sat in silence for a moment, staring at the road.

"That's your life story?" she asked.

He looked over at her and then he laughed. Nadia felt the awkwardness between them begin to disappear.

"No. My father was a doctor who was killed by a stray bullet in 1948. I was studying in the United States. My mother came to live with me in Cairo when I graduated from Princeton in 1950. I have a degree in History.

"My other four brothers were killed with the Arab irregulars during the battles for the Latrun Pass. I have three younger sisters, also in Cairo. I spent two years as a Lieutenant in the Egyptian Army, and I met Yassir Arafat at a student rally while I was doing work at Al-Azhar University in Cairo in 1953. Now I'm convinced that the only future for us Palestinians is *futuwwah* [guerrilla warfare]. It has become my life."

"Does it fill your life, Hassan?" She looked at him and he turned his head slowly to meet her gaze.

"Until today, I never really thought about it. I have been totally absorbed. At the moment," he turned back to watch the road, "I think it is clear that there is another dimension to my life which is stirring me, which has just been awakened."

They rode again in silence.

"You'll like my son Hamdi. He is full of life and energy, and I'm sure he'll be delighted to make a new friend."

"I look forward very much to meeting Hamdi."

She smiled at him, no longer the cowed soldier with the charismatic commander. Just a woman who was beginning to feel a primordial stirring in her flesh.

When they reached the el-Rashid house, it was well past midnight. Samir and Widad were sitting in the interior courtyard and Samir was drinking arak, the harsh, potent liquor made from dates.

Nadia introduced Hassan to her sister and brother-in-law, and they sat on wicker chairs across from Widad and Samir. Hassan took a small glassful of the arak, but Nadia—like Widad—was offered none. They drank tea. They chatted pleasantly for a few moments and then Munif returned. After a bit more of the typically flowery graciousness of the hosts to their guest, they all went to sleep. There was no guest room, and Hassan simply slept next to Munif in Munif's large bed, a common manner of treating guests.

In the morning, Nadia and Widad and Hamdi were up early squeezing ripe figs and placing them on palm frond trays to dry in the sun. When the men were finished with their prayers, they ate breakfast at the long dining room table. It consisted of hard boiled eggs and pita and cheese called lebeneh. The lebeneh was sort of a tart yogurt which was served covered with olive oil in a small cup. The eater picked out a small scoop of it, rolled it into a ball and let the oil drip off, and then ate it with the pita and eggs as a sandwich. The women and girls ate standing up in the kitchen, making absolutely no noise and only coming into the dining room to serve the men. Hamdi and his two boy cousins sat with the men. After breakfast, Samir and his brother Khalid left for work. Widad left a little later to go shopping and Nadia remained behind to supervise the household staff and care for Hamdi.

Hassan and Munif went into the courtyard with some maps and blank paper and spent a couple of hours planning the fedayeen's first raid. Next week, early in the morning, they would attack Kibbutz Gan Artzi, about fifteen miles into Israel from Gaza.

At about eleven, Munif left for the construction company. Hamdi was playing with his dog in the courtyard. Nadia was curing olives, sitting on a stone bench next to the splashing courtyard fountain.

"Hamdi's a fine little boy, Nadia," said Hassan.

"Yes, he has adjusted well to this refugee life we lead. Someday, he will lead our *hamula*."

"Maybe if you are finished here, we could take a walk through the olive groves."

"Let me finish this one jar. I'll meet you on the hill in a few minutes."

When Nadia came to the hill behind the villa, she was wearing a thin red cotton flowing caftan, clinging to her bodice and falling to the tops of her sandalled feet. The caftan was almost transparent in the bright sunlight and she saw that Hassan was staring at the curve of her inner thighs as she walked toward him. They walked into the thick olive grove blanketing the small rocky hill. Nadia carried a wicker basket with her, and after about ten minutes, she spread a towel on the ground in the shade of an ancient, expansive olive tree. She brought out a jar of olives, a string of dried figs, and a bottle of lemonade. The towel was only three feet long, so they sat close together, their backs against the tree, their arms and legs touching.

Hassan was obviously not experienced with women. Nadia could feel it by the way his body tensed next to hers. She knew that he had probably had intercourse with women, but only prostitutes. In Palestine, premarital sex with any non-prostitute was liable to get a man killed by the girl's father or brothers. And Cairo was no different, she knew that. She was equally sure that whatever experiences he had known had possessed only a physical aspect and none of the emotion that she knew that love should hold. Nadia was by contrast very experienced. She had been married at the typical age of sixteen and had nine years with her husband before he was murdered. He had been a sensual lover, a slow and caring lover. And she had missed him and his body these last lonely six years. Now she had found another real man and she felt a deep hunger for his body.

Nadia tilted her head toward Hassan and kissed his cheek. He turned and she kissed him softly, running her tongue inside his lips. She saw the bulge in Hassan's pants and was amused—flattered—by his excitement and she wanted to touch him, feel him inside. But not here, not this way.

They ate a few olives and figs and drank some lemonade. Nadia started to pack the picnic things in the basket.

"*Chelleek kemaan shway* [stay a little longer]," Hassan implored her.

"*Deroori 'aroo hal'eet* [I have to go now]," she replied reluctantly, also wishing that they could be together as man and woman. They strolled back to the house. For over two hours together, they had not spoken a word.

A little while later, the rest of the family came home for the afternoon break. They all sat in the large parlor and chatted as the children played on the floor. At five, the men again returned to work and Nadia and Widad busied themselves preparing dinner. At eight o'clock, while the women ate soundlessly in the kitchen, the men and boys ate a huge meal of lamb roast and fresh fish and fried eggplant and the ever-present lebeneh. At nine, the children went to bed, and the adults sat in the warm Mediterranean breeze in the courtyard. Samir and Widad chatted for a few minutes with Nadia and Hassan. Then Samir stood and yawned and stretched, indicating that the evening was over.

Hassan stayed at the el-Rasid home all week. He and Nadia would steal off for a picnic each day and they would go to sleep when Samir signaled the evening's end. By the end of the week, neither Nadia nor Hassan could see enough of each other.

Chapter Four

On Wednesday morning at three, Hassan, Nadia and Munif drove their jeep to the Gaza border. The twenty-five hand-picked fedayeen had camped there overnight. They had six additional jeeps and a Russian halftrack armored car mounted with an 85 mm. cannon. They drove in a column toward the kibbutz. They had practiced the assault maneuver for seven hours yesterday, so everyone knew his job. Their allies would be complete surprise and the kibbutz's lack of any defense organization.

Many of the Israeli border kibbutzim were run by Nahal, a paramilitary organization of soldier/farmers who fulfilled their two years of mandatory military service by working in military-like units to protect the border settlers from fedayeen raids. These Nahal kibbutzim were numerous and well defended. But Gan Artzi, this morning's target, was not a Nahal settlement. It was a very old farming village which Palestinian intelligence reported to be essentially unarmed.

At three forty-five, the halftrack took a stationary position on a ridge overlooking the kibbutz about one hundred yards away. It was a dark, cloudy night. The outlines of the six wooden barracks buildings of the kibbutz could be seen well enough for the gunner to adjust his range. The rest of the jeep-borne fedayeen rode to the edge of the kibbutz. They left their jeeps and formed a firing line fifty feet wide, which would spray the path down the center of the kibbutz as the frightened kibbutzniks were forced out of the barracks by the shelling. Or so the plan went.

Nadia and Hassan and Munif sat in the command jeep next to the armored car. Nadia was anxious to start the slaughter, to repay the debt. Munif was on the walkie-talkie with his assault leader. At four o'clock, he received word that the fedayeen were in position. Then he signaled to the gunner to open fire.

In quick succession, ten 85 mm. rounds screeched into the sun-bleached and dehydrated wooden buildings of the kibbutz, creating ear-piercing explosions in the black and silent desert night. Flames leapt up from every building, and the kibbutz was immediately lit up like day.

Out of a building at the far end of the path people began running, several of them on fire and screaming. The machine guns of the fedayeen cut them down. There was no other movement in the town. The fedayeen waited.

Nadia felt a deep thrill, a pervasive pleasure at being able to begin her return to 'awda. She had dressed to kill for this very special occasion. Widad had tailored a fatigue outfit tight to her shapely breasts and hips, and Nadia could see the heat in Hassan's eyes each time he stole a glance at her.

It took over an hour for the tinder dry barracks of the kibbutz to be devoured by the orange flames. At almost five in the morning, the sun began to rise over the charred ruins of Gan Artzi and the seven bodies lying in the street. The fedayeen held their positions. Nadia and Munif and Hassan were determined to know why there were not three hundred settlers here as their intelligence had reported. Nadia had been blooded, but she was expecting much more.

The ringing blast of a howitzer shell obliterated the armored car next to their jeep. They jumped off the jeep and hit the ground, peeking over the ridge toward the small hillock on the other side of the kibbutz. Through binoculars, Nadia could see the barrel of the howitzer protruding from a cement bunker, almost hidden by pampas grass and thorny acacias. In the side of the hillock, just now beginning to glint in the rising sun, were steel doors. She disgustedly gave the glasses to Munif who looked, nodded grimly to Hassan, and then passed the glasses back to Nadia. The kibbutzniks had built fortified concrete bunkers in the small hill and were living in them. They had abandoned the tinderbox kibbutz buildings, probably because the Israeli military forces had instructed the kibbutzniks on the border in the tactics of resisting fedayeen raids, which their intelligence must have reported were about to begin in earnest.

A few of the old-time settlers, the stubborn ones, had died in the raid. The rest of the kibbutz was safe. Several .50 caliber machine guns began raking the fedayeen from slits in the artillery bunker on the hillock. Munif radioed his assult leader to withdraw his men to Gaza Square. They simply did not have the firepower to engage the enemy in its concrete fortress.

None of the fedayeen was killed or injured except for the halftrack driver and gunner. Munif and Hassan talked glumly as they sped back to Gaza. It had been a small success, not a complete disappointment. But they had encountered an Israeli defensive technique which was a complete surprise to them: a whole village living in semi-subterranean reinforced concrete bunkers. Against such a defense, the fedayeen simply lacked sufficient offense. They would obviously have to change their tactics. They would have to attack the Nahal kibbutzim, which had troops stationed in them, because at least there the Israelis had apparently not seen the need to move the kibbutzniks out of their houses and into bunkers. The resistance would obviously be much greater. But this was for 'awda, for homeland, and this would be the way of the fedayeen. At the moment, it was their only way.

The automatic response to any fedayeen raids from the Gaza Strip or Jordan or Syria or Lebanon was an immediate reprisal raid by an elite Israeli paratroop contingent called Unit 202, com-manded by Major Aryeh Verred, who was widely reputed to have but the slenderest reed of affection for the Palestinians.

The Arab refugees were accustomed to these reprisals and there was simply no way they could guard their camps against them. It was the price they paid for the way of the fedayeen. Living in the squalid camps was no greater pleasure than dying in the struggle for 'awda.

Chapter Five

After the raid, Hassan was gone for about two weeks. Nadia was like a schoolgirl, chattering to Widad constantly about him— Hassan this and Hassan that. Nadia could hardly wait for Hassan to return, to see him again, to touch him. Widad was delighted. A widow with a son was of almost no stature in Arab society, and it was time that Nadia should get married again.

When Hassan finally returned, he said he could stay a week. Nadia resumed her pose as "mysterious Levantine beauty" and tried to hide the giddy thrill she felt at seeing him again. The third evening after supper, when they sat in the courtyard, Samir was different. He and Widad yawned and said they were sorry that they were tired so early, but they were going to bed. Why didn't Nadia and Hassan just stay up and go to bed when they felt like it? Then Samir and Widad went inside.

After a half hour, Nadia went inside and packed a small basket, took Hassan's hand, and they walked once again into the olive grove. She spread a large blanket on the ground and they knelt on it facing each other.

"My family likes you and holds you in high esteem. They approve of you," Nadia said.

"I am humbled by the honor they do me."

Nadia was through with the traditional Arab voluptuous and flowery polite formality. She wanted him. "Are you serious with me?"

"I am serious."

Nadia unbuttoned her blouse and took it off. She pulled her skirt off over her head. She had on nothing underneath. She unbuckled his military web belt, and he lay back and she pulled his pants off by the cuffs. He took off his underwear. She lay beside him. Under the olive branches it was almost pitch black.

They turned toward each other and kissed long and hard. She held him in her hand, stroking him softly. "Ooh, you are so big," she cooed, knowing the need that a man had to be told this, especially at that oh-so-delicate moment when first he revealed his precious secret.

Hassan rolled onto her and entered her, and she gasped and thrust up her loins to envelope him deep inside her.

They lay perspiring in the soft breeze and rested. Then again she held him and stroked him, and they joined in love.

Long before the family awakened, they walked back to the house, she to her room and he to the bed he shared with Munif. Soundlessly.

Hassan stayed at the el-Rashid home all week. The marriage contract between Nadia and Hassan was signed on Saturday. Traditionally, her father or brothers should have signed for her. But since they all had been murdered by the Jews, Samir signed. It made her feel worthless, rootless, to be an "orphan." Even the word itself hurt. And she was stingingly aware that in the old days in Palestine, the ceremony consisted of a magnificent banquet at her parents' home, at which all of the guests and gifts came, followed by an even grander banquet at her new husband's home where all the guests and gifts and dowry were displayed. But Nadia had no family of her own left, and Hassan's home in Cairo consisted of himself and his widowed mother.

Where treasured tradition would have called for Hassan to bring Nadia to live in newly-erected quarters built onto his family home, tradition had been deprived of meaning, because they were refugees. The best that Nadia could have were three new rooms built onto the Gaza el-Rashid home, a bedroom for Hassan's mother, a bedroom for the married couple, and an expansive parlor for their entertaining. And even more embarrassing to her, the only dowry that she could offer was all of the occupied lands of Deir Yassin, the miles of watermelon fields and olive groves, once owned by her family.

Hassan's mother, Sara, arrived from Cairo three days before the wedding banquet. Her new bedroom was already built. She was a scrawny, withered woman in her seventies and wore a traditional long black dress, her hair covered in a black kerchief. She looked askance at Nadia, studying her with hooded eyes, and Nadia believed in her heart that the old woman was thinking, "This *orphan* will marry my Hassan!"

Hassan had gone to Cairo the week before to discuss General
Union of Palestinian Students matters with Yassir Arafat. The
defensive bunkers of the Israelis were a major stumbling block to
the General Union's plans, and the need to attack Nahal kibbutzim
raised the quality and quantity of weapons needed by the fedayeen.

The marriage banquet began Saturday afternoon at four o'clock
under a pellucid sky. It was the third week of September, and the
breezes off the Mediterranean licked deliciously at the open
windows of the el-Rashid villa. It had been newly painted on the
inside in honor of the occasion, and the three new rooms for the
abu-Sittahs were on display. In the courtyard, gifts began piling up
on the tables set up for them. None of them was wrapped, but
brought openly to display the magnitude of the esteem in which the
guest held the bride and groom. There were spits set up all over the
courtyard, and lambs were being turned by little girls. In the
spacious kitchen inside, the fresh fried fish was being prepared in
the ovens. On small mosaic-inlaid coffee tables outside were bowls
of humous and stacks of pita, and at another table, a man carved a
side of lamb and made small *kebaabs* [shish kabobs].

The greatest gift of all was the howitzer and the mortars which
had arrived the day before. Arafat had come along in one of the
trucks, so that he could honor the wealthy el-Rashids and their
brilliant new family member, Hassan abu-Sittah. Arafat was
related to the el-Husseini family of the former Grand Mufti of
Jerusalem, one of the most prominent families of Arab Palestine.
He had been private secretary to Abdul Khader el-Husseini, the
legendary military hero who had been killed at Kastel just before
the Deir Yassin massacre. Arafat had then left Palestine and studied
engineering at Cairo's Fuad I University. He met Hassan in Cairo
in 1953. Arafat's relationship to the el-Husseinis gave him entree
into virtually all of the drawing rooms of real power in the Arab
world. His presence at the wedding banquet was a great honor, and
he had brought the personal best wishes of Premier Nasser and
General Sadat to Hassan and his stunning bride.

The el-Rashid house and courtyard and the olive grove beyond
filled with the notables of the Gaza Strip, the mukhtars of all the
cities and towns, the qadis and holy men, the wealthy businessmen
of the Strip, and many of the fedayeen officers and leaders. It was a
fete straight from the Arabian nights, with arak flowing like water

and strolling musicians and singers and food fit for a caliph. The Muslim law forbidding strong drink was boisterously joked about and stringently ignored. The revelry lasted well into the night, as tradition demanded, and the last well-wisher did not leave or stumble or get carried home until three in the morning.

Tradition also dictated the entrance of Nadia abu-Sittah, attended by the women of her family, into the heart of the festivities at nine o'clock when everyone was happy and high and well fed—but not yet drunk. She was dressed in a full length wedding gown of sheer mauve silk, tight and form-fitting and slightly flared below the knees. She wore the gown over a pink body shirt of thin cotton. The effect was one of subtle nudity, displaying her fulsome figure and sending gazes of envy through the crowd of men and women alike. Nadia's shiny black hair fell about her shoulders. On her feet were seed pearl encrusted slippers and around her neck was a quadruple rope of opera pearls, all gifts from Samir who had them specially flown in from Paris. On both arms were golden bangle bracelets, without which she would not be the well-dressed Arab bride. They glinted against the mauve lace ruffles on the ends of the long sleeves. The bracelets were the gift of Hassan's mother, Sara.

Nadia paraded behind the gift tables in front of the guests, accompanied by her proud and beaming sister, Widad, and her mother-in-law, Sara. In the courtyard crowded with the elite of the Gaza Strip, the fashionably dressed and decorated wives and daughters of the rich and powerful, Nadia looked like a gracious blooming calla lily in a meadow of wildflowers.

After about fifteen minutes of strutting, she retired to her bedroom with her retinue to await her husband. He came in two hours later and the attendants bowed backwards out of the room, showing traditional kingly honor to the newlyweds. The banqueters sang and drank and ate in the courtyard and the olive grove and the parlors of the sprawling house.

Hassan undressed a little hesitantly, embarrassedly. Nadia lay on her side and watched him in the candlelight. He walked toward her and stood next to the bed. She did not roll over to give him room to lie down next to her.

She picked up a vial of almond oil which she had earlier placed next to the bed. She poured some in her palm and rubbed her hands together. She reached out and caressed him with long delicate fingers, and he pulsed in her hand. She stroked him eagerly. Then she lay on her back and closed her eyes and opened her legs wide and rubbed her oiled fingers over the insides of her thighs and her silken ebony swan's down. And he came to her.

Chapter Six

From Hassan's years as an officer in the Egyptian Army, he knew that you do not just walk up to a 155 mm. howitzer and pull the trigger. It weighs several tons and must be trucked to where it will be used. It takes two men to lift and load each shell. When the shell is placed in the receiver, the breech door must be slammed home with the inevitable clanging of a dungeon door slamming shut. It must be sighted by coordinates which require at least an elementary grasp of trigonometry. Any resighting of the piece requires a spotter, located nearer the target, to call in to the sighter and give him the corrections, also in terms of trigonometric coordinates. The sighter just cannot wet his forefinger, test the air, and wing it. It is not easy to shoot a 155 mm. howitzer, and there was not one soldier among the fedayeen who had any training in artillery.

Heavy mortars, Hassan knew, were a different matter. The sighting is done in terms of meters of distance rather than trajectory, and therefore minimally-trained soldiers can zero in a mortar by "Kentucky windage" (wet finger and squinting) within three shots.

Because of the need for training, Arafat had brought orders from General Sadat for the artillery commander at the Egyptian Army post in Gaza City to provide howitzer training to six select fedayeen. All artillery training took place deeper in the Sinai near the Mediterranean coastal city of El Arish, where Egypt's principal Sinai fortress was located.

In mid-October, Hassan and five fedayeen reported to the medieval stone fortress near El Arish to begin artillery training. They started small and worked up, piece by piece. Much of the time was spent in the classroom, learning the functional trigonometry and spotting techniques necessary for sighting the big gun.

Since El Arish was only a bit less than fifty miles from Gaza City, Hassan spent the weekends, Thursday afternoon to Saturday afternoon, at home with Nadia. There he could also continue the minute planning of the Nahal Oz attack with Munif. As the training was completed, they selected a date for the attack: February 15, 1955.

In the two weeks between their return from El Arish and the attack date, Hassan and his five trained artillerymen trained eight teams of mortarmen. Two mortar teams would be used against each of the guard towers just to make sure one of the mortars hit the target. They would attack the settlement at five-thirty in the evening, when almost everyone would be in the eating hall. It had to be timed exactly, so that they could attack just before dark and escape in the ensuing darkness. They had no training in night firing and Hassan remembered the instructor's warning. Stay away from night shelling, he had said. The lights from buildings loom out of the dark and create optical illusions which prevent proper distance spotting without special night training.

This was a tricky attack plan, because the timing was dangerously critical, but that did not deter Hassan or any of his men. The fedayeen were restless, miserable in their fetid huts in the sprawling treacherous refugee camps, and they needed to fight for their own sense of meaning, for their souls, for 'awda.

Munif was in command of the infantry force of one hundred fifty men with machine guns. Their mission was to make a perimeter around the south and west of Nahal Oz to prevent any pursuit of the fedayeen by the Israeli military unit. They would hold the perimeter for half an hour after the howitzer and mortar shelling to give the artillery plenty of time to return to the Gaza Strip. Then they would return in their five stake trucks and four jeeps. The stake trucks were provided by the el-Rashid Construction Company. The logos on the doors were covered with masking tape to avoid identification.

Nadia was now a married woman and could not accompany men on such a mission. It was unseemly, a violation of Muslim law concerning the mixing of sexes. So she stayed behind reluctantly, begging Allah for her new husband's safe return.

The attack force of fedayeen assembled outside Gaza City on the dirt road six miles from Nahal Oz at four-thirty in the afternoon of February 15. It was a lovely sunny day, about seventy-five degrees, and quite still. The convoy sorted itself along the road and took off slowly toward the kibbutz. The howitzer halftrack did only ten miles an hour.

Suddenly there was the loud clanging of metal on metal, then a shearing sound, and the halftrack screeched to a halt. One of the track plates had become dislodged by a rock on the road. They had no spare track parts, so one of the Palestinians who was an auto mechanic banged and wrenched and sweated over the track for forty-five minutes. Finally it was jerryrigged. But they did not arrive at the orange grove two hundred yards south of Nahal Oz until about ten minutes to six. It was almost dark.

The mortar teams took their supplies out of the truck and made wide sweeps to get to their positions near the four guard towers. The infantrymen left their trucks and jeeps and formed a southern and western enclosure perimeter around the kibbutz. The howitzer spotter climbed a tree with his binoculars and walkie talkie. It was now quite dark.

Hassan stayed in his jeep at the edge of the orange grove, in contact by walkie talkie with the howitzer and the eight mortar teams and Munif, who was leading the men on the ground. On Hassan's signal, the mortar and artillery shelling would begin simultaneously. Hassan was very excited, without fear, in love with the danger and the anticipation. It was like making love with Nadia. When he was in her, moving and rubbing himself in her orifice of love, he was in another world, another place, another time, transported by the sheer physical and emotional pleasure of loving. And then, after he came and jerked and groaned and held her so tightly she could hardly breathe, he was empty and spent and back on earth. A battle was like making love.

He knew that they should cancel this mission because of the darkness. But his hunger for the killing was too ravenous, his lust for revenge too rapacious, unbearable, to put it off even one more day. He decided that he could figure out the night problems. He would not delay this moment of triumph.

At six-thirty, Hassan gave the signal to open fire. The howitzer breech rang shut and a deafening blast sent the first shell sailing toward the eating hall. The sound of mortars popping like bursting paper bags filled the air. Through his binoculars, Hassan could see three of the guard towers already aflame. He also saw the howitzer shell hit at least thirty yards in front of the eating hall, in the kibbutz square. The second shell hit about ten yards closer. The third shell hit about fifteen yards behind the hall. Hassan could hear the confused panicky directions of the sighter. But Hassan himself had no idea what to do. A fourth shell screeched toward the eating hall and hit to the right of it about twenty yards. Israeli bazooka and machine gun fire began raining in on the orange grove. One of the stake trucks was ablaze from a shot through its gas tank and a bazooka shell shattered the engine of another of the trucks. The battle was already twelve minutes old, and the eating hall was surely empty by now. All four guard towers had been destroyed, but the fedayeen were not in position and had no contingency plan to attack the kibbutz on the ground. Hassan called through his walkie talkie for a general withdrawal.

The withdrawal plan worked exactly as figured. The artillery halftrack and mortar truck reached the hiding garage in darkness in Gaza City within forty-five minutes. The infantry men then abandoned the perimeter and piled into the remaining three stake trucks and four jeeps, sped back to the Gaza City Square, and blended into the darkness.

The next morning, Hassan went to the news vendor in Gaza Square for a *Jerusalem Post*, the only English language newspaper from Israel. The *Post* reported that Nahal Oz had suffered nine deaths in its military unit, that its guard towers had been destroyed, and that fourteen other men, women and children had been killed by artillery shelling. An additional fifty-six soldiers and kibbutzniks were wounded.

Well, thought Hassan, again not a great triumph, but certainly no great loss. Two stake trucks were a small price to pay for so many Jews dead and wounded. And each time they fought, Hassan was learning valuable lessons. Soon they would be a real commando team, well equipped, well trained, and well blooded. He felt good.

Chapter Seven

In the frigid pre-dawn of February 25, Unit 202 massed in battalion strength on the Israeli border across from Gaza City. The stake trucks which the Palestinians had left behind at Nahal Oz had revealed the logo of the el-Rashid Construction Company. Intelligence reported that both Samir and his brother Khalid worked fulltime at the company. However, the other brother, Munif, was often absent for days or weeks at a time. Some reports had it that he was Yassir Arafat's lieutenant in the Gaza Strip. In any event, he had surely provided supplies for the fedayeen raid on Nahal Oz.

Major Aryeh ("Arik") Verred detailed a company of men to destroy the el-Rashid Construction Company and to hunt out and destroy Munif at his home. The other six companies of paratroopers would assault the Egyptian Army fort in Gaza City. This would not be merely a typical reprisal raid. This would be potent proof that Israel had turned a new and savage leaf in dealing with terrorism.

A platoon surrounded the el-Rashid home at dawn. Hassan was in Cairo consulting with Yassir Arafat, and Nadia was with him. Samir, Munif, Khalid, six-year-old Hamdi, and Samir's sons were at morning prayers in the courtyard, kneeling on their individual prayer blankets, their open palms held up beside their faces, their eyes closed, when three paratroopers silently slipped over the courtyard wall. From intelligence photographs, one of the paratroopers recognized Munif and sprayed him with a long blast from his Uzi. The bullets shattered his open palms and obliterated his face. The other praying men and boys were paralyzed with shock and fear as they watched the Israelis leap back over the wall and heard several jeeps speed away from the house. The horrible quivering crimson flesh of Munif's decimated face was indelibly etched on Hamdi's soul. The garish, blood-soaked image of his uncle would not leave his mind's eye. The top of Munif's skull had been blown off, and the inside looked to Hamdi like a broken open pomegranate. But Hamdi did not cry, he did not run and hide from the hideous sight. He knelt beside Munif and held his dead hand. Nadia had taught Hamdi not to cry, that only girls cry, that a boy no matter how small is a man, and a man must not cry, he must not be weak. And Hamdi was not weak. He had learned his lessons well. He was filled with hatred of the Jews, the slaughterers of his family.

At the Egyptian fort, the headquarters building and several barracks were blown up as well as a number of trucks and armored personnel carriers. At least forty of the troops were killed and an equal number wounded. Unit 202 then headed leisurely out of the Gaza Strip, watched furtively from shuttered windows by the tight-jawed townspeople, showing them that the Israelis could strike with impunity anywhere and anytime in the Gaza Strip.

Chapter Eight

As the memory of her mourning ululation for her revered brother-in-law Munif receded into the past, Nadia began to realize that Munif's death and the virtual failure of the fedayeen attacks in Israel were the fault of the General Union of Palestinian Students, of Hassan. Little mistakes which became major blunders: not sanding the el-Rashid logos off the stake trucks, but merely covering them with tape because they were so rapturously confident of victory; not realizing that night artillery attacks required special training; not having any kind of reliable intelligence system in Israel. The way of the fedayeen had become the way of fools, reduced to slaughtering small Orthodox boys at prayer, throwing grenades at tourist buses, attacking families strolling on the beach. Each time, Hassan would say that he had learned another lesson from the latest attack, and "soon they would turn the corner, soon there would be a real war of liberation." But the corner was not in sight, and lessons like the death of Munif weren't worth learning.

The evening after a massive Israeli retaliation raid against a Jordanian police fortress, Qalqilia, the abu-Sittahs and the el-Rashids sat in the courtyard of their home in Gaza City and listened to reports of the raid from Jordanian State Radio on the wireless. Amman reported King Hussein's implementation of the Anglo-Jordanian peace treaty of 1948 to bring in English troops, and Jordanian officials predicted war with Israel based on all the available evidence. The Israeli raid itself had killed and maimed and wounded more Arabs in one massive blow than all the fedayeen raids for months had scored against the Jews.

Nadia was grim and frustrated as she listened to the news. None of the el-Rashids had talked to Hassan about the muffed raid which had resulted in Munif's death eight months ago, but Samir's younger son still had recurrent nightmares and an aura of sadness pervaded the household. Not merely because of the death. Death was not a stranger to these Arab refugees. But because of the needlessness of his death, caused by the General Union's carelessness.

"The British will not aid Jordan. No one will," Nadia said slowly. "Hussein is isolated, orphaned by everyone in the Arab world except Nasser. And Nasser signs pacts with anyone who speaks Arabic. The Saudis have the greatest influence over England's oil from Qatar and Kuwait. And Jordan has no oil at all. So the British will not help Jordan any more than they helped us in 1948 and 1949."

It was Nadia making this political analysis and everyone—including her husband—watched her and listened with respect. She had been reading avidly for several years, everything she could find on Middle Eastern international relations, history and politics. Particularly since the death of Munif, she had spent days on end immured in her room, reading and making notes and reading some more. Nadia was in a pensive mood and her pent up frustration was beginning to bubble out.

"Each time the fedayeen attacks Israel, it finds a new surprise that it had no idea about. Either the Israelis are inside cement bunkers, or they're gone on holiday, or our guns won't hit them, or our trucks break down, or the Israeli Army is waiting for us even before we arrive. And then in retaliation for whatever foolish little damage we do, they mount a tenfold effective reprisal which invades precisely the camp from which the fedayeen raid originated and seeks out and destroys the very leaders involved in the particular raid. Just as with Munif." Nadia looked around slowly at her family. Hassan's head was bowed. His black hair fell over his forehead and partially hid his eyes from his wife's lacerating glance. An Arab woman did not talk so boldly about her husband's mistakes in front of others, not unless she wished to be beaten to death by her husband later in their bedroom. But Nadia was right, and even Hassan knew it, and these things finally had to be said. Samir, as head of the household, did not stop her. In fact, he had the same need Nadia had to unburden the bitterness that had arisen from Hassan's poor planning that had killed Munif. Nadia continued, emboldened by Samir's grim condoning frown.

"The fact is that our 'army' is a rabble and our 'intelligence service' is a joke. Our intelligence consists of reading the Cairo newspapers and the *Jerusalem Post* and listening to Israeli radio broadcasts which we can hardly understand because none of us speaks Hebrew well enough! We have no intelligence coming from within Israel itself. And do you know why? Because the Arabs of Israel—just like us who used to live there for generations on end—refused to learn the Hebrew language. It was the enemy's tongue, the defiler's tongue, so we avoided learning it as a sign of our hatred of the Zionists. Even today, the Arabs of Israel refuse to attend regular public schools but insist on providing their own Arabic speaking schools for their children from kindergarten through high school. And the result? Virtually no Arab in Israel speaks Hebrew well enough to get into college in Israel, let alone to infiltrate any of their government services, or the Army, or to steal their documents, or to intercept their wireless transmissions.

"But how about Israeli intelligence? Almost half of the Jews in Israel emigrated there from Arab countries where Arabic was their native tongue. Many of the native Israelis grew up side-by-side with Arabs and learned to speak fluent Arabic as a matter of course, while Arab mothers were beating their children for repeating even one word of Hebrew. So the Israelis can infiltrate every Arab country and every fedayeen camp—and they can even read the logos on our construction trucks."

Hassan looked up sharply at his wife as she made this sarcastic, piercing remark. Her eyes met his, and her eyes were dancing flames. She was afire with anger and frustration and hurt. He slowly lowered his head again, gritting his teeth so that his jaw muscles stood out like peach pits.

"Even their Chief of Staff speaks fluent Arabic! His mother didn't spank him for playing with the Arab boys when they grew up at the Sea of Galilee. So our intelligence consists of newspaper clippings while theirs has penetrated to our very core. The way of the fedayeen has become a farce!"

This time, even Samir was stunned by Nadia's vitriolic comment. He caught her eye and shook his head, warning her to watch her tongue lest her husband cut it out. She sat for a few moments to let her temper subside and her heat dissipate. The family was hushed. Nadia realized that she had waxed too hot, gone too far. Her husband was looking at her with eyes so wide that the black pupils were mere pinpoints on a sea of white. His tongue flicked dryly at the corners of his mouth.

She continued very subdued, very softly. "Our aspirations are genuine and just. *Al-tariq al-fida'i*, the way of the fedayeen, is the sacred Muslim way of combating infidels and it is the way of honorable men. And our fight for *'awda*, homeland, is the only honorable thing for us to do, for this is *jihad*. But we can no longer use simple terrorism and Second World War weapons and small unit tactics to defeat the Jews. They have a modern, highly equipped and trained military with mobility and weaponry that we can only dream of. We too need such an army. The General Union must change with the changing world. No more terrorist bands, no more groups of untrained, unskilled farm laborers with guns. The General Union must turn the fedayeen into a real army. You Hassan, you must go to Yassir Arafat and tell him these things. Only you are close enough to him and powerful enough to create the new organization that we need so that we can return to our *'awda*."

Nadia had tried to save his face. Hassan looked at his beautiful wife, but his eyes showed that his resentment was not entirely gone. She had spoken hard words. The General Union would have to change. But it was not fitting for an Arab wife to say these things in front of other people. Yet it had been done with Samir's approval as head of the *hamula*. Therefore, Hassan could do nothing about it, he could not even beat her. His twitching eyelids and cheeks betrayed his anger, and he wordlessly left the courtyard and the house to escape his humiliation.

Chapter Nine

Hamdi was seven now, old enough to see his *'awda*, to visit the precious land that had for centuries past been his ancestral home and soon would be again. Nadia implored Hassan to take their son to Palestine. Since the recent Israeli retaliation against the fedayeen had halted their activity for the time being, Hassan made plans for the trip. He and Hamdi would drive to Cairo, pick up a freighter to Beirut, and take a bus down through Lebanon to the Israeli border city of Rosh Hanikra. There was essentially free travel through that border area. They could rent a car in Israel. Both of them had forged Israeli identification cards listing them as Arab Christians from Maghar. Hassan had a very old friend in Maghar who would back up his false identity, so there should be no trouble.

Six days later, they rented an auto from an Arab used car dealer in Acre. They drove to Haifa and spent an entire day driving around the port visiting the sights of the city. Hamdi was more excited than he had ever been in his life. He chattered constantly and pointed at everything. Hassan took him to dinner at a fine restaurant in the huge Arab section of the city. Everyone spoke Arabic, just like back in Geza City, and Hamdi was confused. He thought there would only be Jews speaking a funny language like at Rosh Hanikra. They went to bed at nine, in a hotel on Mount Carmel, and Hamdi fell instantly asleep, exhausted from all the excitement.

In the morning, they drove eastward through carefully harrowed fields of lettuce and onions and potatoes and groves of yews and eucalyptus and trees fecund with bright yellow-orange apricots to Nazareth, then down steep rocky slopes to Tiberias on the Sea of Galilee. Hassan parked near the white sand beach and he and Hamdi walked along the row of shops and restaurants and sat in small wicker armchairs at a scarred wooden table overlooking the shimmering emerald sea. Again, the waiter and many of the patrons spoke Arabic. Hamdi felt very much at home here.

Then Hassan and Hamdi walked to the ruins of the Crusader church about half a mile away. It was built of huge rough-hewn, square-cut boulders which must weigh several tons each. It had stood guard over the harbor of Tiberias a thousand years ago.

"See this great church, Hamdi? The Christian Crusaders from Europe built it to help forcibly to convert all of our people from the true faith of Muhammad."

Hamdi listened hard to Hassan. But he didn't know what "Crusaders" were, he didn't know what "convert" meant, and he wasn't quite sure what a "Christian" was, although he had heard the word before.

"And just like this church," Hassan continued, "Christianity shall crumble and die out among our people. We're going to Maghar, about ten miles from here. They're all Christian Arabs there, Hamdi, but they are good people. They don't give help to the Jew scum, and they don't fight in the Jew Army. I have an old friend in Maghar, Jussuf Abood. Have I told you about him?"

"I can't remember, Daddy," said Hamdi very seriously.

"Well, I met him in Jerusalem, when we were both studying English, before I went to Princeton in the United States. He was studying to be a teacher. We became very close friends. He has a big, big family in Maghar. You'll like them."

"Oh, goody! Are we going now?" asked Hamdi. This heavy talk about Crusaders and Christians was boring him to death. He wanted to get back to the car and play with the tiny toy trucks that Hassan had bought him in Haifa.

They drove on a narrow winding road through the Galilean hills for twenty minutes, through the myriad silver green olive trees crowded on the lush grassy slopes, to a little whitewashed village which seemed to arise like a profusion of mushroom caps out of a huge rolling meadow of red flowering ice plants. The first building was a tall, steepled, white stucco church with mosaic tile all over the front and windows of stained glass. Then past several houses to a huge, sprawling villa where Hassan parked the car. The freshly-painted white plaster villa was perched on a small knoll and spilled over it on all sides. Attached to the front was a small room with an open wooden door. Hassan took Hamdi by the hand, and they walked inside. It was not more than fifteen feet square and its walls were stacked floor to ceiling with canned goods, housewares, small tools, battery radios, phonographs, little gas stoves and small appliances of every description. This was Maghar's General Store.

"Kamel! *Marchabbah!*" Hassan greeted the shopkeeper, who was kneeling on the floor, stacking one of the shelves.

"Hassan! *Alle wassele feek!* [Welcome and again welcome]," said the fat shopkeeper, rising off the floor and hugging Hassan. They kissed cheeks three times.

"*Neharkum sa'id* [May your day be prosperous]," said Hassan.

"*Neharkum sa'id w-mubaarak!* [May your day be prosperous and blessed]," responded the shopkeeper. "*Awhashtuuna* [We have been desolate without you]," continued Kamel in the practically endless greeting ceremony of the Arabs. Hamdi watched and smiled as the two old friends held hands and exchanged the string of required greetings. Finally, Hassan backed away and took Hamdi by the hand, pulling him forward and introducing him proudly to the shopkeeper.

"Come. It is time to close the shop," said Kamel.

His villa was luxurious by village standards. It had a long wide parlor with several low divans covered in colorful throws. Its floor was pinkish marble tile with oriental carpets adorning much of it. The huge dining room had a long wooden table and sixteen chairs. In the corner sat a very old woman in a black robe and headdress. She was sqeezing ripe figs and placing them on wicker platters to be dried in the sun. She nodded as they walked silently past her, and they went out into a spacious, terra cotta-tiled courtyard with a water fountain in the center around which were several stone benches, shaded by the overhanging branches of an immense aleppo pine which embraced the courtyard like a doting mother with its low sloping branches.

At two o'clock, they went inside to the dining room to enjoy the luscious feast of roast lamb and turtle doves and spitted goslings and fried perch that had been prepared for the honored guests. All of the men, down to the four-year-old, sat at the dining table. The daughters of Yussuf and Kamel were the servers. When the serving was over, the girls went back to the kitchen to eat silently with their mothers and grandmother, forbidden to disturb the menfolk during their meal.

"Yussuf is the principal of the school now," said Kamel proudly, smiling at his younger brother. Kamel's bushy walrus moustache almost completely hid his mouth.

"Congratulations!" said Hassan. "What did you do, kill the other guy?"

They all laughed. "No," said Yussuf. "He got a better job driving a cab in Haifa. He's making $200 a week off the American tourists alone!" Yussuf's swarthy, thin face was bitter. He was tall and slender and had literally no resemblance to his very fat brother Kamel.

"Well, maybe if you do a good job as principal, you'll get an offer to drive a cab," Hassan kidded him.

"So how shall we celebrate the pleasure of your company, Hassan?" asked Yussuf.

"I thought we'd stay tonight. And then I'd like you and Kamel to come with me up to the Golan Heights, like the old days. We can hunt boar and partridge and roast it at the Sea of Galilee, have a real family picnic. What do you say?"

"Terrific!" answered Yussuf, and Kamel nodded and smiled. "We'll leave tomorrow morning early."

That night, after Hamdi had been put to bed with two of Yussuf's youngest sons, the three men drove to an Arab bar on the waterfront in Tiberias, surrounded by fishing skiffs and the smell of salt wet wood and decaying cement. They sat smoking nargilahs and drinking arak, and they talked about old times.

Early in the morning they set off to the Golan Heights in Kamel's Land Rover. They drove around the northern end of the Sea of Galilee, brooding still and purple in the meager dawn light, and through the Syrian border checkpoint near Almagor. Then they drove northeast to the hills around Khushniya. The dense underbrush of the pine forest hid the savory wild boar that had provided food for the Christians and sport for the Muslims for centuries. Using the hand-engraved double barrel shotguns belonging to the Abood family, they bagged three small boars before noon. They also shot a dozen partridge. Hamdi got to fire the shotgun once, but it hurt his shoulder and almost knocked him down.

They returned to Maghar in mid-afternoon and loaded the entire family in the Land Rover and a stake truck and drove to the beach on the Sea of Galilee near Capernaum. Next to the ancient Roman ruins they set up spits and dug barbecue pits, and the women and girls set about preparing the food while the men and boys swam and splashed in the Sea. Hassan took two of the partridges and traded them to an Arab fisherman for three St. Peter's fishes, a delicious species of perch, since he and Hamdi were forbidden by Islam from eating pork.

Hamdi had never had such a happy time in his life. The sea air was cooling and sweet. The gentle hills of Galilee were studded with lush meadows thick with grass and wildflowers of red and cream and yellow and blue, and the Heights of the Golan, below towering snow capped Mount Hermon, were forested and rich with wildlife. It was like being in paradise.

Hassan sat with Hamdi at the edge of the Sea and looked gravely at the little boy. "Do you like it here?"

"Oh yes, Daddy! It's fantastic!"

. "Look about you, my son. See this place and the valley and the hills and the mountains. Feel this air and taste this fish and this partridge. This is what they stole from us, my son. This is what the Jews have done to us. They have cast us into a wasteland and they have stolen our paradise, our homeland, our *'awda.*"

Hamdi felt miserable. All he could think about was having to leave his new friends tomorrow, having to go back to bleak, brown, barren, boiling Gaza City. All because of the Jews....

Chapter Ten

David got out of the cab in front of the flat on Geulah Street. Leah had been standing impatiently at the kitchen window for over an hour waiting for her brother. She ran downstairs and hugged him as he entered the apartment house foyer. He was gaunt, and his eyes were puffy, and his hair was thinning and becoming pure white.

He returned the hug disinterestedly, quickly. He followed her heavily up the stairs and into the flat. He smelled stale and had not shaven for a couple of days. He was still dressed in the soiled blue workshirt and shorts of the kibbutz. He sat on the edge of the couch.

"What's wrong David?"

He looked at her for a few moments and then stared vacantly at his hands. "How did you do it, Leah? How did you lose everyone and still manage to hold onto life?" He looked at her and his eyes were tormented.

She sat down next to him on the couch and put her arm around him. "Is it still Deena and Jacob?"

"They come to me sometimes at night," he whispered to her, as though he were telling a dark secret that no one else must know. "It wasn't bad at first. It was good. We would sit and talk and I would hold Jacob, and Deena and I would make love. But then they started coming bad. Deena without eyes, slit open, Jacob without his head and emasculated. And they say nothing to me. They just sit on my bed and bleed and make a mess on everything." He rubbed his hands hard on his sleeves, washing off the blood that only he could see, and his body shook convulsively.

Leah held him tightly. "I think you need help, David. Tomorrow we'll go to Freud Hospital. Maybe you need a rest. You've been working very hard on the kibbutz bringing in the cotton."

"The cotton was in weeks ago, Leah. And what can they do for me at a hospital? Just help me live with it. I don't think I want to live with it." He spoke matter-of-factly.

"Enough of that talk now, David! Matt and Joshua will be home soon. They just went up the street to the cleaners to pick up our outfits for the graduation. I want you to shave and shower right now and put on clean clothes. Did you bring your uniform?"

He nodded resignedly.

"Good. You were always so beautiful in your uniform. Everyone will be looking at you instead of me and its my graduation." She stood up and laughed lightly, trying to lighten his mood, and she took both of his hands and pulled him to his feet. He picked up his canvas bag and walked into the bathroom, closing the door behind him.

Leah walked to the kitchen window and stared down at the street, seeing nothing. She lit a cigarette and inhaled deeply, feeling slightly dizzy as the smoke filled her lungs. Matt hated her to smoke, said it was unladylike. But sometimes when she got very nervous, it seemed to help.

She didn't see Matt and Joshua enter the building and didn't even hear the living room door shut behind them. But then she heard five-year-old Joshua's giggles and his footsteps running.

"Mommy! Mommy! Is Uncle David here?"

"Yes, Joshele. He's just getting washed and dressed now. You go into your room and put on those clean clothes Daddy just brought home."

Joshua ran out of the kitchen and down the hall into his room. Matt came into the kitchen and saw Leah's drawn face, the cigarette. He was suddenly frightened.

"Is it as bad as Giora said?" he asked in a whisper.

She nodded slowly and took another long drag of the cigarette.

"Oh my God! What can we do?' he said to her, looking helpless, his shoulders slumping.

"I think he's suicidal again."

"Giora told me he thought so, too. He said he's been acting the same way he did last time, two years ago, when he holed up in his cottage for three weeks and refused to eat or drink or take care of himself. We'd better take him over to the hospital again."

"I told him, but he doesn't want to go. I think he just wants to die," she whispered, and tears filled her eyes and flowed over the lower lids and wet her cheeks.

"Okay, I'll talk to him as soon as he's out of the bathroom. We may have to bring him over there tonight yet," Matt whispered, put his arms around his wife and hugged her tightly. "You okay?" Matt's craggy face was deeply furrowed, the lines drawn tightly from the sides of his nostrils to the corners of his tensely pursed lips.

"Yeh, I'm okay," she sniffed.

"Come on, let's get dressed." They walked into their room and closed the door. Matt put on a starched white shirt with stiff French cuffs, a burgundy tie with tiny blue polka dots, and his navy blue linen suit. It was too warm for wool in Jerusalem in late May.

Leah put on the new clothes she had bought just a week ago. After all, college graduation happens just once in a lifetime, so there was every reason to splurge a little. She buttoned and zipped the tight, kelly green velvet skirt and tucked in the wispy mint green raw silk scoop neck blouse. Matt sat on the edge of the bed watching her, as he often did.

Matt is the work of God, Leah thought, the kind of person you point at to prove the handiwork of God on earth, the otherwise unexplainable perfection. But David, too, is the handiwork of God. And God has for some terrible reason abandoned David, visited him like Job with boils, scabs and unhealable, unbearable wounds.

"How do I look?" Leah smiled at Matt, basking in the look he gave her.

"Like Pallas Athene when she got her first good look at the size of the centaur's cock!"

"I guess you've been reading classical poetry again and getting horny," she sat down beside him on the bed, and they both laughed, good strong laughter, trying to wash away their growing dread over David. She put her hand on his leg and sighed deeply. "What are we going to do, Matthew?"

"Let me talk to him alone for a few minutes. If he's really despondent, I'm going to take him over to the hospital right away. But if he seems all right, I think we ought to just wait and see. He's always better after he spends some time with us, especially with Joshua. Let's just see, okay?"

"Okay," she said, her voice resolute, and they both walked out of the bedroom. Leah went into Joshua's room. He was lying on his back on the floor trying to tie his sneaker shoelaces, but he had them knotted up as usual.

Matt poured three glasses of brandy and sipped distractedly at one. David came out of the steamy bathroom, and he looked like the David of old. He was wearing the stiffly starched "dress" fatigues of a *Tat Aluf* [Major General] in Tzahal. He was clean shaven and his deep bronze farmer's tan stood out against his white hair. Matt breathed a sign of relief as David walked up and they hugged.

"Want a drink?" Matt held up one of the glasses for him. David took it and swallowed the brandy in one gulp.

"I see you're still drinking that shit from Rishon le-Zion!" David said, laughing, putting down the empty glass.

"Tell Sharett to give me a raise and I'll drink French cognac from now on." Both men laughed easily.

"Seriously David, how do you feel?"

"Much better. Being with you all makes me feel much better. It always does." He paused and looked apologetically at Matt. "I'm really sorry for giving Leah a scare. I know I did. But I'm okay, really."

"Good. I want you to stay with us for a while. Now that Leah's finished with school and Joshua's out of kindergarten, they'll want you to stay here and spend some time with them. Okay?"

"Sure, I'd love it."

"Good. Let me get Leah and Josh and we'd better go to dinner or we'll be late for the graduation."

Matt walked into Joshua's bedroom, and a moment later they came out, and Joshua ran toward David and leapt into his outstretched arms.

"Uncle David! Uncle David! Daddy said you're staying with us."

"Yep. For just as long as you want," said David, holding the sparkly-eyed boy in his arm.

Leah could literally read her brother's thoughts in his tortured gray eyes: Oh Jacob, Jacob, Jacob. Why couldn't this be you. Oh God, why my Jacob. . . .

They walked down to the Land Rover parked in the small garage behind the flat. They drove to downtown Jerusalem to the Europa Delicatessen, the only restaurant in Israel where you could get real mandelbrot and stuffed kishke and knishes and gefilte fish with beet sweetened horseradish, all the delicacies of the old world, that other life.

Menachem and Aliza Begin were already seated in the small restaurant. He was after Leah again, now that she had had her four years of being a mother and a wife and a college student. Menachem wanted her to join Cherut so that she could run for a seat in Parliament in the next election. They shook hands and hugged all around the table, and they ordered.

They ate the steaming chicken soup with kneidlach, and David looked strong and self-assured. Leah glanced at him again to reassure herself, and then she resumed listening to Menachem's insistent arguments.

"—and this time you don't have to worry about alienating the Labor Party, Matt. Ben-Gurion's retired—at least for the moment —so Leah can be a member of Cherut and no one will say 'boo' to her."

He was right, and they all knew it. Matt nodded in agreement and shrugged his shoulders. "It's up to her, Menachem, not to me. Leah makes her mind up all by herself about everything else and she'll make the final decision on this too."

"I *have* decided," Leah said quietly. "I am going to run. The Labor Party has its Golda. Cherut will have its Leah!"

They all lifted glasses of fruit juice and drank a toast. Joshua was

busy picking up a kneidl out of the chicken soup with his fingers
and taking bites out of it. David had a distant look, disattached.

The Hebrew University graduation was outside this year, in the
Valley of the Cross just west of the site where the new campus was
under construction. The original campus was on Mount Scopus in
East Jerusalem behind the Green Line, under Jordanian control.
And although the Jews were supposed to have rights of protected
access to the campus as well as to Hadassah Hospital next to it, it
had become too dangerous for Jews to go into Jordanian Jerusalem.
So Israel simply started carving a new campus out of the rolling
hills next to the Valley of the Cross. Classes had been held since
1948 in various government and communal buildings in downtown
Jerusalem, and the capacity of the University was therefore quite
small, and its Baccalaureate class was but a few hundred.

Five thousand people sat on folding chairs set up in neat rows
beside the Monastery of the Cross and huge spotlights on posts
illuminated the ceremonies. There was no procession of graduates,
just a series of speeches by various faculty leaders. Joshua's
attention span had evaporated only a few minutes after they had
been seated. It was nine-thirty and well past his bedtime, and he
was cranky. So Leah had to take him in her arms and soothe him,
and he finally fell asleep.

David sat rock still between Matt and Menachem. He was
torpid, vacant, his earlier pleasant mood having fled as quickly as it
came. Now he was obviously in his own world.

The last speaker was Yigal Armon. He had risen from Palmach
commander in 1948 to Chief of Staff of Tzahal in 1953, a meteoric
career, a womanizer with fabled gifts, Ben-Gurion's toady, his fair-
haired boy. David stared at the speaker, far away at the podium, and
Leah could see her brother's rage. She, too, could not fight away the
memory of the *Altalena* fiasco, when Armon had almost killed her.

"Our armed forces shall be the mightiest in the entire Middle
East," Armon was saying. "No nation shall dare threaten the Jews
or the Jewish State again. We have learned the most tragic lesson of
history, that while we are God's chosen people, He has not chosen
to defend us. That we must do ourselves. We will never lay down
the Bible and the Talmud. But they will no longer be our artillery
and machine guns. The people of the Book shall be the people of
the Book and the sword. Never again shall we pray to God to

preserve us. We shall preserve ourselves by our own hand. And we shall cut off the hand of any oppressor who dares to threaten even one among us."

Leah listened absently to the impassioned rhetoric and the appreciative applause of the audience. But she was growing more and more concerned with David. He was literally lost in his own mind now. Even Menachem noticed, and he looked with concern at Leah and Matt.

"We'd better go," said Matt. They had come late and were sitting toward the rear, so there was little fuss as they walked up the grassy slope out of the Valley of the Cross. When they reached the end of Aza Street where they had parked, they shook hands with Menachem and Aliza. David simply stood dumbly. Matt was carrying Joshua, and Leah held David's hand as they walked to the land rover. Suddenly, as abruptly as his torpor had begun, David laughed good naturedly and said, "Can you believe that son of a bitch Armon? Ben-Gurion makes him the Chief of Staff, just because he never had a goddam independent thought in his brain that Ben-Gurion didn't plant there and approve!"

They reached the Land Rover and got inside, Leah taking Joshua on her lap. Matt turned around in the front seat and looked at David. "Are you okay, David?"

"Oh sure! I just got kinda moody there, listening to that bastard talk. I'm fine." He smiled broadly at Matt and patted his shoulder reassuringly.

"Maybe it would be better to take you over to the hospital tonight. What do you think?" Matt asked softly.

David spoke slowly and carefully. "No, really Matt. I'm fine now. I just got to thinking a little too hard about some things. Really, I'm just fine now." His voice was strong and convincing.

Matt and Leah looked at each other and she nodded almost imperceptibly. Matt started the car, and they drove through the quiet streets to their apartment. Leah undressed Joshua as he lay sound asleep, and she put his favorite teddy bear in the crook of his arm and covered him with the light quilt. She closed his bedroom door softly. Matt poured three glasses of brandy and they all sat and sipped, chatting and yawning. Matt and Leah went to the bedroom. David stretched out on the softly padded sofa.

Was it a dream? Leah lifted her head off the pillow. And then she knew, instantly. Matt was already running through the bedroom door into the living room. She jumped out of bed and raced behind Matt. The moonlight streaming through the windows was all the illumination they needed. David was lying on his back on the sofa, his right arm hanging over the side, a British service revolver on the floor under his hand. There was a bloody hole in his right temple.

"Mommy, Mommy, is something wrong?" Five-year-old Joshua came out of his bedroom rubbing his eyes, dragging his teddy bear by one floppy ear. He could see his uncle lying limply on the sofa in the murky darkness.

Leah ran to him and swept him into her arms and put him back into his bed and tucked him in tightly.

"Did Uncle David hurt himself, Mommy?" he asked, looking at Leah intently.

"No Joshele. I think he just ended all his hurt," she said, smoothing the covers over him.

"Is he with God now?" he whispered.

Let him believe, she thought bitterly. Soon enough he will learn. "Yes, Joshele. Uncle David is with God."

She sat on the edge of the bed and watched him fall asleep. And she continued to watch over him as she heard the ambulance attendants come and take her brother away. She rocked softly, but she did not cry. She was all cried out from the years of death and loss. She was suffused with tearless hatred for the scum who murdered her brother David. There was only a shell left of David Brod when they were through with him: the Palestinians. First the Nazis, then the British, now the Palestinians....

Chapter Eleven

In the elections in May 1955, Leah was number two on Cherut's list, behind Begin himself. Begin's political savvy worked well, and Cherut won fifteen seats, second only to the Labor Party's forty seats. Cherut had become Israel's major opposition party to the Mapai coalition.

The Knesset session in August began with a violent debate over the status of the Arab refugees and the Absentee Property Regulations, as well as the abuses being practiced against the Arabs by the Custodian of Absentee Property. Amos Almogi arose and went to the podium to address the Knesset. He was short, wiry, and had black eyes and blue-black curly hair. He was very Arab looking and strikingly handsome.

"Fellow members of the Knesset. World opinion is increasingly reproving the Jews of Israel for the injustices that we have perpetrated against the Arabs who once lived in our State."

There was some scattered applause from the members, some catcalls, and a good deal of booing. The Israeli Knesset was not the austere and somber Congress of the United States. It was a loose, informal and boisterous body of people who expressed openly and loudly its taste or distate for what any particular speaker was saying. Almogi continued speaking.

"Between 1948 and 1953, of the three hundred seventy new settlements in Israel, three hundred fifty of them are on lands formerly owned by Arabs. In addition, the State of Israel and the Jewish National Fund have 'purchased' from the Custodian of Absentee Property three hundred eighty-eight towns, villages and parts of other cities and towns which once belonged to the Arabs. Consequently, sixty percent of Israel's total land area consists of property 'bought' by us through the Custodian of Absentee Property, all of which once belonged to the Arabs. And nearly one-quarter of the buildings in Israel, including ten thousand shops, businesses and stores, were 'purchased' by us in the same way through the Absentee Property Regulations."

Boos and catcalls, clapping and cheering thundered through the Knesset. Almogi waited until the tumult had subsided and then continued.

"In 1953, this Knesset passed the 'Land Acquisition Law' and created a Commission to evaluate the claims of the Arab refugees for their confiscated land and property. The problem with the law is that land values were set as of January 1950, and since then the Israeli pound has suffered a six to one inflation. So the Arabs have been offered only fifteen or twenty percent of the value of their property. Also, the Commission unilaterally has seen fit to disallow many hundreds of claims as being frivolous, without so much as investigating the claims. Our government has only been able to settle about a thousand claims, and there are well over two thousand more that are simply being disregarded."

More boos, more catcalls, more cheering and applause. Some members got out of their seats, threw their papers on their desks, and stormed dramatically out of the hall. A normal Israeli Knesset debate. Once again, Almogi waited patiently for order to be restored.

"I would like to read to you an article from the *New York Herald-Tribune* which describes the situation of the Arab refugees in two of their camps. Please forgive my pronounciation. My English isn't too good:

> "The tent camp in the Jordan Valley on the approach to Jericho had perhaps twenty thousand inhabitants.... I looked at their filthy habitations—brush for mattresses, a torn blanket or two, a larder empty except for a pinch of meal, a pat or two of lard. The camp was talking about an Arab businessman from Haifa. The day before he had taken his two sons behind the tent, shot them through the head, and turned the gun on himself.... [T]he [Jews had taken] his home and business, and refused to allow his return even to liquidate. He was penniless and couldn't stand watching his children's bellies bloat. The tent camp at Ramallah was even worse. Icy winds off the Judean hills whipped through the torn flaps. The widow from Ramle wore an old flour sack, and her legs were blue with cold. Her five children emitted a monotonous wail; she was on the move perpetually, swabbing their runny noses. Her husband, a Ramle carpenter, had been killed in the war.... Agonized, she asked me what happened to her home...."

Leah could not understand Almogi's heavily accented English so she listened through her translator headset as a simultaneous translation was done. Everyone listened grimly. There were no catcalls or boos or clapping this time. Just silence.

"When I saw this article about the Arab refugees, I thought back to the Holocaust. No, we haven't killed them like rats. Yes, we fought a war in which some of them were involved—although most were not, they were simply victims of the war. No, we have not created concentration camps for them and kept them there. Yes, they have mostly their fellow Arabs to thank for keeping them isolated and poverty stricken and disease ridden in the rat holes they call refugee camps. Yes, it is the Arab nations themselves that refuse to permit the refugees to be integrated into their national mainstreams, in order to keep them a dagger aiming at our heart.

"But I beg all of you to recognize our need to deal with the problem of the Arab refugees *now*, even if the Arab nations will not. Already our border towns and kibbutzim are being subjected to terrorist attacks from fedayeen bands from the Gaza Strip and Jordan and Syria. If we do not seek to do justice on behalf of the Palestinians, we will never have real peace in our land. Yes, the Arabs have committed grave wrongs against us, but we have in turn delivered unto them even more severe blows. And they have been rendered helpless by us."

Leah was shocked at Almogi's speech. He didn't have the vaguest notion what it really meant to be helpless. He was the head of a new party called the "Mizrachim" [Easterners], made up almost entirely of immigrants from Arab countries. He himself was from Morocco and had come to Israel in the flood of some four hundred thousand Sephardic Jews who had left or been forced to leave their Arab homelands after Israel's War of Independence had rocked the Arab world. Some of them were more Arab than Jew, spoke better Arabic than Hebrew, and some even harbored a certain nostalgia for their Arab homelands. And just a few of them were like Almogi, conscience stricken over the injustices that the Jews had perpetrated against the Arabs. Injustice by the Jews! Leah shuddered with anger. Sure, she had seen one horrible tragedy at Deir Yassin. But just one. No one could point to another. And the one Jewish excess was meaningless when compared to the hundreds of Palestinian terrorist attacks against the Jews. Deena, oh Deena. And Jacob. And David. No different than what the Nazis had done to her family, what the Prince of Darkness had done to Jonathan and Nachman.

Leah watched Amos Almogi leave the Knesset podium, and she heard the clapping of many of the ministers and her anger boiled over.

"Helpless" was not a word that applied to the way that the Jews treated the Arabs. It simply had no relevance, no meaning in the context of Israeli-Arab relations. Leah knew what "helpless" really meant. She knew that no wrong, none of what Almogi called "severe blows" by the Jews against the Arabs, none could come near to what Europe's Jews had been through. They had suffered *real* wrongs, *real* blows, *real* helplessness. Involuntarily, as she seethed over Almogi's speech, she was taken back, back to the time of her own helplessness, her deepest fears. She rested her elbows on the desk and her head sunk into her hands as the unwanted memories surged before her mind's eye.

Leah Arad pedals the bicycle along the paved road until she begins to see the outline of the hills in the fading night. She takes the first dirt path she finds and pedals quickly down it. She rides for an hour through the forest and coasts for miles down the long slope into vast fields of barley. While it is still barely dark, she pedals through a tiny hamlet. No one stirs. A dog barks from somewhere. One of the thousands of villages of East Europe, untouched by time or technology, medieval, superstitious. She pedals a little farther, to a wide stream that runs straight across the disappearing path. It is light now, the sun is up. She has no idea where she is, and she does not care. She sips water from the stream and lies down next to it.

She awakes to someone prodding her with a stick. She looks up, but the high sun blinds her. She sits up and looks into the face of a boy, eight or nine years old. He is carrying a long staff and tending a small flock of sheep drinking at the stream.

"Czy pan sie dobrze czuje? [Are you all right?]" the boy asks.

"Pomocy [Help]," she says.

The boy runs after a stray lamb, shooing his sheep together in a group.

"Are you lost?" he asks.

"Sort of."

"Come, I'll take you home."

She picks up her bicycle and wheels it beside the boy and his scurrying flock of sheep. She is exhausted and dirty. Dried flecks of blood and flesh, looking like caked dirt, are all over her arms and face. The nightmare of last night is like a veil covering her eyes. She constantly sees her baby Nachman being swung into the wall. Everything else is fuzzy, unfocused.

They come into the village and the boy drives the sheep into a wire enclosure behind a cottage. He goes inside the hut. Leah remains in front, holding her bike, beginning to be aware of where she is and the danger she is in. If these Poles realize she is Jewish, she will be killed. In a moment, a tall peasant woman comes out wiping her hands on her apron. She has long, blonde hair like thick straw. She is probably in her mid-twenties, plump, pretty, and old before her time. "Who are you?" she asks Leah.

"Nazywam sie Lara. *I am from Warsaw. I was kidnapped by German soldiers who had their way with me. I have run away from them and I must hide. My family was killed in the German invasion. I have nowhere to go.*"

"*We have nothing here in Brzka. Just the food and meat we grow. Our men who were not killed by the Germans are in the forest with the* Armia Krajowa *[Polish Partisans]. Just the women and children are here and a few old men.*"

"Prosze me pomoc *[Please help me]. I am so tired. I cannot go on. Please let me stay here and rest.*"

The woman looks her over from head to foot. She calls to the boy standing at the door to come over. "Open the shepherd's shack and bring her a pail of water." Turning to Leah, she says, "My husband used to sleep in the little shack behind the cottage when he got too drunk and I kicked him out of bed. The Germans killed him. You can use it. Voytek will open the door for you. We nailed it shut. I am Marja."

"*Thank you for your kindness.*"

She wheels the bicycle behind the stone cottage to a wattle and daub hut, perhaps eight feet square. She lays the bicycle against the side of the hut. Voytek has ripped some crossboards off the decaying wood slat door and is pushing it open. It is tied with hemp to one side of the wattled door jam, and there is no knob or lock. She has to stoop to walk inside and can barely stand. The floor is packed dirt and there is a rag bed in the corner. Light comes through a foot-square opening in the side wall. Leah flops down on the rags. Voytek comes in and puts a pail of water, a hunk of brown soap and an old kerosene lantern on the floor. Leah immediately falls asleep.

When she awakens it is deep night. She crawls outside the hut. A full moon brightly illuminates the village and fields in the small valley bounded on all sides by the crests of pine covered hills. The stream sparkles in the moonlight.

She takes the soap and walks through the barley fields to the stream and lets her frock drop to the edge of the water. Her only underclothes are panties, which she wears into the stream. It is less than two feet deep, and she sits in the cool crystal water and lets it wash her with its current. She takes off her panties and washes them with the rough soap. She lays them on the grassy bank and scrubs her dress in the cool water. She stands in the stream and rubs the soap all over her body, scouring until it hurts her, abrading her skin, trying to wash away the filth of her memories along with the blood and flesh of her murdered son. She lies back on the bank and stares at the brilliantly starry sky in the soft breezy warm night. Again she sleeps, and the Angel of Death's bloody eyes stare at her from under a grotesquely cleft forehead.

She awakens unrefreshed at dawn and puts on her still damp clothes. She walks back toward her hut. Voytek waves at her as he dawdles with his sheep on a grassy knoll. Marja is scattering corn for some clucking chickens. Other peasant women and children putter around the small cottages. The milkman is driving his aged, fat, arthritic cow down the center path of the village and milking her into the pails brought to him by the little girls who wait in front of their cottages.

Marja looks at Leah walking through the field. She is beautiful, Marja thinks. But so sad. Her eyes are empty. I have seen such women, who have lost everything in the war. Walking dead.

A siren, still far away, bellows in its unique Nazi hee-haw. Leah stops in the field of tall pale yellow shimmering barley about fifty feet from the hut. None of the villagers seem to take notice. Sirens on the highway are commonplace. The sound comes closer up the other side of the hill leading to the village. Marja sees Leah kneel down below the level of the barley tops. She is completely hidden.

The siren crests the hill, and down the cart path bounce two soldiers on motorcycles followed by a jeep with a mounted machine gun. In the jeep is Captain Hans Fricke, Adjutant to the slain Kommandant of Treblinka, Colonel Karl Mencken.

The little girls flee with the milk cans back into the cottages. Their mothers stop in the middle of their chores and watch the Nazis. This is unusual; these scum ordinarily stay on the main road and do not come to the isolated village.

The jeep clatters to a halt in a cloud of dust in front of the old dairyman. Fricke walks to him, halts and strikes him in the face with a short riding crop. The old man teeters slightly but remains standing.

"We are looking for a pretty blond girl, about twenty years old, a Lithuanian. She has murdered a German officer." Fricke's Danzig Polish is odd to these peasants, but they understand him.

"She is not here, Pulkownik *[Colonel]," answers the old man through toothless gums. "We only have very young Polish girls and old hags here."*

Fricke strikes the dairyman again with the crop. And again the ancient peasant does not move, seeming only vaguely to feel the blow.

"There is no such girl here, Pulkownik.*"*

Fricke scans the cottages in this tiny hamlet. The two motorcycle soldiers have searched one of the places already and are coming out of a second. Fricke walks over to Marja. Voytek is hiding behind her, peeking out around her arm. Fricke grabs Voytek by the ear and twists it. The boy lets out a howl. His little flock of sheep scatter bleating.

Still twisting the ear, Fricke demands, "Where is she boy, the blonde she-devil?"

"I have not seen her. She is not here," Voytek cries, twisting his head and stretching his neck to ease the hold on his ear.

Fricke looks sneeringly at Marja and the boy and lets go of his ear. He walks briskly back to the jeep and calls the soldiers to end the search and get back on their motorcycles. The Germans bounce away back up the path and over the hill. The hee-hawing siren fades into the distance.

Leah stands up and runs to the hut. The peasants are back at work in their fields and vegetable patches. They do not look at her. She knows everyone in the village saw her walking in the grain and then saw her duck down and hide. She goes inside the hut and closes the door. Marja has already started hoeing weeds in a potato patch between the cottage and the hut. Voytek is rounding up his scattered flock. A cricket saws loudly somewhere in the wattled roof of Leah's new home. A flock of bluejays sing and flutter over the village,chirping hungrily at the fragrant golden fields of ripening grain.

The long days of summer brown the grass by the side of the stream. The weather turns hot. Leah often sleeps with the door wide open and the rag covering the "window" pulled aside. She plays for hours with Marja's two-year-old daughter, Kessi. The baby toddles around in the garden, playing with the tiny bugs and occasionally tasting them. Marja and Leah laugh and grimace and say "Ech!," and a delighted Kessi giggles and eats another bug. Voytek is much more taciturn. He saw the Nazis shoot his father two years ago on the first great German sweep to pacify the countryside, and he did not speak for months afterwards. He is nine years old and dark like his father was. Frequently he brings Leah little delicacies, a rabbit he has snared in the fields, a little fish he has caught with his hands in the stream, a small shirt loaded with wild berries.

Leah and Voytek sit owl-like by the stream for hours and throw pebbles into it and watch the ripples. Two mourners.

Time is kept by the moon and the seasons in the village. There is no newspaper or electricity for radios. No one owns an automobile. Once every couple of weeks, a huge peddler's cart rattles down the hill path into the hamlet, drawn by a gaunt horse. The women trade grain and slabs of salt pork and chickens and lambs in return for the manufactured goods and bolts of cloth they need. Leah does not remember what day she left Treblinka, what day her son was murdered, where she buried him. She does not know what month it is, except that the scorching summer days are burning out and getting cooler, and the nights are breezy and pleasant. It must be fall.

Leah and Voytek are ambling behind the grazing sheep at the edge of the forest behind the fields. A group of eight or ten men come toward them. The leader is a short bald man, filthy and emaciated, wearing the tattered gray and black striped pajama uniform of Treblinka inmates. The others are all as dirty and starved, some taller or shorter or hairier. They hang back at the treeline as the leader warily approaches Leah. He speaks to her in Polish, assuming that she is a peasant girl from the village below. On the pocket of his pants is stitched a yellow Star of David.

"Please, Miss, give us some food. We are starving to death," he says to her.

She immediately recognizes their clothes and knows that they have escaped from Treblinka. She also realizes that they could not know who she really is, because she was never inside the camp. She wants to reach out to them, to touch them and reassure them that they are now safe. But they are not, and she cannot. If Voytek gets the idea that she is a Jewess or a Jew lover, she is dead. She remains silent, choked with fear and helplessness.

"Where have you come from?" Voytek asks.

"We broke out of Treblinka four days ago. All the Sonderkommandos *rioted and burned down the camp. We have been wandering in the forest ever since. Please help us, little father."*

"You are Jews. Get away from us! Get away from our village!" Voytek screams. He grabs Leah's hand and starts running with her down the hill into the barley field. The startled sheep are bleating and running behind them. The cadaverous Jews disappear into the forest.

Voytek runs up to Marja, on her hands and knees in the vegetable patch. "Mama, Mama. Some Jews from that prison up the road. They were here Mama, they escaped!"

Marja is alarmed. She tells Leah and Voytek to be on the lookout, then runs off to warn the dairyman of the danger so that he can alert the rest of the village. That night, the villagers pound posts into the ground behind the cottages and place lanterns on them to keep the Jews from sneaking into the village and poisoning the livestock or putting a spell on the vegetable gardens. They know all about Jew magic. When the Jews in the villages were rounded up and marched off by the Nazis years ago, the townspeople knew that God was reaping his rightful vengeance upon the killers of His Only Begotten Son.

At dawn, two of the emaciated Jews creep out of the forest and run slowly to Voytek's sheep pen next to the cottage. The sheep bleat, frightened by the strangers. Two neighbor women stealthily emerge from their cottage carrying pitchforks. Marja leaps from the front door at a run and picks up the scythe lying against the cottage. She approaches the filthy Jews slowly. The other two women come toward them from the side.

The Jew stops struggling with the fence latch and looks at Marja, terror and starvation mixing in his wild eyes. With a quick sweep, Marja decapitates him with the eight-foot long scythe. The other two women plunge their pitchforks repeatedly into the other Jew.

From the tiny window of her hut, Leah watches in terror as the women murder her fellow Jews. She is sickened. She vomits into the chamber pot beside her bed. But there is nothing she can do to help these starving wretches. She too would be killed. She—they—are absolutely helpless. She sits on her bed and rocks back and forth, her body shaking uncontrollably. May God forgive her, she prays, for her cowardice in not trying to aid her own people. But her own will to survive has become her only code of conduct.

The three Polish women drag the bodies and the head to the cart path in front of the cottages and lay them across it. That afternoon, the expected sirens invade the pastoral village, this time with two trucks of SS soldiers. They lumber up to the sun-swollen putrid bodies of the Jews and look, not bothering to get out of the trucks. No one hiding in this village. No problem here. This is a peace offering. They turn the trucks around with difficulty and waddle out of the valley.

Leah and two other women dig holes for the Jews and bury them. That evening, Marja kneels before her ikon in the cottage and lights a candle. She has never before killed anyone and she is moved. She recites aloud the prayer for the dead and prays that these Jews will be forgiven their sins in purgatory and be permitted to take Jesus as their Savior and enter Heaven. Leah kneels beside Marja and prays silently, yiskadal v'yiskadash shmay rabah.... Tears run down her cheeks. Marja cannot imagine why Lara is crying. After all, these are only Jews. Marja pats her dear friend Lara on the back and soothes her. It has been a hard day for all of them.

Leah pushed away the memories. She had sat quietly in the Knesset for over two months now, and she had never taken the podium to make a speech. She was too self-conscious, too timid. But suddenly she was overwhelmed by the need to set the record straight, to silence the clapping of the Knesset ministers over the fictitious "helplessness" of the Arabs and the imagined Jewish "injustices" against them. She stood up and walked slowly to the podium. She opened the small Bible that she always carried in her purse. Her soft voice was amplified by the microphone through the Knesset chambers and enveloped the ministers.

"The Bible tells us of David and Bathsheba, a story which expresses both our understanding of the presence of good and evil in all human beings as well as our striving for justice—for the triumph of good.

"'And it came to pass in the evening, that David arose from his bed, and walked upon the roof of the king's house. And from the roof he saw a woman washing herself, and the woman was very beautiful to look upon. And David sent and inquired about the woman. And someone said, "This is Bathsheba, the wife of Uriah the Hittite." And David sent messengers and took her. And she came in unto him, and he lay with her. And she returned to her house.

"'In the morning, David wrote a letter to Joab, his general, saying, "Set Uriah in the forefront of the hottest battle, and get away from him, that he may be killed." And it came to pass, Joab assigned Uriah unto a place where he knew that valiant men were. And the men of the city went out, and fought with Joab, and there fell some of the servants of David; and Uriah the Hittite died also.

"'David sent and fetched Bathsheba to his house, and she became his wife and bore him a son. But the thing that David had done displeased the Lord.

"'And the Lord sent Nathan the Prophet unto David. And he came unto him and said: "There were two men in one city, the one rich and the other poor. The rich man had very many flocks and herds, but the poor man had nothing, save one little ewe lamb, which he had bought and nourished up; and it grew up together with him, and with his children. It did eat of his own food, and drank of his own cup, and it lay in his bosom and was unto him as a daughter. And there came a traveler unto the rich man, and he was unwilling to take of his own flock and of his own herd to prepare food for the traveler. So he took the poor man's lamb, and he slew it, and he prepared it for the man who had come to him."

"'And David's anger was greatly kindled against the man; and he said to Nathan, "As the Lord liveth, the man who has done this thing shall surely die. And he shall restore the lamb four times over, because he did this thing, and because he showed no pity."

"And the Prophet Nathan said: 'Thou art the man!'"

The Knesset chambers were silent. No one stirred. Leah's blond hair glowed golden under the bright Knesset lights, and she stood rigidly tall before the rows of ministers. Her voice gained strength, and she looked about the chambers at the silent ministers. No longer was she timorous.

"We are like unto the poor man with only one ewe. But the Palestinians have many flocks. We asked nothing more from them than that they let us live in peace. But they would not. They attacked us and slaughtered our people. We begged them to leave us in peace on our tiny ribbon of land, in the last *malineh* for our people. But the Palestinians refused. The Arab nations refused. With all of their millions of square miles of land and their oceans of oil, they refused to let us keep our one tiny ewe lamb, and they wrought death and destruction upon us from every direction."

The ministers were entranced by the impassioned eloquence of this stunning woman. They all had heard her story, what she had been through. Israel was too small for secrets about its political leaders. And they listened in awe to the fervent words issuing from the lips of this beautiful prophetess of Israel.

"We must never let one Palestinian refugee back into our land until the Arab nations agree to live in harmony with Israel! We must never lower our guns or our guard until we have peace! As long as the Arab leaders keep threatening us to turn the Jordan into a river of Jewish blood, we will leave the refugees in their camps along the Jordan, and it shall remain a river of Palestinian tears!"

BOOK FOUR

ERETZ YISRAEL

"If I forget thee, O Jerusalem, let my right
    hand wither away,
Let my tongue be stuck to the roof of my
    mouth, if I do not remember Thee,
If I do not set Jerusalem above my highest joy."

—Psalm 137:5-6

Chapter One

April 1957

In the Gaza Strip, the festering Arab refugee camps from which
the fedayeen were recruited were Israel's military objectives during
the Sinai Campaign. Israeli armored personnel carriers rolled down
the fetid paths of the camps, firing their machine guns into the air
and occasionally into groups of men who were foolish enough to
show their machismo by standing around in defiance during the
attack. In some of the camps, the young fedayeen staged defensive
actions. They were pitifully powerless against the armor of the 12th
Brigade. After less than two days, hundreds of refugees had been

killed and there would not again be mounted a major fedayeen raid from the Gaza Strip. The Israelis had sanitized it.

Hassan abu-Sittah had left for Cairo at the outbreak of the War, and he was serving as an Egyptian Army officer at the Canal defense lines. Yassir Arafat had done the same thing. Nadia and the el-Rashids sat behind shuttered windows in their home in Gaza City and prayed that the Israelis would pass them by this time. Their prayers were answered. When the war drew to a close and it became clear that they were completely out of danger, they once again lounged in the courtyard one cool evening after supper.

"The Israelis outfoxed all of the Arab nations as usual," said Nadia. "They stage the beginning of a fake war at Qalqilia to make us think they will attack Jordan and then they really take part in attacking the Gaza Strip and the Suez Canal. But even their attack on the Suez Canal is a fake, because what they really want is the Strait of Tiran, so they can open up their Port of Eilat and not even need the Suez Canal. In eight days, they not only defeat the mighty army of Egypt, but they thumb their noses at the British and the French and pursue their private war plans. So tiny Israel, the merest pawn on the chessboard of nations, suddenly becomes the strategic king in the English-French chess game of canal occupation. And even though the United States rapidly forces France and England to remove all of their forces, King David Ben-Gurion of Israel flatly refuses to withdraw! The Hebrews have a new King David on an imperial march across Arab lands, intent on rebuilding the Biblical Kingdom of David and Solomon of three thousand years ago. And we are helpless to block their path!" She paused and looked at Samir in desperation. "What is left for us here in Gaza City, Samir? What do we do now?"

It was the question foremost in everyone's mind. For as the reality of their pathetic weakness in the Gaza Strip had become more and more crystal clear over the past several months, they had all wondered what to do next. Where could they go to be safe?

"Three months ago, I went to Jordan to have a chat with the Minister of Interior," Samir answered slowly. His mild blue eyes were narrow slits, his brow tightly knit. "I knew him when we had our business in East Jerusalem. I also talked to some businessmen I know in Amman. I had almost decided to move all of us there, until the Qalqilia raid made it look like Jordan would be in a war. Now I have decided. We will go to Amman."

"How do we get our possessions there, our business equipment? Do we simply drive straight across Israel?" Widad's question was in a tone of complete incredulity, and she wore a look of utter defeat.

"Exactly," answered Samir. "The Israelis don't care where we live as long as it isn't in Israel. When I was in Amman, I got Jordanian passports for everyone of us including Hassan. I also got bills of lading and identification documents to cover all of the equipment we need to transport to Jordan to restart our construction company. In a few months, when the Sinai War is completely settled, Israel will once again open traffic over the Allenby Bridge and we will simply drive across Israel into Jordan. I'm sure of it."

"And suppose we do make it, Samir. What of *'awda*, what of Deir Yassin and Ein Kerem—our homes—what of *al-tariq al-fida'i?*" Nadia asked.

"That will wait until I have provided complete safety for my family, including you, Hamdi, Hassan and Hassan's mother," responded Samir with finality, stifling Nadia.

Jordan was a cruelly alien land. A steady, knifing wind blew off the clay hills like the breath of a perpetually angry dragon. It filled Nadia with a deep sense of despair. Their new home was by refugee terms a mansion, but the land was baked and brown. Mold-smelling dust infiltrated the air and clung to their nostrils. Certainly not the verdant hills of Deir Yassin. Not even Gaza City with its Mediterranean beaches close by. Nadia was thirty-three years old and she had just been forced by the Israelis from her home for the second time.

They came to Amman in July 1957 just as Samir had said—straight across Israel. And everywhere they looked in Israel, there was an explosion of new housing and new villages and the cities were mushrooming, and there were whole new sections of Jerusalem which had been built by the Israelis. It was no longer sleepy traditional Palestine. The Jews were rapidly turning Israel into a modern, technological hustle and bustle country. They drove down the new road between Tel Aviv and Jerusalem and none of the old Arab villages remained. They were gone, demolished, melted into the rocky hills. Nadia had to suppress a sense of admiration for what the Jews had accomplished in so short a time and even a greater sense that she no longer recognized her own country.

For Hassan, it was quite different. He seethed as they drove through the cities and towns along the new highways, and he hated the Jews for the changes they were imposing on his *'awda*. And only after they entered Arab East Jerusalem through the Mandelbaum Gate did he begin to relax. This was where he had been born and where he had lived. And nothing had changed. It was now part of Jordan, having been incorporated by King Abdullah in 1950. But someday, Hassan swore to himself, all of East Jerusalem and the West Bank and the Gaza Strip and the rest of Palestine would once more be the Palestinian *'awda*.

Amman, for Hassan, was just another place where he had to wait before going home. It was barren and bleak, but they lived well and comfortably, and from this center he could help Yassir Arafat build a new *fedayeen futuwwah* of self sacrificers committed to guerrilla war. The leaders of the General Union of Palestinian Students decided on a new and more appropriate name: *Fatah*. It was the reverse acronym of *al-Harakat at-Tahrir al-Falastin* [the Movement for Palestinian Liberation], and if you reversed the acronym *HaTaF* you had *FaTaH*, which meant "conquest," a fitting code name for the movement.

Hassan painstakingly began the rebuilding process, going to the many refugee camps and seeking out the fedayeen. And just as before, they reinstated their practice of small unit terrorism, indiscriminately murdering soldiers and civilians, adults and children in the many towns and villages on the West Bank border with Israel, placing bombs in buses and in the Jerusalem souk and in parks and playgrounds and parked cars and paint cans and refrigerators. And this time, when Israel staged its inevitable reprisal raids against the refugee camps, it was striking at the nearby camps in the West Bank and not at the truly offending fedayeen bases in Jordan. Because for the Israelis to have crossed the West Bank into Jordan with land or air forces would have been a major act of war, which the Israelis had no interest in pursuing. So one of the major consequences of Israel's reprisals against essentially innocent West Bank refugee camps was that in those camps the Jews were creating fedayeen out of otherwise peaceful and non-hostile Arabs.

The one thing—the most important thing—that Hassan failed to achieve was the establishment of a true Fatah army. To do so, he needed significant aid from the Arab nations, both for weaponry and training facilities. But the Arab world was in bitter internal ferment and it was fearful of letting the homeless, rootless Palestinian terrorists become an independent military force in the midst of the already turbulent Arab states.

Nadia could never completely divert her mind from her constant brooding over Palestine and Fatah and her fear for the safety of Hassan and Hamdi. She slavishly pursued a goal which she had promised herself she would do: she studied Hebrew. At the Teachers College in Amman was an old professor who came from Jerusalem and spoke fluent Hebrew. He became Nadia's private tutor. She studied avidly and would teach Hassan and Hamdi phrases. In 1960, Hamdi was eleven years old, and she made him study Hebrew along with her.

She would listen to *Kol Yisrael* [Israel Radio] for hours on end, training herself to understand the formal language of the news, the colloquial language of interviews, the slang quips and asides of the announcers, even the words of the songs, the hardest thing to understand in any language.

In 1961, the el-Rashids and abu-Hassans bought their first television set. Jordan had a state run station which broadcast various kinds of programs, mostly news and commentary, several hours each day except Friday, the Muslim sabbath. In Amman they could also pick up Israeli Broadcasting System programs from Jerusalem forty miles away. Jerusalem broadcast every day except Saturday. So Nadia often watched Israeli TV while doing her housework.

One afternoon, she was ironing some things with the TV on, when she thought she recognized the woman on the screen. Out of the dim recesses of her memory came the face of a woman pulling her from the village, helping her to escape Deir Yassin. It was an Israeli political interview program she had seen many times before. The lovely blond woman with the interviewer was older—after all, almost thirteen years had passed—but it was her. Nadia sat on a footstool close to the TV and watched closely and listened. The woman was named Leah Jordan, a Minister of Knesset in Begin's Cherut Party and apparently a well-known personality in Israel. The other interviewee was Amos Almogi, a Knesset Minister in the ruling Mapai coalition. He looked like an Arab. Nadia was fascinated.

"Mrs. Jordan and Mr. Almogi, you both gave famous speeches to the Knesset several years ago which made quite a stir in Israel and in your own parties. I'm going to play back some highlights of those speeches to familiarize our audience with what you said, and then I'll have some questions for you."

Nadia listened in rapt attention to the excerpts from the Knesset speeches that Leah and Amos had made in 1955.

"Well, Mrs. Jordan, do you have any comment on that today? Have your views changed?"

"My views have remained absolutely unchanged."

"And you, Mr. Almogi. Is your attitude toward the Palestinians still so conciliatory?"

"I must admit, Aaron, that I am probably even more of a dove than I was then. My opinion is that we have failed to help solve the problems of the Arab refugees and our government is at this very moment accentuating the problem rather than attempting to solve it. Israel is now strong enough and secure enough to turn our attention to those many Arabs who were merely victims of the War for Independence and would be perfectly good and decent citizens of the State of Israel today. We employ many thousands of them from the Gaza Strip and the West Bank to come to our farms and cities every day and provide the labor which our own Jewish population is insufficient in size to provide. Why shouldn't these Arabs also live here? I grieve that the tragedy of South African apartheid and the way their native negro population has been moved into separate 'colonies' like Soweto, is beginning to parallel the way that Israel is treating the Palestinians."

Nadia listened in fascination to the words of Amos Almogi. She had never before heard such a conciliatory tone taken by an Israeli politician. She could see the strain on the face of Leah Jordan, listening in obvious disgust with Almogi, waiting impatiently for her opportunity to respond.

"The critical difference that Mr. Almogi always fails to recognize," said Leah acerbically, "is that the Palestinian refugees are in a declared constant war with the Jews of Israel. That is certainly not the case with the blacks of South Africa. We have absolutely nothing against the many thousands of good and decent Arabs who live here in Israel and are our honored neighbors and friends, and we don't practice apartheid against them. But the refugees are entirely different. When they stop their acts of war and terrorism, we will gladly take down the barriers to their return. But we have an absolute historical right to possess this land of ours and to restore the Land of Israel to its rightful place as a Jewish State in the family of nations. As long as the Palestinian refugees persist in trying to destroy us, it is they who shall be destroyed."

Almogi squirmed in his chair, chafing at the oddly incongruous words of violence issuing from the red cupid's bow lips of the beautiful woman sitting across from him. His black eyes narrowed and he gritted his teeth.

"Mrs. Jordan refuses to see the forest for the trees," he responded. "There is a chilling parallel between the Palestinian Liberation Movement, Fatah, and her own liberation movement to which Mrs. Jordan belonged fifteen years ago. The Irgun's symbol was a hand holding a rifle over the map of Palestine. Do you know what Fatah's symbol is? It is a hand holding a rifle next to a *keffiyah* [Arab headdress] over the map of Israel! Are these Palestinians yearning for anything different than what we ourselves once longed for and killed for and died for: their own national identity?"

"We did not take away their identity," said Leah. "We did not disperse them from Israel. Their own leaders did. And now they want to come back and start all over as though nothing happened, as though there was never a war which they themselves started."

"That's ridiculous," snorted Almogi. "Most of them are just villagers, peasants who fled from warfare all around them. They have every right to return to their homes."

"And then how do we protect ourselves from them, Mr. Almogi! How do we keep them from committing terrorist raids on us day and night!" These weren't questions, they were bitter accusations.

"I just don't believe that that is a genuine problem. It's just an excuse we use to keep them from returning. But I strongly believe that if we integrated them into our economic society, they would be far less dangerous than they are now."

Leah glared at the small dark man sitting across from her. Her disgust with him was palpable in the stiffness of her body, in her downturned mouth.

"Some of us have become guilt ridden," she said, "filled with a sense that we have wronged the Palestinians. I think that is absolute nonsense. We have hurt them far less than what they did to us. It was their terrorism, their war, which caused their exile. Not anything we did. We only acted in self-defense.

Almogi was quick on the uptake. "It is an important element of our law that when someone commits an act in self defense, the violence of the defense cannot exceed the violence of the first attack. That is why it says in the Bible, 'An eye for an eye, a tooth for a tooth.' The law of retribution has always been to set things *equal*. But in response to Palestinian terrorism against us, we have increasingly come to require ten eyes for an eye, a hundred teeth for one tooth. And our reprisal attacks against the Palestinians have dramatically emphasized this deviation by us from our own biblical code of conduct. I am deeply troubled by the effect this is having on what has always been supposed to be the soul of the Jewish people: 'Let justice roll as a wave, and righteousness as a mighty stream.' Are these words of our Prophet Amos still what we truly believe?"

Nadia abu-Sittah was so fascinated and disarmed by this interview between the two violently opposed Israeli Knesset members that she couldn't even blink.

"Well, Mrs. Jordan, do you think there is some remedy to this impasse that the rest of us may be missing?" The interviewer asked the question with a shrug and a smile, but not sarcastically. It was obvious from his manner that he felt deep respect for Leah Jordan and that she was a person of real significance in Israeli politics. Her face was sad, grim, and she shook her head slowly. Her loosely chignoned hair bobbed.

"Aaron, before we Jews ever came to the Land of Israel, we spent forty years wandering in the desert. And when that was almost over, God ordered Moses to send spies into the promised land to see who lived in it and what it was like. Moses sent the leaders of the tribes into the promised land on this sacred mission. After forty days, the spies returned to Moses and reported that it was truly a land flowing with milk and honey, but that it was filled from one end to the other with fierce warriors living in fortified cities.

"Moses wanted to enter the promised land immediately, but the spies warned him against it. And they spread the report among the Israelites that there were fierce people living in the land. The Israelites wept and moaned, and they begged Moses not to lead them into deadly warfare in the Land of Israel. For the spies had told the people that the Land of Israel was '*eretz ochelet yosh'vehah hee*' [a land that devoureth the inhabitants thereof].

"Indeed, Israel is a land which devoureth its own inhabitants. We Jews have proved the truth of the biblical warning. But unlike the Jews of Eastern Europe waiting pitifully to be devoured, we have fought back this time. And we have fought with such ferocity that even many among our own people are shocked at the absoluteness of our determination to protect our Land of Israel and ourselves from the Palestinians who wish to devour us—"

The interviewer held up his hand to indicate that the time was up. He thanked both participants. Leah frostily refused even to look at Almogi.

Nadia watched the program end, but she didn't move. She was glued to the chair, thrilled by the sight of the woman who had saved her life those long years ago, but terrified by the woman's words reeking of violence and hatred.

Chapter Two

Ramadhan is the Islamic holy month. It is an adaptation of the Jewish High Holy Days and transforms the fast day of Yom Kippur into the fast month of Ramadhan. During the entire month, from sunrise to sunset, the Muslims neither eat nor drink. But after sunset each day, they eat especially elaborate feasts. The month ends with the '*eed al fitr*, a magnificent banquet, which celebrates Allah's gift of the Koran to Muhammad and the Muslims, just as the Jewish High Holy Days culminate in the holiday of Simchat Torah, "Rejoicing of the Law," celebrating God's gift of the Torah to Moses and the Jews.

Hamdi Attiyah attended a traditional Madrassa school in Amman supported by affluent Palestinian refugees. There were no girls. He studied the Koran four hours each day, learning to chant it by heart. He was constantly drilled in the basic elements of their Sunni Muslim faith. Then he spent another four hours studying mathematics, Arabic grammar, and history. Particularly during Ramadhan, when there was no food or drink during the days, he was lengthily and stringently drilled on the Koran and the life of Muhammad. The day before the *'eed al fitr*, Hamdi sat in the living room of the el-Rashid villa, while Hassan and Nadia cermoniously drilled him on the lessons of the Koran.

"Who are three great prophets of Islam?" asked Nadia, her cobalt eyes flashing with pride at her beautiful, wavy black-haired son.

"Abraham, Moses and Jesus," answered Hamdi.

"And who is Allah's messenger, His greatest prophet?"

"Muhammad!"

"And when did Muhammad leave the city of Mecca and go to the holy city of Medina?" asked Hassan.

"The *'hijra'* was in the year one," responded Hamdi.

"What is the *'jihad'*?"

"It is the 'striving' of the *fedayeen*, the self sacrificers, against the infidels; and it is the duty of every Muslim to convert the infidels to the true faith of Allah or to strive against them—to destroy them."

"What is a *'Muslim'*?"

"He is one who has 'surrendered' to the will of Allah."

"And what is *'Islam'*?"

"It is 'surrender' to the true faith as revealed by Allah's messenger, Muhammad."

"And what is a woman's place in Islam?" Nadia asked.

"It is to serve her husband and to rear his children in the true faith."

"What is the sin of the Jews?"

"The three Jewish clans of Medina refused to accept the truth of the Koran, so Muhammad and the fedayeen slaughtered most of them and drove the few survivors from the holy city."

"What is the obligation of all true believers?"

"We must continue the *jihad* against the Jews. We must once again make Jerusalem the third great city of Islam. As Muhammad said in his *Hadith* [Sayings]: 'O Jerusalem, the choice of Allah of all his lands! In it are the chosen of his servants. From it the earth was stretched forth and from it shall it be rolled up like a scroll. The dew which descends upon Jerusalem is a remedy for every sickness, because it is from the gardens of Paradise.'"

"And what is the 'Promised Land?'" asked Nadia, studying her son.

"The Yahudun falsely claim that it is their Israel. This is a lie.

The Yahudun are actually European Crusaders who have invaded our homeland Palestine. Palestine is the land promised to the faithful of Allah by his sacred prophet Muhammad, and al-Kuds [Jerusalem] is its holy center from which Muhammad ascended to the heavens."

"And what is the holocaust?"

"It is what the Yahudun have done to us. It is the destruction of our people which began with the perfidy of the British, when they groveled like cowards to the Zionist pigs and agreed to partition *our* land to the Jew scum, and then it is the forced exile of our people from our promised land beginning with the massacre of our family at Deir Yassin and continuing to the treacherous attacks on us even today." Hamdi's passionate eyes sparkled.

Nadia and Hassan beamed with pride at Hamdi. He had learned well.

In Ramadhan 1961, Hamdi was thirteen years old, no longer a child, but now entering into his years of young manhood. He was already taller and stockier than Hassan. He was an excellent student, very intense and fervent, and a leader among his friends. He was for Nadia the only link which she had to the old, rich and gracious life of Palestine, where she had been so happy and secure. She doted on him, the seed of her former life, for he would herald their rebirth in *'awda*, their homeland. He was *Salach al-Din* [Saladin], destroying the infidels in a holy war and restoring Jerusalem to the true believers. As the feast of *'eed al fitr* arrived, the nights were quite cold. The feast was held indoors, with special sweets prepared for the occasion and gifts exchanged by everyone.

Hamdi's gift, from Hassan and Nadia, was a Kalachnikov submachine gun, the symbol of the fedayeen and the principal symbol of a Fatah boy's manhood. Hassan proudly handed it to him and watched the boy's face break into a broad smile. Now he was truly a man. Soon he would take part in the raids against the Jews which constituted *al-tariq al-fida'i*, the way of the fedayeen.

The next day, Hassan and Hamdi, and Samir and his youngest son Isam, drove over the barren dusty Judean Hills to East Jerusalem. As they entered the high-walled Old City, their excitement rose. It was a rare treat for them to go to the "third pearl of Islam," the sacred city of Muhammad. Both Hassan and Samir had lived there years ago, but now it was a dangerous place of bombs and Jewish terrorist attacks. And Jordan's King Abdullah and his grandson King Hussein had discouraged the reverence of the Palestinians for their former first city, hoping to suppress the growth of a Palestinian chauvinism which could endanger the stability of Jordan. Times like this, however, these special turning points in the life of a Palestinian Arab, required that he reassert his connection with 'awda. Hamdi had become a young man, and it was time for him to visit the golden Dome of the Rock and el-Kas Fountain and colorfully tiled al-Aqsa Mosque. They were all built on the ruins of the Second Temple of Jerusalem in the heart of the Old City, and one day the Arabs would destroy the "Third Temple," the newly reborn Jewish State which had become their tormentor and oppressor.

They toured the Haram on Mount Moriah where the mosques were located and then browsed through the teeming exotic souk. They sat on wrought iron chairs at a small and rickety round metal table at an outdoor Armenian cafe and drank tiny cups of heavily sweetened cardamom coffee. Then Hassan bought a poster of David Ben-Gurion, and they drove back toward Amman. About halfway, they stopped off the road in the Judean Hills and Hassan tacked the poster up on a tree stump. He got out the Kalachnikov, a box of cartridges, and unloaded clips.

"Hamdi, you load the clip like this," and he showed his stepson how to press the cartridges into the clip with his left thumb.

"Now hold it with your elbow slightly bent and aim with your right eye," and he demonstrated. He took careful aim at Ben-Gurion's broad forehead about twenty-five feet away and shot two bursts in rapid succession. All but one shot pierced the Israeli Prime Minister's skull.

"Okay, let me now," Hamdi said very excitedly. He pressed the button, extracted the clip, and slapped a loaded one into the submachine gun. He pulled back the extractor as Hassan had showed him and let it snap forward automatically chambering the first cartridge. He took careful aim and missed the tree.

"No Hamdi, shut your left eye and sight over the top of the barrel with your right eye. Breathe deeply and then hold your breath."

Hamdi followed directions and his first shots hit Ben-Gurion in the nose. His next shots were in his right cheek. He then let out his breath with a gasp, rested for a moment, held his breath again and fired a long burst. Seven of the shots went into the Prime Minister's face. Hassan, Samir and Isam clapped and hooted. Then Samir shot a clipful and Isam had his turn. They kept shooting until all hundred cartridges were spent and David Ben-Gurion was obliterated.

"Someday, if you are lucky, it will not be just his poster that you destroy," said Hassan.

Chapter Three

Joshua's thirteenth birthday was February 6, 1962, and Leah and Matt planned a big party for him and his friends as well as some of their own. The Jordans were no longer poor, since Matt had gone into private practice as a lawyer two years earlier. So they could afford to splurge a bit on a party, something that would have been too expensive when both Matt and Leah worked in the government.

In Israel, among the great majority of essentially secularized Jews, there was no synagogue ceremony marking the thirteenth birthday. These Israelis were not "observant"; they had shed the Orthodox adherence to the 613 Commandments. For them, the boy's thirteenth birthday was still a special day because of the customs surrounding it in older traditional Jewish life, but the celebration of it was simply a big birthday party without religious overtones.

Neither Matt nor Leah was observant. Leah's childhood and young womanhood in Vilna were burned out of her like soot during the Holocaust. The same with Matt. Many thousands of Jews had gone to the gas chambers singing, "*Ani ma'amin be'emuno shlemo be'vios hamoshiach, be'vios hamoshiach ani ma'amin* [I believe with perfect faith in the coming of the Messiah, in the coming of the Messiah I believe]." How many millions had perished with these words on their lips, but still He had not come. And the Land of Israel, the last refuge for the shattered handful of European Jews left barely alive, had been built not by the Messiah, but by Jewish terrorism and bloody opposition to British rule and battle after battle with the Arabs. By killing had Israel risen from the ashes, not by prayer.

The Jordans now lived in a stone house near the Old City of Jerusalem, in the Yemin Moshe Quarter. It was not a very large house, but it was comfortable and had a nice little grassy garden with two hearty tangerine trees and a thriving fig tree. Joshua's big day finally arrived, and more than forty of his friends descended on the quaint old house. They sat in the garden listening to records, the girls on one side giggling and the boys on the other side trying to look grown up and bored.

Matt and Leah entertained a few close friends in the small parlor. Menachem Begin was there with his wife, Aliza. And Ami Carmel, now also a Minister in the Knesset for the Cherut Party, was there with his wife. Matt had bought two bottles of fine brandy, and everyone was having a good time.

When the party had been going on for a few hours and the adults were becoming well mellowed by Matt's cognac, a girl ran into the parlor from the garden, her ponytail bouncing.

"Mrs. Jordan, Mrs. Jordan!" she ran up to Leah crying. "Joshua and two other boys are fighting!"

Leah jumped up and followed the girl outside. Matt ran out behind her and pulled Joshua off of another boy, a very close friend and classmate. The other boy's nose was bleeding and Joshua's was obviously broken. A third boy was sitting and crying, holding one hand over his right eye.

"What the hell has gotten into you?" Matt stormed at the thirteen-year-olds.

Begin looked after the boy on the ground. He would have a black eye, nothing serious. Someone helped the other boy stand up and swabbed the blood off his lips and chin.

"Well, I guess the party is over," said Leah to the unhappy looking group of boys and girls, and they began trailing out of the garden gate back to their homes. Leah tried to look cheery, standing by the gate saying good bye to the children she had known for years, all longtime friends and classmates of Joshua's.

While they were leaving, and Menachem and Ami were cleaning up the other two boys and making sure they were okay, Matt drove Joshua to Stephen Himmelstein's home a mile away. He had been their family doctor for many years. Joshua had to continually cough the blood out to keep from choking. An hour later, his nose set and taped, his eyes beginning to develop black raccoon rings, they got back in the car to drive home.

"Well, Josh, my dear lad, that was a hell of a nice way to treat your friends at your own birthday party."

Joshua stared out the window silently.

"Come on, son, how about an explanation?" Matt was a devoted and loving father, but he had no desire to be his son's pal, his buddy. He was his father, and that meant that when he asked a question, he got an answer. Still Joshua said nothing. Matt's brown eyes were lusterous with anger, his face becoming florid. He reached over and shook Joshua's shoulder.

"I'm talking to you, Joshua!"

The boy turned his blond head away from the front window and stared down at his feet, tears spilling from his eyes and falling off his cheeks.

"They called Mom a Nazi whore," he said in gasps between sighs and sobbing.

Tears immediately obscured Matt's vision, and he pulled the car to the curb and parked. He slid over on the front seat and put his arms around his son and they both cried.

"We'll talk when we get back home with Mom," he said to Joshua, and he slid back behind the wheel and drove to their house in Yemin Moshe. They walked through the front door and the adults were still in the parlor, polishing off the last of the cognac. In the hallway, Matt told Joshua to go on to his bedroom. They'd get rid of the guests and be in in a few minutes. Matt walked into the parlor, his shoulders slumped, his face flushed.

"What is it, Matt? What happened?" asked Leah fearfully, seeing his waxen eyes and defeated slouch. The others all looked at him with concern.

"One of the kids told him something about what happened to you in the Holocaust."

Leah was stunned and her eyes searched her husband's craggy face to see if he meant that Joshua had heard the really bad part, the filth. Matt nodded at her grimly.

"*Oy vey iz mir*," she groaned, slowly putting her hands over her eyes.

Matt sat down heavily in his armchair.

"Well, he's thirteen years old. That makes him a man to us Jews," said Begin. "Better he hears it from you than in the streets. God willing, he will understand, or at least trust you enough to store it up until he does understand."

"Leahleh, go to him now," Aliza said, getting up and taking her by the hand and pulling her out of her chair. "Tell him. He's a good boy. There's nothing else to do."

Matt got up and took Leah's hand, and they walked slowly to Joshua's room. Joshua was lying in bed, staring at the ceiling. Matt and Leah sat down on the edge of the bed. She took her son's hand in both of her own and spoke very quietly.

"We haven't told you before because you were too young. Now our tradition says you are a man. I am sorry you had to hear bad things from your friends. I am going to tell you myself. It is hard to understand these things, Joshua, but please try." As Leah told her son of her years in the Vilna Ghetto and Treblinka, Joshua looked at her in open-mouthed shock.

"There is no need to fight with anyone who says bad things about me, Joshua. It is only because they really do not understand how it was in the Holocaust. If they understood, they wouldn't say bad things. There is nothing I can do to undo what happened. We must all live with these things."

Joshua rolled over on his side, away from his parents, and his body shook with sobbing. Matt pulled Leah up off the bed and they left the room.

"He'll have to work it out for himself," said Matt to his wife. They went back into the parlor and joined their guests. They all talked quietly, somberly, dredging up memories that had long been shelved. Begin talked about his months in Lukiszki Prison in Vilna and more months in exile in Siberia. Leah listened to the familiar stories, and her mind dragged her unwillingly back to Vilna, back to Colonel Karl Mencken, the Angel of Death, the Prince of Darkness. Nazi whore....Jewish whore....

The slaughter at the Gaon Synagogue in Ghetto Two on the eve of Kol Nidre, the murder of her husband Daniel, is not just an isolated Aktion. It is the beginning of the liquidation of Ghetto Two. But the killing does not spill over into Ghetto One.

Leah does not report for work at the Ghetto One soup kitchen for several days. After a week, a Jewish policeman knocks on the door. "Mrs. Arad? Police Chief Krens requests that you come with me to his office."

Leah puts on a heavy overcoat. She picks Nachman up and wraps him in a small blanket. The policeman walks with them to the Judenrat.

She knocks on Krens' office door and enters. Nachman is asleep in her arms. Krens comes over to her and gently lifts the baby and puts him on the couch.

"I am, of course, totally sympathetic about you missing work this last week, but there is a problem with your mother, brother and baby. The Gestapo demands that all non-productive Jews be turned over to them for 'resettlement.'" The euphemisms "resettlement" and "special handling" mean extermination. And everyone knows that Krens is in charge of making the selection.

Still Leah says nothing. She waits for what she senses is coming.

"Of course, if your family were to be under my protection, they would be perfectly safe." Krens walks to his office door and slides the bolt closed. He walks over to her and pulls her to her feet. His breath is rancid. He feels her breasts and runs his hand over her flat stomach. He rubs the mound between her legs and runs his hands around her and fondles her buttocks and hips. She is petrified. He kisses her lightly on her forehead and smells her hair. Even in the Ghetto she manages to get soap and keep her body and hair clean.

He smiles pleasantly at her. "Return here this evening, Leah. You will live with me. I will get a crib for Nachman. Your mother and brother will stay at their apartment, and they will have my protection."

Leah puts on her coat. She walks to the couch and picks up the gurgling Nachman and walks through the door into the hallway and out of the Judenrat.

Rachel cries quietly when Leah tells her that she and Nachman are moving into the Jewish Police Chief's apartment. Leah does not tell her what happened with Isaac Krens, but Rachel knows. She can see it in her daughter's eyes. Leah is becoming the Police Chief's kurveh [whore] to save her mother and Nachman and Jonathan.

Leah is too beautiful and ripe to be lucky enough to live in anonymity in the Ghetto. Rachel knows that sooner or later this is bound to happen. At least they will now be under the protection of the Ghetto's most powerful Jew.

In early November, Gestapo headquarters gives orders to the Judenrat that there are to be issued a total of twelve thousand passes to the approximately twenty-eight thousand Jews remaining in the Ghetto. Each yellow pass holder can select "dependents" who will receive an equally official blue pass. The blue "family" pass holders can not include parents of the yellow pass holder.

The passes are delivered to Chief Krens' office for distribution. Leah *knows that she and Nachman and Rachel and Jonathan will receive the blue passes for Krens' yellow one. Rachel comes to the Judenrat and Leah makes her up heavily and pulls her hair back and combs it and covers it with a kerchief. Her pass picture is taken. Her pass identifies her as Krens' wife. He is forty-three years old. Rachel's pass says that she is forty-two, and Leah and Nachman and Jonathan have passes as their children. Not a very likely looking family, but many of the Ghetto's families are born in just this way during distribution week.*

Isaac Krens has slightly different plans, however. His younger widowed sister, Katerina, needs a blue pass. Krens has only been allotted four blue passes for his own use. He discards Rachel's picture and places Katerina's picture and description on the pass. He gives it to one of his police officers to deliver to Katerina.

The German Aktion *begins at midnight. Armored cars carrying soldiers of* Einsatzkommando 3 *enter the three gates of the Ghetto with hundreds of other soldiers running beside the cars. They flood the streets of the Ghetto. Spotlights are turned on and loudspeakers blare, "Attention! All Jews without yellow or blue passes assemble on the streets in an orderly fashion."*

Rachel is awakened by the noise and looks out her window to the street below. German soldiers scurry everywhere. They climb the mounds of dirty snow piled on the sidewalks and enter her apartment building. She hears the banging of rifle butts on the doors below. Terror grips her. She has not yet received her blue pass.

She throws an overcoat over her nightdress and runs out of the apartment to the back stairway of the building. There is a hiding place in the basement that had been used by some of the Jews during a previous Aktion. *The basement is pitch black and freezing, and she can hear other people's hushed voices from the tiny* malineh. *She gropes in the dark to a wall covered with shelves, which in better days has held stored flour and cornmeal and sacks of vegetables. She kneels at the bottom shelf and pushes the wood panel behind it. It clatters free. She rolls onto the shelf and into the closet-like hiding place dug into the earth behind the shelves. Two other Jews are there. They pull her in roughly and press the board back into place. They breathe shallowly, afraid of making any noise.*

It is twenty-three degrees below zero. Rachel shivers and slowly becomes numb. The other two are a young couple. They huddle together rubbing each other continuously to keep as warm as possible.

The Aktion *ends at dawn. The Germans herd over twelve thousand men, women and children out of the Ghetto and into the Ponar Forest for execution. But the roundups have not been completely successful. Almost four thousand of the doomed have hidden safely in every nook and cranny of the Ghetto. The Gestapo knows that it will have to smash the* malinehs *if it wants complete control of the Ghetto.*

Leah holds Nachman, hugging him to her chest, as she watches the diggers. Tears stream down her cheeks and turn to tiny ice crystals in the freezing wind. It is mid-morning, but the black overcast imparts a dusky pall to the courtyard of Rachel's apartment building.

Isaac Krens stands next to Leah. His gray face is grim. He calls out instructions to the two policemen digging the hole. The ground is frozen solid, and the hole grows slowly. Then it is finally finished. The two sweating policemen pick up Rachel. She is frozen stiff and wrapped in a canvas shroud. They place her in the grave.

Within two weeks, the Gestapo has another plan to ferret the illegals out of the malinehs *and trim the Ghetto to the permissible twelve thousand. Standartenführer Karl Mencken comes to the Judenrat to meet with Chief of Police Krens. Mencken was a Lutheran Minister in Nuremberg before the War and taught Old Testament Hebrew at the* Institut Für Evangelische Lutheran Studien, *the centuries-old Lutheran seminary. His expertise in Jewish affairs has made him invaluable to the* Totenkopfstandarten *[the "Death Head Regiment"], the elite troops specially selected to administer concentration camps, and he has rapidly risen in rank since he joined it in 1934.*

Mencken sits at Isaac Krens' desk in the Judenrat. Krens stands at attention in front of this handsome officer. Krens trembles.

Leah translates for the Colonel as he spells out his plans for a "pink pass aktion" to rid the Ghetto of slackers. Then he stands and comes around the desk and tells the trembling Krens to wait for him on the street below. And then he rapes her, forces her to do things she had never done before, degrades her. When it is over, when Krens comes running back into the apartment and sees her, he is ashamed. He is the top Jew in the Ghetto, but he cannot lift a finger to protect Leah from any German or Lithuanian, let alone a Death Head Regiment Colonel.

The "pink pass aktion" begins at noon three days later. It is bitter cold and snow falls heavily. This is the most thinly disguised of the liquidation roundups. The "registration" is in the large courtyard behind the Judenrat. A convoy of trucks drives up to the courtyard entrance. The loading of the three thousand Jews begins, shepherded by hundreds of German soldiers. The trucks make round trips to the Ponar Forest, returning to pick up more human cargo until the courtyard is empty, except for the fifty or so Jews who have been shot to keep the others in line.

Chief of Police Krens and Colonel Mencken walk into the dark and deserted courtyard to inspect the day's work. Only a squad of Death Head Regiment soldiers remain near the Judenrat.

As they walk toward the rear door of the Judenrat, Mencken draws his Mauser machine pistol and shoots a short burst point blank into Isaac Krens' temple. Krens sprawls flat in the frozen snow. Mencken doesn't miss a step. He enters the deserted building and runs up the stairs to Krens' office on the third floor. He goes through the office and into the apartment. Leah is sitting on the couch and rises uncertainly as he enters. Her mouth opens and she gapes at him in fear. He holsters his Mauser.

"Come with me. Bring a blanket."

"But where? My son. I can't leave my son." She is frantic. She points to Nachman, sleeping in his crib.

"I said come with me now, goddamit!" he screams at her.

"If I can't take my baby, shoot me here!"

Mencken looks hard at her. She is not bluffing. She does not appear to be terrified any longer.

"Okay, bring your baby. Wrap him in a blanket."

The Colonel walks into the bedroom and takes the quilt off the bed. He leads Leah by the hand into the darkened hallway and down the steps to the front door. He pushes her and Nachman into the corner of the foyer and drops the quilt on the floor.

He walks outside alone.

His driver snaps to attention in front of the command car, a Mercedes limousine. The streets are pitch black and deserted except for the ten Death Head soldiers standing by their truck near the courtyard entrance.

"Schnebel. Go back to the barracks with Krueger's squad. I'll drive myself."

"Jawohl, Herr Kommandant." Schnebel clicks his heels and walks over to the other men at the truck. They get in and drive quickly down the street to the Ghetto's main gate. When the street is empty, Mencken runs back into the Judenrat, picks up the quilt, and leads Leah to the car. He opens the backdoor, tells her to lie on the seat, and covers them with the quilt. He drives through the Ghetto gate and for about fifteen minutes through dark streets. "Leah, uncover yourself and your baby. We will walk quickly and calmly into my house."

They get out of the car. He holds her hand, and she carries Nachman.

*They walk in. He closes the door behind her and leads her into the parlor,
turning on the light as they enter. He sits Leah down and lectures her,
carefully, emphasizing each fact. "Your new name is Lara. Your baby is
Milos. You are a Lithuanian girl whose husband was killed in the bombing
of Vilna. No one will be able to question this or trace your story, since many
vital records were destroyed in the fire at Government House during the
bombing, and your apartment building at 10 Borozowa Street was
demolished with most of the tenants in it."*

*Leah has lead a cloistered life until the Ghetto. She is not known to
anyone but Jews and two or three Lithuanian policemen, so there is almost
no likelihood that anyone will recognize her. She will stay in the house at all
times. If for any reason she has to go outside, she speaks perfect Lithuanian
and German. Her blond hair and gray eyes make her look like a Christian.
There should be no problem.*

*Weeks pass and become months. Karl never talks to Leah. They do not sit
and chat. That is not why she is here. She is a piece of meat, fragrant and
beautiful and tender and succulent, but still just meat. If anything goes
wrong, anything than can harm Karl's world, he will kill her and Nachman
without a flicker of his eyelids. She knows that unquestionably. He often
gets drunk sitting late at night in the parlor drinking Steinhäger. And then
his usually gentle lovemaking turns brutal. And he is unable to ejaculate,
and he stuffs his penis up the other hole because it is tighter. She screamed in
pain the first time, and only the first time, because then he severely beat her.
So she has learned to let him do anything he wants to her and not to scream
or cry. Then he might not beat her. And she can keep on living, and so can
her baby.*

*In early May, Mencken comes home and tells her that they are leaving.
He has been given a new assignment, a real career maker. He is to direct the
construction and staffing of a vitally important detention center for enemies
of the Third Reich. He shows her where the place is on the map he spreads out
on the bed. It is in Poland northwest of Warsaw, where the picturesque Bug
River flows through pine forests, a quaint rural village named Treblinka.*

*That evening Leah lays Nachman down in his crib. She is frightened even
more than usual. Nachman begins to cry. She sings him a little lullaby, her
favorite, which her mother had sung to her as a baby:*

> *"Unter yiddele's viegele, shtayt a klor
>   veiss tzigele,
>   Dos tzigele iz gevoren handlen,*

Dos vet zein dein beruf,
Rozhinkes mit mandlen,
Schlof'zhe Yiddele schlof."

[Under my baby's crib is a pure white goat,
The goat will pull a peddler's cart
That will be my baby's trade,
Peddling raisins and almonds,
Sleep, my baby, sleep.]

A peasant's lullaby of a different world, she thinks. Oh God, let my baby
live. Please God, my shield, my protector, please let my baby live—

Leah pressed her eyes with her hand, trying to blot out the
memories. Joshua, looking as though he'd been beaten with a
baseball bat, pattered in stockinged feet to Leah, his head down,
and curled up in her arms in the big overstuffed couch on which she
was sitting. He cried softly. She hugged her son's head to her
breast, and silent tears flowed down her cheeks and wet his hair.

The others quietly tiptoed out of the parlor, leaving mother and
son to heal each other.

Chapter Four

"I am asking you this as a favor. No one else can defend this
man," said Farid Qahmel to Matthew Jordan.

"But Farid, I'm not a criminal lawyer. You need someone who
knows the criminal law. I've been practicing international law for
fifteen years."

"It's you we need," Qahmel insisted. His blue eyes were flat and
hard. He was a short man, very fat, in his mid-fifties, with a
carefully combed and coiffed bouffant of brown hair graying at the
temples. He spoke cultured and perfect Hebrew, gesturing with
exaggerated effeminate hand movements.

Matt was very uneasy. He squinted at the Arab as if to squeeze
him out of the room. The Knesset had just two weeks ago repealed
the emergency restrictions applying to the Arabs living in Israel,

and already there was a test case, a major cause célèbre. All of Israel was talking about it. Two days ago, an undercover policeman in Jaffa had seen several Arab men entering and leaving a small house in the Arab section. He had become suspicious that something was afoot, but he didn't know just what. So he had watched the house for an hour and the activity was constant. He decided to see what was going on. So he simply pried open the back door of the small house and crept inside. The owner of the house took him for a burglar and shot him. He died in surgery a few hours later.

Under the old emergency regulations, the policeman would have had a right to enter the Arab's home furtively to investigate "suspicious activities which the policeman had reasonable grounds to believe may be inimical to the State of Israel." It was a hangover from the British Mandate period, when house to house searches by the British occurred with regularity. The Jews had adopted these same regulations with respect to Arab citizens.

Two weeks ago, however, these emergency regulations had largely been abrogated. On such flimsy grounds for suspicion as were involved in this case, where no obvious crime was being committed right before his eyes, a Jewish policeman could not simply sneak into an Arab's home. He had to go through the same procedures that he would if he were intending to search the house of a Jew: he would have to supply facts to a magistrate supporting his supposition that a serious crime was being committed, and if the magistrate were convinced of the nature of the crime and the identity of the criminals, he would then issue a search warrant for the house. Despite the new law, however, there was an outcry in Israel against the Arab killer of the Jewish policeman. It was learned that the Arab had been the leader of a suspected Palestinian terrorist group called the "Heroes of the Return," and the traffic in and out of his house was assumed by everyone to be related to terrorist activity.

"Listen Farid, my friend. In a couple of days, the son of a bitch will probably be lynched, and I can't even say that I'd blame anybody for it. I really don't think that I can help you."

"What the hell kind of hypocrite are you?" Farid sneered at Matt in disgust. "The Knesset abolishes the apartheid legislation, and the first goddam time an Arab exercises his right to protect his home from an apparent burglar or worse—just as every Jew is granted that right—you tell me it's okay if the Jews string him up by the balls!"

"Now, listen, dammit! That Arab is a terrorist, and there aren't too many of us Jews who have much sympathy for him killing one of our policemen."

Farid Qahmel glared at Matt with a look of incredulity, of utter disbelief and disgust. "Do you hear what you're saying, my friend? You and I both know that we are dealing with a principle that transcends the otherwise mundane facts of this case. The point is that when your policeman broke into this Arab's home, he had no probable cause to believe that terrorism was afoot, he had no warrant, and he would have been shot the same way if he entered a Jew's home! And no one would have uttered a peep!" He slashed the air with oddly long and slender fingers.

Matt knew that Farid was right. They had been friends since 1949, since the bloody War of Independence had ended. Farid was from an old aristocratic family of Jaffa, and he had chosen to remain in his home rather than flee from Israel like so many others. He was a wealthy man and one of the leading lawyers of Arab Israel. Matt had needed him many times for favors, to help work out problems between the Arabs and Jews. Farid had never let him down. Now he was calling in his marker.

"Why me, Farid?" He looked at the Arab with pleading brown eyes. His tousled brown hair fell over his forehead, and he ran his fingers through it nervously, smoothing it back. "I have to work six days a week just to stay up with my own caseload. I have to go to New York or London at the drop of a hat. I really don't have the time for this. Maybe I could let you have one of my associates," Matt said lamely.

Farid simply sat in front of the desk, staring at Matt. His look said everything. Matt finally shrugged his shoulders resignedly.

"All right. I'll talk to the son of a bitch." What else could he say? "But if he really is a piece of garbage, I promise you that I will not represent him."

Farid was all smiles, all Arab politeness again. The two old friends chatted lightly for a few more minutes, and the Arab lawyer left. Matt called the Tel Aviv jail and informed the officer in charge that he would be visiting his potential client later that afternoon. At a little after three, one of Matt's associates drove him from

Jerusalem to Tel Aviv jail and waited for him outside in the car. During the entire hour ride, Matt studied the old emergency regulations which had been superceded by the new "civil rights" legislation. The law had clearly changed. There was no legal question about it. Arabs were now protected by the warrant requirement. Unless the policeman had reasonable grounds to believe that a serious crime was being committed before his very eyes and that there was some pressing need for him to search and arrest immediately, he had to go to a magistrate and apply for a warrant. This policeman had not done so, and by his own statements before he died, there were insufficient facts to support any pressing need permitting a warrantless search.

Matt sat in the bare stone interview room. It had no windows, its lighting was poor, and it had two straight backed wooden chairs with a small card table between them. They don't do much to make defense lawyers comfortable here, Matt thought to himself.

The Arab was brought in menacled with a belly chain that had a segment attached to both ankles and another segment attached to handcuffs. He shuffled into the room and clinked into the empty chair, looking suspiciously at Matt.

"My name is Matthew Jordan. Farid Qahmel has asked me to talk to you to see if I'll take your case."

"Fuck you and all your Jew bastard brothers! An Arab can't get a fair trial in front of Jews." The prisoner scowled at Matt, savage and sullen. He was about thirty years old and very dark, and his several day stubble made him look even darker and even more forbidding. He was tall, slender and intense.

"Well, we're off to a very good start," said Matt, looking the prisoner in the eye. "If you're really thrilled about spending the rest of your life in prison, keep it up." Israel had no death penalty. Its penalty for capital cases was life imprisonment. The Arab's face changed from black hatred to a look of deep fear, and his black eyes clouded with forboding.

"I thought he was a burglar or a robber. He wasn't in uniform, he had no badge or anything. I had no way of knowing." The Arab's Hebrew was fluent, educated.

"You sound like you've had some college?" Matt said to him questioningly, trying to draw him out, to relax him so they could really talk.

"I graduated with a history degree from the Hebrew University of Jerusalem. Now I sell shoes in Tel Aviv. It's not easy for an Arab to get a job." The last was said without malice, rather matter-of-factly.

"Yes, particularly if he's a terrorist," said Matt slowly, scrutinizing the young man's reactions.

"I am not a terrorist."

"Well, what is this report I have here?" Matt shuffled through his papers and pulled out three mimeographed sheets, a report from the Tel Aviv Prosecutor's Office. "Hamid al-Alami. Reputed leader of 'Heroes of the Return,' no visible means of support, constant activity in his home from confirmed members of anti-Israel groups." Matt ticked off the facts and once again studied Hamid.

"It is all true," said the Arab with a shrug. "Except that I sell shoes at a store in Tel Aviv, on Dizengoff Street, and that's how I earn my living. The rest is true."

"So you really think that I'm going to defend an Arab terrorist for murdering a Jewish policeman?" Matt asked him in disgust, beginning to rise from the table.

"My group has never engaged in violence. We do oppose the Jewish usurpation of our homeland, but we do not commit terrorist atrocities. To the Jews, every Arab who longs for a Palestinian 'awda is a terrorist. But that is not true. I lead a group of others like myself, sick of the dual laws—one for Jews, one for Arabs—sick of selling shoes after we beat our brains out and pauperized our families for a University degree. But we are not terrorists. I want Israel to change, I want my people to have the homeland that was promised us by the United Nations in 1947, but my group doesn't kill anyone."

Matt sat back down in the uncomfortable wooden chair. He listened.

"I took several classes from Professor Jacob Tal, the greatest historian at the Hebrew University. He lectured about the Jewish biblical concepts of social justice, the gift of the Jewish people to the world, the social conscience of the great Prophets of Israel. You know what Professor Tal's favorite line is from the Bible, Mr. Jordan?" Matt shook his head, drawn to this Arab's intensity, his disarming candor. "His favorite line is from the Prophet Micah: 'It hath been told thee, O man, what is good, and what the Lord doth require of thee: only to do justice, to love mercy, and to walk humbly with thy God.'" Matt listened in rapt attention. Hamid al-Alami stared at him, glum and sullen.

"But it really isn't true today, is it Mr. Jordan? Where Arabs are concerned, you Jews no longer care about justice and mercy." He paused again. "The day that policeman broke into my home, I had been meeting with my friends—other members of my organization —all day. We want to join Rakach, the Israeli Arab party, and we were planning our strategy. That's all, Mr. Jordan. I killed that policeman, and under the same circumstances you would have killed him too. But you wouldn't end up sitting here in shackles."

Matt shook his head resignedly and frowned. "Mr. al-Alami, I don't know what I can do for you, I really don't. But I will represent you." The Arab showed no emotion. He simply nodded. Matt left the room and walked out to the waiting car. *You jackass,* Matt kept saying to himself on the ride back to Jerusalem, *you're the one who's going to get lynched!*

Al-Alami stayed in jail pending his trial. For serious crimes in Israel, there was no such thing as a bail bond. But the trial was held just three weeks later. There also wasn't any such thing as a "jury of his peers" in Israel. His jury would be the standard tribunal of three Jewish judges who would hear the case and decide the Arab's fate. The public response to Matt Jordan defending the Arab terrorist killer was acidic. He received many calls, both at home and at his office, calling him a traitor. There were even a few obscene telephone calls to Leah and two run-ins that Joshua had in school. It was not the best of times.

As the trial day neared, demonstrators carrying posters calling for repeal of the new civil rights legislation vied with other protestors carrying placards calling for the death penalty for Arab terrorists. They marched in front of the Jordan home as well as many public places. Matt was accompanied by a unit of Tel Aviv policemen who ushered him into the District Courthouse through the unhappy mob outside. The trial was very short. The Arab admitted everything charged against him, except he denied being a terrorist. In any event, the statements of the policeman before his death clearly indicated that he had not had reasonable grounds to enter the house without a warrant, and indeed, he didn't even have sufficient evidence of illegal activity to support the issuance of a warrant. Under the new civil rights legislation, the Arab had the same right to protect the sanctity of his home by the use of deadly force as did any Jew in Israel.

A tense and disturbed tribunal delivered the verdict of the Court late in the afternoon of the first day of the trial: Hamid al-Alami was acquitted. His shackles were removed. He was escorted out the back of the courthouse and whisked back home. The three judges also ducked out the back. Matt had to go through the mob of angry Jews in front of the building. They were on the verge of violence over the verdict and Matt's part in it. As the policemen assigned to protect him hustled him to his car, a reporter for the television news service pressed near him and asked him to come to the studio for an interview. Matt directed his driver to take him to the Israel Broadcasting Authority's studios. He went on TV in a live interview a half hour later. Virtually everyone in Israel watched the evening news anyway, and the magnitude of the day's events had drawn all of them to their television sets. Leah and Joshua watched him in their Jerusalem home. Matt had called her earlier and told her he might have some trouble getting back to Jerusalem for a few days. Leah and Joshua were frightened, fearful for his safety.

"We present to you tonight one of Israel's leading lawyers, Matthew Jordan, who today successfully defended Hamid al-Alami, the Jaffa Arab charged with murdering a Jewish police-man." The interviewer asked several questions of Matt concerning the background of the case and the facts involved as well as the application of the new civil rights law.

"And what do you really think of the verdict, Mr. Jordan, in the context of Israel's continuing problems with Palestinian terrorism? What effect will today's verdict have on our ability to curb terrorist activity before it is permitted to occur? Don't *we* have the right of self-defense anymore?"

"It is not a question of self-defense. It is the much more fundamental question of human rights. Why shouldn't Israel's Arab citizens enjoy the same legal protection that the Jews have always had? We cannot treat them as second class citizens and still retain our moral standing among the civilian nations of the world. That is what our new civil rights act is all about. And if affording our Arab citizens the equal protection of our laws results in some increase in our internal security problems, then that is the price we must pay for being a democracy that believes in the fundamental equality of all human beings.

"When the Nazis passed the Nuremburg Race Laws in 1935, making Jews second class citizens of Germany, not a cry was raised in protest by the many good people of the Third Reich. They just let it happen. It was but a short leap from legal inequality to out and out repression, and then to the gas chambers and the ovens. We Jews know better than any other people in the world the fundamental corruption that destroys a society which permits the human rights of some of its citizens to be amputated, just because of their race or creed or religion. Once you cut off their rights, it becomes increasingly easier to cut off their heads." Matt spoke slowly, and his voice was shaking with emotion.

"You know something I am a bit reluctant to admit? It was this young Arab, Mr. al-Alami, who had to remind me how we Jews are supposed to conduct our lives. He confronted me with the great line from our Prophet Micah, about what the Lord requires: 'to do justice, to love mercy, to walk humbly with God.' Do you know what that really means?" Matt looked hard at the interviewer, who was captivated by the lawyer's magnetism. Then Matt once again looked into the eye of the camera.

"I learned Hebrew as a foreign language when I was a young man, because I was born and reared in the United States. Hebrew is a Semitic language, entirely different from English which is an Indo-European language. English is a language of nouns and adjectives. Hebrew is not. It is a language of verbs, transitive action words, and most of our nouns and adjectives are simply forms of verbs, forms of action. When the Prophet Micah asks, 'What does the Lord require of you?' he gives the answer with action verbs: '*asot mishpat*' [*to do* justice], '*ahavat chesed*' [*to love* mercy], '*v'hatznaya lechet im elohecha*' [and *to walk humbly* with thy God].

"Micah does not tell us that to be a Jew requires us to *believe* in justice or to *have faith* in God or any dogma. Other religions are based on these premises. 'Believe in me and thou shalt be saved' is an entirely non-Jewish concept. To Jews, it is not what we say we believe that matters, it is how we *act*, how we *do justice*, how we *love mercy*. The Prophets of Israel require us to *demonstrate* that we walk humbly with God by what we *do*, not by what we say or pray or tell people we believe.

"And we have demonstrated that today. We have *done* justice to a fellow human being. The Bible repeatedly call us Jews 'a stiff necked people,' a very contentious bunch. We have all kinds of beliefs, from the ultra-orthodox to the atheists, from democrats to communists, from Hasidim with long caftans and fur-trimmed stremels to men and women in shorts and tee shirts who have never even been in a synagogue. But we are all Jews. Other religions have splintered over tiny differences in beliefs, they have become warring factions and enemy camps over vague differences of faith and theology. Not the Jews. With all our disparity, with all our contentiousness, with all our squabbles and fights, we have through two thousand years remained one people.

"This is so because at the bottom of our sense of peoplehood, the fundamental thread which ties us all together and makes us into the 'Jewish People' is the absolutely inviolable demand of the Prophets of our Bible that we actually *live* God's laws, that we do justice and do mercy to every person in our midst, whether he is a Jew or a 'stranger'. It is that plain, that basic. And that is what happened today. Nothing more, nothing less. We *did* justice."

Matt's eyes were ardent, glistening. The interviewer's mouth was partly open as he stared at the lawyer.

"I'm sorry for going on like that," said Matt. "I don't mean to lecture like some pompous professor, and I don't have the qualifications to."

The interviewer regained his composure. "Not at all, Mr. Jordan. I'm certain that our listeners are interested in what you say. But one thing bothers me. While we afford the Arabs the highest ethical commitments of our faith and our way of life, they seem to be rewarding us only with skepticism and terrorism. The situation is asymmetrical, to say the least."

"Well, I guess there's no easy remedy for it, no facile answer." Matt paused a moment in thought. "It's like the story by Peretz, '*Im Lo L'mallah Mizeh*' [If Not Higher Than That]. There lived a saintly rabbi, a *Tzadik* [Righteous man] in the village of Nemerov. And every year just before the High Holy Days, the *Tzadik* would disappear and not return until Rosh Hashanah. And he wouldn't even go to the synagogue to lead his flock in the important prayers preceding the High Holy Days. The Hasidim, the pious ones, said that he went to Heaven each year to implore God to be good to His people. The Litvaks, the skeptics, said that he was really an evil man who used this time to steal from the houses of those who were at prayer in the synagogue.

"There came a Litvak to Nemerov who decided to resolve the mystery once and for all. He hid in the *Tzadik's* closet one night before Rosh Hashanah and waited for the *Tzadik* to awaken. The *Tzadik* got out of bed, dressed in rags, put a bandanna over his face, took a gunny sack and an axe, and went into the nearby forest. Snow was thick on the ground. The Litvak followed stealthily behind, now strong in his conviction that the rabbi was really a thief and probably even an axe murderer.

"The rabbi cut wood, bundled it in the gunny sack, slung it over his shoulder, and went to the tiny shack of a poor sickly Christian widow. Her son was a vicious anti-Semite who lived on the other side of the village. The *Tzadik* knocked on the window and called out, 'Firewood for sale.'

"From the shack came a weak thin voice, 'But I have no money, and I am too weak even to get out of bed to start a fire.'

"The *Tzadik* went into the freezing house and the Litvak crept to the window to listen. 'This wood is only one prutah a sack,' said the *Tzadik*, 'and I will tend your fire for just one more prutah.'

"But I have no money,' wailed the sick woman. 'I'll never be able to pay. And I can tell by your accent you're a Jew. Why would you help me?'

"Because you need a fire so you won't freeze to death,' said the rabbi as he busied himself making a fire in the frigid shack.

"The Litvak went to the synagogue and the people were once again discussing the *Tzadik's* puzzling absence. How could he not be present for such a vital thing as reciting 'Slichos,' the Prayers of Forgiveness? 'He must be a crook!' yelled the skeptical Litvaks.

"To drown out their yells, the pious Hasidim bellowed, 'He is in Heaven! He is in Heaven!'

"And the Litvak walked to the podium, quieted the congregation, and said, 'Yes, if not higher than that.'"

Matt Jordan looked again at the interviewer, and this time the man had nothing to say. He just listened.

"We cannot expect the Arabs to embrace us like brothers. We have all been through too much. But despite their skepticism, despite *anything*, we must give them justice, we must act righteously toward them. That is what it means to be a Jew, to be a Jewish State."

Matt waited in the studio for about an hour after the interview ended. He visited with an old friend who was one of the directors of the Broadcasting Authority. Then he ventured slowly out the front door, not knowing if he would be mobbed by demonstrators. No one was there. His associate drove him back to Jerusalem and the pickets were gone from the sidewalk in front of his house. An old man and someone else, maybe his son, were on their hands and knees on the sidewalk near the entrance to the house, and in the beams of flashlights, they were using steel wool to sand off the swastika which had been painted there just two weeks before.

Chapter Five

Dalia Almogi had black almond shaped eyes and olive skin and long black gleaming hair. When she spoke, it was with the soft guttural speech of the Sephardim. Ashkenazim, Jews of European descent, did not speak Hebrew with these soft gutturals and other Arabic sounds, as did the Sephardim, "Oriental Jews" from the Arab countries. She was Moroccan.

Her family had come to Israel from Morocco's capital, Rabat, in 1953 when Dalia was three years old. Her father had taught French and Arabic in a private high school in Rabat until the resentment against Israel and the Jews had become so fierce that his life was threatened several times. They had been able to take very few of their belongings with them from Morocco, and the government forbade transfers of money by Jews leaving the country, so they came penniless.

They lived in a tent village on welfare money for about sixteen months, supported meagerly by the resettlement section of the Jewish Agency. Then her father had become disenchanted with the Ashkenazic prejudice which was keeping him from finding a teaching job. He had had a religious upbringing, so his Hebrew was fluent. That was not the problem. The problem was that he was a *"Marakai,"* a Moroccan Jew, and the European Jews did not permit *Marakai'im* to integrate easily. With a sense of bitterness and resentment, he studied the Israeli system of government and decided to start his own political party.

Amos Almogi was an attractive and vibrant man and a captivating speaker, and he very quickly succeeded in gathering around him leading oriental merchants and professionals. He formed a party which was called "Mizrachim" [Easterners] and became its salaried leader. They were then able to move out of the tent city to a small house in Jerusalem. Dalia had three younger brothers and a sister, so it was cramped, and they didn't have a lot to eat. But it was far better than a tent.

In the same election in 1955, when Leah Jordan was elected to the Knesset on Cherut's list, Almogi and four others were elected on the Mizrachim list. He and his colleagues then helped form the coalition making Mapai the lead party. Almogi had then been made Assistant Minister of Education, a rather elusive job but a nice title, and he had continued to serve in all of the Mapai coalition cabinets including the present one, in which he was a full-fledged Minister Without Portfolio, commanding a large coalition block of nine other Mizrachim members of the Knesset. He had become a powerful force to be reckoned with in Israeli politics, one of the spokesmen for the Sephardim.

Many Sephardic Jews had become Israel's lower class. Ashkenazic parents did not urge their children to take up with the Sephardim. For one thing, many were poor and unskilled. For another, their sexual morality was slum Arab or French-Moroccan, and that was even far looser than the general laxity of Israeli morés. So Askenazic mothers often blinked and swallowed hard when their children brought home a Sephardic boyfriend or girlfriend, and fathers gave little heart-to-heart talks about "sticking with your own kind." But Joshua did not hear this talk at home, not ever, not from Leah and Matt.

Dalia Almogi was a junior in the same high school that Joshua attended. They lived about a mile apart in Rehavia, Jerusalem's diplomatic quarter, which housed many foreign embassies and where many of Israel's government leaders lived.

More and more during Joshua's senior year, he would bump into Dalia in the hallway at school, he would sit down across from her at lunch, nonchalantly, acting as though he didn't notice her. But they both noticed, and when Joshua looked into her deep black eyes, he always lost his tongue.

Maybe it had started as just the inner thrill a teenager gets when he puts one over on his parents, that first induced Joshua to ask her out on a date, and then another and another. And perhaps it was the same thing that motivated her to accept—at least at first. The children of two mortal enemies in Israel's Knesset dating behind their parents' backs. It was exciting, dangerous, funny.

After all, Dalia was well familiar with the vivid French and Arabic expressions which her father periodically used to describe Leah Jordan. The Oriental Jews didn't swear in Hebrew, Hebrew being the "holy tongue." They swore in French or Arabic or Italian or Persian or Berber, depending on where they were from. Her father's favorite description of Mrs. Jordan, which Dalia had overheard him use several times while entertaining close party colleagues at their home, was a viciously elegant Arabic slur: "She is the offspring of a camel, whom her father met at a desert mirage, and while it was chewing its cud with its back turned, sodomized and fucked; it is as yet unknown from which orifice Leah Jordan emerged." Dalia snickered at the image. Joshua's grandfather may have been a camel fucker, but Josh sure was a doll.

And Joshua too was steeped in his mother's stories of her many bitter encounters with Amos Almogi. At home she often unloaded her repertoire of Yiddish dirty words to describe him: "*schmuck*" [prick], "*tuchus*" [asshole], "*mumzer*" [bastard], and a special one she reserved only for Almogi, "*kackerleh*" [little turd].

Joshua and Dalia's meetings were more and more frequent during the school year. Their partings became longer, more lingering and sweeter. One Saturday evening, they met downtown and talked until after midnight. Then Joshua drove them on his Vespa to the Valley of the Cross, a huge field next to the Hebrew University, and a favorite spot for lovers to melt into the shadows of the small hill marking the university's northern border. They lay next to each other in the grass and they kissed. He touched her breasts under her light sweater and blouse. Her nipples were large and firm like blueberries. She pressed herself against his body and her hip rubbed the bulge in his pants.

"Joshua?"

"Yes."

"Do you like me?"

"You know I do."

"Let's wait a bit."

"I can't. I'll go crazy."

"I think you'll be all right."

"I swear I'll die."

"Joshua, I don't want to add to the stories everyone tells about Moroccan girls. Let's wait a while." She sat up and began straightening her skirt and blouse and sweater and hair. Joshua lay in the grass, bemoaning the black fate that had done this to him, wanting to make love to her, to hold her and make her his. But he didn't want to hurt their relationship. This was not just a passing crush.

They sat together for another ten minutes in silence, and he wrapped his arm around her and hugged her to him and kissed her hair and her forehead and her eyebrows and her eyes and her ears and her nose. It was late. He drove her to within a block of her home and dropped her off. They would meet again next Saturday night.

Sunday morning is Israel's Monday, and Joshua got up late for school. By the time he got down to breakfast, his parents were almost through. His father was as usual reading the newspaper at the table, and his mother was sipping a cup of coffee. Joshua sat down and caught his mother's angry glance.

"Good morning, everybody," said Joshua cheerfully.

"Morning," grunted Matt.

"I got a phone call last night from Essie Haberman. She says she was shopping and noticed you out with a very pretty girl," said Leah slowly, quietly.

Oh shit, thought Joshua. Here it comes.

"Essie said she recognized the girl."

Matt kept his face glued to the newspaper, the way he did when he was ignoring Leah because she was in one of her pissed-off moods. Aw shit, Joshua thought, she's gonna beat my brains out with her coffee cup.

"Essie said she once met the girl at a Mizrachim party reception, and that she was introduced by her father—" Leah paused, curling her lips as if to show that the mere saying of the name was like trying to swallow donkey shit, "Amos Almogi."

Joshua looked at his empty plate. He glanced up to his father for help. Still reading his goddam paper. No help there.

"Of course, she could have been wrong. You know Essie," Leah said slowly, waiting for her dear little boy to answer before she castrated him.

"Mom, I was meaning to tell you. Her name is Dalia, and she is really—"

"*Bist di mishugga?*" [Are you crazy?], screamed Leah at him in Yiddish. She always lapsed into Yiddish when she was screaming at Matt or Joshua.

"*Er iz a mumzer fun gehenna!*" [He is a bastard from Hell!] She was at high pitch now, full swing.

"Now Leah, take it easy. Joshua didn't do anything terrible," soothed Matt.

"Nothing terrible!" she shrieked. "Nothing terrible! My own son goes out with my worst enemy's daughter and makes me the laughingstock of my friends! Nothing terrible?"

"Now Leah, just cool down. What is between you and Almogi in the Knesset has nothing to do with Joshua or me or any of your friends. And you know it. Now just cool off." Matt stroked her shoulder and she began to calm down.

"She's really a very nice girl, Mom, and I—"

"Shut up and get out of here. You're late for school," said Leah disgustedly.

Joshua, pleased to escape so easily with all his parts intact, quickly left the house.

Across town, the same scene was being played out, except this one was in gutter French. The informant had been one of Amogi's observant friends who ran a candy store on Ben-Yehuda Street.

"*Mais non, Papa. Il est un tres brave garcon, tres—*" [But Daddy, he's a very nice fellow, very—]

"*Merde!*" he screamed at Dalia. "*Est-ce que tu folle?*" [Are you crazy?] I have been so humiliated! You and that bitch's whelp!" His black eyes blazed with indignation.

Finally, her mother calmed him down and Dalia fled off to school.

Well, she thought to herself as she walked to school, that's over. And I'm still alive. God, I hope Mrs. Jordan didn't find out, too. At least now she's a bitch instead of half of a she-camel. I wonder if that's a step up?

* * *

His mother would not be home from the Knesset until at least six o'clock. She never was. His father had finally gone to Haifa on business for a couple of days. So Joshua and Dalia were going to be alone in the big Jordan house with a whole afternoon to themselves. Joshua was very excited.

He picked Dalia up on his scooter at two-thirty. She wrapped her arms around him and pressed her cheek against his back all the way back to his house.

Joshua led her by the hand up the stairs to his room. She followed eagerly. She too was very excited. They had been planning this for weeks. Dalia had already ruined several nice outfits on the dewy grass at the Valley of the Cross.

He closed and locked the door. She had never been in his room. It was small and had a twin bed. There was a red and blue University of Arizona pennant tacked to the wall over the small desk. Joshua's father's alma mater. Next to the pennant was a group photograph of Joshua's soccer team. In the corner was a small bookcase with the Bible, a few history textbooks, and the ubiquitous volume of collected poetry by Israel's poet laureate, Chaim Nachman Bialik. Dalia walked up to the bookshelf and thumbed one of the volumes, suddenly bashful at being alone with Joshua in his bedroom. It seemed so grown up, so serious. Scary.

Joshua pulled off his polo shirt and sat down on the edge of his bed. He untied his sneaker laces and kicked them off.

"Dalia."

She was now glued to the bookcase, her back to him. He got up and walked to her and caressed her from behind softly fondling her breasts. Her scent tantalized him. It was like a faint warm spice coaxed out of a thicket of clove trees by a radiant sun. She turned around and they embraced and kissed deeply. Their breathing came quickly, excitedly. She unbuttoned her blouse and reached around her back and unhooked her bra. She stood still in front of him letting him undress her. She stepped out of her skirt and lay on top of the bedspread in her lacy beige panties. Joshua unbuttoned his levis and pulled them and his shorts down together.

Joshua slid the delicate panties down Dalia's tawny buttocks and over her silky brown slender legs.

"Do you have a thing for protection?" she whispered as he rubbed her.

"No. But don't worry. I'll be careful."

But he was not careful, because he couldn't make himself be. And it didn't matter to her by that time either. She needed him so deeply, so interminably. And each time they joined it was like the first time for both of them, and it almost was. For three hours they lay together, touching and rubbing and massaging and learning each other, intoxicated by the newness and uniqueness and unparalleled pleasure of love and loving. And then Dalia lay in a luxuriant bath which Joshua scented with a few drops of Leah's treasured Nina Ricci perfumed bath oil, and he washed her. He sat on the edge of the tub with his feet in the water, and she washed him. They felt very grown up. They dressed and went downstairs. It was almost six o'clock.

"I'm going to make dinner for you and your mother."

"Maybe that's not such a good idea yet, Dalia."

"Look, she has to get used to me, and the sooner the better. I'm going to be around a long time."

Joshua had no argument with that, and he smiled and nodded to the dusky black haired beauty. Her cheeks were flushed with the excitement of the last few hours. Her black almond eyes glistened.

She went to the kitchen and opened the refrigerator and studied the contents. She took out an eggplant, a bell pepper, two small onions, and a small bud of garlic.

"I'll make Moroccan style eggplant salad," she called from the kitchen. Joshua came in and watched her busy herself at the counter. He fished the stove top eggplant roaster out of one of the unruly cluttered lower cabinets and got her the grater. She put the whole eggplant on the roster on a medium lit burner and covered it and then went to grating and mincing and chopping the other ingredients. After a few minutes, she came back out into the dining room wiping her hands on one of Leah's aprons.

Joshua was sitting at the dining table, a book opened before him. "I thought we'd study a little *Shulchan Aruch*, Dalia."

"Do you really think your mother will believe we've been here studying all afternoon?" she laughed.

"You don't think so?" he said to her with mock consternation. "Oy vay!"

Both of them laughed. She sat down beside him. "This is my favorite section of the *Shulchan Aruch*, Dalia." He pointed to

Chapter 150 of the large book. The full six volume set of Jewish laws had been compiled by Joseph Karo, a Spanish rabbi, in the sixteenth century. It contained all of the minute rules of everyday life surrounding the 613 commandments which every orthodox Jew was expected to observe. This one volume abridged *Shulchan Aruch* was one of his mother's "nostalgia books"—Joshua called them—one of several books she kept around to remind her of the Old World, the long past world of east Europe, now so foreign and unbelievable to the modern young Jews of Israel.

Joshua read aloud, forcing himself to sound serious like a strict old yeshiva teacher:

> "Men of strong constitution who enjoy the pleasures of life, having profitable pursuits at home and are tax exempt, should perform their marital duty nightly. Laborers who work in the town where they reside, should perform their marital duty twice weekly; but if they are employed in another town, only once a week. Merchants who travel into villages with their mules, to buy grain to be sold in town, and others like them, should perform their marital duty once a week. Men who convey freight on camels from distant places, should attend to their marital duty once in thirty days. The time appointed for learned men is from Sabbath-eve to Sabbath-eve. One must fulfill his marital duty even when his wife is pregnant or nursing. One must not deprive his wife of her conjugal rights....
>
> "When having intercourse, his intention should not be to satisfy his personal desire but to fulfill his obligation to perform his marital duty, like one paying a debt.... Sages say (Sukkot 52b): 'A man has a small organ, if he starves it, it is contented, and if he pampers it, it is hungry.' But one who has no need for it, and he deliberately arouses his lust, is following the counsel of the Evil Impulse."

Dalia cackled with delight. "I want you to be a scholar so we have to do it from Sabbath Eve to Sabbath Eve!"

"Wait! Wait!" Joshua held up his hand solemnly. This is even more important, Paragraph 17:

> "Semen is the vitality of man's body and the light of his eyes, and when it issues in abundance, the body weakens and life is shortened. He who indulges in having intercourse ages quickly, his strength ebbs, his eyes grow dim, his breath becomes foul, the hair on his head, eyelashes and brows falls out, the hair of his beard, armpits

and feet increase, his teeth fall out, and many other aches besides
these befall him. Great physicians said that one out of a thousand
dies from other diseases while nine hundred and ninety-nine die
from sexual indulgence. Therefore, a man should exercise self-
restraint.

Both of them were laughing so hard they didn't hear Leah close
the front door and come into the dining room.

"What's so funny?" she said to her son walking up to him and
pecking him on the cheek.

"Oh, hi mom," he said, suddenly becoming serious. This was
not a moment he had long cherished. "This is Dalia Almogi."

Leah had had an inkling of it as soon as she saw the sultry beauty.
The girl is really gorgeous, she thought to herself, and she extended
her hand to the blushing girl.

"I'm very pleased to meet you, Mrs. Jordan," said Dalia,
suddenly very shy. "I've heard so much about you."

"Oh yes, I'm sure you have, dear." Leah smiled knowingly at
Dalia. "Your father and I are such good friends."

"Yes, I've heard," Dalia replied, and all three of them laughed.

"What are you children doing?"

"Oh, just studying the *Shulchan Aruch*, mom. That's what Dalia
and I love to do," said Joshua looking away.

"Yeah, I can imagine," said his mother.

"Dalia fixed some Moroccan hatzilim for dinner, mom."

The enticing smell of garlic simmering in oil wafted from the
kitchen.

"Oh, how very sweet of her," said Leah, glancing at her apron
which Dalia was wearing. Dalia was looking away. "I'll just go
upstairs and change."

Leah walked up the stairs and down the hallway. She smelled the
Nina Ricci scent from the bathroom and saw the still glistening
drops of oily water not yet dried on the sides of the bathtub. She
passed by Joshua's room and peeked in quickly. Her gray eyes
twitched unhappily. The bedspread was tousled, not tight and
straight like she had made it that morning. Oh, my little boy
Joshie, she thought to herself. My sweet little innocent Joshie. And
there's *that* girl downstairs in *my* house, wearing *my* apron, cooking
dinner! Oh God! I'm going to be a grandmother!

She came downstairs a few minutes later, and Joshua and Dalia were deep in whispered conversation at the dining table. "Dalia, did you call your parents and tell them you would be late. I don't want your father to think that you've been kidnapped and murdered by the Jordans."

"Oh, it's okay, Mrs. Jordan," said Dalia. "I called my mother, and she said they wouldn't call the police as long as I checked in every half hour." She said it very seriously, softly, purring like a kitten with the hint of a smile.

Leah looked at the girl sternly, and then she let out a long laugh. This girl is really something, she thought to herself. No wonder my little boy is hooked like a walleyed pike. Dalia smiled broadly at her, not a little girl or a blushing maiden. A woman, obviously in love with her son, yearning to replace Leah as the woman in Joshua's life. But so soon?

Leah walked to the china cabinet and set three places with the good stuff and the silver. She sat down at the table across from him and Dalia.

"So what have you been studying in the *Shulchan Aruch?*"

Joshua turned the book around and pushed it across the table. She read it intently and said, "Good advice." All three of them laughed.

"You know, thirty years ago we didn't think that was so funny," she said them, becoming serious. "Before my marriage to Daniel, my mother actually had me study these things. It's really true. I know that it's hard to believe it now—even for me. But in those days, this was what we believed and how we thought."

Dalia got up and brought in the steaming serving dish of eggplant and a bottle of milk.

Leah had been put in a reflective mood by reading the familiar passages from the *Shulchan Aruch*. She started to reminisce.

"I guess all of that stuff sounds ridiculous today. But it was serious then. Joshua's grandfather Saul, my father, was very devout." Leah was talking to Dalia now. Joshua had heard the stories many times. "Till the day he died, he followed the laws of the *Shulchan Aruch*." As she said the word "died," Leah's deep gray eyes moistened and her cheeks reddened. She decided she'd better change the subject so she didn't make a scene in front of her son's new girlfriend. Dalia appeared embarrassed by the tears in Leah's eyes, and she looked away. Leah had no idea whether Dalia knew about Daniel and Vilna, about Krens and Treblinka and Mencken. But it was better to let Joshua tell her about these things.

"So when's dad coming back from Haifa?" Joshua asked brightly.

"Oh, he called today. Maybe one or two days more," Leah answered, regaining her composure.

"Our *Gadna* group is planning a weekend trip down to Hazor, mom. Middle of next month for three days. Is it okay?"

"Sure, Josh." The Zionist high school youth groups had periodic excursions to biblical excavation sites and other famous places in Israel. "We'll have to get the zipper on your sleeping bag fixed."

"Right. I forgot. And by the way, I thought maybe Dalia could go along." He glanced at Dalia and then shyly at his mother. A little smile flitted on his lips.

"Well, that's not up to me, Josh. It's up to the Almogis."

"I know, mom, but we thought that maybe you could call Dalia's mother and tell her it would be okay."

Leah stared at her son in disbelief. "Are you serious? I have enough trouble with Mr. Almogi. I sure am not going to run interference for you!"

"Please, Mrs. Jordan," pleaded Dalia. "My mother is really very different than daddy. She's not interested in politics and she has nothing against you. I promise. If you'd just talk to her and tell her that it's okay with you, she'll take care of daddy. I really want to go to Hazor."

Leah saw visions of her little boy Josh and this beautiful girl jumping behind a big rock and the dust rising from their frenetic activity. She studied the young lovers in front of her and she hadn't the heart to say no. Israel was a new world, vastly different from the one in which she had grown up. Joshua was a good boy, eighteen years old, just a few months away from entering the Army for his mandatory service. And this girl was old enough, that was perfectly obvious.

"Okay. What's your number? I'll call your mother."

Joshua and Dalia waited worriedly while Leah went into the study, where the only telephone was, to make the call. She came back a few minutes later.

"Your mother is very sweet, Dalia. She says that it will be okay."

"Oh, thank you Mrs. Jordan," Dalia gushed. She jumped up from the dining table and ran around the table and hugged Leah. Leah was totally disarmed by the girl's youthful exuberance and pleasure and loving warmth. She suddenly felt very happy for her son.

"Well, I've got some work to do. Then I'm going to sleep early. Big day tomorrow." Leah smiled at the two and walked upstairs. A few minutes later, she heard Joshua's scooter start up and sputter down the street. He must be taking Dalia home. Leah took a long bath and stretched languorously in the warm water. She hadn't read the *Shulchan Aruch* for several years, and she hadn't thought of her father's death for even longer. Now the memories began to swim before her eyes. She got out of the tub and toweled herself roughly, rubbing away the images. She got into bed and missed Matthew. She hated to be alone. And as she fell asleep, the dybbuks and golems invaded her dreams.

Chapter Six

"Josh! Hey Josh! Over here!"

He heard Dalia calling and finally spotted her waving at him from a group of some twenty-five milling teenagers. The Jerusalem main bus station was teeming with travelers, as usual, and Joshua made his way through the crowd, carrying his heavy duffel bag on his shoulder. Dalia ran up to him and gouged him playfully in the ribs. He dropped the duffel bag, and they hugged happily.

"Three whole days together!" she gushed, smiling at him.

"And two whole nights," he said quietly, and they both giggled conspiritorially.

He dragged his duffel bag over to the group of teenagers waiting for the charter bus to Hazor. The bus was called for boarding, and they all carried their bags and suitcases and backpacks to the luggage loading platform and then boarded. Because they couldn't travel through the West Bank, the trip was a long one. They first went to Tel Aviv and then up the coastal road to Acre, then east through Safed to Hazor. What would have been a two hour trip up the Jordan past the Sea of Galilee was actually almost six hours.

The *Gadna madreech* [leader] gathered his young charges together in the descending darkness of the hilly Huleh Plain and marched them into the camp area. It was May, and warm and dry, and they would sleep in their sleeping bags on the ground. The *madreech* was a handsome young man just out of the Army who had been doing this for several months. As darkness came and the group got settled into their chosen areas, he called them together around a large campfire. The air was tangy scented from the burning pine logs.

"Now, my little dears," the twenty-one-year-old *Gadna* leader addressed his seventeen- and eighteen-year-old charges, "there are a number of rules to get straight."

Dalia and Joshua sat cross-legged, holding hands. Most of the others had also paired off.

"Your mommies and daddies sent you here to make *good* little zionists out of you. They did not send you here to make *new* little zionists!"

The group rocked with laughter. Several of the boys hooted with delight.

"In other words, my little sweets and sweetesses, in case I am not making myself absolutely clear, I am not intending to conduct a lovefest here!"

The teenagers exploded with laughter. The *madreech* was also smiling broadly.

"So I will conduct a zipper check when you all get tucked in tonight. All sleeping bags are one to a customer. All zippers will be closed tight. And I will sleep with one ear open for the sound of zipping!"

Girls giggled, boys chortled.

"Okay, tomorrow morning at seven, the Army mess truck will be here for breakfast. We'll hike all morning and have bag lunches at Hazor, we'll go to Lake Huleh in the afternoon, and then the mess truck will be back here for supper. We'll spend tomorrow night here, too, and then leave Sunday morning for Jerusalem. Now who has that guitar?"

One of the girls lifted up the guitar she had brought and then started strumming the familiar folk ballads of Israel.

"Dodi li, va'ani lo,
haroeh bashoshanim . . ."

They sat around the campfire for two hours, singing song after

song, clapping hands, now and then jumping up to dance a hora.
"Hava, nagila hava, nagila hava,
nagila v'rannana...."
And as they tired, and the campfire burned down, they sang the softer ballads they all knew so well.
"Hana'avah babanot,
ana ha'iri pana'ich aylai...."
Some of them knew a few of the Yiddish folksongs of the east European stetls, and they joined in the poignant love songs.
"Shayn vi di livone,
oon lichtig vi di sterren...."
The fire died and they left for their sleeping bags, looking quickly around to find the *madreech*. But he had left earlier to spend the night with his fiance at Kibbutz Ayelet Hashachar nearby.

Dalia and Joshua were in heaven. They lay in each other's arms and counted the stars and made love and stayed awake almost all night with the tirelessness of young lovers. And when the light began to creep along the horizon, and they heard a car coming toward the camp on the long dirt road—probably the *madreech* sneaking back from trying to make a new little zionist—Dalia reluctantly tiptoed back to her sleeping bag. They slept for a couple of hours before sunrise.

Few of the teenagers were bright as daisies in the morning light, but several of them were rosy cheeked. The campground had a row of outhouses and wash basins for the boys, and just over a small hill was another group for the girls. At a few minutes after seven, scrubbed and brushed and ready, they passed by the mess truck and filled their aluminum trays with tomatoes and cucumbers and herring and white bread.

The *madreech* assembled them and gave a short speech about the history of the mound of Hazor, an ancient site which was being excavated by archeologists from the Hebrew University of Jerusalem. Joshua was particularly fascinated and listened in rapt concentration, for it was in the Book of Joshua that Hazor was described.

"Hazor is one of the vitally important areas of ancient Israel," recited the *madreech*. "It dominated the main trade route across the Jordan Valley from Egypt to Mesopotamia. It was the chief Canaanite city-state when the Israelite conquest began in the late

13th Century B.C.E. It actually consists of two separate cities. The first began in about 2750 B.C.E. and lasted until 150 B.C.E. The second started in about 1750 and lasted until the Israelite conquest in the 13th Century B.C.E. The conquest was under the command of Joshua, who had replaced Moses as the leader of the Israelites and had led them from Jordan into the Promised Land and laid claim to the biblical Land of Israel. The King of Hazor was Jabin, and he assembled several other Canannite kingdoms with their horse drawn chariots to do battle with Joshua's soldiers. The Bible tells us, in Joshua chapter 11: 'And Joshua turned back at that time and smote its king with the sword; for Hazor formerly was the head of all those kingdoms.' The mighty Israelites then subdued all of the Galilee."

Joshua Jordan was enthralled. As he and Dalia traipsed through the rolling yellow grass hills of the Huleh Plain toward the two hundred acre site that was ancient Hazor, they could both hear the clash of desperate armies fighting for mastery over the promised land. And as they walked gingerly in the excavation area, they were muted by the nearness of biblical history, as though they were there and could hear the great leader Joshua's voice ring out as he proclaimed the Israelite victory from the city's tower. Then the mighty warrior Joshua had performed the act that created biblical Israel. He had apportioned the land among the twelve tribes: Asher and Naphtali in the north, Ephraim and Manassah in the east, Judah in the south, and Dan in the west....

They ate lunch sitting on a mossy granite casemate wall that King Solomon had built when Hazor was one of his "royal cities" in the 10th Century B.C.E.

"Joshua conquered the Canaanites almost thirty-three hundred years ago on this very spot, Dalia," Joshua said in a tone of genuine reverence. "Isn't that fantastic! God, I really feel weird."

Dalia took his hand and laid her cheek on his shoulder. They were both awestruck by the grandeur of this place and their role as inheritors of the heritage of ancient Zion.

"And King Solomon made this place one of the great cities of the golden period of our history. We're sitting right in the middle of all of it! God, isn't it somethin'!" Joshua said.

Dalia hugged him tighter and felt tingly with loving him. He was her brave warrior, he was her Joshua, leader of the Israelites.

Chapter Seven

By the time Joshua graduated from high school, he and Dalia spent all their spare time together. The two families accepted the inevitability of young love with resignation, knowing that it would probably dissipate and disappear when Joshua went into the Army in August 1966. He would have two months of basic training in the Negev during which he would be restricted to base. Then, after three days leave, he was going to do Reconaissance training for another three months. The Recon Units were the equivalent of the British Commandos and American Special Forces and were the cream of Israel's armed forces.

But when Joshua came home from basic training, his three day leave was entirely with Dalia. It was on a Monday, Tuesday and Wednesday, and she took off from school, and they went down to Kibbutz Na'on and stayed in one of the visitors' cottages. It was not a shocking event for the parents, since it was common for soldiers and their girlfriends to do this in Israel's new society.

Joshua came back from three months training in Reconnaissance in the beginning of January 1967 to spend his next ten day leave, and there was no question left that Dalia and he were far from dissolving. During the months that Joshua had been away, Dalia would stop from time to time and visit Leah and Matt. They came to see what Joshua found in her, a wisdom beyond her years, and the unintentional but intrinsic seductive magnetism possessed by some of the oriental girls, a very different sensuousness than that exuded by Europeans. She was also a happy girl, clearly from a nice family.

During Joshua's second leave, Dalia decided that the two families ought to have a gathering so that they could meet and break the barrier between them erected by the political impasse between Amos and Leah. It was a bitterly cold Jerusalem winter night, with winds from the Judean hills whipping stinging sleet into everyone's faces. The little party was at the Almogis' home, and Matt and

Leah drove over in the perilous weather which put a frost on Leah's already chilly mood.

By the time the Jordans were inside the Almogi house, Leah was half drenched. She dripped into the parlor on Dalia's arm to meet Amos and his wife, Shulamit.

"How nice to see you again, Mr. Almogi." Leah forced a dazzling smile and held up a limp hand for her host to shake. She could hardly repress her revulsion when the little turd took her hand.

"Oh, please call me Amos," he said to her with an extreme effort to be polite. "I am very pleased to introduce you to my wife Shulamit."

The women picked up on each other's vibes instantly. Leah couldn't hide the intensity of her distaste for Shulamit's husband. It was too palpable. Leah also noticed the way Amos moved next to her, like he was hopping gingerly on tiptoes to avoid stepping in cow dung in a pasture. The situation had to be remedied before the evening became a disaster. After all, Dalia and Joshua were going to marry, and the families had to get along.

"Please come with me Leah and we'll get you dried out," said Shulamit sweetly. Leah could instantly see where Dalia had inherited her beauty, her willowy seductiveness. If Leah was a lioness, then Shulamit was a Siamese cat. She led Leah into a small room adjoining the master bedroom, a sewing room which also had a makeup table covered with the usual array of brushes and combs and cosmetics and perfumes. The house was a large and comfortable one, the third one the Almogis had lived in after leaving the tent city and one befitting the status of a cabinet minister. Leah was impressed by the comfort of it, Shulamit's subtle hand in decorating and arranging it.

"Sit right here Leah, and use anything you like. Let me get you a dry sweater to put on. That one's half soaked."

"Oh, no need to bother—"

"It's no bother, but I think my sweater will be a little small for you," said Shulamit, assessing Leah's ample bust. "But if it's a little too tight, it's not so bad, huh? It will take my husband's mind off politics."

Both women laughed.

"I think you're a better politician than I am, Shulamit. Maybe you should run for the Knesset."

"No thank you. One nut in any family is enough."

Again both women laughed. Leah drew the wet sweater over her head and Shulamit handed her a lovely pink cashmere sweater to put on. Shulamit hung Leah's on the drying rack in the bathroom. When she returned to the sewing room, Leah was standing in front of the mirror putting the last primping touches on her hair.

"Lovely," she said to Leah.

"Well, a big snug."

"Lovely, believe me. When Amos sees those marvelous tits, he'll forget about politics and we'll all live through this evening in one piece!" She and Leah looked at each other and laughed. This is some woman, thought Leah. I'm glad my son will marry her daughter.

The little party, if not a smashing success, at least became a pleasant get together among friends. Amos talked mostly with Matt, about the latest threats from Nasser, and the saber rattling of Syria and Jordan. Shulamit and Leah talked for hours and entertained the Almogis' three sons and other daughter. They had not even noticed that Joshua and Dalia were gone for over an hour, until the two came into the parlor looking a bit damp and chilled and ruddy cheeked. Probably been making love in the garden, thought Leah and Shulamit, catching each other's eye and grinning. Well, they too were young once, and young lovers once. Let them drink their cups full of each other. Because Joshua was leaving to start officer's training school in two days, and he would be gone for another four months.

Early May. The Negev Desert Officers' Training Base reminded Joshua of the movie set for one of those old French Foreign Legion films. Stone fortress, sand, shimmering haze of heat, clumps of bedraggled thorn bushes. Zinderneuf! And the son-of-a-bitch Drill Sergeant must be the infamous Lajaune.

"You hear me shitface?"

"Sir, yes sir!"

"Stand straight when you talk to your superiors!"

"Sir, yes sir!" Joshua braced his entire body in front of the mammoth Sergeant standing only six inches in front of him.

"You think you're a big shot because you got a politician mommy?"

"Sir, no sir!" The Sergeant's breath could pickle tomatoes. Joshua stared straight ahead, careful not to focus on the Sergeant's face.

"My mama washed floors, shitface! My papa died in the Sinai Campaign, so I didn't have no chance to become no cunt. You a cunt, shitface?"

Joshua said nothing, just gritted his teeth. It'd be heaven to castrate this bastard with a blowtorch, burn out his eyes. Steady, Legionnaire Geste! Only two more weeks.

"Hit it, Jordan! Gimme fifty!"

Down Joshua went on his hands and toes and started doing rapid pushups. Forty other officer trainees were in various stages of being humiliated by one of five Drill Sergeants, leaping to the ground, doing pushups, or leaping back to their feet.

"Double time, double time, run in place! You there! Quit standin' around with your thumb up your ass!"

They ran in place, knees high to touch their hands outstretched at waise level.

"Column a twos!"

Joshua ran to the lines quickly forming, happy for the relief from the individual attention. They double timed to the tactics class which was in a barracks classroom. Colonel Harkabi, one of Israel's foremost experts on Arab tactics, was the lecturer. He riveted the group with hard black eyes, a mirthless frown and a rasping voice.

"Despite the fact that the Israeli ground forces are enormously outmanned, and our tank corps is generally slower than the Arabs', our military planners count on one critical thing: the very nature of Arab societies vis-a-vis the society of Israel.

"Modern mobile warfare requires teamwork and risk taking. When one infantryman advances on an objective, he does so only because he knows that his buddies are behind him providing covering fire. The advancing soldier takes the risk of exposing himself to danger because his social links with his buddies have proved to him from infancy on that they will not simply abandon him and let him 'swing in the wind.' The risk taker must be deeply imbued with the feeling that his thrust into danger is being solidly backed up by all of his comrades.

"The social fabric of Israel has carefully been woven into this precise pattern for years. That is why it is an absolute rule of the armed forces that an entire battalion of soldiers will risk the lives of all four hundred men just to save the life of one trapped soldier—even just to recover his body if he is already dead. This is the ultimate expression of the group solidarity that has developed in Israel.

"Arab society is entirely different. The *hamula* system is the core of the social structure of every Arab nation. The average *fellah* in the ranks distrusts the effete officers' corps which hold their positions mostly by virtue of social status. And under the extreme pressures of war, the social fabric of the military unit loses its temporary glue, and the unit disintegrates into a motley group of individuals fighting for their own lives, because their background and experience tells them that when push comes to shove, one man from *hamula X* is not about to risk his life for another man from *hamula Y*, and neither of them will follow the questionable orders of an officer from *hamula Z*.

"This fundamental principle of Arab societies is what sociologists and military planners call 'amoral familism.' The amoral familist fights as well as any soldier in the world when he is given a static position to defend. This requires him only to stay put and fight next to his officers and his comrades, and not to take any greater risk than any of them.

"So in Maginot Line-type static defenses, cement bunkers and forts and reinforced trenches, the amoral familist is a fierce opponent. For this reason, the Israeli tactic is to move mobile armored infantry and paratroop forces rapidly through and around the static defense lines and then to sweep back and attack them from their unprotected rear. This should force the Arabs into defensive flight from which they are incapable of organizing mobile offensive counterattacks or creating mobile lines of containment."

Colonel Harkabi looked ruefully at the officer candidates. "At least we hope that this will work. If it doesn't, we're all in deep shit!"

Uneasy laughter rippled through the soldiers.

It was a proud day for Matt and Leah and Amos and Shulamit and Dalia when they drove down to Massada to attend the graduation ceremony for Lieutenant Joshua Jordan. The ceremony was always held on the heights of the Masada fortress, where two thousand years ago a small band of Jewish zealots had held out to the last man, woman and child against the onslaughts of the entire forces of the Roman Legions in Palestine. This was the symbol of Tzahal, the Jewish Army: that a small, tightly knit and determined army could protect tiny Israel against the onslaughts of vastly larger forces.

Dalia graduated from high school at the end of May, and she too would be entering the Army in August. Girls did not serve in combat units, but filled all of the many support roles for the combat forces. The principle behind this was a very old Yiddish proverb: you can have a circumcision without a woman present, but you can't have a circumcision without a woman. A single woman could produce a squad of soldiers. But no battalion could produce even one. So women were kept out of combat roles. In any event, during the two years of mandatory service, the young soldiers were not permitted to get married. So Dalia and Joshua had two full years in which they mostly would have to stay far apart. But this was the Israeli Way—their way—and they would make it just fine.

Chapter Eight

Hamdi Attiyah had grown into young manhood the way every boy envisions it. He had wavy black hair and yellow flecked black eyes and a face that set girls' hearts pounding. He was well over six feet tall and muscled like a fabled Arab warrior of old. Nadia saw him through a mother's eyes, a caliph with a scimitar in his sash, leading his brave people in a *jihad* to regain their *'awda*. Hamdi had been orphaned by the infidel Jews, his *hamula* had been destroyed, his traditional birthright stolen from him by the Yahudun. And although he and his mother lived under the protection of the powerful el-Rashid *hamula*, he was not its rightful heir apparent: Samir's eldest son was. The Yahudun had planted a knife in Hamdi's heart and he was reared in hatred for the usurpers of his heritage.

When Hamdi was fourteen, he had joined a para-military organization of boys who practiced small unit military tactics with sticks and dummy rifles. They spent many days bivouaced in the

Judean Hills east of Jerusalem, learning the terrain, readying themselves for the inevitable conquest of Palestine, for that was Allah's will. Now, at the age of seventeen, his madrassa schooling completed, he was ready for serious training.

Algeria since 1962 had been a haven for Palestinian groups training in terrorist tactics. The Algerian dictator Ben Bella had been among the first Arab leaders to recognize the Palestine Liberation Organization (PLO) when it was founded under Egyptian auspices in 1964. And several training camps had flourished since that time. It was to the best of these training facilities that Hassan sent Hamdi. Hamdi arrived by airplane in Algiers late in the afternoon and was met by Ismail Jaffi, an old friend of Hassan's and the head of the training camp. They drove four hours southeast through the Atlas Mountains and then into the desert, isolated and remote, and came to a tent encampment by the Melrhir salt marshes nestled among protective hills. Hamdi was assigned a cot in a tent with three other boys, two Jordanians and an Egyptian. They kissed in greeting and then they lay in apprehensive silence in the frigid summer night in the austere tent in the barren desert.

At four in the morning, someone blew a whistle in the tent and whacked Hamdi across the soles of his feet with a night stick. He leapt out of bed with a shocked howl and realized that the others had also been awakened this way. They ran outside and he followed. There were outdoor wash basins about thirty yards away, one for each of the thirty-two trainees. In the gathering light of sunrise they splashed a little water on themselves. Hamdi ran back to the tent for his shaving kit and toothpaste. Too late. Several men were walking through the encampment blowing whistles. The trainees ran to their tents and dressed immediately. Hamdi put on the fatigues and combat boots that Jaffi had given him yesterday. He then joined his three tent mates at attention in the formation in the center of the camp.

Ismail Jaffi blew a whistle at the head of the formation. "Attention! Attention!" he cried out.

All of the boys had had years of paramilitary training, and they sprang swiftly to attention.

"You will learn the chant of Palestinian revolution." Jaffi spoke in literary Arabic, far more formal and grammatical than the dialects of the various Arab nations and subregions which were essentially

different languages, like German and Swiss, or Spanish and
Portuguese. The only common denominator for these Arab boys
from all over was literary Arabic. It sounded very stilted—very
strange—to Hamdi to be doing a military maneuver in literary
Arabic.

"Chant this after me," Jaffi commanded. "*Al-qawmiyya al-
arabiyya, wataniyya, iqlimiyya* [Arab nationalism, patriotism, re-
gionalism]." The boys chanted the same words and repeated them
several times.

"*Al-watan al-kabir, al-watan al-saghir* [The Great Homeland, the
Small Homeland], *Nachnu al-fida'iyyun* [We are the self-sacrificers]!"
The boys chanted the segments over and over, prompted by Jaffi.
Then he led them in chanting the entire set of slogans, clapping
their hands in martial rhythm:

> "Al-qawmiyya al-arabiyya,
> wataniyya, iqlimiyya.
> Nachu al-fida'iyyun.
> Al-watan al-kabir,
> al-watan al-saghir.
> Nachnu al-fida'iyyun!"

The chanting and clapping went on for almost half an hour. Then
Jaffi held up his hand, signaling a halt.

"We are the self-sacrificers," he called out to the assembled boys.
"We begin with allegiance to the entire Arab world, and to this we
add allegiance to our leaders and especially to Palestine. This is our
iqlimiyya [regionalism]. We give allegiance to all Arabs of *al-watan
al-kabir* [the Great Homeland], while always giving our ultimate
allegiance to Palestine, our *al-watan al-saghir* [Small Homeland].
These are the articles of our faith! We are the self-sacrificers!"

It was getting lighter, but it was only about forty degrees. The
boys stood shivering in their thin fatigues. Jaffi and his cadre of
eight trainers stood facing the formation. They were dressed
exactly as the boys, but Hamdi could not detect any of them
shivering. Jaffi was of medium statute, stocky, and he stood stiffly
at attention, haranguing the trainees.

"We in Fatah have learned that the Palestinians will not embark
on the course of struggle and cannot change its conditions unless
we practice revolution. Revolutionary struggle is the only way for

the recreation of the Palestinian nation, the reformation of its soul, and the reactivation of the Arab masses. Those of you from the West Bank have been told by King Hussein's henchmen that 'regionalism' is an evil concept, and that 'the Small Homeland' means allegiance to Jordan. These are lies! For us, we have but one ultimate goal: Palestine! It is our 'regionalism,' it is our 'Small Homeland.' We must practice our revolutionary struggle against anyone—Jew or Arab—who tries to crush the soul of the Palestinian people!"

With that, Jaffi turned on his heels and strode away from the group. The eight trainers called out orders to the formation, dividing the boys quickly into eight groups of four. Then they started on their morning jog around and through the Melrhir salt marshes. Hamdi was glad for the exercise. At least he wouldn't freeze to death. He was in a group of boys from his tent, and after a few miles, one of the Jordanians fell back. A mile later, the Egyptian fell by the side of the trail and vomited. Hamdi and the other Jordanian ran strongly behind their trainer, a wiry, dark, small man who didn't even puff after miles of hard running. They reached the camp and Jaffi wrote down the name of the trainees who had not fallen back. There were only seven of them. They would be the trainee leaders. Hamdi was the tallest of them, so he was given two small crowns to pin onto his epaulets. The other six trainee leaders received small tin diamonds for their epaulets.

Breakfast consisted of sitting cross-legged around a campfire and eating stale pita, lebeneh and sardines, along with the ever present cardamom-laced coffee. And as would happen at every meal during the months of training, Ismail Jaffi harangued the group.

"The enemies of the Palestinians are Israel, world Zionism, imperialism and Arab reactionism! We must fight all of them with equal zeal. *Nachnu al-fida'iyyun!* We are the self-sacrificers! We are the self-sacrificers!"

Over and over, Hamdi would hear the same slogans throughout the months of training, and he would chant them and clap, again and again and again until they became the first words he thought of upon awakening and the last words that passed through his mind as he fell into exhausted sleep each night. And every day was the same. Long hours with the Kalachnikov and the heavy machine guns and the heavy mortar. Hour after hour, day after day, learning not to blow himself up by accident while shaping a plastique explosive and learning the numerous ways to detonate it.

Only nineteen of the original group of thirty-two graduated. The others had dropped out or been weeded out in the first few weeks. But the real graduation was the exercise planned for Nahariyya Israel. Specifically, the target would be tourists visiting the ruins of the Phoenician temple of Astarte near Nahariyya beach. Hamdi would lead a group of six soldiers in the attack.

But first things first. Hamdi was just two months away from his eighteenth birthday, and he had proved himself a man. And as with the rite of passage of all boys to manhood in virtually every culture everywhere, two things are necessary to mark the passage: he must get drunk and he must get laid. Some of these young men were more experienced than others. Hamdi had never touched a woman and he had only had sips of Arak at ceremonial occasions. But Farouk, his Egyptian tent mate who had turned into a first-rate soldier and friend despite his slow start, had been reared in a Cairo slum and knew his way around women and booze. The nineteen graduates were driven into Algiers Saturday afternoon. They would fly to Beirut tomorrow to plan and execute their graduation exercise in Israel. But tonight. . . .

"Come on, this way," called out Farouk over his shoulder to Hamdi and three others. They were shoving their way through the teeming outdoor marketplace near the beach in Algiers.

"Come on, I can hear the music!" Farouk yelled. "I would know that sound anywhere!" He followed the high pitched almost monotonal sound of belly dance music and led his friends through the market down a winding alley as the music became louder. They walked through a bead curtain into a large smoke-room filled with men at tiny tables, drinking, smoking, watching an almost nude belly dancer on a small stage dance to a blaring phonograph record. Several topless waitresses circulated among the tables.

Hamdi stood enthralled, drinking in the scene, his mouth open in awe.

"Come on, Come on!" Farouk yelled from across the room. "I got a table."

Hamdi edged his way through the crowd, brushing up against the bare breasts of one of the waitresses. She didn't even seem to notice. She was chatting in French with one of the men at a table.

Hamdi and his four friends sat on low stools around the small table.

"Fantastic, huh?" Farouk beamed at the others.

"I've never seen anything like this!" said Hamdi.

Farouk stood up and waved his arms. He caught the attention of a waitress and she came over to the table. She was slender and dark, black hair and eyes, and her breasts stood out, and her swollen nipples fascinated Hamdi.

"Five cognacs," ordered Farouk. The waitress walked to Hamdi and nearly gouged his eye with one nipple.

"You want to come with me for a little fun, sweetie," she said to him in French. He couldn't understand a word. She repeated it in Algerian Arabic. He was too embarrassed to speak. His pants were bulging. She put her hand on him and massaged the swelling. "Maybe a little later, huh?" She smiled sweetly to him, revealing three gold teeth, and swayed away to get the drinks.

"She loves you, Hamdi! She'll fuck you for love!" Farouk laughed and slapped his leg, delighted at Hamdi's total embarrassment. "The big tough soldier is a pussy!" chortled Farouk. Hamdi blushed deeply.

They watched the dancer gyrate on stage and press her muff into the hungrily waiting mouths of the men at the tables ringing the stage. They watched the waitresses hustle the patrons and go off for brief minutes into a room or series of rooms behind a brocaded cloth curtain. They drank and watched, drank and watched.

It was almost midnight. The waitress who had propositioned Hamdi had made at least ten trips behind the curtain with a variety of customers. She came back to the table and put her arm around Hamdi's shoulder and pressed her voluptuous breast to his cheek. He had drunk five, six—he had stopped counting—cognacs, and his head was swimming. Farouk was drunk and singing loudly with the music. Two of the others had staggered out earlier. The other boy was slumped dead drunk on the table.

"Come with me sweetie," the waitress said to Hamdi, pulling him off of his stool.

He staggered behind her, drunk and nauseous from the cognac, and followed her through the curtain into a small cubicle covered by a beaded curtain. There was a foam mat on the floor. She led

Hamdi to it, and she sat down. He stood next to her. She unzipped his pants and pulled out his throbbing erection. "A stallion," she breathed throatily. She knelt in front of him and slid him into her mouth. But standing up and walking had made him suddenly very sick. Quickly, shakily, he stumbled to the pissoir at the north wall of the corridor. The thick ammonia stench of years of urine over-whelmed him. He vomited on the floor. He ran water into the wash basin and rinsed his mouth out. He felt slightly better and went back. The waitress was lying nude on the mat, her legs spread invitingly. She smiled at him and licked her lips.

Hamdi kneeled down on the mat between her legs, and he felt deathly nauseous once again. He jumped up and ran back to the pissoir and vomited repeatedly. His head was swimming painfully. He was soft now, and he zipped his trousers. He staggered back to the table and grabbed Farouk by the arm.

"Wasn't it fantastic?" Farouk beamed drunkenly at Hamdi. "She did it for love, right? She didn't even charge you?"

"Yes," said Hamdi.

He pulled his friend to his feet, and both of them took their passed out companion by an arm and staggered out into the alley.

Hamdi and his five comrades drove down from the soft greens and blues of Beirut to the harsh dusty browns of the Palestinian refugee camp just outside of the coastal town of Rashidiye and about fifteen miles north of the Israeli border. They changed into fatigues and cleaned and oiled their Kalachnikovs. They pinned grenades to the holders on their breast pockets and sharpened their knives. Hamdi was ready, excited. This was his debut.

After a sleepless night, they loaded into a rubber assault boat at the pier. It was five o'clock, Tuesday morning. The two hundred sixty horsepower outboard engine carried them the twenty miles to Nahariyya's deserted northern beach in less than an hour. They moored the assault boat out of sight behind a rock outcropping and two of the soldiers carried the box of plastique explosive between them. They walked silently to the rubble site which over three thousand years earlier had been a Phoenician temple to the Goddess of Fertility, Astarte. They waited. The first tour bus from Acre would arrive at eight o'clock. They scattered among the fallen pillars and lay on the ground waiting. It was mid-September and the weather was balmy.

At five minutes to eight, the Egged tour bus pulled into the parking area in front of the temple portals, which resembled pregnant women, narrow on top and bottom with softly swollen bellies. Hamdi heard the motor go off. The door was opened. The driver was reciting the history of the place over a microphone to the tourists, still seated in the bus. Then Hamdi heard them begin to exit the bus.

"*Allahu akbar!*" he screamed, the signal for the attack to begin. He and his five men surrounded the bus and the stunned tourists in less than a minute.

"Back in the bus!" Hamdi screamed at them in Hebrew. They were too terrified and stunned to move. There were several old couples and a few teenage girls. Only about a dozen people.

"Back in the bus!" he screamed again and pointed his kalachnikov at the driver. His heart pounded wildly with excitement. The frightened tourists quickly began scurrying back into the bus.

One of the Palestinian soldiers crawled under the bus and located the main fuel tank. He molded a plastique explosive to its underside and attached an electrical detonator to it. He unwound the detonator wire and came out from under the bus. The Palestinians quickly backed away as the frantic tourists all got back into the bus. On a nod from Hamdi, the soldier with the detonator wire touched the end of it to a metal knob on a small radio transmitter. An enormous explosion rocked the bus and it was immediately engulfed in a ball of orange flame.

Hamdi ran with his men to the assault boat. There was a young couple strolling on the beach nearby. As the two saw the Arabs running toward them, they began to run back up the beach. Hamdi stopped and sprayed them with his submachine gun, but they were out of range. The Palestinians untied the boat, pushed it out into the mild surf, and sped uneventfully back to a cheering group of friends at Rashidiye pier. Israeli radio was reporting eight dead and five severely injured. It was a perfect attack, well planned, flawlessly executed. They were blooded.

Nadia had been predicting for months that Egypt's Nasser, who had long smarted from the acidic denunciations of him by his fellow Arabs, would finally take action. The Syrians and Iraqis had called him a coward for allowing United Nations Emergency Forces to occupy the Southern Sinai to keep the Israeli port of Eilat open. And Nadia could see in every television newscast about him that Nasser had endured enough chortling about his womanly cringing. In early June 1967, he ordered the United Nations Secretary General to remove the UNEF forces from the Sinai. And as if on cue, it was done immediately. At the same time, the head of the Palestine Liberation Organization gave a "victory" press conference at which he boasted to the world that his people were ready to "march to liberate... our country. Those [Jews] who survive will remain in Palestine. I estimate that none of them will survive."

Nadia was very proud of her husband. Hassan and his newborn Palestinian army, al-Asifah [The Storm], had a major role to play in the *jihad* against Israel. Part of al-Asifah would be stationed in the Gaza Strip and man major artillery batteries. The cream of his army would be sent along with the Jordanian Legion to liberate all of Jerusalem, the third holiest city of Islam. Hassan himself would head the commando forces in the battle for Jerusalem. And at his side would be his Lieutenant, Hamdi Attiyah, eighteen and a half years old and a natural leader of men.

Nadia had insisted that he become fluent in Hebrew, and he had. Even Hassan had learned enough to carry on a simple conversation. They would need this weapon to defeat the Israelis and reclaim their homes in Palestine. By the time Hamdi returned from Algeria, fickle and unpredictable Syria was supporting the Palestinians and he attended officer's training school for the Syrian Regular Army. When he was commissioned a Lieutenant in May 1967, he joined the cadre of skilled officers around which al-Asifah had been molded.

In the early morning stillness of June 4, 1967, when the *jihad* with Israel was imminent, Hassan and Hamdi and the el-Rashid men and boys gathered in the courtyard of their home in Amman, and they fervently intoned the morning prayer service.

Hamdi touched his ears with his hands. He then clasped his left hand with his right and held them in front of his face. He bowed and knelt down, touching his forehead on his private prayer rug, an act of contrition which had long ago created a prayer mark on his forehead, and recited the *al-fatihah*: "In the name of Allah, the merciful, the compassionate...." He sat back and looked over his left shoulder and then his right, acknowledging the messengers of

Allah who recorded all of his deeds, good and bad. Hamdi continued the ancient rituals in deep prayerfulness.

The morning prayers over, Hassan and Hamdi drove their Syrian Soviet jeep to join al-Asifah in East Jerusalem. Their exile was almost over.

Chapter Nine

A little after dawn on June 5, 1967, Israeli airplanes swept below the Mediterranean radar screen protecting Egypt's airfields. In a massive preemptive strike, the Israelis destroyed three hundred nine of Egypt's three hundred forty combat aircraft on the ground and bombed the runways into unusable rubble. Another twenty Egyptian airplanes were destroyed in aerial dogfights. Later that morning, Syrian bombers attacked the oil refineries at Haifa, the Jordanians strafed a small airfield, and Iraqi jets attacked the coastal resort town of Natanya. By nightfall, the Israelis had completely destroyed the Jordanian air force, two-thirds of the Syrian air force, and the principal Iraqi airbase of Habbaniyah.

The ground attack into the Sinai and Gaza Strip started only an hour and a half after the air strikes, at eight fifteen that same morning; and by darkness on June 8, the entire Sinai from the Gaza Strip to Eilat to the Gulf of Aqaba and back to the edge of the Suez Canal, was in Israeli hands. Battles were still raging with Syria at the Golan Heights and with Jordan in the West Bank and Jerusalem.

In East Jerusalem, which had been incorporated into Jordan in 1950, there was a Jewish enclave called Mount Scopus where the Hebrew University and Hadassah Hospital were located. It had been agreed during the Israeli-Jordanian armistice talks in 1949-50 to maintain Mount Scopus as a demilitarized zone and to permit Jewish traffic to it through the Mandelbaum Gate, at the barbed wire border between Arab and Jewish Jerusalem, but it had long since become deadly dangerous for Jews to travel freely to Mount Scopus.

On June 5, the Jordanian Legion occupied the three principal strategic areas of Arab Jerusalem: U.N. Headquarters, the Hill of Evil Counsel and Ammunition Hill. The Legion massed for a strike into Jewish Jerusalem. The only strategic area it did not command was the Jewish enclave on Mount Scopus, the highest point in all Jerusalem and the perfect place to unleash a devastating artillery barrage on the Jews.

Hassan abu-Sittah was in charge of a brigade of al-Asifah at the Hill of Evil Counsel, readying a strike into the heart of Israel. Hamdi Sharifeh commanded a battalion, and his mission was to overcome the eighty-five man Jewish police station on Mount Scopus so that the Jordanian Legion could bring up artillery. Mount Scopus came under attack at noon on June 5. In response, the Israeli Command detached a paratroop brigade from the Sinai and helicoptered it to Jerusalem. The Recon Platoon assigned to the brigade was under the command of Joshua Jordan. They reached East Jerusalem late in the afternoon.

The vitally important battle, involving the al-Asifah unit shelling Mount Scopus, began shortly after dawn. It was led by Joshua's Recon Platoon followed by a squadron of tanks and half a battalion of paratroopers. The ten jeeps and forty men of the Recon Unit headed north on Nureddine Street to the edge of the quarter called Sheikh Jarrah, where the street turned sharply to the right for the steep ascent to the Hadassah Hospital and then to the old campus of the Hebrew University. At the base of the Mount, two hundred al-Asifah soldiers were dug into trenches to stop the attack and protect the other two hundred soldiers above who were shelling the crest of the Mount with heavy mortars. Hamdi Attiyah was in a sand-bagged command post about twenty yards behind the lower trenches.

As the Israeli Recon Unit rounded the curve to ascend Nureddine Street, the machine gunners in the trenches opened fire on them, about fifty yards away. Through his binoculars, Hamdi could see the blond Recon Unit Commander, helmetless in the first jeep, sitting high on the jeep's rear gate and wearing headphones, obviously in contact with his other units and his own commander. When the machine gun fire began, the blond officer dived off his jeep, his headphones flying off his head from the impact, and scurried for cover underneath the jeep. The driver was killed by a fusillade which shattered the windshield. The two other soldiers in the jeep scattered to cover in the gulleys on both sides of the road.

Hamdi had seen this Jewboy's face well, probably the same age as he, and he grinned at converting this proud Israeli officer into a scared rabbit in a matter of seconds. The rest of the jeeps pulled to the sides of the road and the men jumped into the gulleys. Several bodies littered the road. One jeep was on fire. The Arab machine gunners stopped. Hamdi surveyed the stilled roadway through his binoculars.

Suddenly the blond officer cowering under the first jeep scooted out five feet to grab his headphones and dived back under before the staccato blasts from two machine guns could get his range. Damn, Hamdi swore to himself. Now that son of a bitch is back in contact with his troops and his commander. Hamdi walkie talkied his closest mortar team to descend the hill to his command post. A few minutes later, three Palestinians ran down to the CP, two of them toting the crate of shells between them, the other cradling the mortar.

"I want that lead jeep knocked out. There's an Israeli officer under it," Hamdi ordered the mortarman. "Set your piece up right behind here. The sandbags will give us cover."

The mortarman elongated his tripod to level the gun, and the two other soldiers rapped six-inch steel pins into the ground through the holes in the tripod feet to stabilize the mortar. In minutes they were set.

"Commence firing when ready," ordered Hamdi.

The first shot hit twenty feet to the right and a little in front of the jeep. The gunner quickly adjusted his range and windage. The second shell hit level with the jeep and about five feet to the right, throwing a cloud of dirt and asphalt over the jeep.

An Israeli Super-Sherman tank abrubtly rounded the curve of Nureddine Street, and Hamdi saw the smoke curl from the end of the long 85 mm. cannon before he felt the impact of the explosion just fifteen feet to his right and above the CP. A recoilless rifleman below in the trenches fired two shells, missing both times. The explosion had covered the mortar team behind Hamdi with dirt and they were shaking the dirt off themselves and the mortar gauges, readying for the next shot. Another cannon shell from the tank hit even with the CP about twenty feet to the right.

Before they could move, another 85 mm. shell burst just above the mortar position, killing two of the Palestinian mortarmen on impact and burying the third alive under a crushing mound of rock and dirt. Hamdi ran from the CP down the hill and jumped into the nearest trench.

Under cover of another cannon shell aimed at the trenches, the blond Jewish officer crawled out from under his jeep, jumped atop it, and started fanning the trench area with the mounted .50 caliber machine gun. Hamdi ducked for cover in the trench. He could hear several tanks rolling toward them on Nureddine Street. Once again the Palestinian recoilless rifles popped and the resulting explosion pulled Hamdi upright in the trench to see the lead tank burst into a smoke ball from a direct hit. The second tank simply rolled the smoking one into the gulley, and the line of tanks continued up the steep hill, shelling the Palestinian trenches with increasing accuracy.

Hamdi called out for his men to fall back up the hill to their second line of defense, where the mortar teams were firing on Mount Scopus. He would simply turn the mortar fire around and decimate the column on Nureddine Street before finishing the capture of the Mount. The two hundred Palestinians jumped out of the trenches and scrambled up the hill two hundred fifty yards to the second defense line.

The Israelis regrouped below. Once again, the Recon Unit got back into its jeeps to lead the tank column up the road. Hamdi could see the beginning of the Israeli maneuvers through his binoculars. They were out of range of small arms fire at this distance. He saw the blond Jew officer talking on the radio. Then he saw him hand signaling to separate his Recon Unit in two, sending the halves up Mount Scopus' rocky dirt side roads to flank the two ends of the Palestinian defense line and enclose their outer perimeter, while the tank column attacked the middle of the trenches supported by the two hundred paratroopers running alongside the tanks. Hamdi understood the tactics at once. The Israelis were outmanned by the Arabs, who had a battalion entrenched on the Mount. But the Israelis had heavier guns, and the tanks would have free rein if the Recon Unit could knock out the Arab recoilless riflemen, because mortar shells would simply bounce off the steel skin of the tanks.

The Recon jeeps disappeared in angry puffs of dust into the scrub brush on each side of the road as Hamdi watched the Israeli column begin moving up the hill. Hamdi ordered the mortar teams to open fire on the road in front of the tanks, a hundred yards down the hill, to create an impassable anti-tank trench. He signaled the recoilless rifle squad leader to disperse his ten bazooka men along the three hundred yard defense line. Within moments, the mortars began cracking and the pops began going off from the recoilless rifle shells. But Hamdi had not been aware of the speed and mobility of the Israeli tanks, and as the giant Super-Shermans gained speed at the bottom of the hill, they began literally racing toward the middle of the Arab lines, impervious to the potholes left by the mortar shells and going too fast for the recoilless riflemen to take good aim.

Suddenly from both sides of the defense line, the Recon jeeps opened a fanning fusillade with their .50 caliber machine guns. Hamdi realized that his battalion was trapped. As the tanks came within twenty yards of the trenches, the paratroopers ran ahead, leaping into the trenches and fighting hand to hand with the Palestinians. Bodies of Jews and Arabs alike were strewn everywhere. The screams of the wounded pierced the air along with the roar of the weapons.

Hamdi was ten yards behind the main trench, hidden by a huge boulder. He saw an Israeli paratrooper break through the trench and whirl around just five yards below him and fire back into the trench. Hamdi readied his Kalachnikov and stepped out from behind the rock, screaming *"Allahu akbar, Allahu akbar, Allahu akbar!"*

The Israeli soldier spun around and Hamdi blew his face off with a blast from his machine gun. Hamdi then rushed to the dead Jew and pulled him by the feet behind the boulder. The Jew's fatigue shirt was covered with blood. Hamdi ripped off his own shirt and carefully unbuttoned and removed the Jew's shirt and put it on. He pulled his pants off and put the Israeli's uniform pants on. Their boots were the same, paratroop boots of French issue. Hamdi threw away his Kalachnikov and slung the Jew's Uzi over his shoulder. He watched the battle in the trenches come to a rapid end, and then he started groaning and walking slowly down the hill, joining the stream of wounded Israelis walking and being carried to the aid station at the foot of Mount Scopus. The high sun was virtually blotted out by a fog of smoke and dust.

Hamdi walked past the blond Israeli officer in his Recon jeep, who was now standing up on the back of the jeep, surveying the small mopping up action two hundred yards away near the other end of the trench.

"We've won. Mount Scopus is ours!" Hamdi called out to the young officer in the fluent Hebrew his mother had made him learn, *alhamdillah* [thanks be to Allah].

The blond Jew officer looked down at the young paratrooper who was holding his immobile left shoulder and grimacing with pain, his fatigue shirt covered with blood from the wound. "Do you need a stretcher? I'll get stretcher bearers for you," the Jew called down to Hamdi.

Hamdi studied the Jew's face, memorizing it, the brown eyes, ruddy skin, hair the color of ripe summer corn. "No, Lieutenant. The job isn't done here. I'll make it fine." And he continued his slow halting walk down the hill with the other wounded to the chaos of the undermanned first aid station. A few moments later, he simply slipped away to a nearby olive grove, waited for nightfall, and walked to the Jordan River and swam across.

One day, I will kill that Jew bastard, thought Hamdi, someday I will blow his fucking head off.

The Radio Amman announcers bubbled with extravagant reports of Arab victories, skirmishes and battles won, stolen territory reclaimed, the heroism of their fighting warriors. But Nadia listened also to *Kol Yisrael* and Israeli reports were just the opposite. The truth began to filter through Amman like the moldy dust, as the tattered remnants of the fleeing battalions crept back to their homes.

Nadia stood with an ocean of shaddured women in the main square and ululated in mourning. A hemorrhage of tears spilled from her red lids as she bemoaned the fate of her son, her husband, her homeland.

But finally they came back to her, *alhamdillah*, and her fear turned first to gratefulness and then to despair. They were still refugees, beaten, degraded, without face. She felt the emptiness of homelessness more than she ever had before, because it now seemed truly permanent. She had planned her return to the Jerusalem hills for years, and in the last month it had appeared far more substantial than just a wispy dream. Her mind roiled with passion and confusion.

"I must go back and visit my family."

Hassan looked at her and frowned. "What family? They are all dead."

"I want to visit them where they are buried, Hassan. I want to minister to their souls."

"What burials? What gravesites? The Yahudun just blew them up with the village!" Hassan was sick with his loss in war, tortured by the look of shame in his wife's eyes. He shuddered at her accusing look of humiliation.

"I must visit my '*awda*," she said darkly.

Hassan threw up his hands in frustration and looked for support from his son. Hamdi simply sat, head downcast, as though he weren't even listening.

Nadia rose slowly from the living room sofa. "Drive me to the Jordan River, Hamdi, to the shallow ford near Aricha [Jericho]."

"You cannot do this, Nadia. It is far too dangerous." Hassan's voice was almost whiney.

She looked coldly at her husband. "I cannot *not* do this. If I wait for you to make it possible, I will be a very old woman with no eyes left to see."

Hassan gritted his teeth and walked out of the parlor. Nadia walked to Hamdi and gently laid her hand on his slumped shoulder. "I will pack a small carpetbag."

He opened the Mercedes door for her when she came out. She had changed from her blue gauze caftan to a pants suit of light gray wool and an open necked white cotton blouse, in the Israeli style. She got in the passenger seat. Hamdi was in a short sleeve plaid sports shirt and Levis. They were both quite nondescript, in the event that they were spotted by an Israeli patrol across the narrow river.

"You can't go over there, Mama. There are swarms of Israeli soldiers all over the West Bank. How will you get through? Where will you stay?"

"I speak Hebrew like a Jew and I can walk to Jericho and get a bus to Jerusalem. I'll stay in a hotel like any tourist and take taxis wherever I want to go. Don't worry about me."

He looked over at her and she smiled at him reassuringly. They drove in silence for thirty-five minutes.

"Park in that stand of trees over there." She looked at her watch. "It'll be dusk in a half hour and no one will even see me cross over."

They waited almost an hour, until it was almost dark and there was no movement on the highway. Hamdi drove to the ford and they could see the lights of Jericho just a few miles away.

He put his hand on hers. "I know we have failed you, Mama. Please forgive us. Please come back to us soon."

She looked at his suffering face and felt deep hurt. She hugged him close to her. "You have not failed me. We are simply not strong enough yet. But we will be." She drew away and looked softly at him. "I know we will be. But this is just something that I must do. I can wait no longer."

She picked up her carpetbag, left the car, and in a minute she had disappeared from his view. She pulled off her shoes and put them in the bag. She folded the legs of her pants up a foot. The mighty Jordan of Bible and song was but a twenty-foot-wide rut in a shallow sandbar at this place. She walked down a gentle slope, crossed it quickly, and emerged on the other side. Whatever Israeli patrols were guarding the border were far from here, and she walked straight across low rolling hillocks to Jericho.

At the bus station, the disinterested manager told her that the Jews had requisitioned all the buses, but there were taxis up the street. She walked to the stand a block away and told the Arab driver to take her to the Old City.

He dropped her off on the Arab side at the tiny village of Silwan, and she walked through the Valley of Kidron through the Dung Gate and the Armenian Quarter to Jaffa Gate where she got an Israeli taxi to the Sheraton Hotel.

In the morning, she breakfasted on the dates and raisins and almonds which she had brought with her. She took a cab at eight in the morning to the bright little Jewish town of Motza. Behind the town she found the ancient Roman road she had trodden a thousand times and started walking up the hill to where Deir Yassin once had been.

She heard the sound of running feet and turned around. A little girl scurried through the back porch screen door of one of the village houses. "Mommy, Mommy!" she called excitedly.

Nadia stopped, not wanting to be shot for a burglar or trespasser.

A tall woman with red hair bright as a cherry tomato came

quickly out of the house, through the thin green patch of lawn, and stopped a few feet in front of her.

"*Shalom, shalom, boker tov,*" said the woman. Her countless freckles wrinkled up in a friendly smile. The little girl stood watching from the open screen door.

"*Boker or,*" responded Nadia easily. As she said the words, she immediately knew that the many years she hadn't spoken Hebrew had just caught her. The "r" of a Sephardic Jew would be a soft guttural rasp. The Arabic "r" that had just come out of her mouth was a quick tongue trip.

The woman squinted and eyed Nadia warily. "Where is your car? How did you get here?"

"I have no car, I came by taxi."

"Why are you behind my house?"

Nadia saw an old man walk through the back door of the house onto the lawn. He stood still, carrying an Uzi. Well, if she was going to die, she thought, it will be with honor alongside her family.

"I am not here because of you or your house," she said, keeping her voice and face bland. "I used to live up there."

The woman looked up the hill to where Nadia was pointing, and suddenly she stepped back a foot and stiffened, her eyes fearful. "Why did you come?"

"To see my home. To talk to my family. Only that." Nadia looked straight into her soft blue eyes.

A minute passed. "Let me see in there," the woman gestured toward the carpetbag.

Nadia separated the handles and held the bag open. Toothbrush, toothpaste, a soiled towel, balled up panties and bra, a bag of dried fruits.

The woman nodded and relaxed her tensed shoulders. "It was bad what happened there," she said slowly. "I lived in Tel Aviv then and we never even heard of it. But it was war and there was evil on both sides." She paused, a doleful look clouding her eyes. "You will find nothing of your home or family. It has all been scraped away." She turned and walked back to her house.

Nadia had steeled herself for this moment, but the enormity of the utter evaporation of her past clutched at her. The Roman rock-cut tombs were the only man made things still standing. The village was simply gone and in its place was a barren square of hard packed dirt studded with stones like worn-down teeth. Where her house had once been, the Mukhtar's expansive rock villa with the fancy tile and the terra cotta roof, not even one of the wall blocks was left to remind her of its opulence. Bulldozers and graders had culled all of the town from the hill of which it had once been an integral part, and only piles of rubble rested at its fringes. There was otherwise no vestige of what had been a place of Arab heartbeats and sinew and hair and bone and yearnings for more than a thousand years.

She walked to the meadow of wildflowers across which she had fled to save her life on that last day, the last time she ever saw her family and her home. Down the slope she went, looking for the spot, the only place she knew that the soul of one of her loved ones had been laid. But it was too long ago, and she was uncertain. Did the Jewess Leah Jordan bury Sami here? Over there maybe? Or right there, where an especially fragrant and deep red patch of wild roses drank the blood of her baby to impart the glossy vermillion to its petals. She knelt by the roses and put her nose to them, trying to find her baby. Tears trickled through her tightly pressed lids and fell on the blooms, and the rays of the fresh morning sun sparkled off the dew-like droplets.

She knelt there for an hour, perhaps two. And then she scooped out a little hole in the soft loam, and she put the rest of her dates and raisins and almonds in it. She covered it lovingly with the loose rich soil.

On the ridge she saw the old man from the house limping up the Roman road toward her. He was empty handed. Each of the scarred ruts of the road was replicated in his etched leathern face. He came to the edge of the slope and looked down at her. He smiled at her and nodded, and he looked around the emptiness as though he too had lost something here. His innocence? she thought. His once so certain knowledge of right and wrong? We have all lost that here.

He looked again at her and she felt his own pain in those tired black eyes. Then he turned and walked back down the hill.

She stood up slowly, looked around her for a moment, and then retraced her steps to the highway.

Chapter Ten

All Jewish Israel was euphoric. They had lived through the third major war of their twenty year history, and they had triumphed beyond anyone's dreams.

The "Land of Israel" suddenly encompassed twenty-eight thousand square miles of new territory. It also had a population boom: six hundred-five thousand Arabs in the West Bank; sixty-eight thousand in East Jerusalem; three hundred fifty-two thousand in the Gaza Strip; thirty-five thousand, mostly Bedouins, in the Sinai; and six thousand Druzes on the Golan Heights.

Israel had become the sprawling biblical empire of old—Eretz Yisrael—and the Jews were giddy with the exultation of military victory. When the Israelis captured East Jerusalem and the ancient biblical towns of the West Bank, Jericho, Bethlehem and Hebron, Naomi Shemer rewrote some lyrics of her popular ballad "Jerusalem of Gold," and it instantly became the anthem of the Six Day War:

> "We have returned to the wells
> And to the ancient marketplace,
> And the ram's horn sounds on the Temple Mount
>   in the Old City.
> From the caves in the cliffs
> Shine a thousand suns.
> Again we shall go down to the Dead Sea
>   by the Jericho Road.
> Jerusalem of gold, and of copper
>   and sun fire,
> To all thy songs I shall be the lyre."

Not a Jew in Israel would ever abandon Jerusalem again. Not under any circumstance.

It was finally possible for Leah Jordan to fulfill the pledge she had made twenty-two years ago, in her other life. God had sent

Yussel Pinsker to her to heal her soul, to enable her to live with what had happened to her and what she had done to survive. Yussel had yearned to pray at the Wailing Wall, Judaism's holiest shrine, to supplicate before God and to repent of his sins. But he had died so that Leah might live, and since the War of Independence, the Wailing Wall had been part of Jordan and forbidden to the Jews. Now, she could finally go there.

On Shabbat, Leah and Matt walked from their home to the Old City. It wasn't far, just a couple of miles, and it was warm and sunny. They entered the sacred city at the Jaffa gate near the Tower of David, almost three thousand years old. There were numerous Israeli soldiers in the Old City, patrolling the Arab souk. The Arabs and Armenians sat outside their tiny shops, smoking their nargilahs, playing sheshbesh interminably on little game boards, glowering sullenly at the Jewish infidels invading their ancient city.

Leah and Matt meandered through the tiny alleys and finally reached the Wailing Wall, a huge section of stone wall some fifty feet high and a hundred feet long. Hundreds of Jews were there, Hasidim rocking in their prayer shawls, beating their breasts, crying out fervently for God's mercy; others, soldiers and policemen and tourists and many just like Leah and Matt, were gazing in awe at the ancient relic of their people.

It was a centuries-old custom to write a short prayer on a piece of paper and to pray at the Wall and stuff the little piece of note paper into a crack between the blocks, so that it would repose in the heart of this sacred shrine. Matt waited for Leah.

She was overcome by trembling, awed by the presence of God in this holy place. She covered her head with a scarf and walked slowly to the Wall, once again just an orthodox Jewish girl from Vilna.

She pressed her body to the Wall and kissed it, and she wept. She had written a prayer for Yussel Pinsker and herself on a small piece of paper, and she stuck it into a crack: "Praised be Thou, O Lord our God, King of the universe, who sent forth the soul of Yussel Pinsker to join with the soul of Leah Arad, and thus to taste a Jewish orange, to feel the Jewish sun, and to come here to pour out our heart and beg forgiveness for our sins."

She could see him again, as though it were yesterday, emaciated, crippled, barely alive.

The War ends. Finally she leaves Brzka and walks to Warsaw. But she cannot stay in Poland. There is nothing for her here, no family, no job, no hopes for a future. Just more festering hatred of the Jews. After two months of eating garbage scraps and sleeping in doorways, she knows that her only chance for life is to go west, away from the Poles and the Russians and the Germans.

She walks for hours away from Warsaw to where the railroad tracks are still intact. Many of the tiny shattered remnant of the Jewish people leave East Europe. Afoot and on trains and in carts and wagons, they flee from the Russian Army.

After three days without much water or any food, Leah is dehydrated and shrunken by starvation. She gets out of the boxcar in Konin. The Warta River flows peacefully behind the railway station. She stumbles shakily up to the edge, splashes water on her face and neck, and drinks deeply, bending low on her hands and knees over the river and lapping the water.

There are others along the banks, gaunt and dirty and haunted, pausing in their journeys to nowhere.

"Vayomer Adonoy el Gidon, bishlosh mayos ha'ish hamlak'kim oshia es'chem. . . ." [And God said to Gideon, by the three hundred men that lapped will I save you. . . .]

Leah hears the voice speak the only Hebrew she has heard since the night of Kol Nidre, three years ago, when Daniel was murdered. She stands slowly and looks around. An old man smiles at her, sitting back against a tree. He looks away, lamenting that this poor Polish girl will never get the cuteness of his little quip.

Leah walks toward him a few steps, slowly, stops in front of him, and finishes the passage from the Book of Judges, Chapter 7: "Venosati es Midyan beyodecho, vechol ha'am yaylchu ish limkomo" [And deliver the Midianites into thy hand, and let all the people go, every man unto his place].

The old man stares at blond, gray-eyed Leah in surprise. And then a grin spreads over his face. He lifts his bent body with great effort, his left arm uselessly hanging at his side. Atop his bald head is a black wool yarmulke surrounded by a gray, unruly fringe. He is Leah's height and extremely emaciated.

"A Yiddishe tochter?" [A Jewish girl?], he says to her in amazement, staring at her blond hair and gray eyes. "No wonder you survived. You're one of the lucky ones. I obviously am not so lucky." He laughs, pointing at his face. He is quite homely, made even more so by the deep sunken cheeks and hollow dark bags below his eyes. Starved, haunted.

"Please help an old man, my child," he says, and hooks his good arm in Leah's arm. He walks with her painfully up the bank and across the tracks to the little town of Konin. They go silently, since the effort it takes the old man to walk is exhausting, and he can hardly catch his breath. They reach the small city hall and sit down on the curb in front of it to rest.

"I am Yussel Pinsker, late of the Warsaw Ghetto, before that from Lublin and Shenyava."

"I am Leah Arad, late of the village of Brzka, and before that Vilna."

"Oy vay, a Litvak!"

"Oon di, Reb Yussel, a Hasid?"

They both laugh. He gathers his strength. It is hot and muggy. She helps him hobble to the railway station. She and two other women lift him into the boxcar. There is plenty of room. Several of the cars are empty and there are only four or five people in some of them. They sit against the back of the car, facing the direction they are going, looking out at the blurred countryside.

Leah and Yussel are on the train for two days. Finally, it rambles into Poznan, the largest city in this part of western Poland. They will have to change trains, bellows a switchman, walking down the platform. This one is needed immediately to convoy a company of Red Army soldiers to Berlin.

The forty or fifty Jews get out of the boxcars and sit on the railway platform against the wall. The Russians mill about, some of them looking enthusiastically at the little group of Jews. Here is a bit of sport to help pass the time, they think. Several of them walk over to the Jews and begin taunting a young Hungarian Hasid wearing a filthy long black caftan and a stremel, a black hat with a wide fur band.

"Hai, Zhid!" the soldier yells, kicking the Hasid on his outstretched feet. "Dance for us, Jew!" The soldiers all laugh uproariously at the great joke.

One of the soldiers, a huge gorilla-like stump of a man, walks down the row of Jews looking the women up and down. He stops in front of Leah. Her heart stops beating. Oh please God, not again, she thinks. Please keep this filth away from me. Yussel starts to stand up and the soldier kicks him in the stomach and sends him reeling back against the wall. Yussel slumps on the floor.

The Russian studies Leah. She was once pretty, he thinks, maybe even more than just pretty. But now she is a corpse, matted filthy hair, emaciated, hollow eyes and cheeks, no tits, cowering like a simpering mongrel bitch in her stinking rags. Nothing here to quicken a man's heart and harden his rod.

An officer breaks away from the jumble of troops down the platform and hollers orders at the four soldiers taunting the Jews. They slowly straggle away, back down the platform.

Yussel is breathing very shallowly. The kick has surely broken his rib cartilage, maybe even a rib. He is in severe pain. A trickle of blood comes out of the side of his mouth. His lung has been injured. There is nothing to do, just sit there all day and night waiting for the next available train. It finally comes at mid-morning and the Jews struggle aboard. After another day, they are in Zbaszyn. They get off, and there is a boy waiting at the station, as he does every day, who leads the Jews two blocks to the Jewish Welfare Council transient hostel. Yussel is immediately brought to the infirmary, a room with two small beds and a white metal cabinet. The doctor is at least eighty years old. He is as wrinkled and tiny as a prune on toothpicks. He taps Yussel's chest with arthritic hands.

"Your heart is very weak. You have a bruised lung, but no broken ribs. You will have to rest here in Zbaszyn. You will not make it even another two or three days on the train."

"But Doctor, I must go on. I must go to Eretz Yisrael. I will not die on the soil of the killers of our people."

"I cannot and certainly will not prevent you from leaving, Herr Professor Doktor Pinsker," says the doctor, who speaks Yiddish with the Germanisms of the aristocratic German Jews, "but again I warn you, you cannot survive the journey at this time. Please stay with us for a few days."
He gives Yussel a shot of something in his stringy arm, and Yussel soon drifts off to untroubled sleep. Leah waits her turn with the other women and takes a tepid shower. She scrubs her hair and skin vigorously trying to cleanse the stains from her soul. It has become a habit with her, a need. She picks up an old but clean blouse from the pile of used clothes donated by the "Jewish war relief". A little sign next to the clothes says they are from the Brooklyn branch, wherever that is, and she goes back to the infirmary to see Yussel. Leah sits with him all day and night, dozing and dreaming and shaking herself quickly awake from her constant nightmares and dozing again. At about two or three in the morning, Yussel awakes, somewhat revived by the long sleep. He looks very peaceful.

"Ah, Leahleh my child. Go inside and sleep. I will be all right here. You need rest."

"No zaydeh [grandpa]. I will stay with you. I feel fine." She holds his hand and pats it. He looks at her, and he feels her deep suffering. "Leahleh, I have told you all about myself, for hours I have told you. It is for catharsis,

for the cleansing of my soul. To face these horrors, to speak of them, is to conquer them and to be free in your soul. Tell me about yourself, Leahleh.

She starts slowly. She tells a little, but then she cannot find the voice for the really bad things.

"And then, Leahleh? After the Ghetto? Come, release the chains that crush your heart. Tell these things that destroy your soul."

She is unable to speak, reluctant even to think of these horrors. But then she suddenly feels as though she has to say them, to get them out of her. And she tells him everything. Her body shakes, and her voice is a gasped whisper.

"Come here," Yussel pulls her by the arm out of the chair and into the bed next to him. He hugs her to him. Trembling with sobs, she presses against the old man.

"We Jews are the People of the Book, Leahleh, the Book of God's laws and judgments, the Tanach *[Bible], which is also the early history of our people. But it is not only a story of good things and nice deeds, it is the story of real people and their sins and evil as well as their goodness.*

"You know about our great King David, the unifier of our people, and you know the story told of him by the Prophet Samuel. When David saw Bathsheba for the first time, he was smitten with her beauty and he wanted her. But she was married to one of David's soldiers, Uriah the Hittite. So David gave orders to his commander to place Uriah at the head of the troops so that he would be killed in the next battle. And that's just what happened. Then David took Bathsheba as his wife. But the Prophet Nathan found out about this evil act of the King, and he confronted him openly with it and denounced him and pronounced God's curse on the King. So the firstborn son of David and Bathsheba died at birth to punish David for his sin.

"The world would not have known this terrible evil deed of one of our greatest leaders if we had not written of it ourselves in our greatest book, the Bible. Why did we do it, Leahleh? Because our sages have always known that knowledge of good requires knowledge of evil, and our duty is to separate out the bad as much as we can and strive for good. To be perfectly without sin is the province of the Lord our God alone." Leah lies quietly beside Yussel, and he continues in whispers.

"We have lived through the worst of times, Leahleh. Who among us has not been tainted by our own efforts to survive, to clutch for life and hope. It cannot be an act of evil to hide and beg and pray that we will be spared, even while they slaughter those closest to us.

"There is no human being, no people, who is not made up of both good and evil," she barely hears him say. She falls asleep. Yussel hugs her closely to him

and also falls asleep. For the first time in years, she sleeps without being awakened by a nightmare.

In the morning, a hand lightly shakes Leah's shoulder. She awakes. It is the doctor.

"Herr Pinsker is dead," he says to Leah with sadness.

She looks at Yussel, next to her in bed. His eyes are closed, his face relaxed, maybe even smiling. She swings her legs over the edge of the bed and stands up. He has died softly in his sleep. She knows that the soul of Yussel Pinsker has passed into her own to help make her whole again. She kisses his forehead. And with a determination she has never before had, she starts walking westward.

Chapter Eleven

After the Six Day War, with al-Asifah in ruins, Hassan and Nadia decided that it was appropriate for Hamdi to go to college in the United States. There was nothing for him in Jordan at the moment, and a stay in America would be a broadening experience. There were a number of schools that would be suitable for Hamdi, but the best was clearly the University of California at Berkeley, the eye of the hurricane of every radical cause imaginable, a place where Hamdi could blend right in almost without notice. Many other Palestinian boys had gone there over the preceding few years, and Hamdi would have a solid well-knit community of Palestinians to fall back on as a support group. The only problem was that his English was almost non-existent. So they decided that he should go to Berkeley right away and spend a year with English tutors. He was exceptionally bright and he would learn quickly. He could then be admitted into the foreign students program and be pampered along for another year or two, until his English was fluent, and then switch into a regular academic curriculum.

Hamdi was reluctant to leave his family, but he too realized the value of the educational experience that was in the offing. So in mid-July, just a month after the Six Day War ended, he boarded an airliner in Amman for the long flight to New York and then to San Francisco. He was met at San Francisco Airport by his long time friend Nayif, who had been attending Berkeley for two years. They drove up the peninsula to the interchange approach to the Bay Bridge, across the bridge into Oakland, and another few blocks to a small apartment building on Alcatraz Avenue on the sourthern edge of Berkeley. From the living room window of his one bedroom apartment, he could look down Alcatraz Avenue to its dead end at the freeway on the edge of San Francisco Bay and then directly to Alcatraz Island lying cold and forbidding in the frigid water. It was a spectacular view, like nothing Hamdi had ever seen before, especially at night when the glittery lights of San Francisco lit up the hills across the bay.

The next day, Nayif drove Hamdi down Telegraph Avenue to the edge of the Berkeley campus. Hamdi opened a checking account at the small Bank of America branch, with the $10,000 letter of credit that Hassan had given him drawn in American currency on the Banque du Liban in Beirut. Then Nayif drove him to a used car lot, and Hamdi bought a 1965 Volkswagen beetle for $1,000. He had an international driver's license which was good for a year.

That night, Nayif brought Hamdi to Professor Farid Selim's house for dinner. The house was an old and picturesque three story Victorian in the Berkeley Hills above the campus. Farid's wife Victoria met them at the door and treated Hamdi with great deference. Victoria Selim spoke almost no Arabic. Nayif had told Hamdi about Farid's background, and also about his wife Victoria, things that Hamdi thought that her husband surely did not know— particularly how well Nayif had known Victoria long before Farid had met her.

She was a Baptist girl from Nashville who had wandered out to San Francisco in search of free love and free drugs and meaning in the Haight-Ashbury district. After three years of sleeping around and searching for any cause she could adopt with typically excessive passion, she had met Farid at a student rally against Israeli imperialism in 1966. Farid was an Associate Professor of Engineering at Berkeley, thirty years old, and a native of Haifa, Palestine, which he had last seen in 1948. His family had fled to Beirut where his father became a Professor of Chemistry at the American University. Farid had graduated with honors and ul- timately received his doctorate at MIT in Boston. He had then taken a position in the Berkeley Engineering Department. He also became a leader of various Palestinian causes.

Victoria was a whole new experience for him. She had clung to his intensity and his passion for the underdog Palestinians with an almost worshipful diffidence, while at the same time she attacked his body with a hunger he had never before experienced.

Nayif told Hamdi about his own numerous Arabian nights with Victoria, both before and after her marriage to Farid. And he described with a wistful smile her attributes, undoubtedly the same ones that had so smitten Farid. She sucked him and fondled him like no Arab girl was ever likely to do. She got high on pot and acid and all kinds of pills, and she would take off her clothes and writhe gleefully in front of him like an Egyptian belly dancer, rotating her slender buttocks and shaking her heavy, big nippled breasts and pressing his face into her, enveloping him with the sweet musky smell and overwhelming animal lustiness that were her special gift.

Farid too was entranced by her, not knowing how many other men had come under that same spell. They married, and she studied Islam so that she could convert. She wasn't much at languages, however, and Arabic was extremely difficult. So she knew only a few phrases. Since Hamdi knew no English, she and Hamdi could do nothing but smile at each other across the dinner table.

"There are several Palestinians at Berkeley majoring in English," said Farid Selim. "Here are a list of names and telephone numbers of some of them. They do English tutoring on the side. If you aren't happy with one, try another. You'll find one who can help you learn."

Hamdi took the list from the professor, folded it and put it in his pocket.

"This Saturday night is a meeting of the 'Palestinian Student Union' here in my house. Come around seven and you'll meet some other students, Americans as well as Arabs, who are after the same things we are. Then we'll put you to work. You can sit at one of our information tables at Sather Gate and hand out literature on our legitimate rights and the Arab-Israeli dispute. Most of what the Americans hear is Jewish and Israeli propaganda. We're trying to balance the scales."

"Are there any really activist groups here?" asked Hamdi.

Farid studied the handsome newcomer closely. "Exactly what do you mean?"

"I mean a group which fights the Jew scum with more than words."

Nayif laughed at the surprised look on Farid's face. "You see, Farid! I told you that we had a real bombshell here with Hamdi. He's the son of Hassan abu-Sittah, and calm debates are not what he's after."

"Hamdi, I know how you feel," said Farid seriously. "But we have to be very careful here. Berkeley is full of Jews. We can't be starting riots or the University police will bar us from the campus. Be patient. Go slow. Learn about these Americans. They love underdogs and hate terrorists. At the moment, we are the underdogs and they are flocking to support us, even some of the Jewish students! We can't do anything at the moment to ruin our image."

They finished the lamb stew dinner and Farid brought out a bottle of Arak. But it wasn't the real thing, it was not made from dates but was merely flavored alcohol, and it depressed Hamdi with its phoniness. He was a little homesick, a little lost. Berkeley was totally alien to him. He could hardly understand a word of English. And he could only look forward to years of learning and studying and being away from his family and his *'awda*. He felt like he had been exiled.

In the morning, he slept late and then took a walk around his neighborhood. It was foggy and chilly and he went into a little cafe around the corner from his apartment. An old Chinese man was cooking eggs and some sausages on a grill, and several customers sat at the counter reading newspapers. The Chinese cook came up to him and said something which didn't even sound English, and Hamdi pointed to the plate sitting in front of one of the other customers. A few minutes later he got two pieces of toast and three strips of bacon and three eggs over easy. He ate it having no idea what the strips of meat were but loving the taste. Eating pork was a violation of Muslim dietary laws, but he had never before seen bacon, and he had no reason to believe that these savory strips were from a forbidden pig.

At about ten o'clock, he walked back to his apartment and took out the list of tutors so he could get down to learning English. The first two numbers rang and rang and no one answered. As he was dialing the third, there was a knock on his door. He opened it.

Victoria Selim stood in the hallway smiling at him. Her chestnut hair fell loosely around her shoulders and her enticing blue eyes smiled at him.

"Hi," she said, walking into the apartment.

"Hi," he said, closing the door behind her.

She walked over to the couch, pulled off her raincoat, and threw it over the arm. She was wearing a wool miniskirt and a soft sweater, and her big breasts jiggled as she sat down. She smiled sweetly at Hamdi and patted the cushion next to her. Hamdi sat down. Her perfume was delicious. He had never been alone with a woman before, except his mother and grandmother, and that time in Algiers.

Victoria reached into her purse and pulled out a little baggie with a dried grass-like substance in it. She also pulled out a small envelope with cigarette papers. She proceeded to roll a joint and light it, holding the smoke in and swallowing it rather than inhaling it. She handed Hamdi the small cigarette and he did the same thing. He coughed harshly and his eyes teared. He had smoked before, but he had never heard of marijuana. Victoria laughed at him and gestured for him to take another drag. He did and managed to swallow it down without coughing again. It made him a bit light headed. After the fourth drag, he was tipsy and giddy. Victoria giggled at him as she stubbed out the end of the roach. She pulled her sweater over her arms and tossed it on the floor. She pulled Hamdi's head to her chest and he began sucking on her nipples, and then he felt her undo his zipper.

She stood up from the couch and unzipped her skirt. It fell to the floor and she stepped out of it. She was naked. She walked to Hamdi. He was intoxicated from the marijuana cigarette and the pleasure of his first lovemaking and she rocked on him and let out a short scream as she climaxed during his orgasm.

She rolled another joint and they smoked it and giggled and made love again. She left at noon. Hamdi felt much more at home in America now.

Victoria visited him often, and as his English improved from day to day, they were able to talk more and more. But it was not talk that she came for, and it was not conversation that he wanted, and they got along wonderfully well.

When Hamdi's English became sufficient for a small conversation, Farid put him to work at the Palestinian table at Sather Gate, the entrance to the University off Telegraph Avenue. He would sit there four or five hours a day, handing out leaflets to anyone who stopped. Occasionally a passerby would talk with him about this or that aspect of the Israel-Arab conflict. For one entire week in January 1968, a group of Israeli students marched with placards in front of the table, blocking passersby from picking up any of the Palestinian literature. Hamdi taunted them in his fluent Hebrew and one of the Jews taunted him in fluent Arabic and the march ended when Hamdi broke one of the placards over a fat ugly Israeli Jewess' head and shattered the nose and jaw of the Jew scum who tried to come to her rescue. Hamdi ran down Telegraph Avenue and drove back to his apartment before the police came, and he didn't return to the table for two months. It was too damn cold to sit out there anyway.

In April, he was back behind the pamphlet table at Sather Gate. The Vietnam War had made anti-American terrorists out of a number of student radical groups. Latching on to the war as their *raison d'etre*, these kids from some of America's middle and upper class families had begun planting bombs in bank buildings and utility company buildings and post offices and courthouses, as their protest against the stolid military-industrial complex which ran American life. The "Students for a Free Society," as one of these nut groups was called, reached out to slum blacks and Iranian dissidents and displaced Palestinians to supply the brutality and terrorist techniques around which the group was molded. Hamdi was asked to go to a meeting by another Palestinian who had been in the States for six years and was a hanger-on to a number of such groups. Hamdi's knowledge of small demolition tactics and his Algerian training in insurrection techniques was well known to the Palestinian, who knew that it would be invaluable to these American boys and girls from the finest families.

Hamdi had no idea what the meeting was to be about. It was held at a fine apartment just two blocks from the North Campus in an oak tree lined lane of expensive student housing. The girl who asked him to become their "bomber" had straggly blond hair and a narrow marmoset face. She wore a loose muu-muu which she called a "dashiki" and which showed her bulbous nipples and pendulous breasts. She wore no makeup and smelled of dried perspiration unameliorated by such bourgeois taints as deodorant or perfume.

Hamdi was turned off by the woman and insulted by her proposal and he told her that his talents were not for sale but were for the benefit of his oppressed Palestinian brethren. She took away the cordial she had offered him and sneered at him as she poured it back into the Calvados bottle.

In late July, Hamdi was sitting in the warm sun behind the table at Sather Gate, when a lovely girl walked up and spoke to him in Arabic. He could tell instantly from her accent that she was from Algeria. She wanted to know if he had any literature in Arabic.

"Yes, of course," he said, pulling a box out from under the table. He took out a few pamphlets and handed them to her. She studied the covers and walked away.

Two days later, she came back. "Do you have any more on the Arab-Israeli conflict?"

"Listen, why don't we go out to dinner and we'll talk about it?" answered Hamdi. "I have some books. I can bring them along. My name is Hamdi Attiyah."

"I'm Miriam Aljeziri. Okay," she said, smiling sweetly. She took a piece of scratch paper out of her purse, wrote her address on it, and handed it to Hamdi. "Pick me up at seven?"

"I am honored," he said, rising. She smiled at him and walked away. He spent the rest of the day anxiously wishing that seven o'clock would come quickly. And finally it did. He parked in front of her duplex apartment in North Berkeley and rang the doorbell. She opened it and asked him in. She was wearing a long indigo blue gauzy caftan with a ruby beaded v-neckline that set off her shiny black hair and olive skin. She had on a delicate spicy perfume, an aroma like hollyhocks in a spring meadow, that wafted to him as she led him to the sofa.

"I thought we might eat here," she said, pointing to the kitchen table set with dishes and a candle and a bottle of red wine. "May I get you a glass of wine?"

"Yes, I'd love it."

She brought over two glasses of wine and set one on the side table by the couch. She sat next to him, close, sipping the wine.

"You're from Algiers?"

"No, from Oran. How did you know?"

"I could tell by your accent. I lived in Algeria for a while."

"When was that?"

"Oh, before the Six Day War, before the Jews made weeping women out of all of us." Hamdi looked deep into her black eyes. She was as lovely as any woman he had ever seen and she had that special softness of the North Africans. She lightly brushed her hair back from her face with her delicate long fingered left hand and took another sip of wine.

"Where are you from, Hamdi?"

"Palestine. But my family is living in Jordan now. We will return someday."

"Is your family part of the fedayeen?"

It was not an odd question to be asked, but Hamdi did not know Miriam well enough yet to talk about these things. "Come, enough about me. I want to talk about you," he said smiling.

"Well, I'm here getting my degree in English literature. I intend to go back and teach English in Algeria. How about you?"

"My English wasn't good enough to get me into school last year, but I'll be starting in September. I expect to major in Middle East History and Politics." He paused and looked at her seriously. "Listen, maybe you could become my English tutor. I need constant help."

"Do you think we'd ever study?" They both laughed. Hamdi put his arm around her shoulders, and she turned her face to him and kissed him deliciously, softly, and then nuzzled her face in his neck. He was very excited. He put his left hand lightly on her chest and rubbed her small breasts. She didn't stop him. He took her wine glass and put it on the corner table.

"Aren't you hungry," she said.

He didn't answer. He fondled her breasts and her breathing was fast and shallow. He kissed her and slid his hand down her thin caftan and massaged her between her legs.

"Wait, Hamdi. It is too soon," she said very softly, pulling herself up on the couch. "It is not fitting. We have all the time in the world. We must wait."

He said nothing and slowly straightened up. She kissed him, her tongue searching out his and probing his mouth. Then she got up and went into the kitchen and started getting the meal ready to serve. He sat and made himself relax, waiting for his pulse to slow down. He was euphoric with her taste and smell, the sense of the beginning of something rich and valuable and deep, a new element to add to the fullness of his life.

In the second week of August, she moved out of her duplex and into his apartment. Victoria was a little irked, but she was also happy for him. She would pick out another young stallion from the new crop of Palestinians. Hamdi was grateful for what she had done for him, all that she had taught him. But now he was doing those things with Miriam and discovering how much more spectacular it was when there was also love.

Shortly after she moved in, he brought two friends home for dinner. One was a great big Iraqi whom Hamdi called Bobby. The other was Hamdi's Palestinian friend Nayif. They ate dinner, and then Miriam cleared the table and excused herself. She went into the bedroom to study.

"We want to rob the payroll from the Safeway in Hayward," said Bobby. "The brothers say that this Saturday night the Hayward store will be the collection point for all of the Safeway payrolls in the Bay Area, so they can be distributed out on Monday." The "brothers" Bobby referred to were the "Palestinian Revolutionary Front," a tiny splinter group of an Iraq backed Palestinian refugee organization, composed almost entirely of Iraqis claiming Palestinian forebears. Their task was to conduct terrorism against Americans, the supporters of the Jew pigs, cleaving to the ancient Arab proverb that "the friend of my enemy is my enemy." They had asked Professor Selim if they could borrow Hamdi for a night so he could blow the steel back door to the Safeway. A pleasant side benefit of revolutionary terrorism in the United States was that it could be very lucrative.

"And how do we do the safe?" asked Hamdi. "I've never blown a safe."

"Don't worry about the safe. We're going to put it on rollers and take it with us!" The three men laughed.

"Well, shouldn't be a big problem," said Hamdi looking at the rough sketch of the market before him on the table. "When do we do it?"

"We meet you there at midnight. Come alone. Just park behind the store. It'll be dark, because there are no lights back there. We'll be there in our truck. Nothin' to it. As soon as you blow the door, leave. No problems."

"How about the burglar alarm?"

"We'll take care of that before you get there."

"Okay, see you at midnight," Hamdi stood up. Bobby reached into his back pocket and pulled out his wallet. He counted out ten $100 bills and laid them on the table. Hamdi nodded and smiled. He didn't need the money, but one didn't look a gift horse in the mouth. Bobby and Nayif left.

Hamdi picked up the money off the table and walked into the bedroom. Miriam was lying on her stomach over the bed reading a book. It was a very warm night, and she was only wearing panties. Hamdi threw down the money on the bed beside her. She reached for it and held it up.

"Ooh," she squealed. "A few new dresses?"

"Anything you want. Always."

"Oh honey, I love you so." She got off the bed and pressed herself to him and he slid his hands under her panties and fondled her slim buttocks.

"I love you too, Miriam. I need you very much."

That Saturday night, he told Miriam that he and Nayif were meeting some other Palestinians at Professor Selim's house and he would probably be quite late. It was better not to involve Miriam in these things, Hamdi thought to himself. It was safer for her that way, and she wouldn't worry about him. She had been in the bedroom so she hadn't heard the plans for the Safeway. All the better.

The Safeway demolition job went off like clockwork. It took exactly four minutes. He waved to Bobby, got back into his Volkswagen and returned to his apartment. Miriam was sleeping like a baby. In the morning, Miriam was already puttering around the kitchen when Hamdi awoke. He went into the living room yawning and stretching and sprawled on the couch.

Miriam brought the Sunday *San Francisco Examiner* to him and laid it beside the couch. She kissed him lightly on the forehead, said "Good morning, honey," and went back to the kitchen.

Hamdi picked up the newspaper and glanced disinterestedly at the headlines: "Two Arabs Killed in Burglary." He sat up stiffly on the couch and read the story. Apparently the van had been speeding on the freeway at about twelve thirty in the morning and had been stopped by a Highway Patrolman. The officer had become suspicious of the three men in the van and asked them all for identification. He was shot in the shoulder. Another Highway Patrol car in the area had also arrived on the scene just as the shooting happened, and he had called for help. A high speed chase ensued and then a shootout. Two of the Iraqis had been killed. The police then discovered the Safeway safe in the back of the van. It had over $300,000 cash inside. The only one of the "Front" that Hamdi knew was Bobby, and Bobby was dead. Hamdi didn't think the police would have any leads to him. If they had, he supposed, they would already be knocking down the front door.

Three days later, Nayif came to dinner with another "Front" member named Khaliq.

"Listen, we still need the money," said Khaliq. "This time it's going to be at the main store in San Leandro. Same plan." Khaliq laid a thousand dollars on the table.

"The last safe had $300,000," said Hamdi looking hard at Khaliq. "And you guys are dangerous to work with," he paused to let Khaliq fully digest this. He didn't want these Iraqis to buy him too cheaply. As undependable as Iraq had been in its support of the true Palestinian fedayeen, Hamdi wanted to rub their faces just a little in their need for him.

"I want $5,000," he said. He actually didn't care about the money, but he cared about face. The only reason these Iraqis needed him was his facility with explosives, and the only way they showed respect was by what they paid. Among the Iraqis, your price indicated your status, and no one cared where your head was at.

"I'll have to talk to the brothers," said Khaliq, very pissed off, and stormed out of the apartment.

The next day, an envelope with $4,000 in cash was slipped under the apartment door. Miriam and Hamdi found it when they came home from shopping. They had just spent most of the first $2,000 on clothes at Saks and I. Magnin's in Union Square. Miriam was thrilled. Hamdi knew that her family was not wealthy like his, and she was now probably looking at more money than she had ever before seen at one time.

"Hamdi, you have rapidly become the man of my dreams, my 'Prince Charming' as the Americans call it." She stared lovingly at the forty $100 bills in the envelope. Hamdi was very proud, very happy to have this girl and to be able to give her everything she wanted.

"Come, money makes me horny," she said to him, leading him into the bedroom.

Again, Hamdi's part of the Safeway job went off in minutes without a hitch, and he returned quickly to his apartment. And again Miriam was sleeping peacefully. Hamdi undressed, and he was stimulated from all the excitement of bombing the Safeway and now seeing Miriam lying on her stomach over the covers, nude, gorgeous, glistening in the moonlight coming through the open drapes. He loved this girl very much. He got into bed and woke her gently.

In the morning, he was stunned by the newspaper story about the Safeway job: "Second Safeway Burglary Foiled." This time, a private security patrolman had happened upon the Arabs as they wheeled the safe out of the store to the van. He radioed for backup and several police vehicles surrounded the parking lot. There was a short shootout with one of the burglars slightly wounded. The others had quickly surrendered.

Hamdi was frightened. Khaliq was alive and if he identified Hamdi it could buy him leniency. The "Front" would never give away a brother, but he was no brother, he was a Palestinian who had demanded more money for a job. Hamdi went into the bedroom, closed the door and telephoned Nayif.

"Nayif, contact the 'Front' and make sure that I'm going to be safe."

"Don't worry, Hamdi. They would never give any information to the police. Any one of them who did that would be killed. Take it easy. But I just got a call from one of their leaders. He thinks there's a leak somewhere. He doesn't think that it's just bad luck two weeks in a row."

"Well, then tell them I'm out of it. I don't want any part of them until they clean up their act."

"They know that. They're going to cool it until they find the snitch. I'll stay in touch with them and keep you posted."

"Thanks, Nayif."

Hamdi was very agitated, apprehensive, and he stayed in the apartment for the next two days. He didn't even go with Miriam when she went into San Francisco at noon on Tuesday to spend another $1,000 on some new winter clothes. It was already September, and cold weather was on the way. At two o'clock, Hamdi got a call from Farid Selim. He wanted Hamdi to come over to his house at five. Very important.

When Hamdi arrived, Farid and Nayif were sitting in the living room looking extremely upset. Victoria wasn't home. Hamdi took a glass of Arak and sipped. They exchanged the mandatory pleasantries, and then Farid got down to business.

"Do you know what Miriam's background is?"

"What the hell does that matter?" snapped Hamdi.

"Look, I know this is not going to make you very happy, but we think Miriam is an FBI plant."

"That's bullshit!" said Hamdi. "Those fucking Iraqis blow two jobs and they're trying to blame it on us!"

"Take it easy, Hamdi," said Farid soothingly. "It's not them who thinks Miriam is a plant, it's me."

Hamdi looked at the professor with alarm. He tensed and said nothing.

"I talked to the Algerian consul yesterday. They do not have a record of any Miriam Aljeziri on a student visa at Berkeley. I asked him to check further. He made some inquiries with the Saudi embassy in Washington and they asked around. Just before I called you today, I spoke with the consul again. Miriam Aljeziri does not exist. We don't know who she is."

Hamdi was trembling, speechless.

"None of your operations failed until she moved in with you. Now, in the three or four weeks you've been living together, both of your jobs have been blown. It seems to add up. You are the leak."

Hamdi covered his eyes with a trembling hand. He was deeply shaken. His head was splitting with pain. "I can't believe it," he said to Farid, shrinking into the arm chair. "I just can't believe it."

"There's an off chance we're wrong," said Farid, knowing full well there was no chance. "But she is most likely a Jew born in

Algeria. The FBI is using Sephardic Jews to infiltrate Palestinian groups in the States, just as Israel's Secret Service uses them in the Middle East. You're going to have to find out, Hamdi. Until we know for sure, we are all in grave danger."

Hamdi stood up abruptly and walked out of the house. He still couldn't believe it. There had to be another explanation. He drove around Berkeley for two hours, mulling over the possibilities, trying to figure out what had to be done. He drove and thought and forced himself to be calm. At about seven thirty he went home. Miriam had apparently just returned from shopping, because she was taking clothes out of bags and laying them on the couch, admiring them.

"Oh honey!" she said with pleasure, running up to him and kissing his cheek. "Come see what I got." She took his hand and led him to the couch.

"That's beautiful, Miriam. You'll look like a million dollars in it," he said hugging her. "Come on, let's go out for dinner."

They went to a small restaurant near the Berkeley Tennis Club. The lighting was soft, the atmosphere romantic, the food good, and the wine dulling. He drank less than she and kept refilling her glass. She was radiant with the romantic dinner and the wine when they finally got back to the apartment.

She lay on her back and he loved her passionately, bringing himself to orgasm, careful not to bring her along too. He rested for a moment, still in her, and then started to thrust himself deeply into her, this time rubbing against her and bringing her to climax. And as she came and pressed her knees tightly around his hips, he whispered in Hebrew, "*Ani ohev otach, ani ohev otach, Miriam.*" [I love you, I love you, Miriam]. And she groaned in response as she came, "O Hamdi, *atah fantasti,*" Hebrew slang meaning, "you're fantastic."

He stopped moving in her, and suddenly she stopped. Her body settled back on the bed. He switched on the lamp beside the bed, and she gaped at him, her mouth open. He put a pillow over her face and dug his right hand into her throat, smashing her larynx in his powerful grasp and cutting off her breathing. Her slender body writhed under him, her arms tore at the pillow. And then she stopped fighting, and her arms fell limply on the mattress.

He got out of bed and showered quickly and shaved. He put on a business suit and white shirt and conservative tie. He went down to his car parked in the dark lot behind the apartment building and took out the army duffel bag he had bought that evening at the Army-Navy surplus store. He went back into the apartment and put Miriam inside the bag. With her legs folded back at the knees, she just fit. He carried her down to the car and put her in the trunk. He drove about forty minutes north to Suisun Bay, a deserted bay past the little town of Martinez. He drove along the bank looking for what appeared to be a very deep section and stopped beside the road.

It was a darkly overcast night. He opened the trunk and opened the duffel bag. He put a piece of rope through the center holes of the two twenty-five-pound barbell weights he had also bought earlier that evening, and he tied the weights securely around the now rigid waist of the dead girl. He closed the duffel bag again, lifted it onto his shoulder, walked to the edge of the small bay, and heaved the bag into the water. It submerged instantly. A flock of sleepy egrets fluttered their wings and squawked a short protest and then went back to sleep.

He got back into his car and drove to San Francisco Airport. It was almost three in the morning. He had $3,000 in cash. He boarded the early flight to New York City. A day and a half later, he was back in Amman, safe in the protection of his powerful family. His foray into the world outside had been a dangerous one, and he had let his head be turned by its many temptations. But he would never again stray from his true destiny, the fight for his homeland, the way of the fedayeen.

Chapter Twelve

"Captain Jordan," snarled Lieutenant Colonel Heimetz through gritted teeth, "I didn't ask for your fucking views on right and wrong. I give the fucking orders here, you take them!" Heimetz was short and stocky and had a steel gray crewcut. His small green eyes squinted over steel rimmed glasses. His face was scarred and pitted from smallpox. He clenched a cigarette in the corner of his mouth.

Joshua stiffened to attention before his battalion commander's desk. "Yes sir."

"Now get the fuck out of here!"

"Yes sir." Joshua turned on his heels and marched out of the command tent.

He got into his jeep, just outside the tent entrance, and the bitterness and disgust in his drawn face silenced his driver. The driver put the jeep in gear and headed over the rocky dirt road to Recon Company B's bivouac area a few hundred yards from the Jordan River near the West Bank village of Kafr-Qasim.

"Pick up Rav Segens Temani and Kresnitz and bring them here," Joshua said to his driver as he jumped out of his jeep and walked into his tent. A few minutes later, the two First Lieutenants assigned to Joshua's Recon Company came into the small tent. It was late October and a very cold and blustery day, and Joshua was stoking a pot-bellied wood-burning stove in the center of the tent.

"What's up?" asked Uzi Temani, flopping down on the wooden chair beside the cot. Uzi was willowy and of medium height with curly brown hair and black eyes. He looked like a delicate teenager, although he was 24 years old and was the company hand-to-hand combat instructor.

"We got curfew patrol duty in Kafr-Qasim for the next three days," said Joshua, still trying to coax some warmth out of the crackling wood in the stove.

"What the hell for?" asked Kresnitz.

"Because Heimetz says so," Joshua answered, walking over and sitting dejectedly on his cot. "That son of a bitch pock-faced prick! He looks like a woodpecker tried to feed on his face!" They all laughed derisively.

"Anyway," continued Joshua, "Intelligence is reporting that the Arabs are going to commemorate October 29 with terrorist attacks all along the border. We attacked the Suez Canal twelve years ago on the 29th, they'll attack us the day after tomorrow. Kafr-Qasim is supposed to be a staging point for the fedayeen."

"That sleepy little village? Those farmers don't even know *how* to use a machine gun or a mortar," said Temani.

"I told Heimetz that. He doesn't give a shit. He's imposing a four in the afternoon to eight in the morning curfew and we're to see that it isn't violated."

"But Joshua, they don't come out of the fields until dark and they start before sunup. With the freeze about to start, they need every minute of daylight to harvest their crops." Kresnitz was saying what Joshua well knew. A three day curfew at this particular time could mean the loss of a large portion of the harvest, a devastating blow to this ancient impoverished Arab village.

"Our commanding officer suggested to me that my interest in such things as the Arabs' harvest was not very impressive. He wants the curfew for the next three days, and that's that," Joshua said with resignation. He looked at his two First Lieutenants and they shrugged their shoulders.

"Okay, Uzi will post notices in Arabic on the communal buildings in the village tomorrow morning. They'll see them when they come back from the fields in the evening. We'll encircle the village on the 29th and keep the curfew. Understood?

"Yes sir," replied both men and left the tent.

Joshua lay back on his cot and pulled the thin wool blanket around him. This is exactly how you create trouble, he thought, not how you avoid it. Heimetz was an old timer and he hated the Arabs. Not an uncommon trait in Israel. Their comfort, their harvest, their rights, none of this meant a thing to Heimetz. To him, every Arab was a terrorist, an ex-terrorist, or a future one.

The next day, Uzi Temani and some other Arabic-speaking soldiers posted hastily written notices in Arabic on several of the village buildings. Everyone was in the fields except the small children and women. Before dawn on October 29, as Joshua was readying his Company to encircle Kafr-Qasim, a message came over his radio: "Fedayeen activity at abu-Musa. Send all available personnel." Joshua took A and B Platoons toward abu-Musa some six miles away and ordered Temani and Kresnitz to take C and D to Kafr-Qasim. Nothing was going to happen there anyway.

Late in the afternoon, Joshua's scouts reported spotting fedayeen in the hills south of abu-Musa. A and B Platoons rushed to the area, but the terrorists—if there had been any—were gone.

At Kafr-Qasim, four o'clock came and went and none of the villagers returned from the fields. Uzi Temani, the senior officer in charge of the curfew, became extremely nervous. Four thirty, five o'clock, five thirty, the sun began to go below the hills and dusk obscured Temani's ability to see movement around the village. It was cold and still, and the deepening darkness became eerie. Still none of the village men returned from the fields. A small grove of mulberry trees loomed in the murky darkness like wicked specters.

Joshua was out of range for Temani's field radio, so Temani could not ask him for futher instructions. He decided that he'd better contact Lieutenant Colonel Heimetz and get orders about how to handle the curfew violation.

Heimetz was truculent as usual. "Well, find those fucking bastards!"

"Sir, it's too dark already. We can't maneuver our jeeps in these hills in this darkness."

"You stupid asshole. They may have surrounded your men already. There were major terrorist movements all over your area all day today. You'd better be damn sure you have cover!" raged Heimetz over the field radio.

"Yes sir. What do we do about the curfew violators?" There was silence on the other end of the radio for a moment. Then Heimetz spoke slowly.

"The curfew order comes from Headquarters. Our own protection is paramount. Are you sure the villagers were warned about the curfew?"

"I posted the notices myself yesterday. But the Arabs came back after dark last night and left again at dawn this morning. Maybe they didn't see them."

"But you *did* post the notices in full view yesterday?" insisted Heimetz.

"Yes sir, I did."

Another brief pause. "My orders are that curfew violators in your sector will be shot."

"I don't understand," said Temani, thinking that he hadn't heard right.

"You fucking understand, Temani! Don't give me any bullshit! If you lose one goddam man in a terrorist attack I'll have your ass in a sling! My orders are to shoot curfew violators. Those are your orders! Understand?"

"Yes sir. Understood. Out." Temani was desolate, cold, frightened. The darkness was almost complete, except for a little periodic glow from the half moon peeking out now and then between the cumulus clouds. Temani passed the order around C and D Platoons to shoot at anything that moved. Still it was quiet.

Then they heard muffled voices moving along the ridge on the left toward the village. The Israelis could barely make out the silhouettes of the Arab men walking toward Kafr-Qasim. They were all carrying things, but it was too dark to tell whether they were weapons or farm implements. Temani gave the order over his walkie talkie to all squad commanders: "Open fire."

Machine gun fire came from the mounted .50 calibers on the jeeps. It was over in less than a minute.

Joshua and A and B Platoons returned to their bivouac at about seven, after a full day of wild goose chases. He had expected his other two platoons to be back already from curfew duty, but the camp was deserted. He sent his scouts to Kafr-Qasim to see what was going on, and he went into his tent to get the fire going in the stove. A few minutes later, the radioman ran into his tent.

"Sir, you'd better come! There's been trouble at the village!"

"What kind of trouble?" asked Joshua, rising off his knees next to the stove.

"Some of the Arabs broke curfew. They've been shot."

"Aw shit!" Joshua zipped up his field jacket and wrapped his muffler around his face and ran to the radio shack behind the radioman.

"We got orders from Heimetz to shoot to kill," said Uzi Temani over the crackling short wave. "They were almost three hours past curfew, we couldn't tell if they were armed, it was too dark to—"

"How many are dead?" Joshua cut him off.

"We're not sure yet. We're counting now."

"Were any of our men hurt?"

There was a long pause on the other end. "No sir. There was no return fire," said Temani slowly.

"I'll be right there!" Joshua yelled into the phone. He ran to his jeep and sped over the bumpy road to Kafr-Qasim. He was there in less than ten minutes and drove up to the edge of the ridge where the Recon jeeps were parked with their lights illuminating the dirt trail leading to the village on which lay dozens of bodies of Arab men and boys. Joshua ran up to the jeep in which Uzi was sitting. He was weeping, his shoulders convulsing. Joshua shook his shoulder.

"Uzi! Uzi! Cut it out! What the hell happened here?"

Temani looked up slowly. "Forty-three dead. None of them was armed, even with a pocket knife."

"How the hell did it happen? Come on! Come on! Talk!" he yelled at Uzi, again shaking his shoulder.

"Orders from Heimetz. I swear to God, Joshua. Those were his orders."

"That lunatic!" Joshua pulled away from the jeep and looked at the bodies of the harmless Arab farmers. He was sick with anger and frustration and disgust. He ran back to his jeep, drove to battalion headquarters and went directly to the command tent. Heimetz and two other officers were sitting glumly at a table in the middle of the tent.

"What the fuck did you do?" screamed Joshua at Lieutenant Colonel Heimetz.

"Take it easy," said Major Horowitz, standing up from the table and walking over to him.

"I said what the fuck did you do, you crazy son of a bitch!" screamed Joshua, red-faced, trembling.

"You're under arrest," said Heimetz quietly, getting to his feet. He worked his cigarette furiously at the corner of his mouth, puffing a cloud of smoke.

"Come on, Josh, come on!" Horowitz was much bigger than Joshua. He wrapped an arm around his shoulders and pushed him outside the tent. "Get the hell back to your unit, Josh. What do you think you're doing?"

"That crazy bastard murdered forty-three unarmed Arab farmers tonight," said Joshua to his long time friend, Shlomo Horowitz. He got a grip on himself and stood staring at Shlomo in disbelief. "How could he do that? How the hell could he do that?"

"Listen Josh. He says those were his orders from Headquarters. The Inspector General is on his way down here. Now you get back to your company right now. That's an order!"

Joshua walked back to his jeep and drove to Kafr-Qasim. The village women were kneeling beside the bodies of their men and weeping and ululating in the eerie moonlight. He ordered the two platoons back to the bivouac area. Uzi Temani was taken into the Hadassah Hospital Mental Health Center. He was in deep shock.

In the morning, the Inspector General and two Headquarters

Generals took Joshua's statement. That afternoon, Lieutenant Colonel Heimetz and First Lieutenant Temani were arrested for murder and incarcerated in the military prison in Jerusalem. Four enlisted men from Company D were also arrested and charged with murder.

Friday evening Joshua drove into Jerusalem to his parents' home. Matt and Leah were sitting in the living room watching television.

"What is it, Joshele?" asked Leah, getting up from the couch and turning off the TV, obviously alarmed by the look on her son's face.

Joshua sat down heavily in an armchair. "Dad, you have to defend Uzi Temani. He only followed orders. It's Heimetz who ought to be tried for murder. Uzi and the four machine gunners had no choice." He looked pleadingly at his father. Leah and Matt glanced at each other, their faces haggard.

"I won't defend him, Joshua. He committed cold-blooded murder," Matt said slowly.

"Goddam it, Dad! It was orders! Heimetz forced him to do it. I've known Uzi for two years. He's a decent guy and a good soldier. He grew up with Arabs. He doesn't hate anybody. This wasn't his fault!"

"I'm sorry Joshua, you're wrong. It was his fault."

Joshua stared at his father, shocked, wounded. "What the hell do you think would've happened if I had been the one at Kafr-Qasim?"

"You wouldn't have followed his orders to shoot curfew violators. That's what I think would have happened."

"I'm not sure, Dad."

"I'm sure," Matt looked deep into his son's eyes. "I'm very sure."

"But Uzi just followed orders. That's all. They *can't* convict him of murder for that."

"Joshua, your mother and I met at the Nuremberg trials, as you well know. The Nazis all claimed the 'defense of superior orders,' claiming that the death camps were run under orders from Hitler himself, and they had no power or authority to countermand or refuse to follow superior orders. Do you know what the ruling of the Nuremberg Tribunal was?"

Joshua shook his head slowly from side to side.

"I remember the judge's words. He said 'No law of war provides that a soldier will remain unpunished for a hateful crime by referring to the orders of his superiors, if those orders are in striking opposition to all human ethics.'"

Joshua listened in pain, clenching his jaw, feeling his blood rise in his face.

"I talked to the Inspector General two days ago, Joshua. He had your statement as well as Shlomo Horowitz's report about your confrontation with Heimetz. We are very proud of you, Joshua. You did the right thing. Temani did not."

"But Dad, Uzi is from a poor Sephardic family. He had no education. He has had to do everything for himself. He is a fine officer. How in God's name does anyone expect him to refuse to carry out the orders of his own battalion commander?"

"The same way we imposed that responsibility on the Nazis. Are we Jews somehow immune from the law? Are we not to be judged by the same standards humanity forced upon the Nazis?"

"That's different, Dad. That was concentration camps, mass murder of Jews just because they were Jews. This is not—"

"You're dead wrong, Joshua," Matt broke in. "This is the same thing. Mass murder of innocent civilians just because they are Arabs and broke a curfew. And the evidence is clear that they weren't even aware of the curfew and Uzi knew it."

"Joshua. Your father and I have been talking about this for days. We know that Uzi is a close friend of yours. And there is nothing that your father would like better than to help him. But the defense of superior orders is one of mankind's worst jokes, worst fallacies. It is just an excuse for lawlessness. No one knows that better than the Jews. We must show the world that we will not condone genocide. Our problems with the Arab States and the fedayeen are the fault of the Arabs. That does not give us the right to slaughter Arab civilians. We can't let ourselves become animals."

Joshua was confused, forlorn. He didn't know what to say.

"You are our future," said Matt. "Israel has men like Heimetz and some of them are unfortunately in positions where they can do tragic harm to all of us. We depend on men like you to keep us human—humane. We can't kill all the Arabs. We have to live with them, to befriend them, to help them learn to trust us. Then maybe we can have real peace. And you and your generation must be the leaders, Joshua. Our generation has already failed. And the massacre at Kafr-Qasim will scar us for years to come. I'm sorry, Joshua. Uzi Temani and the four enlisted men must be tried for murder. It is the only way we can show the world that we are a decent people, that we aren't Nazis."

A few weeks later, the accused soldiers were tried for murder and convicted. Joshua testified on Uzi's behalf, but it didn't help. Uzi's appeal to the Supreme Court of Israel was denied. The Court held that his "defense of superior orders" was not a valid defense to the commission of an atrocity.

Chapter Thirteen

Dalia Almogi was released from her two year stint in Tzahal at the end of July 1969. Joshua Jordan had chosen to remain as a career officer in Tzahal, and he was a Seren [Captain] commanding a Recon Company in East Jerusalem.

Their wedding was planned for late October.

Two weeks before the wedding, early in the morning, Joshua was on patrol duty with his Recon Company on the Amman road in the Judean Hills about ten miles from the Jordan River. It was a routine patrol, to check for signs of foot traffic on the dirt side roads, a sure indication of guerrilla activity in this remote unpopulated area. Suddenly one of his men shouted to him from about thirty yards away.

"Joshua! Over here!" First Lieutenant Adan, in charge of A Platoon, was signaling to him with his arms held high. Joshua was about fifty yards off the Amman Road, rolling over the rocky ground in his jeep, and he ordered the driver to go toward the First Lieutenant. The rest of the Recon Company halted their jeeps where they were, on radioed orders from Joshua. Joshua's jeep bounced up to where Adan was pointing, and there was the remains of a campsite where as many as two hundred men must have bivouacked. The charcoaled wood in several of the campfire pits was still smoldering and smoking.

"We must have come on at least a company of fedayeen," said Joshua to Adan. "Their lookouts must have picked up our dust off the roads. They're probably still in these hills."

Both men looked around cautiously. They were eighty or ninety yards over rough terrain from the rest of the Recon Company near the road. The surrounding area was covered with small brush. About twenty yards north of the bivouac area was a narrow gully giving way to a steep shrub-covered hill looming on the other side. It looked like a perfect place from which to stage an ambush.

"Do not converge on us," Joshua spoke quietly over his radio to the three other platoon leaders near the road. "It looks like a company or more of fedayeen have set up an ambush from the steep hill to my north. Adan and I are coming out slowly. We'll then flank the hill and see what's in there."

Joshua gave a head shake to his driver, who put the jeep into gear and started rolling slowly toward the road. Adan's jeep followed close behind. The familiar crack-crack-crack of a Kalachnikov burst through the morning stillness. Adan's jeep shuddered to a halt. The driver was dead, and Adan was clutching his blood soaked left arm, staring at it in confusion. Several more Kalachnikovs opened up as Joshua and his driver dived off the side of their jeep. Joshua ran to Adan, and as he was pulling his stunned friend out of the jeep, another short blast blew Adan's chest apart and covered Joshua with blood and gore. Joshua crawled back to his jeep and reached quickly for the radio microphone.

"Do not converge on us! Repeat. Do not converge on us! Platoon A go behind to the far side of the hill and Platoon B remain at the road. When A is in position, A and B will attack the flanks. Then C and D are to come in for a frontal assault."

The fedayeen had still not shown themselves on the hill. They must be thinking that I'm radioing for help, thought Joshua, and they're waiting for the rest of the company to come in to be ambushed. Good, wait a little while longer, just until A gets into position. Joshua heard the pop of a recoilless rifle and Adan's jeep burst into flame. Aw shit, come on A Platoon, now's the time, now's the time. . . .

He felt a searing sensation in his right leg at the same instant that his own jeep was going up in flames. The explosion threw him backward to the ground and knocked the wind out of him. For seconds that seemed like a year, he couldn't breathe, he couldn't feel, he couldn't shake the fuzziness and puzzlement from his mind. Then he began gasping and regained consciousness and saw the bloody wound in his thigh. It was jagged and was apparently from a piece of metal blown off the jeep or shrapnel from the bazooka shell. But for some odd reason it didn't hurt. He couldn't understand it. It hurts to cut yourself shaving, he thought to himself, but a big bloody hole in your leg doesn't hurt. The leaping flames from the two jeeps were concealing Joshua from the hill, and the firing stopped. He sat and stared at his leg in a reverie, as though he were alone in a rowboat on a placid lake fishing for bass and staring at the shimmering water.

Firing started from both sides of the hill as A and B Platoons executed their attack from the flanks. Then he felt himself being moved, and voices around him, and then there was darkness, and then there was nothing.

Chapter Fourteen

It was Shabbos, and Dalia was standing on a footstool filing her fingernails while Leah hemmed her wedding dress. Leah heard a car door slam, and through the picture window she saw a military messenger coming to the front door. He rapped loudly. Leah walked to the door and opened it. The messenger gave her a small envelope, saluted and walked back to his jeep parked at the curb. Leah tore open the envelope and read the note. She stood frozen, and the note fluttered to the floor. Dalia stepped off the footstool, ran to Leah, and picked up the small piece of paper from the carpet:

Seren Joshua Jordan has been severely wounded in a terrorist encounter in the Judean Hills. He is in critical condition and is being taken to Hadassah Hospital. My heartfelt wishes go with you all for his complete recovery.

Chaim Bar-Adon
Chief of Staff, Tzahal

Leah could not move a muscle. All she could do was keep repeating to herself over and over the words of the prayer which she had once before repeated—in that other life so long ago—when Nachman had been murdered: "*Ayl molay rachamim, Ayl molay rachamim, Ayl molay rachamim* .... [God full of mercy ....]"

"Mama! Mama!" Dalia shook Leah's shoulders.

"Come Mama, let's go to the hospital! He's still alive!"

Leah shook her head hard, chasing away the leering gargoyles. "Okay, I'm okay," she said. "I'll find my keys." She ran upstairs and got her purse and pulled out her keys, taking the stairs two at a time coming down. Dalia had changed out of the wedding dress into levis and a tee shirt.

Both of them jumped into the Ford Mustang and Leah gunned the car toward Nureddine Street and Mount Scopus. There was little traffic in Jerusalem on the Sabbath, so in less than ten minutes they careened into the small parking lot next to Hadassah Hospital's emergency entrance. There were three military ambulances near the entrance. They ran through the double swinging doors and entered the hallway in which at least fifteen soldiers were lying on stretchers, with varying degrees of injury. Leah saw all the blood, the torn flesh, and she began to feel nauseous. She clasped her hand over her mouth to press back the vomit.

In the first large receiving room, several doctors and nurses were administering to three more soldiers, but Joshua was not among them. They ran to the second room, and as they swung the doors inward to enter, they almost knocked over Dr. Stephen Himmelstein who was coming out of the room.

"Take it easy, Leah. Joshua's just fine," said Himmelstein. "Thank God it's not too serious. The Recon Unit medic saw all the loss of blood and the size of the wound and got a little scared that it was more serious. But don't worry, Joshua's going to be just fine for the wedding." Himmelstein, the Jordan family doctor and friend for years, smiled benignly at Leah and Dalia.

Joshua was lying on an emergency gurney at the far side of the room, laughing about something with a very pretty young nurse who was adjusting a drip bag in a stand next to his bed.

"Joshua!" Dalia ran over to him as he turned his face toward her and smiled. It wasn't quite clear whether Dalia's flood of tears came entirely from the release of emotion when she realized that Joshua was fine, or whether a few of them were being shed because she was angry with him for flirting with the nurse while she—Dalia—was in so much pain.

"Oh, Joshua," Dalia buried her face in the pillow next to his and wept. He put his untaped arm around her and patted her.

"I'm okay. Just a shrapnel wound in my thigh muscle and a scratch on my arm. But I lost a lot of blood so I blacked out. Don't worry, we're getting married on time."

"Hi, Mom," he smiled up at her. "Nothing to worry about. "I'll be home for the wedding."

"Okay you two, now wait outside," said the doctor. "We have to prepare him for surgery to get the shrapnel out and close the wounds. You can both wait up in the surgery lounge on the second floor." He gently steered Leah and Dalia toward the door.

They sat in the surgery lounge and shifted nervously on the sticky, hot naugehyde armchairs. Leah tried several times to call Matt, but he had not returned home yet. Finally, after over an hour, she reached him and told him what had happened. He came into the lounge about ten minutes later, looking pale. They all sat silently, squirming in the warm waiting lounge. Other parents and wives and sweethearts of the wounded men had begun arriving.

First Lieutenant Dan Hacohen, a very close friend of Joshua's, came in to see Matt and Leah and the families and friends of the other wounded men. He told them that the Recon Company had suffered nineteen dead and forty-six wounded. They had routed the fedayeen in a two hour hand-to-hand fight that cost the Arabs seventy-eight dead and ninety wounded.

After about two hours, Dr. Himmelstein came into the lounge in his surgical greens. "He's okay," he smiled at Matt and Leah and Dalia and shook Matt's hand.

"How long will he be down, Steve? Will he be disabled from it?" asked Matt, not entirely believing his friend.

"He'll walk with a cane to stand under the *chuppa* [wedding canopy], and he'll be back with his unit in a month at most. And that's the absolute truth. There will be no disability."

They breathed deeply with relief. Then Matt and Leah and Dalia walked among the other scared families and friends, and they chatted comfortably with them, knowing their fears, trying to soothe them. Two of the soldiers died on the operating table. Another died before they could get him off the stretcher into surgery.

Major General "Bren" Guran, Commander of all West Bank forces, came in with his adjutant to help comfort the families. He shook Matt's hand warmly and patted Leah on the back.

"Your son undoubtedly saved his company from a real massacre," said Guran. "He refused to call down help for himself when they were ambushed, and he staged a counterattack instead. It was a marvelous show of courage and tactical instinct, and all of his men know what he did for them. You have quite a son."

Dalia spent most of the following days at the hospital keeping Joshua company—and making sure that none of those cute nurses got too familiar. He came home on Thursday morning, healing with the speed of youth. Friday morning he went to Dr. Himmelstein's office to get the stitches out of his leg and his arm, and he also got the doctor's blessing not to postpone the wedding. Joshua was quite able to march down the garden path with his bride, as long as he spent the next day and a half elevating his leg on a sofa, and was sure not to bang it at night.

Joshua hobbled back into the waiting room on a cane, his face drawn. "Dalia, Dr. Himmelstein says that the wedding will have to be postponed."

Dalia blanched. "But I thought you were okay. All the guests and food, how do we let them know so late?"

"Well, we'll just have to do it somehow," Joshua looked down, trying to suppress a grin.

"You jerk! You're just trying to upset me," Dalia snapped at him, seeing his broadening smile.

"Well actually I have a date with one of the nurses tonight, and I was just wondering...."

Joshua ducked as a magazine came toward his head. Then Dalia jumped up and hugged him.

"There's no one here. You want to just lie down on the couch for a few minutes?" Joshua gestured to the waiting room sofa with his cane.

"Come on, you horny animal. We're getting married tomorrow. Then we can do it on the couch and the floor and the bathroom sink if you want to," she giggled in the same old way that he'd always loved.

They walked out of the office arm in arm, and he limped slowly to the car.

Dalia dressed in Matt's study upstairs, and Leah and Shulamit and two of Dalia's closest girlfriends fluttered around her like headless chickens. The guests began arriving below, and then the caterers set up their tables in the garden, covering them with platters of delicatessen. Joshua and three of his friends sat in his bedroom, listening to a Beatles record and watching out the window as the garden filled up. A little after seven, Matt knocked on the door and looked in.

"Well, this is it. You sure you want to go through with it?" He grinned at his son. "Come, mom and I are going to walk you to the chuppa."

Joshua stood up, wincing slightly from the pain in his thigh. He was using a cane to help keep his weight off the injured leg.

Joshua walked slowly down the path, limping slightly, and Leah and Matt walked on each side of him. They walked up to the chuppa, which was a broad prayer shawl spread over four poles. Rabbi Shlomo Gonen was waiting under the chuppa. It was set up in front of a backdrop of blooming white rose bushes and orange and lavender crepe myrtles. Joshua stood fidgeting at the side of the Rabbi under the chuppa, and Matt and Leah stood next to their son, facing the guests.

Leah watched Dalia coming down the path, on the arm of her father, Deputy Prime Minister Amos Almogi, with her mother, Shulamit, on her other side. Dalia was regal in her white satin low-cut wedding gown. And Leah looked at Dalia's sylphlike mother, and in her memory stirred the poem from the Song of Songs:

> "Who is this that looks forth like the dawn,
> fair as the moon, bright as the sun...
> I went down to the nut orchard, to look
> at the fruits of the valley, to see whether
> the vines had grapes, whether
> the pomegranates were in bud...
> Return, return, O Shulamit,
> return, return, that we may look upon you."

Leah was transported by her memories, by the beauty of the mother and of the daughter, the girl who would be her son's "fairest among women." Leah was under the spell of the love poetry of the Song of Songs she had read so many times as a girl and memorized, waiting for her time of fulfillment, waiting for her beloved. What would these two young lovers whisper to each other on their wedding bed, in the passion of their youth and the heat of their lovemaking?

> "How fair and pleasant thou art
> O loved one, maiden of delights.
> Thou art stately as a palm tree,

And thy breasts are like its clusters.
I will climb up the palm tree and take hold
of its branches."

The cracking of the wine glass as Joshua stomped on it brought Leah out of her daydream. Dalia and Joshua kissed briefly. Then they turned to face the crowd in the garden, and Dalia glowed with the beauty reserved only for the brides, and Joshua blushed with pleasure.

Joshua was too exhausted and in too much pain to remain standing for long. He sat on a folding chair and put his leg up on another folding chair. After a few chomps of salami and thick rye bread and a couple of shots of Slivovitz, he had to go to his bedroom and sleep. The intense excitement of the morning and the wedding, coupled with his weakness from his wounds, flattened him. While the party went on below, he slept for two hours. When he awoke, he listened to the noises below in the garden as the last guests left. Dalia came in to see him, as she had done several times that evening, and she sat on the edge of the bed stroking his hair.

"Ready to go to our own home?" he asked his wife. She was still flushed with the excitement and overflowing love of their wedding day.

"I'll change right now. Are you okay?" she asked.

"Yes. I just needed some rest for tonight." He smiled at her, and she giggled.

She left the room and he put the last few of his things away in the suitcases. He pulled on a pair of Levis and loafers and buttoned on a plaid shirt. Then he took one last look at the room he had lived in for most of his life and limped slowly downstairs.

The newlyweds' wedding gift from Matt and Leah, a "new" car, was a 1963 Fiat, a tiny little box of a thing, but it ran well and did not guzzle precious gas. After the last hugged good-byes from the Jordans and the Almogis, Joshua and Dalia drove the five minutes to their new apartment in Hakirya.

Joshua's leg was very sore, and he couldn't put any pressure on it. So Dalia helped him undress at the edge of the bed. She got into bed, and they kissed and petted and purred and fell asleep.

* * *

Late the next morning, they started out on their honeymoon trip to Eilat. Dalia drove, since Joshua's leg was still stiff and sore. They drove east on the Amman Road twenty miles to the village of Nahal Qalya at the head of the Dead Sea and then turned south for the hundred sixty-five mile drive to Eilat. The sun's warmth filtered softly down through the diaphanous cottony clouds. The road was almost deserted except for an occasional military patrol. The road paralleled the Jordanian border for more than seventy miles north of Eilat. But they felt quite secure, since in this deep desert region there was very rarely any terrorist activity. They drove for hours through the bleak desert of limp white thorn acacias, and endless yellow-gray sand, and flowerless, glaucous green broom, and straggly, spiny cacti.

They reached their small pension on the beach in Eilat late in the afternoon. They spent the next ten days swimming in the undulating gulf, picking up shells on the beach, drinking beer in a loud discotheque at night, and making love in every possible place they could find. On the veranda of their room, under the starlit aubergine sky, in a motorboat out in the water, on the beach behind rocks—day or night—and even in bed. The cool salt water helped heal Joshua's wounds, and he gained in strength over their honeymoon. After ten days, they checked out of the pension before daybreak for their drive back to Jerusalem. This time, they would take the inland route through Beersheba and the West Bank biblical towns of Hebron and Bethlehem. November 9, 1969.

Chapter Fifteen

The fifth annual Congress of the Palestine Liberation Organization had been held in Cairo in February 1969, and Yassir Arafat and Hassan abu-Sittah had made their moves. A new Congress of one hundred delegates was elected, with Fatah and its army, al-Asifah, achieving a plurality of thirty-three seats. *Sa'iqa*, supported by Syria, and the Popular Front for the Liberation of Palestine, supported by Iraq, each received twelve seats. The Syrian Palestine Liberation Army and the Popular Liberation Forces received a total of fifteen delegates. Various other fedayeen groups received a few seats.

The plurality of Fatah became Arafat's key to the executive suite, and he was elected chairman of the eleven-man executive committee of the PLO, which included five other Fatah members as well as al-Asifah's commander Hassan abu-Sittah. They had finally succeeded in uniting the PLO and becoming the majority of its leadership. It was time to rebuild Fatah's Army.

Hamdi Attiyah helped Hassan build the cadre of al-Asifah. But Jordan's King Hussein forcibly limited the terrorist activities of the Palestinian fedayeen from within Jordan. The King was not willing to suffer the brutal destructive retaliatory raids mounted by the Israelis. He had his own people and their economic interests to preserve, and he repeatedly announced that reckless fedayeen terrorism and the resultant Israeli reprisals were a threat to the stability of his regime.

Hassan was straining at the restrictions imposed on al-Asifah. And November 9, 1969, was Hamdi's twenty-first birthday. So he and Hassan planned something very special to mark this day. Hamdi hand picked a squad of fedayeen who spoke Hebrew. They would infiltrate across the Jordan River into the West Bank under cover of darkness on the night of November 8, and they would change into the uniforms of an Israeli Recon Unit. They would pick up two stolen Recon jeeps where they had been hidden in a garage on the outskirts of Jericho. Then they would drive the rough back roads through the Judean Hills south to Hebron. In Hebron was an ancient synagogue near the Tomb of the Patriarch, the Cave of Machpelah which the Jews revered as the burial place of Abraham, Isaac, Jacob, Rebecca and Leah. Over the cave, the Muslims had built the *Haram el-Khalil* ["The Sacred Precinct of the Friend of the Merciful One, Allah"], and there had been Jewish-Muslim riots over various claimed desecrations over the years. The last major violence had occurred in August 1929, when a crowd of Arabs incited by the Grand Mufti of Jerusalem had descended upon the Orthodox Jewish community of Hebron, killing fifty unarmed men, women and children and wounding another sixty.

Hamdi reached the town just before dawn and drove to a two-story mudbrick apartment house in the Orthodox section. At daybreak, he split the fedayeen into two units of four men each. Hamdi's unit went into the entrance on the ground floor, and the second group soundlessly climbed the stairs to the second story.

Hamdi kicked open the frail door of the first apartment and all four fedayeen rushed into the single room firing their Kalachnikovs at the people under the blankets in several beds. It was over in seconds. Hamdi heard the firing from upstairs as he ran to the second apartment and kicked in the door. He repeated the same slaughter and ran down to the third apartment. Hamdi kicked in the door, and his three men leapt into the room. Suddenly, Hamdi recognized the light rat-tat-tat of an Uzi submachine gun, quite different from the cracking of the fedayeen's Kalachnikovs. He braced back against the hallway wall next to the door, and when the Uzi had stopped for a few seconds, he burst into the room firing his machine gun. There was nobody in the room. The outer window was open and the curtains were fluttering. Two of his men were dead on the floor. The third struggled to stand and steady himself. Blood was coming slowly from a flesh wound in his side.

"The fucking Jew was standing there in his prayer shawl and his phylacteries holding his submachine gun. He grabbed a baby out of the crib and jumped through the window."

"Go after him!" yelled Hamdi. "Don't let him get to the military post near the synagogue!"

The Palestinian jumped through the window after the escaping Jew and his baby. Hamdi looked around the room, puzzled. There

was no woman here. He couldn't understand why, but he didn't
have time for riddles. He ran out of the apartment and up the
stairway to the second floor, yelling for his other fedayeen to clear
out. They were finished here and had to get out before the Israeli
soldiers were alerted. Hamdi and the four men ran down the stairs
to their jeeps and jumped in. Hamdi heard a Kalachnikov cracking
across the street. He looked over and saw his soldier in the alley.
The Jew, still wrapped in this prayer shawl, was in a heap at his
feet. The soldier bent over and picked up a bundle which began to
cry loudly. He pulled the blanket from around the little child, held
him by his ankles, and swung his head into the alley wall. He
threw down the mess and ran back to Hamdi's jeep. Both jeeps sped
south out of Hebron.

Israeli soldiers reached the apartment building a few minutes
later. They looked through the rooms for survivors. Several people
were still alive though severely wounded. Twelve people were dead.
In one apartment, there were no Jews. A soldier cautiously opened
the closet door, and huddled inside on the floor was a young woman
hugging a tiny infant to her chest.
"It's okay now. It's all over. You can come out with your baby,"
said the soldier to her gently.
The woman stared at him blankly. She looked down at her baby
and slowly took him from her bosom and laid him on the floor
between her and the soldier. The baby was blue, dead. She had
kept it from crying, to keep them from being discovered in the
closet by the fedayeen. She had smothered her baby to death. She
rocked back and forth on her knees, neither crying nor speaking nor
moving her facial muscles. She had retreated within herself to
escape the horror and no longer knew what was happening.
The young soldier walked to the window and vomited through it.
He covered his tear-filled eyes and spat out again and gasped for
breath. He heard shouts from other soldiers across the street and
looked at where they were standing and staring. That's why this
room was empty, he thought. There is her husband, still in his
tallis. And there is her other child. He vomited again.

At Beersheba, Joshua and Dalia stopped for breakfast. It was a
little after seven, and they had driven for three hours. When the

news of the Hebron massacre came over the radio, the cafe keeper turned up the volume so everyone could listen. Joshua and Dalia listened to details of the latest terrorist atrocity with a sense of anger and hatred. They could not finish their breakfasts.

They got back into the Fiat, with Joshua driving this time, and he pulled his ever present Uzi out from under the seat, checked the two thirty-round clips taped back to back, and chambered a 9 mm. cartridge. He put the gun on the seat between them and drove toward Hebron.

About midway up the forty mile stretch between Beersheba and Hebron, Joshua saw two Recon Unit jeeps coming toward them on the highway. As they came closer, he could see by the designation painted on the front bumper of the lead jeep that the Unit was stationed in Hebron. He thought it was a little odd that after a terrorist attack in Hebron, a Recon Unit centered there would be heading south some twenty miles away. Oh well, he thought, he and Dalia had passed the Dead Sea turnoff a few miles back. Maybe this Recon Unit had intelligence that the terrorists were going to cross back to Jordan over the Dead Sea narrows at Cape Molyneux.

Joshua slowed the Fiat by the side of the road so that he could hail the Recon Unit and find out what was going on. He parked his car off the road since there were kibbutz produce trucks on the highway at this hour. He stepped out of the Fiat leaving the driver's door open and waved down the lead Recon jeep which was carrying a captain and a corporal. It stopped on the road opposite him about ten yards away, and the second jeep screeched to a halt behind it.

"Hello, I'm Captain Jordan, East Jerusalem Recon," he called out to the Captain. He thought he recognized the officer, but he couldn't quite place him. "What's going on in Hebron?"

"The fedayeen massacred unarmed civilians in an apartment house," called out Hamdi Attiyah to the Jew. "We've been ordered to cut off the escape route to Cape Molyneux, in case they try to go that way." Hamdi's eyes twitched as he recognized the Jewboy officer who had ruined al-Asifah's Mount Scopus attack two years ago. He strained to keep emotion and recognition off his face.

Joshua stared at the captain, trying to remember where he'd seen him. He looked at the other four soldiers in the second jeep. None of the Recon Unit members had Uzis—they all had Kalachnikovs.

That alone was not particularly suspect, Joshua knew, since Tzahal had seized huge stores of Egyptian arms in the Sinai during the Six Day War, and many Tzahal units were supplied with the Kalachnikovs. But these men were oddly edgy. And he had the feeling that the captain's eyes were too wary, that he had recognized Joshua. But from where?

A produce truck zoomed by. Suddenly it seemed very strange to Joshua that part of a Recon squad, commanded by a Captain instead of a Second Lieutenant, would be sent forty miles from Hebron to the Dead Sea, when Tzahal had an infantry battalion stationed at Masada just five miles from the crossing point to Cape Molyneux.

"Is Sgan Aluf Hanavi in charge of the Units looking for the terrorists?" Joshua asked the Captain, knowing full well that Lieutenant Colonel Hanavi, his former commanding officer, was now stationed far north on the Golan Heights. Again those very wary black eyes scrutinized Joshua's face.

"Yes. Our orders came from him." Hamdi had no idea what else to say and studied the Jewboy's reaction warily.

"Okay, good luck," Joshua waved at them, and they started pulling away down the highway in the jeeps. Joshua leaned into the car and pulled out his Uzi. "Get down," he said to Dalia, and she immediately lay down on the seat.

He leveled his Uzi against his hip and shot a long burst at the rear jeep, now about thirty yards down the road. The jeep swerved off the road and two of the soldiers fell out of the back. They lay still in the dirt. The lead jeep picked up speed and was too far away for the Uzi.

The other fedayeen terrorists in the stopped jeep shouldered their Kalachnikovs and sprayed the Fiat in short bursts. Joshua dived into the front seat, covering Dalia with his body. He heard the jeep screech away.

Joshua and Dalia sat up, and he tried to start the Fiat. It sputtered and died, sputtered and died. He got out and saw the puddle of gasoline at the back of the car, crouched at it and saw the jagged hole ripped by the Kalachnikov bullet in the bottom of the gas tank. He gritted his teeth in disgust and frustration.

Nadia abu-Sittah sat watching Israeli TV all that day, listening to the continuous news bulletins about the Hebron raid, worrying

about her son. By late afternoon, the Israeli military censor had
released the story of Seren Joshua Jordan and his new wife Dalia,
returning from their honeymoon, chancing upon the terrorists and
killing two of them, as yet unidentified. The broadcasts were full
of the heroism and quick thinking of the son of the famous Leah and
Matthew Jordan. Nadia was once again entranced, fascinated by
this Jewish woman Leah and her family. But she was having trouble
suppressing a deep fear that her son Hamdi was one of the two dead
fedayeen.

At nightfall, Hamdi came home, and Nadia hugged him and
shed the tears of a mother's joy and relief. True, she thought to
herself, these acts of terrorism were brutal, some might call them
barbaric. But the Jews had brought this curse down upon their own
shoulders by their evil treatment of the Palestinians. The Arabs
would never stop killing the Jews as long as one Palestinian
remained a refugee. This was *jihad*, the way of the fedayeen.

Chapter Sixteen

News of the terrorist raid reached Leah at her small office in the
Knesset building. It was circulated by military messenger to all
officials in the building. She switched on the radio and listened to
the accounts of the atrocity. At four in the afternoon, the military
censor sent to the Knesset copies of the dispatch which would be
released publicly at five o'clock. As Leah read the account of the
killing of the two-year-old boy by bashing his head against the wall,
she sickened. The vision of Nachman being murdered by the
Prince of Darkness flashed in her mind and made her shudder.

She looked out of her window toward the beautiful and placid
new campus of the Hebrew University, and she fought away the
memories that surged up in her. She continued to read the military
dispatch. The child's mother had smothered her other baby by
hugging it too tightly while they hid in the closet. The woman had
been taken to the mental ward at Hadassah Hospital in a catatonic
state. Oh my God, my God, why hast Thou forsaken us?

Leah could hardly keep reading. Tears filled her eyes, and her
knowledge of this woman's pain made her heart beat wildly and her

head ache. She forced herself to read on, and her mouth fell open as she read the account of her own son coming upon the terrorists and killing two of them. She reached for the phone and called his apartment, but they were not yet home. She sat staring out the window, aghast at the magnitude of the bestiality of these Palestinian terrorists, crushed by the inescapable recurring vision of Nachman's head shattering against the wall.

Menachem Begin came into her office and found her weeping quietly.

"Leahleh, Leahleh. Your son is a hero. You must forget the rest. Our people have faced tragedy, senseless murder and bloodshed, for two thousand years. We cannot stop those who hate us. All we can do is cut off the hands of those who harm us. Go home, Leahleh, go home to Matt. Here, let me call him."

"No Menachem, no. I just need to sit for a while, to shed the horror of this day. I'll be fine." Her face was gray and ashen.

Begin slumped into a small armchair.

"Leah, I have always told you, and now you may not think that I am so far wrong, that the pain caused by the fedayeen to us and us to the fedayeen is so piercing, so pervasive in both of our own hearts and theirs, that we can never sit and negotiate with them like decent menschen. Either we will kill them or they will kill us. I see no other way." Begin stared out the window.

Leah studied the care-worn face of the oldest and closest friend she had in the world, and for the first time in many years her mind was filled with a jumble of conflicting thoughts. The barbaric atrocity committed today by the Arabs was but one in a long series of terrible acts committed by both peoples for decades.

She had taken part a generation ago in the bombing of the King David Hotel, killing and injuring hundreds of innocent human beings. And she had justified it in the name of the Jewish right to their homeland. She had witnessed the tragedy at Deir Yassin, and even that she had ultimately accepted as one of the sad episodes in building the Jewish state. She and Matt had been terrorists, they had executed two innocent British Sergeants, they had fought for Israel in one war. Their son had fought in another war, and now he too was a part of the cycle of terrorism that had begun to characterize their daily existence.

Acts of barbarism like today's had wrung out of the Israelis—

even the most compassionate and compromising among them—the desire for repatriation of the Arab refugees. And the gnawing hatreds had been accentuated by the constant terrorist raids of the War of Attrition following the Six Day War. Today was for Leah the last straw. These people who shattered a little baby's skull against a wall were not worthy of anyone's compassion. She had once killed a Jew, a fellow soldier, who had wantonly murdered an Arab family. She had always hoped and believed that her son would do the same. To do otherwise was to join the beasts of prey, the jackals who roamed the desert. But now she was beginning to feel different, less sure.

"Menachem, all I want to do is kill every one of those vicious animals." Her face was pinched and she was emotionally drained. "I know that we have helped to create the kind of killers who attacked Hebron today, and we people of Israel have a portion of the blame for each human life that was wasted today and last week and last year. But where once I thought I knew the answer, now I know that there is no answer. As I get older and come to grips with what I—we—have had to do just to survive, I only have more questions. And the one question that will not leave me day or night is how we stop this spiral of terrorism before it consumes us all, before we end up crushing Arab children's heads against a wall?"

The two old friends sat silently in the deepening dusk, staring at the placid campus of the Hebrew University through the window, their souls in torment.

Leah handed Matt the military dispatches she had received that afternoon, providing more details than the television newscaster knew about the Hebron terrorist attack and their son's role in its aftermath.

"Did you talk to Josh?" he asked her, finishing the last page.

"No, he went to West Bank headquarters for debriefing. But I got a hold of Dalia. She was fine. They're okay."

"Thank God."

They were both sitting in the living room on an overstuffed sofa. She gave him a questioning look.

"What's God have to do with it?" she asked.

He studied her to see if she was kidding. "All right, let's not have this discussion again, Leah. I don't feel very philosophical right now."

Leah got up, switched off the TV, and returned to the sofa next to
Matt. She turned toward him and kissed him on the cheek. She
rested her hand lightly on his shoulder.

"I'm sorry, honey," she said. "I'm just shook up over today. That
Arab bashing the baby against the wall. It makes me sick. I've had
visions of Mencken all day."

Matt stroked her hair. "You know, you're still a great looking
broad."

She snuggled against him. "Thanks, honey."

Minutes passed. She sat up and her face became more serious.

"You know, I was thinking of that Arab's trial you did a few years
ago. What was his name?"

"You mean Hamid al-Alami, the murder case in 1965?"

"Yeah, right, right. I've been trying to remember his name all
afternoon."

"So?"

"I feel *tzedrayt* [confused], *farblunjit* [lost and wandering]."

Matt looked closely at Leah. "What are you talking about,
honey?"

"I remember when you won that case, how proud we were,
Joshua and me. And you gave that great speech on television, and
everybody talked about it for weeks."

"Yes, so what's the point."

"The point is you were wrong. You should have let that bastard
die." Her voice was a choked hiss.

Matt drew away and scrutinized his wife. "I didn't set that Arab
free, our Civil Rights Act did. And it would have been plain
illegal—murder—to have convicted him for something no Jew
would have been convicted of. We couldn't let a thing like that
happen."

Leah's eyes were narrowed slits, her lips tight and white across
her teeth. "How can we follow a self-destructive policy of equality
under our law when these Palestinian animals shoot us down like
dogs and smash our little ones against the rocks!"

"My God, Leah. I can't listen to you talk like this."

"There you go with God again."

"Leah, what is it with you? The al-Alami family has lived in
Israel about three hundred years longer than we have. How are we
supposed to deny them the equal protection of our laws? And he

was no terrorist, he was just guarding his home the way you or I would."

"They're all terrorists or potential terrorists. And we have to start realizing that and treating them like they treat us."

"Leah, that's pure nonsense!"

She studied her husband. "Today did something to me, Matt. I guess it was just the last straw for me. Those animals have wrung all the compassion out of me. It's horrible to say, I know it," tears welled in her eyes. She sniffled. "But I just can't help it. We have to hunt them down and destroy them before they kill all of our children."

She trembled and began to weep. Matthew hugged her to him. Tears misted his eyes.

Chapter Seventeen

The retaliatory raid was an air strike that evening into the Palestinian refugee camp located nearest the Dead Sea.

King Hussein breathed a sigh of relief that the Israeli raid had not been against his own people in one of Jordan's cities. Two more terrorist attacks from Jordan into Israel, in March and June, the second one of which precipitated a devastating Israeli bombing raid on Jordan's potash and salt works twenty miles south of Amman, proved to Hussein that he would soon have to tighten the noose around the Palestinians.

On September 15, 1970, Hussein declared martial law. For two days, he negotiated with Arafat and abu-Sittah. The negotiations got nowhere. Over the next three days Jordanian units battled with Palestinian units in ever increasingly bloody confrontations. Then, almost two hundred Syrian tanks, painted with the insignia of the Palestine Liberation Army, moved toward Amman to back the Palestinian revolution against King Hussein.

Hussein ordered his entire military into an all-out offensive. The Jordanian Air Force destroyed every one of the invading Syrian tanks and Jordanian Legion troops decimated Palestinian strongholds in and around Amman. Over three thousand soldiers died on both sides in the week long civil war, and another ten thousand were wounded.

Fatah's official army, al-Asifah, had stayed out of the Jordanian civil war. Hassan abu-Sittah had correctly and shrewdly judged that the time was not ripe for Hussein's defeat. There had been another more personal factor which had also colored Hassan's thinking. Samir el-Rashid now had the largest construction company in Amman, and he was the head of the *hamula* under which Hassan and Nadia and Hamdi lived.

Their lives were very comfortable, and Samir and Widad were not filled with the fervor of *al-tariq al-fida'i* as they once had been. Even the memory of their murdered son Zuhayr had faded. In fact, during the stirrings preceding the September civil war, Samir had warned Hassan on several occasions not to be involved with any actions against King Hussein, since the el-Rashid Construction Company required the King's good will. It had not been a difficult decision for Hassan to make, to keep al-Asifah out of the conflict, since Syria had obliged by taking up the Palestinian cause and sending the PLA tank corps to confront Hussein's troops.

So al-Asifah had held its fire, though many hotheads had left the ranks and joined the invading Palestine Liberation Army in the civil war. All of the Palestinians who had taken part in the war suffered Hussein's wrath beginning in late September 1970—"Black September" they called it: they were expelled from Jordan.

They began to trickle and then to flood into southern Lebanon, where over a hundred thousand Palestinian refugees had settled after fleeing from Israel in 1948-49. The Lebanese camps run by the United Nations Relief and Works Agency were principally located in the spacious fertile agricultural valley of south Lebanon, and they were a far cry from the generally squalid- and disease ridden camps of the barren dusty plains of Jordan where no employment was available and the UNRWA dole was inadequate to provide more than the meagerest daily food requirement for these desperate refugees.

Lebanon was entirely different. The first wave of Palestinian refugees had been gladly received into Lebanon more than twenty years ago and had generally become well-integrated into the national society and economy. A large class of wealthy Palestinian merchants developed in the west Beirut quarter called Basta. A great many other Palestinians found employment in thriving Lebanon, which had to import transient labor from other Arab countries to meet its labor needs. It was these transients—mostly Shi'a Muslims from the Persian Gulf—who filled the city slums and became the lower class of Lebanon, not the Palestinians.

In April 1971, King Hussein commanded all remaining Palestinian fedayeen to evacuate Amman and to be concentrated under Jordanian Legion control in the remote forested area between Jarash and Ajlun, forty miles north of Amman. Samir el-Rashid called his closest friend, the Jordanian Minister of Interior, and requested a meeting with King Hussein.

Two days later, Samir went to the palace, met with the Minister, and they walked together to Hussein's enormous reception hall. The King was sitting on his ornate gilded throne, wearing his usual tan military uniform, meeting various petitioners and supplicants and reading and signing documents handed to him by the several advisors standing beside his throne.

The Minister of Interior caught Hussein's eye, and the King clapped his hands together indicating an end to the morning session. He walked behind the throne to a set of intricately carved wooden doors and walked through them. Samir and the Minister followed him into the room.

Samir walked up to the diminutive monarch and kissed him below his collar bone, the ancient Arab sign to swear the subject's *bay'ah* [allegiance] to his ruler. The three men sat in large over-stuffed burgundy velvet armchairs around a tiny inlaid mosaic coffee table. A military houseboy brought in a silver tray with a coffee server and three tiny silver cups. Hussein elaborately poured the cardamon-laced coffee, the traditional drink to start off important meetings like this. After the ceremony of pouring and offering the coffee was over, and after the three men had exchanged the voluptuous greetings and regreetings required by Arab politeness, Samir got down to business.

"You are my King, and I have sworn my *bay'ah, ya Malik* Hussein," said Samir, looking into the monarch's eyes. "You must not wish for your servant to leave Amman."

"I have no problem with you and your wife and children, *ya sayyid* el-Rashid. It is with Hassan abu-Sittah and his family that I find some distress."

"Hassan has not taken part in any of the agitation against you, *ya Malik*. He has been scrupulous in maintaining his and al-Asifah's loyalty to you."

"I know that. But we both know that it is only a matter of time before the PLO and Yassir Arafat plan an all out war against me and my government. After the Palestine National Congress in Cairo in February, Arafat announced that the PLO was intent on the overthrow of Jordan's 'puppet separatist authority,'" the King snarled the words at Samir. "It will not be long before Hassan abu-Sittah is called upon to put those treacherous words into action."

Samir was being forced to make his choice, and it was no longer difficult for him. He had made it long ago, when their construction company had made them rich, when he realized that peace and comfort for his family in Jordan was far preferable to *al-tariq al-fida'i*, constantly pitting his own life and the lives of his wife and children against the insuperable might of Israel for the old dream of *'awda*, the empty promise of return to a homeland which was no longer their home and no longer their land. Samir's once rock-solid body had surrendered to years of lavish living, and his ample girth bulged in his five hundred dollar London-tailored blue serge suit.

"My *hamula* shall not protect Hassan abu-Sittah and his family, *ya Malik* Hussein. I have sworn you my *bay'ah*. My family wishes to remain in Amman and retain your good grace. I shall sever Hassan's family from my fold." His soft blue eyes were imploring and sincere, his voice resonant with conviction.

These were very strong words and Samir could see that he had convinced Hussein that he meant them. As the King stood, so did Samir and Khalid. Hussein stepped to Samir and kissed him on both cheeks. He took Samir's hand and held it in both of his own, the sign of brotherhood.

"Hassan abu-Sittah is an idolator, ya Samir," the King addressed him informally, showing his friendship. "He has abandoned Allah and the way of the Prophet, and he has adopted Arafat as his new prophet, and they conspire against me. As it is written in Surah IX of the Koran, 'Will you not fight against those who have broken their oaths and conspired to banish the Apostle? . . . Make war on them: Allah will chastize them through you and humble them. He will grant you victory over them and heal the spirit of the faithful . . . .'"

"I will ever remain faithful, *ya Malik* Hussein," said Samir earnestly, and he once again kissed the King below the collar bone. Khalid and Samir bowed backwards out of the room.

Chapter Eighteen

Hassan and Hamdi were at al-Asifah's main camp near Ajlun all the rest of that week and the next, so Samir had ample time to plan the way that he would cut them off from the el-Rashid *hamula* without being murdered in the process. First of all he told Widad, and he instructed her to drop hints to Nadia over the coming days. Then he himself would talk to her before her husband and son returned.

The talk with Nadia occurred in the courtyard garden a week and a half later after dinner. It was a lovely spring night. That day, the Amman newspaper had carried headlines about Arafat's latest speech and a long story described the speech and the gathering momentum toward another civil war led by the PLO against King Hussein. Arafat was quoted as saying, "We demand a national rule in Jordan, because on the one hand Jordan is a geographical-historical extension of the occupied Palestine homeland, and on the other, because of its masses Jordan is the base and springboard for any effective move against the occupation enemy and forces." This was too much for King Hussein. Early that afternoon, Samir received a telephone call at his office from his friend the Minister of Interior. Now is the time, he had told Samir. The King will wait no longer.

Nadia had picked up on the hints dropped by Widad. And at dinner this evening, she had seen the grim drawn face of Samir as she helped Widad serve the el-Rashid men. She too had read the newspaper headlines and the story and was aware that her world was about to go topsy-turvy again. Later in the courtyard, sipping Arak nervously, Samir told her what she already knew.

"Nadia, you know that I have loved you as a sister and treated your family as part of my own."

She sat quietly, looking at him in the dim light from two lanterns, saying nothing.

"I have striven for twenty-three years to build the el-Rashid Construction Company into the kind of business that my beloved father intended it to be when he founded it in Jerusalem in our other life. Now, King Hussein himself has demanded that I show my loyalty to him. If I do not, he will crush us and our Company like so many toothpicks, like he destroyed two hundred Syrian tanks in 1970."

Still Nadia said nothing.

"The el-Rashids have given up their UNRWA refugee cards. We are now full fledged Jordanian citizens. You and your family must do the same." He knew well that this was an empty demand of Hassan and Hamdi. They would never abandon *al-tariq al-fida'i*. It was their very lives, their souls. And Nadia knew that Samir was fully aware that his demand as head of the *hamula* could not be followed.

"Samir, you know that Hassan and Hamdi will not abandon the *jihad*. They cannot comply with your wishes."

"Then you will have to leave my home," Samir said, his eyes flat, no longer just having a conversation, but now entering his role as head of the *hamula* whose word is law.

"Then we will leave." Nadia said. There could be no backing down. She and her family were now and forever Palestinians. There was no other way.

"I will give you and Hassan plenty of money to settle wherever you wish. Please leave in the morning." Samir stood and walked into the house. His wife Widad did not move.

Nadia remained sitting in the courtyard. The breeze was cool, the stars twinkled brightly. For the third time in her life, she was being torn from her home. But this time, it was not the Jews. It was her own people, her own family!

"You have grown fat with the luxury of this alien land," Nadia growled at her sister.

"I have to do as my husband commands," Widad whined. "You know that, Nadia. You know that his business is his life. What can I do?"

"A true Palestinian makes the *jihad* for *'awda* her life, not a few silk sheets and feather mattresses and nice cars."

They sat quietly, Nadia feeling too sick to move. Her own sister was siding with King Hussein against her, against Hamdi and Hassan. She felt like crying out to Allah to flay these enemies of the fedayeen.

"I could kill Samir myself for his treachery," Nadia whispered through clenched teeth. "But I have seen that your manservants have been carrying pistols in their sashes for the last few weeks. I guess Samir had this planned for some time."

Widad was crying softly. "Please Nadia, just leave. Do not destroy us. All we want is peace and quiet. We have had too much suffering." Her heavily rouged lips were an ugly smear, distorted with pain and dread. She looked to Nadia like a sulky fat girl caught pillaging strawberry jam jars in the kitchen.

Nadia cast Widad a withering look. Her sister had become nothing but a contemptible cur. Nadia went inside the house and packed Hassan's small wardrobe in a single valise. Hamdi's clothes were with him at his tent home near Ajlun with al-Asifah.

She sat on the edge of her bed, her body shaking uncontrollably. She was almost fifty years old, no longer a fetching young beauty capable of rebounding boldly from all of life's shocks. She was getting old, tired, and she needed a solid home, this home. But now it had been torn from her, and she had nowhere to go. Like all of the true Palestinians, they were victims of the Israelis by day and the Jordanians by night. Forced from their homes by the Jews and the Arabs alike. Only the blood of all these enemies could avenge the Palestinians' pain.

BOOK FIVE

LAMENTATIONS

"Thou, O God, hast cast me into the mire,
  and I have become like dust and ashes....
Thou art become cruel unto me; with the might
  of thy hand dost Thou oppress me.
Thou liftest me upon the wind, Thou makest
  me to ride upon it,
  and Thou throwest me about as in a tempest.
Yea, I know that Thou wilt bring me unto
  death...."

—Job 30: 19-30

Chapter One

May 1971

In the flood of Palestinians was the family of Hassan abu-Sittah.
They did not walk; they did not ride to Beirut on donkeys. They
drove their new 1971 Mercedes sedan to the Lebanese capital,
Beirut—the Paris of the Middle East—and Hassan's first stop was

at the Banque du Liban where he deposited the $200,000 in American currency which Samir had given Nadia when she left Amman that morning.

Nadia had arrived at the al-Asifah camp near Ajlun and found Hassan and Hamdi at eight o'clock in the morning. They had raged over the treason of the el-Rashid clan, but they knew that they could not go back to Amman. Only death awaited them there. They also could not stay in the forest, surrounded by Jordanian Legionaires. For they had been dishonored and emasculated by the Jordanians, prevented from any forays into Israel and reduced to a band of embittered, squabbling, undisciplined, homeless and rootless orphans. Al-Asifah must move, Hassan decided. So by noon the army had broken camp and loaded all of its equipment and belongings and themselves into the canvas covered Soviet stake trucks supplied by Syria. Al-Asifah would set up its new camp near the village of Yaatar, in the Janoob Valley of southern Lebanon controlled by the Palestinians, just five miles from the northern border of Israel.

The al-Asifah convoy spent the night camped just west of Damascus, guarded closely by a division of Syrian troops. They drove into Lebanon the next morning and turned south to the Janoob Valley at the crossroads of Majdal Anjar in the heart of Maronite Catholic Lebanon. From behind shuttered windows, alarmed Maronite mothers and children watched the convoy of over ten thousand Sunni Muslim soldiers rumble through the center of the ancient slumbering villages where the followers of St. Maron had lived since the seventh century.

The abu-Sittah family drove directly to the sumptuous home of a Palestinian friend who had become a wealthy importer in Beirut. They were provided the hospitality of his house and his pledge of full support for the way of the fedayeen. It took them about a week to locate and purchase a three story villa in Beirut's Basta quarter, with a spectacular panoramic view of the Mediterranean white sand beaches across the street. The street was studded with marvelous holly oaks and English elms. The melodious songs of larks, nestled in the protective branches and rich foliage, replaced the howling of the stinging winds of Jordan.

Nadia began to feel more and more at home, though her malignant hatred of the Israelis was now almost matched by her bitterness against the Jordanians and her own sister and brother-in-law. But Beirut was vastly nicer than Gaza City and Amman. It was a modern sophisticated city with a comfortably warm climate and outdoor cafes and Parisian boutiques and a cultured community of rich successful Palestinians. Over the months, Nadia came to feel quite at home. Life had once again become sweet for her, as sweet as it could be away from her *'awda*.

Chapter Two

Hassan devised a training plan for his new young fedayeen which tested them and trained them in a less dangerous way than against the Jews. The treacherous Yahudun were as venomous as vipers and always sought to exact double or triple vengeance for Palestinian raids on their people. But the infidel Maronites were far less capable of defending their small mountain villages against attacks. The Maronite Militia was mostly stationed near the Israeli border in the south. So the scattered farming hamlets of the mountains were ineluctably enticing to Hassan as places for training his young fighters. Seventeen of these villages had served as guinea pigs for his trainees without one death among the fedayeen, without even one incident of retaliation.

The Palestinian cadre took turns leading two- or three-man squads into the languourous medieval hamlets to kill a few hapless shepherds or farmers or girls out for a stroll or blow up a barn. It was Hamdi's turn to lead, and his squad consisted of two fedayeen. One was a pimply faced fourteen-year-old with freckles and hair the color of a rooster's comb, who was too tall to be called a boy and too spare and stringy to have developed a man's strength. The other was twenty years old, a tough from Rashidiye Camp who had been let out of jail for assault, on the Mukhtar's orders that he join the fedayeen. He was of medium height, well fed, dark and brooding and distrustful. He had disliked Hamdi from the beginning, because Hamdi was one of the officers, one of the rich city boys who didn't know what it meant to really be a refugee.

Hamdi drove the jeep a hundred yards off the highway and parked behind a small hill some half mile from Tanoun, a tiny village of Maronite Christian pig farmers, nestled by a shimmering topaz lake of snow melt from the surrounding mountains. The dawn air was crisp and bracing. Several little girls were filling water buckets at the lake. Sunlight had just begun to spill over the eastern hilltops and spark the soft rippling water.

"There it is," whispered Hamdi. "It's the barn on this end of the street, on the left side."

The three men crouched in a meadow of tall wild irises with waxy glistening white and yellow blossoms that reached all the way to the edge of the hamlet, providing excellent cover for their approach and departure.

"Here, Malik." Hamdi handed the skinny fourteen-year-old the satchel with C-4 explosive. "Now remember," Hamdi looked sternly at the boy, "find the first weight-bearing beam and mold it around the bottom."

The boy's eyes were flat, his eyelids twitched and mucous trickled from his nostrils. Hamdi shook his head grimly at the other man, who grimaced.

"Okay, Malik, nothing to it, Hamdi soothed. "Just fast in and fast out. Khalid will cover you."

Hamdi remained crouching in the high irises. The two others slithered toward the barn about thirty-five yards away, Malik moving gingerly with the satchel hung around his neck. Khalid cradled his Kalachnikov on his forearms.

Like all of the dozen or so structures of the village, the barn was a log cabin with a thick yellow thatch roof of elephant grass. Hamdi watched as the two men crept out of the irises and ran low to the side of the barn away from the rest of the village. Meadowlarks sang lustily nearby, squabbling over a delectable worm or grasshopper.

Suddenly, the bucolic repose was shattered by the stutter of a light submachine gun. Hamdi tensed in the irises like a cornered panther. He saw Khalid lying on his back motionless. The young redhead, Malik, was standing back against the barn wall, his hands outstretched over his head.

From a small rickety woodshed beside the barn stepped a man carrying an American M-16. He was wearing the dark green fatigues and hard round French fatigue cap of the Maronite Militia.

Christian Militia aren't supposed to be this far west in the Mountains, thought Hamdi. This is something new. He raised his Kalachnikov and took careful aim at the soldier walking toward Malik. Then he felt the point of a knife blade on the back of his neck. He carefully lowered his submachine gun and dropped it in front of him. He slowly stood and turned. Another Militiaman stepped back from him and trained the bayonet fixed M-16 at his stomach.

"*Sabach alchayr* [Good morning]," said the Christian Arab to the Palestinian and smiled broadly, displaying a wickedly rotten array of teeth. He flicked the rifle up twice, quick gestures, and Hamdi turned carefully and raised his arms and started walking toward the barn.

Curious villagers were coming out of their shacks, men pulling filthy white flannel shirts over wide billowing once white trousers tucked into rubber knee boots, women swathing their heads in broad kerchiefs of faded red wool, their long full black skirts almost trailing in the mud that oozed through their toes on the hamlet's only street. They gathered silently in a half-circle at the barn.

Hamdi joined Malik against the wall. "Be a man," he growled to the shivering boy, whose eyes twitched with terror. Khalid sprawled dead on the muddy ground in a wide pool of blood. His white eyes gaped, his mouth was twisted, frozen, and his purple tongue protruded swollenly.

Two little boys ran forward and spat on Hamdi and Malik. Giggling, they ran back to join the adults in the half-circle. One of the village men walked up to the older soldier, closest to Hamdi. The soldier chortled delightedly as he listened to the farmer's whispered words.

"Let's go," the soldier said to his prisoners, gesturing with his M-16 for Hamdi and Malik to walk to the mud path. The villagers followed closely behind.

A thick pole in the ground in front of one of the shacks was fitted with fist-sized iron rings at top and bottom. A hitching post. The soldier told them to stop and stand at the post. The villager who had spoken to the soldier pulled two long leather thongs out of his pocket. He knelt in front of Malik, tied a tight loop around the terrified boy's right ankle, and then threaded the other end through the iron ring at the bottom of the post, leaving a six-inch leash from post to ankle. The villager turned toward Hamdi's left ankle with the second thong. Hamdi lowered his arms, and his hands became menacing fists. He pulled his leg away.

"You want to die right now?" asked the older soldier conversationally, pointing his M-16 at Hamdi's face.

Hamdi slowly released his fists and brought his arms up over his head again, looking into the soldier's black unsmiling eyes. He felt the villager tie the thong around his left ankle and secure it to the post ring.

One of the young women gaily pulled the red kerchief off her hair and tore it in half. She handed it to a man who blindfolded first Hamdi and then the sniveling Malik. The villagers were chattering excitedly now, and Hamdi could hear the squealing of an angry pig close in front of him.

A shoat had been collared by a six-foot leather thong, and one of the soldiers tied the end of the thong to the same bottom ring of the hitching post.

Hamdi felt the handle of a knife being pressed into his right hand. "Stick the pig!" someone yelled. "Stick the pig!" came a chorus of shouts. Hamdi stood motionlessly. Above the obscene shouts of the soldiers and villagers were the outraged squeals of the pig.

"Stick the pig or we stick you, Palestinian!" hollered the older soldier and prodded Hamdi roughly in the ribs with his bayonet. Hamdi felt warm blood trickle down his side from the bayonet gouge. He could hear Malik yelp miserably, and he assumed that the other soldier had also cut the boy with his bayonet.

Hamdi bent toward the sound of the squealing pig and took a weak swipe at the sound. Suddenly he felt the blade of a knife slash through the meaty underside of his left forearm. He straightened in pain and turned to his left, toward the whimpering gasping sounds of terror Malik was making as he slashed wildly through the air. Again he felt searing pain as Malik's knife drove into the top of his left foot, the one tied to the post.

In self-defense, Hamdi struck downward and to his left and felt the knife bury itself to the hilt. He pulled off his blindfold and saw Malik slump forward lifelessly on his belly. The villagers leaped and hooted gleefully.

Blood rolled down Hamdi's arm and his fingers were paralyzed.

But he could see that it was not spurting, no severed arteries. The pain in his foot suddenly radiated upward and he felt himself getting weak and nauseous. He fell to his knees and remained there dazed.

Two village men grabbed him by the shoulders. A soldier cut the thong binding his injured leg to the post. The men dragged him on his stomach into a pig sty close by and laid him in the putrid slop. One of them bound his hands with a rope and tied the end of the rope to one of the pig sty railings three feet off the ground. Hamdi struggled to roll over on his back and pulled himself up against the rails so that he was almost sitting, his arms tethered above and behind his head.

Some of the men and women had gone to tend their own pigs. Most of them, however, stood around the outer rails of the fifteen-foot-square sty. The children were whistling and giggling and pointing as they watched two great sows root at Hamdi's bloody foot. Luckily his boot lace was tight and the wound was up between his toes, so the blood was ceasing to flow. He kicked his feet wildly, scaring away the sows.

A soldier brought the shoat on its thong leash from the hitching post to the sty railing. A villager expertly severed its throat with a clean swipe of a long slender knife. It wriggled frantically for a moment and then stilled. The same villager turned the shoat on its back and slit it open from its throat to its anus. He pulled out the pile of sticky, oozing, stinking entrails and threw them over the railing onto Hamdi's head and face and chest.

Hamdi gagged from the stench and the horrible transgression of being touched by the flesh of an unholy animal detestable to Allah, forbidden to Muslims. The sows came back viciously grunting and rutting at the profligate feast awaiting them.

The soldiers had dragged the bodies of Malik and Khalid to the sty. They picked up one and then the other and flung them like so much garbage into the sty. The sows immediately left the struggling, screaming Hamdi and busied themselves with the human offal.

Hamdi passed out from loss of blood and from the exhaustion of fighting off the pigs.

* * *

Hassan was alarmed. Ten o'clock already, and his son was not back. Tanoun was only thirty-five miles away, and they had left over four hours ago. He assembled twenty of the more experienced older fedayeen and they drove toward Tanoun in a column of five jeeps. They pulled off the highway and parked behind the same hill that had hidden Hamdi's jeep earlier that morning, but all they found were tracks in the grass and an oil stain.

The heavily-armed men crawled expertly through the meadow of wild irises bordering the topaz lake. Two men remained behind as a rear guard. Hassan studied the hamlet with binoculars. He quickly located most of the villagers around the pig sty and could see why Hamdi had not returned.

The retribution was exceedingly swift. The preoccupied villagers did not even see the approach of the Palestinians until they heard the crackling of fire and turned around to see the barn and several of the houses disappearing in hungry flames. The fedayeen quickly began to shoot every man, woman, child, dog, cat, pig and donkey. Every structure was torched. Hassan knelt beside Hamdi and cut his bonds. One of the men brought two pails of fresh cool water from the well and Hassan poured them over his son, washing the foul unholiness from his body.

Hamdi asked Hassan to spare the two Maronite Militiamen.

He struggled to his feet, his left arm hanging uselessly by his side, unable at first to walk because of the stab wound in his left foot. He hobbled slowly with the help of his father to the middle of the street where the two soldiers were sitting on the ground, their hands tied behind them, a circle of fedayeen around them.

Hamdi carefully picked up one of the bayonet-fixed M-16's from the ground, hobbled in front of the older soldier, and said, "*Sabach alchayr* [Good morning]." He smiled at the Christian Arab and plunged the bayonet through the soldier's eye and out the back of his head. Hassan walked directly in front of the younger soldier, open-mouthed in fear, his tongue lolling, and sprayed his face with the Kalachnikov.

Nadia thanked Allah that Hamdi had not been seriously injured by the infidel scum Maronite Catholic men and women and children of that evil village that Hassan had righteously cut off from the earth. Hamdi's wounds were only in the muscle of his forearm and the sinews between two toes, and he had healed rapidly and completely. The scar on his arm he would wear with pride, the badge of the Palestinian freedom fighter.

It was three o'clock in the morning and she could not sleep. Something kept coming back to her, preying on her mind, jolting her out of sleep. The hands of a strange man touching her body, the soft face of the Madam, the whore of whores, the fat Maronite in the emerald green evening gown with the bleached blond hair who had tried to sell Nadia's body. The Maronite whore who had called Nadia "Palestinian scum." Nadia reeled with the memory, so distant, so long ago, yet brought stingingly back to her by what the Maronites had done to her son Hamdi.

She walked out on the balcony and looked over the purple sea, murmuring with soft soughing sounds carried on the spring breeze. There was only a half moon strumming its yellow beams on the glinting water. Allah had saved Hamdi from the Maronites. But oh so close had they come to destroying him whom she held most dearly in this world, flesh of her flesh, heart of her heart, bone and sinew and blood of her own loins. She suddenly felt the absolutely burning need to set matters aright, by herself, with her own hand, to settle the score. This was not a task for others to do— no, no, no. This was an act of redemption and resurrection and retribution which she herself must perform. No one else could do it. May Allah will it that the Maronite whore has been spared for this moment, that she has lived so that I might see her again.

She went silently into the bedroom to change from her night-dress to an old black caftan and *shaddur*. Hassan and Hamdi were both at the training barracks in Yaatar. Careful not to wake the servants, she padded into the kitchen and selected a long thin filet knife from the drawer, wrapped it in a small kitchen towel, and tucked it in her belt under the broad *shaddur*. Silently she left the villa, walking along the beach road in the darkness. The Maronite quarter was a long way up the beach and she walked for almost two hours. It was still deep darkness when she reached Khartoum street and turned right to enter the residential district where she remembered the house to be.

There it was. A thin white light hanging from one of the fake Roman pillars was the only illumination. It was almost five-thirty and the slumbering neighborhood was still. Nadia walked up the broad front steps and through the polished wooden doors into the reception room. It was exactly as she had seen it twenty years ago, Persian carpets and red plush, but much more seedy. Several candle stubs glowed weakly on the counter.

Nadia walked toward the room behind the counter where a ribbon of light showed below the door. It was where the fat woman had come out the first time they had met. There was no sound in the brothel. All of the ladies of the night had undoubtedly plied their trade up to an hour or two ago and were now resting from their labors.

The doorknob turned freely and Nadia carefully pushed the door open. A small lamp burned on a bedstand. The room was small, crowded with an immense bed pushed up against the far wall. On the bed sat the fat Maronite whore, her back and head against the wall.

May Allah be praised, thought Nadia. Her heart felt light with joy and eager anticipation. He has preserved this evil woman for her moment of destiny.

She was incredibly the same, only fatter and more dissipated. Her bleached strawy hair was disheveled. Her jowly cheeks were heavily pinked with blusher and sagged onto four rolls of chins. She was swathed in a great puce silk gown which fell open, baring her immense breasts. On her chest was a box of chocolates, and four Siamese cats slept on the bed around this puddle of decaying flesh.

On the wall behind her, directly over her head, was a large crucifix of wrought iron with a plastic Jesus hanging from it.

"Who are you?" asked the fat whore, squinting through aged eyes and poor light at the intruder.

"I am one whom you sought to defile."

She squinted harder.

"I have come to you after many years to reward you for your evil act."

"What are you talking about?" The whore sounded very tired, cranky, not fully comprehending.

"I was here many years ago." Nadia slowly unwrapped the *shaddur* from her face and let it fall.

"Come closer, you, I can't see you."

Nadia walked to the side of the bed and stood in the lamplight.

"Here, have a chocolate," said the whore in that same soft purr of a voice that Nadia remembered. She handed a candy to Nadia.

Nadia did not take it. The woman slowly dropped her hand. "Get out of here. I don't want you here." She had become petulant. "I must go to sleep."

"I want you to look at me very hard. I want you to remember me."

The old woman squinted closely at Nadia. Her eyes looked more awake now, more intent, and her mouth slowly drooped open with her effort at concentration. "I do not know you. You have made a mistake. Get out of my house."

"You called me 'Palestinian scum.' You tried to sell my body," Nadia muttered through jaws clenched in hatred.

The old woman peered closer. Then she shrugged. "Do you think I can possibly remember all of the Palestinian sluts who have come to my door? Do you think you are the only one? I have seen rivers of scum flow in and out of my door. And I've seen enough of you! Get out now!"

Nadia stared at her, saying nothing, but her eyes spoke an unmistakable message to the old whore.

"What is it that you want here? You should not be here." Her voice had become a whimper. "You leave here! I want you to get away from me!" She reached for the telephone on the bedstand.

Nadia quickly pulled the wrapped knife from her belt and let the kitchen towel fall to the floor. She pressed her left hand harshly over the fat Maronite whore's mouth and nose and shoved the knife through the center of her throat and out the back of her neck. She watched the blood come. She watched the light fade from the eyes and the body relax on the bed. Only a few seconds.

Nadia wrapped the *shaddur* around her face and shoulders again and went out into the cool dawn. She walked to the beach and casually retraced her steps. The songs of larks in the great holly oak in front of her villa heralded her return. Tomorrow night, she knew, she would sleep much better.

Chapter Three

Hassan and Hamdi were away from Beirut for weeks on end. The recruits for al-Asifah were drawn from the Palestinian sup-purating sores called refugee camps. Tell Zaatar, Rashidiye, Sabra, Shatila and many smaller camps were breeding grounds for the dozens of Palestinian terrorist groups that began to make almost daily raids into the agricultural settlements and kibbutzim of Northern Israel.

After they had spilled the blood of Jew scum in these small attacks, al-Asifah would take the best of the terrorists into its growing ranks, and they would be trained in conventional small unit warfare, tanks and artillery. But the heart of the fedayeen movement was still the constant slaughtering of Israeli civilians, for this was the quintessential method of terrorism: indiscriminate brutal slaying of civilians, especially children, to spread panic among the general population, ruin the morale of the Jews, and paralyze their capacity for unified resistance. But no major terror-ist raid on Israel had been carried out in years, not since Hamdi's brilliant operation in Hebron, and Hassan could sense Nadia's growing restiveness.

They sat on their terrace overlooking the softly rolling Mediter-ranean and sipped heavy spice-laden coffee out of delicate pale rose eggshell porcelain demitasse cups.

"Do you know what next Wednesday is?" Nadia asked.

He looked quizzically at her. It's not her birthday, he thought quickly to himself. It's not our anniversary. He couldn't think what it was.

"September 10, Hassan. September 10."

He stared at her, creasing his brow, and then suddenly he realized what she meant. "Oh! Right! The anniversary of Deir Yassin."

"Exactly," she said slowly. "And I think the fedayeen should plan something special for that day. It's the twenty-fifth anniversary of the destruction of my family, my entire *hamula*. It is the day which marks the beginning of our wanderings in the wilderness, and I want the Jews to remember the day forever."

Hassan nodded slowly, thinking how meaningful and symbolic a full scale raid into Israel would be as a commemoration of the Jewish annihilation of Deir Yassin. He instantly thought of S'de Dan, an Israeli "development town," a showpiece of Israel's policy of encouraging settlements near the dangerous Lebanese border to show the world that the Jews had no fear of Palestinian terrorism.

"I have just the place, Nadia. Hamdi and I have talked about it several times, and we have a good deal of intelligence on it. S'de Dan, a pretty little town with new housing developments and a lovely new school building on its northern end. There isn't a military post within twenty miles. Just waiting for us."

Nadia beamed.

Hassan's ink-black hair had long since turned gray, and his once lithe and sinewy body had given way to a thickening in the waist, but he still felt like a lion, still a warrior. Nadia walked over to him and knelt between his legs and wrapped her arms around him. Hassan stroked her hair, and he put his head on hers and closed his eyes, and he remembered the first time he had touched her so long ago, the first time he had experienced her love. He knew that next week he would feel this same surge of pleasure at S'de Dan, when he killed Jews and avenged the murders of Nadia's family and so many other innocent Palestinians.

Hamdi was in Libya undergoing advanced artillery training, so Hassan decided to lead this operation himself. It would be a great morale booster for the men of al-Asifah, to know that their leader had not grown too soft to lead an attack, to get his boots scuffed, to kill Jews. Hassan drove to Bishra the next day. It was a fortified encampment of al-Asifah troops eight miles from the Israeli border and only ten miles from S'de Dan. Hassan ordered the Bishra commander to assemble fifteen of his best men in the briefing bunker immediately.

A half hour later, Hassan outlined the attack plan on the large chalkboard in the bunker. The Palestinians were thrilled that they had been chosen to accompany the great Hassan abu-Sittah on this historic raid. They raised their Kalachnikovs high over their heads and chanted, "Deir Yassin, Deir Yassin, Deir Yassin!" and a virtual frenzy enveloped them. They danced for joy and spilled out of the briefing bunker to tell their friends the good news. Just four more days and they would be heroes.

September 10 finally came. At nine in the morning, Hassan got into the lead jeep beside the driver, and the four jeeps and sixteen Palestinians drove toward S'de Dan. They drove slowly past the border, which was nothing more than a sign in Arabic and Hebrew, and continued southward. None of them took particular notice of the line of fresh asphalt across the narrow road just inside the Israeli border. It looked like a bit of patching.

The idea flickered through Hassan's mind for just a split second that the Jews might be using "sensors" on the Lebanese border, just as they were using them in the Sinai, near the Suez Canal. But he pushed the thought away. There was plenty enough to think about right now.

The Israelis had just begun using the experimental devices on the Lebanese border which—if they were tripped—were supposed to set off a beeping sound in the listening post at the military headquarters in Metulla twenty miles away. Sometimes they worked, sometimes they didn't.

This time the bored Tzahal private sitting in the control booth with his headphone sat stiffly upright in his chair as the beeping started. He located the tripped devices on the sonar-like screen in front of him and pinpointed the nearest town to be S'De Dan. Two Huey helicopters, each carrying a platoon of Golani Brigade paratroopers, took off for S'de Dan twelve minutes later.

The Palestinians reached the Netiv Meir school building without a hitch. The four jeeps split up, each one stopping in front of a different one of the square cement-block building's walls. The drivers manned the jeeps' mounted heavy machine guns to prevent anyone from escaping. The other members of the team ran inside the school. The teachers and students were held at gunpoint while Lino, Harbi and Kamal expertly planted the charges. They were almost done when they heard the familiar roar of a helicopter overhead and heard machine gun fire from one of the jeeps.

Hassan raced outside and saw a helicopter landing in an athletic field about a hundred yards away and another one hovering overhead and spraying the jeeps intermittently with its machine guns. The Arab attackers began pouring out of the school building and ran toward the jeeps. They were quickly cut down by the helicopter fire and the soldiers who were now nearing the school through the grassy playing field.

Hassan ran back inside the school building. The explosives were already planted, and Harbi and the two other remaining Palestinians were herding the terrified students and their teachers out of the four classrooms and into the auditorium. They were mostly teenage girls, crying and gasping, white with fear.

Hassan mounted the platform at the front of the auditorium and shot a blast from his Kalachnikov into the ceiling. A terrified silence settled on the hostages.

"Be seated and keep your mouths shut!" Hassan screamed at them in Hebrew, menacing them with his submachine gun. The other Arabs stood in back of the auditorium and levelled their Kalachnikovs at the frightened hostages. The milling about stopped, they all took seats.

"Anyone who moves will be killed!" Hassan yelled. He walked quickly down the aisle and out of the auditorium. He walked cautiously to a window which opened out on the back of the school and the playing field, and he braced against the wall and peeked out. It looked like half the Israeli Army was out there. Three more helicopters had landed and there was a swarm of soldiers deploying at the edge of the school.

Hassan had no idea what to do. But at least he had an auditorium full of Jew scum to negotiate with, and he felt certain that he would be able to buy his way out of this mess in exchange for their lives.

"We want to talk to someone! We want to talk to someone!" came the blare of a Hebrew voice over a hand held megaphone outside. Minutes passed. "We want to talk to someone!" came the voice again.

Hassan shattered the window with the barrel of his Kalachnikov and stood braced against the wall. After a minute, he laid the submachine gun against the wall and stood in front of the window. The soldier with the megaphone was kneeling at the edge of the playing field some thirty yards away. He stood slowly and put the megaphone to his lips.

"You are completely surrounded and there is no possibility to escape. Order your men to put down their arms and come out peacefully. You will not be harmed."

"Fuck you, you Jew scum!" screamed Hassan back at him. "I have a hundred boys and girls, and this building has been planted with enough explosives to obliterate everyone." He waited for his message to sink in. "I will only speak to someone in Arabic. No more Jew talk!" Hassan stood in the window, emboldened by the scores of hostages in the auditorium whose lives were in his hand. As long as he had the school children, no harm would come to him. The Jews were soft about their children.

The same Israeli handed the megaphone to another soldier and walked toward the window. He stopped about twenty feet away.

"I'm Major Avneri," he said to Hassan in Arabic. "Who are you?" Avneri was short and heavy. He appeared to Hassan to be in his mid-thirties, with a great mop of wavy black hair and glistening black eyes.

"Let's dispense with the bullshit, Major. I have an auditorium full of boys and girls in here. If my men and I aren't permitted to leave untouched, we'll kill them all." Hassan spoke conversationally, as though he were talking over the back fence with a neighbor about the high price of turnips.

"I have no authority at the moment. We are waiting for General Geva to arrive from Tel Aviv. He should be here momentarily."

Hassan walked back into the auditorium and whispered to each of his men in turn, telling them to stay put and alert. He left the auditorium door open and sat in a chair just inside it. Ten minutes passed, twenty, an hour. Two hours. The children shifted uncomfortably in the metal folding chairs. A short, bald man, one of the teachers, stood up in the midst of the seated children. He turned around to face the four Arabs in the back of the auditorium, and then he edged his way slowly past the seated children in the row and stepped into the aisle.

"The children must eat, it is past lunch time for all of—"

Smoke curled from the barrel of Hassan's submachine gun as the burst destroyed the teacher's face and chest. He slumped in a bloody heap in the aisle. Screams broke out among the children.

"Shut your mouths!" Hassan screamed at them. "I told you that if anyone moved you'd be killed! Now shut up!"

The children gasped and pressed their hands over their faces to suppress their crying. Silence slowly descended like a shroud.

"What is the shooting?" blared a voice in Arabic over the

bullhorn from outside. Hassan didn't budge. A few moments later came the same question again. Hassan didn't move from his chair. An hour passed.

"This is General Geva. This is General Geva. Where is your spokesman?" The amplified Hebrew voice broke into the auditorium. Hassan rose stiffly from the metal chair and walked to the shattered window. As he got to the window, Geva lowered the megaphone. He was standing directly in front of the window with Major Avneri.

"I only speak Hebrew. If you want to talk in Arabic, Major Avneri will translate for us," said the emaciated-looking General. He was of medium height and had thin, graying, once-brown hair, and his back and neck were arthritically straight. He squinted at Hassan with watery hazel eyes, and his tensely pursed upper lip looked to Hassan like a tiny parrot's beak.

Hassan thought for a moment. The waiting had gotten on his nerves. His Hebrew wasn't perfect, and he was afraid of misunderstanding or causing the Israelis to misunderstand. "I only speak Arabic to Jew scum," he spat back, looking into the General's icy eyes.

"The General wants to know what that shooting was a while ago," said Avneri.

"One of the teachers disobeyed my orders. He is dead."

"What about the children?"

"None of them has been harmed. Give us two jeeps. We will take two hostages in each jeep with us. When we pass the border, we will let them go."

The Israelis mumbled together for a moment. "We have no authority to let you leave," said Avneri.

"Have two jeeps at the front door in five minutes," said Hassan through gritted teeth.

Hassan walked back into the auditorium and waved for the three other Palestinians to come over to him. They whispered together for a minute. Then Hassan walked over to the last row of children. There were about fifteen boys and girls, the oldest probably seventeen, the youngest thirteen.

"You four girls," said Hassan in Hebrew, pointing his submachine gun at the four nearest him next to the aisle. "You come with me."

The girls stood slowly, terrifiedly. One of them had her hand in the hand of the boy sitting next to her, and he would not let go.

"Let go of her!" screamed Hassan.

The boy leapt up from his chair and lunged toward Hassan. Hassan sprayed him with the Kalachnikov and two of the girls were also hit. Some of the other children began to get up from their seats. Hassan shot a burst over their heads and restored order quickly. The boy and one girl were dead. Another girl, a pretty thirteen- or fourteen-year-old, groaned from the wound in her shoulder and lay sprawled in the aisle. She was petite, and Hassan dragged her out of the auditorium. He picked her up like a bundle of rags and dumped her through the shattered back window. Two medics with a stretcher came running up to her and quickly carried her away.

At the edge of the playing field Major Avneri knelt and lifted the bullhorn. "If any more hostages are harmed, we will assault the building."

"Then all of them will die!" screamed Hassan through the window.

Avneri and Geva came slowly to the window. Avneri spoke in Arabic, translating the General's words: "No ransom will be paid, no terrorist will leave with a hostage. If just one time we permit ourselves to be blackmailed by a hostage situation, then no Jew will ever be safe. You must believe without the slightest doubt whatsoever that if you try to take even one of those children hostage, you will either surrender or you will die. There is no other way."

Hassan wheeled angrily and walked back into the auditorium. He sat again in the metal chair and tried to think what to do. He began to realize, as hour by hour ticked by without a sound from Major Avneri, that he had been wrong about the Jews. They were not just talking tough. They would not negotiate, not even for all of their children. A sense of desperation began to grip him. He realized that the only possibility was an escape plan. Darkness fell slowly. Hassan switched on the overhead lights. None of the hostages had been permitted to go to the toilet, and many of them had relieved themselves, either from fear or necessity, in their seats. The still hot air and the stench of the auditorium was stifling. Hassan walked into the corridor outside the auditorium, and huge spotlights shone through the outer windows of the building, eerily lighting up the school house in brilliant patches. He took several gulps of air to rid his lungs of the stench and went back into the auditorium.

"Harbi, Lino, Kamal, come over here," he called out to the three explosives experts. They came to him in the back of the auditorium.

"We have no alternative. The Jew scum will not negotiate."

Hassan saw fear in all of their faces. The earlier bravado of expectant victory had been replaced by glazed eyes and twitching cheeks and flaring nostrils, like frightened foxes sniffing the scent of hunters.

"We only have one chance. Reset your charges to blow the auditorium and the front wall of the building. We'll kill all of the hostages and run for it through the dirt and dust and debris of the explosion. Maybe we'll make it."

Hassan stood in back of the auditorium as the three other Palestinians ran to where they had planted their explosives over twelve hours ago. All of them returned about five minutes later. Kamal went down the corridor to the front wall of the building and laid a large canvas satchel against it. The others placed stringing wires from all of the reset explosives back to the detonator box on a chair at the back of the auditorium.

Some of the older children, realizing what was happening, began rising from their seats and calling out to the others in terror. Hassan shot a burst into the ceiling. The murmur of the children did not die down this time, and many of them began to cry. They were panicked beyond control. They began to scramble over each other to get to the aisle and run out of the building. Hassan lowered his Kalachnikov at the group of children nearest him and pulled the trigger. Suddenly, Hassan heard yelling from outside the building and long bursts of heavy machine gun fire, and then he felt a sudden white heat at the base of his skull.

Chapter Four

Nadia sat in the traditional black mourning gown and wept as she listened to the *imam* chant suras from the Koran. Hamdi sat beside her, dry-eyed. Men did not cry, and certainly not over a martyr's death like Hassan's. Hassan had killed two dozen Jewish boys and girls in commemoration of Deir Yassin. To die thus was to assure one's place at the Fount of Selsabil, in the Camphor Garden, in the Kingdom of Eternal Bliss. Hamdi got up slowly and tiptoed out of the room. He had to go to a meeting at the Melkart Hotel with Yassir Arafat and two of the leaders of the Lebanese government. The Lebanese were frightened over the Palestinian terrorism and the Israeli reprisals.

Four days ago, when Hamdi had flown back from Libya as soon as he had been notified of Hassan's death, Arafat had come to the abu-Sittah villa to pay his respects to Nadia. He had also brought great news. In honor of the martyrdom of Hassan abu-Sittah and the superb record of his stepson Hamdi, Hamdi Attiyah was appointed commander of al-Asifah.

Just two days after that, the Israelis had executed their retaliatory attack. A squad of naval commandos infiltrated at night from the Mediterranean into the heart of Beirut. In a period of hours, they blew up three of the principal PLO administrative buildings and assassinated four Fatah leaders as they slept in their beds. The commandos escaped untouched.

The central government of Lebanon was in panic. The President and Prime Minister called for an immediate meeting with Arafat. The meeting took place at the Melkart Hotel in Beirut. The Lebanese demanded that the Palestinians cease and desist forthwith from armed attacks on Israel. The constant brutal Israeli retaliatory attacks were beginning to affect the stability of the Lebanese economy and to frighten the Arab businessmen around the Middle East who had made Beirut the financial and banking capital of the Islamic world.

Yassir Arafat and Hamdi Attiyah, already reeling from the

intensity of Israel's retaliation against the PLO and the death of Hassan, grudgingly signed the Melkart Agreement. They pledged to engage in no further military strikes against Israel. They also agreed to permit a watchdog group of Lebanese army officers to monitor fedayeen activities to insure that the Palestinians would abide by the pacification agreement. Once more, the Palestinians had been emasculated. And again, as in Jordan, it was at the hands of their fellow Arabs. But this time, the betrayers of the way of the fedayeen were led by Maronite Christians. This had a particularly grating effect on the Sunni Muslim Yassir Arafat and Hamdi Attiyah. They had lost face to Christian infidels.

When Hamdi returned from the Melkart Hotel to the villa, he was in a sick rage. Nadia was sitting on the sofa in the living room, drinking tea, staring. Her face was sallow and drawn. Her once shiny black hair was now gray, protruding in unkempt wisps from under her black lace kerchief. Hamdi sat down next to his mother and took her hand in his lap. The first tears he had shed in many years, since he was five or six, trickled down his cheeks. He had just lost his stepfather, and his first act as heir to the command of al-Asifah was to be humiliated by Christians, the same enemy who had humiliated him just a short time ago with pigs. They had threatened him with the Maronite Militia's vengeance if he continued to lead al-Asifah in the way of the fedayeen, the *jihad* against Israel. He had been forced to capitulate, for the fedayeen were too weak to fight back at the moment. His body began to shake with sobs, impotent rage and frustration.

Nadia slapped him hard across the face, leaving blood-red welts on his cheek. "I have always told you a man never cries! He is never weak, not a true man!" she screamed at him.

Hamdi took a deep breath and forced himself to stop crying.

"I have brought shame upon the fedayeen," he said quietly. "I have been forced to turn our soldiers into scared sheep." He told her what had happened at the Melkart Hotel. She listened with clenched teeth.

"They must not do to us what the Jews and King Hussein did," she said. "They must not destroy our people and our fight for 'awda. If the Lebanese fight against us, then they are against the *jihad* and against the will of Allah, and you must destroy them." She took both of his hands in her own and looked at him savagely.

"You must destroy them!" she screamed at him. She put her head back and screamed at the ceiling, closing her eyes, her voice exploding and ricocheting against the walls, repeating it over and over as she clenched her son's hands, "You must destroy them!"

Hamdi received a letter—actually it had been addressed to Hassan abu-Sittah—from the English Journalists' Foreign Affairs Bureau requesting that he agree to be interviewed about the murky origins of Fatah and al-Asifah and his rise to power. These organizations had always intentionally been cloaked in secrecy, since they operated more or less clandestinely and always at the whim of their fickle Arab patrons. But Hamdi felt that it was time to seek at least the appearance of legitimacy. He called the Bureau and set up the interview for his home two days later.

Her name was Julia Flynn, and Hamdi instantly knew that she was not only going to interview him about Fatah and al-Asifah and the PLO. He was sure that she was also here to seduce him if that was the only way to get a story. It exuded from her like soft candlelight. He had heard many stories, that it was a common practice for journalistic organizations to send their prettiest and most willing and eager young women to do interviews with Arab leaders. Here she was.

Julia sat in a straight-backed wicker chair on the balcony. Hamdi sat uneasily on a small low wicker divan across from her. She was all polite business, but she was exactly what he had expected: probably in her mid-twenties, very liberated British independent type with a short, bone-colored leather skirt and a cream angora sweater, quite snug over hard, little, pointy breasts with no bra. Very long and slender legs were crossed, and she sat slightly turned toward Hamdi so that he would be sure to have an almost wonderful view of the treasure trove where the tight skirt gapped. She was red haired, green eyed, wore almost no makeup, and the opposite of the average Arab girl.

She asked many questions.

He told her of Black September in Jordan, how Hussein had treacherously tried to destroy the Palestinian national movement, how he had finally forced them to come to Lebanon. He told her in glowing terms about his stepfather Hassan's heroic attack on the Jew scum and his martyrdom.

All the while, for over two hours, Julia sat entranced. She had spent almost two years in the Arab Middle East, had interviewed many leaders, but was never so captivated by any of them as she was with this handsome charmer. His English, even his accent, was excellent. He told her about being a student at Berkeley, but he didn't elaborate.

Nadia came out on the balcony and sat down next to Hamdi on the divan. Hamdi introduced her diffidently. Julia sensed from the tone of his voice and the way he looked at his mother that this striking woman was the real power in the abu-Sittah family. And she looked it. Even in the plain black shift of mourning and her hair wrapped in a black lace kerchief, she was regal, powerful.

"Do you believe that the Palestinians will really be able to drive the Jews from Palestine?" Julia directed the question to Nadia, wanting to hear her speak. Hamdi translated into Arabic.

"*Na'am*, nodded Nadia slowly, simply.

"Can you really hope for a military victory over the Jews? Aren't they too powerful?"

"*La*," was Nadia's laconic reply, shaking her head.

"Wouldn't negotiations be a more likely solution, negotiations for your own state in the West Bank and Gaza?"

"We cannot abandon the way of the fedayeen, the *jihad* for our *'awda*," translated Hamdi.

"But really, Mrs. abu-Sittah," Julia cajoled her softly, trying to get her to say something more than this doctrinaire, formulistic Palestinian jargon that she had heard time and time again. "Look around us. You have a marvelous villa here in Beirut, your balcony has a view of the loveliest beach in the world. There is a big Mercedes parked in the carport downstairs. You have at least three servants that I have seen. That Persian carpet I saw in your parlor has to be worth £3,000 or £4,000. What more could you possibly have in Palestine?"

Nadia listened to the translation of this girl's question, and her eyes narrowed. Why didn't this girl understand?

"These *things* have nothing to do with the quality of our lives," answered Nadia. "Could any woman have a more wonderful son?" she asked rhetorically, looking at Hamdi and then back at Julia, who seemed entirely to agree. "But my life was destroyed by the Jews in 1948, and I was resurrected only by my will and Hassan's will to wreak Allah's vengeance on the Jew scum."

"What was your life like in Palestine, Mrs. abu-Sittah?"

"It was rich so that we did not need money and *things*. We had the sweetness of life. I was a woman of sixteen when I married Hamdi's father, Farid. He was magnificent, like Hamdi." Her eyes glistened.

"His family had tilled the rich soil for a thousand years, and it had always yielded up abundant fruits for all of us. And Farid was a lion among men. No woman could have wished for more or found it. Our home was rich because it was full of our *hamula*, thirty people lived there. We were rich with family and the earth and the wealth of our honor as a family, a clan, a people."

"And now," her voice became bitter. Hamdi translated for his mother. "And now the Jew scum have left me with only *things*. You cannot be rich with such things. A Persian carpet cannot make you feel like a human being. A Mercedes in Beirut, alone with my servants in this great house overlooking the Mediterranean, is not as rich as a donkey cart in the sprawling stone villa in the bosom of my loved ones, all murdered by the Jews."

Nadia sat quietly for a moment. The pain of Hassan's death was close about her. But at least he had died a hero's death, making the Jews pay dearly for his life. Farid had not been so lucky. Snuffed out, crushed like a cockroach even before he had reached the full flower of his manhood. She could still see him as he was on their wedding day.

"That Persian carpet was a gift from my first husband's father on our wedding day," Nadia spoke wistfully, and her features softened as she reminisced.

"They had gone to Baghdad to buy it, Farid and his father Muhammad. You couldn't buy such a nice carpet in Jerusalem, and it was dangerous for an Arab to go to Iran at the time. It was right at the outbreak of the Second World War. But Iraq was safe under British protection the same as Palestine. I remember they were gone for weeks, and when they returned with the magnificent Qum carpet, all of Deir Yassin gave them a hero's welcome and there was a banquet. And they brought me many bangle bracelets, and I was the proudest woman on earth.

"My Hamdi is Farid's duplicate, like a photograph. That's how handsome was my husband." Nadia looked at her son and smiled, and she took his hand in hers.

Julia Flynn was surprised by the tenderness of this woman and her son. The legends growing up about her and Hamdi Attiyah were of violence and hatred and ghastly acts of depravity. Like that "martyrdom" of Hassan abu-Sittah at the school in S'de Dan. These people may call it anything they want, but insane murder of children is all it was. But this was something she had never expected to see, this depth of tenderness between mother and son. She listened and watched in fascination.

"At the wedding feast, Farid looked like a caliph from the old stories. Every girl in Deir Yassin wanted him, but I got him," she said with a broad smile. "I took him to me and loved him, and he never went to another bed as long as he lived. He did not have to, because I was all he ever needed.

"He could have taken four wives, you know," she looked at Julia and winked, "but he didn't need four, just me." She boasted proudly in a rich soft voice, seeing it all again through the smoke and fire and pain of over thirty years.

"Our fields around Deir Yassin were like voluptuous botanical gardens, rich and fertile and giving off the scent of a million flowers. And they were ours. They were all we ever wanted. We never stole a tomato or a chicken from the Jews."

Whatever Nadia's inner thoughts had now turned to, her face hardened. The softness faded from her voice and suddenly a palpable change seemed to occur in the atmosphere, as though a cooler wind blew over the balcony.

"A Mercedes, Miss Flynn. I don't want a Mercedes. I want my home in Deir Yassin. I want my son to till the fields and harvest the fruits of Allah's beneficence. I want to deliver an appropriate reward to the Jews who have oppressed us. How many times will Allah permit them to wreak havoc on my loved ones, before he lets me visit them with His vengeance?" Her cobalt eyes glittered with tears. She got up quickly and walked inside the house. She had had enough of this journalist. She could speak no more of these things to a stranger, a foreigner, a European.

"I hope I did not upset your mother," Julia said to Hamdi with genuine concern.

"Well, she'll be all right," said Hamdi. "It is my stepfather's death. She revered him, and now she feels all alone."

The atmosphere had changed. Julia could feel that the sensual bond she had forged between herself and Hamdi had broken.

Temporarily, she hoped. Hamdi sat up straight in the divan to signal the end of the interview.

"I really would like to meet with you again, Mr. Attiyah." She almost purred.

Hamdi did not want her to come back here. His mother had had her fill. But he did want to see more of this flame haired beauty with the freckled, turned up nose and dancing green eyes.

"Perhaps we could meet on the beach tomorrow afternoon," he said, pointing toward the beach directly outside the balcony and across the street.

"Lovely." She smiled at him with obvious pleasure. "Two o'clock, then?"

Hamdi showed her to the door and then walked back through the living room. He could feel the heat of his mother's withering stare.

"Are you crazy?" she said.

He stopped and faced her. "What do you mean."

"That English girl could be anyone. You cannot be safe with her. None of us can. Remember Miriam."

"But Mama, I have no one. I need someone. I feel like my life is empty."

"Empty!" she screamed at him. "*Al-tariq al-fida'i* is the only lover you need for now! It is all that any of us need until we return to Kafr Yassin!"

Hamdi saw her from the balcony. She laid out a beach towel and took off her white loose shirtwaist and folded it, carefully laying it on the towel.

He slung his long towel over his shoulders and walked to the beach. He laid the towel down beside her and took off his beach shirt. She shaded her eyes and looked at his muscular body.

She was wearing a two piece swim suit of simple soft black nylon, and her nipples showed her excitement.

He had not been with a woman for six years, not since Miriam. . . . The mention of her yesterday for the first time in years had jolted him. He rolled over on his side and looked hard at Julia, as if he could penetrate her skin and make sure where her heart was. She loved being looked at by this god straight out of the Arabian Nights. She turned her head toward him and saw his serious studying look.

"I'll tell you anything," she answered his look.

Her long red hair was pulled straight back in a pony tail, and her square jawed, frank face was unpainted. She rolled toward him and propped herself on an elbow. The top of her swim suit gapped.

Everything she wears is trained to gap, he thought to himself.

"Let's swim," he said.

He stood up, took her hand and pulled her up, and they ran into the warm water. The sun streamed down like a flamethrower, making the water feel cooler than it actually was. They joined hands in the surf and jumped together and touched and bumped into each other. She felt his hardness against her, and she was excited. She looked into his dreamy black eyes.

They walked along the beach, dripping dry under the intense sun. Then they started walking back toward their towels. Others on the beach gazed at them in envy.

"So what will be your next move, Hamdi? Do you have any operations planned?" she asked, always the journalist.

Hamdi looked toward his villa. His mother was standing on the balcony looking out, arms folded, just standing. He could feel what she was thinking, what he was thinking. One Miriam in a lifetime is enough.

He picked up his towel and shirt and kept on walking away from the beach. Julia stood on her towel in surprise.

"Hamdi," she called after him.

He kept walking.

She called that afternoon, but Muna, their servant for twenty-four years, told her that he was out. She called twice the next day, but he would not talk to her. He was afraid. The aching need in his loins and his heart could not overcome the fear.

She stopped calling.

Chapter Five

Israel was the Biblical Empire Reincarnate. It was mightier than the Ammonites, Jebusites, Philistines, and all the warlike tribes which surrounded it. The Labor Party of Golda Meir was the "old guard" of Israel, the original Zionist pioneers who had forged a modern nation out of the swampy clay and sun brittled dust of the Land of Israel, the Promised Land.

The elections for the Eighth Knesset, scheduled for October 31, 1973, were in full swing. Golda Meir was the Labor Party peacemaker, Israel's grandmother, and at her side stood Israel's most popular war hero, Defense Minister Yigal Armon, heir apparent to Golda's crown. The Labor Party displayed on its party list an entire constellation of war heroes and famous men. Isaac Rubin, hero of the Six Day War, which he had masterminded as Chief of Staff. David Shaltner, the immortal David Ben-Gurion's closest confidant for many years. Abner Even, Israel's spectacularly eloquent Foreign Minister, a real favorite of American Jews. Everywhere across Israel billboards extolled the virtues of the Labor coalition:

> "The Bar-Lev Line. There is peace on the banks of the Canal, in the Sinai Desert, the Gaza Strip, the West Bank, Judea, Samaria, and on the Golan. The lines are safe. The bridges are open. Jerusalem is united. New settlements have been established and our political position is stable. This is the result of a balanced, bold, and far-sighted policy.... You know that only the Mapai [Labor] Alignment could have accomplished this."

Joshua Jordan came home to Jerusalem on a seven-day leave starting October 5. Most of Israel's standing army was on leave for the week, because October 6 was Yom Kippur, the Day of Atonement.

Joshua had been stationed at the Bar-Lev Line for a year, and he had only been home four times. The Bar-Lev Line was an immense complex of concrete bunkers and fortifications like the Maginot Line. As the Maginot Line had formed an impregnable barrier between France and Germany before the Second World War, so did the Bar-Lev Line seal off the entire east bank of the Suez Canal, the Israeli side, from the possibility of frontal assault by the Egyptians.

Joshua got home at two o'clock in the afternoon, and Dalia was waiting impatiently for him. He took a quick shower to scrub off the Sinai dust, and he went into the bedroom. Dalia was already on the bed and the months of longing and wanting and frustration melted away as they became one body.

Hours later, but still too soon, they washed each other in the

shower and then dressed to go to Kol Nidre dinner at his parents'
house. It was an important evening in the Jordans' lives, because it
was both the eve of the most intense holy day of the Jewish year as
well as the anniversary of the death of Leah's first husband. They
never discussed it, but it always hovered over this evening like a dire
warning, a hushed brooding murmur constantly repeating, "Never
again, never again, never again...."

The Almogis were already there when Joshua and Dalia arrived,
and they all went straight to the dining room. Though none of
them were observant Jews any longer, they still fasted on Yom
Kippur as a national celebration, and they had to finish eating
before sunset. Matt Jordan and Amos Almogi had been in deep
discussion for over an hour and they continued it at the table. There
had been an emergency Cabinet meeting that afternoon which
Amos, as Deputy Prime Minister, had attended. He was extremely
agitated.

"The Chief of Staff has requested that we put all of Tzahal on a
full-scale alert. He believes that an Egyptian attack is imminent,"
said Almogi. "But Defense Minister Armon and all of our intelligence staff believes it's just more of Sadat's saber rattling. So
Golda has only declared a Class C alert. We'll have to see what
develops."

"I can't believe that Sadat really wants to risk a war with us," said
Leah. "His favorite image is wearing that *gallabiah*, that striped
peasant's robe, and sitting on his prayer rug telling his problems to
Allah!" Everybody at the table chuckled. "Starting a war with us
wouldn't do much for his image as a peacemaker."

"I'm not sure his image isn't just a carefully fostered deception,"
said Matt. "The Egyptians have a standing army of over eight
hundred thousand men as well as thousands of the best Russian
tanks, aircraft and artillery. What the hell do they need that kind of
military for if not an offensive war? Our military isn't even a third
that size including all our reserves, and our arsenal is half that size."

"I've been watching Egyptian maneuvers on the Canal for a year
now," Joshua said, "and it sure looks like an offensive buildup to
me. They don't remove nearly as many troops as they bring up, and
they've been engaging in constant war games. I'll tell you the one
that bothers me the most. Our aerial reconnaissance has photos of it
happening literally every week for months. They send amphibious

assault barges from one end of the Great Bitter Lake to the other, and then they roll out these huge hoses that look like giant fire hoses, and they pump water out of the Lake through them." Joshua paused and looked around the table at his family. "They know they can't knock out the Bar-Lev Line with artillery. But what if they flooded the bunkers? They'd drown us like gophers in hole."

"Well, all we have to rely on are our intelligence people, and they say no war," shrugged Almogi.

"I really think they're wrong," insisted Joshua. "Chief of Staff Elazer believes there should be total mobilization against an impending Egyptian attack, and he's the best soldier Israel has. Why don't we follow his advice instead of Yigal Armon's. Armon has lost contact with military reality."

Everyone at the table knew what Joshua was referring to. Many professional military men believed that Yigal Armon's celebrity had destroyed his former military brilliance, and he was now singularly intent on creating a strong political image and following so that he would be assured of succeeding Golda as Prime Minister. The generals complained that he was neglecting his defense ministry. He had become an indiscreet womanizer and a lover of high living. And his example had paved the way for a creeping malaise in Israel's professional army, a laxity and lack of discipline that was corroding the spirit of solidarity that had always glued Israel's soldiers together.

"We also have to face the reality of Isreal's economic situation, Joshua," said Almogi. "Last May, when the Syrians had full war games with their two hundred fifty thousand troops near the Golan Heights, we called a Class A full mobilization. It cost us $200,000,000 and almost devastated our economy. Full mobilization means that every able bodied man under the age of fifty-six is called up, the shops and businesses in every city and town in Israel are locked up, the produce and poultry trucks stop their deliveriers from the farms and kibbutzim, the housewives haven't enough savings to buy even two weeks of groceries. The men are off in the Army getting paid $50 a month, so they can't pay their mortgages or their apartment rent, they can't pay off their business loans to the banks, they can't pay taxes to support the government.

"If we were to call a full mobilization every time Syria or Egypt looked like it was getting ready to attack, we'd destroy our entire economy in a hurry. It just can't be done."

"Money! Politicians always talk about money!" Joshua practically snarled. "What you really mean is that the elections are just three weeks away, and if the Labor Party calls for a full mobilization, and God forbid no war breaks out, Labor will lose the election and you'll be out of power!"

Dalia gave her husband a scorching look. Her father and Leah Jordan had buried the hatchet for six years, and she didn't want Joshua starting a war between the families.

"Take it easy, Joshua!" chided Matt. "Being a twenty-four year old Tzahal Major doesn't qualify you to be Prime Minister of Israel!"

"Yes, Joshua darling," said Leah sweetly, impaling him with a glance, "why don't we talk about something else. Like what you're going to name the baby."

Dalia was three months pregnant and just beginning to show. She blushed.

"How about Amos Junior for a boy and Shulamit Junior for a girl," said Shulamit laughing. The others chuckled, too, and the tension began to dissipate.

"I've been thinking Saul for a boy and Rachel for a girl," said Dalia softly, looking at Leah.

Leah's eyes filled with tears.

The sun lowered behind the rocky hills of Judea and Samaria. Yom Kippur began, the Day of Israel's Atonement.

Chapter Six

The avalanche of death catapulted down upon the stunned Israelis at two o'clock in the afternoon. For the first time in Israel's history, the sanctity of Yom Kippur was broken by televised announcements for an immediate call-up of all reserves.

Golda Meir addressed the people of Israel on television that afternoon. "Citizens of Israel. At around two o'clock today, the armies of Egypt and Syria launched an offensive against Israel. The Israel Defense Forces are fighting back and repulsing the attack. The enemy has suffered serious losses. They hoped to surprise the citizens of Israel on the Day of Atonement while many were praying in the synagogues. But we were not surprised. Our forces were deployed as necessary to meet the danger. We have no doubt about our victory."

Yigal Armon came on camera after the Prime Minister's speech. "We shall smite the Egyptians hip and thigh," he boasted to the people of Israel.

But it was all a fraud. The Bar-Lev Line had been totally overrun. Israeli soldiers on the Line and behind it near the Mitla and Gidi Passes were dying by the score, helpless to repulse the massive onslaught of the Egyptians. By nightfall, over thirty thousand Egyptian troops had secured control of the Suez Canal, crossing over to the Sinai on landing craft followed by hundreds of tanks crossing on pontoon bridges. The Israeli airforce was powerless to halt the surging Egyptians, since most of the Israeli jets were downed by deadly accurate Soviet SAM missles.

On the Golan front, the Syrian assault was catastrophic. Eight hundred tanks and three divisions of Syrian infantry in armored personnel carriers swept through the Israeli lines. At the base of the Golan Heights, in the Chula and Jordan Valleys at the edge of the Galilee, kibbutzim were being evacuated of their women and children. There appeared no doubt that the Syrians would burst from the Golan into the very heart of Israel.

As the Israeli reservists reported to their units in increasingly greater numbers over the first three days of the war, they discovered the incredible laxity that had corroded the military establishment under Yigal Armon's tenure as Defense Minister. There were insufficient uniforms to go around. When they tried to start the troop trucks and jeeps, they found that the vehicles had been stored at huge depots for years and no one had bothered to keep the batteries charged. When they got into their tanks to drive them to the fronts, the tank engines burned up after a few miles because no one had bothered to change the oil or add any for years. Many of the tanks could not even be taken to the fronts, since there were insufficient transports available, and the tanks were unable to travel two hundred miles over hard terrain on their own tracks.

The people of Israel were in deep shock over the magnitude of the Arab threat and Israel's total unpreparedness. "Battle fatigue," the nervous breakdown of a soldier under fire, a hitherto unknown malady in Israel's armed forces, was filling a Tel Aviv hospital with its haunted victims. The Lord God of Israel, a wrathful God, had visited upon His chosen people an awful vengeance on their Day of Atonement.

Joshua was called by telephone at three o'clock on Yom Kippur and told to report to the Sinai staging point near al-Auja. He took a bus there with forty reservists and they reached it late in the evening.

The staging area was pure chaos. There was no transportation for the one hundred-eighty mile trip to the Egyptian front. There were no tank transports. There was no artillery. There was only a pervasive feeling of fear and disgust among the thousands of troops, stranded far from where they could be of any help to Israel.

Finally, after two days, Joshua reached General Verred's headquarters in the Sinai. The abrasive, insubordinate Major General Aryeh Verred had left Tzahal less than a year ago, in a huff at being pased over for Chief of Staff. He had retired to his farm in the Plain of Sharon—the largest privately owned farm in Israel—and become a restless gentleman farmer tending to his lambs, sheep and horses. But now the General Staff needed his military genius. He was recalled and assigned a division of armor across from the Egyptian positions on the Israeli side of the Great Bitter Lake.

That night, at a staff briefing at Verred's command post, Joshua Jordan listended as the General outlined his counterattack plan. He would send an armored spearhead into a break in the Egyptian lines at the north end of the Great Bitter Lake. Years ago, when he had been in charge of the Southern Command, Verred had split the Bar-Lev Line fortifications at that point and built a four-hundred-by-hundred-fifty-yard flat area known as the "Compound," which could be used if necessary as a tank crossing point. It was barricaded on the sides by a high earthen ramp. The Egyptians had occupied the fortifications near it, but the Compound was an unoccupied seam between their forces. Joshua would command one of the paratroop battalions which could cross over the Canal by helicopter and drop onto the Egyptian side to create a pincer movement to the rear of the Arab troops.

The next morning, Verred's tank corps sped through to the Canal and began to cross the water on the Egyptian pontoon bridges, while another armored column mounted a diversionary attack directly on Egyptian forces north of the Compound. But the Egyptians had strongly reinforced their positions around the Compound, and Verred's division came under a deadly crossfire. They fought through the night, and by morning, thirty Israeli tanks and two thousand paratroops had crossed the Canal to Egypt.

Joshua Jordan's paratroop battalion was finally able to land deep in Egypt and to destroy most of the Egyptian anti-aircraft and SAM missiles batteries. Within two days, Verred's division cut off and surrounded the remaining twenty thousand men of Egypt's elite Third Army. Eight thousand of them had already been taken prisoner by Israel and additional thousands were dead.

On the eastern front, the Syrians had been driven from the Golan Heights. Both sides had suffered terrible losses. Jordan had never energetically entered the War. Israeli troops were once again in control of Judea and Samaria, the West Bank.

Israel had again won a war with the Arabs, but this time there was no glory in victory. There were only grieving cries of anguish from the families of the two thousand five hundred slain soldiers and the three thousand wounded, a vast number of victims for tiny Israel.

Port Ibrahim lay in its centuries-old squalor at the base of the Suez Canal where it joins with the Red Sea, perhaps at the same place where more than three thousand years earlier God had parted the Red Sea to permit the Israelites to escape from the treacherous Egyptians. But the Israelites had not needed the staff of Moses to part the Sea in 1973, for they had simply flown over it and galloped through it, and this time it was the Egyptians who fled in panic. And when the smoke cleared and the dust settled and the booming artillery fire stopped, the new Israelite warriors in their deadly Merkava Tanks—"Chariot Tanks" —had surrounded Pharaoh Sadat's legions.

Major Joshua Jordan's paratroop battalion was bivouacked just north of Port Ibrahim, to cut the southern escape routes off from the trapped Egyptians. Ships were laying in rows off the squalid port waiting day after day for the Canal to reopen so that they could resume their journeys. Sailors of every nationality spent tedious evenings in the port getting drunk and exercising the whores and the boys for whom the sudden influx of sailors was a rich harvest. Rabble bands of Palestinians from the Gaza Strip gathered in Port Ibrahim, humiliated over the tragic loss they had once again suffered at the hands of the scum Jews. They were restless for revenge, seething with hatred. Unable to vent their anger on the Israelis, they attacked sailors in bars and in whorehouses and on the docks. The port's small police force was unable to cope with the enormous flood of violence. A week after the War ended, a small oil freighter was dynamited a hundred yards from the entrance to the Canal, turning the Red Sea into a black oily cesspool. A Palestinian group calling itself "Fighters of the *Jihad*" boasted of its accomplishment to the adoring whores and idolatrous boys in the seedy waterfront bars.

Late the next afternoon, Joshua led a company of paratroopers down the main street of Port Ibrahim in search of the "Fighters." They parked their jeeps and armored personnel carriers in a staggered line down the middle of the two blocks of bars and brothels. The street emptied. Shutters closed. The bustling piers were deserted. An eerie silence reigned. Darkness fell like an opaque umbrella enveloping the port.

Shots began ringing out, coming from the cracks between shutter slats, from behind barrels in the crooked alleys and hidden doorways. The Israelis left their jeeps and APC's and spread out along both sides of the street. It was a pitch black night, heavily cloudy, cold and damp from the mid-November wind whipping in from the Red Sea. A Kalachnikov rang out in a long burst and three Israeli soldiers fell. Joshua could barely see the men fall, and he led a squad at a run to the spot. They fanned out in a circle around the lifeless bodies. Suddenly, firing broke out all around him and Joshua saw four or five shapes emerge from a blackened doorway. He swung his M-16 toward them and then fell unconscious from a blow to his temple. He came dizzily awake, his head spinning painfully, and found himself lying on a long wooden table in a dimly lit basement. He was face down straddling the table and his arms were tied tightly by a rope which encircled both wrists and went underneath the table. He looked around carefully and saw two men, two women and a young boy sitting at another table watching him stir. They were drinking from several arak bottles.

"Hey motherfucker! You done sleeping?" One of the men stood up uncertainly from the table, slung his Kalachnikov on his shoulder and walked to Joshua's head. He was short and squat, stubble-bearded, maybe forty years old. He swung the barrel of the submachine gun forward and struck the top of Joshua's head. The pain was lancing, excruciating, and blood rolled onto his face and puddled on the table.

"Hey motherfucker!" The man prodded Joshua's shoulder with the gun barrel. "Don't fall asleep again Jewboy. We want to have a little fun." He was speaking heavily-accented, ungrammatical Hebrew. "Come here, Miri. See if he likes girls."

One of the women, an aging whore, stood up drunkenly and swayed toward the table. She stumbled and leaned against the side of the table a foot from Joshua's face.

"Come on, Miri! Let's see if he likes you!" The stubble-bearded Arab broke into loud guffaws. His thick lips twisted back from brown filthy teeth.

"You like Arab ladies, Jewboy?" she said in Arabic. Joshua couldn't understand a word. She lifted her full skirt and bundled it above her waist. She had on nothing underneath, and she spread her thick legs and thrust her black pubic patch over the edge of the table toward Joshua's face. Her smell was pungent, rank.

"That good pussy, huh Jewboy?" said the Arab as he swung the Kalachnikov into Joshua's skull again. Joshua blacked out for an instant, awoke, and fought to maintain consciousness. He was in too much pain to think coherently. What was happening was like shards of reality, jagged, ill fitting. He could only barely remain conscious. He knew he was going to die, and he wanted to kill these filth, he did not want to die without shoving a knife into their eyeballs, without tearing out their livers with his teeth.

"He don't like pussy," said the Arab to the man and boy at the table. "He likes boys. Selim, come here and let him suck your cock."

The young boy stood up excitedly. This was fun. He had an erection from the violence.

"Come on Selim, get on the table, let the Jewboy have his pleasure," said the Arab.

Selim walked to the head of the table and pressed his penis on Joshua's bloody forehead and rubbed it on Joshua's bloody cheek. Joshua jerked his head away.

"Oh, so that's it! Now I know what he likes," said the stubble-bearded Arab. He unzipped his fatigue pants and pulled out his heavy erection. "Here, Miri, make me hard for the Jewboy." He walked to her and she fondled him expertly, both of them watching Joshua's face. She knelt in front of the Arab and took his tip in her mouth and it swelled and filled her and she stroked it. All the while she leered drunkenly at Joshua.

The Arab walked to the foot of the table. Miri reached under Joshua's stomach and undid his belt buckle and unzipped his pants. The Arab leaned across and pulled Joshua's pants and shorts down below his knees to his boot tops. Joshua felt the Arab climb on the table. Then his buttocks were pulled roughly apart, and he gasped with the stabbing pain as he was entered, torn, violated as the Arab's big penis went into him. Joshua struggled and screamed, and the Arab crashed his fist into Joshua's kidney. The pain made it impossible for Joshua to scream or move. The Arab moved in him, faster and faster, and the thrusts were deep. Joshua had an orgasm. He was soft, but he could feel the burst of ejaculation. And then the Arab came in him, deep in his bowels, and Joshua vomited from the pain of the incredible degradation. He lay on the table and wept.

"You liked that, huh Jewboy?" Miri said in Arabic. She reached under his belly and rubbed her hand in the small pool of Joshua's semen. She wiped her hand on Joshua's mouth, and her body shook with peals of laughter.

"I knew we'd finally find something you like," said the Arab zipping up his pants and walking around to the head of the table. "You want to die, right Jewboy? You want me to kill you so you can have peace, huh motherfucker? But we don't kill you. We put a little note up your ass for all your friends to see when they find you. And then you go home and tell your mama and your wife and your sons and daughters that the best fuck you ever had was Rasulallah's cock up your ass." He roared with laughter.

He walked behind the bar and got a sheet of paper and wrote something on it, rolled it up and walked behind Joshua. He pressed the end of the paper into Joshua's anus and pain radiated through his body in searing waves. The Arab walked to Joshua's side and clubbed him in the kidney with the butt of the Kalachnikov.

Joshua woke up as one of his officers cut the ropes off his hands. He did not know how long he had lain there. He was in too much pain to move. The squad that found him stood around shuffling their feet, embarrassed, not looking at their commanding officer, and he could not bear the shocked expressions on their faces. His men had all been in the War, they had seen death, they had seen terrible wounds. Six of their comrades had died this evening and eighteen others were injured. But this was different. What they saw when they finally found their CO made them cringe and shrink away. What the Arabs did to Joshua's body a Jewish doctor could cure. But what they had done to him this way, this was different. Joshua did not speak, he did not groan or cry. He just lay on the table as the medics ministered to him, and he could not look at anyone.

His perforated kidney healed in two months. His ruptured spleen was removed and the scar healed quickly. His blond hair again grew over the two spots on his scalp that had been shaved and stitched. His torn anus and bruised bowel and prostate gland healed in weeks. He looked like the same handsome soldier who had gone to the Sinai front last October. But Dalia knew that he wasn't the same.

When Joshua came home from Hadassah Hospital the second week in December, he smiled and kissed her and said all the right things to her. But when she lay with him and touched him, he didn't get hard. He told her that it was just an after effect of the general anesthesia. And when she bathed in scented bath oil and washed herself for him and came to him, moist between her legs and nipples tingling, he rolled away from her and told her that his pain here or there was acting up.

Dalia came into the bedroom after her bath at about ten. The small vanity light was on, and she sat on the padded stool and brushed her long black hair. Joshua was in bed as usual. She had come to expect him to be in bed asleep when she got into bed.

She stood and took off her robe. She didn't notice that Joshua was watching her. She looked in the mirror at her round belly— seven months pregnant—and caressed it with her hands. She slid her right hand under her belly and between her legs and rubbed her velvet hair. She was deeply, piercingly lonely. He hadn't touched her since he came home from the hospital over two months ago.

She got into bed, and he was lying on his side toward her. She kissed his cheek and his shoulder and nuzzled her lips lightly on his chest. She touched him tenderly and began to massage him softly. She needed him so much.

Joshua's hands were on the top of her head, pushing her away. He rolled over, away from her. His body was tense and stiff.

"Joshua. Let me help you," she whispered to him. She put her hand on his shoulder, but he shook it off. She lay on her back, tears flowing from her eyes. She forced herself to relax and stifle the sounds of her crying. She lay there for an hour, two, and listened to Joshua's slow and soft breathing, and she slipped into sleep.

Dalia woke up with a start, like a bad dream. Joshua was screaming, sitting up in bed, holding his hands over his eyes and screaming "I'll kill you! I'll kill you!" She got to her knees and took hold of both of his wrists.

"Joshua! Joshua!" She pulled on his wrists, "Joshua, it's okay!"

He stopped screaming and put his arms down, staring blankly at her. Suddenly he jumped off the bed and ran into the bathroom and slammed the door. Ten minutes later he came out of the bathroom, took a blanket out of the bottom drawer of the dresser, and walked into the living room closing the bedroom door behind him.

She lay back heavily on the bed and the pain in her heart felt real, too real. Then she realized with panic that it wasn't in her heart but in her belly. A knife cut into her back and revolved in her kidneys, and she felt a rush of hot fluid burst from her womb. She screamed in agony and comprehension. The door swung open and Joshua turned on the light and rushed toward her.

"Oh God!" he gasped. "Dalia, Dalia."

She could do nothing but groan. The pain was too great. Her face was distorted, and her lips were drawn white across her clenched bared teeth. She screamed again and her back arched with the splitting pain of the baby's head forcing open the not-yet-ready cervix.

Joshua pulled on his trousers and shirt. He wrapped Dalia in a blanket and carried her out of the apartment to the car parked outside at the curb. He laid her on the back seat and ran around and jumped in the driver's seat and sped toward Hadassah Hospital's emergency room. Dalia screamed again, a long shattering scream which died off into a strangled gurgling sound. Then there was silence. Joshua drove to the emergency room double doors and ran into the hospital. Seconds later he ran out beside two attendants pushing a gurney. A red glow from the neon "Emergency" sign spilled out like a bloodstain. Joshua lifted his still wife and laid her on the cart, and the orderlies pushed her quickly inside to an examining room.

The blanket fell off of her and hung over the sides of the cart. She was perfectly still. The tiny head of the baby was out of her, face up, sticking out of her womb. It was blue and still. Joshua was paralyzed with the horror of it. He collapsed to the floor in a heap.

Seconds later, minutes later, he awoke with a snap of his head as the ammonia fumes from the capsule held under his nose jolted him back to consciousness. The gurney was no longer in the room. An orderly pulled him to his feet. He stood shakily.

"My wife?" he mumbled half in a fog.

"She's in the operating room."

"Is she dead?"

"No. She's okay."

"My baby?"

"We'll know soon. Come, sit down over here." The orderly helped Joshua to a chair. He sat and stared at the clock, not because he cared or understood what time it was, but because it gave him something to focus on. He asked an orderly to call his and Dalia's parents. He sat there an hour, not moving.

Matt and Leah rushed breathlessly into the examining room. Leah walked to her son and knelt in front of him. He looked at her with empty eyes. Matt stood next to him, his hand on his son's slumped shoulder.

"Joshua. Dalia's fine. And the baby is perfect," Leah said to him very quietly.

He burst into tears and buried his head in his hands.

At four o'clock the next afternoon, Rav Seren Joshua Jordan put on his major's uniform and straightened it in front of the bedroom mirror. He was still on extended sick leave and had no orders to report to duty, but he had something important to do which required his uniform. He rolled up some civilian clothes and shoes and put them in an overnight bag. He put his Browning Hi-Power 9-mm. automatic under his pants in the small of his back with the handle sticking out as usual and shouldered his M-16.

Dalia would be all right. He had spent most of the day with her at the hospital. And their tiny daughter Rachel was fine. They were both healthy and strong. Now it was time for Joshua to become healthy and strong.

He drove to the East Jerusalem military headquarters. He went to the Intelligence Section and asked the junior officer for the last week's reports on terrorist incidents. It was not an unusual thing for officers from various units to check these confidential intelligence reports from time to time. Joshua sat at a school desk and made some notes. Last Monday, a woman and her two children had been killed when they passed by the Atara Cafe on Jaffa Street, where workmen were repairing the interior ceiling. A paint can outside had exploded.

The suspect was George Hawatmek, a Palestinian from Ramallah. He was well-known to Israeli authorities and was the prime suspect in two other recent bombings in Jerusalem. Hawatmek had been arrested and detained for two days after the Atara Cafe killings, but as usual he had an excuse. His brother-in-law was the Mayor of Ramallah, and he swore that George was in his office that very morning discussing some problems with a viaduct. George was the town's engineer. He was forty-seven years old and lived with his wife, seven sons and the unmarried four of his nine daughters in a sprawling villa in Ramallah. Joshua wrote down the address.

He left the military headquarters and drove to a fashionable Arab restaurant just a block from the East Jerusalem District Courts Building. The Arabs here were used to Jewish patrons, and the food and entertainment were good. Joshua was very hungry. He ate the kibba avidly, soaking up the savory gravy with heavy dark rye bread. He drank several tiny cups of the rich coffee. He needed it. He would be up all night.

He watched the belly dancer with pleasure. She was a pretty woman in the Arab way, bleached blond, a little overweight, lovely melon breasts, and she smiled at Joshua and danced around his tiny table, and he stuffed a ten lira note in her G-string. She shook her hips at him with spectacular speed like a delighted cocker spaniel greeting her master and bumped off to the next table in quest of another reward.

At nine o'clock, he left and took the highway north to Ramallah about ten miles away. Slushy snow covered the dark streets in this ancient Arab town, but he knew it well from having patrolled it years before. He parked a half block away from George Hawatmek's villa. He quietly got out of the car, opened the trunk, and put the M-16 and Hi-Power into it. He took out the MAC-11 .380 machine pistol with the foot-long silencer attached and closed the trunk gently. He got back into the car, changed from his uniform into slate gray trousers, a black sweater, gray woolen jacket and black watch cap. He didn't even feel cold, despite the fact that his breath fogged the windows of the car. Ice crystals formed in the the corners of the windshield, glowing like phosphorescent cobwebs in the muted yellow sheen of the quarter moon He felt himself almost happy, invigorated, more at peace with himself than he had been for months. Since that night...

A little after daybreak, Hawatmek got into his Volvo and drove away slowly through the iced slush. Joshua recognized him from his photo in the intelligence file. He followed about two blocks behind. There was enough traffic as the workday began so he was not out of place.

The Palestinian drove north of Ramallah to the small farming village of Deir Dibwan. Joshua was very excited. The intelligence dossier had a report in it that Hawatmek's group operated out of Deir Dibwan, but there had never been any confirmation. There were several cars on the muddy village street and several produce trucks. Joshua trailed far behind and saw the Palestinian pull into a shed next to an adobe house on the edge of the village. The shed door closed.

Joshua circled around several of the streets and then drove slowly past the adobe house. It was fifty yards from its nearest neighbor. Joshua pulled up next to the shed. No windows from the house or the shed overlooked where he parked. He took the MAC-11 off the seat and left the car door open as he walked around the back of the house where a lettuce field stretched for at least a mile.

Joshua slid along the back wall and peeked through a filthy window. The house was one large room with six cots in it and several crates stacked in one corner. George Hawatmek sat at a kitchen table with three other men. They were all drinking coffee and chatting like old friends.

Joshua ducked under the window and went up to the rear door. It was made of thin planks held together with two crossed two-by-fours. With a surge of delight and energy, Joshua kicked the door open easily and ran inside. The Arab's mouths dropped open in surprise and fear. Joshua riddled the four men with the entire forty round clip, sput-sput-sput-sput....

He walked over to the crates against the wall. There were six boxes of dynamite and blasting caps, a crate of hand grenades, and a large assortment of automatic weapons. Joshua felt elevated, reincarnated. He walked calmly out of the house, got back into his car, and drove to Hadassah Hospital to pick up his wife and daughter and bring them home.

They lay together in each other's arms.

"I'm sorry, Dalia. I'm sorry for what I've put you through."

"Don't be sorry, Josh. I understand. But we've never talked about it, and I think I just have to tell you something."

Joshua said nothing.

"You are no less a man because you were raped. Dr. Rosen explained that you ejaculated because of the pressure on your prostate gland. You have nothing to be ashamed of, and it's time that you go back and face the world."

Joshua was morbidly silent.

"And it's not to the Army you should go," she said quietly.

He turned his face toward her. "What do you mean?"

"Your father and I have talked about this several times in the last couple of months. We both think that you've been a soldier long enough. Resign your commission, go to the Hebrew University Law School, and you can practice law with your father. I've been without you long enough over the last few years, and now we have a little baby, and I want you to be with us."

Joshua sat up stiffly in bed. "I'm a soldier, and I'm going to stay a soldier."

"Joshua, please just think about what I'm saying. You don't have to decide now or tomorrow. Just think about it," she implored him. "This is the second time in four years you were injured. Next time you could die. Please Josh, I want you alive, not just your memory and your photograph and your child." She began to cry softly, and Joshua lay his head on her breast and stroked her belly.

"Okay, honey. Please don't be upset. I'll think about it, I promise." But his words were only to soothe his wife. He would not leave the Army. He wanted to do only one thing as a career, as a daily pursuit, and he could only do it legitimately as a soldier: kill the Palestinians who had debased him. Or, in the likely event that he never saw those particular Arabs again, then he would kill the others—so many others—just like them. It was the only goal that Joshua strove for.

Dinner at the Almogi house was unusually tense. Amos Almogi was grim, almost sullen. The Agranat Commission, appointed to study the causes for Israel's unpreparedness preceding the Yom Kippur War, had just published its first report. And it had hit Almogi's Labor coalition like a bombshell. Many army officers, from the Chief of Staff down to Colonels and Lieutenant Colonels, had been forced to resign. And the outrage and blame had reached into the very heart of Israel's government. The Labor Party itself had held a caucus at which the old guard of Israel had been defeated. Golda Meir and Yigal Armon were gone from the government. Amos Almogi would no longer be Deputy Prime Minister. He was in deep dispair, withdrawn, lost in thought. His once wiry, taut body was now soft and stout and slumped. His hair was silvery gray.

"Your daughter is the spitting image of you, Dalia," said Leah, smiling at the radiant new mother.

"We drink a toast to Rachel Jordan," said Shulamit, passing among them with a tray of brandy snifters.

"You're about ready for rotation, aren't you Josh?" asked Matt casually.

"When I got the promotion last month, I also got notification that I would be sent back to Jerusalem in June." Joshua was very young for promotion to Lieutenant Colonel, but the forced retirement of so many upper echelon Tzahal officers in the last few months had left a vacuum which urgently needed to be filled.

"Tzahal is now requiring its field grade officers to get college degrees," Joshua said. "That's why I'm being transferred here, so I can start on my B.A. at the Hebrew University next fall. I've decided to get my degree in Arabic studies so Dalia can do all my homework." He laughed lightly. Dalia had received her bachelor's degree in Arabic literature last summer. She had taken this year off to have the baby, and she was planning to begin studying for her M.A. in the fall.

"What made you choose Arabic studies, Josh?" asked his father.

"Know your enemy," Joshua answered.

"Well, that's fine, Joshua!" Leah said. "But how are you ever going to learn to read Arabic? It looks like two worms shtupping."

Matt and the others roared with laughter. "A poet as always, Leah darling!" said Matt.

"Seriously," said Leah, "how are you going to work out your class schedule?"

"I'll have classes on Monday, Wednesday and Friday, and I'll do my Army duties on Tuesday, Thursday and Sunday. It's already been approved by Central Command."

"I was kind of hoping you'd rethink staying in the Army," said Matt. "You could go to Law School and join me when you get out." He looked deeply into his son's eyes. Dalia had planned this moment with Matt and her parents. She had not talked to Leah about it, however, because she knew that Leah shared the same hatred of Palestinians that had gripped Joshua and was fast becoming an obsession with him. The smile left Leah's face and the blood drained from her cheeks.

"Dad, I've talked it over with Dalia a couple of times. I'm a soldier. I like being a soldier. I've got a chance for rapid advancement now, and I may be one of the senior staff some day. That's what I want." Joshua's voice was almost apologetic as he sought support from each of his family.

"Joshua's absolutely right," said Leah. "Someday he'll be a General, and maybe he'll even be Chief of Staff. Our son! Your husband, Dalia! Hasn't the fiasco of the Yom Kippur War taught us anything?" She looked around at the others in disbelief. "It is men just like Joshua who must *not* leave the Army. We have plenty enough hand wringers and gutless bastards to get us killed by the Arabs! We need men like Joshua to make sure we don't get killed!" Leah was almost yelling, deeply angered by what looked to her like a carefully planned conspiracy to make her son leave his chosen career as a soldier.

"Quit being so goddam melodramatic, Leah!" Matt was equally annoyed. "What the hell has happened to us? It's almost like we needed to get a little shit kicked out of us last October just to make sure we wouldn't become a nation of shopkeepers and scholars like we used to be. We hate that old ghetto Jew so much that we'd rather be dead!"

Leah stared darkly at her husband. "Have you forgotten what we've lived through, Matt? Have you forgotten that it wasn't us that started this killing and war making?"

"Of course not, Leah!" Matt's voice was gruff. But this goddamed war hero mentality that we've all developed is going to destroy Israel!"

"Now who's being melodramatic?" Leah spat at her husband.

"Okay, okay! Take it easy, everybody," soothed Shulamit.

She poured more brandy for them.

"You know," said Matt deep in thought, "I have always had a passion for classical literature. I studied Latin in high school and college, because in those days you either took Latin or Greek, and Greek was too damn hard." Matt laughed, and the others laughed along with him, happy to get away from the confrontation that had developed.

"The other day, I was reading Virgil again. And I came across a line that I've never really understood until now: '*Quisque suos patimur manes.*' You know what that means?" He looked around at the others. "It means, '*We make our destiny by our choice of gods.*'"

"And I think Israel's Generals have become our gods. In 1956, it was Yigal Armon with the Sinai Campaign. In 1967, it was Isaac Rubin with the Six Day War. And last October, when the leadership of Yigal Armon proved so defective, we replaced him with a new god, Isaac Rubin! We turn from one General to another and back, wishing for a hero. We no longer believe in God, because he abandoned us in the holocaust. Now we have a pantheon of gods: our Generals. And what is our destiny?" Matt looked slowly from face to face.

"We have made our destiny by our choice of gods. We are a nation of warriors engaged in constant warfare, losing our sons and husbands one by one. I grieve over the destiny that we have made for ourselves."

Rachel stirred and cried in her bassinet. Leah lifted her and rocked her and cooed her back to sleep.

"We are slowly poisoning ourselves with hatred of the Palestinians. We are becoming obsessed with our own *jihad* against them. Their brutality is contagious, and we have caught the virus." Matt stared at Joshua.

"Remember Heimetz, Joshua? Remember what that one man's hatred cost at Kafr-Qasim?" Matt studied his son. "We can't let his actions become acceptable to us. We were all appalled by it five years ago. Would we feel different about it today?"

"God damn you, Matthew!" Leah hissed at her husband. "What the hell has gotten into you? I better take you home before you whip out your staff and try to part the Red Sea!"

The look she gave Matt in the car going home was pure acid. "What the hell was that about?" she stormed at him.

"Dalia and I have talked about it several times. She is tired of being afraid, of being scared he won't come home one night." He glanced at her and added slowly, reluctantly, "And so am I."

"Did that pussy of peace Amos Almogi have something to do with it?"

"Poor Amos. He used to be the 'little turd.' Now he's the 'pussy of peace.' I don't know which is more lovely! You're a goddam silver-tongued orator, Leah," he smiled, false and sarcastic.

"Goddamit, Matthew! I asked you if that goddam Almogi had something to do with this conspiracy against my son!"

"No, Leah darling. It was strictly Dalia and me. Since the War, Amos has been too preoccupied with his political problems to even talk to him about it."

They drove in silence for a few moments. Leah stared ahead at the dark familiar street, angry over what had happened. "How the hell can you and my daughter-in-law gang up on our son like that?" She gave Matt a venomous look.

"Nobody ganged up. We'd just like him to get out of the Army and do something better."

Leah looked at him in disbelief. "Better? Better! What the hell could be better? He's a brilliant officer in the Israeli Army!"

"Take it easy, Leah! He's my son, too!"

They continued in silence, not looking at each other.

"Listen, Leah," Matt tried to placate her, "what happened to Joshua has seriously affected him emotionally. Dalia told me. He's not the same man he was. Now he's filled with hate and a need for revenge that is eating away at him. Dalia and I were just trying to help him. Maybe we were wrong, but we did it out of love for him and no evil motive."

Leah was weeping silently. "Every time I think of what that Palestinian did to our son, I want to kill every Palestinian for all the hurt they have caused us. I can totally understand why Joshua is staying in the Army. And anyway, the decision is his to make, not ours or his wife's."

They drove in silence, and Leah stopped crying. "We have changed, Matt. At least I know that I have. In 1948, I killed one of our own soldiers at Deir Yassin. And I saved the life of an Arab woman, a beautiful young woman, very pregnant. Remember how devastated I was that our soldiers had murdered women and children?" Matt nodded at the memory of the tragic massacre.

"But I feel different about it now," she went on slowly. "That Arab woman gave birth to a child, and our Intelligence reports that child is Hamdi Attiyah, the leader of al-Asifah! Can you believe it! I saved her life, and she went on to marry that animal Hassan abu-Sittah, and she gave birth to the devil himself!

"And she probably had fifteen more children, and they are all terrorists or will be. And maybe one of her sons was the animal who hurt Joshua at Port Ibrahim," she shuddered as she said the words. "I could have saved Joshua from harm if I'd killed that Arab woman. That's what eats at me, Matthew," she said in a whisper.

"Jesus Christ, Leah! That's crazy talk! That's goddam crazy talk: the only good Arab is a dead Arab. What's happening to you?" But she wasn't listening to him any longer. She was looking out the car window, adrift on a sea of memories. oblivious to her husband's anger.

That night, like an increasing number of nights, Leah told Matt that she had a headache, and she was going to sleep in the spare room. A black mood gripped her. She was fifty-two years old, and the years were beginning to tell on her, to take their toll. She felt the transformation of age, she felt her face and body change, inevitably, inexorably. Her hair was streaked with gray. Her cheeks sagged just a little, and her high smooth forehead was just a bit lined. And now Joshua was a grown man, and she could not protect him from pain and suffering, from the predators who fed on Jewish blood.

One generation of Jews follows another, and nothing changes.

The only thing different is the names of the dead. The Holocaust goes on. Only men like Joshua could stop it, put an end to it once and for all. They would destroy the offenders, smite them hip and thigh, kill them by the tens and the hundreds and the thousands, until finally the Arabs would know that to take one Jewish eye would cost them a hundred eyes, a thousand eyes. Only then would there emerge the possibility of peace. Why could Matt not see it? Why had he grown so unsure? Oh, Matthew! Why can't it be like it was, like we were, young and fresh and certain about ourselves and our futures. What has happened to us....

Chapter Seven

September 10, 1975, was the Sunday that Hamdi Attiyah had long planned for and anxiously awaited. It was a day of profound historic significance to all Palestinians—and especially Hamdi—because it was the memorial day of the slaughter of his grandfather and father and his ancestral village of Deir Yassin, and it was the Memorial day of his stepfather's martyrdom at S'de Dan.

In Beirut's Maronite Christian suburb of Ain Rummaneh, Pierre Gemayel, leader of the Maronite Phalange Party, was driven in his chauffered limousine to consecrate a new church. During the ritual, ten al-Asifah commandos led by Hamdi burst into the church and opened fire on the participants with machine guns. Four Maronites were killed and a score wounded before Gemayel's bodyguards could repulse the attackers. Hamdi escaped with all of his men.

At noon, a bus carrying heavily-armed Palestinian fedayeen drove into Ain Rummaneh. It was stopped by Bashir Gemayel's Militia and all twenty-two fedayeen were killed. The long planned PLO civil war had begun.

The Gemayel family was Lebanon's most prominent Maronite leaders. Pierre was seventy years old and the leader of the Christian community as well as Lebanon's principal political party, al-Kataeb, the Lebanese Social Democratic Phalanx. It was a moderate party, responsible for most of Lebanon's progressive social legislation guaranteeing equality under the law irrespective of race or religion. It had its own militia, a private Maronite army led by Pierre's son, Bashir Gemayel. It was but one of the country's militias, along with the Druzes in the mountains and the central government's small army, that made up Lebanon's armed forces. There was no unified command for the various private militias. They acted essentially as protectors of their own people.

Hamdi well knew that this was the fundamental weakness of Lebanon's government, and this was the basis for his intricately planned PLO civil war strategy. The fedayeen would stir up religious hatreds that would fragment the nation, collapse the ruling coalition, and unleash the better armed Muslims in a unified war against the Catholic Maronites. Hamdi Attiyah had planned the strategy for two years. Lebanon, unlike Jordan, could not field a strong central military under a supreme commander to destroy al-Asifah.

Massacres of whole communities of Muslims rotated with massacres of entire Christian villages as the complete dissolution of Lebanon succeeded according to plan. But then a hitch developed. Syria, unwilling to lose its control over Lebanon, sent several armored divisions into Lebanon in June 1976. The civil war slowly began to grind to a halt under the repressive restraints imposed on the fedayeen by the weaselly Syrians.

In early July, Hamdi and a battalion of al-Asifah troops occupied the Maronite village of Shikka and dispatched every one of its nearly one thousand inhabitants to their eternal reward. The Maronites retaliated with a massive strike against Tell Zaatar, the main Palestinian refugee camp in East Beirut. Almost three thousand refugees were ruthlessly slaughtered. Syrian troops again began creating lines of containment around the Palestinian-controlled areas. Hamdi was fully aware that the Syrians were fearful of the potential total anarchy threatened by the Palestinians. Such anarchy would hinder Syria's long coveted dream of absorbing Lebanon into "Greater Syria."

After almost two years of civil war, the once magnificent capital city of Beirut was in many places reduced to rubble and divided into two armed camps, Muslims and Christians. The "green line" separating the two became a devastated no-man's land of snipers and mortar shelling and exploding cars and terrified orphans seeking shelter in the rubble. Hamdi's plan had worked spectacularly, even though the Syrians had prevented him from achieving total victory—his treasured goal of killing all of Beirut's Maronite leadership.

The Christian-controlled Republic of Lebanon had literally been fragmented into a medieval morass of warring tribes, a seething witches' cauldron of religious hatreds. Al-Asifah could now return to its central task. Unfettered any longer by the humiliating Melkart Agreement of 1973, Hamdi Attiyah's PLO army began almost daily terrorist attacks into Israel from its strongholds in southern Lebanon.

Chapter Eight

Screaming Katyusha rockets from Shaqra in southern Lebanon smashed into the northern Israeli village of Kiryat Shemona. The Jews rushed into the familiar bomb shelters. The Katyushas smashed buildings for an hour. Then there was silence.

A battalion of Israeli paratroopers dropped into the hills behind Shaqra and set up a mortar barrage from the rear of the al-Asifah fortifications. More paratroopers swept down on the surprised Arabs like rabid falcons unleashed in fury and destroyed the Katyusha missile batteries and the Soviet 130 mm. artillery planted in reinforced concrete bunkers. The Palestinians fled into the nearby pine forest.

Hamdi had been visiting the Shaqra missile and artillery installations, and the shelling of Kiryat Shemona had been a demonstration for him. In the ensuing attack, Hamdi had been wounded in the buttocks and the rear of his right thigh while running from the missile batteries. Shrapnel from a rack of the Arabs' own 130 mm. shells, detonated by a hit from an Israeli mortar, had blown lethal fragments two hundred yards in every direction. Hamdi felt the heat of the jagged metal enter his rear, but he kept running with his aide into the thick Aleppo pine forest. He collapsed headlong into the prickly cones and pine needles carpeting the forest floor. His right leg would hardly move and was bleeding profusely, and his buttocks ached. He was in too much pain to move. His aide kept running and finally found an al-Asifah medic. The medic sprinkled sulfa powder over the wounds and applied pressure bandages, and then his expertise was exhausted.

After the attack, several of the men loaded Hamdi and six of their other seriously wounded comrades into a Lebanese Red Crescent ambulance for the long ride to the Sunni Muslim hospital in the Basta section of Beirut, just a mile from Hamdi's home.

He woke up two days later, dopey from the morphine and grimacing with the undrownable pain. He was lying face down on the bed, and as soon as his mind unfogged, he felt down his side for his leg. It was still there, *alhamdillah* [thank god].

Nadia watched him awaken and breathed a deep sigh. She hovered over him and told him he would be fine and stroked his tousled black hair. Then she buzzed for a nurse.

"Please tell Dr. Huri that he is awake," she said to the nurse who came through the swinging door into the small private room.

Five minutes later, the doctor came in.

"How are you feeling now," came a woman's voice from above him.

"Please get the doctor," said Hamdi, wincing in pain, turning his face toward the voice.

"I am the doctor," said the woman. "Do you need something for pain?"

"Yes. Right away."

He felt the left sleeve of his pajama shirt being pulled up and the tiny pin prick in his arm, and in a few minutes he slid off to almost painless sleep. When he awoke it was dark, and the stabbing pains had started again. He reached for the buzzer pinned beside his head on the bedsheet. A nurse came in, and Hamdi asked for more painkiller. Another pin prick, more ethereal sleep. He awoke in daylight. The severe pain was gone. There was a dull throbbing in his behind and his right leg and a burning in his crotch. He reached down again, this time to make sure that he still had his manhood. He did, but there was a tube in it.

A nurse came in and puttered around his bed, washed his back with a sponge, changed his urine bottle, adjusted the drip bottle on the stand, and took his temperature. He felt much better. It was three days since he had been wounded. His body was beginning to heal. A few minutes later, he heard a woman's soft voice above him.

"Good morning, *ya sayyid* Attiyah. Are you feeling better this morning?"

Hamdi strained his neck to see her, but he couldn't. She took a chair and put it by the head of his bed and sat down. She was now at eye level with him.

"Who are you?" asked Hamdi, confused by the young woman wearing a heavily starched white doctor's coat and a stethoscope.

"I am Dr. Huri. I have been treating you since you came."

Hamdi's eyes opened wide in disbelief. "You operated on me?"

"Yes."

"You put the tube for the urine bottle in my thing?"

"With these very two hands," she grinned at him, holding up her slender hands in front of him and turning them over and back.

"*Ya Allah!*" [Oh my God!] he muttered into the mattress.

"Don't be so upset. I'm a surgeon, a real doctor. You're not my first male patient."

"You're my first female doctor."

"Believe me, *ya sayyid* Attiyah, you have nothing to be ashamed of," she said to the grieving man and patted his arm.

It was always this way with new male patients. Arab men lost face if a woman saw their parts in anything but a love encounter. It was unseemly for a woman to touch them there, they would say, and refuse to be treated by her. But Hamdi had had no choice. He had needed the best general surgeon available at the Basta Hospital, and she was it. Many of the doctors had left Beirut during the civil war, never to return. The wife of the legendary Hassan abu-Sittah had herself asked Dr. Huri to save her son's life. And she had. She had operated on the strong, virile, violated body of al-Asifah's leader, and she had saved his leg and stitched up his wounds with skillful hands.

"Do you need anything for pain right now?"

"Not at the moment, doctor. I want to be able to think for a while. I'm feeling better."

"Good. I'll call your mother and tell her you're okay. I'm sure she'll want to visit you this morning."

Nadia came in an hour later. It was eight in the morning. Hamdi had eaten some soup for breakfast, and the annoying needles for the drip bottle were taken out of the back of his hand. The generalized pain invading his entire body had faded, and he could now feel the specific pains from his wounds. He still could not move, lying flat on his stomach, except to raise his head and shoulders weakly by propping himself up on his forearms. But it took too much energy, and his happy mother's visit tired him, and the wounds in his lower body began thudding heavily. He buzzed for a pain shot, and his mother left. He slept again, on and off, all day and night. The painkiller was switched from morphine, which made him sail on clouds and feel slightly nauseous, to demerol, which did not mask the pain as well but also did not blow his mind. He felt much better in the morning.

Dr. Huri came in with a male nurse after the nurse's aide had given Hamdi a sponge bath.

"Good morning, *ya sayyid* Attiyah," she said cheerfully. "It's time to get you back to normal." The nurse rolled a stand up next to the bed. It had various instruments and a kidney shaped porcelain pan with some liquid.

"What are you going to do?" asked Hamdi warily, having a frightful inkling of what was coming.

"The doctor is going to remove your bladder tube," said the male nurse matter-of-factly. Dr. Huri busied herself at the small stand putting on rubber gloves. She gritted her teeth hard to suppress a smile, God forbid a laugh.

"*Ya Allah, ya Allah, ya Allah!* groaned Hamdi into his mattress, and he turned his head away from the doctor so she would not see his shame while she handled his limp, numb, manhood.

She uncovered him and the male nurse rolled him slightly on his side. The pain shot through him. Deft fingers pulled the tube out in seconds. Then the doctor sponged his groin with the solution from the tray on the stand. Hamdi recited a Sura from the Koran to divert his mind. How could his mother let this happen to him?

"All right. You're just fine now," said the soft sweet voice to him. "I'll get you a shot for the pain, and I'll see you later this afternoon." Hamdi did not look around at her. He couldn't.

The next morning, he ate well and felt good. Dr. Huri came in at ten o'clock and checked his stitched-up behind.

"Not a very noble wound for a Palestinian fighter, is it Dr. Huri?" he said, lying face down as she changed the dressings.

"Far more noble than it would have been if you were turned around, *ya sayyid* Attiyah," answered the sweet soft voice.

He grinned and then laughed into the mattress. She too began laughing, and it took minutes for them to control their recurring bursts of laughter. When she was done changing the dressings, he rolled over on his side and looked at her.

"You'll be going home tomorrow."

"I'm delighted. But I would be more delighted if I might have the honor of seeing you again, doctor."

"You'll have that honor, more than once. I will be over to check your behind every two days."

Both of them exploded with laughter again. Her black eyes twinkled and her long silken hair shook around her delicate shoulders. *Wallahi!* She is beautiful he thought to himself, she is as graceful as a swan and as ephemeral as a dream.

"I will be back to check you again before you are released tomorrow," she said, walking lightly out of the room.

The next morning she was in surgery, doing an emergency operation on an al-Asifah soldier who had accidently detonated a land mine. Another doctor checked on Hamdi and gave him his release papers. Hamdi was very disappointed not to see Dr. Huri.

Nadia helped him limp down the hallway and out the front doors to their Mercedes limousine. The Basta quarter had not suffered much damage during the civil war, because it had been protected by an entire al-Asifah division under Hamdi's personal command. So they drove in the cool fall air through the tree lined avenues to their villa.

The strain of walking, the stabbing pains in the back of his leg, and the general excitement of coming home took their toll on Hamdi. At two o'clock, he took a couple of pills, lay down in bed, and did not awaken until the next morning when the sun streamed into his bedroom through the windows open to the azure Mediterranean. While he was still half asleep, his mother knocked and peeked into the room.

"The doctor has come to check on you."

"Oh good. Send her in."

Nadia noticed how the doctor's visit brightened her son's face. And she looked closely at the petite, lovely doctor who strode businesslike into Hamdi's bedroom and closed the door.

"The wounds are healing very well, *ya sayyid* Attiyah."

"Why don't you call me Hamdi. And your name is Karima, if I'm not mistaken."

"That's right. Okay, I'm going to take out the stitches now. It shouldn't hurt."

She snipped quickly and deftly. Only twice did Hamdi wince, when a bit of the scab was torn away by the stitches. Karima Huri wet a large cotton ball with peroxide and swabbed the wound areas.

"Okay, all done," she stood up beside the bed. "You should heal with very minor scarring. You won't have any limp or any disability. You're a lucky man."

Hamdi rolled over slowly on his back, taking a very long time to pull up his pajama bottoms. He glanced at her, and she was looking at him.

"Won't you have a seat. I'll ring for some coffee." He reached for a cord attached to a button on the wall and gently pulled it twice.

"Well, maybe just for a few minutes," she said, sitting in the armchair beside the bed.

The servant Muna came in with a tray of coffee and two cups. There was also a platter of small hard rolls and two heaping dishes of orange marmalade. The old woman put the tray down on the bedstand between Hamdi and Karima and walked silently out, casting a withering glance at Hamdi. Hamdi could read her mind in her eyes. She had raised him from a pup, she had been his nanny and watched over him since he was two months old. He was a good boy, a pious Muslim, and now he had a *woman* doctor who saw his private parts and sat in his bedroom with him in his pajamas! In was unseemly, it was disgraceful. A woman's place was at home, suckling her babies, not touching strange men's behinds. Lebanon was shameless. Things were different in their *'awda*, even in Jordan. The old woman slammed the door as she left.

"You must forgive Muna. She doesn't approve of woman doctors."

"Not many people do, Hamdi. It is something that will have to change, but only time can change the old traditions."

"What made you become a doctor?"

"My parents owned a dress shop in Haifa, and when we left Palestine in 1948, they were able to open a dress shop in Beirut, and they did quite well. I was a good student, and I always wanted to be a doctor. So when I was eighteen, they sent me to school at the University of Brussels. I went to medical school there and did a surgical residency at the hospital of the University of Paris. I've been back in Beirut since 1974, just before the civil war. My parents' dress shop was destroyed in the civil war. And they are now old. They're living in the Shatila refugee camp in southwest Beirut. It's not bad."

Karima poured coffee for both of them and heaped marmalade on the hard rolls, passing one to Hamdi.

"I hope it was not the fedayeen who destroyed your parents' shop."

"No, the Maronites."

"Doesn't it make you hate them?"

"Yes," she said seriously, simply, looking into his eyes. "My parents have always believed in *al-tariq al-fida'i* to restore our *'awda* in Palestine. And so do I. Otherwise I wouldn't stay at the hospital here in Basta."

Hamdi was very taken with her.

"Well, I've got to run. I'll be back in two days to look in on you again. I don't think there will be any complications. You should be entirely healed in five or six weeks."

Before he could say anything or ask her to stay for just a few more minutes she was gone. She stopped in front of Nadia, having coffee in the spacious sitting room, and told her that the stitches were out and Hamdi would be just fine. Then she left.

I see the look in her eyes, the flush on her cheeks, thought Nadia with a mischievous grin. *She has him in the palm of her hand. Yes, in more ways than one,* she thought to herself and laughed.

The leader was a man naked but for a bloody loincloth, with wooden foot-long spikes driven through his flesh in a dozen places. He rhythmically chanted "Hussein, Hassan, Ali," oblivious to his wounds. Behind him were four men carrying the *naql* [replica sarcophagus] of the *Imam* Hussein, the third Shi'ite *Imam* [legitimate successor to Muhammad].

Then came the procession of the *dastas*, a score of men marching abreast followed by thousands of men in rows. They chanted "Hussein, Hassan, Ali," over and over. Each one had a chain or a stick and wore a white handkerchief headband. They struck their heads with the chains and sticks until the handkerchiefs were bloody, and then ceremoniously and steadily flagellated their backs and chests. This was the tenth of Muharram, the great Shi'i holiday of Ashura mourning the murder of their martyr Hussein at the hands of Sunni Muslims thirteen centuries ago.

The huge parade of mostly slum dwelling Shi'ites snaked past the American Embassy, down the beachfront avenues, and toward the Basta quarter where the Sunni rich lived.

Hamdi stood on crutches on the corner of the balcony looking around the side of the villa to where the street bent. He saw the mob a quarter of a mile away slithering forward like a gigantic, ungainly millipede. He hobbled to the phone and tried to call Karima. The nurse at the hospital told him that she had already left. He knew that she would drive here from the west and would probably not see the procession until it was too late.

"What is all the noise out there?" asked Nadia, coming out of the kitchen wiping her hands on a dish towel.

"The flagellation march of Hussein's faithful. They're coming down our street."

"Karima?" gasped Nadia.

"I don't know," he shrugged, feeling helpless.

"Call Maneer."

He dialed the al-Asifah headquarters in the Fakhani section of Beirut about twenty minutes away and spoke animatedly with his aide.

"Okay, Mama. It's okay. Maneer has already sent a squad to our villa. They'll be here any minute."

Hamdi and Nadia walked out on the balcony. His leg throbbed too much to stand. He settled gingerly in the wicker armchair.

The procession was now fifty yards away around the bend in the street. Hamdi saw Karima's car approaching from the other end of the boulevard.

She couldn't see the mob. She pulled up slowly in front of the house and opened the door. She heard the mob and then saw it emerge around the bend thirty yards away. It was too close for her to reach the door of the villa set far back across an expansive lawn.

"Get back in the car! Lock it!" hollered Hamdi. She looked up uncertainly at him and Nadia, then jumped back into her Volvo and rolled the windows up.

Hamdi leapt up as quickly as he could and ran to the hall closet, pulled out his Kalachnikov, and ran, almost falling, down the stairs onto the front lawn. He was in pajamas. His leg gave out and he sprawled on the grass. He scrambled to his feet. The mob was ten yards from the car. From the fringes broke off several flagellants. They ran to the car and started beating on it with their chains.

"*Allahu akbar!*" screamed Hamdi, shooting a burst from his submachine gun into the air.

The Arabs around the car ducked and began running back to the main procession. Karima was petrified with fear. But seeing

Hamdi with the Kalachnikov emboldened her for just long enough. She slid over on the seat to the passenger side and came out of the car at a run to Hamdi.

A canvas-covered troop carrier careened to a screeching halt in front of the villa. Eleven Palestinian soldiers jumped out carrying a variety of weapons including bazookas and heavy machine guns. They formed a protective barrier on the lawn as Karima helped Hamdi limp back into the villa.

The mob continued its march undaunted, under its self-generated manic spell. Nadia and Hamdi and Karima watched it for an hour from the balcony, eyes narrowed, nostrils flared, their lips twitching with hatred. Karima trembled uncontrollably. Then as the procession waned, her fear began to drain away and she felt only empty, impotent.

"We haven't enough trouble with the Jew scum," said Nadia acidly. "Think how easy it would be if we all would join forces united against them. We could defeat them in a week."

"Just wishful thinking," said Hamdi. "About as easy as getting the Irish to stop killing each other."

Karima stood in front of Hamdi and helped him up. "Come on. I better make sure your leg wasn't injured."

Karima closed the bedroom door and softly slid the bolt. She needed him now, now, now. She needed his strength, his strong protecting arms comforting her.

She helped Hamdi to the edge of the bed. He lay back wincing with pain. She pulled his pajama bottoms off. He started to roll over on his side to let her examine his wounds.

"No, you're okay," she said softly and put her hand on his hip, rolling him on his back.

He looked into her eyes, glowing black embers, and forgot that his leg hurt. She unbuttoned her blouse and it fell to the floor. She unhooked her bra and it slid off her arms next to the blouse. Her skirt and slip joined the pile. She pulled the pink silk bikini pants off slowly. Hamdi breathed deeply. Her nipples puckered like strawberries.

She straddled him and they kissed long and hard. She sat up on him, and she squeezed her knees hard on the bed and clasped a hand over her mouth and stifled the throaty breathless groans. Hamdi clutched the sheets and raised his knees and could not stop the gushing which burst forth from his wellspring.

Both families were fully aware that this was not a passing romance. She was twenty-seven, he was twenty-eight. They should get married. He visited the Shatila camp and sat on a pillow in the stone cottage while he talked with Karima's seventy-year-old mother and seventy-five-year-old father. He drank three tiny cups of the potent cardamon-spiced coffee, and he asked *sayyid* Huri for the honor of his daughter in marriage. And the Huris were delighted, for this was Hamdi Attiyah, the commander of al-Asifah, the warrior hero who would restore their *'awda*. In gray, barren Shatila Camp, and in destitute Sabra right next to it, there were many old people. And all day they would sit and smoke their nargilahs and talk about the treachery of the Jews who had forced them from Palestine, and the malignancy of the Maronite Christians who had ruined their shops and homes in Beirut. Their heroes were the fedayeen. Maybe they were too old now to return to Palestine, but their children must go back. It was their land.

They married in March, when the weather became warm enough to make an outdoor wedding banquet pleasurable. It was held in the spacious courtyard of the abu-Sittah villa. And at nine o'clock, Karima strutted behind the tables of gifts, accompanied by her younger sisters and her mother and Nadia. The crowd of half-drunk revelers looked at this petite smashing beauty in her flowing white silk wedding gown, and the men wished that they were Hamdi, and the women hoped that they had looked this way at their own wedding banquets, but they knew that they had not.

Hamdi went in to his new wife at ten-thirty, and her courtiers bowed out of the room. She undressed, a little shy. He undressed. She was small, and he filled her, and she could hardly breathe with the tightness of herself around him and being engulfed by his body and feeling him pressing down into her deepest love place. And then he groaned and came hard in her and deep and plunged in and out, and she wrapped her arms around him with a strength she had never before had and opened herself even wider and deeper for him, and she did not want him to stop ever.

A moist Mediterranean breeze cooled the room, fluttering the Belgian lace curtains. An incandescent moon ignited the amethyst sea. They lay there touching, holding, whispering, loving.

Chapter Nine

Leah sat on the twenty-foot-square wooden platform in the center of Tel Aviv's Dizengoff Square. The Square was a tapestry of huge, well-tended trees and lush newly-cut grass and neat rows of red and white rose bushes. The platform was draped with bright blue and white bunting. It was a Cherut Party rally, and Menachem Begin and Major General Aryeh Verred were with her. Verred had become the new darling of the Cherut after the Yom Kippur War, when he achieved the distinction of being almost the only General praised by the Agranat Commission for the brilliance of his strategy and his tactical operations, rather than being scored for incompetence. The hippopotamus-shaped former General was standing on the platform, waving his arms to the crowd and throwing kisses as the thousands of onlookers began chanting "Aryeh, *melech yisro'el, chai, chai v'kayam.*" It was a play on the old Zionist marching song: "David, King of Israel, live, live and rise again." Aryeh Verred was the new warrior god of Israel, like King David had been in 970 B.C. Leah was amused by the antics of the buoyant, irreverent Verred. And both she and Begin were counting on his popularity to bolster the Cherut Party list at the polls just two days away.

Leah had been at several of these rallies throughout Israel during the past weeks. They were genuinely uplifting to her, a sea of smiling cheering Israelis fired by Menachem's and Leah's speeches and always chanting "Aryeh, *melech yisro'el*" as the sandy-haired ex-General merrily pranced his mammoth bulk on the stage. Leah could feel the difference in the crowds, she could sense that this time it would be different. She believed that Cherut—now part of the Likud bloc—was going to beat the scandalized Labor Party for the first time.

Likud had stepped into the leadership breach and was giving the Israeli voters a chance to elect a group of leaders who harked from the days of Israel's creation, but who had not been tainted by power and money and corruption over the twenty-nine years of the State's existence. Tonight, at the last mass rally before the election, Leah gave a vintage Jordan speech to the roaring crowd.

"Israel is the land of Bible times. Our borders stretch from the Mediterranean Sea to the River Jordan and rightfully include Yehudah and Shamron [Judea and Samaria], the West Bank."

The crowd clapped and cheered. This was the kind of courageous hawkish voice which they needed to grind out the last vestiges of Labor Party shame.

"Whoever is ready to hand over Judea and Samaria to foreign rule is laying the foundation for a terrorist Palestinian state forever intent on killing us all. We denounce any such plan. We recognize and respect the cultural and religious autonomy of our Arab brothers, and we offer them their choice of Israeli citizenship with full rights, or the retention of their citizenship as Jordanians or whatever else they choose. Just one thing we promise: until the PLO lays down its guns and comes to the peace table, there can be no talk of a Palestinian state in the West Bank. And under no circumstances will we ever permit Jerusalem to be partitioned again. The city of King David is the indivisible capital of the Land of Israel!"

The crowd roared with approval. Many started to dance the hora and clap and sing. The politicians on the platform looked at the huge outpouring of proof of their popularity, and they had visions of victory, of finally leading Israel down the right path. Leah and Menachem and Aryeh did their own little hora on the stage to the whistles and claps and cheers and affection of the crowd.

Leah drove back to Jerusalem late that night, and she was infused with a new sense of purpose, of Israel's rebirth. She was fifty-five years old and still stately and impressive. But over the last few years she had lost her vitality and energy that had once been her special quality. Too many problems, wars, terrorism, death, political scandal after scandal. The Prime Minister's wife had been discovered to have an illegal bank account in Washington, D.C., and he had resigned in disgrace. Doctors at Hadassah Hospital's prestigious cancer clinic were convicted of taking bribes to treat Israel's elite and ignore the humbler patients covered under the comprehensive State Socialized Medicine Plan. Speculators in land were manipulating government agencies to buy up parcels in the

West Bank and get priority to build government subsidized housing. The scandals had rocked Israel to its very soul, crushing the pride of the Israelis and bringing them to yet another crisis of agonizing self-appraisal in just three years.

Leah had fought back the cynicism that had threatened to overwhelm her. Now she was being reborn. Israel was about to become a nation of ideals again. She felt exuberant, young, fresh and hopeful.

The next day was the lull before the election storm. Dalia and Rachel spent the day with Leah to keep her calm. They puttered around the house and took a short walk to the little park nearby and returned home and listened to phonograph records. Dalia was heavily pregnant, full term, and she waddled exhausted out of the Jordan house at six o'clock. Election day, May 17, was extremely tense for Leah. She and Matt voted at mid-morning and then went back home and watched TV. At four o'clock, Joshua telephoned excitedly. Dalia was in labor.

They all met at Hadassah Hospital's obstetrics clinic. At nine that night, Dalia gave birth to a son. They immediately decided to name him Saul. Leah beamed with pride, unable to keep the tears from welling in her eyes. Joshua and a sleeping Rachel drove over to his parents' house to watch the election returns on TV. He put Rachel in her crib in his old upstairs bedroom and sat on the couch with his parents.

The polls closed at eleven that night. Long before their close, Israeli pollsters had forecast a Likud victory from the spot interviewing that they had conducted at the polling places. By midnight, the mobile television crew had been dispatched to the obviously-winning party headquarters on King George Street in Tel Aviv. There they interviewed various of the party stalwarts and waited for the entrance of the victor. At about one in the morning, Menachem Begin pushed through the crowd with the two secret service guards who would from now on be his constant companions. He shook hands all around and drank a champagne toast with the hundreds of cheering Party workers. Then the crowd hushed, and he spoke to the people of Israel.

"Today is a historic turning point in the annals of the Jewish people and of the Zionist movement—one such as we have not seen in the forty-six years since the Seventeenth Zionist Congress, in

1931, when Zeev Jabotinsky suggested that the objective of Zionism should be the establishment of a Jewish State in our time. Zeev Jabotinsky devoted his whole life to that aim. He did not live to see the establishment of the State or the turning point that has taken place today. His students who in the name of his doctrine and for its realization fought for the liberation of the nation, and continued patiently and with absolute faith in democracy to aspire to change the shape of things in our country by means of the ballot slip—and the ballot slip alone—have arrived this far.

"My first thanks are to my wife, to whom more than any other person on earth apply the eternal words: 'I remember thee, the kindness of thy youth, the love of thine espousals, when thou went after me in the wilderness,' to which I add, sown with mines."

He paused to kiss his wife Aliza, then thanked his son and daughters and his sister.

"Some of the men and women who will be the new leaders of Israel are with me tonight. Let me introduce the new Minister of Defense, the new Speaker of the Knesset, and our Minister of Agriculture, Aryeh Verred."

The TV camera panned to the three men in turn, and the crowd cheered and whooped.

"The only new Cherut cabinet member not with us tonight is my dear friend Leah Jordan. She is the new Foreign Minister of Israel."

The crowd of Party celebrators roared their approval.

"And now I want to thank my friends and comrades of the underground, of the Irgun Tzvai Leumi and of the Fighters for Freedom of Israel [the Stern Gang], the vaunted heroes. We have come a long way and they never ceased to believe that a day like this would come, that a night like this would come."

Leah watched the victory celebration with tears in her eyes. On one side of her on the couch was Matt, sniffling back his emotion, and on the other side was Joshua, beaming with pride.

"Well, Madam Foreign Minister," said Joshua, kissing his mother on the cheek. "How does it feel to finally be in the cabinet after all these years."

"Tiring Joshele, very tiring for an old woman like me. Go home sweetheart, it's late. We'll take care of Rachel for a couple of days."

Joshua left. It was almost two in the morning. Matt and Leah switched off the TV and sat on the couch, too excited to go to sleep yet, just wanting to sit together, to talk about the years of the past, the distance they had come, and the distance they could now go. Finally, Leah could reinject Israel with some of the pioneering zeal which had given it birth so many long years ago. She could help to put the people back on their feet again, restoring to them a sense of their old Jewish morality and cleaving to it for strength and nobility, rather than the quest for money and things which had soured Israel.

They went upstairs to their bedroom and undressed, as usual, sitting on the edge of the bed. Leah stood up and looked at herself in the full length mirror. Thirty-five years ago she had never thought she would get old, she had never even thought she would live past today, tomorrow. But somehow she had, and then the years had begun to march and then to jog and then to run. And now the slender firm beauty of youth had become heavier and much less firm. And the once long wavy blond hair was now graying and cut short. But her face was still the same, strong, and her deep gray eyes still sparkled. Well, not exactly Marilyn Monroe any longer, she thought to herself, but not yet Golda Meir! She chuckled and smiled at the new Foreign Minister in the mirror, and she turned a little to examine her once round hips which time was squaring. She looked over at Matthew, already asleep on the bed. He was balding now, and his hair was not quite brown, sprinkled with gray. He had kept trim, and he still held the same attraction for her that she had first felt many years ago. So many years ago....

She got into bed, switched off the lamp, and took his hand in hers. He slept quietly. She drifted into deep, dreamless, happy sleep.

Chapter Ten

Karima was pregnant. And in early October 1977, she bore a son, and they were proud, and they named him Muhammad in memory of Nadia's martyred father-in-law, the mukhtar of Deir Yassin who had been slain by the Jew scum. Hamdi vowed that his son would know the verdant hills around Jerusalem, that he would play in the wadis and the gentle hills and the forests of Palestine, that he would not be a refugee.

But the very next month, as Karima suckled her newborn, they sat in disgust and surging hatred and watched television pictures of Anwar al-Sadat and Menachem Begin hugging each other in front of a cheering crowd of Jews! Sadat had sold out the Palestinians, he had opted to exalt the petty needs of his peasants over *al-tariq al-fida'i*, over the way of the fedayeen, over the *jihad* against the Jew infidels whose very existence poisoned the Arabs' guts. As Karima watched the treasonous strutting and posturing of Sadat, hatred welled in her, and her milk turned sour and her suckling baby cried.

Nadia sat in a chair watching the broadcast. Karima sat next to her on the sofa. Hamdi was standing. Sadat had arrived the night before, November 19, 1977, and he was shown kissing—kissing!—Golda Meir and pumping the hands of Menachem Begin and Leah Jordan and Moshe Yadlin and Isaac Rubin and Yigal Armon.

Nadia spat on the floor.

In one of the news clips of Sadat's arrival, Hamdi stiffened when he saw the blond Israeli officer next to the Egyptian President, standing very close and looking around, wearing remote earphones. It was him! The Jew bastard who had stymied Hamdi twice. He was unmistakable. Then the news clips of Sadat's arrival ended, and the Jordanian reporter did a live commentary on Sadat's resounding welcome as he entered the chambers of Israel's Knesset. The Palestinians stared at the television screen in shock and disbelief. And there was that blond officer again, holding Sadat's left arm and walking him through the applauding, cheering gang of Jew pigs.

The traitor made a speech, merely paying lip service to the legitimate rights of the Palestinian people and the complete repatriation of the refugees, never once asking for the payment of the war reparations which Israel owed the Arabs. Instead, he gushed with talk of peace with Israel! In four wars in thirty years, the Egyptians had lost eighty thousand soldiers, and fourteen thousand Israelis had been slain. The economies of both great nations had been severely damaged. Peace was the only answer. Give back the Sinai, give back the Abu Rudeis oil fields, and Egypt will make peace, Egypt will recognize the State of Israel!

What about the West Bank, Sadat, you fucking traitor? What about Jerusalem, one of the pearls of Islam? Sadat had abandoned the Palestinians.

It was a hard and terrible thing to watch, this love affair of Sadat with Jews and imperialists. Hamdi swore an oath to kill this traitor. Egypt could not be permitted to make a solid peace with Israel.

The cacophony was uniquely Cairene. The loudspeaker blared with the clanging martial music of the Egyptian army. Hawkers sold kebaabs and hard candies and orange drink. Street clowns cavorted and children shrieked.

The parade was the biggest military spectacle that President Sadat had ever provided for the world. It wound down the broad boulevard across from the pyramid-shaped monument to Egypt's unknown soldier. This was the commemoration day of the brilliant and heroic defeat by Egypt of the Jews on the Day of Atonement nine years ago. Now it was a national holiday, a day when all of the fellahin could feel like conquering heroes.

Sadat sat in his bright blue Field Marshal's uniform with a broad green sash, bedecked with gold braid, puffing conscientiously on a Dunhill pipe. He listened in one ear and then the other to his Vice President and Minister of Defense, both assuring him as always that Egypt's might was equal to any challenge, that the Muslim Brotherhood and the Libyans and the rabid Khomeini shi'ites could be suppressed, and that he was the beloved of his people, the chosen of Allah, the statesman of statesmen.

And steadily lumbered the huge artillery pieces on halftracks down the broad boulevard. And goose-stepping soldiers turned eyes right sharply and saluted their leader.

The tanks were coming, buzzing raucously on freshly oiled tracks. American M-60's, Russian T-72's. Sadat was ecumenical.

Hamdi and Karima sat on the end of the bleachers with a small coterie of PLO dignitaries. How long they had yearned for this moment, how painfully they had waited. Hamdi wore the fatigues of al-Asifah, and Karima was resplendent in a magenta silk sheath.

A small portable radio was in his lap, an earphone in his ear, and he appeared like so many others to be listening to the radio commentary on the parade. But the voice was not the announcer's. The broadcast frequency could only be picked up by special crystals supplied by Hamdi to the Muslim Brotherhood team specially selected for this historic occasion. He had also supplied the six Chinese anti-personnel grenades that were so well suited to events like this.

The covered truck marked D-16 approched the grandstands, and Hamdi watched it intently. It towed a Soviet 130 mm. antitank gun. As it drew abreast of Sadat and his entourage, Hamdi switched the radio off, creating a soft beeping signal in the earpiece of the truck driver. Three black-uniformed army officers leapt out of the rear of the truck and started spraying the center of the grandstands with their AK-47 assault rifles. Another soldier slid out of the passenger side of the truck and threw the Chinese grenades into the now jumbled melee of screaming, frantic spectators.

Hamdi jumped off the side of the grandstand about six feet to the ground. Karima leapt into his outstretched arms. They melted into the hundreds of terrified running spectators. But unlike the others' faces pinched with fear, their faces were contorted uncontrollably with broad smiles.

Muhammad had been just a bit sad on his birthday that his mommy and daddy weren't at the party. After all, a kid didn't turn four every day. Nadia could hardly tell him that his parents were far off in Cairo going to try to murder General Sadat in two days at a big military parade, so he should be proud, not sad. So she just told him that they had gone to a big Eygptian parade as representatives of the Palestinian people, and they'd be back real soon. On October 4, the villa overflowed with four-year-olds and their mothers, and they all ate cake and ice cream and blew horns and played tag and hide-and-seek. And then Nadia's silent, lonely, fear-filled wait for Hamdi and Karima resumed.

The weather on the sixth was unseasonably hot, and the air in the villa hung like dank mist. Nadia put a new bright red swimming suit on Muhammad, and she wore a light yellow sundress and a broad-brimmed white straw hat. She packed the beach bag, and they walked across the street to the white fine sand.

"Hello, Nadia." A woman, sitting on a beach towel, called over to her and waved. The little boy next to her jumped up from the towel, picked up a little plastic pail and shovel, and ran to Muhammad.

"Gramma, did you bring my pail?" asked Muhammad.

Nadia stopped and fished in the big blue and white canvas bag and pulled out the yellow pail and shovel. Muhammad and his friend Khalaf went trotting to the water's edge to dig clams.

Nadia walked up beside Khalaf's grandmother, her next door neighbor, and laid out her big red towel with the yellow duck on it.

"Jennifer still not back?" asked Nadia.

"No, tomorrow I think. This birth caused her more trouble than Khalaf's. But she looks much better this morning. And wait till you see tiny Annette, Nadia, she's as pretty as a picture!" The old woman's gray hair was wrapped in a great white gauze scarf which wound around her entire body as she sat on the towel. She was very fat, and her round cheeks stood out like sun-darkened leather pouches.

"Hamdi and Karima?"

"Still in Egypt. Be back maybe tomorrow, the day after."

Nadia reached into the beach bag and pulled out a small battery powered radio. She switched it on and the familiar high pitched sounds of a wailing trumpet accompanied by a clarinet radiated from the little plastic box.

"Such a nice honor for you, Nadia, to have your son head our people's delegation to Egypt." She said it earnestly and without a flicker of jealousy.

"Thank you, Clara. Our family has been greatly honored by Sadat's solicitude." Nadia said "Sadat" in the same way she always did, with a slight curl of the lips and a tug of distaste in her throat.

A flock of voluble seagulls landed on a piece of flotsam out in the water and raised squawking havoc, contesting with each other over some gem.

"Did you see the new car that Laila Mahmouda woman is driving?" Clara said, wrinkling her nose in disgust.

"Yes, sure. The biggest Cadillac in Lebanon," Nadia chuckled.

"You know how her husband—that traitor—is making all his money now?"

"He's a butcher, no? I heard that he had a string of butcher shops all over Beirut."

"That's not all," said Clara, conspiratorial in her knowledge. "He just got the contract to supply the Maronite Militia of Pierre Gemayel with meat. I hear that he is slaughtering *pigs* in the shops on the same tables he uses for mutton and beef!"

The bunch of seagulls left the water in a flurry and fluttered noisily over the beach.

"You can't be serious?" Nadia was genuinely aghast. Such a treachery was a defilement of Allah's law of cleanliness.

"I heard it from Mahmouda's own son-in-law at the hospital. You knew that their daughter gave birth yesterday?"

"No, really? But hasn't she been married only six or seven months?" Nadia pursed her lips in thought. "Wasn't their wedding just last April?"

Clara nodded up and down triumphantly with a broad smile and a wink.

Muhammad and Khalaf came scampering up to their grand-mothers, giggling gaily, and dumped out their little pails of clams and wet sand on the towels.

"That's wonderful, dear," said Nadia.

The boys ran back to the beach.

"You should have seen that Laila Mahmouda woman's face when I told the son-in-law how much I had enjoyed the wedding banquet at his father's villa *last April*," Clara smiled. "Her ruby red lips and heavily rouged cheeks turned white before my very eyes!" Clara slapped her thigh and snickered with delight at being able to share all her latest delicious gossip.

"You know how her face stays without a single wrinkle?"

Nadia shook her head.

"A Paris plastic surgeon!"

"Really?" said Nadia feigning enthusiasm. She cared not one whit for all this talk, but Clara was a dear friend, and it was a way to pass the afternoon without constantly brooding about Cairo, what might happen to her son and his wife.

The tide began coming in, and the frothy white lip of the surf faintly sprayed over Nadia. A stronger breeze began to wash away the humid burning air. The endless stream of Clara's gossip went on and on. She had a tidbit about everyone.

"That randy goat will never latch on to a man like him," Clara was saying.

"Who knows?" said Nadia. "A man gets old and his brain gets soft. All he wants is a pretty young thing to touch him and make him feel like a boy again."

"But Hala Ziyadi? She has been with half the men in Tyre, and she only stopped with *half* because she got a disease and the rest of the men would no longer touch her!"

"Clara, you are wonderful. With you I need no newspaper." Nadia was getting worn out from the two-hour storm of the old woman's words.

"Thank you, Nadia." She smiled sweetly. "It is good for an old grandmother to be appreciated."

The music from the Palestinian-owned radio station stopped in mid-song and there was an uncharacteristic silence. A minute, two. Then the voice of the announcer: "We have received a Reuters News Service bulletin concerning Egypt. I will read it to you. 'Earlier today, while viewing a military parade on the ninth anniversary of the Arab victory over Israel in the October War, President Anwar al-Sadat of Egypt was assassinated, together with several of his government's highest officials and many other spectators. Three of the attackers were killed by soldiers on the scene, and the Military Police are continuing to seek out the conspirators. At this time there is no known motive for this act of murder. Unidentified government sources have indicated their suspicion that Libya's Muammar Khadafy is implicated in the plot.' We have no more information at this time, and we return to our music program."

Unlike after the death of a revered Arab leader, when a *faqih* would replace the regular announcer and would recite endless suras from the Koran, the wailing music resumed from the small plastic box.

"May Allah protect your son, Nadia." Clara gave Nadia a look of sorrow.

"Let me try to get more news on another station," Nadia said, her face contorted with worry. She picked up the radio and turned the dial slowly. It went from music station to music station and then there was the well-known voice of a Beirut newsman. Sketchy pieces of information were coming in, and he was trying to make coherent sense of it. It seemed that the dead and wounded had been at the center of the grandstand around Sadat. Nadia was sure that Hamdi and Karima would not have been that close. In the first place, the Palestinians were distasteful to the Egyptian president. And more important, she was sure that Hamdi would have been

smart enough to stay as far away as he could while still assuring
that the plan was carried out.

Nadia still felt a twinge of fear in her stomach, but she was
actually quite confident of her children's safety. The news had
thankfully silenced Clara, and they sat listening intently and
watching their grandchildren play in the sand.

Groups of Palestinians began forming in excited knots on the
beach. This was the Basta quarter of Beirut, almost purely
Palestinian, and they didn't have to contain their smiles and
whoops of pleasure as they heard the news of the execution of that
vile traitor.

"Gramma, Gramma! What is everybody dancing and yelling
about?" Muhammad ran up to Nadia, his little pail spilling over
with precious beach booty, clams, shells, smooth rocks.

"Everyone is just very happy, Muhammad. Mommy and Daddy
will be home tomorrow, and they've just been to a very nice
celebration."

Perhaps it was the tone of Nadia's voice or the look in her eyes
that made Clara study her, scrutinize her face. Perhaps there was
not enough fear in her liquid cobalt eyes, not enough true concern
in her voice. Clara studied her old friend with an expert gossip's eye
and ear.

"So, Nadia, this is maybe not such shocking news to you, after
all?" Clara eyed her friend with the beginning of a wry smile.

Nadia knew better than to say a word to her old friend and
neighbor. She busied herself shaking the sand off of the yellow duck
on her beach towel and folding in into the bag. She gathered up the
radio and took Muhammad by the hand. She smiled at Clara, she
just couldn't help herself, and then broke into a hearty laugh.

Clara stood up slowly, nodding her head knowingly. "Then it's
true what they've been saying, Nadia. Hamdi is our true leader,
our Salach al-Din, and he is leading our *jihad* against our enemies."
She spoke the words quietly, with deep and genuine reverence.
"May Allah always protect him." She kissed Nadia respectfully on
both cheeks and then under her collar bone.

Nadia smiled softly and began walking back to the villa. She had
always known it would be his destiny. Hamdi had finally proved
that he truly was the mighty Muslim warrior of old, the destroyer

of the Crusaders who had occupied holy Palestine and expelled Allah's enemies. It was finally happening: they would soon return in bloody triumph to Jerusalem.

BOOK SIX

NO MALINEH

"I will tell you what I will do to my vineyard: I will take away the protective hedge, and the grapes will be eaten up, and break down the wall thereof, and the vines shall be trodden down. And I will lay it waste. It shall not be pruned nor hoed, but there shall come up briars and thorns. I will also command the clouds that they rain no rain upon it. For the vineyard of the Lord is the house of Israel, and the men of Judah His most pleasing plant. But when He looked there for justice, behold violence, for righteousness, behold a cry."

—Isaiah 5:5-7

Chapter One

April 1982

Joshua received orders on April 21: evict the settlers from Yamit. He flared with indignation and hurt and immediately drove to Jerusalem, straight to his parents' house. It was late. He didn't see any lights burning. He let himself in with his key and walked through the living room. In the library, there was a reading lamp on, and Matt was asleep in his chair, his favorite book of Latin poetry open on his lap.

"Dad," said Joshua quietly, touching his father's shoulder. Matt awoke with a start, saw his son and rubbed the sleep from his eyes.

"Joshua! What the hell are you doing here?" he asked with alarm.

"Don't worry, Dad. No family problems. I just wanted to talk to you and Mom about the orders I received today."

"What are you talking about?"

"I've been ordered to evict the Jewish settlers from Yamit."

Matt looked at his son soberly and pointed to the light switch. "Why don't you turn on the light and have a seat. We'll talk. It's midnight," he said, looking at his watch. "We'll let your mother sleep. She didn't get home from the cabinet meeting until ten o'clock." Joshua switched on the overhead light and sat in the big leather armchair.

"Look Dad, we fought and died for the Sinai in three wars. And after 1967, every government of Israel promised the settlers that if they built a town in the Sinai, we would support them and never make them move. Now I get orders to move them by force, because our government is so anxious to please Egypt and the United States that we're willing to screw our own people. And I'm ordered to be the screwer!" Joshua spoke bitterly, his face flushed. He jabbed his thumb at himself, and his tense jaw muscles striated his cheeks.

"Don't be so dramatic, Josh. No one is being screwed. Every settler at Yamit will receive more than ample compensation and will be resettled wherever he wants. They'll all be fine. But unless Israel gives up the Sinai, we will violate the peace treaty with Egypt. That we cannot do."

"Sure! And then the Muslim Brotherhood will murder Mubarrak just like they killed Sadat last October, and Egypt will get another Nasser, and they'll have their tanks planted on the border of Israel ready to blow our brains out again!"

"Maybe so," said Matt with a shrug.

"Dad! How can you be so goddam lethargic? The blood of our people has colored the Sinai sand for over thirty years, and you just say 'piss on it'!"

"My dear Colonel," said Matt, glowering at his thirty-two-year-old son. "Do not lecture me about blood. I have seen enough blood to last six lifetimes!"

Joshua sat back in the armchair, silenced by his father's intensity.

"Israel is not a nation of warriors, Joshua. Despite the tragic fact that we have been forced for decades to be soldier-citizens, we are not a military dictatorship. We are a suffering little country, composed of the cast-off peoples of the whole world. Almost none of us would be here if we had really been welcome in our native lands. Our people—from the Zionist pioneers of eighty and ninety years ago—came here to escape repression and hatred. First it was tsarist repression in Russia and east Europe. And then it was the Holocaust, which brought your mother and me here. And after that it was Arab repression which brought the Sephardim here—your own wife and her family. And the only thing that we want is peace, Joshua. Not constant war. And if we have to give back the Sinai and the West Bank and Gaza and the Golan Heights, we will do it!"

"Well, I know that isn't the way Mom feels about it," said Joshua.

"Maybe that's why she's upstairs asleep and I'm down here in this chair." Matt's brown eyes glinted hard at his son. "Your mother and I love each other, Joshua. We always have. We always will. And not too many people who've been married for over thirty years can say that. But that doesn't mean we see eye to eye on everything, as you well know. I have grown more and more convinced that we have just plain avoided many opportunities for starting the peace process with the Arabs, and we have chosen military might as our ultimate protector rather than diplomatic might. And that has drained away much of our support from the United States and Europe.

"The peace treaty we made with Egypt in 1979 is the best thing that has ever happened to Israel. And it was only because of Sadat's insistence—not ours—that the treaty was made. And we must preserve it like a jewel. And yet, your mother voted against the treaty. Her hatred of the Arabs is so intense that she is totally unwilling to believe that we have any chance of lasting peace with any of them."

Matt looked at his son with tenderness. "You too, Josh. What happened to you was a terrible tragedy. Not because of what the Arab did to your body, but what he did to your soul. He made you hate. That one Palestinian made you lose your compassion for all of the Palestinians."

Joshua stared at his hands, shuddering at the always fresh memory of his debasement. Matt's eyes moistened. They sat silently for several minutes.

"It is a universal problem with professional military men,

Joshua, they thrive on war, not peace. That's why all democratic governments everywhere require civilian control of the military. If our heroic Defense Minister Aryeh Verred had his way, we would have tank battles with all comers every two weeks just to keep our swords sharp. But Israel cannot survive that way, Joshua. We are too small, we are too poor, we are too dependent on the good will of very fickle friends. We must make peace or we will die. It is that simple. And to do that, the settlers must leave Yamit."

"Dad, you know I'm not a warmonger. And you know that despite my profession, I would always choose peace. But to evict hundreds of our own people from their homes of fifteen years, where we promised them they could stay? And for what? A fragile half promise from a weak and temporary Egyptian leader that maybe we'll have peace."

"That half promise is all we have to work with, Josh, and we'll break our backs to fulfill all of *our own* promises to Mubarrak. It is our only chance for peace."

Matt and Joshua sat quietly, studying each other. It was almost one in the morning. Joshua stood up slowly, grimacing, and walked out of the house. Matt could not suppress the tears falling from his eyes as his son left to return to the Sinai. So much pain, so much suffering. Too much for one family, too much for one people. How can it end? When will it end?

At eight o'clock in the morning, fifteen Tzahal stake trucks pulled into Yamit. Over a hundred of the settlers had refused to leave. Some of them stood in the square in their prayer shawls and phylacteries and prayed the service of mourning. Others had barricaded themselves in the barn and the chicken coops.

Joshua had carefully selected a unit of soldiers to remove the settlers. Most of them were orthodox Jews, wearing yarmulkes instead of helmets. None was armed. And none wanted anyone to get hurt. By nightfall, the last of the holdouts had been put on the stake trucks and driven across the border into Israel.

Anti-government demonstrations incited by the Gush Emunim [Bloc of the Faithful] broke out all over Israel and filled the news for days. They denounced Begin and Aluf Mishne Jordan as Nazis. The wounds were deep in Israel, and the government and the Army smarted from being described by the worst word in the Jewish lexicon: Nazi. For week after week, the ugly demonstrations went on and the virulent shout "Nazi Jew" rent the air.

Joshua received leave from duty for the last week of May. He had not had as much as a week off at any one time since the birth of Saul five years before. Rachel was now eight years old and growing like a wildflower. Joshua had been away from his Jerusalem home for much of the time these last few years, and he longed to spend time with Dalia and the children. He drove up to the apartment in his jeep and ran inside to the kisses and hugs and happy giggling of Dalia and Saul and Rachel. They too had been stung by the news reports about Yamit and the demonstrations and by their own people calling Joshua a Nazi. Rachel didn't exactly know what that meant, but she knew it was a bad word. And they shouldn't say that about her daddy.

Joshua and Dalia made love like newlyweds that night. He needed her to envelop him, to love him, to protect him. He needed her smell and her taste all around him, the wetness of her, the buttery softness of her breasts. He was in pain from the wounds caused by his own people, hurting from the word they had called him. And Dalia touched him and kissed him and took him inside of her and held him tightly. And they slept in each other's arms, and he could not take his arms from around her because he needed her so deeply. And Dalia shared with her husband the sweet nectar of her soul. And she healed him. And when they awoke, he could be Colonel Jordan again and slay dragons and do battle with evil beasts. Because he had Dalia to live for and to protect, and his daughter Rachel and his son Saul.

They made love again when they awoke, early in the morning, for they could not drink enough of each other. And then they arose and sat on the terrace in the cool morning breeze and drank coffee, looking for the thousandth time in awe at the splendor of the Old City, which they could see from their terrace, and marveling at the sparkling Dome of the Mosque of Omar and the pristine rock cupola of the Tower of David.

Then Rachel bounced awake and Saul came out rubbing his eyes. It was Sunday, and Rachel had to get ready for school. She was in the third grade.

"Daddy, I haven't seen you in so long, do I have to go to school?"

"Ask Mommy."

"Mommy, do I have to?" implored Rachel, looking very sad at Dalia. When she looked at her like this, Dalia saw her own face, her own eyes. She was Dalia, only in a little girl version.

"Well, let's see what we can do. Maybe Daddy wants to go to Eilat so we can spend a week at the beach." She turned to Joshua with a wistful look in her eyes. "Remember that pension we spent our honeymoon at, Josh? Maybe we could go there for a few days. It's still not too hot to have a good time there."

"Hell of an idea," said Joshua. I'll call Rachel's principal in an hour. We're all going to Eilat for a week!"

Eilat was much more built up than it had been in 1969, but the pension was the same. They had remembered it a little better than it really was, but nostalgia cured its deficiencies. And it was off the tourist track and quiet, since vacation time had not yet begun.

Each day they would go out on the beach at about nine o'clock. Saul and Rachel would take their pails and little shovels and run up and down the water's edge looking for shells and crab bubbles. Saul would trail behind his older sister, doing whatever she did, learning from her, very serious in his pursuit of aquatic gems.

Dalia and Joshua would mostly lie on their big beach towels and get browner. Or they would jump together, hand in hand, into the surf. At noon, they would unpack the food from the pension's kitchen, rolls and hard-boiled eggs and fruit and eggplant salad and herring and sardines. They all would eat and sit around on the towel for a while. Then, they would do the same thing until mid-afternoon that they had done all morning.

Joshua played with Saul and Rachel the games of all fathers and their children on every beach everywhere. He uncovered a tiny sand crab and chased squealing Rachel with it. He helped Saul build sand castles and mold the turrets and escarpments and moats. He buried Rachel in the sand with only her head and her toes sticking out. They walked up and down the beach, each child hanging on one of daddy's hands. And Saul or Rachel would break away and jump in delight on a piece of seaweed and pop its pods, and show Daddy the pretty seashell that had just washed up or the smooth rock or the little dead fish. And they would hold on to him again, because he was their protector, and he made them safe, and he made Mommy smile so pretty and glow.

Evenings were quiet. They would watch television in the parlor of the pension, chatting easily with the few other guests. Then at nine or ten, when Rachel was yawning and denying that she was tired, they would go back to their room. The children went to bed and Joshua would read them a fairy tale, and they would fall asleep. Joshua and Dalia would drink a little wine on the starlit veranda. At about eleven, glowing with the wine and the urgent need for each other, they would go down on the beach again and find the same places they had found thirteen years ago, and they would re-invent love all over again as though they were its authors and it sprung anew from them each time they merged. They were the center of the universe, and God had hung the stars in His heavens so that they would glint off the dusky curves of Dalia and the ruddy hard body of her only love.

The week ended too soon, and they drove north to Jerusalem. This time there was no terrorist attack in the south, no chancing upon fedayeen, no killing. There was only quiet warm desert, and ancient biblical villages and towns, and the rising rolling Judean hills as they neared Jerusalem, and the cool air as they rose from the desert and the low hills into the eternal capital of the Land of Israel.

Chapter Two

The thick gray smoke from Amos Almogi's obscene brown cigar thickened the cabinet room air as usual, and Leah Jordan peered at him in disgust. Aryeh Verred was beaming and voluble, a happy hippopotamus. Begin called his cabinet colleagues to order, reciting the litany of the last few days.

"On June 3, 1982, Israel's Ambassador to London was seriously wounded in an assassination attempt as he left a dinner party at London's Dorchester Hotel. Scotland Yard detectives shot his would-be assassin and captured the two accomplices. They were an Iranian, a Jordanian and an Iraqi, members of a Syrian supported Palestinian terrorist group. Their apartment contained a stash of illegal arms and a list of prominent Israeli and British Jews selected for assassination.

"On June 4, the Israeli Cabinet met and approved a reprisal raid.

Israeli jets were unleashed against PLO targets around Beirut and southern Lebanon. The PLO have now struck back with a devastating heavy artillery barrage on the northern Galilee villages and kibbutzim.

"We are faced with serious provocations abroad, as we were prior to the Yom Kippur War. We are faced with attacks from entrenched artillery positions in southern Lebanon which our air force is powerless to silence. The Galilee, the agricultural heart of the Land of Israel, is in mortal danger. I met with Defense Minister Verred and Foreign Minister Jordan and Chief of Staff Cohen yesterday and again this morning. I believe that we must engage in a major pacification program for southern Lebanon—"

"What the hell does 'pacification' mean, Menachem?" broke in Amos Almogi, chewing viciously on his cigar. "That glint in Aryeh's eyes tells me that 'pacification' has to mean 'war.'"

Leah stared at Amos and could hardly hide her disgust. He was always like that, she thought, always shying away from action, always timid when it came to cold, hard, military confrontation. Thank God that Menachem has learned just to ignore him.

"Let's hear it from Aryeh himself, Amos," said Begin.

"My mouth waters at the prospect," muttered Almogi.

Verred began his recitation. "We call it operation 'Peace for Galilee,'" said the Defense Minister, smiling broadly at his colleagues around the Cabinet room. "We intend to send four separate strike units into southern Lebanon tomorrow beginning at eleven in the morning. Our air force will soften up the PLO. The Golani Brigade, is under the command of Aluf Mishne Joshua Jordan," he paused and glanced victoriously at Leah. She beamed with pride. Almogi gave them both a vitrolic look. Leah wished that God would turn Almogi into a fat pillar of salt. "The Golani will attack the Beaufort Crusader Fortress and destroy the heaviest of the PLO artillery fortifications. Our three other units will take 'Fatahland' around the western slopes of Mount Hermon, the southern Beqa'a Valley, and Tyre on the Mediterranean coast.

"The Syrians have a division of the Palestine Liberation Army in the Beqa'a on the Syrian-Lebanese border. They are covering a heavy concentration of surface-to-air missile batteries. The Syrians also have three hundred tanks there, and they have virtually seized Lebanon as a vassal state.

"It is our goal to destroy the Syrian deployments in Lebanon and to rout the PLO from the southern twenty-five mile strip along our northern border. When we have pacified the south and brought peace to the Galilee, we will turn the south of Lebanon over to Major Sa'ad Haddad, the commander of the Maronite Christian Phalange Militia in the south. He will be able to keep the PLO out once we get them out."

Leah had heard this at the private meeting yesterday, so none of it was a surprise. The other ministers sat in uneasy silence and digested the plan. There had been recurring whispers of such an operation for over a year, ever since the al-Asifah units in southern Lebanon had greatly increased their attacks on Israel. But until Israel's own air raid into Lebanon yesterday, the PLO attacks had been relatively minor incidents, and the Israelis had learned over many years how to exist and thrive despite the terrorism.

"I am troubled, Aryeh," spoke the Minister of Justice quietly. "How do we justify a full-scale invasion of Lebanon based upon the *almost* assassination of one of our ambassadors and yesterday's artillery attack of the PLO set off by our own reprisal raid?"

"We don't need to justify anything to anyone. We are a sovereign nation, and we have the same right of self-defense that we had in 1967, when we preempted Egypt's attack against us."

"Of course we have the right of self-defense, Aryeh. But where is the evidence that Israel is about to be attacked by anyone?" insisted the Minister of Justice.

Leah was fed up with all the shrinking hesitation around the table. "The truth is that the PLO threat to King Hussein in Jordan is preventing him from joining with us in negotiating our plan to create a controllable Arab state in the West Bank," she said. "Destroying the PLO should bring Hussein to our peace table."

Menachem Begin studied the thoughtful faces of the Ministers. "I assure you that we are not intending to engage in a full-scale war in Lebanon. We will limit our strike to the Awali River and the coast up to Beirut, only for the purpose of routing the Palestinians from the strongholds which have enabled them to kill our people and destabilize the Kingdom of Jordan day after day."

The discussions went on for another hour, and only Amos Almogi could not be mollified. When the vote was taken, only he raised his hand against war in Lebanon.

* * *

Matt came home late from the office. His face was deeply furrowed and he looked tired.

"Rumors have been flying around all day Leah. And then Josh called me forty-five minutes ago and told me he was reporting to Metulla tomorrow and would be gone for awhile. What's up?" He sat down in his favorite armchair next to the couch his wife was sitting on.

"The Cabinet adopted a plan for the pacification of southern Lebanon. Josh will lead the capture of Beaufort Castle. We should be able to terminate the PLO threat to our northern settlements in a day or two." Leah looked at Matt and wished she didn't have to go through this with him. If only he would understand, if only he would finally realize after all these years that the Palestinians only understood one language—guns. And the Palestinians only understood one kind of negotiation—war.

Matt stared at her in amazement. "And what the hell is the provocation for a full-scale invasion of Lebanon? The wounding of our ambassador in London?"

Leah nodded slowly. "And also the constant shelling of our north and the constant terrorist attacks."

"Leah, Leah, Leah," he chided her like a wayward child. "We've been dealing with that for years. Our reprisal attacks against their positions have always been more severe than their attacks on us. And the Maronites in the south are getting strong enough to police the Palestinians for us. What the hell is suddenly such an emergency that we have to start a goddam war in Lebanon?"

"We have to show the Arabs that we can't be murdered one by one. We have to prove to them, once and for all, that Israel will not be destroyed or weakened by terrorism."

His voice was steadily rising. "I think what we're doing proves exactly the opposite, Leah. It proves that Israel *is* being destroyed by terrorism, so deeply infected with virulent hatred of the Palestinians that we are losing our own humanity because of their inhumanity. We have become carnivorous just like they are, unable to control our frustrations, thirsting for revenge. Have the oppressed become the oppressors?" he screamed at her. "Do you hear me, Leah? *Have the oppressed become the oppressors?*" He glared at her, and neither of them spoke for minutes.

"The god of war rules in the council of the Jews," said Matt bitterly. "The god of war is our savior, he heals our wounds and eases our frustrations. Have we learned nothing from the past? The mighty Soviet Union with its great army rushes headlong into the jaws of the civil war in Afghanistan, and the soldiers are swallowed up and eaten in great gulps by a flock of primitive tribesmen. The mighty United States with its great army rushes headlong into the gaping abyss of the Vietnamese civil war, where just ten years before the French had been destroyed, and the greatest army on earth is eaten alive and spat out in bloody tatters by peasants wearing black pajamas." Matt stared darkly at his wife.

"And now you and Menachem, with the aid of Aryeh *Melech Yisrael* [King of Israel], want our tiny suffering nation to jump tooth and nail into the bloody morass of the Lebanese civil war. What in God's name do you think we can accomplish there, except to lose the respect of the world and to lose hundreds or thousands of our own sons and kill hundreds or thousands of Arab sons?" Matt was again screaming, enraged.

Leah had had enough of listening to Matt's glib and eloquent speeches. Damn him! He has grown old and cantankerous and full of his own moral importance and certainty. Oh Matthew, Matthew! What has happened to you? What has happened to us? She got up heavily from the couch and walked upstairs to the bedroom she now generally occupied alone.

At six o'clock in the evening, when Joshua had just gotten home, a military messenger came to the door with his orders. He was to be detached immediately from the West Bank and would report at 0800 hours 6 June to Major General Jesse Amir, Commanding Officer of the Northern Command, at NC temporary headquarters just outside of Metulla.

Dalia and the children were very subdued all evening. Rachel was particularly affected by her mother's mood and cried when she went to bed. Josh hugged her and kissed her and assured her that Daddy would be just fine.

Dalia and Joshua sat on the sofa in the living room.

"I'm getting the Golani Brigade," said Joshua, "our best unit of mixed infantry, armor and reconnaissance."

Dalia smiled at him, feeling his deep sense of pride. She put her hand lightly on his leg and pressed close to him.

"What do you think it means?" she asked. "How long will you be gone?" She could not entirely mask the fear in her voice.

"I don't know for sure. The talk is just a couple of days. Then we'll turn the mop-up over to Major Haddad's Maronites. Probably be back here in a week." He smiled at her reassuringly.

"But I don't get it," she said very quietly. "A full invasion of Lebanon?"

Joshua's eyes lost their luster. His shoulders slumped and his voice became somber. He could never maintain for long a false front to his wife. She always saw through it.

"I don't know. It's been bothering me all day," he said slowly. "The Israel Defense Forces have always been strictly that, *defense*. Even the Six Day War of 1967 was generally accepted by the international community as a 'preemptive strike' against Egyptian and Syrian threats to our very existence."

He looked earnestly at his wife and she saw his deep misgivings. "But Lebanon is different. The PLO threat against us is what it's always been, just hit and run terrorist tactics, and our Maronite allies in southern Lebanon are rapidly developing the ability to deal with the PLO. This Lebanon invasion just doesn't make much sense when you think in terms of preemptive or defensive warfare."

"Yes, in fact it looks exactly like the opposite, like an aggressive war, which is what our people have always denounced."

Joshua blinked hard and shook his head resignedly and shrugged his shoulders. "I'm a soldier. The rest is for the politicians."

Dalia was worried and anxious. And Joshua kissed her and petted her and consoled her and told her he would stay in an armored personnel carrier at the rear of the battle. Dalia knew that he was lying, for he was Joshua Jordan and he would be at the head of his troops. But she let him console her and did not let on that she knew how much danger he would be in, because she did not want him to worry about her. They made love hungrily on the couch, and they fell asleep at midnight. At three in the morning, he quickly got up, showered, shaved, and left the apartment without disturbing his family.

He drove in his jeep to Jericho, then northwest on the Jordan River highway through Bet She'an and Degania to Tiberias, then straight north from the Sea of Galilee to Metulla, right across from the Lebanese border at one of Israel's northernmost bulges. He reported to the bustling Northern Command headquarters and shook hands with numerous officers he knew well. He went into General Amir's office.

"Joshua! Good to see you again!" said the General ebulliently, pumping Joshua's hand. He was standing with two other senior officers at a large map on a mechanical draftman's¹ stand.

"Very happy to be here, Jesse," said Joshua, shaking hands with the other men, Colonel Aaron Eli and Major General Yanosh Ben-Galil. They all turned to the map.

"Joshua, your brigade is just south of Metulla. You will move straight toward Beaufort. Aaron, pick up your unit at the coastal border at Rosh Hanikra. Yanosh, you will proceed east from just north of Tel Dan."

Amir traced the general battle plan for the three commanders. Yanosh's units would split in two at the Anti-Lebanon Mountains, one of them following the eastern slopes to the Beqa'a Valley where the Syrian forces and missiles were massed, the other unit going through the mountains directly into the PLO fortifications and the Druze villages. It was not yet known how the Druzes would react, on whose side they would fight. Amir then traced Joshua's attack through Beaufort to the coast linkup with Eli and push north to Beirut. The Ein Hilwe refugee camp near Sidon was the principal PLO concentration below Beirut. It would have to be neutralized. Joshua's misgivings faded. Finally after nine years of brutal sense-less terrorism and frustration by the Palestinians, they could now strike back at the fedayeen and still their swords forever. It was a great day for Israel.

Joshua drove to the Golani Brigade encamped just ten minutes away. He pulled up to the command post, a large tent, and went inside. He shook hands with the officers who were waiting for him. He knew most of the senior ones. It was nine-thirty. They gathered around the large battle map on the table and Joshua outlined the attack plan. Quite simple. Just head straight for Beaufort and see what kind of resistance they encountered. Based on the nature of the resistance, Joshua would improvise appropriate tactics. This was the Israeli officer at his best, and he had the best unit in the army for the job.

At eleven o'clock, Joshua, in the lead armored personnel carrier, radioed the move out signal to the other commanders, and the APC's and tanks and jeeps crossed the border into Lebanon. Beaufort was seven miles away perched atop the highest hill in the area and covered on all sides by defensive bunkers. Joshua rode on the lookout step of his APC, the upper part of his body exposed, studying the terrain through binoculars. When they were a mile and a half away, they crested a small tree-lined hill and Beaufort came into view. Joshua studied its approaches carefully. Tanks could not climb the steep hill and would be sitting ducks for the artillery if they came out into the open. He quickly decided on a plan of attack and radioed the two Lieutenant Colonels in command of the infantry and Recon Units and the Major commanding the tanks. The infantry and Recon would split in two and flank the Fortress on the sides. The tanks would line up across this hill under cover of the pine trees. The 105 mm. cannons of the tanks could reach the fortified artillery bunkers at the front of the Fortress. They would engage the fire from the bunkers while the rest of the Brigade would flank them and take the Fortress. Then they would come down from the Fortress and attack the bunkers from the top.

Joshua led one of the infantry columns through the tree-studded hills in a wide sweep to the right of Beaufort. He monitored the radio signals of the other units as they took up their assignments. The tanks had moved into position on the hill. It was almost one o'clock. Joshua gave the order for the tanks to begin shelling the hill.

Clouds of dirt arose from various parts of the hill as the fifteen tank gunners got the range and windage. The heavy artillery boomed from the bunkers, but the al-Asifah unit had still not located the source of the shelling. After ten minutes, when the tank and artillery duel was in full swing, Joshua gave the order for the flanking units to attack the fortress itself.

There was a fifty-yard seam between two bunkers on the side of the hill. These were not fortified concrete artillery bunkers like the ones at the front of the hill facing Israel. These were defensive machine gun emplacements to protect the fortress from assault on the ground. Joshua led the APC's straight for the seam while the Recon jeeps headed for the edges of the bunkers on each side. The sudden approach of the infantry soldiers had taken the Palestinians by surprise. They had thought they were only in for an armored attack, which they knew from experience would not be enough to take Beaufort. Suddenly the Recon jeeps, their .50 caliber machine guns blazing, came at an angle toward the edges of the defensive emplacements. Sappers jumped out of the jeeps and ran toward the Palestinians' guns, carrying saddlebag charges of plastique explosives. It was almost suicidal for the Recon units, a pure and simple matter of throwing soldiers into a rain of fire hoping that just one 'would have the chance to swing the explosives into the emplacement before he died. It worked, at great cost. The defensive machine gun bunkers lay in smoking silence. Bodies of Israeli soldiers littered the side of the hill.

Joshua's column sped to the highest point on the hill that the APC's could carry them. They then jumped out of the APC's and began an infantry assault on the Fortress. It was heavily defended. Al-Asifah machine gunners, covered by two-foot-solid stone walls, peppered the Israeli soldiers as they came up the hill. Joshua called for them to fall back to cover in and around the APC's. They would have to wait until darkness concealed their approach.

Joshua radioed the commander of the unit on the other side of the hill. They had encountered precisely the same problem and had fallen back to their APC's. Joshua ordered him and the tank commander to hold fire until deep darkness at nine that night. Then he wanted the tank gunners to shell the Fortress itself while the foot units climbed the hill.

Hours passed. Occasional machine gun bursts from the Fortress brought a peppery response from the Israelis. Otherwise, no one moved. The sun set behind the hills a little after seven, and darkness descended slowly. The Palestinians had a few huge spotlights which they crisscrossed down the sloping hill, but Israeli sharpshooters quickly put them out of commission. At nine o'clock, Joshua gave the order to begin the assault.

A steady shower of 105 mm. cannon shells burst into the Fortress. Joshua and his men ran in the deep darkness up the hill and grouped along the outer wall of the old Crusader Fort. Cannon explosions lit the darkness like a surrealistic fireworks display. There were two massive wooden doors on the side of the wall. Joshua sent a demolition team to blow the doors. His soldiers crouched by the wall, waiting for the explosion, waiting to enter the Fortress.

Light machine gun fire suddenly startled Joshua, and a second later a muffled explosion sent three of the demolition team soldiers into the air like clods of dirt. In the glow of the explosion, Joshua could see that the al-Asifah sniper had blown the charge before the sappers even got to the wall. He whispered orders to his runner who disappeared into the darkness as he ran ahead down the wall. Minutes later, an Israeli soldier stood out from the cover of the wall and slowly sprayed the top of the wall with his Uzi. He drew the sniper's fire, and ten Uzis opened up on the area around the short leaps of flame at the end of the sniper's machine gun.

Another demolition team edged toward the doors. They planted the charges on the huge hinges and the bolt heads studding the center of the two doors. After a minute, a roaring explosion deafened everyone for an instant, and then the crouching soldiers ran through the still smoking hole where the doors had been. Joshua radioed the tank commander to cease the cannon barrage.

Joshua and his five hundred men ran into the Fortress. The hail of fire from the al-Asifah defenders was torrential. Joshua's men were dying by the score. It was the most elemental of all battles, just as the Crusaders had fought from this same place hundreds of years before. Men throwing themselves on their enemies, pure mass overcoming entrenched positions, wholesale death. Many of the Israelis ran through the courtyard to the living quarters while others climbed the ladders and steps to do hand-to-hand combat along the parapet of the massive wall. The other half of the Golani Brigade had also breached the wall to the rear of the Fortress, and the Israelis began to overrun the al-Asifah defenders.

Joshua ran through the central quarters of the Fortress trying to find the command center. Six infantrymen ran closely behind him. They ran past one empty room after another and then came to a locked steel door. Joshua radioed for a sapper. In minutes, a charge was molded around the doorknob and the bolt, and the soldiers pressed back against the stone corridor wall as the door was blown.

Joshua was the first one through the door. It was the command center, lit up, with electric control panels covering one entire wall and maps on another. Suddenly he felt a severe pain on the side of his head and he fell face down on the stone floor. But he did not lose consciousness. Machine gun bursts deafened him in the stone command center but in moments there was silence. He struggled to his feet, weaving slightly. His face was covered with blood and he could not see out of his left eye. One of his men sat him in a chair, and a medic ran up. It was only a flesh wound, a crease above his temple, but the profuse bleeding had obscured his vision. The medic cleaned his face and taped the wound.

The battle was over. Demolition teams crawled down the front of the hill and blew up the entrenched artillery that had relentlessly pounded Israel for years. The Golani Brigade had suffered hundreds of casualties. Hundreds more bodies of Palestinians lay everywhere and those Arabs who were not dead or too seriously injured to move had fled into the hills.

When Beaufort was secured and shots were no longer ringing out from hidden areas and undiscovered hiding places, the exhausted Golani Brigade slept. Joshua radioed news of the victory to Northern Command headquarters. Then he received an ampule of morphine from a medic and jabbed the needle into his thigh, squeezing the tube of pain killer into his body. In fifteen minutes he was asleep on a bunk where last night some Palestinian had slept. It was two in the morning.

At seven o'clock, he was shaken awake by his adjutant. He rubbed his eyes and felt his bandaged head gingerly. It ached slightly but nothing serious.

"What the hell is it?" he asked, feeling as though he needed to sleep another six hours.

"Prime Minister Begin and Defense Minister Verred are arriving by helicopter. I just got the message from the NC headquarters."

"Aw shit! That's what we need is a goddam inspection the morning after the worst fucking battle I've ever seen!" Joshua rubbed his eyes again and jumped down from the bunk. "All right. Has graves registration tagged and bagged the bodies?"

"Yes sir. They're finishing up now. They're piling them out on the east ramparts at the head of the road down the hill so the trucks can take them back to Israel."

"How about the Palestinians?"

"There's a mass grave behind the Fortress. The trucks brought up bags of sulphur to spread over the bodies. They had three hundred thirty-four dead."

"How about us?"

"Seventy-four dead, three hundred six disabled wounded."

"Son of a bitch! Son of a bitch!" Joshua was sickened by the high cost of Beaufort Fortress. "Okay, let's go out and wait for them."

As Joshua and his adjutant walked through the courtyard, support units were continuing to arrive from Israel. Some were loading the Jewish dead into stake trucks and recording their names in a log, others were laying out the Palestinians and pouring sulphur over the bodies. A column of ambulances was picking up the wounded and taking them back to Israel. As Joshua walked outside the main gate, the helicopter came into view and landed in a clearing. Aryeh Verred bounded out of the helicopter first, like a drunk hippopotamus, and held out a hand for Begin. Behind him came several photographers and newsmen. Begin and Verred were beaming with pleasure. The Prime Minister held out his hand to Joshua.

"Wonderful job, Joshua, wonderful job. Aryeh, you chose the right man for this job."

Verred pumped Joshua's hand and hugged him. "Fantastic! Beautiful work! We're all proud of you!"

The photographers were clamoring for a picture of the war hero, Colonel Jordan, being greeted by the victorious Prime Minister and Defense Minister.

"Come, Joshua, a picture for your mother," Begin smiled and broke into laughter.

"Not with this bandage on my head, Mr. Begin. If Mom sees it, she'll be up here on a bus tomorrow to take me out of summer camp."

All three men rocked with laughter.

"Medic!" Verred called out. "Get a medic up here!"

In seconds a medic ran up, awed by the Prime Minister and the Minister of Defense.

"Change his bandage," ordered Verred, pointing to Joshua. "Give him a little pink one."

With Joshua still standing, the medic carefully unrolled the gauze which had been wrapped around a pressure bandage. The gash was not bleeding. The medic applied salve and three large pink bandage squares over the long gash.

"Good, now we'll have our picture taken," beamed Begin, signaling the photographers to go ahead. The cameras clicked from various angles for several minutes, with Begin and Verred and

Jordan taking various stances and positions. Then Begin took a sheet of paper out of his suit coat inside pocket and delivered a short statement about what a great day this was for Israel and what a step forward his people had made by ridding the Galilee of the PLO artillery that had killed them and destroyed their homes and farms for years. The mobile TV cameraman recorded the historic moment on video tape for the people of Israel to see and hear on the news this evening. After the short speech, they all loaded back into the helicopter for the ten-minute trip to Metulla. Joshua walked over to an ambulance and had a medic bandage him properly again. It was about time to regroup and move across Lebanon to join Eli's unit at Sarafand.

At noon, Joshua's brigade moved out on the twenty-five mile unimpeded scenic drive through the expansive vegetable patches of the fertile valley, across the sun pinked Zahrani River, and on to the Mediterranean highway above Sarafand where Eli's hundred-tank armored brigade was waiting. It had met light resistance in Tyre and had left twenty-five tanks and three hundred infantrymen to deal with the PLO enclaves there and in Rashidiye.

Joshua's troops reached the linkup point at five o'clock and made camp for the night. They would press toward Beirut the next day.

During the week following the capture of Beaufort, the Israelis closed in on south Beirut and linked up with Bashir Gemayel's Maronite Christian Militia in east Beirut. Fighting continued in the fortified al-Asifah camps all through the corridor from Sidon north to Beirut. More fighting erupted between Israeli and Syrian troops along the Damascus highway. Heavy Syrian resistance was broken and the road to Damascus lay open before the Israelis.

Al-Asifah's "impregnable" fortifications in southern Lebanon lay in ruins under the onslaught of the Israeli Army. The Israeli trademark mobile improvisational tactics had outmaneuvered and defeated al-Asifah and its Syrian ally at every confrontation. The Israelis and the Maronites had west Beirut in a vice, and on July 14 the President of Lebanon called for the exile of all PLO armed soldiers from the embattled nation.

A "Peace Keeping Force" of French, Italian and American soldiers was agreed upon by the Great Powers, and eight hundred United States Marines stepped ashore at the Port of Beirut to insure the safe evacuation of the Palestinian fighters. In the midst of everything, the Lebanese Parliament held elections for the Presidency of the Republic of Lebanon. The lucky, happy winner was thirty-four-year-old Bashir Gemayel, number two son of the founder of the Kataeb Party, Pierre Gemayel. Bashir had made himself famous by killing Muslims, as the Supreme Commander of Lebanon's Maronite Christian Militia. He publicly called for a peace treaty with Israel and pacification and exile of the armed soldiers of the PLO.

Chapter Three

Joshua sat at his card table desk in the Golani Brigade headquarters tent in the Port area of northeast Beirut. He thumbed through the dispatches looking for the only one that really mattered to him and his men, orders to withdraw from Lebanon and go home to Israel. No such luck. September 6, 1982, three months to the day since they had invaded Lebanon and still no sign of leaving. Joshua's eye caught one of the dispatches, formal notification of the arrival of the American Marine "Peace Keeping Forces." Colonel George Zaleski, in charge of the eight hundred man Marine contingent, was described as a "forty-seven-year-old Polish Catholic from Chicago, a strapping six foot six inch, two hundred forty-pounder, a graduate of the Naval Academy at Anapolis."

The dispatch continued with a short description of the ceremony between the American Ambassador and Zaleski as the Marines came ashore. They were outfitted in jungle camouflage fatigues. Where the hell do they think they are, Joshua thought, the Belgian Congo? They had only M-16 rifles, M-60 machine guns, and a few anti-tank rockets. When asked why his men were so lightly armed, Zaleski assured the reporter that he was "not anticipating any use of weapons, because we are here as peace keepers." As an aside, he added, "we'll use whatever we have in the unlikely event that we must defend ourselves."

Joshua doubled up laughing. His adjutant looked over from the hot plate where he was brewing instant coffee and stared at the cackling Golani Brigade Commander.

"David, come read this report about the U.S. Marine Colonel," Joshua waved his arm at his adjutant and slapped his hands on his knees with glee. David Bar-Elon walked over to the card table and quickly read the dispatch from Israeli intelligence. As he finished, he too chortled.

"Where does he think he is, in downtown Chicago chasing around a group of college boys and girls protesting against the school administration?" Joshua shook his head in disbelief. "Those naive bastards are going to get their balls blown off." He was no longer laughing. It wasn't funny. Beirut was a zoo, but the cages had all been broken open and the ravenous lions and tigers and jackals and wild dogs were loose on the streets. Unless you spoke Arabic, as many of the Israelis did, you were totally lost in this jungle city. And even with the Arabic, you still had trouble telling the Shi'ites from the Maronites from the Druzes from the Sunnis from the just plain nuts.

"We have eighty-five thousand soldiers in Lebanon, and we've been totally incapable of keeping the peace. What the hell do the Americans think a handful of Marines can do?"

The Brigade clerk came into the small tent at a trot. "Tat Aluf [Brigadier General] Gilni wants you at headquarters on the double, Aluf Mishne Jordan."

Joshua jumped up from the table, grabbed his M-16 and his helmet, and ran out of the tent followed closely by his adjutant. They ran across the huge asphalt loading square behind the dock warehouses to a small cement block building at the head of the row of warehouses. Both men removed their helmets and went inside. Joshua was told to go into General Gilni's office. Bar-Elon waited in the anteroom.

Aram Gilni glanced up quickly as Joshua came in and then resumed reading. His face was drawn, angry.

"We have to let them out with their weapons," Gilni said quietly between clenched teeth. Joshua said nothing, still standing in front of the desk.

"I'm sorry, Joshua. Sit. Sit."

"Thank you, Aram," said Joshua as he eased himself into one of the wooden chairs in front of his commanding officer.

Gilni sat back and clasped his hands on the arms of his chair. "Can you believe it? We have to let the scum out with their weapons. After all we've been through, this is our gift from the United States."

"I don't exactly understand."

"The Americans have assured the PLO that its fighters who leave peacefully this week will be able to keep their weapons. We cannot disarm them before we ship them out. I've just gotten confirmation from Defense Minister Verred." Gilni was tense and angry, spitting out the words.

"Just how much of their equipment can they take?" asked Joshua.

"Everything they can carry," answered Gilni, shaking his head in disgust. "We lose hundreds of our men and get thousands wounded to finish the PLO threat once and for all, and then the goddam politicians damn well guarantee that the whole thing was in vain." Gilni slammed the desk with his hand and growled, "I just can't believe it!"

Joshua said nothing, feeling slightly nauseous. Minutes passed. Gilni calmed down.

"All right, Joshua. I'm putting you in charge of the evacuation of the PLO leadership from Fakhani. You'll escort the scum from the PLO headquarters to the Port. The American Marines will get them onto the ships. You just make damn sure the Maronites don't pull any attacks while you've got custody. Clear?"

Joshua nodded, grinding his jaws.

"You start tomorrow morning at 0700. Mass your Brigade at the Museum crossing. The Palestinians will be waiting."

Gilni stood and looked very solemnly at Joshua. "Make damn sure there's no trouble. We can't kill the bastards anymore, now we have to assure their safe conduct!"

Chapter Four

Most of West Beirut lay in ruins. The once beautiful Mediterranean villas and gardens of the Palestinian and Lebanese Sunni Muslim rich were piles of rubble and earth. In the Basta quarter, the remaining fedayeen were trapped by the Israelis and the Maronites. Israeli aircraft screamed like savage vultures through the skies unleashing missile after missile into the already devastated heart of the fedayeen movement.

Hamdi Attiyah had flown to Tunisia with Yassir Arafat to visit their new patron, President Habib Bourguiba. The President promised them splendid villas in Tunis and money and provisions for as many of the PLO fighters as they could bring with them. When Hamdi returned to Beirut, to the basement of the bombed out villa where his family lived, Nadia was deeply bitter.

"Why don't we just stay here and die as true believers, as fedayeen, Hamdi? Why must we be uprooted again and start all over? I am almost sixty years old. I cannot start all over again. I will stay right here." Her eyes were defiant. She sat on a folding chair by a small wooden table and pared a withered apple. A rat scurried after a cockroach in the corner of the squalid damp basement.

"Mama, Mama," he said to her softly. "Our lives are not over. There is much for us to do. Finally our people have found a real friend. President Bourguiba will help us rebuild even stronger than before." He took her hand in his across the table.

"Mama," Hamdi said, his voice slow and hesitant. "Karima and I and Muhammad are staying." Nadia looked at her son in alarm. "We must, Mama. Karima's parents are in Shatila Camp, and they're too old to leave. She can't leave them. Shatila is safe, there aren't any armed al-Asifah units there—I have seen to that. So it won't be attacked by the Jews or the Maronites. Karima and I and our son have UNRWA refugee cards giving Shatila as our home camp. And Karima can work at Gaza Hospital in Sabra. She's needed there. We'll be okay, and we'll join you as soon as the war is over." Hamdi was drained, vacant, his eyes muddy with despair.

"You mean I must leave my fourth home, I must now be separated from my only son, the only family I have left."

"Mama, I will join you soon, I promise."

"It is no good for us to be separated, you hiding in Shatila, cowering with all the old men like a whipped cur. You must come with me. You must rebuild al-Asifah in Tunis. If that is where I must go, then you must come with me at the head of our Army."

"I cannot, Mama." Hamdi almost whimpered. "I must protect Karima and our son and Karima's parents. It will just be for a short time. And I am not hiding out, Mama. I am still al-Asifah's commander, and I will never demean Hassan's memory, I will not live for one day or even one hour without thinking of Deir Yasasin and *'awda*. I swear it."

Hamdi's eyes met his mother's, and she could see the effort of will that he was exerting to make his eyes shine strong and bright again, trying to convince her that he was still hard and courageous and undiminished. She could feel his determination not to lose his composure in front of her, not to let her see the depth of his despair, the true anguish of his pervasive fear. For when he had let her see into his heart two weeks ago, she had been so sickened that she had slapped him. Karima had seen it; Muhammad had seen it and cried. Her son had lost face, and she had been ashamed for his cowardice.

Nadia picked up the paring knife and pressed the point into her palm, wanting to feel the pain in her hand to distract her from the pain in her heart. Blood dripped down her hand.

"You can't stay here, Mama," Hamdi pleaded. "The rats will take over. You have only a hole in the ground for a toilet. There is no fresh water except what we bring in buckets. This is no home, Mama. This is just a bombed out shell."

In his mother's eyes was emptiness.

"Thousands of our fighters have already left, Mama. They will protect you in Tunis. You will have a nice villa again. You cannot stay here in this holocaust. You will die."

Hamdi walked over to Nadia and bent and kissed her on the cheek. Blood dripped from her hand, and he took the paring knife from her and put it on the table.

"I have to go now, Mama." He turned away from her to hide his smarting eyes. "A car will be here for you at six o'clock in the morning to take you to our headquarters in Fakhani. This is the only way, Mama. You will be safe in Tunis."

He walked quickly out of the basement. A rat crept up to a piece of apple peel by Nadia's foot. She didn't move, just watched it.

Bright sunshine greeted the Golani Brigade as it massed the next morning at the "green line" separating Christian dominated and controlled East Beirut from Muslim West Beirut. Maronite militiamen of Gemayel's pro-Israel Phalange were manning the rubble-strewn checkpoint near the Museum. Beyond the barricades, the remnants of the PLO and al-Asifah leadership and hundreds of Palestinian soldiers in a motley array of tattered uniforms sat or stood glumly in their Soviet armored personnel carriers and jeeps and tanks.

The woman on the lead tank was regal, like a queen leading her fawning courtiers. Her aquamarine caftan unfurled behind her like a flag of valor carried gently by a caressing breeze. Her hair was long and slate gray, falling down her back. Her head was high, her back and shoulders braced. Nadia abu-Sittah would lead her people from the nether world to the sunlight of a new and spectacular day.

Joshua watched the woman slowly approach, and he felt a sudden rush of unwanted respect for her, for her glowing face and straight back and iron spirit. He had the odd feeling that it was his mother on that tank, like an indomitable warrior at the head of her troops.

The procession began. The tanks and recon jeeps of the Golani Brigade split into halves, one leading the PLO column and the second bringing up the rear. The column proceeded slowly, quietly, and reached the Port embarkation area after some forty minutes. Reporters and news photographers from a hundred places were waiting at the Port. Joshua noticed the regal Arab woman's reaction when she saw the cameras. He heard her scream out to the fedayeen to be men, to look like the redeemers of Palestine. They erupted into smiles and cheers and began shooting off their beloved Kalachnikovs in bursts. The terrorists would convert the PLO's march to oblivion into a triumphal departure, weapons and all, to new bases in the Arab world.

Joshua, in the lead Recon jeep, led the column up to the boarding gate of the freighter. A contingent of the French Foreign Legion's Second Parachute Regiment crouched behind sandbags on both sides of the embarkation area. Standing in front of the huge loading ramp, flanked by a company of camouflage-clad American soldiers, stood a giant of a marine Colonel. Joshua's jeep rolled to within ten feet of him, and Joshua jumped out and walked toward the American.

"Colonel Jordan, I presume?" said Zaleski extending his hand.

"Colonel Zaleski, I'm sure," answered Joshua smiling. David shook Goliath's hand. The Marine was almost a head taller and sixty pounds heavier.

"Let's load 'em!" called out Zaleski to the junior officers standing at the head of their men.

"Colonel Zaleski, please tell the Palestinian drivers to leave the keys in the vehicles so my men can remove them, otherwise we'll be here for days bringing up tow trucks," said Joshua as Zaleski began walking briskly away. The Marine stopped and turned slowly toward Joshua. His feet were wide apart, his hands on his hips.

"What d'ya mean?"

Joshua felt like saying "What do you mean, what do I mean?" but he restrained himself. Instead he said, "My orders are that the men go on the freighter but the vehicles and heavy weapons remain." Several of the jeeps were hauling anti-aircraft missile launchers, and some others were pulling artillery pieces. The two tanks were Soviet T-72's, the best.

"Sorry Colonel," said Zaleski evenly. "My orders are to load the whole lot, and that's what I'm goin' to do." He turned again and hollered, "Load 'em up!"

Joshua turned back toward the group of Israeli recon jeeps behind him and yelled, "Cover everybody!" A radioman in one of the jeeps transmitted the order to the tanks and within seconds the tank turrets both in front and behind the PLO column were wound toward the Palestinians. The bolts of the mounted .50 caliber machine guns in the lead jeeps slammed shut and chambered live rounds, some pointing toward the Marines, others trained on the French Legionnaires.

Zaleski went white with rage and walked back toward Joshua shaking his fist, sputtering, "You shrimpy little Jew bastard! I'll beat yer fuckin' brains out!"

"Somebody better explain to you who the enemy is here, you fucking horse's ass!" Joshua said between blanched lips. His guts were churning with anger.

Colonel Zaleski stopped in his tracks and color began to come back to his face. He gritted his teeth and dropped his hands to his sides.

"Yer an eloquent motherfucker, Colonel Jordan. Been hangin' around Americans?"

"My father was born in the States. He gave me his passion for poetry."

Colonel Zaleski walked up to Joshua. He looked lost, frightened by this strange land, these strange people. "So what the fuck d'we do now?"

"I'll ask for further orders from my headquarters," answered Joshua.

"Listen pal, I really am sorry I said that," said Zaleski looking genuinely contrite. "It fuckin' slipped out. The situation's been kind of fuckin' tense here the last few days. In this goddam place, it's hard to tell the players without a program, and I ain't got no program. Everybody looks and sounds the same. I better radio for orders myself." He walked over to a Marine radioman, and Joshua went to the Recon jeep with the radio. The Palestinians stood silently in their vehicles, careful not to set off the Israeli cannons and machine gunners. Nadia stood fiercely on the lead tank, hands on hips, her cobalt eyes aglow. Fifteen minutes passed.

Brigadier General Gilni sped into the loading area in his jeep and jumped out before his driver had fully stopped it. He was seething. He stormed up to Joshua.

"As far as I'm concerned, the PLO bastards can go back to Fakhani and we'll scuttle this whole goddam exercise!" he raged at Joshua.

"Take it easy, Aram! We're about to start a war with the Americans and French. Did you contact Cohen?"

"Yes. He's getting orders from Aryeh Verred." Gilni sat down in the back of the radio jeep, and he and Joshua stared gloomily at Colonel Zaleski who was stalking his own radioman fifty yards away. More tense moments passed.

The roaring whip-whip-whip of helicopter rotors bore down on the Port, and the Marines stepped back, clearing a landing area between themselves and the Israelis. Down came the Cobra gunship and out stepped an American Admiral. He ducked and ran toward Colonel Zaleski. The massive Marine saluted and stood smartly at attention, staring over the Admiral's head. The Admiral spoke to him animatedly, and then they strode briskly up to the Israeli Recon jeep, Colonel Zaleski to the left rear of the Admiral.

"I'm Admiral Sherman," said the distinguished looking elderly man conversationally, extending his hand to Gilni sitting in the jeep.

Gilni shook hands with the Admiral and said in Hebrew, "This guy looks a lot more like a damn politician than a soldier." He smiled politely at the Admiral.

"General Gilni says that he's very sorry about the mixup, Admiral Sherman," Joshua translated for the Americans. "The General doesn't speak English, sir. I'm Colonel Jordan. I'll translate."

The Admiral shook hands with Joshua. "Well son, we'll just have to wait a bit until our Ambassador gets this straightened out. Sorry for the problem."

Joshua translated for Gilni, who really needed no translation because he had spent all of 1980 as a student at the U.S. Army Staff Officers War College in Leavenworth, Kansas. After listening to Joshua's translation, Gilni muttered, "The Americans will sell us out for a single can of thirty-weight oil." Joshua translated it for the Americans: "We'll simply have to wait a few moments for further orders."

The Admiral and the Marine Colonel walked back to the stilled helicopter and sat inside. As the minutes passed, the wives and children of the PLO fighters began to arrive in the square. The families had walked from Fakhani to see their men off, and now they began to flood around the vehicles, weeping and moaning and ululating and tugging at their men and throwing flowers. The Kalachnikovs once again began to crack their victory chorus. Clip after clip they shot off, riddling the sky with a million paroxisms of their pain. The scene was madness, deadly mindlessness. Misguided bullets struck dozens of PLO men and women and at least twenty-five children. No one bent to help them. The two thousand women and children danced and yelped and howled as their hundreds of men exhausted the available ammunition.

Silence gradually descended on the Port as the weapons were emptied. The Israelis and the Americans and the Frenchmen picked themselves up warily off the ground and from behind bunkers and under jeeps and behind any available post. Seventeen Arabs lay dead, forty-six were wounded.

Joshua saw that the Arab woman in the turquoise caftan had not moved. She stood ramrod straight on the lead tank, surveying the area like a Wagnerian heroine. A smile curled the edges of her mouth, flames danced in her eyes.

The radioman gave the phone to General Gilni. Gilni grunted into it a few times. Then he gritted his teeth and growled, "What the hell—"

He listened again silently. "Yes, sir. Yes, sir. I do understand, sir." The radioman replaced the phone in its cradle.

"Pull your men out, Joshua. The scum keep all of their weapons and their vehicles, too."

Joshua stared at the General, stunned.
"Pull them out now! That's an order!"

Chapter Five

Joshua went into his tent and sat down at the table. He pulled open the middle drawer of the rickety desk and took out the photograph that Dalia had sent him a week ago. He touched it like it was fragile and delicate and turned it over for the hundredth time to read what Dalia had written on the back: "Worried Dalia, unworried Rachel, oblivious Saul." Then he looked at the faces again. His spectacular wife looking very earnestly into the camera lens and the smaller reflection of her standing next to her smiling broadly and little blond Saul with his hand up waving at Daddy.

Joshua took out the pad of paper he wrote letters on and the ball-point pen which was starting to get a little scratchy and started to write. "Dear Dalia. We got fucked good again today," he thought to himself. No, you don't write that kind of shit to your wife. She'd rip open the letter at the mailbox and read it avidly and stand there and cry while all of the neighbors peeked out their windows at her. He was a lousy letter writer, he could never think of anything to say. What do you write to your wife whom you haven't seen for over three months? "Dear Dalia. The sky is blue, like the magnificent Mediterranean. The birds sing sweetly in the trees, except when our planes come over and rocket the shit out of west Beirut and leave two and three year old kids sitting in rags on their moms' and dads' corpses, crying, filthy faces, having no idea who is fighting who for what. And neither do I." And neither do I, Dalia, he thought to himself. But he didn't write any of that to send to his wife.

"Dear Dalia," he wrote. "I am frightened all of the time. I am terrified. I want to get out of here as fast as possible. I want to come home to you and hug my daughter and my son. And then I want to lie in your arms and love you and I want you to love me and I never want to stop. Because nothing else in the world matters. I am blown away. I am shriveled up like a dehydrated apple core. I have no sense of humor left. I have no love for my country. I have no feeling of duty. I have no pride because I am a Colonel and will someday be a General and maybe even Chief of Staff. I am a burned out shell. I love nothing but you and Rachel and Saul. I want no one else, nothing else. 'Vanity of vanities, saith the preacher. All is vanity.' All except you."

He wrote intensely, rapidly, knowing that he could not send this letter either. He crumpled up the sheet and threw it into the waste paper basket. And then he started writing again slowly. "Dear Dalia. I love you all more than anything in the world. Tell Rachel and Saul that I love them and kiss them and hug them for me. And tell them that I am coming home soon. We won't be here much longer, because the PLO soldiers have all been shipped out. And I'm coming home, and I'm going to go to law school and join Dad in his practice, and we're going to live happily ever after. I love you. Josh."

Chapter Six

Hamdi drove his Mercedes sedan to the "green line" checkpoint between East and West Beirut. He was dressed smartly in a blue wool suit. He showed forged safe conduct papers to the Maronite guards. The papers identified him as a Maronite businessman who had been in the west zone at the University for just two hours, and now he was returning to his home in Baabda, the fashionable Christian suburb where Lebanon's Presidential Palace was located.

Hamdi was waved past the "green line." Finally he was doing something he would remember with infinite pride, that would bring a gleam of great joy to his mother's eyes. Finally.

He drove to the headquarters building of the Phalange Party where President-elect Bashir Gemayel was holding a highly publicized council session with his newly selected advisory staff. Hamdi showed other papers to the guards in the basement garage at the Phalange building, identifying him as a news reporter for the Maronite controlled Central News Agency of Beirut. He parked in the middle of the garage, took the elevator to the first floor, walked down the back steps, and caught a bus going to Ashrafiyeh in northeast Beirut, once fashionable, but now a bombed-out slum.

At eight minutes after four in the afternoon, a mountainous explosion from the bomb in Hamdi's Mercedes caved in the Phalange Party headquarters building.

Hamdi faded into the Christian slum of Ashrafiyeh where al-Asifah had a safe house lost in the maze of tiny alleys and crumbling hovels. Hamdi stayed inside watching TV, smiling at the news reports of the shambles and death toll he had caused at Phalange headquarters. He ate sardines and lamb stew and humous from the plentiful stock of canned food in the pantry. He drank a little Arak in the evening to help him get to sleep. He heard a news bulletin and grimaced. It was a Cabinet statement from Israel's government about Israeli Army units taking up positions in West Beirut "to prevent the danger of violence, bloodshed and anarchy." *Ya Allah*, Hamdi sneered. Everywhere the pig Jews go there is nothing but violence and bloodshed against my people. Who are they trying to fool?

The Israeli Cabinet room was filled with the ministers and their principal aides. The vote eight days ago to accede to American pressure and to permit the PLO terrorists to evacuate Beirut with all of their light and heavy weapons had been far from unanimous. Rancor had infused the debate. But what could they do? The government of the United States had delivered its most serious ultimatum in years to Israel, since Kissinger's "don't preempt" in 1973. Begin had personally been told that if the exile of the PLO did not go as ordered by the U.S., the multi-billion dollar military aid package would be stymied by the Pentagon. Reagan had already clamped down on the delivery of scheduled F-14 and F-16 fighters. Begin had no doubt that Reagan would fulfill his new threat. The Cabinet had grudgingly approved the U.S. evacuation plan which literally preserved the PLO intact. Begin had himself radioed the orders to General Gilni at Beirut Port eight days ago.

Defense Minister Aryeh Verred was now briefing the ministers on the situation in Beirut. The week long evacuation had just been completed.

"President-elect Gemayel has been holding meetings with our representatives on a comprehensive peace treaty with complete recognition of Israel as a sovereign Jewish State coupled with reciprocal trade and defense agreements. The Maronites are consolidating their control over all of Beirut as well as the coast and southern Lebanon, which we have pacified for them. As soon as Gemayel formally takes office, a little more than a week from now, we will issue a joint announcement calling for full scale treaty negotiations." Verred smiled with pride.

"Can Gemayel maintain power once we withdraw?" asked Leah Jordan. The events of the last week had severely shaken Leah's confidence, and a creeping sense of unease—of guilt—was beginning to afflict her. All the loss of life, and for what? Instead of destroying the PLO, they had let them go free to renew their war against the Jews.

"There is a problem with that." Verred's broad smile gave way to a frown. "The central government is too fragile to hold up against the Syrians at this time. We have attempted to secure agreement from Syria for joint withdrawal of all of our forces, but so far we have been unsuccessful. For the time being, we cannot lessen our protective presence in Lebanon."

"But just what does that mean?" pressed Leah. "Do we have a timetable for withdrawal? Do we have plans for turning over our positions to Gemayel's troops?"

Verred was obviously becoming uncomfortable. He cleared his throat nervously. "I am sorry to say that the present situation is too shaky for us to be able to pinpoint a program for withdrawal and a complete timetable. If we pull out, Lebanon will be thrown into complete anarchy. We must maintain our support of the Gemayal government until Syria agrees to withdraw."

"And if Syria does not agree to withdraw, Aryeh?" Leah insisted. "What then? The Syrians have wanted to annex Lebanon since the French left in 1943. Now that they have a foothold there, do we have any genuine reason to believe that they can be induced or forced to withdraw?"

Verred shifted nervously in his chair. He cleared his throat again, but he said nothing.

"I truly no longer understand why we remain in Lebanon," said Amos Almogi, looking slowly around the table at the other ministers. "When we got into this war over three months ago, Mr. Verred assured us that it would be over in seventy-two hours. After our troops cleaned out the major fortified positions in Fatahland and along the coast, they were to withdraw below the Awali River and turn over control of south Lebanon to Major Sa'ad Haddad's Phalange militia. But none of that has happened. Instead, we became flushed with the excitement of military conquest, we pressed to Beirut, and instead of withdrawing, we sent more and more troops to occupy the city. Now it looks like our occupation will never end."

Leah had voted to invade Lebanon. In fact, she had strongly supported the invasion. But now it was out of control, and Amos Almogi's words were beginning to make sense to her. This alone increased her uneasiness and confused her.

"Look at this," Amos said. "I'm sure you've all seen it this morning." He held up the front page of the morning newspaper and pointed to the article about the "mothers' peace march" in Jerusalem's Central Park yesterday. "Never before have our people been so disunited over the action of their government. They carried signs reading 'Give us back our sons' and 'We bore children, not cannon fodder.' We have achieved a true milestone in Israel's history: we have pursued a war which even most of our own people cannot understand and cannot condone. And then we made all the deaths and suffering of our soldiers pointless when we let thousands of PLO soldiers leave in triumph. We are creating a Vietnam for ourselves!"

"I can't disagree with Mr. Almogi," chimed in the Minister for Minority Affairs. "Professor Leibowitz at the Hebrew University has termed our policy 'Judaeo-Nazi' and called for our soldiers to refuse to serve beyond Israel's borders. This isn't just crank talk. For the first time in any of our memories, we have reservists willing to face court-martial rather than report for duty. And now we appear to have won the battle and lost the war. We buckle under to American pressure, and we send off the whole PLO Army in victory atop their tanks and artillery, shooting their guns in celebration. Our dead and wounded young men seem to have suffered in vain. What have we achieved in Lebanon?"

"Minister of Defense Verred assured us we would win this war in a matter of days," said Leah, looking at Begin. Her voice became bitter. "Now we are suffering increasing casualties, and still the war does not end. It looks like the only ones winning this war are

the undertakers." Her gray eyes were flat with confusion, with her
growing loss of conviction and mounting fear.

"Look at our image in the rest of the world," said Amos Almogi,
holding up a sheaf of newspaper clippings. "Every day they print
photos of what our bombs and missiles have done to the women and
children in Lebanon. Armless, legless, faceless five-year-olds cradled by their weeping blood-soaked mothers. Bombed out hospitals
with insufficient beds and medicine to treat the hundreds of
innocent victims—"

"The PLO terrorists hide behind their women and children,"
broke in Begin heatedly. "There is nothing that we can do. Our
weapons are not selective, and like usual the Palestinians distribute
these pictures to everybody to show that the Jews are animals and
purposely destroy innocent civilians. It is libel! It is calumny!
They are terrorists, not we! This is a war of self defense!"

"That's right!" Now it was Aryeh Verred's turn. "In war, civilian
populations always suffer. Look at the Allied bombing of Dresden
and Berlin, and the American bombing of Hiroshima and
Nagasaki. Hundreds of thousands of innocent civilians were killed
or maimed. But no one calls that 'terrorism.' Only when the Jews
are involved does the rest of the world yell 'terrorist child killers.'"

Leah Jordan looked hard at the Defense Minister. "How
wistfully we yearn to oversimplify the growing tragedy of
Lebanon, to make it a contest between good and evil the way it was
thirty-five years ago. The answer was so easy to grasp then, so easy
to define, when I first stepped off the ship in Haifa after the
Holocaust. It was us or them, good or evil. And we had no doubt
who was good." She paused and looked somberly around the table
at the other ministers. "But now it is not so clear to me. Lebanon is
terribly different.

"What is 'terrorism,' and what is 'self defense'? The Palestinians
attack our women and children and unarmed men in schools and
movie theaters and buses and on beaches. They leave bombs in cars
and restaurants and on the streets. Innocent people die. And this
we call 'terrorism.' Then we send our airplanes over their camps and
towns and bomb them and strafe them, and innocent women and
children die in schools and movie theaters and buses and on
beaches. We kill and injure unarmed civilians, boys and girls and
mothers and fathers, while they ride in their cars or sit in

restaurants or walk on the streets. But *this* we call 'self defense.'
Who are the terrorists in Lebanon? Is it us or them? Or is it both of
us?" Leah was deeply shaken. Had Matt been right? Could Matt
have always been right?

Begin held up his hand to silence the debate. He had just been
handed a note by a military page: "President-elect Bashir Gemayel
and twenty-five members of his government-in-waiting have been
assassinated in a terrorist bombing at Maronite Phalange headquarters in Beirut," he read to the ministers around the table.

The ministers sank deflated into their chairs. Begin read the rest
of the message to himself and then addressed the Cabinet. "Our
military headquarters is recommending that we immediately deploy several thousand troops inside the 'green line' in West Beirut
to assure that there is no orgy of Maronite retaliation and then
Palestinian re-retaliation."

Aryeh Verred looked defeated. His best plan for Lebanon had
just literally gone up in smoke and ashes. None of them had
anything to say. Begin looked around the table.

"All right. Chief of Staff Cohen's recommendation is that we
establish observation posts at the Palestinian camps in west Beirut
and the rest of the Muslim zone and that we deploy units to keep
the Christians from carrying out any terrorist reprisals. Any
problems?"

Again the ministers sat silently, glumly. What else could they do?
Events were now controlling them. The situation was slipping far
from their grasp. Begin directed the Cabinet Secretary to draft a
one-liner for distribution to the news services. When the Secretary
finished, Begin read the press release to the Cabinet for discussion.
There were no objections:

> "The Israeli Defense Forces have taken positions in west Beirut to
> prevent the danger of violence, bloodshed and anarchy."

Thursday, September 16, was a balmy Mediterranean day. In
Israeli staff headquarters for Lebanon, at the Port of Beirut in the
northeast section of the city, things were winding down for the
coming holidays. Tomorrow evening would be the beginning of
Rosh Hashanah, the Jewish New Year, the beginning of the "Ten
Days of Awe" which would culminate with the austere fast day of

Yom Kippur. The Israeli staff had issued orders to its occupation troops to be vigilant but to permit all observant soldiers to be released from duty to attend religious services by military field Chaplains. Staff headquarters was itself lightly manned.

Major General Jesse Amir was visited at noon by Lebanese Army Chief of Staff Fady Frem and Maronite Militia Intelligence Chief Elias Hobeika. The Christian Arabs were fuming over the Palestinian terrorist bombing which had killed their President-elect two days ago and killed and injured most of the Maronite political aristocracy of Lebanon. The Arabs remarked that they would be sending militiamen into the Shatila and Sabra refugee camps for a "*kasach.*" When General Amir's Arabic translator said that it would be a "chopping," Amir turned to him and asked, "What the hell is a 'chopping'?"

The translator asked Frem and Hobeika to elaborate for the General on what they meant by a "*kasach.*" They shrugged their shoulders as though it weren't really very important and said, "Well, you know, a 'chopping,' a 'cutting.'"

The translator again explained it in Hebrew to Amir: "*Zot omeret 'kitzootz,' 'chitoof,'*" [It means 'chopping,' 'cutting'] and the translator also shrugged his shoulders, not knowing exactly what that really meant in Arabic or Hebrew, though both of them were his native languages. Amir watched the off-handed gestures of the two Arab leaders and decided he wouldn't make a mountain out of a molehill. Anyway, the Lebanese might as well watch the refugee camps while the Israelis were busy with the holidays. Amir approved Elias Hobeika's proposal to bring two Maronite Militia battalions to the Israeli observation post at the entrance to Shatila and Sabra and let them enter the camps that evening.

After the Arabs left, General Amir telephoned Aryeh Verred in Jerusalem. "Aryeh, our friends are moving into the camps. I coordinated their entrance with the top men."

"Congratulations!" said Verred. "The friends' operation is authorized."

Two battalions of Militiamen massed at the Israeli observation post at the entrance to Shatila. Sabra and Shatila adjoined each other, but unlike Ghetto One and Ghetto Two of the Vilna Ghetto, there was no fence separating them. The first group of Arab Catholic Militiamen began infiltrating the Sunni Muslim Palestinian refugee camps at five o'clock that afternoon.

The next night, Israeli Chief of Staff David Cohen became concerned over piecemeal intelligence reports of firing being heard from Shatila and Sabra. General Cohen drove to the observation post outside the camps. It was dark and neither he nor his aides could see anything in the blackened camps. They heard desultory firing, but the Maronite officer in the observation post assured them that it was a simple peacekeeping operation against isolated pockets of armed resistance. There was "no military operation" in Shatila or Sabra, as evidenced by the fact that the second battalion of Maronite Militiamen was still below in the streets and wasn't even being used. Reassured, Chief of Staff Cohen left the area. He told his adjutant to ignore the reports from several of the senior staff that there was a massacre going on. Anyway, it was Arabs against Arabs in there, and the Jews weren't involved.

On Sunday morning, Hamdi switched on the television set in his hideout in east Beirut. News bulletins began to interrupt the regular programming. There had been some Maronite attacks on the refugee camps in West Beirut. At ten-thirty, he froze in his chair as the news reports became more descriptive, more certain. Phalange Militia had entered the Shatila and Sabra camps three nights ago and engaged in mass murder of the unarmed Palestinians. Red Crescent [Arab Red Cross] and International Red Cross officials had gained access to the camps earlier this morning and reports of a mass slaughter were being confirmed.

"*Ya Allah!*" groaned Hamdi over and over as he watched the growing evidence reported on TV all day long. "Karima and Muhammad. My wife, my son," he moaned again and again, digging his aching fingers into the arms of the chair, his head throbbing with pain.

He walked to Ein Rumani, the main route across the "green line," and bribed an Arab Red Crescent ambulance attendant for his identification card and his tee shirt with the Red Crescent logo on the front and back. He rode in the back of the ambulance to Shatila and jumped out and ran to the house of Karima's parents. The brutal, suffocating stench of decomposing bodies putrified the air. The Maronites had killed every living being. Bloated decaying bodies of men, women and children lay in piles in the narrow streets. Hugely bloated horses and donkeys lay like fur covered balloons, still attached to their wagons. Dogs littered the ground by the human bodies.

Hamdi ran with his hand covering his mouth, gulping for air. He found the Huri cottage and ran through the open front door. There they lay, Papa and Mama in the bed in the main room, swollen, decomposing. Karima, holding Muhammad tightly in her arms, was sprawled on the floor in the small back room. Her face was gone and maggots were feasting in this orgy of death. Muhammad was riddled with bullets. Hamdi fell to his knees beside the rancid bodies of his loved ones and choked on the stench of death and the vomit that spewed forth from him.

He wiped his face with the back of his arm and spat out the filth from his mouth and stumbled uncertainly out of the cottage. And then he ran, to escape the horror of his family's slaughter, to get away from the agonizing stink of the hundreds of bodies. He climbed on the running board of a departing ambulance and jumped off again in Mazraa a mile away, still in west Beirut. He walked to the al-Asifah hideout there, where there were other fedayeen holed up and food and weapons. He would kill them for this—all of them: Jews, Christians, whoever let this happen. It was the only meaning left in his life.

The next morning, before daybreak, Hamdi strapped a stinger missile launcher and two shells on his back. He crept through the dark streets and the looming shadowy piles of rubble to a block away from the entrance to Shatila. Any Israeli or Phalange units sent into the camps to investigate the atrocity would come out this way. He took cover behind the half wall of a bombed out building facing directly on the street, and he loaded the missile launcher. And he waited.

Colonel Joshua Jordan was telephoned at Golani Brigade headquarters at three o'clock that morning. General Amir ordered him to take a Recon unit into Shatila and Sabra and find out what the hell had happened. Joshua spoke Arabic, he would get the straight story, and he would report immediately to Amir. Highest priority.

At four in the morning, Joshua got in the lead Recon jeep and led the ten jeep column toward the Israeli observation post outside Shatila. They snaked slowly through the potholed rubble strewn boulevard leading to the camps. It was well before sunup as they passed the observation post and drove into the camps.

The only time that Joshua had ever seen anything like this before was in Holocaust photographs of the concentration camps and killing centers. The stench was overpowering. The heavy floodlight beams played on the bodies unsteadily and made them appear to quiver. Pulsating swollen apparitions. Joshua held his hand over his nose and pressed his mouth to try to keep back the vomit. There were bodies everywhere, old men and women. But most of the bodies looked like children's rag dolls, little boys and girls and babies, blood spattered, cut open, emasculated, disembowelled. Arab against Arab, Catholic against Muslim.

It began to get light. Joshua knelt by the bodies of three infants, their skulls shattered, their bodies strewn like garbage on the ground. And he wept.

He stood up shakily and slowly regained his composure. His father had been right, he had always been right. The only fruits of hatred were these broken and mutilated bodies of babies. It could be Rachel and Saul lying there. He walked back to his jeep and signaled his men to pull out. It was sunup now, and the colors of death were even grimmer in the daylight. Joshua knew that this was the turning point. He could stand no more of this. He would report to General Amir, and then he would resign his commission and go home just as soon as he was permitted. He had to get away from here, from the death and destruction and pure lunacy that pervaded Beirut, from the ignorant wide-eyed Zaleskis and the virulent Palestinians and savage Maronites and medieval Druzes, from the constant fear and interminable doubt. Oh God, let me go home to Dalia, to Rachel, to Saul. Oh God, keep me alive in this butcher shop.

His mother had once told him, when she tried to explain the Holocaust, that even though the Jews were God's chosen people, if God had ears he didn't hear the cries of pain, if God had eyes he didn't see the suffering, if He had a tongue He spoke no words of comfort, if He had a soul, He showed no pity. Oh God, please God, for once show pity and let me get out of this madness alive.

Hamdi Attiyah heard the sounds of the engines approaching and shouldered the stinger missile launcher, propping it on the half wall in front of him. He crouched and waited. The first Israeli Recon jeep came into view a block away. Could it be? It was. It was! The blond Jew officer who had fucked him twice! That same fucking

Jew bastard! Praise be to Allah, Lord of the worlds, the Beneficent, the Merciful....

An Israeli sharpshooter, riding in the second jeep, saw the movement of the man behind the piece of wall. "Look out! Over there, on the right!" he hollered as he quickly shouldered his M-16 and took aim at the Arab.

Chapter Seven

Monday, September 20, 1982. A chill wind presaging a bitter winter bit at the flags lining the walkway to the Knesset. The yellow gray stone government buildings clinging to the crest of Giv'at Ram brooded stoically like frigid sphinxes.

The preceding two days were Rosh Hashanah, so no newspapers had been published, and television and radio only broadcast for a couple of hours late Sunday evening. Most Israelis had not heard the news. Early Monday morning, however, it glared from every news stand: "Israel Is Blamed in Massacre." TV and radio were full of the reports from the International Red Cross.

At ten o'clock in the morning, an emergency session of the Cabinet began. It was an acrimonious meeting, an unusually stormy session even for Israel's notoriously contentious leaders. It had gone on for over two hours already, with Begin pounding the table in rage, calling the Red Cross representatives anti-Semitic scum and pro-Arab liars and ranting about Israel's innocence, while other ministers waved the latest intelligence briefing reports, distributed to them by military messengers from time to time, and pointed to the growing unimpeachable confirmations from legitimate sources that a massacre had indeed taken place and the Jews had simply let it happen. The only minister absent was Aryeh Verred, who had gone to Lebanon to investigate the matter personally.

The intensity of Begin's attack on the defamers, the "blood libelers" who had made such terrible accusations against the Jews, had chastened the Cabinet ministers. "Gentiles kill Gentiles,"

Begin raged, "and the Jews are blamed!" The Cabinet was considering Begin's proposal that he go on national TV and categorically deny that the Jews had had any knowledge of the Christian Militia's true intentions in Sabra and Shatila.

A military messenger entered the room and distributed a set of photographs to each of the ministers. The photos had just been received over the wire from Beirut. They were pictures of the slaughtered victims in the Sabra and Shatila camps. The ministers were stunned at the carnage, at the bestiality of the attack on unarmed civilians.

Leah Jordan sat in silence, guilt beginning to overwhelm her. The Israeli Army had gone into west Beirut to prevent just such atrocities. But instead, the Maronites had murdered these helpless men and women and children while the Jews stood by and did nothing. Leah had passionately denounced the Germans and the Lithuanians and the Poles who had painted crosses on their doors and hid in their apartments while their Jewish neighbors were slaughtered by the Nazis. Were the Jews to be judged differently? Leah was suddenly seized with dread. Matt had been right. *"Quisque suos patimur manes." We make our destiny by our choice of gods.* Matt's words from years ago rushed over and over through her mind. Leah had played a major role in enthroning the god of War, and now all Israel was being devoured by it. She wanted to run to Matthew, to tell him that she was sorry, that she had been wrong, that she loved him and needed him. Why had she let bitterness creep up between them, to spoil the years they had left? Oh God, oh God, oh God, I'm sorry....

A military messenger again entered the Cabinet room. He went to Leah Jordan, Amos Almogi, and Menachem Begin, and he handed each of them a folded note.

Begin glanced at the note briefly, annoyed by the interruption, and then he abruptly stopped speaking. He put his elbows on the table and his face fell into his hands. The minister next to him picked up the note, read it, and then passed it down the table.

Leah read the note again, slowly, to make sure she wasn't mistaken.

"Ayl molay rachamim," Leah repeated over and over in her mind, "God full of mercy...."

She wept bitterly. She was standing next to Matt, bracing against him, and his trembling body seemed more bent and frailer than she had realized.

They drove slowly from the Military Cemetery on Mount Herzl to the Jordan house. Amos and Shulamit, Dalia and her sobbing children. They sat around the patio table in the back yard, and soon Dalia took her children inside, to sit with them alone, to try to make them understand. Understand? But how? She didn't even understand.

Silent tears fell from Leah's cheeks to her black jacket. She began speaking, not much louder than a whisper, like the soliloquy of someone mortally wounded, transfixed by visions of her own mind, in a time and place beyond now.

"You know, I never quite shook the habits of my youth. When I grew up in Vilna, good Jewish girls read only the Bible in their free time. There were no paperbacks to read. Novels weren't considered worthwhile. So I read the Tanach every day. And when I was a girl, I would memorize first one part and then another. You know the first story I read and memorized? It was the great love story in Genesis about Jacob and Rachel. And I dreamed of being as beautiful as Rachel and finding my true love while I watered my flock of sheep by a well." Leah looked up, trying to gain control of herself. She looked at the sad faces of her family.

"When I got older, when I got more mature and my mother explained to me a woman's parts and a woman's great privilege, to experience love and to create life, I found *Shir Hashirim*, the Song of Songs, and I read it a thousand times and memorized every line of the magnificent sensual love songs.

"And then I met Daniel, and I loved him, and we were married and had a beautiful baby boy, Nachman. And you know something? Every word of the Song of Songs was true. It wasn't just foolish poetry. It was really the way you felt when you were in love. I guess that's the reason they put it in the Tanach, because it's the truth." Leah looked at Matthew, and his eyes bore into her with deep compassion, deep grief.

"Do you know what I have been reading now for over thirty years? Over and over I have read it, because it is *our* truth: Psalm 137. Everyone at this table, every Jew in Israel, probably every Jew and Christian in the entire world, knows the *first part* of Psalm 137, because it has been the theme song of the Promised Land for two and a half thousand years, since our first refugees were exiled from their homes in Jerusalem by the Babylonians:

'By the rivers of Babylon, there we sat, we
wept when we remembered Zion. . . .

If I forget thee, O Jerusalem, let my right
hand wither,
Let my tongue be stuck to the roof of my mouth
if I do not remember thee,
If I do not set Jerusalem above my highest joy.'

"That's the part of Psalm 137 that everyone knows. It is our own Biblical claim to the restoration of our dispersed people to their beloved homeland, the Land of Israel. Here we lived once until we were banished by foreign oppressors. Here we rebuilt our lives anew, on the holy soil of our ancestors, and our rallying cry was, 'If I forget thee, O Jerusalem, let my right hand wither.' And we did not forget, and our right hand became an iron fist. And when we finally became a nation again, and the Arabs attacked us, we fought and suffered and died and overcame enormous odds. We made the entire world gasp in awe at the miracle of our rebirth as an heroic and idealistic people. The despised Ghetto Jews, the pariahs of the western world, had transformed themselves after centuries of imposed purgatory, and we became proud and strong and free.

"But then came Lebanon. Oh, what a desecration we have committed! And we got drunk on victory, on the blood of our enemies, and we basked in our new role as a military colossus astride captive lands and peoples." Leah stopped speaking. She reached into the pocket of her jacket and pulled out a folded handkerchief. She slowly wiped her eyes with it and put it back. She sat a moment longer, needing to rest.

"You know, it's odd that no one seems to know the *other part* of Psalm 137:

'Remember the children of Edom, O Lord,
On the day that Jerusalem lay in ruins
When they cried 'Demolish it! Demolish it
down to its very foundations!'

O daughters of Babylon, whom we shall destroy.
Happy shall be he who repays you for all you
*   did to us,*
Happy is he who shall seize your children
And smash thy little ones against the rocks!'

There was a deathly hush around the patio table.

"I have experienced in my life the wrath of the Babylonians, the destroyers. I am still haunted by a vision which burns crystal clear through the haze of forty years: I still see the Prince of Darkness smashing the head of my little one against a rock—" She broke into shudders. She could not speak. No one moved. They sat minute after agonizing minute.

"And now the Palestinians have destroyed my second son, they have smashed his head upon the rocks." She covered her eyes with her hand and pressed back the tears, forcing away the surging grief which threatened to choke her, to envelop her. She got hold of herself and looked at Matt.

"But it is *I* who became a Babylonian, crying 'Demolish! Demolish!' Psalm 137 is now the rallying cry of the *Palestinians*. It is they who weep by the rivers of Babylon. I helped to exile them there, I pursued them, and I rained death and destruction upon them until they had no *malineh*. And now they are smashing *our* little ones against the rocks, avenging the day when we demolished *their* Jerusalem down to its very foundations."

Tears rolled down Matt's cheeks and his arms hung lifelessly at his sides. Amos laid his head on his folded arms on the table. Shulamit, her eyes glassy with tears, walked to Leah, stood by her side, and put a hand lightly on her shoulder.

Chapter Eight

The fish hawker waved a sea bream at Nadia, squawking in that incomprehensible Tunisian dialect about something, its great taste, no doubt, and the minuscule price that he was demanding for such a delectable morsel. Nadia kept on walking, detesting the cloying sweetness of the morning fresh fish now beginning to turn in the sweltering afternoon sun.

"And for you, Madame, the most elegant of precious silks." Another of the souk's endless merchants waved a wispy bolt of mauve taffeta at her. At least this one spoke an Arabic that she could understand. Grateful for his polite, deferential voice, Nadia stopped and fingered the silk and made a few mumbled appreciative sounds. She walked slowly on.

The badinage of two more merchants didn't stop her, and she finally found the tiny closet-sized nook of a shop that specialized in picture frames and scrapbooks. The wizened woman shopkeeper peeped something at her in dialect, saw through squinting cataract-opaqued eyes that a richly clad aristocrat looked at her puzzledly, and said in the closest thing to standard Arabic that she could muster, "May I be of service to the Madam?"

"I wish to see your finest scrapbooks."

"Oh yes, Madam, I have just the thing." She hobbled on two black-scarred wooden canes to a glass counter and rummaged in a set of boxes in the lower drawer. She pulled out a thick scrapbook with red simulated leather covers.

Nadia flicked her hand, dismissing it as garbage. "I wish to have one of those kind with the hammered silver covers that have embedded turquoise stones like Jerusalem Stones."

"Oh, yes, yes."

"I have seen one here before. Perhaps a month past."

"Oh yes, I remember. A Yemenite trader came. I bought a few of them in several sizes." The old woman struggled to remember if she still had any, where she might have stored them.

"I will pay you handsomely."

"Oh yes, yes, yes. I think I remember where I put that last one," she said, hobbling behind a curtain to a dusty jumble of boxes and cloth sacks.

She emerged in triumph a moment later, an object wrapped in a blue velvet bag squeezed under her arm.

Nadia took it from under her arm and laid it on the grimy counter. She pulled out the silver covered scrapbook, hammered with an intricate edge design and a geometric pattern in the center, studded with rich veiny Jerusalem Stones, a traditional piece of Yemenite craftsmanship. The paper was thick blue vellum. Nadia gave the shopkeeper a bill which the old lady brought one inch from her right eye, scrutinized sideways toward the light, and folded quickly into her caftan pocket.

Nadia walked out of the souk to the vegetable market on the edge of the beach. Muna was arguing heatedly with a greengrocer over the quality of two plump eggplants. As Nadia approached, Muna called out to her, "This thief of a madman wants more money for two stringy, bruised eggplants, than I paid for an entire kilo of tomatoes."

The grocer was all Arab politeness and insult, wringing his hands and whining and pointing to himself and the sky and to the other nearby vendor's inferior produce. After the appropriate amount of haggling, Muna carefully dropped the two eggplants into her large string bag, and she and Nadia began walking back to their villa.

Two little boys were playing on the beach, at the water's edge, and Nadia stopped and looked at them. She walked slowly toward them and stopped a few feet away. Muna stayed up the beach, watching from afar.

With a giggle and a yelp, one of the boys threw a little plastic shovelful of salt wet sand at his pal and ran a few feet away. "Can't catch me! Can't catch me!" he sang out to his little friend.

The other boy quickly scooped up half a yellow plastic pail of muddy sand and ran after his friend. He was too slow and had to throw the sand too far. They both returned to the water's edge and resumed digging for clams.

Has it been *that* long, thought Nadia to herself. Was it all the way back around Muhammad's birthday in 1981, an entire year and a half since she'd been on a beach to loll back and have pleasure. No, not that long. Several times the next summer. Oh yes, and remember the week that Karima was dieting, late last summer, and she was swimming a half-hour every day, and she and Muhammad came to the villa, which by then was bombed out, and they went to the beach, and Nadia had played for hours at the water's edge with her grandson.

The searing pain of it all immediately returned to her, and she saw again how Muhammad looked as he found his precious clams, how beautiful petite Karima was, wearing an absolutely sinfully skimpy red bikini. And she saw Hamdi's look of love mingled with no longer well hidden fear when he came to pick them up. Most days then, she saw her son's fear.

The Palestinians were doomed by then, but Nadia had upbraided her son for looking defeated. She had railed at his loss of heart. "A caliph must not lose his nerve," she had chided him, "he must keep his scimitar at the ready and his courage undiminished."

"But I am not a caliph, Mama, only in your heart. I am just a saddened man who has led his people to their death. Everywhere are our enemies and everywhere they prevail against us. When can our people ever have peace, when can our souls ever have rest?" He had almost wept.

And instead of giving comfort and succor to her son, as a mother must, and instead of hugging him and kissing his cheeks and telling him that it was alright just to be a man, to be human and feel fear for himself and his wife and his son and his mother, instead of that Nadia had slapped him.

Oh, how she had disgraced him in front of his wife and son. Allah, Allah, how could You have let this happen. She wept now at the memory, at the cruel sound of her hand crossing her son's face. At the look of ineffable sadness that he had given her. He was so tired. All he wanted to do was rest, to stop tempting death, to rescue his imperiled family. But she would not let him.

A trenchant wail came from her lips, getting louder, and she raised her face to the heavens and screamed at Allah for having let his obedient daughter hurt her son, kill her own son. And she beat her breast with her fists in agony.

A flock of terns, which had been industriously pecking away at the water's edge, swooshed suddenly upward in loud flapping flight, cawing clamorously at the harsh intruder upon their serenity. And the two little boys turned around in shock and dread and gaped at the old lady in the traditional black caftan bellowing at the sky while tears fled down her cheeks.

Nadia sat at the elegant walnut dining table in the immense formal dining room and shuffled through newspaper clippings in a folder. It had become her daily ritual, but today would be a bit different because she would put the clippings into her new rich scrapbook. Her servant Muna sat at the table and read the PLO newspaper. Sunlight streamed through the huge picture window embracing the plangent azure Mediterranean. The villa occupied the entire peak of a small hill overlooking Tunis several miles to the west. A steep cliff plunged from directly under the picture window to a rocky wave swept cove some two hundred feet below. Sea spray driven by screaming winds ran in rivulets down the picture window.

"Did you see this?" Muna asked, pointing to the lead story.

Nadia shook her head.

"There is going to be an Israeli Knesset debate over the commission of inquiry report on the causes of the Sabra and Shatila massacre," said Muna, shoving the newspaper toward Nadia.

Nadia read the article. "The report lays moral blame at the feet of the Prime Minister and the Foreign Minister, Leah Jordan," she said, shaking her head. "I never understand the Jews. They seem to have a deep need to take the blame for everything that goes wrong. The Maronites murder our people, and the Jews beat their breasts and rend their garments."

"The vote of confidence debate is going to be February 17th," said Muna. "That will finally be the end of Begin's government."

"Who knows any more, Muna. Begin has nine lives. He'll probably survive." Her voice lowered. "But Hamdi had only one."

She again shuffled through the file of clippings, some from Israeli papers, some from Arab, regaling the poignant story of Leah Jordan saving Nadia Attiyah at Deir Yassin, and how Nadia's son Hamdi grew up to be the killer of Leah's son Joshua. She read in the PLO paper about the death of her son, reading for the hundredth time the almost memorized story about how he had heroically killed Colonel Joshua Jordan before he himself had been killed. But the pain of Hamdi's death had never been softened by knowing that this Jewish soldier had also died. Somehow, the murder of Leah Jordan's son had never seemed to her a noble or heroic act. She knew with lancinating, scalding sadness that this was one act that was gravely wrong, that Allah would not reward Hamdi for the death of *this* Jewish soldier.

"I must see this woman Leah Jordan again," she said slowly.

Muna wrinkled her brow and looked sidewise at Nadia. "Are you crazy? She is the Lioness of Judah. She will cut your heart out with a paring knife! You, the mother of her son's murderer."

"It does not matter. I must look into her eyes. I must tell her that

I know her grief." She stopped abruptly, and her voice was hoarse, weak. "I must tell her that I am sorry."

Muna stared at her in disbelief. "Sorry?"

Nadia nodded. Tears filled her eyes, and her skin was taut and mottled over her cheeks. She walked slowly into her bedroom and closed the door.

Muna did not understand. But there was so much she could never understand about all of this. So much death. So much loss and suffering. She got up heavily and went into the kitchen to begin dinner. They would eat alone again, as always, because there simply was no one else. They were all alone in this huge mansion, empty, forlorn.

A week later Nadia crossed the Allenby Bridge on a forged work permit identifying her as a West Bank Palestinian domestic worker in Jerusalem.

Chapter Nine

Matt shook the frigid rain from his overcoat and stamped the dripping water from his soaked shoes. His black woolen trousers were saturated to the knees, giving off a faint camphor odor. He helped Leah off with her coat. She was oblivious to it, to her wet muddy shoes. Matt hung their coats on a rack. They walked down the corridor of the Knesset Building to the private members' entrance at the rear of the huge chambers. The MP saluted smartly.

"It's a real flood out there today, isn't it Mrs. Jordan," said the MP smiling familiarly, resuming a stiff at ease by the door.

"Kind of matches the mood, doesn't it," answered Leah glumly. "What's going on now?"

"A real great speech by Minister of Defense Verred, ma'am. He's really givin' 'em hell!" The soldier nodded and smiled confidently. "He's not gonna let 'em pin this one on the Army."

Matt squished his shoes on the brown cement floor trying to squeeze out more of the rain. "Goddam shoes are ruined," he muttered to nobody.

The MP opened the door, and Matt and Leah entered the back of the Knesset chambers. Matt went up to the visitors' gallery. It was standing room only for this vote of confidence debate.

A woman sat in the corner of the gallery, in the topmost row. She was wearing the traditional black caftan of mourning. Her face was hidden by a *shaddur*, and wisps of gray hair fell over her forehead, a crown over her lambent cobalt eyes.

Leah took her seat at the front row of tables, to the right of Menachem Begin, directly in front of the podium. Verred smiled briefly at Leah and concluded his speech.

"Nothing in the Commission of Inquiry Report, nothing that happened at Sabra and Shatila, nothing permits the conclusion that I was derelict in my duties. I had no idea that there would be an attack by Catholics on Muslims. Our soldiers played no part in the tragedy. And under no circumstances will I resign from the Cabinet, notwithstanding the recommendations of the Commission!"

A small volley of clapping was met with an explosion of catcalls and boos from the majority of Knesset members and the visitors in the huge chambers. The boos echoed off the walls as Verred returned to his seat to the left of Begin. Begin worked his jaws nervously and his cheek muscles stood out like welts.

He turned to Leah and whispered, "We are fighting for our political lives, Leah. You are next. Be very careful."

He eyed her cautiously, as if to divine what she was going to say. But her face was immobile. She slowly got to her feet and walked heavily to the podium. Angry catcalls and profanity raked the chambers.

Leah surveyed the faces of her colleagues and friends, the leaders of Israel, and her voice was hoarse and faltering.

"The Commission of Inquiry says that the Prime Minister and I are morally to blame because of what occurred in Lebanon." She stopped and looked at Begin, who was staring fixedly at his hands.

"The Commission is correct."

The spectators gasped. Begin glowered at her.

"We have been suffering for nine months in Lebanon, wreaking indiscriminate destruction on the Arabs and our own soldiers alike. There is an orgy of death there and we are feeding like vultures on the blood. And thousands of our soldiers remain in Beirut, but somehow we cannot muster the courage to stop the carnage and bring them home.

"First Sabra and Shatila send us reeling, and hard on that, score upon score of our own sons die, and still we are no nearer our goal of destroying Palestinian terrorism than we were before all this devastation began."

A sepulchral silence descended on the Knesset chambers like a foreboding thundercloud.

"But now we are like addicts of violence, craving punishment. One tragedy is not enough. We are oppressed by terrible guilt. We want more and more self abasement, more and more painful punishment. So we leave our soldiers in Beirut, even though no useful purpose is served, and day by day we must suffer the anguish of the death of another of our husbands or sons."

Her voice became stronger, louder. The Ministers and visitors alike were listening in silent awe to the fervent words of Israel's Foreign Minister.

"In the Talmud is the story of the rich man and his servant. The rich man sends him to buy fish at the market. The servant is neglectful, and the fish he brings back is rancid. 'Okay,' says the rich man, 'you must choose one of three punishments. Either you will eat the fish, or I will give you ten lashes, or you must pay me the five drachmas which you wasted.'

"So the poor servant thinks about it, and decides the least punishment is to eat the fish, and he starts eating. He gets three quarters through it and becomes so sick he simply can't finish. 'Okay,' he cries, 'flog me.' After the seventh lash, the servant screams out, 'Stop! Stop! I can't take any more! I'll pay you the five drachmas, my entire life savings.'"

Leah paused and her face became taut. She raised her arms by her side above her head, fingers outstretched.

"We are the servant!" she roared, a lioness before her pride. "We cannot resolve to suffer only one punishment!"

No one stirred in the chambers. Leah shuddered and her shoulders slumped. Her voice lowered and faltered again.

"Thirty-seven years ago, an old ghetto Jew saved my life. He made me able to go on living, despite all that I had seen, all that I had done. And some of those things I did to survive were so degrading, so sickening, that it horrifies me to think of them even today, so many years later." Leah looked down at her hands and swallowed deeply, steadying her quavering voice.

"And that old ghetto Jew told me something that I always try to remember but is so easy to forget: we are all made up of both good and evil, we are composed not only of decent and noble deeds but of our indecent and evil ones as well. That is why the greatest book of our people, the Bible, has in it the story of our greatest hero, King David, conspiring to have Uriah the Hittite killed in battle so that David could steal Uriah's wife Bathsheba. Only a people like us, with the most intense and powerful moral code that the world has ever known, could face itself with that much honesty, that much naked self-scrutiny.

"And the Bible tells us that the Prophet Nathan visited a terrible vengeance on the people of the house of David because of the King's evil deed: 'Because thou hast done evil in the eyes of God, *never shall the sword depart from thy house.*' And this has been our burden ever since. For three thousand years, the sword has never departed from our house."

She stopped and looked at the cabinet members in front of her. Her eyes fell on Menachem Begin, and he was looking back at her. His eyes had softened, and she felt his piercing grief. She looked up at Matt, and his face was aglow with pride.

"Now we must change that. Now we must sheathe the sword and pick up the Book once more. The People of the Book must once again shine as a light unto the nations. We will defend our beloved Land and our people with all the might of our sword. Never again shall anyone oppress us. *But never must we let ourselves be the oppressors!* Let not one more Palestinian be hunted down like an animal until he has no refuge, no hope, no *malineh!*"

Suddenly she noticed the woman in the corner of the gallery, and those unforgettable cobalt eyes lacerated her—bore into her soul. Nadia let the *shaddur* slowly fall, and her cheeks were glistening with tears.

The Prophetess of Israel stood weeping, her shoulders trembling. She looked at Nadia, and her voice was a haunted whisper echoing funereally in the huge chambers. "We have failed our soldiers, our sons, and their blood is on our hands." Nadia gritted her teeth and nodded softly—almost imperceptibly—to Leah.

The people in the chambers were silent and motionless, totally engulfed by Leah. And then her tears stopped. And her abyssal gray eyes became calm. And from her came the dulcet soothing voice of a mother to her child. And her voice grew louder and fuller from deep within her as she spoke the ancient healing words of the Prophet Isaiah:

> *"Nachamu, nachamu ami*
>   *yomar Elohaychem....*
>
> Comfort ye, comfort ye my people,
>   saith your God.
> Speak tenderly to Jerusalem,
>   and cry to her
>   that her warfare is ended,
>   that her iniquity is pardoned,
> That she has received from the
> Lord's hand
>   double for all her sins."

THE END